THE PRODIGY SLAVE

Book Three:
The Ultimate Grand Finale

Londyn Skye

The Prodigy Slave

Book Three:

The Ultimate Grand Finale

Londyn Skye Novels

ISBN: 978-0-578-24041-1

Library of Congress Control Number: 2020920199

Copyright © 2020

Reference information for Slave Codes: District of Columbia Slave Code Manual of 1860.

Reference information for Constitutional Amendments: Constitution of the United States of America.

Reference information for The Cornerstone speech excerpt: Alexander Stephens' "The Cornerstone speech."

Editor: Luceele Smith

https://www.linkedin.com/in/forensicproofreader/

Table of Contents

Prologue

April 15, 1863
Three years after escaping Adams Plantation

At the stroke of midnight, the most erogenous part of James was standing at full attention; it was eager for a more erotic sort of stroke. Innately knowing what sentimental day it now was, his internal body clock alarmed him to wake up for a sensual celebration. James quietly rolled over and lit several candles on the nightstand. They illuminated the bedroom enough to allow him to gaze at the stunning woman he was eager to celebrate with. Expressing appreciation for the fact that she was his woman, James wrapped his arms tightly around Lily and let a loving kiss linger on her cheek. She slowly roused from her slumber, moaning lightly over the soft feel of his lips. She turned toward her husband, opened her eyes, and smiled at him. The sight of the beautiful expression began to arouse James even more as he descended on her lips. Lily parted her mouth, inviting his tongue to delicately play with hers. He happily accepted the invitation, deepening the kiss while gliding his hand slowly down the side of her warm body. The feel of his hardened flesh pressed against her thigh suddenly had Lily wide awake as well. After years of complete sexual satisfaction by this man, she now reacted no differently than an addict who was about to make the climb to the ultimate high. Blood began pumping at a rapid rate through her body as James slid his hand down into her underwear and slowly massaged her hidden pearl. A pleasure-filled sigh escaped Lily's lips when he then glided his fingers into the wetness of her insides, slowly dipping them in and out of her. James then withdrew his fingers and slowly slid them into his mouth for a taste. Lily moaned as she carefully watched him suckling each one. The sight turned the heat up in her body another degree, making her just as eager to feel his erotic strokes as he was.

Eager to feel James inside her, Lily sat up and rolled him onto his back. She then straddled him, slid his shirt off, and tossed it onto the floor. As she leaned down to kiss him, she began grinding against the rock-hard bulge in his pajama pants. She sucked in air through her teeth after the feeling sent a jolt of electricity ricocheting through her body. She purred when James then reached inside her silk panties, grabbed on to her firm cheeks, and delicately squeezed. She sat back up after their brief kiss, slowly rubbing her swollen nub hard against his crotch. The feeling further ignited her nether region and awakened her sensual lioness, making her all too eager to strip. She kept her lowered bedroom eyes glued to his, wanting to be sure he did not blink as she erotically danced her way out of her pajama top. While watching him watch her, she slowly exposed her breasts to his eager eyes and tossed her shirt on the floor. James's view was short-lived, however. His eyelids reflexively closed, and his rigid flesh began to pulsate over the intense sensation of Lily grinding against it. When the pleasure caused his mouth to fall open, Lily seized the opportunity and guided one of her hardened nipples inside it. Like a starving lion cub, James instinctively clamped down and began ravenously suckling. The sweet sound of Lily's moans triggered James to gently bite her nipple, hoping to turn her purrs into deepthroated lioness growls.

The pleasureful currents set Lily's body aflame, but she regained control of herself and pulled her breast from James's mouth, evoking a sigh of disappointment from him. She slithered down his body, placing a series of kisses on his torso along the way. She gripped onto his pajama pants, pulled back the waistband, and began softly suckling the tip of his swollen flesh, seasoning her tongue with his sweet and salty flavor. The sudden, intense sensations hit James with force, reflexively causing his hips to thrust toward the pleasure. He sucked in air hard through his teeth, then let out a deep-throated moan as the joyous sensations spread through his body. After the intentional quick tease, Lily released James from her mouth, evoking another sigh from him. She smiled at her devilish teasing as she continued descending down James's body, pulling his pants completely off along the way. She then stood up near the end of the bed as she dropped his pants. She paused and took a moment to gaze at the ripped, muscular body that was hers to play with. She then slowly danced her way out of her panties, keeping her eyes on James the entire time. The way he intensely watched her every move set her entire core on fire with desire.

Once nude, Lily provocatively crawled back into the bed, kissing and sucking the interior of James's thighs as she made her way up. She stopped when she was even with his pulsating erection. As if she was being enticed by candy, Lily's eyes widened, and she began to salivate. She glanced up at James with hungry eyes, loving the anticipatory excitement on his face. While continuing to watch him, she slowly glided her tongue up the length of his hardened flesh, just as if she was indeed enjoying the flavor of a candy cane. She then sucked hard on the tip, causing James's body to tense again over the acute jolt of pleasure. As the feeling spread, his body relaxed, and he let out a long satisfying breath. Craving more, he thrust his waist upward. Lily happily responded, sliding her entire mouth around him, moaning over the taste as she slowly swallowed him whole. The hot sensations caused a savage growl to roar from the pit of James's stomach. Lily took her sweet time slowly releasing him, keeping her lips tightly constricted around his flesh the whole way up. After releasing him completely, she raised up to see the look on James's face, wanting to be sure she had left him lingering between bliss and desperation for more. His parted lips and heavy breathing left her confident that she had indeed achieved her goal.

The wanton look on James's face had Lily ready to massage his hardness with a much more tantalizing part of her anatomy. She grazed her breasts across his torso as she made her way toward his face, seductively biting his nipple, his right ear, and his lower lip. Like it was an irresistible dark, sweet berry, she then dangled her right nipple just inches from James's mouth and waited for him to bite back. He indeed bit lightly then sucked hard, sending a rush of heated moisture streaming down between Lily's thighs. The sensation had her beyond ready to ignite the rest of her body. But as she began lowering herself onto James's hardened flesh, he grabbed a hold of her buttocks and stopped her. His sudden move made her look down at him puzzled.

James gazed at her for a moment before responding to the questioning look in Lily's eyes. "I wanna take my time lovin' you tonight," he whispered as he caressed her face. The way he gazed at Lily as he touched her sent an intense surge of butterflies fluttering through her stomach.

James loved that Lily always wanted to be in control and to dominate him during their bedroom endeavors. But whenever she did, he always had to fight hard to maintain control. On this special night, he did not want to have a battle with his body. He wanted all his focus to be spent on pleasuring the woman he loved. This time, he wanted Lily to submit to his loving ways for a change. He wanted to express his joy, his appreciation, and his love for her in an extremely slow and passionate manner.

James started those expressions with a tender kiss. He carefully rolled Lily onto her back and descended on her lips, gently parting them to allow his tongue to softly caress hers. His tender affections had immediately changed the mood from highly erotic to beautifully sensual. With the emotion he exuded while tasting her lips, James could have stopped there, and Lily would have been thoroughly convinced of how deep his love for her was. That alone made her feel a sudden need to cry. But James was not nearly finished … not on this special morning.

After nearly bringing Lily to tears with a long loving kiss, James finally pulled away from her mouth. Continuing in an unhurried pace, he then began kissing her body. His lips made a slow trail along her neckline, delicately tickling her skin with the tip of his tongue. He then softly dragged his tongue along her clavicle bone. From there, he glided it down between her cleavage and onto her left breast. Lily amassed her hands in James's hair, sensual sighs escaping her as his mouth delicately caressed her nipple. After enjoying the sounds of her soft purrs, James eventually moved on in his slow, loving descent, not missing an inch of Lily's skin with his lips along the way. With great reluctance, he temporarily skipped over the precious hidden jewel between her legs and gave her inner thighs the same tender treatment as the rest of her body. Usually, the intoxicating scent of her pheromones would make him want to hastily satiate himself with the taste of Lily's nectar. But, on this night, he remained patient, taking his sweet time before his intimate meeting with the dripping hot abyss that was just inches from his salivating mouth. Lily was completely enchanted by his tenderness, her legs shuddering, and her soft moans continuously praising his diligent work.

Only after James's lips had perused every inch of Lily's legs did he begin kissing his way back toward his sweetly scented destination. Upon arrival, his watering mouth opened wide and he delicately began French kissing Lily's hidden set of lips. Lily inhaled sharply the moment he stimulated her sensitive folds. She then exhaled his name in a drawn-out breathy cry. With great finesse, James continued suckling Lily's southern corridor, moaning the entire time, as if he had never tasted such sweetness before. Normally, it took the added element of his fingers tickling Lily's insides to drive her to the pinnacle and beyond. But the passion with which James had just gracefully pleasured her southern pathways sent her running and jumping over the edge within seconds. The way Lily orgasmed and breathlessly moaned James's name was just as slow and sensual as the loving actions he had taken to get her there.

After savoring the taste of her erupting honey, James was still not finished with thoroughly pleasuring his exquisite woman. His manhood was begging for an eruption of its own, but he ignored the throbbing as he walked across the room and grabbed a bottle of Lily's favorite body oil. As he walked back over to the bed with it, he took a moment to appreciate the beauty of the luxurious nude body lying there illuminated perfectly by the flickering candle lights. James then leaned down and let another loving kiss linger on Lily's lips, as he silently thanked God for bringing her into his life. "Turn ova', beautiful," he whispered after pulling back from their sensual kiss.

Lily happily did as she was told, eager for more of his loving touch. She could indeed feel the love in James's strong hands as he ran them along her curves. He slowed down when he graced the suppleness of her posterior and gently squeezed them. The soft moan it elicited from Lily made him even more eager to submerge himself inside the paradise hidden between her perfectly rounded cheeks. But, still, he ignored his throbbing erection and miraculously maintained his patience. He poured the body oil into his palm and vigorously rubbed his hands together to warm them. Standing on the side of the bed, he then began slowly massaging Lily's skin, starting at the very tip of her feet. James's intentional lax maneuvers for this special evening continued as he made his way up to Lily's calves and hamstrings. "Slide toward me," James whispered before moving on to massage her buttocks.

Still enchanted by his touch, Lily happily followed James's commands. She maneuvered her feet onto the floor and laid her stomach flat on the mattress. She intentionally spread her legs on either side of James and centered her sacred cavern just inches away from his swollen member, instantly turning it blue with anticipation. She smiled when he let out the loud groan she was seductively trying to elicit. James reciprocated the teasing and pressed his throbbing erection flush against Lily's skin. He, too, smiled seductively and grappled her buttocks again after she unleashed a loud groan of her own. Now panting heavily, James had to exhale sharply to alleviate the pressure building in his groin. He then swallowed hard to keep himself from drooling as he poured more oil into his shaking hands. The oil came out in quick droplets, much like the eager semen escaping his pulsating manhood and dripping onto Lily's leg.

After thoroughly warming his hands, James began massaging Lily's buttocks. He spread her cheeks in the process and slowly drove his erection into her scorching hot abyss. Every nerve in his body ignited, causing Lily's name to rip through his throat in a raspy tone.

"Yeeesss," Lily moaned simultaneously, gripping the sheets and pushing herself toward James to submerge his erection even deeper.

Still though, James was in no hurry. He took a deep breath to settle himself and continued massaging Lily's buttocks while gently stroking inside her. His oiled hands gracefully glided along her spine as he pulled his hardened shaft back to the very edge of her sex and then slowly filled her again and again. Several times, Lily began to pump against him, wanting to take control as she normally did. But James quickly grabbed her posterior cheeks to remind her that he wanted to take his time loving her on this evening. While in control, he teased her every now and then, suddenly thrusting quickly inside her, just to hear her erotic moans escalate. Twice he even took her to the edge, letting her dangle near the pinnacle of ecstasy, then pulling her back before she took the blissful leap without him.

Even after stroking and massaging Lily for as long as he had, James was still in no rush to put an end to their pre-dawn celebration. He wanted to commemorate this special occasion in a way that was guaranteed to stay imprinted in their minds for a lifetime. After his long sensual massage, he withdrew from Lily and rolled her over onto her back. He filled his hands with oil again and leaned down to lightly suckle her neck while massaging her arms. His hands then followed the path of his lips down to her breasts. Lily's soft sighs proved how much she was enjoying the feel of his lips and hands massaging her skin and nipples in unison. The erotic sounds had James's mouthwatering as he placed both of her legs over his shoulders. He then slowly moistened them with the oils as well. As he caressed her legs with soft touches of his hands and lips, he slowly drove his erection back into Lily's smoldering cavern. The flames of pleasure elicited deep-throated growls that escaped them both in unison.

As James pumped slowly inside Lily, his oil-slick hands glided down her thighs, up her stomach, and onto her breasts. While playfully tugging at her nipples, he slightly increased the speed of his thrusts. When Lily's sighs began to heighten and signal her impending eruption, James quickly withdrew from her. He picked her up and carefully laid her back down in the middle of the bed and climbed in with her. As if he was awestruck by the sight of her, he suddenly paused as he hovered above her. Overcome by the depth of his feelings, he momentarily gazed at her with adoration. Lily's multicolored eyes gazed back at him; the sudden tears in them were a testament to how loved she felt by the strapping man staring appreciatively at her. Her tears then cascaded down the sides of her face as James parted her mouth with a fervent kiss while gliding himself back into the warmth of her paradise. The sensation sent currents of pleasure pulsing through their bodies, the intensity temporarily breaking their loving kiss. Once regaining control, James descended on Lily's lips again, the dancing of his mouth on hers matching the rhythm of his pelvis as he stroked inside of her. After nearly an hour of James's sensual foreplay, Lily could not help but erupt within seconds after his rigid flesh began pounding powerfully in and out of her. The erotic singing of his name immediately caused

James to unleash a tsunami of semen into Lily's womb as he howled her name in return. His body grew rigid as it released all its pent-up pressure. Submerged at the deepest point inside her, he stayed there frozen by the aftershocks of pleasure. When the drawn-out euphoric feeling subsided, the strength in James's arms gave way and he collapsed gently down onto Lily. As he lay there catching his breath, she kissed his forehead, silently thanking him for suspending her body in a state of rapture for the first hour of this special morning.

When James regained his strength, he raised up and smiled down at his wife. "Happy anniversary," he said, caressing her cheek.

"Happy anniversary to you too," Lily replied, her smile illuminating as well.

James kissed her forehead and then abruptly rolled off her.

"Hey, where you goin' so soon?" Lily asked playfully.

James reached underneath the bed. "To get this," he replied, pulling out a gift-wrapped box that he had hidden there.

Lily's eyes widened with excitement when he handed it to her. "Someone's been keepin' secrets," she smiled.

"Hopefully, one you won't punish me for."

"Oh, this most *certainly* warrants a punishment … but one you'll *thoroughly* enjoy," she sensually teased.

Her words elicited a low growl from James, making him want to toss the gift aside and receive his erotic punishment instead. "I'll be eagerly awaitin' that damn punishment," he said, blowing out a breath to release the sudden heat in his body.

Lily seductively smiled at his response. "Well, before then, I'd like to see what this little treasure is," she said, tearing off the wrapper and tossing it aside. The name *Piers LeRoux* artfully embossed on the decorative wooden box beneath the wrapping paper quickly hinted to what lay inside. She took the lid off, but very quickly found it difficult to make out the painstaking details of Piers's beautiful artwork with a mist of tears suddenly blurring her vision.

"You like it?" James whispered.

"I love it," Lily whispered back, wiping away a tear before it landed on the revised version of her and James dancing together in the Manhattan art gallery ballroom. Piers had duplicated the original charcoal sketch as a full color, eleven by fourteen oil painting and placed it inside of a decorative frame. "I've always felt as though this moment beautifully captures how much we mean to each otha'."

"That's *precisely* what I was thinkin' when I asked Piers to do this. I wanted 'em to capture in vivid colors a moment in my life when I was thinkin' about how much I love you."

"Our minds were certainly in sync," Lily tearfully replied, feeling a rush of warmth flow through her body. James's words had instantly infused far more sentimental value into the portrait that she could not stop gazing at.

"And I certainly rememba' feelin' your love while I's holdin' you that night," James commented as he gazed at the portrait along with her. "In fact, I so clearly rememba' *every* thought goin' through my head in that moment," he said, as the glorious memories flooded his mind. "Includin' how badly I wanted to marry you. And now…"

"It's our beautiful reality," Lily finished with a smile.

James nodded. "And I don't think I can eva' adequately express how truly grateful I am for that fact." He took hold of Lily's ring-bearing hand and gently kissed it. "It's been an honor to have you as my wife for these last three years."

His sincere words finally made Lily pull her eyes away from the beautiful portrait and turn toward the incredible man pictured in it. She gently placed her ring bearing hand on his face and tenderly caressed his lips with hers. "Thank you for this gift. I'll cherish it," she whispered, "just as much as I cherish havin' you as my husband."

"You're welcome, Miss Lily," he replied, his body equally igniting with warmth after absorbing her words and her passionate kiss.

Lily smiled at the portrait again. "We have to find the perfect place to hang this lata'," she said, carefully laying it back in the case and placing it on the nightstand. She then turned around and curled up in James's arms. "*Three years*," she said, kissing his chest. "I can't believe it's been that long since our little midnight weddin' unda' the stars. Time flies, as they say."

"Sure does," James replied as he wrapped his arms around Lily. "Won't be long before we've collected seventy more years' worth of unforgettable memories and priceless treasures that'll make every anniversary deservin' of a grand celebration."

"You gonna start off every grand anniversary celebration spoilin' me with slow love makin' like you did today?" Lily asked, nibbling at James's ear.

"You betta' damn believe it," James growled.

"Even when you're ninety?" Lily joked.

"I don't give a damn if I have *two* bad knees *and* a bad back, I'll find a way to please my queen!"

"Is that a promise?" Lily laughed.

"Ironclad!"

"Okay, I'm gonna hold you to that. Don't wanna hear no excuses eitha'!"

"*Excuses?!* I'll be too outta' breath from chasin' you down with my walkin' cane for that!"

Lily burst out laughing again.

"Once I catch ya', I'll probably fracture both of my hips tryna satisfy you," James replied, biting her neck.

"Well, ya' just might fracture more than that, 'cause I'ma need some of your lovin' more than just once ya' know?" she said through her laughter.

"Really now?"

"Mm-hmm," Lily replied, a hint of lust quickly returning to her tone. "Just like I need you again now," she confessed, suckling gently on his neck.

James lowered his eyes and let out another low growl as his erection hardened against her thigh again. Lily smiled, still enjoying the effect that she had over her man after three magnificent years. She let James have his way earlier that night. But now, she straddled him, eager to dominate him once again. James glided his hands down the sides of Lily's illustrious frame and smiled up at her as he happily let her take hold of the erotic reins and ride him in whatever way she desired this time.

Hours after Lily exhausted James a second time, he woke up when he heard the familiar sound of youthful giggling and little feet scampering on the other side of the bedroom door. The familiar noise happened every morning like clockwork. The sound roused Lily from her sleep as well. Still wrapped in James's arms, she turned toward him and smiled at the way his face always lit up over what had become a morning ritual.

"You betta' move fast," Lily said, her voice groggy. "You know she always outruns ya'."

"Not this mornin', she won't," James bragged.

"Mm-hmm, you say that *every* mornin'," she playfully teased.

James kissed Lily on the cheek, scurried out of bed, and threw on some clothes. Lily laid on her side, smiling and shaking her head, knowing he did not stand a chance of conquering his morning mission.

"Hey you, come here!" James said as he flung open the bedroom door. He dashed into the hallway and the morning chase officially commenced.

With her smile still in place, Lily got out of bed, put on her clothes, and went to watch her husband fail like he did every morning. She indeed stepped out of the bedroom to find James in pursuit of their three-year-old. As usual, the toddler had an ample lead on her father, all the while giggling at the playful chase she had initiated. The youngster made her way out the front door and toddled down the porch steps with James still trailing her. Lily stepped out on the porch and leaned on the railing, smiling as she continued to watch. Their swift little daughter still had a commanding lead on her father as she made her way toward a massive treehouse. James finally closed in on her, eager to scoop his daughter up and give her a kiss. When he was just inches away from touching her, though, he suddenly could no longer move ... just like *every* morning. Standing there as stiff as a statue, James could do nothing but watch the back of his daughter as she ran further and further away.

No different than every day preceding this one, James instantly panicked. "ROSE!" he cried out. But, like always, little Rose never bothered to turn around. At shrill levels, James repeatedly screamed her name, but she never even reacted to the sound. Despite all his efforts, he remained frozen and little Rose continued to run away from her father's loving arms.

Still unable to move his feet, James looked over his shoulder toward the porch to find that Lily was gone too ... just like always. He suddenly shouted Lily's name. His voice was once again at shrill levels as he sat up in his cot, sweating and breathing hard after being torn from his sleep by the frustrating dream. His head darted quickly from left to right as he tried to decipher reality from the lifelike visions he saw in his head as he slept. Once the sleepy fog cleared, he realized it was yet another one of his recurring dreams, one that always brought him temporary joy, yet simultaneously tortured him.

Thoroughly aggravated, James exhaled sharply and buried his face in his hands. He wondered why nightmares were the way his mind seemed to enjoy punishing him. His current recurring dreams had now replaced the nightmares that he had dealt with as a teenager after being dragged to his father's torture camp. Now, on a regular basis, he was jarred awake by sweet dreams of Lily that always ended bizarrely as he chased Rose toward the treehouse he had envisioned building her. Over the three years since Rose's death, James's dreams had evolved. Rose had even grown in size, no different than she would have in real life. In every dream, though, two facts remained the same: Lily disappearing and Rose eluding his grasp. He had never even gotten so much as a peek at her little face. Those facts always tore James from his sleep while screaming at shrill levels.

Despite how loud James's shrieking was on this morning, the unkempt man lying in the cot next to him barely roused from his sleep. He, and all the other filthy men lying nearby, had long since gotten used to James hollering the names of flowers in the middle of the night. Their ears had no choice but to adapt to his deafening shrills; they were *all* stuck there with him indefinitely. Some of them would even die there. After so many months trapped together, those unkempt men were now aware of the significance of the names James yelled, as well as the tragedies in his life that had led him to be stuck where they all were now. Every man there even knew to steer clear of James altogether in two days: the anniversary of Rose's death. On that night, they were used to seeing him pacing, fighting all urges to fall asleep so as not to take the chance of being tortured by his nightmares. The impact of not being able to hug Rose or to even see the color of her eyes in his dreams seemed a million times worse on the anniversary of such a heart-shattering day. Sleep was, therefore, not an option on any April seventeenth. For those entire twenty-four hours, the men lying nearby knew that James Adams would be mourning the loss of his daughter all over again.

And today, on this fifteenth of April 1863, the men surrounding James understood why his sorrows were nearly as heavy as they would be in two days. James's misery was already evident by the way he sat on the edge of his cot, in a place he may very well die. He had his face buried in his hands, fighting back tears as he tried to deal with the fact that the only people present during his wedding anniversary were a bunch of filthy men. On such a special day, he ached over the fact that the only way to give his wife a sentimental gift was in his dreams. There was no other way to hold her, kiss her, make love to her, or tell her how much he loved her. Because, just like little Rose, James had lost Lily three excruciatingly painful years ago too.

Chapter One

Wednesday, April 18, 1860
Early A.M. hours after escaping with Lily
from Adams Plantation

"Wake up!" Jesse snarled, smacking James hard in the face.

An unconscious James was tied to the base of a tree with a gag in his mouth and a tourniquet around his wounded right leg. Duke had left him that way while he rode back to the Ghost Rider rally point looking for Jesse. After searching for hours, Duke had finally rallied several of his Ghost Rider brethren, including Jesse, J.R., and Jacob. He then proudly led them to the temporary prison of his ailing victim, one that Jesse continued to inflict more pain on.

"Get up goddamn it!" Jesse yelled, smacking James again. Jesse showed no concern whatsoever over the sight of his son's limp, bruised body. Instead, he dumped a canteen of water on his head and continually nudged him with his heavy boot trying to rouse him. James groaned and his head fell from one side to the other. "I said, wake up damn it!" Jesse suddenly kicked him hard in frustration.

The blow finally jarred James from his pistol whip-induced slumber. He was immediately hit with the severe pain of a migraine and intense throbbing in his right thigh. Being pounded repeatedly in the head with Duke's revolver hours earlier had left him black and blue and severely concussed. James was fortunate that Duke's bullet had only grazed his thigh bone on its way in and missed a major artery on the way out. Despite it, the excruciating pain and loss of blood had crippled him too much to stand or defend himself against his father.

Jesse turned his attention to Duke after seeing the shape that James was in. "Why the hell'd you shoot 'em, ya' hunchbacked sack of shit?! I told ya' to bring 'em to me! I ain't say shit about puttin' a bullet in his ass!"

"He killed three of our brethren and he tried to shoot me! Y'ur lucky I didn't blow that little pussy's head off!"

"I don't give a shit what he did!" Jesse grabbed Duke by the shirt collar with his unbroken hand. "I said to leave 'em to me to handle! That was a fuckin' orda'!"

"I ain't takin' no more goddamn orda's from you!" Duke pulled out his revolver and aimed it at James. "Now, take y'ur fuckin' hands off me! I oughta get justice right now, since you ain't gonna do shit but slap this little pussy on the wrist and kiss his pretty little cheek to make 'em feel betta' afta'wards!"

"You got two seconds to put that pistol down or you'll be pickin' y'ur rotten teeth up off the goddamn ground," Jesse threatened. Duke actually found the courage to keep the pistol pointed at James, but not for long. True to his word, Jesse bashed him in the mouth with a lightning quick jab. He watched Duke crumple to the ground and then turned his attention back to James. "Where the hell is my property, boy?!" he yelled, snatching the gag out of James's mouth.

Still slipping in and out of consciousness, his father's words sounded distorted in James's aching head. Even if he could make sense of what he was saying, he would not have had the strength to answer.

"Where the fuck is she?!" Jesse demanded to know, suddenly kicking James hard in the side again, fracturing his rib this time.

Every ounce of oxygen suddenly exited James's body and the world temporarily went black again. He fought hard to inhale, gasping desperately for air. When he was finally able to fill his lungs, he managed the strength to slightly lift his head toward his father. "I … ain't … tellin' … you … shit," he murmured, fighting for every breath in between his words.

Jesse kicked him hard in the gut again. As James desperately fought to fill his lungs, Jesse squatted down and grabbed his son by the hair, forcing his wobbly head to look toward him. As soon as James steadied his head, he spit a mouthful of blood into his father's face.

"YOU NIGGA' LOVIN' SON OF A BITCH!" His blatant disrespect sent Jesse into an instantaneous rage. He pulled his pocketknife off his hip with lightning speed. Just as he flicked open the blade, a gunshot suddenly went off behind him, startling the whole group. Jesse quickly let go of James. His wobbly head fell back onto his chest, and he faded back into unconsciousness. Jesse turned around to find a sheriff, two deputies, and two civilians on their horses approaching in the distance.

All five men rode closer to the group with the angry eyes of Ghost Riders glaring at them the whole way.

"Y'all mind explainin' to me what in tarnation's goin' on here?" the sheriff asked once he was close enough for everyone to hear him.

The entire Ghost Rider posse just stared at him in silence.

Now that he had a closer look, the sheriff realized he knew every face in the group … a group he did not like. He climbed down off his horse, pulled a rifle from a holster on his horse's saddle, threw the barrel over his shoulder, and marched toward the group with a relaxed confidence in his strut. "Well, well, well, if it ain't Fayetteville's most model citizen," he said sarcastically, looking right at Jesse. The sheriff had once worked as a deputy in Fayetteville and was now a sheriff in a neighboring town.

All of the Ghost Riders recognized him too. "Sheriff Clemens," Jesse greeted with a nod of his head.

Clemens turned his head and glared at Duke who had just gotten to his feet and was wiping the blood off his mouth. "Yet anotha' one of Fayetteville's *upstandin'* citizens is here too, I see," he said, still staring at Duke. Clemens then turned in a circle. "Well now, what the hell do I owe the honor of bein' surrounded by *all* of Fayetteville's finest?" he joked.

Silence.

Clemens suddenly peered over Jesse's shoulder. "Jesse, you wanna explain to me why y'ur son's tied to a goddamn tree?" he asked, finally sounding serious.

Jesse turned and glanced briefly at James and then turned back to look at the sheriff without saying a word.

Clemens glared back at him with lowered eyes. Clemens had never much cared for Jesse. When he was just a deputy in Fayetteville, he refused to believe that Elizabeth's death was a tragic accident. All along, he had been inwardly convinced that Jesse was responsible for taking his wife's life. But with the coroner finding her injuries consistent with having been trampled by a horse, he was unable to press charges against Jesse the way he had hoped. Despite being forced to close the investigation, it was a case that had always haunted him. Clemens never forgot about how frightened young James was when he was questioned about the details leading up to his mother's death. It was obvious that Jesse had instilled that fear in James and had also force-fed him the well-rehearsed story that James kept regurgitating during the questioning. Clemens now hoped that this debacle in the woods would finally give him a way to put Jesse behind bars where he felt he belonged years ago.

Without pulling his lowered eyes away from Jesse, Clemens motioned his head toward the two strange men behind him, still sitting on their horses. "Those two drifta's ova yonda' came lookin' fur me before dawn to tell me they rode up on four dead bodies in the woods." The sheriff peered over Jesse's shoulder again. "Looks to me like James might still have a bit of air left in his lungs afta' all. But those otha' three fuckers are deader'n turkeys on Thanksgivin' Day." The sheriff finally pulled his eyes away from Jesse and turned in a circle to look at everyone again, easily sensing their tension. "My best educated guess is that y'all know who killed all them poor fuckers and why the hell they did it. Anybody wanna save me some trouble and fess up now?"

Silence.

"If none of y'all wanna talk, I'll be glad to lock every one of ya' up 'til I get a fuckin' answer."

Silence.

"Have it your way," Clemens responded, motioning to his deputies to start handcuffing everyone. He turned to glare at Jesse again with a wicked smirk on his face. He marched over, slapped the cuffs on him, more than happy to personally escort him to jail.

James had Sheriff Clemens and those two drifters to thank for the fact that he was able to maintain the little oxygen that remained in his lungs. Their early morning find spared James from the torturous show that his father was about to put on in the midst of his blinding rage. However, Clemens's intervention would eventually lead James to suffer a far different, far more public and salacious form of torture.

The Underground Railroad:

A network of secret routes and safe houses established to help enslaved Negroes escape to free states.

"James Adams, on this fifteenth day of May, eighteen-hundred and sixty, you're bein' charged with felony first-degree murda' of Willard McKinley, Jethro Blankenship, and Jeb McClintock. You are also charged with the assault of Duke Dixon as well as felony violation of slave code article three, section eight, grand theft of a slave, felony violation of slave code article five, section two, intermarrying with a Negro, felony violation of slave code article one, section six, education of a Negro, and felony violation of slave code article five, section seven, impregnatin' a Negro. Do you fully unda'stand the charges bein' brought before you here today?"

"Yes, your honor," James replied, standing before the judge with shackles on his wrists and ankles.

"How do you plead?"

"Not guilty."

"Your trial is set to begin Monday, September tenth. Court is adjourned." The judge banged his gavel and the murmuring amongst all the people in the pews of Fayetteville's district court resumed. As soon as those stunned patrons stepped outside, the shocking news of the James Adams' murder trial began to spread like a sensational wildfire.

Prior to that plea hearing, most citizens of Fayetteville knew nothing about the allegations against James. Even the families of the three men murdered had yet to be told who the alleged killer may have been. After being found in the woods in such bad shape, Sheriff Clemens had the decency to send James to a prison infirmary to recover from a bullet wound, concussion, and fractured bones in his ribs and eye socket. Clemens refused to press any charges against James until he had the wherewithal to answer questions about the case without losing consciousness throughout the process. Decent recovery had taken him nearly three weeks. During that time, Jesse and his posse were questioned and quickly released from jail after it was determined that they were nowhere near the scene of the crime that night. However, James and Duke remained in Clemens's custody since it was clear that they were the only two present during the murders. They would have been transferred to a Fayetteville jail after that, but there was confusion about which town the murder had actually taken place in and which jurisdiction should preside over the trial. Knowing that James did not stand a chance of having a fair trial in Fayetteville, Clemens had fought hard to have the case heard in his jurisdiction. He was, therefore, livid over a judge's ultimate decision to have the trial take place in Fayetteville. He felt as though he had failed James again in giving him a fighting chance at true justice.

Clemens was not the only one upset about the trial being moved to Fayetteville. Jesse had demanded that his brethren remain tight-lipped about the abominable acts his son had committed. He did not want the humiliating news tainting his family name. So he, too, was fuming over the fact that James was dragged back to their hometown and paraded into the district court in front of a town full of people who had known them their whole lives. With his son's sinful secrets now spewing like vomit out of the gossip-happy mouths of every Fayetteville citizen, Jesse sentenced *himself* to imprisonment on his own farm. He rarely left his home and saved himself the shame of being shunned.

While James lay ailing in the prison infirmary, Griff set out on a feverish search for him and Lily. He wrote a letter to William and Landon in Manhattan, stating that James and Lily had failed to show at any of the tradeoff points. By the time William read the letter, Griff and two other bandits were already making their way south through every city along the planned escape route, not knowing that they had passed right through the town where James was recovering. Along the way, Griff and the bandits met up with Elijah, who was waiting patiently at his assigned relay point so as not to raise any suspicion about his devious deeds at Samuel's assigned location. Elijah played his role well, even feigning concern about the fact that Samuel was missing. Once he was confident that his tracks had been covered, he lied and told the group he would start searching for James and Lily at Underground Railroad locations as he made his way back to Manhattan. With his dirty secrets in tow, Elijah parted ways with Griff and the bandits a few days before they arrived in Fayetteville.

Once in Fayetteville, Griff and his men spent a few days inconspicuously trying to find out information on James and Lily's whereabouts. Griff and the bandits watched Jesse's house and even sat for hours in taverns eavesdropping on conversations. But news of the murder trial had yet to make it to the ears of Fayetteville's residents, so nary a word about James was mentioned. They even saw Jesse at a pub, but he did nothing but sit silently sipping his gin as if all was normal.

Before leaving Fayetteville altogether, Griff finally got bold and snuck onto Jesse's plantation while he was gone. He quickly made his way into the slave quarters where several female slaves were getting ready to head out to the fields. The sudden appearance of a brooding white man, dressed in all black with two pistols hanging from his hips, immediately stopped every slave in their tracks. Griff had stayed on the outskirts while guarding the perimeter during James and Lily's wedding ceremony, so none of them recalled who he was. With mouths agape and eyes wide, they stared at him in silence.

"I don't mean anybody any harm," Griff said to them. He had both his hands raised, trying to ease the tension he felt after startling everyone. "My name's Griff. I'm a friend of James and Lily's. Do any of y'all have any idea where they might've went?" Griff scanned all the brown faces staring silently back at him. "This is real important," Griff continued when he got no reply. "Did Lily mention anything about where she might be goin'?"

After the massacre the slaves had witnessed the day James escaped with Lily, they were reluctant to even talk about Lily's tragedy amongst themselves, let alone with an odd-looking white stranger. Jesse had already beaten several of them while demanding answers to Lily's whereabouts. The effect it had on them was literally still on many of their faces and were painful reminders that the consequences of discussing their master's business would be brutal.

With painful lessons still figuratively and literally ingrained in her head, an older slave finally spoke up. "We don't know nothin', mista'," she stated sternly.

Griff looked into her eyes and easily sensed her fear. More importantly, though, he sensed she knew something that she was not willing to share. "Please, if any of ya' know anything, you'll be helpin' Lily. I promise ya'."

The older lady shook her head. "We don't know nothin', mista'," she insisted again.

Griff suddenly looked around and noted the bruises, busted lips, and black eyes that Jesse had given to a few of them. He then realized he was staring at the reason he would never get an answer out of anybody standing there. "Sorry to botha' y'all. Thank ya' anyway," he finally said. He tipped his black Stetson and quickly made his way off the property.

All the slaves curiously watched him leave and then headed out into the fields. The older woman who had spoken to Griff scurried into the house to speak to Corrina. She entered through the kitchen door in a panic. "Corrina, I think Jesse tryna test us," she announced.

Corrina stopped doing dishes and turned around. "Why you say that?"

"He done already beat half of us for claimin' we don't know where Lily is. Now, I think he done sent some strange man here to see if he can get us to talk."

"Hell, that don't sound like Jesse at all. He don't send nobody to do his dirty work. That evil bastard takes too much pleasure in doin' the task himself."

"True."

"What'd the man say?"

"Said his name was Griff. Claimed he was a friend of James and Lily's. Said it's important that he finds out where they are."

"*Griff?*" Corrina instantly had a flashback of Lily calling out that name as she hugged a man at the wedding.

"Yeah, scary lookin' white man, dressed in all black with…"

"His mustache twisted down on the sides," Corrina finished.

The older slave looked at Corrina oddly. "You know 'em?"

"Yes! And so does Lily!" Corrina suddenly bolted from the house and took off running toward the plantation gates.

After recalling Lily's reaction to seeing Griff, Corrina was confident that she could trust him with knowledge of James and Lily's botched escape. She especially wanted to tell him what she happened to overhear the evening before. As she was fixing dinner, J.R. had come by to tell Jesse that James's murder case was being moved to Fayetteville. Jesse flew into a rage over the fact that the town would soon hear about his son impregnating a slave, something that angered him far more than the fact that James was accused of murder. Corrina was now desperate to get all that information to Griff, hoping that it would aid in his search for Lily. At the very least, she wanted him to know James's whereabouts. She screamed Griff's name repeatedly as she ran toward the plantation entrance as fast as her legs would carry her. But her efforts proved to be in vain. By the time she reached the fence, she could see nothing but the dust kicked up from Griff's horse.

After his frustrating search, Griff made his way out of Fayetteville. He hoped James and Lily had just changed their minds about going to the Old World and had *intentionally* vanished without a trace. Griff figured neither scenario was likely, but he preferred to believe that over the thought that Lily may have suffered an unspeakable fate at the hands of her master.

Had Griff stayed in Fayetteville just a few more days, he would have learned exactly where James was, as well as the story being told about him that was now being spread through the town like debris in a tornado:

FAYETTEVILLE DAILY CHRONICLE
Wednesday May 16, 1860
Charismatic town doctor or cold-blooded murder?

That's the question Fayetteville residents are asking themselves this morning. Lifelong resident and new community doctor, James Adams, was charged with second-degree murder yesterday. Dr. Adams, along with Fayetteville resident, Duke Dixon, are being held without bond for the death of Willard McKinley, Jeb

McClintock, and Jethro Blankenship. All three men were gunned down back on April seventeenth of this year, each leaving behind a wife and children. The motive for Dr. Adams actions are said to have stemmed from a dispute with his father, Jesse Adams, over a slave that Dr. Adams allegedly stole and impregnated. Dr. Adams's attorney argues that the murders were committed in self-defense. Duke Dixon has admitted to being present when the crimes were committed but claims to have played no part in the murders. Dixon is being charged for false imprisonment, assault, and the attempted murder of Dr. Adams. Both men will be tried separately with Dr. Adams's case beginning on September tenth of this year. Dixon is set to testify in Dr. Adams's upcoming trial. No trial date has been set for Mr. Dixon thus far.

No trial was needed for the gossip-happy folks of Fayetteville, though. They already had a verdict in the case of Dr. Jameson Michael Adams, thanks in part to a woman scorned who was still raging with vengeful desires. Just hours after hearing about James's indictment, Mary Jo Parker began concocting a story about him that would eventually land her a role as the prosecution's lead character witness.

Even without the rampant gossip and Mary Jo slandering his name with her salacious story, James knew he needed a damn good defense attorney in a town like Fayetteville. Being as cryptic as possible, he wrote a brief letter to Harrison at his law firm's address, using the playful nickname his fraternity brothers had given him as a funny play on words for being a rower, among *other* things, while at school.

Stroker,

I'm in desperate need of your help. Please come as soon as possible to the Fayetteville, Virginia prison. On my behalf, will you please contact the only other person who can help me in a very dire situation. Please ask if they will come as well.

Sincerely,
Southern pretty boy

After signing the fraternity nickname James was given, he sealed the envelope and wrote only Harrison's law firm address on it. He then handed it to the prison guard, praying that Harrison or William, or both, would quickly come to his aid. He was wise enough to refrain from mailing a letter directly to William, not wanting to make known the address where Lily might possibly be.

Before ever sending that letter, the judge had already assigned James to an attorney. Mason Rockefeller was Fayetteville's finest public defender ... and well-known to *every* judge in the judicial system for having very particular prejudices. Mason was not a Ghost Rider, but if it was not for his high-profile job, he would undoubtedly be a regular attendee at their late-night Negro "barbeques." Mason especially hated those who educated or fornicated with slaves. The judge in James's case was well aware of that fact when he "coincidentally" assigned him to James. After just one interaction with Mason, James began to feel hesitant about speaking to him. Mason had a way of appearing to be professional while simultaneously scolding James with his eyes and condescending verbiage. When Mason's disgust became brutally evident while obsessively questioning the details of his involvement with Lily, James immediately ceased talking. He began to suspect that his attorney-client relationship was going to be anything but a privilege. He went back to his cell and wrote yet another letter to Harrison, a man whose loyalty and trust was as solid as the bars surrounding him.

In his second letter, James cryptically asked Harrison to get in touch with William again. He was desperate to know if Lily had made it to Manhattan alive. That knowledge alone would have given him some semblance of peace while he sat idly by in prison awaiting his trial. He thought to write a letter to Gideon, hoping maybe he would update him, but felt it was best not to have any evidence that would incriminate him for his involvement in Lily's theft. He preferred to wait and ask Harrison to speak to Gideon in secret on his behalf. With his letters sent, James had nothing else to do but wait … and think of Lily and Rose obsessively. Rose, Lily. Lily, Rose. They inundated his mind along with all the things he could have done differently that would have kept Lily on the path to her dreams and their daughter still growing and thriving. Tortured by his mistakes, James slowly felt his sanity slipping away.

Losing hope, his mind, and his patience, James began to write letters every day to Harrison. Waiting for a reply from him made the anticipation of daily mail delivery just as much torture as his obsessive thoughts. But the only thing the postman ever delivered to James was a daily push toward the cliffs of insanity. Death threats and letters expressing joy that James would soon burn in hell were plentiful, but not a single shred of mail from his loyal friend was ever received.

Finally, though, after weeks with no reply by letter from William or Harrison, James heard five precious words he had been dying to hear. "Adams, ya' got a visitor," he was told by a prison guard.

James hopped out of his cot at lightning speed. "Who is it?"

The guard opened the cell and put James's shackles on in silence. He grabbed his arm and nudged him forward when he was finished. James's heart nearly pounded its way out of his chest as he was marched through the corridors towards the visitor's quarters. He was praying he was being led to Harrison or William. However, the person he saw sitting at the visitor's table was one he never would have expected.

The guard pushed James down into a chair and shackled his hands to the table across from his visitor. "Carolyn," James nodded, greeting Gideon's young wife. "A-are you alright?" he asked after noting her red eyes and the handkerchief in her shaky hand that was moist with her tears.

Carolyn dabbed at her eyes and then looked directly at James. "Wh-what did you do to h-him?" she asked, sniffling.

"To *whom?*"

"My husband!" she fired back, clearly upset.

"Carolyn, I'm sorry, but I don't unda'stand what you mean."

"You were the last one to see 'em! He would neva' just run off and leave our son this way! You must've done somethin' to 'em!"

"*Run off?* Carolyn, I have no idea what you're talkin' about."

"I read in the newspapa' that you murdered three men the same night you was by my house beggin' Gideon for help! That w-was the last time I eva' saw my h-husband! H-how am I supposed to know you didn't kill h-him too?!" Carolyn accused, suddenly breaking down into heavy sobs.

"Gideon hasn't come home since then?" James asked, looking and sounding thoroughly perplexed.

"Don't pretend like you didn't know!"

"Carolyn, I swear, I knew nothin' of this."

"Because of you, Brandon's been beggin' to see his daddy for weeks! He must be dead! There ain't no otha' way he'd abandon his little boy like this! Pl-please, if you know where Gideon's body is, j-just tell m-me. I at least w-wanna give 'em a propa' burial. I'm b-beggin' y-you," she sobbed. "For the sake of my son, can you please t-tell me where his f-fatha' is?"

James's eyes began to glisten with moisture as he gazed at the heartbroken woman before him. "Carolyn, if I knew what happened to your husband, I swear I'd tell you. But I promise, I had nothin' to do with his disappearance. I mean that."

"You're a liar! You killed 'em to keep 'em from spillin' your despicable secrets!"

James shook his head. "Carolyn, that's not true, I …"

"STOP LYIN' TO ME!" she yelled, springing from her seat. The prison guard ran over and grabbed her when she began flailing and slapping James in the face. "YOU'RE A LIAR AND A MURDERER!" she continued to scream repeatedly as the guard pulled her out of the room.

James's stomach began to spasm violently after he was taken back to his cell. He agreed with Carolyn. Gideon had refused to abandon a town that needed his services, even after they had shunned him for taking such a young bride. So, James knew he was *definitely* not the kind of man who would ever abandon his wife and only son. Much like Carolyn, James was convinced that only one thing would have prevented a caring man like Gideon from returning to the family he adored … one very *permanent* thing. The mere thought of Lily having met the same fate had James on bended knee, vomiting violently into a pail. He felt like the last bit of his sanity finally came spewing out with the little food he had managed to ingest.

After completely clearing the contents of his stomach, James wiped his mouth and sat on the edge of his cot with his sweat-soaked face buried in his hands. The moment his face hit his hands an epiphany came crashing to the forefront of his mind. Gideon had suddenly made him think about the character of the people he knew well. Gideon would never abandon his family. William would never abandon Lily. And Harrison would never abandon *him* … not unless there was one damn good explanation. In that moment, it finally dawned on James that it was not *Harrison and William* who had turned their backs on him but, rather, the *entire town* of Fayetteville. James glanced at the toothless prison guard on duty, suddenly convinced that he and his counterparts had likely never mailed his letters in the first place.

The following day, James demanded that Mason request a change of venue for his trial. Weeks later, the judge smugly denied the request with a ridiculous excuse. When James saw the sly smirks exchanged between the judge and Mason, his suspicions about the entire legal system colluding against him were solidified. James was convinced that the gross negligence Mason was about to commit would *normally* be grounds to have an attorney disbarred, and that the judge's collusion would *normally* have him thrown from the bench. But in the *abnormal* case of the abominable sins of Dr. James Adams vs. Fayetteville, their gross miscarriages of justice would be revered and highly celebrated. That simple truth left James believing that the judicial system was about to honor the letters of every citizen who wished him a torturous death and a trip to the flaming pits of hell.

Chapter Three

September 10, 1860

"NIGGA' LOVIN' KILLA'! NIGGA' LOVIN' KILLA'" was the *heartfelt* chant being repeated by an angry mob of patrons to welcome James to the beginning of his journey to the flaming pits of hell. The trial was set to begin at 9 a.m. sharp, but James began hearing the choir of *God-fearing* townsfolk singing their *lovely* melody at 8:30 a.m., from literally a mile away. The chants grew louder as his paddy wagon drew closer to the town square. James could not be seen inside the covered contraption, nor could he see much out of its small window. But he knew immediately when he had reached the outskirts of the unruly mob. It was not the increased volume of their chants but, rather, the rocks and mud clods that began pelting the sides of the paddy wagon.

Once the dirt-covered wagon halted near the courthouse, a slew of deputies had to forcefully get dozens of citizens under control before they could even open the paddy wagon door to let James out. With shackles on his ankles and wrists, James needed assistance getting out of the wagon. The very second his head was visible, the crowd roared into another ferocious fit of hysteria. Several deputies held back the wild mob, while another one dragged James by the arm across the road toward the courthouse. James had once marched across that very same road and had a town full of women gazing hungrily at him while naughty thoughts rolled through their minds. Those same women now glared at him with lowered eyes of disdain while loudly condemning him instead. A gang of mischievous teenagers expressed their disdain by suddenly launching a hail of mud clods at James. Several deputies rushed over to stop them, but they were far too slow to react. By the time James reached the courthouse steps, his nice, tailored suit was speckled with brown stains. A city that had once deemed him as the town's most desirable man, were now clearly proving in the most despicable ways that they viewed him as the most hated.

James had earned the title of most hated man thanks in part to Mary Jo Parker. She had worked to elevate the town's hatred for James harder than she had ever worked at any other scheme in her life. The attention-garnering, sob story that she had sold to the masses had the town's emotions at a fever pitch by the time the first day of testimony was set to begin. Being that she was one of the star character witnesses, she wanted to be sure that everyone was eager to watch her well-rehearsed, dramatic performance on the stand. Her hard work had certainly paid off. Nearly the entire town was either inside or outside the courthouse. Many had gotten up before dawn to stand in line to get one of the few seats inside the courtroom to witness the drama firsthand. James was marched into a courtroom slap full of people, waving hand fans to ward off the cloud of musty, summer body heat that was stifling the air in the room. He was stunned to see that there was literally not one inch of space to give in any of the pews. He could have easily mistaken the scene for one of Lily's sold-out shows.

James was laughed at as he walked in with a multitude of mud stains on his suit, face, and in his hair. Jesse, J.R., and Jacob were at the front of the courtroom chatting with someone. The minute James walked in, the three men halted their conversation. While the rest of the courtroom patrons snickered and made snide remarks, Jesse and his two older boys silently glared at the black sheep of their family through lowered eyelids. They kept their eyes glued on James the entire time he was marched down the aisle. James walked the entire way ignoring the laughter and reciprocating the hateful glare. Just before entering the swinging door to the gallery, J.R. and Jesse blocked the aisle, refusing to let James get to his seat. James and his father stood with only a foot between them, their intense unblinking eyes speaking of how badly they wanted to torture each other.

"Step aside, gentlemen," the deputy escorting James announced.

Jesse and his boys finally stepped to the side and breezed out of the courtroom to wait in the holding room for their turn to be called to the witness stand. When they were gone, the deputy escorted James to his seat, unlocked his chains, and brought him over a towel to allow him to clean himself off before the proceedings began.

Not long after, the jury was led into the jury box and the bailiff called everyone to order. "All rise for honorable Judge Nathaniel Lucifer."

James scoffed at the adjective used to describe this particular judge. He felt he was the furthest thing from *honorable*.

"You may be seated," Judge Lucifer announced to the crowd after taking his seat.

James was way ahead of the crowd, though. In a blatant show of disrespect, he had remained seated as Judge Lucifer gallivanted to his throne. James had glared at him the whole way there while thinking there could be no better last name for a man who was clearly one of the devil's henchmen. He certainly felt like he was sitting front and center in the pits of hell, surrounded by demons. As opening statements were given by the prosecution, he looked over at the jury of people who were supposed to be his peers. James shook his head and scoffed at the much older men in the jury box. With the way the town had turned on him, he was not the least bit stunned to find that eight Ghost Riders and four well-known staunch defenders of slavery were "chosen at random" to determine his fate. He blew out a breath of frustration and tried to prepare himself to be slaughtered by the so-called justice system.

When the prosecution was finished painting James as a raging homicidal thief, Mason stood to give his opening statement. After colluding with the prosecution to ensure that they had an *extremely* biased jury, Mason now felt free to deliver the stellar defense showdowns that he was known for.

Mason Rockefeller was actually an incredibly gifted attorney … gifted in aesthetics as well. He was a youthful looking fifty-year-old man with salt and pepper hair, always wearing expensive suits over his lean body. His looks and intelligence had bred extreme arrogance and a level of narcissism that left no room for him to love a wife or children, both of which he did not have. He was far too busy loving himself, his career, and sleeping with an array of whores. Despite the hypocrisy of his sinful sex life, Mason considered himself above *everyone*, including every attorney who had ever dared to challenge him. His cases were not about justice but were to feed his ego by proving that he was far more intelligent and cunning than every attorney who crossed him. His ego thrived on such victories. The only exception to that rule was in cases where he was slated to defend any white man who had fornicated with a slave. Mason was a former northerner who had migrated to the south for the sole purpose of legally owning slaves. He, therefore, considered abolitionists and Negro lovers lower than the mud he forced his slaves to scrub from the soles of his shoes daily. Oddly, had James only been convicted of murder, Mason would never have colluded with the prosecution. He was confident he could have *easily* secured an acquittal against those whom he had labeled the M.P.A.F's: moronic, Podunk attorneys of Fayetteville. But hearing that James had allegedly impregnated a slave made him lower than the feces in an outhouse in Mason's eyes. Conspiring to condemn such a man to lifelong torture, or *preferably* a torturous death, was icing on the cake for his narcissistic ego, much more so than any victory.

And so, the courtroom show that Mason Rockefeller was about to put on today was just that ... a show. His theatrics were not about garnishing another esteemed victory but, rather, ensuring that the sort of bottom feeder he loathed would never again see the light of day, all while preserving his image as a stellar defense attorney. With that in mind, Mason strutted back and forth in his high-dollar suit during his opening statement, using his linguistic brilliance to enchant everyone, as he typically did. Even James began actively listening to the final portion of his attorney's opening statement when he became mystified by the words coming from his mouth.

"... and so, gentlemen of the jury, Doctor Jameson Michael Adams is far from a murderous monster, seeking to kill without reason. I will prove that this is a dignified man who was *forcefully* pushed to a breaking point, one which ultimately led to a need for him to defend his life and the lives of helpless people in an unjustified ambush. By the time this trial is over, the evidence will prove, beyond a shadow of a doubt, that James Adams is simply a man whose actions were as instinctive as any charismatic doctor who swore an oath to protect and care for those in need ... regardless of social class or race."

Mason's opening statement was so compelling, James slowly turned his head and stared at him when he was finished, as if a stranger had just sat down beside him. His performance had even managed to spark a bit of hope in James for an acquittal. When he looked back at the jury, however, that spark was quickly doused. It was an instant reminder that there was not a single impactful statement or vicious cross-examination that would sway the cemented racist minds of the men sitting there. He was certain that the "jury of his peers" had signed their guilty votes long before their posteriors were ever seated in the courtroom. Despite that fact, Mason and Judge Lucifer were ready to play their fictitious roles as law-abiding members of the judicial system. And so was Tobias Crumwell, the lead attorney for the prosecution.

When opening statements were over, the judge looked over at Tobias. "The floor is yours, Mr. Crumwell."

Tobias Crumwell was everything that Mason was not. He was a fifty-year-old short, red-faced, no-neck, bald man with the exception of a two-inch line of gray hair barely hanging on around the sides of his head. He could have easily been mistaken as a seventy-year-old man on the verge of death. He was swollen – *everywhere* – with a midsection that had obstructed the view of his penis for over two decades. The buttons on his cheap suits always looked like they were begging to be freed, and he tended to sweat profusely no matter the climate, much like he was now. Tobias dabbed his handkerchief on his forehead as he grunted and struggled to rise from his seat to call his first witness. "We'd like to call Jesse Roscoe Adams Junior to the stand please," he said as he waddled his way to the podium.

A bailiff went to retrieve J.R. from the witness holding room. He was escorted to the stand and took a seat after being sworn in. James shook his head and laughed quietly when he looked at his brother. It was the first time he had seen him with a haircut and clean shaven in years. He was doubly shocked to see that he owned a decent suit and even took the time to bathe and scrub years of layered dirt off his hefty body.

Tobias approached the stand after J.R. was sworn in. "You go by J.R., correct?"

"Yessa'," J.R. replied, actually sounding respectful and polite.

"Can I call you that here today?"

"Sure can."

"Okay, then J.R. Can you take us back to Tuesday, April seventeenth of this year? What were you doin' that day?"

"My brotha' Jacob and I were helpin' our fatha' with some work on his barn, but we needed some more wood. So, I went to Albert's General Store that afta'noon to pick some up."

"And what happened afta' you left the store that afta'noon?"

"I run into Mary Jo Parker."

"Who is Mary Jo Parker and how do you know her?"

"I know'd Mary Jo since she was born. Our fatha's did business togetha'. So, she's always been close to our family. In fact, at the time I run into 'er at Albert's, she was due to become an official part of the family."

"How so?"

"She was my brotha', James's fiancé. They were supposed to be married this month actually."

"So, it's safe to say you know Mary Jo well?"

"Yessa'. She was sorta like a close cousin."

"With the excitement of an upcomin' weddin', you must've found Mary Jo in a ratha' jovial mood that afta'noon at Albert's?"

"No sa'. She was upset and cryin'."

"Cryin' for what?"

"She had just found out that James was havin' an affair."

"With whom?"

"With Lily."

"And who is Lily?"

J.R. turned and sneered at James. "One of my fatha's slaves," he said with disgust in his tone.

His words evoked a low grumble of disgust from the audience as well.

"Quiet!" the judge ordered.

"Did Mary Jo give you details of the affair?" Crumwell asked after the courtroom was silent again.

"She gave me more than that," J.R. huffed. "She gave me a bunch of letters that James and Lily wrote back and forth to each otha' with details about the sort of *things* they were doin' in secret."

"Did you say letters that *Lily* wrote?"

"Yessa'. Lily wrote a letta' to James thankin' 'em for teachin' 'er to read and write."

"What otha' sort of details did you discova' in those letta's?"

J.R. looked over at James. "The fact that the baby Lily was carryin' was his."

Another round of gasps erupted from the crowd. The commotion brought forth a soft tap of the judge's gavel to silence the noise.

"Did Mary Jo also confide in you about that outside of Albert's store?"

"Yessa'. Mary Jo said she confronted James about the letta's when she found 'em. She said he demanded that she keep it all a secret."

"Did he threaten her in any way?"

"Yessa'. He said he had every intention on keepin' that little nig-... that *baby* on the plantation, no matta' what she had to say about it. Said he'd do unspeakable things to her fatha' if she didn't comply with his wishes."

James snickered and shook his head at how blatant his brother's lies were.

"Quiet Dr. Adams!" the judge warned.

James just stared back at the man, fighting the urge to tell him to shut the hell up.

"Continue Mr. Crumwell," the judge said after James's rude interruption.

"Did you tell your fatha' about any of this?" Tobias asked J.R.

"Well, I went straight to my fatha's plantation with the *intention* of tellin' 'em right away, but I ran into a little problem."

"And what problem was that?"

"I went into the kitchen..." He paused and cleared his throat. "Just to, uh, ask Lily for a glass of lemonade ... and she ended up stabbin' me in the arm."

"Lily? The same slave your brotha' allegedly impregnated?"

"Yessa'."

"Do you have any idea why she would do such a thing?"

"No sa', I just asked 'er for some lemonade and she pounced on me. It was like she was sick 'n tired of folks tellin' 'er what to do or somethin'. She suddenly flew into a rage and took it out on me."

The image of his brother in the kitchen with Lily that day had the rage inside of James brewing to near explosive levels, especially after the dismissive way he had just lied about his vile assault.

"What happened afta' Lily stabbed you?" Crumwell asked.

"I's tryna leave so I could get some help for my arm, but she just kept on attackin' me like a goddamn dog with rabies! So, I ended up tryna subdue 'er outside. She was kickin', scratchin', and flailin' so hard, my brotha' and fatha' had to run ova' and help me hold 'er down."

James was suddenly the one feeling like a rabid dog. Face red, jaw clenched, and huffing hard, he made a sudden move to rise from his seat toward his brother. Mason grabbed his arm before he was fully standing and shoved him back down in his chair. The bailiff drew his

41

pistol and aimed at James, leading to another uproar from the audience.

"Dr. Adams! Anotha' move like that and you'll spend the remainda' of this trial in shackles, do you unda'stand me?!" Judge Lucifer warned.

James refused to take his eyes off his brother or acknowledge the judge at first. Not even ten minutes into his J.R.'s testimony, he was ready to kill the man. Even though his homicidal visions continued to run rampant, James somehow managed to settle himself down. He snatched his arm away from Mason and straightened his jacket. "Yessa'," he finally replied, his bloodshot eyes still fixed on his brother.

J.R. returned the icy glare, discreetly licked his lips, and smirked at James as a way of telegraphing how much he had enjoyed "tasting" his woman.

The bailiff holstered his gun but continued to stand near James.

"You may continue," the judge commanded Tobias once all was calm.

"So, what happened afta' you were finally able to subdue Lily?" Tobias then asked J.R.

"It was then that I's finally able to tell my fatha' about Mary Jo's confession and the truth about James bein' the fatha' of the baby Lily was carryin'."

"How did Lily react afta' you told your fatha' about the baby?"

"She suddenly tried to attack me again, but my fatha' stopped 'er."

"Was he able to get 'er unda' control?"

"No! I'm tellin' ya', she was thrashin' like a wild dog. Ain't neva' seen a more disrespectful nig- ... *slave* in all my life! But my fatha' was kind enough to give 'er several chances to calm down. He kept askin' 'er stop, but she started kickin' and scratchin' 'em like a wild banshee."

"What did your fatha' do to stop 'er from assaultin' him?"

"He dragged 'er naked behind ova' to the whippin' tree to give 'er a few stripes across the back."

"How many times was he forced to whip 'er before she settled down?"

"I'd say it was only about three or four times before my brotha' James intervened."

"Intervened? How?"

"He came ridin' 'cross the fields on his horse, firin' his pistol at my fatha'."

"Did James succeed in shootin' 'em?"

"No. My brotha' Jacob and I pulled 'em off his horse and wrestled 'em to the ground."

"So, if it wasn't for you and your brotha's heroic actions, your fatha' might very well have been killed by James?"

"Yessa', that's true," J.R. boasted proudly.

Despite the truth in how he would have blown his father's head off, James did his best to stifle his laughter about the adjective used to describe his brother's actions that day. It came out as an angry snort, only heard by the bailiff hovering close to him.

"What happened in the hours afta' that incident, J.R.?" Tobias continued.

"My fatha' broke his hand while he was punishin' Lily, so Jacob and I took 'em to Dr. Whitfield to get it looked at and so I could get my arm stitched too."

"What happened when you returned to your fatha's plantation?"

"Me, Jacob, and my fatha' found James in the slave quarta's with Lily. He was holdin' onto a baby."

"To whose baby?"

"Lily's."

"So, she gave birth that evenin'?"

"Yessa'." J.R turned and glared at his brother. "But James *killed* it."

Low level murmuring rumbled through the crowd.

Had James eaten that morning, he likely would have vomited over his brother's sickening accusations. Instead, flashbacks of his daughter fading away in his arms flooded his mind and suddenly overflowed out his eyes before he could do anything about it. Pain had quickly outweighed the anger James felt over his brother's egregious lies. He lowered his head in sorrow, hiding his silent tears as they pelted the floor in rapid succession. Had his misery not felt like the weight of a mountain, he was liable to commit another bloody homicide in front of a court full of people.

"Did he say why he killed his own child?" Crumwell asked.

"He was screamin' at my fatha' like a madman, sayin' that he preferred for it to be dead than to be a slave on his plantation."

"So, your brotha' took the life of his own baby just to spite his fatha'?" Crumwell asked.

"Yessa'. He didn't want our fatha' to have what was rightfully his property."

"Did James also take issue with the fact that Lily was your fatha's rightful property?"

"Yessa'."

"Has James eva' gone to any extreme measures to infringe on your fatha's rights ova' Lily too?"

"Yessa'. Twice actually."

"Can you tell us about the first instance?"

"Last year, he lied to our fatha' and said he was takin' Lily to a slave breeda'. Instead, he took 'er to play pianah in some symphony."

"And who taught Lily to play piano?"

"James."

"So, your brotha' not only taught Lily to read and write, but even taught 'er to play piano?"

"Yessa'."

"Did your fatha' eva' condone James teachin' Lily any of these things?"

"Naw, neva'. He don't believe in educatain' nig- ... *slaves*. He abides strictly by the slave codes."

"When your brotha', James, took Lily to play in the symphony, how long was he gone with 'er?"

"Nearly a year."

"Did your brotha' eva' intend to bring 'er back?"

"Naw, my fatha' had to track 'em down and force 'em to bring back his property."

"And can you tell us about the second instance when James was attemptin' to infringe on your fatha's rights to Lily?"

"A few hours afta' James killed his baby, he took Lily and ran off with 'er somewhere."

"Has your fatha' been able to retrieve his property?"

"No sa'. We tried lookin' for her, but ain't none of us seen Lily since that night."

"Thank you, J.R." Tobias turned to the judge. "No furtha' questions, your honor."

James could barely bring himself to look at his brother after listening to a testimony riddled with egregious lies. However, he hoped that J.R. was not lying about the fact that their father had yet to find Lily. Knowing that Jesse had no access to her gave him some semblance of peace.

"Your witness, Mr. Rockefella'," the judge told Mason.

Mason got up from his seat and straightened his expensive suit jacket. He then strutted over to Tobias's table and just stared at him with his arms folded across his chest. Tobias just looked at him oddly, suddenly feeling self-conscious.

"Your witness, Mr. Rockefella'," the judge reiterated.

Mason still stood his ground and continued to stare at Tobias.

"Mr. Rockefella', what in the world are you doin'?" Judge Lucifer asked.

"I'm simply waiting for Mr. Crumwell here to add those incriminating letters to the evidence table," Mason answered. He then finally turned to look at J.R. "One would only assume that letters that carry such a great deal of solid proof would be lying right here," he said, slapping his hand down on the evidence table. "But alas! This table is empty!" He walked up to J.R. "So just where are those incriminating letters you speak of J.R. ... Can I call you J.R. too?"

J.R. did not reply.

"Well? Just where are they?" Mason asked again.

"When I went into the kitchen to confront that nig—" He cleared his throat. "To confront *Lily*, she snatched 'em from me."

"*Confront?* Confront her about what?"

J.R. adjusted in his seat and began to sweat. "I-I meant to say *ask* … not confront. I went to ask 'er for some lemonade and she snatched the letta's from me."

"So, you went in that kitchen just to *confront* … I mean to, uh, *ask* for a glass of lemonade?" Mason mocked.

"Yessa'."

"Well, if that's all you were there for, how in the world did Lily know that you had any letters with you?"

"Huh?" J.R. replied, already confused by his own lie.

"The letters! The ones you *allegedly* got from Mary Jo! Those *damning* letters that Lily *allegedly* snatched from you. How … did … Lily … know … you … had … them?"

J.R. was slowly turning red. "She, uh, saw 'em on the counter."

"You very clearly stated just thirty seconds ago that she snatched them from *you* … not the *counter*. So, which is it?"

"She-she. Well, I-I had laid 'em down then picked 'em up when I noticed she saw 'em. And, uh, that's when she snatched 'em from me."

"So just to be clear. You have incriminating criminal evidence. Instead of going straight to your father, you stop to *confront* … uh, I mean to *ask* Lily for some lemonade. You lay those important letters down right in front of her and she's able to read them while simultaneously pouring your lemonade?"

"Y-yessa'. She saw that I had 'er letta's, got mad, and pounced on me!"

"But a moment ago, you testified that she pounced on you like a rabid dog because it seemed she was sick of people telling her what to do. If it was truly the letters that ignited her anger, why not mention that in your testimony?"

"I, uh, forgot about that part."

"Forgot? If you've completely forgotten about an extremely important part of what happened that day, isn't it fair to say that the details of your side of the story aren't reliable?"

"Huh?" J.R. replied, looking thoroughly confused.

"Let me make the question a little more elementary for you! If you're so forgetful, why should the court believe you?!"

"Because I was there and I'm confident about what happened!" J.R. bit back.

"So confident that you completely omitted why Lily attacked you in the first place?"

"I just forgot for a moment! Everybody has lapses in memory, but for the most part I got an impeccable memory!" J.R. stated, wiping away the stream of nervous sweat now pouring into his eyes.

"Well, let's put that *impeccable* memory of yours to the test, shall we?" Mason smirked. "Since Lily allegedly told James she was with child in those letters, about how far along was she, according to the dates?"

"Uh ... I reckon she was about, uh, five ... no *six* months."

"You *reckon* she was six months along?"

"I had to recall the dates, but yes, accordin' to what I read, she was about six months along."

"And you stated that this six-month pregnant woman stabbed you after you *asked her for lemonade,* correct?"

"Yessa', got the wound to prove it!" J.R. replied confidently about the only true part of his story.

"After stabbing you, you stated that Lily didn't get any further than the front porch as she was fleeing with those letters in her hands, right?"

"Yessa'."

"So just what did Lily do with the letters between there and the front porch that caused them to be absent today?"

J.R. swallowed hard, his racing heart pumping sweat into the pits of his suit in buckets. "She-she, uh…"

"We have more witnesses to roll through, so we could use a lot less st-stuttering and a lot more a-answering here, uh, uh … J-J.R."

J.R.'s face was beet red with anger by the time he thought of a response. "She threw 'em into the fireplace!"

"So, there's a fireplace in your father's kitchen?"

"No sa'."

"Where is it?"

"The livin' room."

"Did she throw those imaginary…" Mason cleared his throat. "I mean, *incriminating* letters into the fire before or after she stabbed you?"

J.R. thought for a minute about how he should lie this time. "Afta'."

"So, I just want to be clear. A six-month pregnant woman puts her pitcher of lemonade down, snatched papers out of your hands, stabbed you, waddled with lightning speed to the living room, and then tossed the letters into the fireplace before you could do anything to stop her?"

"Y-yessa'," J.R. replied sheepishly.

His answer garnered a round of soft laughter from the crowd.

Mason turned toward the laughing audience. "Hell, I think I find it far more funny that a pregnant woman, who'd been slaving over a hot stove all day, had a fire going in the middle of a warm Virginia spring day … don't y'all?" he joked, unable to resist the urge to highlight J.R.'s stupidity.

"Keep it professional in my courtroom Mason," Judge Lucifer warned.

Mason nodded at the judge and turned to find J.R. staring at him with angry, bloodshot eyes. Mason smirked, enjoying the fact that he had put the tight-lipped grimace on J.R.'s podunk face. "So, you claim that Mary Jo Parker gave you those letters outside of Albert's store, correct?" he continued.

"Yessa'."

"How many letters were there?"

"Um, at least two dozen."

"How long did it take you to get to your father's house after Mary Jo gave you those letters?"

"About thirty minutes."

"So, within thirty minutes, you were able to read at least two dozen letters, and recall the details from every single one?"

"Yes! I read fast!"

"All while guiding your horse's reins, huh? Takes an awful lot of talent."

"I'm a talented man with an impeccable memory then I suppose!" J.R. replied, his annoyance now glaring.

"You've proven here today that sometimes you can have *slight* memory lapses about important details. So, I would like to give you the opportunity to run through that *impeccable* memory of yours just one more time. Are you *absolutely certain* that there was nothing else you did to motivate Lily's violent actions? Just asking for lemonade and some imagin– ..."

"Watch it Rockefella'!" the judge warned.

Mason gave his infamous sly smile. "Some *incriminating* letters and *asking for lemonade* suddenly turned Lily into a raging beast?"

"That's all it was!" J.R. replied, huffing and puffing.

"Well then, can you explain exactly how Lily ended up naked?"

"*Naked?*" J.R. replied, wiping another stream of sweat from his forehead.

"Yes, *naked.* Definition ... a person without clothes. Synonyms ... nude, bare, or unclothed," Mason mocked.

"I know what it means!" J.R. fired back.

"Just trying to help. You seemed a bit *ruffled* by the word," Mason sneered.

"Naw! Just don't know what the hell y'ur talkin' about?"

Mason's arrogant strut was suddenly more pronounced as he began pacing back and forth in front of his prey. "After you were stabbed, you say Lily ran and burned those incriminating letters. After which, you say a scuffle ensued that moved the both of you from the living room to the ground in front of the porch outside, correct?"

"Yessa'."

"After that, you told the court that your fatha', and I quote ... 'dragged her *naked* behind to the whipping tree.'" Mason stopped, rested his hands on the bannister in front of J.R., and leaned toward him. "How on earth did Lily end up *naked?*"

J.R. swallowed hard and shifted in his seat. "Don't rememba'."

"That memory of yours certainly isn't proving to be so *impeccable!*" Mason joked.

"It's just th-that it was all a blur. Me and Lily was fightin' awful hard and it all happened so fast!"

"Fought her way right outta every stitch of her clothing!" Mason turned to the audience. "That's the kinda feisty woman I like!"

Every audience member was laughing at Mason as he made light of the details of Lily's assault, but James was seething. Intense rage had gruesome visions of revenge saturating his mind, ones that far superseded the sort of barbarism his father was capable of.

When the crowd's laughter settled, Mason turned and glared at J.R. with disgust. "And you're still *certain* that it was only lemonade that you wanted out of Lily in that kitchen and not something else far more *satisfying?*" he asked smugly.

"I SAID I WANTED LEMONADE GODDAMN IT!" J.R. screamed, jumping to his feet.

"OBJECTION!" Tobias yelled. "He's badgerin' my witness, your honor! He's already answered the perverted question that Mason's insinuatin'!"

"SUSTAINED!" the judge yelled, banging his gavel repeatedly to calm the loud chatter that suddenly erupted amongst the audience. "QUIET DOWN!" When everyone was settled, he pointed his gavel at Mason. "Your first witness and y'ur already walkin' a fine line Mr. Rockefella'! Watch which side of that line y'ur steppin' on in my courtroom!" he scolded.

"Yessa', your *honor,*" Mason replied flippantly.

J.R. had turned to look at James after standing up. He slowly sat back down while still locked in a staring war with his brother. James was not the only one with his eyes fixated on him, though. Mason continued glaring at J.R. in disgust as he finally continued his line of questioning. "So, after your father dragged Lily's *naked behind* to the whipping tree, you claim your brother opened fire on him to try and stop him from whipping her?"

"Yes!" J.R. barked, his respectful facade now completely gone.

"But just like those incriminating letters, you don't have any spent shells here to prove it, do you?"

"No!"

"So, we just have to take your word for it, just like those imagin— incriminating letters."

"I ain't no goddamn liar!" J.R. spat.

"Of course you're not," Mason replied in his infamous condescending tone. "You also stated in your testimony that you wanted to immediately let your father know the contents of these alleged letters, correct?"

"Of course."

"Your brother, James, is a prominent town doctor who serves our community. With the content of those letters allegedly revealing his illegal conduct, why did you not report him to the sheriff first? If Mary Jo gave you those letters at Albert's store, as you stated, you were no more than one-hundred yards from the sheriff's office."

"'Cause Lily's my fatha's slave and James is his son. I wanted to know how he preferred to handle the situation," J.R. replied, sitting up tall after thinking of his lie so quickly.

"As the firstborn son, your father chose you as his namesake. J.R. stands for Jesse Roscoe, correct?"

"Yes."

"Despite being your father's firstborn and his namesake, which of his three sons did your father decide would be the executor of his estate upon his passing?"

J.R. felt his blood start to boil over the question. "James," J.R. answered, his irritation over that fact obvious in his tone.

"Did you agree with your father's decision?"

"No!"

"OBJECTION!" Tobias yelled again.

"For what Mr. Crumwell?" the judge asked.

"I don't see what this line of questionin' has to do with this case."

"There is *indeed* a point, one which I could get to if Mr. Crumwell wasn't so impatient!" Mason replied, turning to burn Tobias with his eyes.

"Overruled … but this betta' be goin' somewhere."

Mason nodded then turned his attention back to J.R. "Now, just who do you believe your father should've chosen to handle his estate upon his death?"

"I've clearly been my fatha's most loyal son. That answer is obvious."

"So, you felt as though it should've been you?"

"Yes."

"Do you think the illegal content in James and Lily's alleged letters would have changed your father's mind about who should be the executor of his estate?"

"If y'ur insinuatin' that I concocted this story for that reason then y'ur outta y'ur damn mind!"

"I'm not insinuating anything about your *lies* … I mean your *story*. I'm simply asking if you believe such information might have persuaded your father to revoke James's executorship?"

"OBJECTION!" Tobias interrupted again. "Your honor this witness is not a mind reader! He can't possibly know what his father would have done."

Mason glared at Tobias with annoyance beaming from his eyes. He then turned to the judge. "Your honor, it doesn't matter how his father would have *actually* reacted to this news. I'm asking this witness what *he thinks* the outcome may have been. Such a question is fair in determining his motives for telling his father about these alleged letters first and *not* the sheriff."

"Overruled. Answer the question Mr. Adams."

Mason glared at Tobias again until he slowly stuffed his wide posterior back into his chair. He then turned back to J.R. with a look of annoyance still on his face. "Again, after your father learned of your brother's illegal conduct, do *you* believe he would have changed his mind about who should be the executor of his estate?"

J.R. glared back at Mason with equal annoyance in his eyes. "No!" he replied, defiantly refusing to give him a truthful answer.

Mason let his glare of disdain linger on J.R. for a few seconds before changing the subject. "You claim that your brother, James, stole Lily from your father's plantation hours after your altercation with her in the kitchen, correct?"

"Yes."

"With your own eyes, did you see your brother take Lily off your father's farm that night?"

"No."

"If you did not see him, how do you know that he was the one who stole her?"

"Lily was unconscious the last time I saw her, and James was there with her. Ain't no way she could've run off without his help."

"Lily was *unconscious?*"

"Yes."

"You claim that your father whipped Lily three or four times that evening for misbehaving, correct?"

"Yes."

"Did your father also punch or kick her while punishing her?"

"He did what he had to do to correct her behavior!"

"I understand that. But I would like the court to have a clearer picture of the way you saw your father *correcting* Lily. So, did he *also* punch or kick her?"

"I don't recall!"

"Well, how exactly did he break his hand during their altercation?"

"I don't know!"

"If Lily was only whipped three or four times, as you testified, how did she end up completely *unconscious* as you just stated a moment ago?"

"My fatha' was well within his rights to punish his property the way he saw fit! That's all I have to say about that, now what's y'ur next damn question?!" J.R. barked.

"Just hours after your father *punished* Lily, you admit that she gave birth, correct?"

"Yes!"

"You also admit that Lily couldn't have been any further than six months along according to those letters, correct?"

"Yes! So?"

"Do you believe that the *punishment* your father inflicted might have possibly contributed to Lily giving birth early?"

"OBJECTION!" Tobias interjected again. "This witness is not a doctor or a midwife! He can't adequately answer a question of that nature."

"Sustained," the judge replied.

"You testified that you *think* James killed Lily's baby because he did not want your father to own it, correct?" Mason asked.

"Yes."

"So, you did not actually *see* him kill the baby?"

"No."

"In your lifetime, have you ever known of any woman who has given birth at six-months gestation and had the fetus survive?"

"Yes! Lily's!" J.R. turned to glare at his brother. "The little mutt she gave birth to was alive until James smothered it!"

A low rumble of whispers suddenly rippled through the crowd. The judge lightly banged his gavel again. "Quiet down please!"

"Your brother is a doctor who swore an oath to save lives, but you still think he would be capable of smothering a baby that you claim is *his*?" Mason asked, sounding stunned by such a notion.

"So what that he's a goddamn doctor! He's also a ragin' *lunatic* who's capable of any damn thing!" J.R. said, continuing to glare at James. "Looney fucker sat there cryin' ova' that damn dead baby afta' he murdered it!"

"He was holding a *dead* baby. I think any normal human being would get emotional over such a thing … Caucasian, Negro, or otherwise, don't you think?"

"Ain't nothin' but a goddamn piece of property far as I'm concerned. I'd cry ova' my dead horse 'fore I cry ova' a worthless dead nigga'!" he said, still staring at his brother.

James used every ounce of his strength to resist the urge to snatch the pistol off the bailiff's hip and shoot J.R. between the eyes.

"So, you admit that you never saw James murder Lily's baby? And you also don't have a confession from James or Lily about the baby's paternity, nor do you have any letters to prove who the child's father really was either?"

"I'm confident about what I read in them letta's, so I'm convinced the mutt James murdered was his!"

"And by the way you like to *ask for lemonade*, I'm just as convinced that that baby could've easily been *yours*."

"OBJECTION!" Tobias yelled, struggling to his feet.

"One more lewd innuendo and I'll hold you in contempt of this court!" the judge warned, pointing his gavel at Mason.

"No need for that, your honor." He glared harshly at J.R. "I'm finished with this witness."

"Any follow-up questions for Mr. Adams," the judge asked Tobias.

"No, your honor."

"You may step down Mr. Adams."

J.R. got up from the witness box and walked toward his seat in the crowd. Everyone in the courtroom could sense the extreme tension between brothers as J.R. made his way toward the gallery exit. All patrons watched his every step in total silence as J.R. got closer to James. Both glared at each other like two lions prepared to pounce. Sensing that a fury-driven explosive fight may be on the horizon, the bailiff took a step closer to James, ready to intervene. The courtroom collectively exhaled when J.R. breezed out of the gallery and sat down in his reserved seat in the pews.

Tobias finally struggled to his feet after the staring war between the brothers finally ended without a bloodbath. "I'd like to call Carolyn Whitfield to the stand," he announced to the court.

Meekly, Carolyn made her way from the witness holding room, through the gallery, and up to the stand. After being sworn in, she sat down, patted the tears from her eyes with a handkerchief, and took a deep breath to compose herself.

"Thank you for bein' here today, Mrs. Whitfield," Tobias began.

"You're welcome," she replied.

"You're Dr. Gideon Whitfield's wife, correct?"

"Yessa', I am."

"How long have you and Gideon been married?"

"Nearly six years."

"And you have a son together, correct?"

"Yessa', Brandon. He's almost three-years-old."

"And how do you know the defendant, Dr. James Adams."

"Gideon introduced me to him when he first came back to Fayetteville nearly two years ago. He worked with Gideon in his medical practice for a while."

"So, Gideon and James knew each otha' well?"

"Yessa'. Gideon helped deliva' James when he was born. He took care of him and his brotha's as they grew up. Afta' he came back from medical school, Gideon wanted James to take ova' his medical practice and to be his successor as the town doctor."

"Did the defendant, James Adams, come by your house the night of April seventeenth this year?"

"Yessa'."

"Can you tell the court exactly what happened when he stopped by?"

"Gideon and I were both startled awake by James poundin' on our door like a madman. Gideon was so startled by the way he was beatin' on the door that he grabbed his shotgun before he answered it."

"Do you know what James was there for?"

"No sa'. I's at the top of the stairs when Gideon answered the door, but I could tell James seemed awfully panicked. Gideon settled him down, then he reassured me that it was okay for me to go on back to bed. Then he stepped outside to speak with James in private, so I neva' got to hear what had him so frantic."

"Did Gideon go back to bed with you afta' James left?"

"No sa'. About twenty minutes lata', Gideon came back in the house and told me that there was an emergency he was goin' to tend to with James and that he'd be back in a few days. He said if anybody asked where he was, he wanted me to tell 'em that he'd gone on one of his usual medical mission trips to trade supplies and help otha' doctors. Then he kissed me goodbye and left."

"Did your husband eva' return home in a few days as he stated he would?"

Carolyn lowered her head. "No sa' … that was the l-last t-time I eva' s-saw him," she replied, her tears instantly returning.

"I know this is difficult Mrs. Whitfield. I'm sorry to put you through this. But do you think your husband would eva' be the sort of man to suddenly abandon you?"

Carolyn immediately raised her head. "NO! NEVA'! He loves me and h-he especially l-loves Brandon! He would *neva'* abandon his s-son!"

"What's the longest stretch of time your husband has eva' been gone on one of his medical mission trips?"

"On two occasions in the past, he was gone nearly four weeks. But he'd write to me at least once a week to let me know where he was and how he was doing and that he was thinking of me and Brandon. He's neva' been gone this long without communicatin', so I know in my heart somethin' ain't right."

"The night Gideon went with Dr. Adams is the same night that Willard McKinley, Jethro Blankenship, and Jeb McClintock were allegedly murdered by Dr. Adams, correct?"

"Yessa'."

"When you discovered that information, you went to speak with Dr. Adams in prison, correct?"

"Yessa'."

"What were you there to ask him?"

Carolyn suddenly turned toward James, her face red with anger. "I wanted to know if he murdered my husband too!" she screamed.

The crowd immediately erupted in low level chatter again. "QUIET!" Judge Lucifer warned, lightly banging his gavel.

"What was Dr. Adams' response?" Tobias asked after the chatter ceased.

"He cowardly claims that h-he doesn't know anything about my husband's disappearance!"

"No furtha' questions at this time, your honor," Tobias said, waddling back to his seat.

"Mr. Rockefeller, any questions for this witness?"

"Yes, your honor." Mason stood and strolled toward Carolyn, his confident bravado even more exaggerated in the presence of a woman. "Mrs. Whitfield, Dr. Adams was not the only person to come by your house on the night your husband disappeared, was he?"

"No sa'."

"Just hours before that, is it true that Jesse, J.R. and Jacob Adams all stopped by seeking medical treatment from Gideon too?"

"Yessa'."

"Were you nearby or assisting your husband in any way as he tended to them?"

"I was actually. I's fetchin' rags, wata', and tincture, that kind of thing."

"What was J.R. seeking medical attention for?"

"He had a stab wound in his arm that needed stitches."

"Did he say how he had sustained his injury?"

"I ova'heard him say a slave had stabbed him."

"Do you recall the name of the slave?"

"Yessa'. Said 'er name was Lily."

"Do you recall the reason she stabbed J.R.?"

"He said he asked 'er for some lemonade and she attacked 'em for it."

"Did J.R. mention anything about Lily snatching letters from him before the altercation?"

Carolyn shook her head. "No sa'. Not that I recall. He just kept sayin' that she erupted ova' somethin' as ridiculous as lemonade."

"Did J.R. mention anything about Lily being naked?"

Carolyn looked perplexed by the question. "Um, no sa'," she replied, her face suddenly red with embarrassment. "He definitely neva' said anything about her bein' nude."

"Do you recall the reason Jesse Adams needed medical attention?"

"Yessa'. Gideon said his hand was broken."

"Did Jesse say exactly how he might have sustained that injury?"

"I rememba' him sayin' that he was punishin' Lily for stabbin' J.R."

"Did he say that he punched her?"

"Not that I recall. He just said he was punishin' her. He didn't elaborate."

"Did you see Jesse's fist?"

"Yessa', actually, I did."

"Were there bruises or swelling on his knuckles?"

Carolyn swallowed hard. "Yessa', his entire right fist was bruised and swollen."

"In your opinion, did the bruising and swelling look to you as if they could have been sustained from excessively punching someone?"

"OBJECTION! She's no medical expert!" Tobias yelled.

"Sustained," the judge replied calmly.

"When Dr. Adams stopped by later that evening, did you ever see Lily in his possession?" Mason continued.

"No sa'."

"Did your husband ever mention that Lily was with James before he left with him that evening?"

"No sa'."

"You said you have a three-year-old son named Brandon, correct?"

"Yessa'."

"There was a time when your little boy was seriously ill back in January of last year. On the verge of death, actually, wasn't he?"

"Y-yessa'. That's true," Carolyn replied, her heart suddenly picking up pace.

"Your husband, who has been a doctor in this town for over forty years, was unable to figure out what was wrong with Brandon, correct?"

"Yessa'."

"Mrs. Whitfield, who was it that finally diagnosed your son's bizarre ailment?"

Carolyn sheepishly looked over at James. "Dr. Adams."

"And isn't it true that Dr. Adams paid out of his own pocket to purchase the necessary drug cocktail to treat your son's ailment?"

"Y-yessa'."

"Isn't it true that he mixed the drugs and administered it to your son as well?"

"Y-yessa'."

"Is your son currently healthy, Mrs. Whitfield?"

"Yessa'."

"Is it fair to say that you owe that fact to Dr. Adams?"

Carolyn swallowed hard. "Y-yessa'," she replied sheepishly.

"You admitted in your earlier testimony that your husband wanted Dr. Adams to be his successor as the town's doctor and to take over his medical practice, correct?"

"Yessa'."

"So, Mrs. Whitfield, please answer this honestly. Do you really believe that a man who has exemplified such compassion and trustworthiness would then maliciously shatter the heart of the little boy he saved by murdering his father?"

"W-well, y-yessa', I … m-maybe." Carolyn lowered her head in shame. "I -I don't know. A-all, I know is that he's the last p-person I eva' saw my h-husband with," she said as she broke down into sobs.

"No further questions, your honor," Mason replied, taking mercy on her.

"Any follow-up questions for this witness, Mr. Crumwell?" Judge Lucifer asked.

"No, your honor."

"You may step down Mrs. Whitfield."

As Carolyn was escorted to her seat, Tobias took a moment to go over his witness list. "We'd like to call Jesse Roscoe Adams Senior to the stand next," he then announced.

Judge Lucifer nodded and motioned for the bailiff to go and get him from the witness holding room.

Once Jesse was sworn in, Tobias began his line of questioning. Jesse was angry that he had not been allotted the opportunity to torture James in the way that he would the slaves at his rallies. He now sat in the witness box trying to torture him with his testimony instead. He responded with many of the same well-rehearsed lies as J.R. to ensure that James wore shackles like a slave for the remainder of his life. Listening to one lie after another made Mason eager to spill more podunk country-folk blood. Tobias's soft questions had guided Jesse to paint himself as an upstanding pillar of the community, but Mason was now ready to gut him and reveal the true monster buried beneath his bulging belly.

When Tobias was finished, Mason stood and looked at Jesse in silence, taking a moment to begin breaking him down with a cold stare. Jesse reciprocated the glare, unfazed by it in the least. Mason then stepped into the center of the gallery. "April seventeenth of this year, you just testified that you had to break up an altercation between your eldest son, J.R. and one of your slaves, Lily, correct?"

"Yes," Jesse replied flatly.

"You also admit that after breaking up this fight, J.R. informed you that the father of the baby Lily was carrying was your youngest son, James, correct?"

"Yes."

"Did J.R. explain how he had gotten that information?"

"Yes."

"How?"

"Mary Jo Parker told 'em."

"Did J.R. mention that he had also read about Lily's pregnancy in a letter?"

"I don't recollect."

"Mr. Adams, did you, yourself, ever see any letters that proved James had impregnated your slave, Lily?"

"No."

"Did you ever see any letters that proved that James taught Lily to read or write?"

"No."

"You just testified that you punished Lily after you learned that she had stabbed, J.R., correct?"

"Yes."

"You admit to whipping her that day as a form of punishment, correct?"

"Yes."

"Do you recall how many times you whipped her?"

"No!"

"In your testimony with Tobias, you said that you had to drag Lily to your whipping tree, correct?"

"Yes."

"Was that because she was unconscious?"

"I don't recollect!"

"Did you ever punch Lily with a closed fist that day?"

"I don't recollect!"

"Did you kick her that day?"

"I don't recollect!"

"Was Lily naked when you broke up the fight between her and your son?"

"I don't recollect!"

"Was she naked when you strung her up to the tree to whip her?"

"I don't recollect!" he fired back again.

Mason paused and glared at Jesse with annoyance when he continued his intentional repetitive defiant reply. "After punishing Lily, you testified that you left to see Dr. Whitfield, correct?"

"Yes."

"What for?"

"To get stitches for J.R. and to have my hand looked at."

"What did Dr. Whitfield say was wrong with your hand?"

"It was broken."

"Was that injury sustained while punishing Lily?"

Jesse scowled at Mason. "I! Don't! Recollect!"

"Was it bothering you before punishing Lily?"

"No!"

"Then is it likely to have occurred while in the midst of punishing Lily?"

"Maybe!"

"Have you ever broken your fist while simply whipping a slave before?"

"No!"

"Mr. Adams, is it possible that you broke your hand while punching Lily in the face?"

"Lily's my goddamn property! I can punish her how I see fit!"

"And I suppose you saw fit to break your hand across her face?"

"OBJECTION! He is way outta line with this questionin'!"

"Sustained! Move on Mr. Rockefella'!" the judge warned.

"Did you ever actually see James take Lily off your property the night she stabbed J.R.?"

"No!"

"Were you there when Willard McKinley, Jethro Blankenship, and Jeb McClintock were allegedly shot by your son, James?"

"No!"

"So essentially, you have absolutely no solid evidence as to any of the claims made against your son here today?"

"I don't need no goddamn evidence to know that he's a nigga' lovin', murderous, thief!" Jesse yelled, turning to glare at James.

"You're not very fond of the Negro race are you, Jesse?" Mason boldly asked.

"They're *property!* Ain't much thought about *niggers* past 'em bein' profitable chattel," Jesse replied just as boldly.

"You've been a lifelong slave holder, Mr. Adams, correct?"

"Yes."

"How do you typically punish any of your misbehaving slaves?"

"I follow the slave code guidelines. Dependin' on the offense they've committed, I give 'em as many stripes as the slave codes allow."

"You seem well-versed in slave punishment. So, is it typical for the slaves you punish to lose consciousness while you're whipping them?"

"They all react differently."

"But have any that you've personally punished ever lost consciousness that you can remember?"

"Not to my recollection."

"Have any of them ever *died?*"

Jesse suddenly froze and locked eyes with Mason.

Mason reciprocated the glare, walked toward the witness box, put his hands on the bannister, and leaned toward Jesse. "Have any slaves ever *died* while you were punishing them?" he asked again.

Jesse's scowl deepened, his eyelids lowered, and his lips pursed tighter. "I don't *fucking* recollect," he replied through gritted teeth.

"Now I see where your namesake gets it," Mason murmured as he walked over to his table. He picked up a document, cleared his throat, and began paraphrasing its contents. "According to this court document, back in 1825 at the age of sixteen, you were convicted of involuntary manslaughter and sentenced to one-month community service after the punishment you inflicted upon one of your father's misbehaving slaves ultimately led to his death." Mason laid the paper down and glared at Jesse. "Does that help you *recollect* that faded memory?"

"*Involuntary!* You read it! The court ruled it as an *accident!*" Jesse fired back.

Mason held up the sheet of paper again and read from it. "Seventy-three bruises, sixty-one stripes, ten missing teeth, two blackened eyes, a shattered jaw, a cracked skull, a missing tongue, and rope burns around the slave's neck were *all ... * an *accident?*"

"OBJECTION!" Tobias yelled. "He's already stated that the court ruled the death as an accident!"

"SUSTAINED!" the judge yelled. He then banged his gavel when the audience began audibly reacting to the savage list of injuries. "QUIET PLEASE!"

James stared at Jesse with his mouth partially agape. It was the first time he was hearing of a crime that proved his father lacked a conscience since birth. James then glanced at the judge and then over at the jurors. From what he was currently experiencing with the judicial system, he was not surprised that twelve soulless men had ruled blatant butchery as an *accident*.

"You testified that James tried to shoot you while you were in the process of whipping Lily, correct?" Mason continued.

"Yes!"

"Do you have any spent bullet shells from his gun to prove it?"

"I don't need no damn bullet shells to prove that nigga' lova' tried to kill me!"

"Well, given your record of *accidents* while *correcting* slaves … can you blame him?"

"OBJECTION!" Tobias yelled, struggling to his feet again.

"No need to rule, your honor," Mason said, still glaring at Jesse. "This witness is *finished*."

"Any follow-up questions for this witness Mr. Crumwell?" the judge asked.

"No, your honor."

"You may step down, Mr. Adams."

The courtroom immediately began buzzing as Jesse exited the stand. Harsh words were whispered about him while even harsher glares were aimed in his direction. But Jesse was oblivious to it all; he was locked in a hateful glare with James. After Jesse exited the gallery, James shook his head, wondering why God had yet to strike his father down.

"Your next witness Mr. Crumwell," the judge announced after Jesse took his seat next to J.R.

"I'd like to call Ms. Mary Jo Parker to the stand," Tobias replied.

When James heard that name, he massaged his temples and exhaled to help soothe his instant annoyance. He refused to even turn and look in Mary Jo's direction, knowing for a fact that she was probably going to enter the courtroom in a fashion that would be just as overdramatic as her testimony.

James's assumptions were spot on. Mary Jo Parker was paraded into the courtroom in a way the town of Fayetteville had come to expect of her. Instead of being escorted from the witness holding room by a deputy, her father was marching her down the aisle with his arm around her. He patted her gently on her arm with his other hand, trying to soothe his emotionally distraught daughter. Wearing an expensive dark dress, Mary Jo was nestled against her father's chest, dabbing at her puffy red eyes with a handkerchief, as if she were being escorted toward a casket. Joseph held his daughter all the way to the witness stand and kissed her on the cheek before turning her loose. Mary Jo then sniffled her way through being sworn in before taking her seat. James still had his forehead resting on his hand, trying to brace himself for the sort of heinous picture she was about to paint of him.

"Ms. Parker, I know it will be incredibly hard for you to testify, considerin' the topics we'll be coverin'. So, we appreciate you bein' here today," Tobias praised.

"I just had to find the strength to be here to help get justice for those poor families who lost their husbands and fatha's."

"And I'm sure they'll appreciate that," Tobias replied with a smile.

James scoffed and shook his head.

"Can you tell us how you know the defendant, Dr. James Adams?" Tobias started out.

Mary Jo exhaled and dabbed her handkerchief at the corners of her eyes before proceeding. "My fatha' has done business with the

Adams Plantation since before I's born. So, I've literally known James since I's a baby."

"Did you spend a good deal of time with Dr. Adams throughout your youth?"

"Yessa'. Several times in any given month, James and his fatha' would have dinna' at our place or we would have business dinna's ova' at their place from time to time. We also attended the same church, so we saw each otha' there on a regular basis too."

"Since you were around him so often throughout your youth, is it fair to say that you know Dr. Adams's characta' well?"

"Yes, I sure do. But…" Mary Jo suddenly began to tear up again.

"But what Ms. Parker? Go on."

"It's just that I wished I hadn't been forced to spend so much time with him."

"And why not?"

"James was as mean as a snake when we were kids. I can rememba' bein' so scared of 'em from a very early age."

"What sort of things did he do that made you so scared of him?"

"It started off as childish things, at first. When we were really young, he'd pinch me or put things in my hair or pull it when nobody was lookin'. He knew I's terrified of snakes and frogs and bugs, but he'd chase me around with 'em if eva' he found any while we were outside. It got to the point that I's afraid to be alone with 'em."

"Did you eva' tell your fatha' about any of his behaviors?"

"No. I's afraid James might take it out on me somehow. I didn't think my fatha' would believe me anyway, because James neva' misbehaved in front of 'em. It's like he knew how to straighten up and be decent when he needed to. Felt like he was always puttin' on a show for folks to make himself look like a gentleman. He was so good at pretendin' to be a little gentleman that my fatha' adored him. My daddy always went on and on about how he hoped James and I would get married one day. He always spoke highly of him … and I partially blame myself for that."

"Why would you blame yourself for James's actions?"

"Because I should've told my fatha' the way James really treated me when folks weren't watchin', so he could've done somethin' about it. If only I'd had the strength to tell 'em the truth, then maybe…" Mary Jo suddenly buried her face in her handkerchief and started to sob.

"I know it's difficult, Ms. Parker, but please, go on," Tobias prompted.

She held her head up again and blew out a calming breath. "If I'd've told my f-fatha' about all the h-horrible things James had done to m-me as a child, then perhaps…"

"Perhaps what?"

"Perhaps he wouldn't have f-forced himself on me when I w-was a teenaga'," Mary Jo sobbed, dropping her face down into her handkerchief again. She wept uncontrollably for nearly a minute as the crowd gasped and murmured amongst themselves.

James pinched the bridge of his nose, closed his eyes, and shook his head. He was damn near ready to give Mary Jo a standing ovation for her award-worthy theatrical performance. Considering the appalling nature of her character-destroying accusations, James should have been just as mortified as the crowd. But, oddly, he found the entire charade amusing. He suddenly leaned back in his seat and waited for the comedy show to continue.

"You kept that a secret as well, didn't you Ms. Parker?" Tobias asked after Mary Jo collected herself enough to continue.

"Y-yessa'," Mary Jo sniffled, dabbing at her tears with her handkerchief.

"Did the problems with Dr. Adams stop there?"

"No, they got worse."

"In what ways?"

"When James got back from university, it happened again."

"What happened again?"

"H-he." She dabbed her eyes again and took a deep breath. "I'm s-sorry, this is j-just so difficult to t-talk about."

"Ms. Parker, I know this is hard. It's okay. Take your time."

Mary Jo exhaled again. "James forced himself on me again afta' I found some letta's in his bedroom. I've neva' seen 'em so angry."

"Why did that make James so angry?"

"Because they were letta's that James had written back and forth with a slave on his fatha's farm, and they revealed intimate details of their love affair."

"What was the name of this slave?"

"Her name is Lily."

"Can you tell us some of the details you read in those letta's?"

"I can't even repeat some of the things they discussed. He and Lily were ramblin' on and on about the sort of inappropriate things that two unmarried individuals should *neva'* talk about, let alone do togetha'. A slave especially should *neva'* be allowed to say or do the sort of things that Lily was with her own masta'."

"I know this may be inappropriate to ask a woman to discuss, but it's necessary for this case. So, just for clarity, did James and Lily confess to havin' intercourse with one anotha'?"

74

"Yes! In the most graphic distgustin' ways possible! Turns my stomach to think about the sort of things they were doin' behind closed doors, in carriages, in hotels, outdoors in the dark, and while in bodies of filthy wata'. They were fornincatin' whereva' they could hide their abominable acts! But what disgusted me most of all was readin' that James was overjoyed by the fact that he had impregnated that nig– ... that *slave!*"

The crowd suddenly erupted in loud chatter again.

"QUIET DOWN!" Judge Lucifer warned, banging his gavel.

"Was that the only letta' regardin' Lily's pregnancy?" Tobias asked once the courtroom was silent.

"No! There were several letta's that they had written back and forth, discussing baby names and such," Mary Jo lied.

"Did Lily eva' mention who taught 'er to read and write?"

"Yessa'. I couldn't hardly make out what Lily wrote because her penmanship was so *god-awful!* But in the very first letta' I read, she was thankin' James for teachin' 'er to read and write. She also said she'd found some otha' book she wanted to stumble through readin' to 'em."

"Were there any discussions of love or marriage between the two of them?"

"James told Lily that he loved her in nearly *every* letta'! And he wrote constantly about his dream of marryin' her!"

"What happened when you confronted Dr. Adams about all these crimes?"

Mary Jo lowered her head onto her handkerchief again and began to weep. "H-he forced himself on m-me again. R-right then and there, he t-tore my clothes off and f-forced me onto the bed. He s-said h-he was gonna p-prove to me that he was in l-love with *me* and *n-not* Lily."

75

"And why didn't you go to the sheriff about this Ms. Parker?"

"B-because James threatened me. He told me to keep the letta's a secret and then demanded that I marry 'em, so that nobody would eva' suspect that he was the f-fatha' of Lily's baby. H-he told me that if I didn't do what I's told that he'd do somethin' to hurt my fatha'. And I l-love my d-daddy with all my heart. So, I w-wanted to do all I could to protect 'em."

James suddenly burst out in a fit of hysterical laughter. In his mind, the comedy show had just reached its pinnacle. He was doubled over holding his stomach, laughing until he damn near depleted himself of oxygen. The entire courtroom turned toward him, looking perplexed at the way he had leaned over in the throes of unrelenting laughter.

"I didn't hear any jokes Dr. Adams!" the judge scorned.

When James's laughter subsided, he looked directly at the judge. "Oh, I'm surrounded by jokes, your honor." He glanced at Mason. "My attorney's a joke!" He turned to the jury box. "The fact that these old racist bastards are supposed to be a jury of my *peers* is a joke!" His tone began to escalate when he turned toward Mary Jo. "The fact that I'd eva' wanna marry that spoiled, pale, self-centered, lyin', bitch is a joke!" He then stood up and turned toward the crowd. "This town is a joke!" He turned back to the judge. "THIS WHOLE FUCKING TRIAL IS A JOKE!"

"DR. ADAMS SIT DOWN!" the judge yelled, banging his gavel.

"THIS IS ALL ONE! BIG! FUCKING! JOKE!" he yelled, suddenly knocking Mason's papers onto the floor.

The bailiff and two deputies rushed over and subdued James just before he flipped the table over. The crowd loudly reacted to his sudden insanity, as they watched the deputies struggle to shackle him by the hands and wrestle him back into his seat. James was huffing and puffing and disheveled by the time they managed to calm him down.

Mary Jo glanced over at James, silently thanking him with a half-second smirk for an over-the-top outburst that helped validate her lies. "That's the exact same monsta' I'd see when everybody's back was turned," Mary Jo stated once her testimony resumed.

James caught sight of Mary Jo's evil glance and then could not bring himself to look at her during the remainder of her testimony. He turned his head and quietly listened to her tearfully succeed at being the character-crushing hero of the case. Mason got up to cross-examine Mary Jo when Tobias was finished, but James just grabbed him by the arm before he could take a step. "Don't botha'," James told him.

"Why not?" Mason asked.

"What's the goddamn point?" James glanced over at the jury and then back at Mason. "You're just delayin' the inevitable."

Mason glanced down into the face of a man who was clearly defeated. Knowing the crimes that he had committed, though, Mason felt not one ounce of sympathy. He snatched his arm away from James and turned to address the judge. "No questions for this witness, your honor."

Jacob testified after Mary Jo, regurgitating the same lies as J.R. and his father. Again, James stopped Mason from cross-examining him. Duke was next, further destroying James's character by retelling the humiliating story of how and why James had stabbed him in the scrotum. He then went on to detail his skewed version of why and how James had shot Willard, Jeb, and Jethro. Despite the outrageous lies in Duke's version of events, James still requested for Mason not to utter a word in his defense. James knew that it did not matter how cunningly Mason ripped each witness's testimony apart and collected mounds of reasonable doubt. Every time he glanced into the jury box full of his father's cowardly brethren, he was reminded that reasonable doubt was irrelevant in the final stages of their witch-hunt to legally hang a white man who loved a slave. James had, therefore, accepted his fate. He could no longer go on actively listening to the charade that was supposed to be a *fair* trial in front of a jury of his *peers*. So as Duke and Jacob helped drag him closer to the pits of hell, James had escaped into his fantasies. He closed his eyes and envisioned Lily at the piano, soothing his troubled mind. As the trial of the century sieged on around him, he was listening to the beautiful song that Lily had written for him. But before the town of Fayetteville gave him the final boot into the eternal pits of hell, James Adams wanted to sit in the confessional to clear his conscience.

When Tobias rested his case, James slid a piece of paper over to Mason. "Ask me these questions," he leaned over and said quietly.

"What?" Mason replied, looking confused.

"Put me on the stand and ask me all those questions," James explained, pointing to the paper.

Mason quickly read what James had written. "I'll have to advise you against taking the stand to address any of this. You'll be vulnerable to Tobias's cross-examination."

"I don't care."

"Well, when he questions you just deny everything. They have no true evidence against you," Mason said softly.

"Don't tell me what to do. Just put me on the goddamn stand!" James replied in a harsh but hushed tone.

"You're just as insane as you are stupid, boy!" Mason whispered back in an equally hushed, harsh tone.

"And you're just as crooked as this bullshit justice system. The eight Ghost Rida's you colluded with the prosecution to get in that damn jury box is proof of that! I'm obviously the only person in this room who gives a shit about my own defense or *true* justice for that matta' … so just put me on the goddamn stand and shut the hell up!"

Mason leaned over and whispered in James's ear. "Have fun hanging yourself … *nigger lover.*"

"The ghost ridin' racist bastards you put in that jury box had my noose ready long before I eva' walked through these doors," James replied smugly.

Mason finally snatched the list of questions and rose from his seat while still glaring harshly at James. "Your honor, my client here would like to take the stand in his own defense."

"Dr. Adams, have you conferred with your counsel about that?" the judge asked, looking at him in a puzzled manner.

"He has, your honor."

"Fine then." The judge turned to the bailiff. "Remove his shackles and escort 'em up here." The bailiff nodded and did as he was told. After being sworn in, James took his seat in the witness box.

Mason stepped to the podium and looked over James's list of questions again. He then approached James in the witness box and stared at him harshly for a moment before proceeding. "April seventeenth of this year, where were you that Tuesday afternoon?"

"Workin' at Gideon's clinic, did some shoppin', and then got an *unwanted* visit by MJ."

"Who is MJ?" Mason asked, genuinely looking confused.

"Mary Jo Parker."

"Do you call her MJ as a term of endearment?" Mason asked, veering from James's line of questioning.

"*Endearment?* There's not a damned thing endearin' about that lyin', connivin' *whore!*" James fired back, turning to look directly at Mary Jo.

The crowd gasped at his harsh terminology.

"Strong words, Dr. Adams."

"*True* words," James quickly fired back.

"Are you calling Ms. Parker a liar because you feel as though there is no truth to any of the claims she's made here today?"

James scoffed. "Yes! Nearly *every* word from her mouth on this stand unda' oath was a damned lie! The one thing in her testimony that Mary Jo and I can both agree on, though, is wishin' that we neva' had to spend a single minute with each otha' ... *eva'!*"

"Well, let's decipher the portions of her testimony that you felt she lied about. Let's start with her claim that you raped her as a teenager."

"A despicable lie!" James answered quickly, still looking dead at Mary Jo. "The mere thought of her nude body would deflate my erection in a heartbeat!"

His explicit honesty garnered another round of loud gasps from the audience.

"How about the second allegation of rape?"

"An even more despicable lie! That whore couldn't *pay* my penis to be erect in her presence!"

This time the audience's gasps were blended with an eruption of laughter. Mary Jo's face darkened into a deep red as she sneered at James. James reciprocated with an evil smirk as he continued to glare coldly at her.

"QUIET DOWN!" Judge Lucifer yelled to the audience.

"How about the claims that she found incriminating letters in your room?" Mason continued.

"That part is true. Mary Jo was *trespassin'* in my bedroom. She dug through my personal belongings without my permission and found them."

"Were the letters written by you and Lily?"

"Yes," James stated boldly.

Tobias suddenly stopped taking notes, pushed his spectacles up, and looked at James. Mason paused and looked at James oddly, annoyed that he had wasted his time proving that there was no proof of any letters exchanged between the pair. "And did you threaten to harm Mary Jo's father if she didn't marry you and keep the secrets divulged in those letters?"

James looked right at Mary Jo. "I'd ratha' shoot myself than marry that woman. It was *Mary Jo* who threatened *me* with those letta's. She said she'd divulge all the information in them if I didn't do what she wanted."

"And what is it that Mary Jo wanted?"

"For *me* to marry *her.*"

"And so, you admit that there were incriminating secrets in those letters?"

"*Secrets?* Somewhat. *Incriminatin'?* No."

"What do you mean?"

"I suppose you could consida' them secret, but only because they were meant to be *privately* shared intimate thoughts between Lily and me. But I don't agree with them bein' incriminatin' because that would imply that I was doin' somethin' wrong. I don't give a damn what the backwards laws state. There was nothin' *wrong* about any of the intimate experiences I shared with Lily. So, while you say those letta's were *incriminatin' secrets.* I say they were *private* and *sentimental.*"

Mason paused again. He had never looked at a client with such aggravation easily readable on his face. "Well, did these so-called *sentimental private* letters mention anything about you teaching Lily to read or write?"

"Yes, they sure did," James replied proudly.

There was a slight murmuring from the crowd over the ease of James's confession.

Mason slowly lowered his eyelids and huffed, beyond annoyed by his client's honesty. Despite how Mason was scolding him with his eyes, James's facial expression softened as he thought of Lily. "Teachin' Lily to read and write is one of the accomplishments I'm most proud of in my life, actually," he admitted, as a faint smile emerged on his face. "Lily's first letta' to me was beautiful. I still rememba' every word. Mary Jo was right. Lily thanked me for helpin' 'er learn to read. She told me she was excited to read a new book she'd found … *Oliva' Twist*. She sat in my arms out by a lake and read it aloud to me lata' that week. It's one of my fondest memories," James said, the lost look on his face proving he was reliving the moment in his mind.

Mason stared at James with his mouth partially agape along with the rest of the crowd. "So, you're openly admitting that you taught a *slave* to read?" Mason asked, a look of disbelief still firmly planted on his face.

"Are you dense?" James asked, finally returning from his memory and glaring at Mason. "I think I was just very clear about that!"

Mason shook his head and scoffed. "So, did any of the letters you exchanged with Lily prove that you impregnated her?"

"No. Definitely not. Mary Jo lied about that part. Lily neva' divulged that in any letta's." James suddenly paused again while recalling the day Lily had accidentally confessed. "She told me herself."

The gasp from the crowd was much louder this time around. Everyone suddenly began looking oddly at each other, unsure what to think. Mason furrowed his eyebrows and pinched the bridge of his nose. "So, you're openly *admitting* that you impregnated *a slave?*"

"A *slave?*" James scoffed. He slowly let his eyes sweep across everyone in the crowd. "That's all Lily is to any of you, isn't she? Just a piece of property?" he asked, as he continued to stare at the audience. "A *slave* ... beneath you, menial, transparent, some meaningless animal not worthy of love or respect ... or even the simple right to learn to read? I wonda' if there's a soul in this audience who eva' thought to view Lily as human." He slowly looked into some of the eyes that stared unblinking at him. "Lily's *human* ... by far the most beautiful I've eva' known, inside and out. She's intelligent, funny, charismatic, courageous ... and fast! *Damn* fast! I could neva' beat 'er in foot races as a kid! She made me feel like a damn cripple! And she's one hell of a fisherman ... I mean, fisher-*woman!* I can hear Lily in my head correctin' my choice of words. She always wanted to make it clear that a woman could reel in more fish than a man. And she wasn't lyin'! She could catch enough fish to feed a family of five while I'd probably die of starvation on the damn boat!"

The audience could not help but to chuckle.

"And *gifted,*" James smiled. "Lily is a truly gifted, brilliant pianist. You could play the most challengin' song for her just one time, and she could play it back flawlessly on the piano. Hell, forget human. Her unique abilities would make you think she was not of this world. She's composed hundreds of beautiful songs inspired by unforgettable moments in her life. Her music was unlike any I've eva' heard before. Her music and 'er talent made a world renowned composa' believe she was deservin' of her own show. He, in turn, made Lily believe in *herself* ... until she built the strength and courage to share her musical brilliance with an audience. With her newfound bravery and 'er incredible creativity, she indeed created a theatrical masta'piece. Every song, every dance, every magical scene in the show was inspired by her dreams and the unforgettable moments of her life. She called it *The Dream Symphony.* Her show became an ova'night sensation. It gained a level of popularity that none of us could eva' have anticipated.

I've neva' seen a phenomenon like it eva' before in my life … doubt I eva' will again. There was such demand to see 'er show that Lily began tourin' around the country, playin' one sold out show afta' anotha'. Hordes and hordes of people lined the streets hopin' to get tickets to see 'er perform. Every single person who was lucky enough to buy tickets would tell you the money and the wait to see Lily was well worth it. You'd neva' get an argument outta me about that … every minute of 'er show was mystifyin'. I have great respect for composa's like Mozart, Beethoven, and William Werthington. But *Lily* will be the beloved musical legend who's talked about for centuries to come … she's just that phenomenal."

James's elegant words about Lily's show alone seemed to have mystified his current audience. As James briefly paused, they sat in respectful silence, looking completely entranced, begging with their eyes to hear more.

"But Lily will be loved and talked about by me for far more sentimental reasons," James continued. "In the midst of a tumultuous childhood, she was the one I escaped with on fantastical adventures. As a teenaga', she always managed to make my hellish surroundin's feel like paradise. Lily's the one whose shoulda' I literally cried on when my motha' died. It was Lily's arms that comforted me in the darkest days of mournin' my motha's loss. Lily's the only reason I didn't put a bullet through my brain afta' I found my motha' dead. In my eyes, Lily's *neva'* been just a slave or a pianist. She's the one and only beautiful reason I felt my life was still worth livin'. She motivates every single thing I do … even breathin'. She's my greatest confidant, the love of my life, and my very best friend. Quite simply … she's the best thing that's eva' happened to me." James glanced over at his father and brothers. "Lily was more family to me than any of you eva' were." He turned to look at Mary Jo. "And she's more of a lovin' and loyal wife to me than you could eva' *dream* of bein'."

"*Wife?*" Mason suddenly spat, his annoyance escalating. "So, you're also openly admitting that you *married* her too?"

"For the beautiful childhood that Lily gave me, for all the times that she made me laugh when I didn't feel like I had any reason to, for comfortin' me in my desolate moments, for givin' me hope when I felt hopeless, for all the times that she's inspired me, for the unconditional way that she loved me durin' times when I didn't even love myself … *yes!*" James looked straight at Mason. "You're *damned* right I married her!

"Lily naturally motivated me to be the best man that I could be for her. I wanted to provide for her and protect 'er with every ounce of strength in my body." James looked directly at his father and lowered his eyes. "The way a *real* man should for the woman he *claims* to love." He turned back toward Mason. "I wanted to fight to give Lily an extraordinary life. I wanted to vow to spend the rest of my life lovin' her the way a beautiful, charismatic woman like her deserves. And so, in a sentimental ceremony, I did just that. Beneath the stars of a midnight sky, unda' God's watchful eyes, standin' in the very place where I first fell in love with 'er, I committed myself to Lily for an eternity."

Staring into nothing in particular, James smiled at the memory. He was so lost in thought that he was completely unaware of the stunned look on every patron's face as they stared at him. Tobias finally dropped his pen after realizing that he wasn't even going to need to cross-examine a man who was so easily divulging the sort of things that he would normally need to torture out of him.

Mason's narcissism had now led his annoyance to escalate into anger after the abysmal waste of his defense strategies were now blatantly evident. "So, I suppose now you'll even *proudly* admit that conceiving an *illegitimate* child with *a slave* was *intentional?*" he asked with malicious disrespect.

"*Illegitimate?*"

"Yes! Your marriage isn't legal, so your baby is indeed *illegitimate!*"

"Why is the marriage illegal?"

"Are *you* dense?" Mason replied smugly. "There's a law on the books against it."

"I unda'stand that … but *why?* You're such a *brilliant* legal scholar," James replied just as smugly. "So, explain to me the *logical* reason why a law was eva' created that makes it illegal for me to marry the woman I love? Am I hurtin' Lily? Will she die? Will I die? Get sick? In fact, will anybody in this room be adversely affected or suffa' in any way because of whom I vow to spend the rest of my life with? Give me just *one* logical explanation, oh *wise* counsel," James stated, sarcasm heavy in his tone.

Mason's brilliant scholarly mind was rapidly searching for an answer or at least a flippant response in return. The way he looked down, his eyes quickly darting left to right, made it look as though he thought he might find the answer somewhere on the floor.

"Oh, *wise* counsel, the court could use a lot less hesitatin' and a lot more explainin'," James replied, mocking Mason's condescending ways.

"I'm not the one on trial here!" Mason finally thought to say, his courtroom professionalism now completely gone.

"No worries, my *genius* counsel. You are not alone in your *failure* to spew your linguistic brilliance upon hearing that question. I have yet to find a single intellectual who has a *logical* explanation for that." James furrowed his eyebrows and leaned toward Mason. "Not *one.*"

"You can *attempt* to be clever and all you want! That doesn't change the fact that, in the eyes of the law, your *dead* baby was an *enslaved mulatto bastard!*" Mason maliciously insulted.

"My baby was not a bastard!" James angrily fired back, glaring hatefully at Mason. "She was a *miracle!* Just like every *human* born on this earth! And yes! I *proudly* admit that I had the great fortune of creatin' that tiny *miracle* with *my wife!*"

James's mind drifted to that very woman again and his facial expression immediately softened, along with his voice. "I's nearly brought to my knees with joy the day I found out I was gonna be a fatha'. Lily had initially wanted to surprise me with the news in the most unique way. She said she had this little sculpture created of me and her sittin' unda'neath the tree we used to climb togetha' as kids. There was a stack of books next to us. I used to read to Lily when we were younga' and then we'd act out the scenes we read. Lily always portrayed one hell of a pirate. If our sticks were real swords, my body would still be covered in old puncture wounds," James laughed lightly, along with the audience. "In the sculpture, we were holdin' onto Wilbur, a turtle Lily and I named and played with all the time. On the base of the sculpture, Lily said she had the artist engrave the words, *as children, we bonded ova' the life of a very special friend and now the beautiful life we have created togetha' will cement that unique bond for an eternity.* Lily wanted to give it to me as a Christmas gift, but she had an altercation with my fatha' backstage afta' he found out about 'er show. He snatched 'er by the arm to drag 'er outta the theata', and she dropped it and broke it. I neva' did get to see it, but I didn't let that take away from the excitement when Lily finally told me I would soon be holdin' my first born," James said, his emotions now beginning to stir.

"I had neva' looked forward to a day with such euphoric excitement runnin' through me eva' before in my life. All day, every day, all I could think about was the moment I'd finally get to hold my little baby, to finally look into the eyes of the miracle my best friend had blessed me with. I's certain my own eyes would be far too full of tears to see clearly, but I knew I'd be ova'come with joy just to hold him or her close to me." James suddenly smiled. "Him or her? I rememba' Lily and I used to playfully argue about who was growin' inside of her. Lily swore it would be our first son. My vivid dreams convinced me it would be our first daughta'. *Daffy*. That's what I used to jokingly call the baby. It was short for Daffodil. Lily found it amusin'. But I truly did want to name all my girls afta' flowa's, just like their motha'," James smiled.

"April seventeenth of this year, I learned that my dreams had literally come true. Rose was the real name I chose. Rose Elizabeth Maya Adams. Her middle names were in honor of both of her lovin' grandmotha's. My firstborn was by far the greatest gift I'd eva' been given. The joy of holdin' her couldn't compare to what I imagined it would feel like. I knew I was gonna love 'er, but I had no idea the love was gonna hit me like a freight train." James wiped a tear out of his eye before it had a chance to fall.

"With the most indescribable love runnin' through me like wildfire, I held Rose in my arms, thinkin' about all the things I wanted to experience and share with 'er as she grew up. I had hoped Lily would teach 'er to play piano. I wanted to teach 'er how to fish. I had hoped she'd be my fishin' buddy. Lord knows I needed all the help I could get to beat Lily," James laughed lightly, along with an audience that was just as entranced by his story as he was. "I wanted to be the first man to eva' dance with 'er and to give 'er her first sentimental piece of jewelry. I wanted to teach 'er how to swim. I wanted to build 'er a treehouse … the biggest damn treehouse you've eva' seen in your life. I wanted to climb up there with 'er and read 'er all the stories that Lily and I had read togetha' as children. I had hoped to buy 'er a telescope, so she could gaze out at the stars at night with Lily, the way Lily and her motha' used to do togetha'." James tilted his head back and closed his eyes to see the visions in his mind more clearly. "While Rose was up there in that treehouse, I wanted 'er to feel like a princess … *my* princess, lookin' down at me from her towerin' castle in the sky." He paused, opened his eyes, and gazed at the floor. His tears pelted his lap, much like dozens of women in the audience who unexpectedly found themselves equally overcome with emotion ... even the wicked eyes of Mary Jo Parker were leaking genuine tears.

"But I'll neva' get to experience any of those moments with Rose now ..." James shook his head to ward off the rising tidal wave of emotion in his chest. "She came into the world three months before she eva' should have. And less than an hour afta' she was born, sh-she took 'er l-last breath in my a-arms. I swear, I c-couldn't breathe eitha'," he said, struggling now to find his breath. "Felt like s-somebody ripped my h-heart clean outta my chest." With his head still hanging low, James paused and exhaled to collect himself. "I was s-so eaga' to g-get to know who Rose was and to l-learn what all her hopes were. I w-was so ready to do a-any and everything I c-could to help 'er achieve her dreams as she blossomed into a beautiful young woman. But none of that will eva' happen now..." James suddenly raised his tear-stained face and glared at Jesse. "Because my fatha' *MURDERED HEEER!*" he suddenly erupted, his face red with rage.

All heads in the audience quickly swiveled toward Jesse in time to watch his eyes lower into hate-filled slits as he glared at his youngest son.

The view of his father started to blur when James's eyes suddenly began to burn with tears. "My fatha' tried to break every bone in Lily's body when he found out her baby was mine! That bastard *killed* my little baby!" he said, still glaring at Jesse. "Rose was anotha' one of his casualties! He added my daughta' to the long list of people he's murdered in his life! Includin' my motha'! It was not a *horse* that trampled my motha'!" He pointed to Jesse. "He's the *animal* who savagely *murdered* her!"

The mouths of those glaring at Jesse began to fall open.

"I stood outside his bedroom as a boy and listened to that monsta' beat every breath outta my motha's body! That sick bastard killed his own *wife!* For twenty years, he beat 'er senseless and cut 'er to pieces with words! He killed her soul! He killed her spirit! He killed her in every possible way that you could kill a person before literally takin' 'er life with his bare hands!" James revealed, as he stared Jesse down. "And Lily was next on my fatha's death list! He tried to stomp the life outta Lily for carryin' my baby!"

"Did you try to shoot your father for that reason?" Mason interjected.

"YOU'RE GODDAMN RIGHT I DID!" James yelled. "That demon doesn't deserve to breathe!" He then turned and glared at his brother. "I'd've shot J.R. next for *rapin'* my wife that day! Lily had every right to stab you! She should've slit your throat, you slitherin' piece of shit!"

Judge Lucifer began banging his gavel when the reaction of the crowd began to sound like an eruption of thunder. "ORDER!" he yelled repeatedly. "Watch your tone and your language in here Dr. Adams!" Judge Lucifer warned once the crowd managed to settle.

James ignored him and continued reciprocating his father's icy glare.

"So, opening fire on your father was solely motivated by a need to defend Lily?" Mason asked.

"Yes! And there's not an ounce of me that regrets tryna' blow that creature away!" James confessed, still glaring at his father.

"*Creature?*" Mason questioned.

"Jesse Adams is *not* a man! He's *Satan* in the flesh! That evil bastard forced me to watch 'em butcha' a slave to death! Piece by bloody piece, he dismembered 'em alive! To this day, I can still hear that man's hauntin' screams in my nightmares!" James yelled, covering both his ears. He then turned toward the jury box. "And every racist bastard sittin' in that jury box was there to witness it! Satan's henchmen were hootin' and hollerin' and firin' guns in the air, like they were celebratin' at a goddamn New Year's party! I've neva' seen such savage barbarism in all my life!" James glared at his father again. "That creature tortures and kills for sport! And its goddamn entertainment for every subhuman piece of shit sittin' on this jury!

"And Jethro, Willard, Jeb … they were all there raisin' their beer mugs high afta' my fatha's so-called justice too! And *they* were the three henchmen my fatha' sent to drag Lily back to his barbaric playground, so her torturous death could be their night's *entertainment!* They were gonna raise their beer mugs high in the air and dance around 'er burnin' dead body like they were at a goddamn hoedown!"

Jesse and J.R. finally began to turn and sneer back at the people in the courtroom as they suddenly began mumbling obscenities to both of them.

"ORDER!" the judge yelled, banging his gavel. "SILENCE!"

Lucifer's repeated demands were drowned out by the loud chatter rippling through the courtroom. Horror was etched on everyone's faces as they verbally reacted to the allegations made against Jesse and J.R. All the while Jesse and J.R. sat as still as statues, their faces fiery red as they glared at James for divulging their family secrets. Everyone there was shocked by the revelations except for Sheriff Clemens. He was wishing James had had this level of bravery as a boy. His graphic testimony would have confirmed what Clemens believed had happened to Elizabeth when he investigated the case. He would have stopped at nothing to put Jesse in a place where he would never have been able to cause James to suffer yet another devastating loss in his life.

When the crowd finally settled, Mason asked the final question on James's list. "Did you shoot Willard, Jethro, and Jeb the night your father sent them to search for you and Lily?"

James took a deep breath to compose himself and turned to look at Carolyn. "I didn't kill your husband, Carolyn. I swear I didn't. Jethro had a gun to Gideon's head, threatenin' to kill 'em if we didn't turn Lily ova' to 'em. It was *Jethro* that I shot to stop 'em from shootin' Gideon. I don't know what happened to 'em afta' that Carolyn, I swear! I'm as devastated as you are about that because my Lily was with 'em."

Carolyn nodded, then buried her face in a handkerchief and began to weep quietly.

"Willard was climbin' in the wagon to take Lily away and Jeb was chasin' us down too," James continued. "So, I did what I had to do to stop 'em all from draggin' Lily back to their torture camp. I couldn't bear the thought of 'em doin' things to her that I've witnessed them do to otha' innocent people. There's not a man in this courtroom that would stand by and allow someone to torture his wife to death in such a way." He turned to look at Jesse. "Except for the demonic creature who fathered me! He'd just do the honors *himself!*"

Jesse pursed his lips tighter and furrowed his eyebrows, deepening the fire-red hue on his face.

James turned to the audience again and blew out a breath. "So yes, I shot 'em all." He turned to the section where Willard, Jeb, and Jethro's families were. "To all of you, I'm so sorry that your husbands, sons, fatha's, and brotha's won't be a part of your lives anymore, but I'm certain that even *they* would not have allowed any of you to be tortured without a fight. They would've defended the people they loved … the way I did."

James let his eyes sweep across the audience again. "I don't regret the way I defended Gideon from men who wished ill will upon him that night. Nor do I regret the fact that I was defendin' my wife from an unjustified torturous death. In fact, there's no punishment you could eva' give me that'll make me regret protectin' and lovin' Lily the way I *always* have and *always* will … not even if I'm condemned to die for it."

Within just one hour after closing arguments, Jesse's brethren gave James that very sentence. The foreman of the Ghost Rider posse read the verdict with an air of pride, knowing James would die by hanging, the way they felt every "nigger lover" deserved to die. James was shackled right then and there to officially begin his stint on death row. The deputy took him by the arm and began guiding him out of the courtroom. Surprisingly, though, the snide remarks from the audience were absent this time. Nothing but James's chains could be heard as they clinked and scraped the ground. The looks of empathy from men and the red puffy eyes of all the women there were proof that James had achieved a small victory after his testimony. The moment of silence seemed to prove that he had succeeded in transferring Fayetteville's hate to the one true man in that courtroom who deserved it. As James was dragged past that very person, he smirked at how explosively angry his father looked. Knowing their father's fuse was short, J.R. and Jacob gripped his arm just to be sure he did not explode with a courtroom full of people watching. The grip they had on him, however, could not stop Jesse's filthy mouth … literally. He spat on James as he walked by.

James yanked his arm free from the deputy and turned toward his father. With his hands shackled, he could not wipe the tobacco drenched spit off the side of his neck. All he could do was look coldly at Jesse, baring his teeth like a rabid dog desperate to attack.

Jesse glared just as coldly back at James. "Don't you eva' address me as your fatha' again, boy. Y'ur dead to me, you nigga' lovin' piece of shit," he spewed.

"You were dead to me the day you murdered my motha'," James snarled. He lowered his eyes and looked at J.R and then back at his father. "You both betta' pray I neva' set foot outside of prison eva' again … because I will stop at *nothin'* to send you *both* back to hell!"

J.R. and Jacob tightened their grips on Jesse when they felt him suddenly try to lunge at the son he had just publicly disowned. The deputies snatched James back and finally rushed him out of the courthouse toward the place where Jesse's brethren had sentenced him to live until the day he dangled lifeless by a noose.

Chapter Four

After being sentenced to death, James was immediately moved to a maximum-security prison. As he was marched through the dimly lit, deplorable building that was now his home, he was pelted in the face with human excrement. His housewarming gift was delivered by an inmate who had saved his bodily waste all day for the honor of painting James's face with it. With only one clear shot, the untamed prisoner had covered nearly the entire left side of James's face with the stinking mound of feces. He let out a loud cackle when it landed just where he wanted. The perfect shot riled up all the other inmates and escalated the laughter and shouting to decibel levels, unlike any other time a new prisoner had been marched down the corridor. The prison guard just kept on marching James to his cell like the vile assault never even happened. With shackles still on his wrists, James could not wipe the disgusting heap off himself. When the laughter and yelling subsided, a familiar two-phrase chant ensued during the rest of the humiliating journey to his cell. After all he had endured with the folks of Fayetteville, James had grown numb to the shouts of "nigger lover," but there was no numbing himself to the stench plastered to his face. When his shackles were unlocked and his cell door slammed behind him, James dropped to a knee and vomited in the corner. He ripped a sleeve off his prison garb and did his best to wipe his face clean with it.

"I see ol' Ernest done got 'em anotha' one. He loves to splatta' nigga' lova's in shit. He figures since ya' love nigga's so much, he'll try to make ya' look like one, especially while y'ur bein' marched in here in shackles with no goddamn shoes on. He figures it's the closest you'll eva' get to feelin' like a real slave."

James turned around and looked at the filthy man who had just spoken. He was lying on his back in his cot, thumbing through a book. The man turned for a moment to return James's glare, flashing what was left of his rotten teeth, which were just as brown as his greasy hair. He reeked of a pungent odor that made James nauseous again. Trying to keep his stomach settled, James turned his attention back to getting feces off his face. Without saying a word, he then laid in the cot with his back turned, trying to get his nose as far away from his new cellmate's stench as possible.

"I'm Dale," the smelly cellmate said, still thumbing through his book.

Again, James did not speak.

Instantly offended by the lack of response, Dale suddenly slammed his book shut, sat up, and looked over at James. "Oh, y'ur one of those, huh?! I know y'ur goddamn type! Ya' think y'ur too goddamn good to speak? Ya' walk in here thinkin' ya' ain't gonna botha' wastin' y'ur time befriendin' fuckers like us 'cause we're beneath ya'! Every man I done met like you walked in here just the way you did. They had their chests all poked out, feelin' strong-willed, and confident in their convictions, convinced they'll neva' speak to a bunch of lowlifes like us … but they *all* break. Even uppity nigga' lovin' *fuckers* like you! It don't take long eitha'. Two 'r three days tops, eitha' you'll break down and cry like a sissified little pussy, or it'll finally sink in that this is home for a long fuckin' time, and you'll realize that you might as well make a few fuckin' friends in the meantime. One way or anotha' … you'll break. I give ya' three days tops, *nigga' lova'!*" Dale snickered, baring his brown teeth. "And you look like a little pussy crier to me. I just know I'ma walk in here in three days and you'll be curled up in the bed sobbin' like a little baby girl, shiverin', and shudderin' with y'ur shoulders heavin', beggin' fur y'ur mama!" Dale started to mimic the motions and pretended to sniffle. "I-I w-want m-my m-ma-ma." He broke out in a fit of phlegm-filled laughter, suffocating the atmosphere with the stench of his breath. He suddenly stopped laughing just as abruptly as he had started, squinted his eyes at James, picked up his book, and laid back down again. "Three days tops, *nigga' lova'* ... you'll talk." He opened up his book again. "They always do," he murmured as he forcefully turned a page.

For nearly three full days, James endured the verbal torment of his prison mates in stone-cold silence. Every day, though, "the feces-flinger" made it his mission to get under James's skin in the lunch line. Ernest was sure to stand behind James talking non-stop in his ear, trying to get him to break. "How'd that shit taste, pretty boy?" he had asked James on the first day. "Bet it reminded ya' of the taste of y'ur nigga's pussy, didn't it? I saw corn in it. Did ya' have you a piece? Ain't neva' figured out how a piece of corn could make it through my whole goddamn body and come outta my ass clean as a whistle."

Everyone within earshot began laughing hysterically while James scooped his prison slop onto his tray in silence.

"You gonna wished you'd've licked y'ur face clean by the time you get done eatin' the food they serve here, 'cause I can promise ya' my shit tastes a whole lot betta'." Ernest then stepped in front of James just when he was finished collecting his meal. "Matta' fact, why don't I just save ya' the misery of eatin' it." He smacked James's tray down onto the floor, igniting a commissary full of laughter.

James still did not budge or say a word. He just stared at Ernest, who was taking a bow after his attention-grabbing comedy performance. James had no appetite anyway. While the guards forced Ernest to clean up the mess, James went back to his cell to lie down. The reason his appetite evaded him immediately flooded his mind the moment his head hit his cot. Thoughts of Lily consumed him to the point that the innate survival mechanisms of his body began to fail. He literally could not feel hunger pangs or thirst. He had no desire to move his body at all. He craved sleep just to give himself a temporary reprieve from his surroundings, but his muddled mind refused to drift into unconsciousness. He spent the majority of his first night behind bars wide awake, staring at the ceiling, crippled by the possibilities of what may have happened to his wife.

On day two of James's death row sentence, every trip to the commissary began and ended the same way. Ernest spat vulgarities into James's ear as they slid their way down the food line. James ignored his rhetoric. Ernest smacked James's tray down at the end of the line, laughter erupted, and Ernest took a bow. He then gladly cleaned up the mess after his comedic performance while James walked back to the solace of his cell in complete and utter silence. However, when James laid down this time, a few tears fell from his eyes. His tears were not for his mama, for being stuck where he was, or because of Ernest tormenting him. His tears were for Lily and the torment of not knowing where *she* was stuck or if someone may be tormenting *her*.

On the third day, Ernest and his minions traded spots with one another just to give him the privilege of marching into the commissary right behind James again. As usual, the vulgarities began immediately. "I sat up all night thinkin' about y'ur little brown girlfriend. I started to think to ma'self … maybe I'm wrong. Instead of shit, I bet that nigga's pussy actually tastes like chocolate. Only somethin' as sweet as that would keep a man as *dignified* as you comin' back for more. Now you got me curious. Tell me about 'er, pretty boy. Is 'er pussy like that chocolate that oozes caramel from the inside afta' you bite it? Do it smell just as sweet?" He put his nose next to James's neck and inhaled long and hard. "Got my mouth waterin' just thinkin' about it."

Even with Ernest's nose a hair's breadth away from his neck, James miraculously maintained his composure as he listened to Ernest's band of nitwits laughing nearby.

"I bet fuckin' her is like submergin' y'ur cock in warm honey, ain't it? Come on and tell me. I wanna dream about 'er t'night. It's got my cock hard as a fuckin' rock right now. Bet a pretty boy like you wants to feel it too," Ernest moaned in James's ear. "You wanna feel my cock stuffed in y'ur ass, don't ya' nigga' lova'?"

Shockingly, James still remained silent despite the heat of Ernest's rancid breath burning his nostrils and his provocative words permeating his nerves.

"Aww, stop keepin' secrets, pretty boy. Come on and tell ol' Ernest what 'er pussy's like," he provoked. "I wanna know what it's gonna feel like when I fuck that little brown whore in my dreams t'night. I'ma have 'er chained up on 'er stomach with her legs spread and 'er pussy wide open. Gonna fuck 'er 'til she bleeds in the cell right next to y'urs, so you can listen to 'er screamin' for help. Heard she was fuckin' you so good, you claimed she was y'ur wife," he laughed. "Don't tell me you was really dumb enough to call y'urself lovin' a nig-
…"

"YES, I LOVE HER!" James suddenly erupted, food and blood simultaneously flying everywhere. With lightning speed, James had smashed his metal tray across Ernest's nose. With ferocity, he then picked Ernest up by the throat with one hand and body slammed him to the ground. He sat on top of him, planted his knees on his arms, and began bashing the edge of the metal tray repeatedly across Ernest's nose until it molded around his face. James then tossed the useless tray across the room and finished the job with his fists, alternating one blow to Ernest's jaw after another.

Normally, Ernest's rhetoric barely registered in James's muddled mind, but upon mentioning the vulgar things he wanted to do to Lily, he instantaneously unraveled. Other than his size and the stench of his breath, Ernest bore no resemblance to J.R. But the disgusting images that his words had painted were enough to make James perceive that Ernest and his brother were one and the same. While in the midst of his mind cracking, James maliciously pelted Ernest non-stop, every blow driven by the vision of J.R. forcefully shoving himself inside of Lily. "TOUCH 'ER AGAIN AND I'LL FUCKIN' KILL YOU, YOU MUTHA' FUCKER!" James hollered at the top of his lungs with every blow, sounding like a man who was undoubtedly in the throes of temporary insanity. James's rage was so animalistic, Ernest could do nothing but lie there helplessly absorbing the violent punishment for another man's actions. By the time the prison guards pulled James off, Ernest had a broken nose, two swollen eyes, and shattered front teeth. Even with five prison guards wrangling him away, James was still nearly impossible to control. "TOUCH 'ER AGAIN AND I'LL KILL YOU!" he continued to yell, as he was dragged out of the commissary kicking and struggling to break free. Despite nearly going hoarse, James could still be heard screaming all the way down the hallway.

Wanting to maintain his status at the top of the prison hierarchy, Ernest was always finding nasty ways to provoke new arrivals into minor fist fights. All the other prisoners always eagerly anticipated what was *usually* a minor showdown between two men exchanging a few cheap blows and rolling around on the floor for most of the fight. *Usually*, there was cheering, laughter, and rowdiness throughout the commissary during the brawl. But the *unusual* sight of James beating a man twice his size into an unconscious pulp, in a matter of seconds, had stunned dozens of hardened criminals into stone-cold silence. When James was gone, they all quietly turned to watch as Ernest's unconscious body was hauled to the infirmary.

"Three days," Dale suddenly boasted to himself, calmly shoveling his prison slop into his mouth. "They all talk … Neva' fuckin' fails."

Ernest would soon be the first in the prison's history to easily eclipse that three-day record of silence, though. His brutal beating left him completely comatose. Whenever his twisted mind healed enough to regain consciousness, he would awaken to a shattered jaw that had been wired shut, leaving him unable to open his filthy mouth.

While Ernest was left in the infirmary to recover, James was left to recover from his emotional breakdown in "the dungeon," a six by six-foot basement room with a dirt floor, no cot, no windows, and no light whatsoever. Being as tall as James was, he could not stand or lie down without touching the walls or the ceiling in the pitch-black cramped quarters. It was hardly the place for someone whose mind had clearly shattered in front of dozens of people. But there James was after being tossed inside with a hard shove. He had rolled over onto his back, his chest heaving. With the memory of what J.R. had done to Lily now fresh on his mind, he was seething. It took him nearly an hour to settle himself down. Once his rage subsided, the side effect was sleep, something James had not had a sufficient amount of in three days. With hardly any food or water in his system, his altercation had quickly drained him of the little bit of energy he had left. For six hours, he slept hard and his dreams were vivid ...

Inside of their beautiful estate manor, James stood behind Lily with his arms wrapped around her waist. He had sidled up behind her while she was cooking his favorite meal and kissed her tenderly on the neck.

"I know what that kiss means!" Lily smiled. "And no! You can't have a bite yet until I'm finished!"

"Damn!" James scratched his head. "None of my tricks work with you anymore, huh?"

"Took you all these years to figure that out, huh? Now, go on and sit yo'self down somewhere," she teased.

"Yes ma'am," James replied, tickling Lily's neck with his lips, igniting her laughter. They both then suddenly turned their heads in the direction of crying down the hallway.

"Sounds like somebody's up from their nap. Now there's somethin' you can do to occupy yourself until I'm done, mista'," Lily said.

"Gladly!" James smiled. "Papa to the rescue!" He kissed Lily again before heading toward the sound of their crying infant. He opened the first door where he heard the crying coming from. The room was bare. The sound of crying had suddenly shifted further down the hallway. James let his ears guide him to another room, only to be met by the sight of the wind blowing the sheer curtains into the air of another empty space. James slammed the door back, confusion now gripping his mind. Chasing the sound of his baby's cries, he picked up the pace, flinging doors open left and right, his heart picking up speed with every empty room he entered. "Rose!" he yelled repeatedly as he began to panic.

By the time James got to the fifth door, the sound of Rose's cries began to sound distorted in his ears. With his chest heaving, he ran and opened the very last door in the hallway. His heart rate immediately began to settle when he finally saw Rose's cradle on the far side of the room underneath an open window. Other than the cradle, the room was completely bare. The very moment he stepped inside, her cradle began slowly rocking on its own and her crying ceased. James began walking toward her soft cooing and her sudden giggling. He, too, began to laugh at the precious sound of her laughter. He stepped closer, eager to see what now had her laughing hysterically. Just feet away from peering into the cradle, though, his body froze. It was as if his feet were suddenly plastered to the floor. No matter how he twisted and turned, no matter how badly he wanted to pick his baby up and comfort her, he simply did not have the power to lift his feet.

... "ROOOSE!" James wailed, as he was jolted awake from what would be the first of many bizarre dreams of that nature. Breathing hard, James shifted his head quickly from left to right. He was thoroughly confused by where he was, and why he had just opened his eyes but could still see nothing, not his own hands, not his surroundings ... and especially not his beautiful beloved daughter. After being deprived of the chance to see her, those shivering, shuddering, shoulder-heaving sobs that Dale had warned about were instant. James was completely heartbroken by the fact that he could not see Rose ... not even in his dreams.

Still confused by where he was, James wailed his daughter's name over and over again at the top of his lungs, until a prison guard slid open a two by four-inch peephole in his door. "Shut the fuck up nigga' lova'!" he yelled.

Startled, James immediately stopped screaming, scampered backward, and bumped the wall. The sudden demand and the sliver of light that lit up the dungeon instantly brought James back to the reality of his surroundings. Panting, he just sat there staring back at the set of eyes that were glaring angrily at him through the small slit. After a few seconds, another flap opened at the bottom of the door and the guard slid a tray with food and water underneath it. He slammed the bottom door flap back and glared at James through the slit in the top part of the door again. "You got twenty minutes to eat!" the guard warned.

Starving and dehydrated, James scarfed down the two pieces of peanut buttered bread and drank all the water in under a minute. It was not nearly enough to satiate a man of his stature. The prison guards were well aware of that; the intentional deprivation of nutrients went hand in hand with a stay in the dungeon. But unlike any other prisoner that was cast down into the darkness, there was something unique added to the unsatisfying meal James received: "You *still* love that nigga'?" the guard asked when he returned twenty minutes later to pick up James's tray.

Sensing the challenging tone in the guard's question, James looked confidently into the glaring set of eyes in the peephole. "More than anything on this earth," he answered without hesitating.

With that answer, the guard slammed the peephole shut and left James to continue rotting in the pitch-black hole where his love for a Negro had landed him.

Chapter Five

"You still love that nigga'?!"

"With everything in me," James conjured up the strength to reply. For a little over a week, three times a day, James could count on two slices of peanut buttered bread and water being delivered to his dungeon cell like clockwork. Six times a day, he could also count on the same glaring green eyes and challenging question as his meal tray was delivered and retrieved. Six times a day, the guard could count on James replying with swiftness and conviction in varying affirmative answers. Six times a day, James's refusal to deny his feelings for Lily was then rewarded with a slam of the peephole door that quickly shut out the only bit of light he got to see on a daily basis.

It was not the size of the torture chamber that James was stuck in that broke men; it was the darkness. It was a thick, pitch-black nothingness that made the room feel more like a coffin than a six-by-six room. The darkness made it impossible for James to even see his hand in front of his face. Nor could he see the massive cockroaches and spiders that were his new cellmates. He had certainly felt them, though. But after days of rotting in the deplorable hellhole, he had become numb to them biting and scampering over his skin, much like his nose was now numb to the suffocating stench of urine and feces, blended with vomit. Many a man had completely snapped while stuck in the confines of those walls, their last bit of sanity swallowed up by the darkness, never to be seen again. If James could see anything, he would have been greeted with the sight of blood-streaked fingernail marks from those who had gone insane and broken their nails off trying to claw their way out. He would have seen circular spots of blood from the dozens of foreheads that had willfully banged against the bricks after their minds had shattered. James had refrained from either of those self-abusive methods, but his constant rocking back and forth was a clear sign that he might be on the verge of an internal collapse. However, it was not the dungeon threatening to cause his implosion; it was his dreams. Ironically, in his dreams James could see light and color, but was robbed of the one beautiful thing he was desperate to see. The chance to touch or see his daughter still eluded him. Each time he had awakened with his arms outstretched, just as they always were in his dreams. "I just wanna hold you," he would wake up quietly repeating to himself. "Please God, I won't hurt 'er," he murmured for upwards of an hour sometimes. "Please God, just let me hold 'er," he babbled, a steady trickle of tears collecting underneath his face, turning the dirt to mud where he lay in a malnourished, weakened heap.

Though his shattered heart somehow maintained a steady beat, James felt his sanity and desire to live slipping away. In those dark and desolate hours, it was Lily's music that kept him from crossing the borderline into insanity and banging his head against the wall until he ceased to exist. James would close his eyes and hum his favorite melodies. His wife's lovely music was the one and only thing to keep him happily dancing with her in the imaginary ballroom of sanity. Lily's music immediately gave way to beautiful memories of the glorious year he had spent with her on the road. Today, after the prison guard shut out his daily glimpse of light, James sat slumped in the corner with his head on his knees and let his mind carry him to yet another precious moment during Lily's journey to Winter Garden …

William did not need to be told that James had finally professed his love to Lily. As they all rode along in the carriage together, William could see that James had obviously expressed that sentiment just by the way he sat with his arm around Lily. His head was gently resting on hers while she nestled against his chest. Both had their eyes closed and seemed content not to say a word while they were lost in the essence of one another. For the first time since meeting the pair, William no longer felt smothered by the tension lingering between them. He, instead, felt happily immersed in the love they exuded. The scene nearly brought William to tears. It reminded him of the peace he had felt after he had professed his love to Emma. Simply by the look on James's face, William knew that he, too, was now experiencing the permanent calming of an inner unrest that only the love of a man's life had the power to unleash.

James, William, and Lily were all on their way to Dayton Ohio. Landon had secured Lily a three-day run at the Victoria Theater there. Though it would be the second theater Lily performed in, James was experiencing it as a first. Having missed her first performance inside a real theater, James suddenly felt hyper-aware of every move Lily made once they arrived. He helped Lily exit the carriage and walked into the theater beside her, paying keen attention to the jovial smile that suddenly graced her face as she absorbed her surroundings. Keeping the sea of emotions in his chest at bay was a constant battle from that very moment. Watching Lily in rehearsals, during costume fittings, and even preparations of her hair and make-up, had a major effect on James. The woman to whom he had just professed his love was doing something that no other Negro woman had ever done in the short history of their country. He realized she was laying the foundation that others like her could walk on in centuries to come. It made every miniscule detail of preparation seem so epically monumental in James's eyes.

James's experience in watching Lily prepare had caused the tide of emotions in his chest to rise to near flood levels by the following evening. At the announcement of five minutes until showtime, Lily stepped out of the dressing room and into the sight of a man who found it nearly impossible to suppress the raging sea of tears she had stirred in him. "Awe-inspirin'," James said, gazing at Lily with adoration. "That's what you are to me." He placed his hand on her cheek. "I'm in awe of you, and I know that audience out there will be too."

Lily's eyes fluttered closed as she melted into James's touch, his words having caused a tide of emotions to swell within her too. It rose even further when she felt his lips gently press against hers. "Aren't you gonna wish me luck?" she whispered, after his kiss.

James shook his head. "You don't need luck. I'm convinced that God has bestowed you with this rare gift for a reason. I'm confident that He will not let you falter ... and I'm just as confident that this audience will fall as madly in love with you as I have."

A single tear trickled from Lily's eye onto James's hand as it rested on her cheek. "Thank you. I needed to hear that," she whispered, "just as much as I needed you here with me this time."

"I think my eyes might dry-up watchin' you. I'll be damned if I blink and miss a second of you up there."

"You betta' not," Lily teased. She kissed James one last time and departed toward the stage.

James turned and watched her with pride as she strutted with confidence to take her place at her musical throne. He then took his seat in the front row, determined to absorb every second of Lily's performance. From the intense beginning, the pool of waiting tears had fortunately moistened the eyes that James indeed refused to blink. Enthralled by the shadowed spectacle and the inspiring music, James could sense everyone around him fighting to keep their unblinking eyes moistened as well. By the time Lily hit the last note in the emotional grand finale, James knew that dry eyes were not an issue for the patrons surrounding him who were giving the Dream Symphony a resounding standing ovation.

The tide of emotions that James had managed to suppress during the show was unleashed in a tsunami hours later. His tears blended with Lily's, christening the pillow of the very first luxury hotel they would stay in together as he erotically glided in and out of the paradise between her thighs. The need to erupt permeated every pore on their bodies from the very first stroke. Within seconds of James dancing within her, Lily had moaned his name into his ear as her insides spasmed around him. James emptied himself upon hearing the melodic sighs of Lily's second grand finale for the evening.

... "You *still* love that nigga'?!" the guard suddenly asked in his usual challenging tone, jolting James from his beautiful memory.

Despite his severely weakened state, James lifted his head toward the glaring eyes and dug deep for the strength to speak. "You can starve me, beat me, leave me locked in here for life, or condemn me to hell, but I'm not gonna change my *fuckin'* answer. If you don't want me to admit how I feel any more, then go on and kill me now, you piece of shit ... because there isn't any otha' way to make me quit lovin' her." James panted hard after his reply. Simply speaking had exhausted him of the strength to hold his head up any longer and it dropped back to his knees.

To James's surprise, he did not hear the peephole slam shut this time. "Hmph." The guard snickered and shook his head. "I knew you felt that way about that woman long before you eva' came to this shithole prison. Didn't figure I'd eva' break a crazy son of a bitch like you eitha'."

James struggled to lift his head again to look into the green eyes that he had become so familiar with. He noticed the anger in them was no longer present for a change.

The guard sighed and seemed to relax. "My fatha'-in-law's farm has had a contract with Joseph Parker for years," he began explaining. "I know you know who that is."

James did not reply. He was using all his strength to hold his head up and listen to where this man was going with his story.

"Joseph Parker invited me, my wife, and her side of the family to Mary Jo's engagement party some months ago. I didn't really wanna go, but for my wife's sake, I went ahead and attended. I's ready to go before I eva' set foot in that damn town hall. Most of the time I's there, I's standin' in the corna', snatchin' whiskey from every servin' tray within reach. I needed it for my sanity. I could only take so much of Mary Jo cacklin' and paradin' herself around like a princess. I just neva' could stand that pasty woman. It's hard to believe that Joseph works in the farmin' industry but his daughta's the most colorless human on earth. I've seen albinos with more color. She looks like one of them damn porcelain dolls I done bought for my niece," the guard joked. "And her gratin' *voice!* I swear 'fore God, listenin' to her talk always has my ears on the verge of bleedin'. I took two shots of whiskey at that engagement party for the poor fucker who was insane enough to spend the rest of his life listenin' to her. Wasn't too long 'fore I realized that that poor fucker was *you*," the guard snickered again.

James would have laughed too, but he lacked the energy.

"Not to my surprise, you looked just as miserable as I did to be there. Ain't neva' seen a man look at his future bride with such disdain. I read right through you in an instant. Somethin' told me you didn't want no parts of marryin' that woman. And I'll be damned if I blamed ya'! I think I'd commit suicide before I spent a second of my life sufferin' with that woman. Hell, the look on y'ur face made me think you were certainly contemplatin' blowin' y'ur own head off," the guard laughed. "Maybe I had too much to drink, but halfway through the night, I's convinced you's trapped into marryin' that cacklin' heathen. It sure as hell was written all ova' y'ur face anyway. All night, I watched ya', feelin' just as sorry for ya' as a shit-covered man … no pun intended," the guard laughed again. "Not one time did I see y'ur face light up with love when you looked at Mary Jo.

"But I finally saw the look of love in y'ur eyes lata' that evenin'. I saw y'ur face light up the way it should when you look at the love of y'ur life. Y'ur eyes lit up and you didn't seem to be able to force the goofy grin off ya' face, no matta' how hard ya' tried. I don't even think I saw ya' blink … but it wasn't Mary Jo you's lookin' at that way."

James could feel himself becoming emotional as he realized who the guard was alluding to.

"You was lookin' at that slave girl that way while she was playin' the piano," the guard continued. "Even as drunk as I was, I knew what I's seein'. I knew because I still look at my wife that way. It's a look like you were mesmerized by the most beautiful work of art you've eva' seen in ya' life. It was like ya' saw y'ur children, y'ur future, and y'ur whole life in 'er eyes. You looked at that woman like you'd take y'ur beatin' heart right outta ya' chest and hand it to 'er if that's what it took to have 'er by y'ur side until the end of y'ur days. Trust me, I know that damn look. And you didn't give it to *Mary Jo* … you gave it to the *slave* playin' that piano.

"Oddly, I rememba' shiftin' my attention to that slave as well afta' noticin' the way you looked at 'er. Just like you, I suddenly couldn't take my eyes off her as she played. For the first time that night, I sat my drink down and just stared at 'er for the longest time. There was somethin' so familiar about 'er to me. Her eyes and the structure of 'er face had me gripped, but I just couldn't quite put my finga' on why she seemed so familiar. It was plaguin' me so much that I didn't even wanna leave the party anymore ... not 'til I figured out where the hell I knew 'er from. I stepped forward scrutinizin' 'er face, her eyes, every motion, every movement of 'er body, and even her finga's as she played. I couldn't believe the way she had memorized that damn song afta' one take. But more than anything, I couldn't believe what my eyes were seein' when I looked at 'er. Then I heard somebody next to me say 'er name ... *Lily.* I remuba' my heart suddenly thumpin' like a stampede the moment I heard it. Afta' hearin' that name while watchin' her whisk her way across those piano keys, I knew I finally had to accept the painful truth..." The guard paused and exhaled. "The woman sittin' at that piano really was my half-sista'." He shook his head in disbelief. "At that moment, I just had to accept that she really was my fatha's daughta'. There was no damn denyin' it anymore," he admitted, sounding pained by that notion. "Lily's eyes, the way her body moved, her expressions, her face, the way she played that piano, it was like I's watchin' my fatha'. She not only looked just like him, but she played the hell outta that piano ... just the way he could."

James stared at the guard in utter disbelief, his heart now the one beating like a stampede.

"My fatha' was an incredible pianist," the guard continued. "His family was too poor to afford a piano. But when he was a boy, he used to sneak onto the piano in the church basement while his motha' was rehearsin' with the choir. He spent hours tinkerin' on it until he taught himself to play. The pastor caught 'em there one evenin'. My fatha' thought he was in trouble, but the pastor was amazed by his talent. Just five years old, and there my fatha' was, playin' like a grown man. He went on to play in that church for decades. He'd put on the Christmas and Easta' concerts every year. It was just him up there by himself, playin' away, commandin' the whole crowd. Most folks wouldn't think that some podunk farma' with a half-ass education, no piano lessons, and calloused hands could eva' play a piano, but my fatha'd make a believa' out of ya' … quick, fast, and in one hell of a hurry. He could've taken a risk to pursue his dream of bein' an orchestra pianist, but bein' a fatha' to us boys was more important to 'em. Instead of travelin' the country, he opted to be a farma' to be sure he had a steady income and a stable life for us boys. So, he neva' put on a single show outside of those church walls. It was the most selfless thing any man could eva' do for his family."

The guard paused and swallowed his swell of emotions. "It's strange. I've got five brotha's and not a single one of us was born with his gift. But *Lily*…" He shook his head and gave a faint laugh of disbelief. "The irony."

"That's an unda'statement," James whispered.

Lily's half-brother exhaled hard after his confession, needing to collect himself. "Not long before that engagement party, I had just found out that Lily was allegedly my half-sista'. For months, I's angry as hell about it. It pissed me off when ya' showed up at my fatha's house askin' about Maya. I didn't think things could get any worse, but there you were askin' me to help reunite a sista' I neva' knew about with my fatha's *mistress!*" He shook his head again. "Talk about rubbin' salt in my fuckin' wounds! If it wasn't for the fact that I's in desperate need of money, I probably would've hauled off and punched you right square in y'ur face."

James now realized that the particular half-brother speaking to him was indeed Wyatt, who was finally answering why he had been so hostile during their first encounter.

"Does Lily know he's her fatha'?" Wyatt asked.

James nodded. "She inadvertently found out the day she was sold."

"Must've been as much of a shock to her as it was for me. For months, I just couldn't bring myself to believe that my God-fearin' fatha' had been unfaithful to my motha' and that Lily was truly my sista'. It wasn't until that engagement party that I finally accepted the fact that she was. There was simply no denyin' it afta' I saw 'er perform. That was the female version of my fatha' playin' that damn piano with the musical gift he had undoubtedly passed on to her. It left no doubt in my damn mind. She was his." Wyatt exhaled again. "As hard as it is for me to admit, I also can't deny that my fatha' sho' did create one hell of a beautiful daughta'. And afta' seein' 'er at that party, it proved that Lily clearly turned out to be special … just the way my fatha' predicted she'd be."

"What do you mean?" James asked, surprised that Lily's father would have said such a thing.

Wyatt heard a noise and turned to see another guard headed their way while making his rounds.

"Why're you tellin' me all this? I don't unda'stand," James prodded.

"You will." Wyatt quickly shoved a plate of food under the door and intentionally left the peephole open to give James a little light. "Eat up. Y'ur gonna need it." He then walked away without any further explanation for his actions.

Despite how famished James was, he did not eat right away this time. The revelation about Lily's father had him far too stunned to move. So, too, did the fact that it had been Wyatt testing the sincerity of his love for Lily with his challenging question every day. The entire scenario had James baffled. He was even more baffled when he looked down at his plate and saw a hearty steak, mashed potatoes with gravy, corn on the cob, a piece of pie, and a candle with matches. And instead of water, his tin cup was filled to the brim with a fine Irish ale.

Chapter Six

After James finished his Irish ale and homemade meal, Wyatt opened the dungeon door and finally let him out. He took James to the infirmary to have his wounds and bug bites treated. He was allowed to bathe, was doused with lye to kill any potential lice, and given fresh prison garbs. After his thorough cleaning, he was then guided back through the dim hallways of the cell block. Unlike the first day James arrived, the ruckus from all the other prisoners was totally non-existent as he was escorted to his cell. All the prisoners held on to their cell bars without making a peep as they watched James walk by. Even James's cellmate, Dale, was standing up when he finally made it back. He did not say a word when James walked in either. The only sound that was made thereafter was the cell door slamming and the jingling of Wyatt's keys as he locked the lock and marched away. Dale and James stared at each other briefly before James laid down in his cot without a word. Dale laid down shortly thereafter. The silence in the entire cell block persisted for another few minutes until Dale rolled over on his side and looked at James again. "Boy, you sho' did lay that shit-slingin' som'bitch out on his ass!" he said. With the silence, his words echoed loudly throughout the facility. In unison, an eruption of laughter broke out from every prisoner in the building. "Wooooo-weee! You whooped ol' Ernest's ass good!" he reiterated through his mucus-filled laughter.

All it took was those few sentences for the hooting and hollering and rowdiness to return to the entire facility. "ERNEST GOT HIS ASS WHOOPED!" was suddenly being chanted in unison by every prisoner ... except for one. Ernest lay in his cot, facing the wall, looking humiliated and mad as hell with his broken jaw wired shut, unable to utter a word in his own defense. James gave a faint smile, shook his head at the insanity, then rolled over in his cot to try and sleep comfortably for a change. Wyatt, in turn, threw his feet up on the desk in his office, put his hands behind his head, and smirked, content to let the insulting chants continue.

The next morning, James stepped out into the sunlight for the first time in nearly two weeks. He had not seen the sun in so long, it physically hurt him to keep his eyes open at first. His skin was nearly as pale as MJ's and his muscles had atrophied from days of lying unused on the dungeon floor. But Wyatt had a solution for that. He had James starting on the ball and chain gang. They all worked long hours, swinging sledgehammers and hauling wheelbarrows full of rocks and lumber to lay train tracks. It was the sort of backbreaking, muscle-building work Wyatt loved to subject his prisoners to ... but *especially* James.

For three weeks, Wyatt gave James the toughest of the railroad assignments, especially those that built his stamina and had him sleeping well at night. A full home-cooked platter was more difficult to sneak to James now that he was no longer in the dungeon, but Wyatt still managed to slide him an extra steak or piece of chicken every night. Wyatt never said a word to James about the reason he continued to break the prison rules on his behalf. James just quietly accepted his kindness with a nod. He figured it had something to do with Lily being his half-sister, or perhaps it was his attempt to make amends for pulling a gun on him while Lily and her mother were saying their goodbyes. But James would soon learn that every extra meal and muscle-building job that Wyatt gave him had a motive far beyond any sort of minor atonement.

It was a week before the presidential and local town elections. Wyatt had three guards who were helping the town sheriff in his final campaign push to be re-elected. Despite being down three guards, Wyatt still insisted on having his prisoners continue their work on the railroad. In fact, he had very much been looking forward to this week when there was a lack of help with the prisoners and an ample amount of attention focused on a major town event. That morning, Wyatt calmly rode along on his horse, trotting behind the slow-walking group of twenty prisoners, who were all chained together. When they made it to their destination, Wyatt began unlocking each prisoner from the group chain one by one. He then attached their individual shackles to a heavy ball and strategically placed every inmate at their assigned duty for the day, saving James for last.

Before assigning his duty, Wyatt marched James way down the railroad track to an area that had already been completed the week before. "Gonna have you re-do this ten-foot piece of track that one of these nitwits fucked all to hell," Wyatt explained to James as he secured the ball and chain apparatus around his ankle. Wyatt stood up and pointed out the repairs needed. "One of these lazy fuckers didn't put enough nails in these rail ties. It won't pass inspection like this." He tossed James a sledgehammer and sat a wooden box of massive nails nearby. "Can you handle it on y'ur own?"

James simply nodded. Wyatt nodded in return and then walked back down the line to mount his horse.

For the few hours thereafter, Wyatt and the other guards all trotted slowly on their horses with their rifles slung over their shoulders. They were spread out evenly, keeping all the prisoners corralled as they worked. Typically, there were eight guards covering the quarter mile stretch of men, but with three guards out for the day, they were pushed to the limits with keeping tabs over everyone ... just the way Wyatt wanted.

"Adams, everybody's breakin' for lunch in a few minutes," Wyatt said, glaring down at James from his horse.

James nodded, laid his sledgehammer down, and was about to pick up his ball and chain to walk back toward the other prisoners. But Wyatt suddenly used the barrel of his rifle and poked him in the chest with it to get his attention.

"You ain't eatin' lunch today, though," Wyatt explained, shoving the barrel harder into James's ribs.

James's heart immediately began to gallop. He swallowed hard and slowly looked up at Wyatt in confusion.

"I'm gonna talk real fast so you need to listen good, ya' hear?"

James nodded again.

Wyatt nervously looked over his shoulder first to make sure the other guard was not making his way around the bend of the hill yet. "Run thirty minutes straight west," he began explaining, motioning his head in that direction. "You'll run right into a creek. Strip y'urself of every stitch of clothin' you got on. Ain't no tellin' when the dogs'll be on ya', but they will eventually. There's a key to the shackle, a canteen, onions, soap, towels, and food in a satchel tucked away in the fireplace of an old burned-out log cabin. Eat quick and wash y'urself good in the creek. Every inch of ya'. Put your clothes and everything else in the creek and let it float away when y'ur through … except the onions. Keep those with ya'. The dogs'll smell the onions and lose y'ur scent. Wade across that creek quick as ya' can. We ain't had much rain. The waters are low. If you make it across, follow a trail of trees with broken tree limbs danglin'. You'll see the pattern. Snatch 'em down when ya' run past. That trail will lead ya' to what ya' need." Wyatt's eyes then drifted down to James's shackles.

James then slowly followed the path of Wyatt's eyes. The whole time he had been working, he did not even realize that one of the links in the chain that led to the heavy ball was broken. It looked as if a sledgehammer had pounded away at it. James would have been even more shocked to learn that it was Wyatt who had taken the time to intentionally damage it that way. He was also the one who had gone through the back-breaking work of removing all the bolts from that hidden area of the train tracks around the bend. James looked back up at Wyatt and saw compassion in his eyes for the first time ever.

"Keep the beard," Wyatt suggested. "I'll make sure that y'ur wanted posta's have ya' clean shavin'. If you get caught, and you mention my name or any of this, I'll see to it that you rot in that goddamn dungeon hole until you cease to exist, you unda'stand me?"

James nodded.

"Wait 'til the next guard passes by here, and you run like diarrhea out of a baby's ass, ya' hear? Run and run hard. And don't fuckin' stop 'til you get to where I just told ya'," Wyatt demanded.

James looked up at Wyatt with a blended look of disbelief and appreciation. Wyatt nodded, removed the rifle from James's chest, and calmly rode off on his horse. James then picked up his sledgehammer and got back to work, waiting patiently for the next guard to pass.

"LUNCH TIME!" Wyatt called out after the guard passed James by. He then quickly handed out lunch duties to all the guards to be sure that none of them doubled back to check on James.

Dale was sitting with a group of his buddies as he ate. They all took turns tormenting Ernest, who had been demoted to fixing lunch and cleaning up because of his mangled state. Near the end of the hour lunch break, Dale tossed some garbage on the ground near Ernest's feet. "Clean that up 'fore I have pretty boy break some more bones in y'ur face," he joked.

Everyone in the group broke out in laughter after overhearing the insult. The wires in Ernest's mouth forced him to endure the torment like an aggravated mute. But the comment got a different reaction out of one of the guards. He suddenly began looking around for "pretty boy." He stopped and looked amongst the scattered bodies relaxing in the shade and suddenly felt his heart rate increase when he did not spot James anywhere. He then prompted his horse to trot over to Wyatt. "Where's Adams?" the guard asked him.

Shit! Wyatt thought to himself. "He's usually ova' in Dale's group," he managed to respond calmly.

"I know, but I didn't see 'em ova' there."

"Didn't ya' double back to get 'em when I hollered for lunch?" Wyatt asked.

The guard suddenly turned red in the face. "N-no, y-yes. I thought I did."

"Well, which one is it, ya' dumb-ass?"

"I-I don't rememba'."

"Well, he's probably still workin'," Wyatt lied, still managing to remain calm. "If he ain't, y'ur ass is up shit's creek! Now go on and check on 'em."

Five minutes later, the guard returned with sweat drenching his face. He nervously approached Wyatt. "A-Adams is gone, sir," he said sheepishly.

"The fuck you mean, he's gone?!" Wyatt yelled.

"L-looks like he h-hammered his w-way outta his ball and chain."

"You dumb fuck! Round up the otha' prisoners!"

With those words, the time for Wyatt to play ignorant had officially ended. Had it not been for Dale's casual conversation, James may have made it until the end of the workday before his absence was noticed. But as it stood, Wyatt was forced to call out the search party and the dogs after only an hour. Wyatt had prepared for this situation as well though. He had taken the filthy blood-spattered clothes that James had worn in the dungeon, tore them into pieces, and buried them in shallow holes headed eastward, far off the trail that he had sent James on. When the dogs were retrieved, he was certain to guide them toward the false path.

James had already taken full advantage of his one-hour lead. He was familiar with the burned-out log cabin near the creek and had made his way there with ease. He snatched the satchel out of the fireplace, ate quickly, tore his clothes off, scrubbed himself in the creek, and let his clothes float down the stream. He put on the pair of boots he was given and dug through the satchel again for a change of clothes. It was then that he realized that Wyatt had not provided him with any. He went back to look in the fireplace again to see if he had missed them but nothing else was there. With his prison garbs now long gone, he had no other choice but to wade across the cold stream nude. After quickly making it to the other shore, he checked around for another bag that might contain something to wear but found nothing. In his search, though, he found the trail of broken tree branches that Wyatt told him to follow. He recalled Wyatt saying that the marked trees would lead him to what he needed. With onions in hand, he began trotting through the woods naked, hoping that clothes would be among the things he would eventually find at the end of the trail.

Completely winded from running so hard, James stopped briefly after a half hour and bent over to catch his breath. At that very moment, he could hear the faint sound of several hounds barking far off in the distance. They could very well have been random hunting dogs, but James took it as a sign that he was now officially a wanted man. That fact gave him another burst of energy and he quickly resumed trotting and hopping over the brush and rough terrain ... stark naked.

Despite being completely exhausted, James had pushed himself non-stop for another solid half hour. He leaned over heaving with his hands on his knees, fighting the urge to vomit as he looked around for the next broken tree limb to guide his path. A slight panic came over him when he failed to find one, nor any sign of the package that Wyatt had promised would be at the end of the trail.

"Since y'ur the only ass-naked man I've seen pass through here, I assume y'ur the person I'm lookin' for," James suddenly heard from behind him.

James briefly looked over at the man and then turned to run.

"Take anotha' step and I'll shoot ya'," the man said, pulling out his pistol.

James stopped and put his hands in the air, figuring he may as well surrender easily.

The man tossed a satchel on the ground near James's feet. "Put y'ur hands down and put those clothes on. I prefer not to see a man's prick while I'm talkin' to 'em."

"That makes two of us," James replied, picking up the bag. He quickly got dressed and looked back at the man.

"Y'ur late," the man said, tossing James a canteen of water. "You should've been here an hour ago."

James looked confused. "Who the hell're you?"

"Colt Collins. I'm Wyatt's younga' brotha'. Sorry he had you runnin' through here ass naked, but he figured it'd give you more motivation to stay on the path he laid out for ya'."

"Damn right about that!" James exclaimed, as he put his boots back on. When he finished, he looked up at Colt. "I'm grateful for what your brotha' did. But I can't help but wonda' why you two are helpin' me?"

"We know you're desperate to find Lily, and my brotha's and I are just as desperate for you to find 'er too."

"You are?" James asked, looking confused.

Colt nodded.

122

"Why?"

"'Cause we need you to help us."

"What the hell could I possibly help eitha' of you with?"

"We need you to deliva' an important message."

"To whom?"

"To *Lily*. We know she's not on y'ur fatha's farm anymore. We've tried lookin' for her recently, but none of us have been able to track 'er down anywhere. Me and my brotha's, we got jobs and families. So unfortunately, we don't have time to dedicate to lookin' for her. But Wyatt assures me that you'd go to y'ur grave before you eva' gave up searchin' for her."

"Your brotha's damn right about that."

"That's why we think it only makes sense for you to be the one to find 'er and deliva' this message."

"What message?"

Colt approached, picked up one of two large satchels on the ground, and pulled out an envelope. "It's our unda'standin' that you taught Lily to read?"

"I did," James boasted proudly.

"Then we need you to give 'er this," Colt said, handing James the letter inside the envelope.

James took a moment to read the contents. He then slowly looked up at Colt when he was finished, the look on his giving away how astonished he was by what he had just read.

"It would mean the world to me and my brotha's if you found Lily and let 'er read that. She needs to know. In fact, it's important to us that she gets *everything* in these two satchels," he said, pointing to them. "Everything in them will help bring more clarity to that letta'. But above anything else, be sure she gets that message," he said, tapping the paper.

James nodded. "I promise, I will," he said as he placed the letter back inside the envelope.

"There's plenty of money, pistols, and ammo in the saddlebags of a horse I got tied to a tree, a few hundred yards in that direction." Colt motioned his head westward. "There's enough can goods and wata' to get you by for a few days too."

"Thank you."

Colt nodded. "See to it that we didn't free ya' for nothin'. Me and my brotha's, we're dependin' on ya', ya' hear?"

"I swear to you and your brotha's that all your efforts will be worth it … and foreva' appreciated."

Colt slapped James on the shoulder. "We'll be prayin' for ya'."

"Thank you. I'll need all the prayers I can get."

James placed the letter inside one of the satchels, picked them both up, and ran off to the horse Colt had waiting on him. He secured the bags to the horse and then rode as far toward the border of Ohio as the stallion could handle for the night. He found a secluded area and hid in a small cave. Once settled, he lit a fire and eagerly opened up one of the satchels that Colt had given him. One by one, he began pulling out the treasures inside, curiously examining each of them. Beneath all the treasures were several journals. He opened the first page of each of them and found the one with the earliest date. He hoped maybe the contents would help explain the significance of the treasures inside the satchels, as well as the motives behind the message from Lily's brothers. James scooted closer to the firelight and began reading the first page of a journal that had been written by the hand of Lily's father.

"I'll be damned," James whispered after the very first passage impacted him hard and immediately began to shift his perspective about Levi Collins...

Chapter Seven

Collins Plantation
August 1834
Ten months before Lily's birth

Maya froze in the chicken coop after turning around to find the drifter that Levi had just hired standing in the doorway. The drifter had his erect penis exposed, stroking it while staring at Maya with his mouth agape. "I wanna feel those thick juicy lips wrapped around my cock," the repulsive man said to her, breathing heavily as he continued to pleasure himself. "I bet you'd have me beggin' for mercy, wouldn't ya' brown suga'?" he moaned.

Knowing she had no other way out of the chicken coop, Maya began trembling. She tried to remain composed but tears suddenly welled in her eyes. The drifter smiled at the fear he had just infused in her. He let out a twisted laugh at the frightened look on her face, pulled his pants back up, turned around to walk away, and was suddenly stunned by all four of Levi's brick hard knuckles.

The drifter's knees slightly buckled, and he stumbled back a step. "What the hell!" he yelled after he regained his balance. He then spit into his hand. "You fucker! You done knocked ma' tooth out!"

"And if you wanna keep the rest of those rotten teeth in y'ur mouth, I suggest you get the hell off of my property! Quick, fast, and in a hurry!"

"You ain't paid me yet!" the drifter had the audacity to reply.

"For what?!" Levi snarled, baring his teeth like a rabid dog. "You ain't done nothin' but drink up my beer and disrespect her from the moment you got here!" he yelled, pointing at Maya.

The drifter tossed his tooth aside and took a step toward Levi. "I ain't leavin' here 'til you pay me my goddamn money!"

Levi fearlessly stepped toward him too. "The only thing y'ur gonna leave here with is a bullet in y'ur fuckin' chest if you don't stumble y'ur drunk ass off of my land!"

The drifter bucked up, threatened Levi with his eyes, and made a move like he was about to lunge at him.

"NOW!" Levi shouted, pulling his pistol from his holster and aiming it at the drifter's face.

The look in Levi's eyes was enough to convince the drifter that he better heed his warning while he had the chance. "B-be easy. Be easy," he said as he backed away with his hands up. He spit more blood out of his mouth, cautiously stepped past Levi, and quickly made his way off the farm.

Levi watched the vulgar man until he was certain that he was no longer a threat. He then turned around to find Maya still staring at him. She was holding her master's gaze for far longer than she knew a slave was allowed. She could not help it. She was stunned that the usually mild-mannered, quiet man she knew Levi to be had just turned into a beast on her behalf. She lowered her head and quickly broke eye contact when she finally realized her mistake. Her heart began to beat rapidly all over again when she heard Levi's footsteps crinkling through the dried hay on the ground as he made his way toward her. With the anger Levi had just emitted, Maya was unsure if he might be on his way to correct her error in yet another heated exchange. Levi stopped close enough for Maya to see his boots as she continued to gaze at the ground.

Silence.

Maya jumped slightly when she saw Levi's hand reaching toward her. "Are you okay?" he asked, gently placing his hand on her shoulder.

"Y-yessa'," she replied nervously, still looking at his feet.

Gently, Levi raised her head to meet his eyes. "You sure?" he asked, needing to see the truth for himself.

The compassionate look in his eyes suddenly brought Maya a sense of calm. "I'm sure."

Levi still would not take his eyes off Maya nor his hand off her chin. He nodded. "Okay then," he replied.

After what felt like an eternity to Maya, Levi finally released her from his gaze and from his gentle grip and walked away.

A few days prior, a sudden summer storm had severely damaged Levi's barn roof. The need for emergency repairs had put an end to his plans to travel out of state with his family to attend the wedding of his wife's brother. Being as poor as he was, Levi had hired the cheap labor of a skilled drifter to help him with the roof repairs. That drifter, however, quickly began putting in the kind of work that he was *not* getting paid for.

While Levi's wife was out of town, Maya had taken over the duty of delivering lunch and drinks to Levi and the drifter as they worked. Unbeknownst to Levi, though, Maya was receiving *unwanted* tips for her service. For two days, Maya had put up with vulgar behavior, disgusting comments, and sexual advances from the filthy drifter. Every time she had delivered his food, he whispered graphic details about the sort of things he wanted to do to her body. When Levi was not watching, the unkempt drifter was constantly groping Maya's posterior while rapidly flickering his tongue at her. Maya's constant disgusting encounters with the man had her petrified and had drastically changed her usual joyful demeanor. After finally discovering why Maya's jubilance was suddenly non-existent, Levi was more than happy to get rid of the problem. He now walked away from Maya in the chicken coop, hoping that the beautiful side of her would finally return. He had *sincerely* missed it.

Hours after his confrontation with the drifter, Levi had cleaned up, changed his clothes, and was ready to eat and relax for the evening. Typically, he did not have a house slave. He could not afford one. He needed the few slaves he had working in the fields, so the household duties were usually handled by his wife, Emily. While she was out of town, Levi greatly appreciated the extra hours that Maya was putting in to help indoors. In all truthfulness, he wished that Maya could prepare his meals all the time. He felt his wife's food was bland in comparison to hers. For that fact alone, Levi was happy to be plodding downstairs toward the wonderful aroma Maya had circulating in the house. He walked into the kitchen and leaned against the doorframe. "Smells good," he said to her.

"Steak, potatoes, cornbread, and green beans," Maya replied as she sat his plate down on the table and wiped her hands on her apron. "Got an extra steak keepin' warm in the oven if that one ain't enough. I warmed up that left ova' peach cobbla' I made yesta'day too … if ya' got room for it, of course," she added shyly.

"Now *this* is a true man's meal," Levi said, staring at the spread of food. "And don't worry, I'll certainly be savin' room for that famous peach cobbla' of yours." Levi turned to Maya and faintly smiled at her. "Thank you for all of this Maya."

"You're welcome," Maya smiled back, feeling unusually nervous around him. She lowered her head quickly when Levi continued to stare at her the same way he had earlier in the day. "A-anything else before I go?" she stammered nervously.

"No. Don't think I could botha' you for much more," Levi replied.

"It's no botha' at all."

"Thank you. But I think this will do."

"I'll leave you to your meal then. Have a nice evenin'." Maya headed toward the door, but suddenly stopped and turned back around. "Masta' Lee, I-I wanted to say thank you … for what ya' done for me today in the chicken coop," she told him, still staring at the wooden planks of the kitchen floor. She heard the floorboards creaking as Levi made his way toward her. Her heartbeat became erratic as he approached, much like in the chicken coop.

"You're welcome," Levi replied. For the second time that day, he placed his hand beneath Maya's chin. He lifted her head and waited for her eyes to meet his. For a few seconds, he just gazed at her. "Please don't look down when you speak to me," he said, suddenly caressing Maya's cheek with the back of his hand. "I can't stand it when you hide this face from me," he whispered. Without once blinking, he continued to admire her beauty. "*Maya*," he said softly, still gazing at her. "Your name means the Goddess of spring." He suddenly began gliding his fingertips softly and slowly down the sides of her face, like she was the most fragile, priceless sculpture he had ever laid his eyes on. "I can't think of a more perfect name for someone as stunningly beautiful as you," he said, looking straight into her eyes.

Levi's spellbinding statements seemed to hypnotize Maya and caused a flurry of butterflies to erupt in her stomach. Her enchanted mind suddenly could not conjure up a single appreciative thing to say in return after being warmed by the graciousness of Levi's words. Her thoughts were completely lost while she stared unblinkingly into the innocent green eyes gazing captivatingly at her. "Masta', I…"

"*Levi*," he interrupted, still unwilling to blink as he gazed at Maya. "Please … just call me *Levi*. I wanna hear you say it," he whispered, insisting she defy slave etiquette.

Again, Maya was too stunned to respond to his simple wish. She swallowed hard and just continued nervously holding his gaze.

Levi softly caressed the side of her face with the back of his hand again. "I lied. There is one otha' thing I's hopin' you'd do before you go."

"Wh-what's that?" Maya managed to reply.

"Have dinna' with me."

"I-I umm, really only made enough for just you."

"You said you made an extra steak. I'd be glad to let you have it and share whateva' else you've made," Levi replied, having yet to take his hand down from Maya's face.

"Thank ya' kindly but…"

"Please?" he begged.

"I just really don't think that'd be a good idea. 'Sides, it's been a long day, and I really would like to get some rest. But thank you."

Levi felt his heart plummet over Maya's decision and finally removed his hand from her face. "I unda'stand." He then took a step back to help put to rest the intense emotions that the feel of Maya's skin had instantaneously awakened.

"I-I think I bes' be gettin' on back to the quarta's."

Levi reluctantly nodded his head. "Goodnight."

"Night masa'."

It slightly stung Levi to hear Maya call him master after his request just moments before.

Maya walked toward the exit, put her hand on the doorknob, and lingered there a moment. She hesitated to open it but refused to turn back around to look at Levi. She could feel his eyes on her and was shocked that she rather enjoyed that fact. But still, she refused to turn back around.

When Maya finally departed, Levi went to the window and watched her continue walking without breaking stride or turning back to look at him. As she strolled into the darkness, Levi's appetite vanished along with her.

May 7th, 1831

Today, my father-in-law gave us one of his slaves. Her name is Maya. Considering the definition of her name, it is so fitting that she has arrived here in this season. She has undoubtedly enhanced the beauty of spring. I never believed in love at first sight, but after what I felt when I first saw her, I'm starting to think that I can't make that claim anymore ...

Those were the first few sentences of a brand-new secret journal that Levi had started the day Maya had moved onto the property years prior. He usually kept that secret journal in a hidden compartment beneath the ground in the barn. But while his wife was away, he had brought it into the house to add his daily entries. He had opened to that first page and read his first passage before finding an empty page to write about the incident with the drifter, as well as his bold statements to Maya in the kitchen.

After finishing his entry, Levi blew out his oil lamp and laid back on the bed with his hands folded behind his head. The latter part of his journal entry had him wide awake staring at the ceiling. He was worried that he had offended Maya with his bold overtures before dinner. He did not understand what had overcome him in that moment. He had gone from three years of successfully suppressing his emotions to letting them erupt all at once. Resisting the unrelenting urge to touch Maya with his hands and with his words suddenly felt like fighting off the urge to breathe. Before meeting Maya, Levi had never felt the sort of deep emotions for a woman that compelled him to act or speak in such a beautiful way without thinking. Not even his wife had ever motivated such boldness.

Had it not been for Wyatt's accidental conception, Levi never would have married Emily. Wyatt was conceived at a church retreat, of all places. While there, a group of teenagers had gotten hold of some liquor. Inadequate supervision for two dozen immature, intoxicated brains proved to be a recipe for disaster. In fourteen-year-old Emily and Levi's case, it was a recipe for a baby. Levi had always considered Emily pretty, but other than what he heard through usual church gossip, he did not know much about her. The following month, however, Levi learned that he was about to spend the rest of his life getting to know Emily extremely well. His knees nearly buckled when she came to him in tears about the fact that she was expecting.

Before Wyatt's conception, Levi had dreamt of going to music school and pursuing a career as a professional pianist. Such motivation was driven by a life-altering trip he had taken to New York to see a symphony live when he was twelve. As dirt poor as their family was, traveling to Manhattan for such an opportunity was a once-in-a-lifetime experience. The unforgettable magical moments Levi experienced the night of that symphony solidified his desire to pursue a career in music. Three years later, however, Wyatt's accidental conception completely changed Levi's life path. Levi's father had taught him well about dealing with the consequences of his poor choices. Levi, therefore, never once questioned what he had to do. Like an upstanding man, he confessed his sins to Emily's father, begged his forgiveness, and asked for his daughter's hand in marriage. Levi then made the selfless decision to put his musical aspirations aside and dedicate his life to being a family man, instead of the esteemed musician he had dreamt of becoming.

Though jolted by the fact that their son would now likely spend his life as a farmer, Levi's family was supportive. His parents scraped together enough money to provide the youngsters with a small farm and a few slaves as a wedding gift. The next gift Levi would receive arrived a few months later on his birthday of all days: his firstborn son. At only fifteen years old, Levi then began his new life as an immature father and husband to a young woman who was essentially a stranger to him.

The perils of two strangers marrying young and caring for a baby began to take their toll within the very first few months of the marriage. Levi quickly realized that he and Emily were not remotely compatible. Being an extremely God-fearing young man, though, divorce was not an option in his mind. He was determined to give Wyatt an upbringing guided by the Lord's word, even if that meant staying in a relationship with a woman that he quickly began to hate with every fiber of his being. He coped with the tortures of his marriage by working long hours on the farm and spending every spare minute with the boys that the couple kept conceiving in the rare moments when they were not bickering.

Emily, in turn, coped with the tortures of their marriage by *secretly* spending money ... lots of it. Most of what she spent went toward liquor. Her first taste of alcohol at the church retreat had been her undoing. She never forgot the way it instantly relaxed and numbed her. She knew immediately it was the medicine she needed to cope with the perils of raising rowdy boys and living in an abysmal, loveless marriage. She was a functioning alcoholic, who consumed more alcohol daily than a man twice her size could handle. While thoroughly intoxicated, Emily would often spend the couple's meager earnings on fancy dresses and purses. She felt she deserved such extravagant items as a reward for dealing with a family she loathed. The more she spent on her addictions, the less time she spent caring for her boys and paying the bills on time like she was charged with doing. Her selfish ways were often the source of massive arguments between the couple that maintained their level of disdain for one another. But *still*, for the sake of his sons, Levi endured every migraine Emily gave him. Like jagged rocks, he swallowed the nightmare of his life and continued to work hard to stay afloat financially and to put food in his children's mouths.

Four years into his tumultuous marriage, Maya was given to Levi by his father-in-law. The very first day she arrived at the plantation, she unknowingly became a source of calm in Levi's emotionally turbulent world. On a daily basis, he and Maya quietly worked with one another in the barn, tending to the animals together like a well-rehearsed symphony. Levi admired the way Maya cared for the animals with such a quiet tenderness ... and the way she quietly cared for *him* as well. Levi never spoke about the disasters of his marriage, but he could tell by Maya's actions that she knew when he was feeling down. She never failed to calmly take over his chores during moments when she sensed his agitation. When the pair did speak, it was usually matters regarding the upkeep of the farm. But Maya's way with words and her ideas to improve production made it clear to Levi that her mind was just as beautiful as her ability to read his emotions. In Levi's opinion, Maya exuded an emotional and intellectual wisdom that far superseded the average eighteen-year-old. They were qualities he was *extremely* attracted to. The uniqueness of her overall being ignited intense feelings within him that he had never felt before.

Ironically, Maya's presence quickly made Levi understand his wife's addiction to alcohol. He finally understood what it was like to have an insatiable craving for something. He understood what it was like to wake up thinking about something, to have it inundate one's every thought every second of the day, to fall asleep with it drenching one's mind, and to have it happily invading one's dreams. He now knew how one's drug of choice had the power to make the most horrible circumstances seem trite. He knew now how if felt to never want to give something up, no matter how wrong it might be. And much like with alcohol, the symptoms of withdrawals immediately set in without the presence of a woman whom Levi had become as helplessly addicted to as a drug.

Levi's *need* for Maya strengthened when he saw that his sons were equally drawn to her warm exuberance. They seemed as instantly addicted to her as he was. Sensing her genuine compassion, they all instinctively flocked to her the first day she arrived. Maya was kind and patient with them as she showed them how to milk cows, brush horses, and collect eggs. Even with a toddler in the bunch, she showed the utmost patience. The boys woke up every morning eager to work with Maya, waddling behind her like little baby geese behind their mother. Even out of her presence, they constantly talked about "Miss Maya" and all the things she was teaching them. Levi certainly understood their extreme enthusiasm. Their mother's alcoholism made her mean, cold, and dismissive. In stark contrast, Maya had a nurturing, loving nature and bathed Levi's sons in it. It made Levi encourage their time with her as much as possible. He knew his boys were naturally desperate for the warm affections that a father could not offer and that their birth mother refused to give. More times than Levi could count, he had glanced over and fought back tears as he silently thanked Maya for filling such a precious, significant role in his sons' lives.

Watching Maya with his boys was not the only reason Levi often glanced at her when she was not looking. Countless times, Maya felt the presence of Levi's eyes on her, but she would turn only to find him concentrating on his work. Levi's stolen glances made her feel as though her intuitions had gone haywire. Unbeknownst to her, though, they were in perfect working order. Levi had always secretly had an affinity for brown-skinned women, but he was utterly captivated by Maya's unique features like no other. Maya never had any idea how hard Levi struggled to quickly pull his eyes away from her in the moments when she nearly caught staring. She never knew how much he absolutely loved the unblemished milk-chocolate color of her skin and the way her light-brown eyes stood out against it. He longed to be trapped in the gaze of those bedroom eyes. He loved the way the tight curls of her afro peeked out of the top of her neatly wrapped scarf. He admired the way she seemed to carry herself like she was meant to be perched on an Egyptian throne with *he* as *her* loyal servant, far too unworthy of being her cherished Pharaoh. The way her full lips perfectly accentuated her face made him feel as though her profile was indeed worthy of painting on the wall of an Egyptian pyramid. Her perfect white teeth, strong jawline, and the evenness of her facial structure made him swear that God had called on his most renowned artist to painstakingly sculpt her. Maya would have been truly stunned to learn that all of her collective beautiful features had made Levi Collins inwardly deem her as a Nubian goddess. Levi's youngest two sons may not have ever been conceived had it not been for that very Nubian goddess playing the lead character in his erotic fantasies while using his wife as an understudy. His fantasies were so powerful, it took an act of God not to moan the wrong name upon climax.

There were far simpler things about Maya that captivated Levi as well. The happy sound of her voice and her laughter as she spoke to his sons would linger in his ears all day like beautiful music. He was especially fascinated by the way Maya would halt her duties altogether and stare out of the barn window in awe of heavy rainstorms, seemingly entranced. In those moments, it made Levi crave to know the secrets of her mind. Even more intriguing to him was the way Maya never failed to smile at the brilliance of the rainbows that often came after those storms. It was for that very reason that he, too, had learned to love the rain. It was not the storm itself that Levi loved but, rather, the clearing of the sky afterward that left a chance to reveal a spectrum of colors as lovely as the smile it would always bring to Maya's face.

Levi never realized how much Maya's rainbow-induced smile had come to mean to him until he was on his way home from picking up supplies in town one day. He looked up and saw a rainbow in the distance after a summer storm had cleared. He immediately stopped his wagon in the middle of the road and stared up at it. He was certain that it stretched over the fields of his farm. He was just as certain that he had missed a rare opportunity to see the phenomenal smile that always lit up his world. He felt his heart sink a little over the thought of missing that beautiful sight. In that instance, Levi closed his eyes and mentally retrieved the perfectly preserved memory of Maya smiling at her precious rainbows. He then opened his eyes and gazed up at the sky again and thanked God for the mysterious wonder that brought such joy to a woman whom he was beginning to care about more than even the strongest man's heart could handle.

After his moment in the kitchen with Maya, Levi now lay in his bed realizing that it was indeed his overwhelmed heart threatening to explode that had caused him to verbally unleash the pressure that had built inside it for years. He could no longer dismiss his feelings for Maya as merely a lustful addiction that would soon subside. Rather, he realized that it was something far more beautiful, yet far more dangerous, considering his circumstances.

After lying in bed for nearly an hour thinking about all the wonderful things Maya had brought into his life, Levi finally came out of his trance and stood up. He walked over to the window of his second story bedroom and looked out at Maya's little cottage in the distance. Despite being in a marriage that was more about obligation than love, Levi was easily able to resist the temptation to indulge with the many beautiful slaves he had known in the past. But Maya had slowly caused his willpower to weaken. Her all-encompassing being had become far too irresistible for even his strong willpower. As of late, nothing seemed to deaden his insatiable desire to see her - all of her - to touch her, to kiss her, to hold her, to be inside of her. No matter what he did, she dominated his thoughts. Maya was a constant on his mind as he slept, worked, and even on the few occasions when he made love to his wife. Watching Maya from a distance had been one thing, but finally touching her the way he had in the kitchen had cemented his strong need for her. It was a feeling he no longer had the willpower or even the desire to run away from. Levi now leaned on his windowpane accepting that in the three years he had worked with Maya, she had slowly and completely seeped into his psyche.

But Levi now feared that his overtness with Maya in the kitchen had scared her. He thought perhaps she would no longer be herself in his presence, much like with the drifter. He questioned whether that fear was at the root of an unrelenting need to see her again. After just a few minutes of staring out the window, Levi suddenly gave into his impulses. He began descending the stairs before he could even think twice about where his legs were guiding him. He did not have anything planned to say to Maya, but that fact did not stop him from opening his front door and trudging along the fields barefoot toward the slave cottages. He was simply determined to settle the unexplainable need to be in her presence again.

Levi crept into Maya's little bedroom in the back of her cottage, surprised to find several candles burning. He gazed at Maya as he quietly closed the door behind himself. He was grateful for the light while she lay there snuggled motionless in her blanket; it allowed him far more time to examine her than he had ever been afforded while stealing glances at her in the barn. The sight of her resting immediately brought him a sense of peace and finally calmed the plaguing need to be near her. Seeing that she too was at peace, Levi shook himself from his trance and turned to leave, not wanting to wake her.

"Don't go," Levi suddenly heard. He stopped and immediately turned back around to find Maya staring at him. He watched her in return as she slowly stood up with her blanket still wrapped around her. They continued to stare at each other in silence for a moment. Those bedroom eyes that Levi had longed to be trapped in were now gazing at him in a way that immediately made his heart start to pound mercilessly against his ribcage. The expression on Maya's face made him curious to know the secrets on her mind. "Is this what you came here for?" she asked as she released her blanket and let it pool around her feet, provocatively revealing those very secrets. Levi's jaw nearly hit the floor along with the blanket. Every drop of blood raced to his pelvis, leaving him as hard as stone after seeing that Maya had just willfully welcomed his eyes to view the luxurious sight of her nude body.

As it turned out, Maya had always found Levi incredibly attractive as well. She loved the way the sunlight created a stunning sparkle in his green eyes. Like a dazzling kaleidoscope, they shifted along a spectrum of beautiful greens, depending on the lighting or the color of his clothes. His unique marble-like eyes were speckled with hints of other colors and were further enhanced by his thick dark eyelashes. The combination made it hard for any woman to turn away from him, either out of envy or because of how mesmerizingly beautiful they were. For Maya it was the latter. She even found beauty in the streaks of red in his blonde hair, which gave away his Irish heritage. He often hid his pale freckled Irish skin beneath a long-sleeved shirt to keep it from burning. But Maya knew all too well that there was a torso layered in pure lean muscle beneath those shirts. She had rarely missed an opportunity to discreetly watch Levi on hot afternoons as he removed his shirt and cooled himself with pails of water. She was as fascinated by his body as her precious rainbows. It always made her curious about what other magnificent wonders his clothing may be hiding.

But, for three years, Maya had talked herself out of the fact that Levi could have ever found her remotely attractive in return ... until their encounter in the kitchen. After that moment, Maya had gone back to the confines of her room feeling far too stimulated to sleep. Much like Levi, their encounter kept her wide-awake thinking about him for the longest time, but not for the reasons that Levi had feared. Maya was in no way offended by the tender way in which he had spoken to her, nor by the gentleness with which he had caressed her face. Those sincere affections were what had ignited her unrelenting urge to strip down and pleasure herself while fantasizing about the way that Levi Collins had touched her in more ways than just the physical.

Their brief intimate encounter in the kitchen had given rise to a multitude of erotic fantasies that Maya was dying to experience. While lying in her room alone, she began envisioning Levi's hands roaming her body, his entrancing green eyes locked on her. Pretending her fingers were his, she slowly slid them inside herself. Just as the pleasure ignited, Levi suddenly appeared in her room. It was as if her aching for him had summoned him at the very moment she had yearned for him most. She froze when she heard him enter. As her heart pounded mercilessly against her chest, she quietly questioned whether to say anything to him. The moment she heard him turn to leave, though, the throbbing between her thighs instantly solidified her answer. Having yet to reach the pinnacle of ecstasy, she now wanted the leading man in her erotic visions to help her finish making the climb.

After being telepathically summoned by Maya's fantasies, Levi now stood before her, his mouth agape. His wide eyes slowly took in every inch of her. From her feet to her toned legs, up to the hourglass curve of her hips, his eyes slowly panned upward. His heart rate increased, and his stones tightened as he gazed at the garden of hair hiding the treasure between her thighs. He continued his visual exploration up her toned abdomen. He paused, yet again, carefully examining the perfection of her perky breasts. The sight of her dark, hardened nipples flooded his mouth with water, no different than gazing at a decadent dessert. From her cleavage to the curve of her neckline, Levi's eyes continued to coast upward. Not one time did he blink as he etched every statuesque feature of Maya into his mind. His watering mouth still agape, his eyes still wide, he looked completely hypnotized by every illustrious detail of her nude body; it was a million times more glorious than his fantasies had ever envisioned.

From her Egyptian-like jawline to her bee stung lips, Levi finished working his way up Maya's flawless face to find her beautiful bedroom eyes still trained on him. "Touch me," she whispered seductively, the very second he looked into her eyes.

Even if Levi wanted to leave, he would not have had the power to make his feet march away while under Maya's spell. She had full control over his mind and his body. *She* now owned *him*. Eagerly obeying the commands of his beautiful seductress, Levi immediately made his way over to her, his eyes unblinking and his heart pounding harder with every step. Despite the short distance between them, he felt as though he could not reach the glorious sight before him fast enough. His breaths became more jagged the very second his hands finally made contact with Maya's smooth toffee-colored skin. Touching her as gracefully as he had earlier in the day, he began gliding his hands along the outline of her curves. From her supple breasts all the way down to her thighs, he delicately touched her skin with his fingertips, his eyes examining every inch of her again. He moaned her name in a drawn-out, breathy tone as he continued to gaze at the wonderment of her body.

Maya closed her eyes, her body and emotions reacting in much the same way as when Levi had touched her earlier. But, this time, she did not try to deny what she was feeling. Instead, she further gave in to the voracious hunger he had stirred inside her. Levi did not dare pull away from her the way he had in the kitchen either. This time, he lacked the willpower to save himself from what he knew he should not be doing. Stopping himself from breathing would have been far easier than overcoming his need to be inside the woman whose delicate skin he now caressed. He *needed* this. He needed *her*. Right here and right now. For Levi, there simply was no other option ... and neither was there for Maya.

Breathing heavily, Levi tenderly slid his hands down Maya's backside and grappled onto the curves of her buttocks. He was instantly addicted to their size and shape. The plushness was unlike anything he had ever felt. His hardened flesh began to ache over the thought of having them flush against his pelvis. Still gripping on tight to each of her perfectly rounded cheeks, Levi let out a subtle groan and gently pulled Maya against him, holding her close enough to feel the throbbing hardness in his pants. Reluctantly releasing her posterior, he then ran his hands back up to Maya's face. He glided the tips of his thumbs across her lips before leaning down to kiss her. It began as a gentle peck but quickly deepened after Maya parted her lips and allowed him to taste even more of her. Their soft moans harmonized as their tongues delicately danced together. Levi gently held the sides of her face, not nearly ready to part ways with the sweetness of Maya's mouth. His mind was still busy filing away the softness of her lips and the flavor of her taste ... and so too was his racing heart.

Levi briefly got hold of himself and pulled back to look at Maya, asking with his eyes if it was okay to proceed further.

Maya responded with a kiss, gently biting his lower lip. "I wanna make you feel good," she reassured him in a sultry whisper. She then turned around and invited him to follow her with nothing more than the sway of her hips. Still under her spell, Levi marched in a hypnotic trance behind her, his eyes locked on the erotic, subtle bounce of her posterior. Maya placed her hands on the wall, seductively leaned over, and invited Levi to invade her insides in a way that she assumed all

143

men preferred it, with very little bodily contact. Levi quickly dropped his pants. Far too impatient to even step out of them, he grabbed Maya's waist and buried his erection deep within her. A savage growl ripped through his throat as the heat of her insides ignited his body. Pleasure exploded from Maya's core, shot through her vocal cords, and came out as an equally animalistic roar.

The intense pleasure overwhelming Levi's body had him scared to move; one more stroke and he knew he would explode. Wanting to ensure Maya's pleasure first, he exhaled to calm himself as he slid his hand down to play with her hidden jewel. She purred as he massaged her; the delightful feeling caused her to slowly grind against his hand. Her slow movements, in turn, began to massage Levi's erection. He exhaled hard once more when he felt his stones threatening to erupt again. As he teased her with one hand, he ran the other up to her breast, and pulled her close to him to cease her grinding. He gently bit the sensitive skin on her neck while tugging playfully at her nipple. Maya's moans deepened, the blend of pleasure and pain causing the moisture between her thighs to flow like a river. Her head relaxed and fell backward. Her beautiful moans drew Levi's lips to hers. The cushiony softness of kissing them brought forth visions of what they would feel like wrapped around a certain part of his anatomy. The images made him turn up the intensity in the way he devoured her lips. The erotic way in which Levi savored her mouth instantly turned-on Maya's hips again. The sudden burst of intense pleasure made Levi break their kiss. He exhaled sharply and Maya's name escaped him in a guttural groan.

Levi finally gave in to the fact that he was now no longer in control. Maya pushed his hands down onto her hips. She steadied her hands against the wall, leaned over, and began slamming herself hard against Levi's erection, swallowing him whole with every thrust. Levi wanted to look down and watch the glorious sight, but the intense pleasure left him far too powerless to even open his eyes. His head fell backward, and his mouth fell open, leaving only his ears to bear witness to the sound of Maya's supple cheeks rhythmically slapping against his pelvis.

"Does it feel good to you?" Maya moaned.

The seductive question nearly made Levi's internal juices break the dam. Just seconds before he overflowed inside Maya, he suddenly pulled out of her and turned her around. With his whole body, he held her against the wall. "*You,*" he breathlessly emphasized, his face less than an inch from hers. "*You* make me feel good," he moaned, descending on her lips again. He closed his eyes and enjoyed them a while longer, waiting for the rising tide in his body to subside. No matter how long he waited, though, he was hopelessly left teetering on the brink of eruption.

Levi did not just want to please himself, though. If he entered Maya again, he knew that would most certainly be the case. Instead, he began sliding his tongue down her body, stopping along the way to sample her breasts again. Maya purred as he sucked and swirled his tongue around her nipples. To add to her pleasure, he glided his fingers inside of her. Her reaction made him drool with the need to taste her nether region. He continued on his descent, kissing and licking his way down her abdomen to her inner thighs. Her constant moaning had him aching with the need to hear the angelic sound of her climax. Working his way up from the inside of Maya's thighs, Levi glided his tongue across her swollen seed. He teased it gently, at first, while tickling her insides with his fingers. He then pulled his fingers out, gripped each of her posterior cheeks tight, and pulled her close. With great force, he then began sucking her pleasure seed. Maya's head fell backward, and her mouth fell open as deep moans began to erupt from her throat. Never in her life had she felt such sensations. Not wanting the feeling to end, she spread her legs, grabbed the back of Levi's head, and forced him to stay put. Her legs immediately began to quiver as Levi sucked hard and gently nipped at her swollen bud.

Within seconds, Maya's internal walls clenched and pulsated. Her knees threatened to give out as she erupted with body-shaking force, piercing Levi's ears with the sounds of her climactic cries.

Levi stood up with those delightful cries still ringing in his ears and the divine taste of Maya's juices still fresh on his tongue. He then lifted her up, let her wrap her arms and legs around his body, and immediately drove his erection back inside of her. He tightly grappled on to her soft posterior again and began putting the muscles in his strong thighs to work. Moaning like a primordial beast, Levi pumped hard inside of Maya, bathing and massaging his flesh with her tight internal walls. The near climactic pleasure of every stroke superseded any feeling he thought was possible inside of a woman. His knees also nearly gave out as he quickly and forcefully erupted inside of Maya's body, crying out for God after feeling as though he had just been catapulted into heaven.

Maya expected that Levi would immediately put his pajama pants back on and walk away feeling satisfied … or possibly guilty. But that was nowhere in his realm of thought. He continued to hold her close, resting his forehead against hers until he caught his breath. He then carefully lifted her from his waist, let her feet touch the ground, and looked deep into her eyes. Although it was over, he kissed her again. It was not a kiss driven by the heat of lust, but because he wanted to. He *needed* to. Maya could feel the sincerity and compassion as his lips softly caressed hers. Tasting herself on him, she moaned and smiled devilishly after their lips parted. Levi smiled in return. His hands were now free, but still, he did not reach for his clothes. Instead, he reached out and caressed Maya's face. He then took her by the hand, guided her to her makeshift bed like a gentleman, and helped her to lay down. Instead of leaving, Levi laid down behind her. Aftershocks of pleasure ricocheted through him when he pulled her nude body flush against his. He gently stroked her skin as his eyes coasted down the side of her body one more time. He was stunned that a woman of her caliber had wanted him as badly as he had been wanting her. Appreciating that fact, he circled his strong arms tightly around her and trailed soft kisses from her shoulder up to her neck. He then stopped to whisper in her ear, "I have a secret."

"Mmm, I guess you most certainly do now," Maya teased as she snuggled into his embrace.

Levi laughed lightly. "Well, that makes two secrets then."

"What's the otha' one?" Maya asked curiously.

"All these years, I've been dyin' to know more about you."

"I suppose you just learned *plenty* more about me," she joked.

Levi laughed again. "And I certainly didn't mind gettin' to know that part of ya' eitha'," he teased in return.

"Well, what more could a man possibly wanna know?"

Levi gently kissed her temple. "I've always been curious about all the fantasies and dreams you have locked away in this mind."

"You just fulfilled one of 'em," Maya easily confessed.

Levi suddenly stopped caressing her arm. "Are you bein' sincere?" he asked, sounding genuinely stunned.

Maya rolled over and faced him. "Seems we've shared an equal cravin' to know more about each otha' all these years, Mr. Collins. I am indeed bein' *sincere* when I say that this is *not* the first time I've fantasized about what lies beneath those clothes of yours."

Levi lifted her chin and softly caressed her lips with his. "I wish I'd've known, I would've come to you years ago."

Maya gazed at him with a wanton look in her eyes. "I'd've much preferred you *cum inside* of me," she whispered seductively.

Her words ignited every nerve ending and gland in Levi's body, causing his testicles to instantly flood with desire all over again. "I'd've satisfied that preference again, again, and ova' again," he moaned, kissing her passionately as his ego swelled to a mountainous size. He then pulled back and looked at Maya like it was the first time he had ever seen a *real* woman. "My God, you've most certainly managed to pique my desire to know about the secrets of your mind tenfold."

"Well, I'm sorry to disappoint, but the rest of the secrets in my odd little mind might only *pique your desire* to drag me to an asylum," Maya joked.

"No worries. Feel free to divulge your secrets. I have a spare strait-jacket lyin' around here somewhere to help protect the masses from your madness," Levi joked in return.

Maya laughed. "Hmm, well, which of my odd thoughts are you eaga' to know?"

"All of 'em. Your hopes. Your dreams. The funny. The serious." Levi touched her temple. "Any and everything locked away in here that you feared revealin' to anyone."

"Well, now I'm curious if *you're* bein' sincere? I've always figured a man would only wanna know what lies between a woman's *thighs* ... not between her *ears*."

"I can't speak for all otha' men in regard to what he wants to know about a woman. And, to be honest, I'd be lyin' if I said that I eva' had a burnin' desire to know the inner thoughts of any otha' women before." Levi propped himself up higher on his elbow and looked Maya in her eyes. "But I am indeed *sincere* when I say that I've been dyin' to know the intimate parts of this beautiful woman named Maya ... the parts that no man can see or touch."

Levi's words instantly unlocked the gates to Maya's vulnerability. She now lay gazing at Levi in awe, equally intrigued by what lies in *his* mind. "I'd ask you not to laugh at my private thoughts, but now I'm suddenly confident that you neva' would."

"*Neva'*," Levi replied, caressing her cheek. "Not unless it was meant for genuine laughta'."

"Well then, get the dusty old strait-jacket ready," Maya joked.

"Will do," Levi smiled.

Maya took a moment to think. "Hmm, well, there is indeed a thought that crosses my mind the very moment I open my eyes every mornin'."

"What's that?"

Maya exhaled and her eyes hovered away from Levi as a twinge of nervousness set in. "Instead of headin' out into the fields or barn to start work, I always wish I's headed to class in some big fancy school."

"Really?" Levi replied, astonishment evident in his tone.

Maya nodded. "I love animals, but I neva' felt like I's meant for farm work. I've always had an unrelentin' desire to learn about all of God's mysterious wonders. I think about it every day. Feels like a burnin' passion, or life callin' or somethin'. I can't really explain it."

"God's mysterious wonders?" Levi replied with genuine curiosity.

"Mm-hmm, I've always been fascinated by nature's phenomenons. Things like..."

"Rainbows?" Levi finished, stating the main thing that had sparked his curiosity about her mind.

Maya looked him in the eyes again and smiled. "How did you know?"

"Just a lucky guess," Levi lied.

"Yes, *definitely* rainbows!" Maya replied, the thought of them broadening her smile.

Infected by her joy, Levi smiled as well. "What else?" he asked, still yearning for more.

"Clouds. I've always wondered why some clouds produce snow, rain, or sleet. Why do some create the sort of thunda' and lightnin' that make it seem like the Gods are at war? Why do some clouds only float like wisps of art paintin' the sky? Weatha' is anotha' thing I've always been curious about. I wanted to unda'stand why the seasons come and go like clockwork. I wish to know what forces are powerin' the sun. Why do we sometimes only see a sliva' of the moon at night, but then see it shine as full and bright as the sun some nights, or some nights not at all. But what I wish to learn most about is the stars. They're by far the most fascinatin' thing in the sky to me."

"Why stars above all else?" Levi replied, hanging on her every word.

"They're the ones I have the most questions about. How did they get there? Why do they twinkle so bright? Does the light shine foreva'? Why are there more stars in the sky than a human could eva' possibly count? Are there otha' animals or people like us livin' somewhere near one of 'em? I'm so fascinated by 'em, sometimes I wish I could make me a floatin' capsule that could fly me up to the moon," she laughed at herself. "I've always wanted to know what the surface feels like. I always imagined it feelin' as soft as powda'. I'd love to nestle into it on my back, stare out at the night sky, and look at all those beautiful twinklin' stars up-close. I bet the view from up there would be so magnificent … it'd probably bring me to tears," she sighed. "Sounds silly I know, but it just all seems so magical and mystical to me, and I can't seem to stop myself from cravin' the answers to all the secrets that only the Lord seems to know."

Levi gazed at Maya silently, his eyes revealing how captivated he was by the secrets of her mind.

Maya looked him in the eyes when he was quiet for too long. "Tryna rememba' where you put that strait-jacket?" she joked.

"An asylum is the last place to trap a mind as captivatingly beautiful as yours."

Not expecting such a reply, a smile emerged on Maya's face that was as grand as her rainbows. "Thank you for that," she replied sincerely.

"You're welcome ... but you certainly make my mind feel so mediocre," Levi joked. "All I've eva' wondered about is the mystery of life?"

"Your musical mind is definitely *not* mediocre!" Maya laughed. "But yes, I'm quite certain there's not a human on this earth who hasn't questioned how we all truly got here ... or *why* we're here. Was it really God? Does he have a plan for all of us? It's certainly crossed my mind. Although, in my odd mind, I've mainly wondered why God created most of us with the ability to produce life ... but not all," she added, a hint of seriousness in her voice.

Knowing why such a thing was a curious question in her mind, Levi caressed her arm. "I can't imagine how it must've felt to learn that about yourself."

"I guess it was a blessin' and a curse as they say. I'm convinced God knew just what he was doin' when he designed me without the ability to make babies. Such a flaw certainly got me outta eva' havin' to go back to those breedin' hellholes."

"I'm so sorry my fatha'-in-law eva' forced you to go there. Those places should be outlawed."

"You owe no apology for his actions."

"I know. But I can't help but apologize for the fact that you eva' had to experience somethin' like that. I just can't fathom what it must do to someone's mind to have such a thing forced on you."

"I can't speak for everyone else, but it helped build a mental strength in me that I neva' thought humanly possible. It's odd the things your mind will do to protect you from goin' insane."

"So, it neva' affected you?"

"A little at first. I cried about it when it was ova' the first few times. But that's when my mind seemed to go to war on my behalf. Afta' a while, I started to just pretend like every man I's with was a man that I loved ... and that he loved me too. It wasn't until then that I learned to enjoy it ... for the *little* time that it lasted anyway," Maya laughed.

"Your beautiful mind hard at work again," Levi replied, gazing at her in awe.

Maya smiled. "Beautiful or insane ... I suppose those descriptions are up for debate," she joked. "But the one thing I know for a fact is how grateful I am that your fatha'-in-law felt I's a waste of his money afta' the doctors told 'em I could neva' have children."

"You're grateful for that?" Levi asked, sounding confused.

Maya nodded. "Because he sent me here afta' all. And helpin' with your boys has filled a motherly void in me. Those handsome little boys of yours have healed me in more ways than any medicine eva' could."

Her confession instantly drew Levi's lips to hers. He let a tender kiss linger there for the longest time. "I'm glad he sent you here too," he whispered, swallowing back an unexpected need to shed a tear over the fact that such an incredible woman ever had to *pretend* she was loved.

When Levi pulled back, he noticed the heaviness of sleep in Maya's eyelids. "You tired?" he asked, caressing her cheek.

"Mm-hmm," she said, her eyelids lowering a bit. "Felt like you drained all the life outta me. Ain't neva' had no man do that little thing you did with your mouth. Thought my legs were gonna give out."

Levi laughed. "Neva' before, huh?" he said, sounding surprised.

Maya shook her head. "The men I's forced to be with only cared about makin' babies ... not makin' me feel good. And they sho' wasn't doin' that little trick you just did with these lips," she laughed, tracing them with her fingertip. "Even if they knew how, I doubt they'd eva' botha'."

Maya seemed to look at such a thing with humor, but Levi was inwardly perturbed by it. "They should have," he whispered, taking her fingertips and kissing them.

"You certainly ain't gonna get an argument outta me about that! Somebody sure could stand to teach those men a thing or two about pleasurin' women!" she joked.

Levi laughed again at Maya's comical nature about such a serious ordeal. "Well, I'm happy to have been the first and even happier that you enjoyed it," he replied pridefully.

"I most certainly did! But it's gonna be two or three days before I get the strength back in my weak knees!" she exclaimed, fighting her sudden sleepiness.

Levi chuckled. "Come here," he said, gently pulling her on top of his chest. He then gathered his arms tightly around her. "Relax," he whispered as he began smoothing his hand up and down her back.

"Don't you have to be up early for church?" Maya asked, grogginess heavy in her tone.

"You tryna get rid of me?" Levi joked.

"Not at all."

"Go on and close your eyes then," he whispered in a very soothing tone, as he continued to glide his hands over her skin. "I'll just stay until you fall asleep." He kissed Maya's forehead and she melted into his chest. Soothed by the comfort of his touch, it was not long before she was sound asleep.

Several hours later, Maya surfaced quickly from her dream state, startled by the strong arms that were still wrapped around her body. Her frantic movements immediately woke Levi up as well.

"You okay?" he asked, gathering her tighter in his arms.

"Well, it's not every mornin' that I wake up in the warm embrace of a man … or *eva'* for that matta'," Maya laughed.

"That's truly a tragedy," Levi replied, softly kissing her on the cheek.

The tender affection sent a surge of butterflies racing through Maya's stomach, causing her to snuggle closer to him.

"You talk in your sleep, ya' know?" Levi teased, his voice sounding deeper than usual just after waking.

"I do not," Maya smiled, sounding just as groggy.

"I swear."

"What was I sayin'?"

"You said, I shooould've eatin' dinnaaa' wiiith Leeevi," he joked.

"I sounded like a ghost?" Maya giggled.

"Sho' did! 'Bout near scared me outta here."

Maya propped herself up on her elbow and looked at Levi, the morning sunlight making the dazzling colors in his eyes easier to see. "You talk in your sleep too, ya' know," she said as she wiped a bit of crust away from his eye.

Levi smiled. "Oh yeah."

"Mm-hmm."

"What did I say?"

"You said, I waaant Maaaya to maaake meee feeel good agaaain," she teased, mimicking his ghostly tone.

Levi moaned lightly, her words immediately causing him to harden. "You must've heard me wrong," he replied.

"Did I now?" she asked, playing along.

"Mm-hmm. Maybe I was mumblin', so let me be more clear this time. I said..." He rolled Maya onto her back, maneuvered himself on top of her and whispered, "I wanna make *Maya* feel good." However, there was nothing sarcastic or silly in his tone this time.

By the tender way Levi kissed her afterward, Maya could feel that he genuinely meant every word of what he had just said. The feeling resonated through her body like a subtle orgasm, and she helplessly moaned as if that was certainly the case. Her response further motivated Levi's desires to stay true to his words. For just a few minutes, all he wanted to do was to taste her and listen to the soft erotic sounds of her pleasure-induced sighs. He then began kissing his way down her body, ready to turn those soft purrs into intense roars of passion. He softly suckled on each of her nipples as he made his descent. He then trailed kisses straight down the center of her stomach. His nostrils flared and his mouth began to water as he closed in on his sweetly scented destination.

All too eager to feel Levi's lips playing in her southern passageways again, Maya spread her legs wide and thrust her hips upward. Her wanton actions caused drool to overflow from Levi's mouth as he suddenly devoured her hidden jewel. The powerful suction caused Maya's breath to catch. She arched her back and tugged hard at Levi's hair as the glorious sensation of his lips and tongue began to rob her of rational thought. But Levi was in no way hurt by her forceful grip. Her actions only made him more eager to suspend his goddess in a state of euphoria. He suddenly eased the force of his suckling and slid his tongue inside her. Simultaneously the pair moaned — she at the glorious feeling and he at her glorious taste. Slowly, Levi then began French kissing her southern lips, wanting to draw out her pleasure. Maya took a hold of his head and gently grinded against his tongue as he ran it along her erogenous corridor. The slight quiver of her legs and the elevating sounds of her cries signaled to Levi what was shortly to come. With every ounce of strength his lips could muster, he suddenly sucked hard on her swollen seed. Maya's back arched, she thrust her hips forward and spasmed again and again, flooding Levi's mouth with the sweet taste of her nectar.

The feel, the sound, and the taste of Maya's body had semen continuously dripping from Levi's hardened flesh. It left a trail on Maya's leg as he kissed his way up her abdomen. When he was lined up with her face, Maya's lips eagerly met his. She immediately parted her mouth, thanking him with a deep passionate kiss. Feeling his pulsating member resting between her thighs, she spread her legs again, erotically begging for more of him. Levi moaned at her wanton actions. More than happy to give her the pleasure she craved, he slowly slid his erection deep inside her. The pair briefly broke their kiss as they simultaneously howled over the searing pleasure now heating their bodies. In unison, they opened their eyes. For a moment, Levi just gazed at Maya. He was simply captivated by everything about her. Wanting to bring her the ultimate pleasure, he descended on her lips again as he began stroking in an extraordinarily slow manner. The gentle way Levi caressed her lips made her feel that she mattered, that her pleasures were a priority above anything else. There were no tricks or movements out of the ordinary in his patient strokes within her. But despite the simplicity, Levi's tender motions made Maya quickly realize that there was an extreme difference between a man who wished to impregnate her and one who wished to *make love* to her.

The passion Levi exuded made Maya eager to reciprocate. She wrapped her legs around him and gripped the strong muscles of his back, wanting his body to melt into hers. She further parted her mouth, happy to let him taste more of her. The experience of being wanted by a woman with such fervent desperation had Levi's stones on the verge of permanent explosion, his mind and body equally on the cusp. He knew now how he wanted to die: inside of this angelic woman as she catapulted him into heaven.

Levi continued the cycle of deliberate slow love making for the longest time. He was striving to bring *Maya* the utmost pleasure, but the intensity was superseding anything *he* had ever felt in his life. The indescribable sensations made him understand how losing a woman to another could drive a man to madness. Maya was not just providing him a means of satisfaction. She was giving him what he had desperately needed for years: knowing what it was like to truly feel wanted by a woman. Maya further proved her want for Levi when his name suddenly escaped her lips in a drawn-out, sultry manner. It erupted helplessly from her, much like the single tear that cascaded down the side of her face. Just hours earlier, Levi had begged her to say his name. He was now hearing it in a beautiful manner, driven by the power of her climactic release. The joy of such a thing brought his ride to an end along with her. The rush of his seed escaping into her felt as intense as their lovemaking had been. The euphoric feeling radiated out to his skin and lingered in his muscles for the longest time, and pleasantly took its time fading from his body.

Maya opened her eyes when she suddenly felt Levi's tears pelting her skin. She looked at him wondering if they were tears of guilt or something more beautiful. He conveyed the answer by the way he passionately kissed her lips. Only his need to breathe forced him to pull away. Even then he remained close, still not ready to part ways. Levi gazed at Maya for a moment as he caressed her cheek. He then tenderly kissed her forehead. "I can't even tell ya' how much I hate to leave you right now but..."

"I know. You gotta get to the church," Maya smiled.

"I'm hatin' myself right now for tellin' 'em that I'd be there today. Wish I'd've let 'em think I's still outta town. But if I don't get there on time, they'll send a search party out lookin' for me," he joked.

"It's okay," Maya smiled. "Go on ahead and get goin'."

Reluctantly, Levi withdrew from her and stood up. Maya watched him the entire time he went about covering his lean strong body with his pajamas. She could not seem to pull her eyes away from him, especially a certain part. A true wonder it certainly turned out to be in Maya's estimation. The length, the strength, and the pleasure it gave her was unlike anything she had ever imagined when she used to gaze at him shirtless across the fields. After the way it had just made her body soar, she felt herself moisten all over again.

When Levi finished dressing, he sat down on Maya's bed. Her nude body was still fully exposed. He let his eyes roam over it again, still feeling the high from being inside of it. He ran his hand down her arm and intertwined their fingers. He lifted her hand, kissed it, and brought it close to his chest. With his other hand, he caressed her face, leaned down, and kissed her passionately on the lips again. He pulled back and momentarily gazed into Maya's eyes. "I lo- ..." He caught himself and swallowed hard, suddenly scared of how easily that phrase almost rolled off his tongue.

Maya looked at him when he paused, and she could see the fear in his eyes. She suddenly became afraid too, afraid of what her reply might have just as easily been.

"I-I'm late," Levi said instead.

"I know. Go on."

He covered Maya up. "Rest well."

"Trust me, afta' that, I certainly will," she smiled.

The words were a further boost in Levi's already heightened ego. He smiled in return and kissed Maya's hand again. He then departed, feeling proud that he had succeeded in his quest to bring Maya as much pleasure as she had brought him over all the years he had known her.

When Levi was gone, Maya rolled over and nestled into the blanket that still had their scent on it. She then fell quickly into a much-needed deep sleep for a good portion of her Sunday afternoon off. When she finally awakened, she went out to the creek to bathe. She stayed there a long while relaxing in the water, unable to stop herself from smiling at the constant recurring memory of her night with Levi. The beautiful visions made her wish that he was wading there with her, holding her, caressing her, and making love to her all over again.

Maya finally made her way back to her little cottage when she was finished bathing. With Levi heavily on her mind, she had a helpless smile on her face the whole way there. She walked into her room and was about to hang her towels up to dry when something laying on her makeshift bed caught her eye. She laid her towels down on a table and walked over to her bed where there was an elongated wooden box with a red bow tied around it. She untied the bow and opened the lid on the box. She gasped and immediately began to tear up when she saw what was laying inside.

Suddenly, Maya heard a noise behind her. Startled, she turned around to find Levi leaning against the doorway of her room. "I put in an orda' to get you one of them floatin' capsules," he began, while gazing at Maya, "but they said it won't be ready for anotha' five hundred years." He walked closer to her, picked her gift up off the bed and put it in her hands. "So, until then, I figured this telescope was the closest I could get you to layin' up on that powdery moon and gettin' a betta' look at all those magnificent stars up-close."

"Thank you," Maya replied with the utmost sincerity in her voice as her waiting tears cascaded down her cheeks. "I'll *always* cherish this," she whispered.

"Just as I'll always cherish you," Levi replied, gently placing his hand on Maya's face. "I appreciate *everything* you've eva' done around here for me and my boys. I'm grateful for you, Maya." He wiped away her tears and then kissed her tenderly on the lips. "Truly grateful," he said, looking her in the eyes.

Maya smiled and nodded, once again, too stunned by his words to reply. Levi wiped away the last of her tears, walked away, and left her alone to enjoy his sincere gift of gratitude.

In that summer of 1834, Levi Collins indeed needed serious repairs to his barn roof. With how horribly his wife had mishandled the finances, he needed every dime to get it fixed. But he now stood staring up at the tarp that he had strategically placed over the hole, content to let it stay there. He suddenly did not care if that barn crumbled into a million little pieces. He felt the money he had spent on Maya's telescope was worth the sacrifice.

... James had to force himself to close an awe-inspiring journal that detailed the relationship of Lily's parents through her father's eyes. The things that he was learning about him had him so intrigued. He wondered why Lily seemed not to know any of this about her mother and father? Considering the dates of the entries he had just read, James was now curious to know what Levi's reaction was going to be when he found out that Maya would soon be giving him a gift that was far more precious than the one he had just given her. He was determined to find the answer, as well as what other startling revelations lay inside the secret journals of Levi Collins. But James was also on a far more important mission. He snuffed out the fire in the cave he was hiding in and tried to sleep before setting out toward Ohio in the dead of night to begin his search for the very gift that Maya had delivered to Levi nine months after their enchanting night together.

Chapter Eight

"Who the hell's in here?!" Harrison yelled, cocking a double barrel shotgun. "I'll blow your fuckin' head off!"

"Harrison! Don't shoot! It's just me! It's James!"

"*Adams?!*"

"Yes, it's just me," he reiterated, as he cautiously stepped out of an empty horse stall with his hands up.

Harrison exhaled a sigh of relief, slowly lowered his rifle, and lifted his lantern. "Jesus! You look like a goddamn mountain man with that beard. What the hell're you doin' in here?"

"I needed a place to hide out tonight."

"To *hide?*"

"Yeah, I'd've knocked, but I didn't think you'd be up this time of night."

"Trust me, I wouldn't be if it wasn't for that new son of mine. Lauren was up feedin' 'em and said she glanced out the window and saw someone dashin' into the barn."

James heard the pride in Harrison's tone when he spoke of his newborn. He was immediately struck with envy over the fact that his friend's baby was alive and well. "Got yourself a son now, huh?"

"Yes, he's finally here." Harrison nodded with a proud fatherly smile. "Zachariah Lee Mitchell. A one-month-old bald-headed wonda'

161

that doesn't believe in sleepin' between the hours of midnight and six a.m.," he joked.

"Congratulations. I couldn't be happier for you and Lauren." James truly meant it despite his envy.

"Thanks," Harrison smiled. "What about you? I know you and Lily were expectin' a few months before us. How's your little one?"

"Dead," James replied bluntly.

The smile immediately faded from Harrison's face and his heart sank into his stomach.

"My little girl is dead," James reiterated, lowering his head and shaking it to ward off tears.

His words felt like a knife in Harrison's gut. He immediately felt regret over speaking so joyously about his newborn. "James, I'm so incredibly sorry," he said, sincere empathy in his tone. "I shouldn't've brought it up. I…"

"No, it's okay. You couldn't've known."

"I'm almost afraid to ask, but wh-what about Lily?"

"That's what I came to ask you, actually. But based on this conversation, it's obvious you know just as little about what's happened to her as I do."

Harrison shook his head in confusion. "What? Why would I know anything?"

"This confirms that you neva' got any of my letta's."

"No. What letta's? I's up in Dayton for several months workin' on a major murda' case. I had my mail forwarded there, but I neva' got any letta's from you."

"I'm not surprised."

"What were the letta's about?"

James ran his hands through his hair and blew out a frustrated breath. "It's a long story."

"Well, come on in and tell it to me. I got all night to listen. Zach's gonna make sure of that."

He slapped James on the shoulder and the two of them went into the house. Harrison immediately gave James a glass of whiskey when they walked in. From the little he had already heard he knew James would need something strong to take the edge off. Harrison then left his buddy alone for a few minutes while he went to the kitchen to warm him up some leftover stew, and to let his wife know that all was okay. By the time he returned, James's glass of whiskey was empty. Harrison grabbed the entire bottle of whiskey from the cabinet and set it on the table to let James refill his glass as needed. No sooner than he sat it down, James indeed picked it up and poured himself another. He guzzled the second shot and exhaled loudly to cool his burning throat. Harrison did not push James to talk. He poured himself a glass of whiskey too and comforted James with his presence while he waited patiently. After drinking his whiskey, Harrison went to check on the stew. As soon as he walked away, Lauren came downstairs with the baby. Harrison was returning with the bowl of food and panicked when he saw his wife walking over to show James their son. He was worried that it might upset him.

"Hi James," Lauren said, swaying side to side with Zachariah in her arms.

James stood up to greet her. "Hello, Lauren. Nice to see you again. Sorry for the late-night intrusion. I didn't mean to scare you. I would've knocked, but I figured y'all were sleepin'."

"*Sleep?* What's that?" Lauren joked. "This little guy doesn't believe in lettin' us do that anymore," she said, smiling down at her son.

"So, I've heard," James replied, caressing his bald head.

Lauren smiled at the way he touched him so gently. "Do you wanna hold 'em?"

"Sweetheart, I don't think that's a good idea," Harrison intervened.

"No, it's okay Harrison. I want to," James replied.

Lauren looked a little confused as to why her husband had just tried to stop her, but she went ahead and gladly handed the baby over to James. James took him gently into his arms, gazed at the wide-eyed little boy, and managed a genuine smile. He sat down on the sofa with him and just stared. He already felt such love for Zachariah for no other reason than the fact that he was the son of a man he loved like a brother. James's tears began stirring as he sat there wishing that it was Rose gazing back at him with bright, curious eyes. He lifted Zachariah up and kissed his tiny forehead. "You two are blessed," he then said to Harrison and Lauren. "Guard this little guy with your life."

"Trust me, we will," Harrison said, reaching over to caress his son's head. "Zachariah, that's your godfatha' you're starin' at, buddy."

James looked up at Harrison, surprised.

"At least that's what Lauren and I are hopin' anyway," Harrison added.

James glanced over at Lauren as well. She smiled and nodded.

"I'd be honored," James replied.

"So would we," Lauren said.

"I'm convinced that you'd guard my son with your life if anything eva' happened to us," Harrison added.

James glanced back down at Zach. "I swear I would."

Zachariah yawned and he suddenly struggled to keep his eyelids open.

"I see you even have the magic touch. He gets good and sleepy in your arms. I need you here more often this time of night," Lauren joked. "I guess I'll take 'em on upstairs and see if he'll actually sleep through the night for a change ... and *myself* for that matta'," she teased.

James stood up and kissed the baby on the forehead. "Good night, little guy," he whispered as he handed him back to his mother. "Good night, Lauren."

"Good night, James. And thank you."

James nodded.

"I'll be up in a bit," Harrison said, kissing his wife before she departed.

James was quiet for a moment as he watched Lauren walk up the stairs. He then walked over and picked up a picture of Zachariah on the fireplace. "I'd truly be honored to be your son's godfatha' Harrison," he said while staring at the photo. "But I don't know if I really deserve it. I didn't wanna say that in front of Lauren."

"Why wouldn't you?"

James walked back over, poured himself another shot of whiskey and sat down. Instead of drinking the shot, though, he just stared at it. "I'm a fugitive, Harrison. I escaped from prison a few days ago."

"A *fugitive?*" Harrison replied, disbelief obvious in his tone.

"Don't worry. I won't stay here long. I don't wanna get you in trouble with the law."

"What were you convicted of?"

"Murda'," James answered bluntly. "And a long list of otha' things."

Silence.

James finally stopped staring at his liquor and turned to look at his friend. "I killed a man, Harrison … three of 'em actually. And what should scare you most is the fact that I don't have a single regret about it."

"James, I've known you for nearly eight years. If you did somethin' that drastic, I have no doubt it was for good reason."

"Then you do know me well." James finally guzzled the shot in his hand. He then began explaining in graphic detail the violent and vile things that transpired the day he tried to escape with Lily and why he ultimately felt the need to commit three homicides. Without once interrupting, Harrison hung on his every word in utter shock over the tragedies that Lily had suffered through that led to the death of their baby.

"Holy shit!" Harrison said, shaking his head. After absorbing the entire sordid tale, he let his body fall back on the couch.

"*Holy shit* is definitely what all this has been," James continued. "So, while I's stuck waitin' on the trial to begin, I wrote several letta's to you and William, hopin' to get some help with my case and with findin' Lily," he further explained.

"You know I'd've done everything I could for you if I'd've known the shit you were stuck in."

"I have no doubt about that. When you didn't respond, it was the first sign that I's up shit's creek from the outset. I neva' stood a chance at that trial. I'd heard stories about entire towns turnin' on a criminal to ensure a conviction, but I neva' believed it was truly possible until it happened to me. They even gave me the death penalty for what was clearly self-defense or, at worst, manslaughta'. But I'm sure that's not the offense they wanted me to hang for any damn way."

"That doesn't surprise me at all when I consida' the fact that you were dealin' with a town full of narrow-minded racists. What does surprise me is the fact that you escaped a maximum-security prison. How the hell'd you pull that off?"

"Lily's half-brotha's orchestrated the whole damn thing, if you can believe that."

"Her *brotha's?* No, I *can't* believe that."

"Yeah, it's anotha' long story, but they have their own good reasons for wantin' me out. They actually want me to deliva' a message to Lily."

"Must be pretty damn important if they were willin' to commit a felony for it."

"Yeah, it's shockin' what they need me to tell 'er. It's gonna rock Lily to 'er core." James shook his head. "I know it rocked mine."

James briefly explained the history of Lily's life and the dynamics between her father, mother, and brothers. He then reached in his satchel and handed Harrison the letter from Wyatt and Colt.

Harrison took a moment to read it and then glanced up at James. "As an attorney, I've heard some of the most outlandish, sordid tales. But I don't think even the greatest author on earth could weave this kind of plot. If it wasn't you who just handed me this and explained this whole story, I'd say you belonged in a goddamn asylum."

"And if it wasn't for Lily's brotha' handin' that to me and livin' through this personally, I wouldn't believe any of this shit eitha'. I guess afta' that crazy trial, Lily's brotha's figured I'd do anything to find 'er and give 'er that letta', which you know is the God's honest truth. That's why I'm here now. The doctor who was helpin' me escape with Lily was supposed to bring 'er here to you, if all else failed with our plans."

Harrison shook his head. "It's quite possible that your doctor friend may have come by here with Lily. Lauren and I left the day afta' your weddin' and went to Dayton. I had a major murda' case I's workin' on that had a change of venue. We went ahead and stayed up there with Lauren's parents afta' the trial, so we could have the baby there. We just got back to town a few days ago actually."

"Damn. That's certainly on par with my bad luck as of late," James replied, shaking his head.

"I know you can't travel back to Fayetteville now, but can you maybe try to write that doctor a letta' and find out where he took Lily?"

"That's the otha' bafflin' part of this shit. His wife came by the jail and told me that he neva' came back home. And that was at least a good two months afta' he left with Lily."

"Damn." Harrison shook his head. "Have you contacted William?"

"I went by his estate, but it's still empty. I assume he's still in Manhattan with his sons. That's part of the reason I'm here too. I's hopin' you'd help me get a letta' to him. I can't show my face at a post office, or any time durin' daylight hours for that matta'. I'm quite sure my wanted posta's are plastered everywhere by now, especially at post offices. So, if I write a letta', can you mail it to William for me?"

"Of course."

"I'm gonna make my way north to Manhattan along the original plotted map that Griff gave us. If my luck turns around, maybe I'll find Lily along the way, or at least some information as to her whereabouts."

"That's a good idea."

"I'm hopin' that Lily is already up there with William, and I'm just ova'reactin' about all of this."

"I gotta be honest with ya'." Harrison leaned forward and rested his elbows on his knees. "First and foremost, your doctor friend is missin'. That sounds suspicious to me. A good, hard workin' town doctor isn't just gonna up and disappear from his family for nothin'. And secondly, if Lily really was safe in Manhattan with William, she would stop at nothin' to come lookin' for *you*, just like you would for *her*. So, don't try to convince yourself that the shit you're smellin' right now is roses. I hate to be so callous, but I think you might need to prepare yourself for the worst."

"I guess I hate to accept that, but you're right. That's exactly what I's initially thinkin'. But it just pains me too much to imagine the worst right now." James let out a heavy sigh. "I tell you what, Harrison, it's eatin' a hole in my soul not to have the slightest clue where my wife could really be."

"I can only imagine. I think I'd crumble to pieces if I eva' lost my wife and son. I honestly don't know how you're holdin' it togetha' right now."

"By a goddamn thread, that's how. And it feels like that thread is bound to snap at any minute."

Harrison was silent for a moment while he thought of something. "Have you considered checkin' out some of those unda'ground secret safe houses? I've heard whispers about more and more of those places poppin' up and helpin' slaves make their way to freedom. A case I once worked on involved an ex-slave who told me he'd been to three different safe houses here in Ohio. He said they were set up just as ya' cross ova' the borda' from Virginia. One was on the outskirts of Watertown, anotha' near Reedsville, and also somewhere around Marietta. He said they were more like makeshift camps than actual houses. All of 'em were in remote locations in the middle of the woods. He said they were hidden really well. I'm not sure exactly how to get to any of 'em, but maybe it's worth checkin' out before you head north."

"Now that I think about it, Gideon once mentioned relayin' supplies for a few Negro infirmaries on the outskirts of Belpre and

Marietta durin' his mission trips. Maybe it's a possibility that he sought help from someone there."

"Sounds promisin'."

"Anything's possible at this point. I'll give it all a shot before I head to Manhattan."

"And I'll see what information I can find on my end. I'll be sure to keep William's address. If I find out anything about Lily, I'll write to 'em and let 'em know."

"I'd appreciate that."

"I'll be prayin' you find 'er."

"Thank you. I need all the prayers I can get." James stood up. "Listen, do you mind if I sleep in your barn tonight? I'll be gone before sunrise, and I'll find anotha' place to hide out until nightfall."

Harrison stood up too. "Hell no, you can't sleep in the barn. You can take your ass in there to the guest bedroom. You can leave wheneva' you're ready."

"But…"

"*But* nothin. I'm a lawya', rememba'? I know all too well about plausible deniability."

"What the hell is that?" James asked.

"Simply put … nobody can prove that I know you're a fugitive, so there's nothin' to worry about." Harrison pointed toward the hallway. "Second door on the left. Get some rest. Feel free to eat whateva' you like when ya' get up. You can take some leftova's with ya' when ya' leave too. I'm off to get some sleep while that boy of mine is down."

James nodded. "Thanks for everything."

"Anytime."

Utilizing Harrison's generosity, James spent the daytime hours hiding out in his house and playing with his new godson. When Zachariah went down for his nap, James wanted to take a nap too, but the pages of Levi's journal had him far too intrigued to sleep. He dug the first book out of his satchel, laid back on his bed, and continued to read where he left off ...

Chapter Nine

September 1834

Levi closed the barn door behind himself and lowered the latch to stop anyone else from entering. Startled by the thud, Maya turned around to find herself trapped there with him. He felt an intense rush of warmth flood his body when she smiled at him. He exhaled as he gazed at her in return. For the remaining three days that his family was out of town, Levi had stayed the night in Maya's cottage, making love to her, talking and laughing with her, and falling asleep with her in his arms. It pained him to abruptly dispense with the beautiful ritual when his family finally returned. Levi had not been himself since then. With Maya constantly on his mind, he was barely able to sleep or ingest food. Oddly though, he was not thinking about what most men would be thinking about after such an unforgettable experience with a woman. There was something else saturating his mind that he knew he needed to speak with Maya about sooner rather than later. Finally having mentally prepared himself to do that, Levi walked over and stood within a foot of her. "Maya, about what happened between us …" he suddenly froze. He had gone over in his head a hundred times what he wanted to say but standing there now with Maya's beautiful doe-like eyes trained on him, he suddenly forgot every word. His throat had gone dry, his palms were sweaty, and his heart began pounding as he watched the joyful smile start to fade from her face.

By the way Levi was looking at her, Maya already knew what was weighing heavily on his pounding heart. "It's alright," she replied. "No need to explain." Feeling embarrassed, she lowered her head. "It was all a mistake."

Levi gently lifted her head. He waited for her to acknowledge him with her eyes. "*A mistake?* Is that what you really think?"

Maya nodded. "But I unda'stand why," she replied, lowering her head again when she felt the sting of impending tears.

"If you think I feel an ounce of guilt or shame about what happened between us, then *no* ... you *don't* unda'stand." Levi lifted Maya's head again. "If there's one thing I've neva' had a single regret about in my life, it was the honor of makin' love to you."

"But I see regret written all ova' your face."

"There's a million emotions runnin' through me right now..." He took hold of Maya's hand. "But I promise ya', regret ain't one of 'em."

"Maybe not. But I sense there's somethin' wrong. I can feel it."

"Ironically, what's wrong is the fact that I *don't* feel an ounce of guilt or regret about what happened between us." Levi let go of Maya's hand, exhaled, and took a step back. He suddenly had a faraway look in his eyes when he finally recalled what he had come to say. "*You'll just know...*"

Maya looked confused. "I don't unda'stand."

"That's what my fatha' told me when I's around thirteen-years-old," Levi explained. "I had asked him how I was supposed to know when I'd found the right woman to spend my life with. He looked at me and said, 'Son ... *you'll just know*. It's nothin' any man can eva' explain. You'll just know.' My fatha' and motha' were happily married for decades, so I thought he'd have some wisdom-filled answer that would solve that mystery for me, but ... *you'll just know*. That's all he had to say. For years and years, I didn't have the slightest clue what he meant by that." Levi returned from the lost land of his memory and looked directly into Maya's eyes. "Not until the day you walked onto this plantation.

"For the last three years, it feels like I've done nothin' but think about you all day, every day ... *nonstop*. Somethin' happens in my life, good or bad, and you're the first person I wish I could tell. I go to bed at night wishin' like mad that I could make love to you and hold you in my arms while we sleep. I fall asleep and I have the most glorious dreams about you. I jump up every mornin' eaga' to see you, 'cause workin' beside you is always the best part of my day. Hell, I can't stand it in this damn barn the minute you walk outta here. I watch you with my boys and wish to God you were their motha'. And that smile of yours. I see you smilin' at my boys, and all of God's precious wonders, and it lights up my world. I ain't neva' felt like this for anyone before ... not eva'. In fact, I didn't know a man could eva' be so strongly affected by a woman. Such a thing was foreign to me ... until you moved here. It was then that I realized my fatha' was right. It's nothin' I had the words to explain. *I just knew* ... I knew almost immediately that there was this incredible woman named Maya that I wanted to spend the rest of my life with. Because you're everything I've eva' wanted in a woman and in a motha' for my children ... *absolutely everything*."

Even after absorbing the genuine tone in Levi's voice as he divulged his sentimental secrets, Maya still did not succumb to her need to cry. She just continued quietly gazing into Levi's eyes.

Levi stepped forward and gently touched her face. "*A mistake?*" Levi shook his head. "I will neva' in life view what happened between us as such a thing. How could it eva' be a mistake to make love to the woman who finally made complete and total sense of my fatha's answer?"

Wanting to protect her emotions, Maya still tried not to let her heart fully absorb Levi's passionate confession. "You say these beautiful things, but you've come to tell me that you don't wanna make love to me anymore … haven't you?" she asked, her voice quivering slightly as she fought to swallow back her tears.

"Maya, I *want you* like I have neva' wanted anything else eva' before in my *whole damn* life," Levi replied with most intense look on his face. "The greatest moment of my life was layin' inside of you. I didn't know it was supposed to feel that way, like no words were eva' invented to adequately describe it." He shook his head and closed his eyes as he thought of it. "I just neva' knew." He opened his eyes and looked at Maya. "And now that I do know, it's got me wantin' you in a way that makes me feel like I'll go mad if I'm denied the honor of makin' love to you … But it's not *just* the pleasures of your body I want, Maya." He touched her cheek again. "I want *you*. I want a life with you. I want a home with you. I wanna raise my boys with you … I wanna marry you. Perhaps that's what you see written on my face. The look of a man who's been wrackin' his brain for days tryna figure out how I could give this incredible woman the sort of life she well deserves. You got my thoughts and desires spiralin' outta control. You make me wanna say to hell with all the rules, to hell with consequences, to hell with society. The things I've been seriously thinkin' about sacrificin' for you make me feel like I'm goin' completely insane. I'm wantin' to give up *everything* to build a life with you, Maya. But how? That one question's got me up at night. It gnaws at me at every second of the day.

"Trust me, if I had the powa' to take you and my boys and flee to a place where we could all live in peace togetha', we'd've been gone years ago." Levi exhaled. "But afta' wrackin' my brain for three days, I realize that I just keep askin' myself a question that there is no answer to. I simply have to swallow the painful reality that I can't make the sort of sacrifices I wanna make for you without severe consequences and destroyin' lives in the process." He caressed Maya's face again. "And I just can't bring myself to lay inside of you every night knowin' that's all I can eva' give you. I can't be a loyal, God-fearin' man and do that to you. You deserve so much more than that. I don't just wanna give you that little *piece* of me. I wanna give you *all* of me. I wanna be the sort of man that gives you *everything* in life. I wanna put you on a pedestal where a woman like you rightfully belongs..." Levi shamefully dropped his head after finding it hard to look Maya in the eyes as he finished his statement. "And it hurts to know that I can't."

Maya also lowered her head to hide her face when the sting of tears began to escalate into a burn. "I unda'stand now," she replied.

Hearing defeat in Maya's tone, Levi finally looked up at her again. "Maya, please, don't look away from me," he begged, gently lifting her head again. "I don't think you truly do unda'stand how hard it is for me to say these things to you. But just know that it takes every bit of strength within me to keep doin' right by my family. Truth be told, I don't know how the hell I'm gonna find the strength to deprive myself of you, and that's the God's honest truth. I feel like I deserve the pain that's sure to come for not givin' you all that you deserve. So please, at the very least ..." He gently touched her cheek. "I beg you not to deprive me of seein' this beautiful face when we speak."

Maya nodded, forcing a smile. "I know how hard it is. And I do believe it's the right thing to do. You have to do right by your boys. Your boys are my world. I'd go to the ends of the earth for 'em and they ain't even mine," she said, managing another brief smile. "So, I can only imagine what you'd do to ensure their happiness."

Levi could not help but kiss Maya's hand for hearing her speak that way about his sons. It further added to the pain of not being able to openly share his life with her.

"Logically, I know you're doin' the right thing," Maya reiterated, feeling the lump starting to tighten in her throat. "That's why I just can't unda'stand why this hurts so bad."

Levi knew *exactly* what force was at work making her feel such pain over the matter; it was the same emotional force that was causing his current pain too.

"I guess I've been ignorant too," Maya confessed. "I neva' realized that there was such a beautiful difference in just makin' babies and makin' love … until the past few nights with you." She looked Levi in the eyes with tears welling in hers. "Ain't nobody eva' made love to me or touched me the way you did," she admitted, her lip slightly quivering. "It's the first time I didn't eva' have to *pretend* to feel loved. I just … I ain't neva' felt so loved."

"That's because you *are*, Maya," Levi responded rapidly. "I love you to your precious stars and back. Despite our situation, don't you eva' doubt that, ya' hear?"

Maya suddenly buried her face in her hands. His beautiful confession caused her to completely unravel. She did not stand a chance of holding back the deluge of tears that suddenly erupted from her eyes. Her tears instantly triggered Levi's. He wrapped his arms around her and held her as she wept. He equally needed her warmth to soothe himself.

When their emotions settled slightly, Levi gently raised Maya's head to look into her eyes. "If there's anything I regret, it's these tears that I've caused," he said as he tried to wipe them away. "Feels like a dagger in my heart."

As always, Maya quickly found the courage to cope with the reality of her life. She thought of Levi's adorable little boys and they instantly gave her strength. She exhaled and stepped out of his embrace. "You're an upstandin', honorable man, Levi Collins. I greatly respect you for that. So, you do what you have to do for your sons. Don't you worry about me … I'll be okay."

Levi believed her, but that notion did not stop him from worrying, nor the excruciating pain in his chest. "Well then, you're a stronga' woman than I am a man. I'll *neva'* be okay with not lovin' you the way you deserve. To not have your words soothin' my ears, to not have the sweet sound of your laughta' healin' me, to not feel the touch of your soft lips, to not feel your bare skin next to mine while I hold you in my arms at night is gonna cripple me ... in fact, it already has."

"It may take time, but I have the utmost faith that you'll find the inna' strength to weatha' this storm too." Maya then cleared her eyes, stepped past Levi and exited the barn.

Levi turned to watch Maya leave. The way he suddenly struggled to breathe, he swore his heart departed along with her.

Chapter Ten

After reading a few more pages of Levi's journal, James forced himself to sleep during the remainder of the daylight hours. At nightfall, he gathered some food and gave Harrison his letter to mail to William, stating that he would be arriving in Manhattan in the coming days. James then said his goodbyes to Lauren, Harrison, and baby Zachariah and set out in search of the safe houses that Harrison had mentioned. After traveling nearly eight hours, he arrived in Reedsville. He found a place to hide during the daylight hours and then spent all night searching every heavily wooded area he encountered. All he found was a series of wind-torn tents, pots, and pans that he assumed were the abandoned remains of a slave safe-house. James slept there and took anything of use before pushing further north five hours to Belpre, only to come up empty there as well. His disappointment also persisted in Watertown. While on the four-hour trek to Marietta, however, James lucked out and came upon a small, impoverished town in the middle of nowhere. From a distance, he watched the well-hidden little town and learned that it was indeed a tiny Negro community. As he sat spying on the outskirts, a two-story building caught his attention. By the sort of people and equipment he saw moving in and out of the place, James assumed it was a small hospital.

As soon as darkness fell, James began making his way toward the tiny community. Not wanting to prance through the town like an authoritative aggressor, he left his horse and weapons tied to a tree and walked down to the clinic instead. Moving briskly, he was able to make it to the hospital without encountering anyone. The run-down building barely had a working door, let alone any locks. He walked right in and was instantly met with the glaring eyes of two women who looked to be in charge of caring for all the sick patients there. They immediately froze when they saw him.

James could sense the fear that had come over the two ladies after seeing his unfamiliar white face. He laid his jacket down and slightly raised his hands in the air to help put them at ease. "I'm not here to harm anyone. I'm lookin' for someone and I'm hopin' y'all can help me."

The two nurses just turned to look at one another. They then turned to look at James again without saying a word.

"May I approach you?"

Again, they remained silent.

James kept his hands up and moved cautiously toward them anyway. He stopped five feet away from them. "My name is James. I'm lookin' for a Negro woman named Lily. Light brown skin. She's about this tall." He motioned with his hand. "She's slenda' with long, dark-brown, curly hair and greenish hazel eyes. She's a very beautiful woman, but she may have been brought here in pretty bad shape with an olda' white man named Gideon … Gideon Whitfield. He's a doctor. I think he may even have relayed supplies to someone for this hospital in the past. They would've been here sometime around mid-April. Any recollection of the two of 'em?"

Both ladies looked at one another and then looked at James again. "No sa', I'm sorry. We ain't seen nobody like that 'round here," one of the nurses replied.

James felt his heart sink. He nodded his head. "Thank you anyway." He picked up his jacket and headed out the door.

"Mista'," James suddenly heard from behind him just as he stepped out onto the dirt path. He stopped and turned around to find a tall, thin, fair-skinned Negro woman with light brown hair and eyes standing there. She looked like she could have been Lily's older sister in some ways. She was standing in the doorway of the hospital, staring at James. She nervously glanced behind her before speaking again. "Did you say your name was James?"

"I did."

"Come with me." The woman led him to a tiny little cottage not too far from the hospital. Once he was inside, she peeked her head outside to be sure that nobody saw them enter before she closed and locked the door. She then turned around and looked at James. "I'm Ava."

James nodded. "Nice to meet you, ma'am."

"Forgive my two nurses for bein' unwillin' to tell you anything in there. We're a part of the unda'ground railroad system. I've trained 'em not to whispa' a word to any outsida's about anyone, no matta' how trustworthy they may seem. Actually, unda' normal circumstances, I wouldn't tell some strange white man anything eitha'. But I'm confident that I can trust you."

"Why the immediate confidence?" James asked.

"Your last name is Adams, isn't it?"

"Yes ma'am. How did you know that?"

"C'mon and have a seat." Ava led him to a tiny kitchen table. He sat down while she poured herself a cup of coffee. "Would you like a cup?" she offered.

James nodded. "Thank you."

Ava walked over with both of their cups and sat down across from him. "I heard you mention a doctor named Gideon."

James's heart started to pick up pace. "Yes, do you know him?"

Ava nodded. "I met him years ago on a mission trip. We got to be decent friends. You're right. I did get supplies from him sometimes like you mentioned. Ova' the years, he'd bring me medications, equipment, or anything else he could spare that he felt my little hospital could use. He'd write me once or twice a year and let me know when we could meet. We always chatted while exchangin' goods. I still rememba' the year he came up here and told me that he'd finally had a son ... little Brandon," Ava smiled. "He was so thrilled. He just went on and on about him. I's so happy for 'em. He deserved it. He'd always been such a kind and carin' man. I rememba' thinkin' his son was lucky to have a fatha' like him. I assume that's the Gideon you're speakin' of, right?"

"That's definitely him. If you've pulled me aside like this then I can only assume Gideon was here back in April," James stated.

Ava nodded, looking down at her coffee cup. She sighed. "He's *still* here."

James perked up. "Where?!"

Ava finally looked up at him. "The cemetery."

The revelation sent a shockwave racing down James's spine and his heart plummeted into the pit of his stomach. "God no," he whispered, lowering his head.

"Gideon indeed rolled in here back in April in a panic. He 'bout near scared the life outta me and my nurses. His right arm was covered in blood. Come to find out, he had a bullet wound in his shoulda'. He was weak and pale as a ghost when we helped him down outta his wagon. I can tell he tried to treat his wound on his own. It was already stitched, but it was red, swollen, and badly infected by the time he got here."

"Did he say who shot 'em?"

"No. I neva' could get a clear answer from him. He just kept on mumblin', '*I tried, but they weren't there. You gotta help 'er.*' Ova' and ova' again, that's all he kept sayin'. I neva' figured out who *they* were."

James quickly concluded that "they" had to have been Harrison and Samuel, Lily's security bandit. As dedicated to Lily as Samuel was, James knew he would never abandon his post intentionally. That fact left him convinced that there was a major mishap at the trade-off spot. "Gideon didn't mention *why* or *where* he was shot eitha'?"

"No. Not a thing about it. The way Gideon was ramblin' and mumblin', I thought maybe he was hallucinatin' anyway. He was in such bad shape, I's more concerned about helpin' him than bombardin' him with questions. But no matta' how I tried to tend to his needs, he just kept on insistin' that we needed to help *her*. 'Where is she?' I finally asked 'em. 'In the wagon,' I heard 'em slur. I went outside, looked in the back of his wagon, and sho'nuff, I found some poor girl lyin' back there." Ava shook her head. "I nearly broke out in tears when I saw her battered body." Ava looked up and saw the anguish on James's face. "That's who you're here lookin' for, right?"

James nodded and swallowed hard, petrified to ask his next question. "Wh-what happened to them afta' that?"

"Ironically, the day Gideon came here, I's hostin' a small dinna' to thank all of the volunteers for helpin' to keep this place up and runnin'. Afta' I had Gideon stable, I went and fixed him a plate too, hopin' he'd eat. Before I handed him the food, I sat on the bed next to 'em, wantin' to say thank you to him for everything he'd eva' done to help my little clinic ova' the years. I tried to wake him, but he didn't move. Just that quick, he was already gone. Infection had already made its way into his bloodstream. He died of sepsis." Ava became slightly emotional. "My good friend died right there in front of me." She exhaled to ward off her tears. "I went outside the next mornin' searchin' through his wagon to see if I could find an address for his next of kin. I opened up a satchel and pulled out a tiny shoebox. I opened it up and my heart 'bout near jumped outta my chest. It startled me so bad, I slammed it back shut and pushed it away."

Already knowing what, or rather *who,* she had discovered, James felt his heart suddenly start crashing against his ribcage.

"I had to let my heart and mind settle before I could open the lid again. I just couldn't believe I's lookin' at a perfectly preserved, beautiful baby, lyin' there all bundled up like she was sleepin'. My mind was racin' to put the pieces togetha'. It answered why the girl Gideon brought here was bleedin'. Figured she'd just given birth not long before. The way Gideon rolled in here in a panic with a bullet wound, it made me wonda' if he was the fatha'. It seemed to make logical sense. It wasn't until the next mornin' that I realized how wrong I was."

"Why do you say that?"

"*Lily?* That's her name, right?"

James nodded.

"Well, Lily finally woke up. One of her eyes was just barely able to peek through the swellin'. She was thoroughly confused by where she was. She was moanin' in pain. Almost seemed she was betta' off comatose. At least she wasn't writhin' in agony. I gave her some morphine and she settled back into sleep for a while. She woke up again at midnight confused and cryin' out for who I now realize is you. Ova' and ova' again, she was hollerin' for you to help 'er."

James blew out a hard breath to fight off his tears.

"The panic she was in and the way she was screamin' your name made it seem like she had just woken up from a nightmare. Me and the nurses ran ova' to settle her down. It took us nearly five minutes to get 'er calm. We put some pillows behind 'er to prop her upright, so she could lie back and catch 'er breath more easily. The very moment she relaxed, she went to embrace her stomach with 'er hands, just as any expectant motha' instinctively does. Somethin' told me to stop 'er ... but I didn't. The second she touched 'er belly and realized her baby wasn't there..." Ava shook her head and looked up at James. "I've worked here for two decades. I've dealt with the beaten, the brutalized, and the broken, but I ain't neva' heard a woman holla' like that in all of my life." Ava placed her hand over her heart and inhaled sharply. "It still makes me lose my breath just to think about the way it crippled Lily to know she was no longa' with child."

James's tears finally pelted the kitchen table.

"When we got Lily halfway settled, she just kept rockin' back and forth for hours, sayin' she thought it was a nightmare. Poor girl just couldn't handle the fact that her nightmare was real, and that 'er baby really was dead. Afta' hours of babblin' about that nightmare, she had cried herself into a trance. She turned and laid on 'er side, starin' into nothin'. I sat down on the bed beside her in the mornin' and asked 'er if she wanted somethin' to eat. She wouldn't even look at me. 'Where's my baby? I wanna see my baby,' was all she whispered. It was like she needed to see the baby to prove it really wasn't a dream. I done learned ova' the years that I ain't the one to be makin' the decision about whetha' or not a motha' sees her dead baby. Some wanna see 'em, some don't. They all have their reasons and it ain't for me to judge or try to change their minds. I just grant their wishes.

"So, I went on downstairs to the morgue and brought that tiny little box upstairs. I neva' know what kinda reaction I'm gonna get from a motha', but I always sit next to 'em for comfort. I put the box in Lily's hands and let 'er open it when she was ready. It took 'er a moment, but she found the strength to do it. To my astonishment, Lily didn't make a sound or shed a tear when she saw that little face. With all the outbursts she'd already had, I guess I'd prepared myself for her to have anotha'. But she was totally silent as she gazed at that little face. It was like she was awestruck by how beautiful her daughta' was. She wouldn't even blink. She finally reached inside and caressed her little cheek. Then she pulled back the little blanket and took a peek. 'Rose,' she said as her tears started to fall again.

"In all my years of doin' this, I neva' can predict what a motha' will do with her deceased infant. But, to my amazement, Lily wrapped the baby back tight in her blanket, picked 'er up, kissed 'er on the cheek and then cradled her in her arms for the longest time. Still, she didn't holla' the way I expected she would. As best she could through her swollen eyes, she just quietly gazed at that baby in awe. To this day, I wonda' what was goin' through her mind that kept 'er so calm. Then just as unexpectedly as Lily had picked 'er up, she laid Rose back in that tiny box. Still, she was calm. But when I closed the lid…" Ava shook her head again. "She cried out like somebody had just set 'er soul on fire. I had a nurse come ova' and take the baby back to the morgue, and I sat there just tryna comfort Lily back to silence.

"While I's comfortin' her, she just kept sayin', 'James'll neva' forgive me for losin' her. He wanted 'er so bad. He ain't eva' gonna forgive me. James'll neva' forgive me.' Ova' and ova' again, that's all she'd say. It's the reason I could neva' forget your name. She sat there for hours, rockin' back and forth, repeatin' that same phrase. She thought that was the reason she was here alone. She was convinced you'd abandoned her here … for losin' your baby. She swore you'd neva' forgive 'er for such a thing."

James suddenly jumped up from his seat, turned his back, rested his hands on the counter, and hung his head low to hide another strong surge of tears.

"When I heard you say your name earlier and describe who you's lookin' for, it instantly took me back to that god-awful night. Just by the passion in your voice and the desolate look on your face when I saw you talkin' to my nurses, I knew beyond a shadow of a doubt you were the James that Lily was talkin' about."

James just stood there quietly with his back still turned, fighting to make his tears cease.

"Did you already know that Rose had passed away?" Ava asked after a moment.

James nodded and finally sat back down, his bloodshot eyes directed at the table. "She died in my arms," he said, shamelessly letting his tears fall in front of Ava. "Ova' eight years trainin' and workin' in the field as a doctor and I couldn't even save my own little baby," he sobbed, sounding as anguished as any man could. "*I'm* the one who doesn't deserve to be forgiven … not Lily."

"I knew you probably felt that way." Ava got up and pulled a trunk out of her closet. "I found this trunk in the back of Gideon's wagon. I didn't mean to be intrusive. I's only lookin' through it to see if I could find Gideon's home address. Instead, I found lots of things with your first and last name on 'em. I also found these." She handed James the picture of him and Lily dancing together, as well as one of the many letters he had written her. "That picture happened to be folded up inside that letta'. The moment I saw you in the clinic tonight, this picture instantly flashed in my mind. It's hard to tell with your beard now, but I figured this was you."

"It is," James responded, staring at the treasured portrait.

"I couldn't help but read the letta' afta' I saw that beautiful drawin'," Ava confessed. "Your words to Lily were just as beautiful. Brought me to tears, actually. Afta' readin' about how much you loved Lily, I knew there was no way you'd be the sort of man who would abandon her or refuse to forgive 'er for losin' that little baby. I didn't believe that for a minute. I tried to convince Lily of that too. I read that letta' to 'er to remind her of your love, but she was too far gone emotionally to listen to any of it. She just wasn't in 'er right mind anymore."

"Thank you for tryin'," James whispered, tracing his finger down Lily's face in the picture. "Do you know where Lily is now?" he hesitantly asked, after collecting himself emotionally.

Ava sighed. "There was a raid on this place not long afta' Lily got here. A bunch of buffoons rode in here on horses, dressed in white robes, lookin' like a bunch of damn ghosts, firin' pistols, and hootin' and hollerin'. They snatched up every single patient in the clinic. Every last one of 'em! They snatched Lily up 'fore she could even get outta bed. They even went door to door in the town and took whoeva' couldn't run fast enough to get away. I've heard that's what them ghostly lookin' cowards do. They find vulnerable communities like this and round up Negroes like cattle. They ain't askin' to see no papers eitha'. They don't give a damn whetha' anybody's really a slave or not. Hell, they know most of these folks can't read or write, and we damn sure can't prove nothin' in no court of law anyway. So, if you're a Negro, you'll always be a piece of profitable property in their evil eyes."

James felt his internal beast starting to awaken after hearing the description of the invaders. "Do you have any idea where these cowards might be takin' folks afta' these sort of raids?"

"I heard they bypass the auctions and sell 'em straight to black market wholesalers or plantations at low prices. They make pure profit that way."

"Any particular plantations, cities, or wholesalers that you may have heard gossip about?"

"Naw, not in particular. I assume they ain't goin' far, though. It'd be hard to wrangle that many folks ova' a long distance without causin' a scene."

"Good point."

"I'm sorry I couldn't be more of a help to ya'."

"You've been more of a help than you'll eva' know, Ava," James said as he got up to leave.

Ava got up to walk James out. She stopped near the doorway. "Listen, James, I just wanna warn ya'. Lily wasn't in no good shape when she left here. I swear that woman went mad afta' we took that baby away. Before then she was gettin' betta'. She was still mighty bruised and swollen everywhere, but 'er feva' was down and she was conscious, obviously. Afta' seein' the baby, though, she wouldn't eat, she wouldn't drink, she got weak, feva' was back up, and she was slippin' in and outta consciousness again. It's like as soon as she knew her baby was dead, she didn't wanna live no mo' ... like she was slowly tryna kill 'erself. She was frail when she left here. Her eyes were sunk in. You could even see 'er ribs. Those men that rode in here stealin' folks only want healthy slaves. The things they'll do to the ones they can't make a profit on..." Ava shook her head. "I don't even wanna speak of."

"Thank you for your honesty."

"She may not have been in the best shape, but I can say for certain that yo' Lily was alive when she left here, if that's any consolation to you."

"It is. Trust me. It *definitely* is. Had you told me she was buried next to Gideon, you'd've been buryin' me there tonight too."

Ava nodded her head. "Speakin' of Gideon, I wrote a letta' to his clinic to try to notify his next of kin. It was the only address I knew, but the letta' was returned to me. I didn't know what else to do, so I went on and buried 'em here for the time bein'. If you could somehow let his family know where he is, I'd be grateful."

"I sure will."

"The nurses and I built a casket for yo' little girl and buried her next to Gideon too. The cemetery is about a quarta' mile north of here. She's up on a hill, unda'neath an oak tree. 'Precious little Rose' is engraved on the tombstone, along with a picture of a single rose."

The tears in James's eyes were fresh again over the kindness of this stranger. "My God, Ava, you have a sort of angelic warmth in your heart that's truly rare in this cold, heartless world. I can't thank you enough for givin' my little girl a temporary place to rest in peace."

Ava blushed. "You're very welcome. It's the least I could do for that innocent little baby," she smiled.

"Listen, you've done so much for me already, so I truly hate to botha' you for anything else. But I was wonderin' if there's some place that you'd allow me to bury that trunk around here?" he asked, turning to look at it. "There's things in that chest that hold a great deal of sentimental value to me and Lily, but I have no way of takin' it with me right now. I'd like to come back for it one day, though."

"Absolutely. That's no botha' at all. Actually, if you'd like, I have a hidden compartment in my barn that I don't eva' use. There's plenty of space for you to put it in there. I got a lock you can use. You can cova' up the compartment with dirt and hay and hide the key when you're done. It'll be safe there. You can come back and get it wheneva' you'd like."

James took Ava's hand into his. "Thank you for this ... and for takin' care of my family while they were here."

"It was my pleasure."

"I won't eva' forget you for this. I don't think I could eva' repay your kindness, but I'm hopin' you'll at least accept this," he said, trying to hand her some money.

"No, you keep that and use it to find yo' Lily. I'll pray every day that you find 'er. I'm sho' she needs ya'."

"Not half as much as I need her."

After locking his sentimental trunk of treasures in the bunker beneath Ava's barn, James made his way to the cemetery, holding a handful of flowers that Ava was kind enough to give him from her coffee table. The moment James set foot in that direction, he could feel his chest constricting as he thought about the fact that Rose had spent her entire life nestled in that very spot. With every step, his need to cry grew stronger. All he could think about was the fact that Rose was supposed to be a four-month-old giggling baby with beautiful eyes like her mother. By now, her chubby face should be lighting up with a smile at the sight of her daddy approaching. But instead, her lifeless body lay trapped by the dirt currently beneath his feet.

James squatted next to Rose's beautifully designed tombstone. His tears cascaded into the grass as he placed the flowers into the cement vase attached to the tombstone. He arranged them neatly, then said a silent prayer before finding the strength to speak aloud. "I know you're in heaven my little love. Every day, I pray and ask the angels to build you the fanciest treehouse in the sky, one with a swing that flies you high above those heavenly clouds and gives you the most glorious view of the paradise you're livin' in. I have faith that they'll take good care of you until the day God calls me home. And when he does, you prepare yourself for the biggest, warmest hug you've eva' had. I love you eternally my little angel," James choked out through his tears.

Unable to bear the thought of leaving just yet, James sat down with his back against the oak tree near Rose's tombstone. He let his tears subside and then lit a lantern. He then took Levi's journal out of his satchel and continued to read the intriguing tale of Rose's maternal grandfather ...

Chapter Eleven

February 15th, 1835

After what I found out today, I now truly believe in miracles ...

In the months following their three-day affair, Levi found it impossible not to smile every time he caught sight of Maya. Just like in the past, Maya would turn in his direction when she sensed that he was gazing at her. Now, though, Levi never bothered to turn away when Maya caught him. She let her eyes linger on him too and acknowledged his feelings with a discreet smile of her own. Levi's body always warmed, and his smile broadened over the return of her simple affection.

Today, while standing in the field chatting with a fellow farmer, Levi's reaction to Maya was no different. Levi glanced over his friend's shoulder after catching sight of Maya emerging from her cottage. The words of Levi's friend faded away from his ears and his eyes instinctively followed Maya. As always, Levi's crooked grin was instant the moment he looked at the angelic woman in his view. Maya turned in his direction and gave her usual smile in return. However, instead of Levi's smile broadening, it quickly faded from his face altogether. There was no warmth running through his body this time either. Instead, he felt as though he had just been submerged in ice. He froze, barely able to swivel his head as he continued watching Maya walk toward the barn.

"You alright, Levi?" his farmer friend asked. "You look like you just seen a damn ghost," he snickered.

Levi's brain did not even register what his friend had just said. He still had yet to blink as he tried to absorb what his eyes were seeing. "Will you excuse me a minute?" he said to his friend, sounding completely void of emotion.

"Sure," the man responded, staring oddly at how the color had drained from Levi's face.

Levi was trying desperately to get his weakened legs to usher him into the barn. But it was not until Maya disappeared inside that he finally got them to work properly. As he quickly made his way there, his mind suddenly flooded with flashbacks of the unforgettable hours that he had spent suspended in heaven with Maya five months prior. Levi had memorized her body backwards, forwards, and sideways on those nights. He had dreamt about that body and fantasized about it constantly since then. That body was imprinted in his memory in stunning detail. So, when the wind just so happened to press Maya's dress flat against her body as she walked by, Levi knew immediately that the slight protrusion in her abdomen was not normally there. The shocking sight hit his body like lightning, causing his knees to nearly give out. It was a miracle that he made it into the barn without collapsing.

The sound of the barn door closing startled Maya. She then turned around to find herself alone with Levi. In his current state of shock, Levi was unable to formulate words. He slowly removed his hat and just stood there looking as pale as a ghost while his heart threatened to beat its way out of his chest. His mouth was partially agape as he stared at Maya with an intensity that he never had before. Maya held Levi's gaze as he had always asked her to do in his presence. This time, though, it was *Levi's* eyes that drifted down for a change. By the look on his face, Maya immediately understood exactly why.

Realizing that Levi was too stunned to move or speak, Maya slowly approached him. With every step, she was reading the look on his face as he gazed at her midsection. To her surprise, she saw tears welling in his beautiful eyes that seemed to sparkle with hope. Maya stopped within a foot of him. But, still, Levi would not remove his eyes from her stomach. The look on his face seemed to be asking a question that he could not get his mouth to formulate. Maya's hand was shaking uncontrollably as she suddenly reached out toward Levi. The intense fear running through her had also voided her of the ability to speak. Instead, she took a hold of his hand. She could not decipher whose hand was trembling worse as she held his. To answer the hopeful question she saw dancing in his eyes, she slowly maneuvered his shaking hand onto her abdomen. The simple act instantly made the welling tears in Levi's eyes overflow down his cheeks. He knelt and kissed the place where his baby was resting, then wrapped his arms around Maya's waist and quietly wept tears of joy.

Levi finally summoned the strength to stand when he felt Maya still trembling uncontrollably. He placed his hands on either side of her tearstained face. "You okay?"

"I am now."

"Why didn't you tell me?" Levi asked, his joyous tears still trickling.

"I was t-terrified. I thought y-you'd be f-furious," Maya replied, her quivering voice proving her sincerity.

"Maya," Levi whispered, tearfully. "We created a *miracle* togetha'. How could I eva' be furious about that?"

Maya lowered her head and began sobbing uncontrollably, his words instantly flushing away months' worth of worry. Levi tightly embraced her, lending a shoulder for her to cry on.

As Maya lay there, Levi felt a sense of sadness that she had been too scared to confide in him sooner. "You've been holdin' onto that fear all this time?" he asked, as he caressed her back.

Maya pulled back from their embrace and nodded as she wiped her tears.

"Well, right here, right now, you let go of every ounce of your fears and worries…" He gently placed his hands alongside Maya's face again and made her look him in the eyes. "Because I already love our little baby … just as much as I love you." He cemented that sentiment in the way he then tenderly caressed her lips with his, the passion in his kiss conveying his gratitude for the gift she would soon deliver. His warm affection indeed raced through Maya's body, immediately exterminating the trepidation that had stolen the joy of being blessed with a gift she thought she would never have. Five months of repressed joy hit Maya all at once, and she felt her entire essence breathe a collective sigh of relief. She then deepened their kiss; it was her way of reciprocating her gratitude for what Levi's love had blessed her body with. Their thankful tears blended together and cascaded down their cheeks, christening the place where the life they had created was growing.

After the intimate exchange, Levi hesitantly pulled himself away from the fantasy world of his mind, where the woman before him was his wife. "I can't wait to hold our little miracle," he confessed, gently caressing Maya's stomach. "You'll have everything you need for the baby before then, okay?"

Maya nodded. "Thank you," she replied, her tears still falling.

"No … thank *you*," Levi smiled. "For makin' yet anotha' one of my dreams come true. I wanted this for you … for *us*. God answered my prayer to bless you with a baby," he said, softly caressing her cheek. "You absolutely deserve to be a motha'."

Levi's words triggered another round of intense sobbing that made it impossible for Maya to verbally reply. She simply wrapped her arms around Levi and melted in the warmth of his embrace.

After holding Maya and weeping with her over the astounding revelation, Levi knew he had to force himself to let go of her again. Before he completely abandoned his fairytale, he tenderly kissed Maya's forehead and wiped the last of her tears. He then cleared his own eyes and blew out a stern breath to settle himself. He put back on his Stetson hat then reluctantly exited the barn and returned to the real world ... and back into the man that the slave-owning south *expected* him to be.

... Every word of Levi's journals had James gripped, his curiosity pinging off the scales. Much like Maya, James's reaction was one of surprise at the way Levi responded to the news of Lily's impending arrival. But he wondered how the same hand that had elegantly scripted such words about Lily could be the same hand that had callously dragged her kicking and screaming from her mother's arms and onto an auction block years later. The two extreme contrasting events did not seem to be able to exist in the same realm of possibility. It made James suddenly wonder if the journals were fabricated or if Levi had gone insane before selling Lily. James was confident that someone would have had to pry Rose from his cold dead hands before she ever set foot on an auction block. He simply could not fathom how a loving father could do such a thing. The entire contradiction had him thoroughly perplexed and continued to keep a stronghold over his desire to turn the pages of Levi's journals.

James's intrigue was further strengthened when he reached into the satchel Colt had given him and pulled out a pink knitted baby blanket and a children's book. They were among the treasures Colt insisted be passed on to Lily. The items seemed to further prove Levi's love for the new miracle soon to come into his life. But James did not recall Lily ever mentioning the children's book he now held in his hands. It left him wondering if she had ever heard it. James opened to the first page of Hans Christian Anderson's "The Little Mermaid" and decided to read it aloud to his own daughter. After reading the plot, James understood why Levi felt compelled to purchase a story about the challenge of loving someone from a completely different world. It was something he currently understood all too well. James placed the book back in the satchel. He then stood up and sighed as he glanced down at Rose and Gideon's grave sites. The sight before him was the ultimate proof of how the world was hellbent on challenging him. The impact, however, was not enough to make him give up on loving Lily, in the way it seemed Levi had.

James turned to Gideon's resting place and said a brief prayer. "Goodbye ol' friend. I'll be sure you make it back home." He then turned and looked at the words on his daughter's tombstone again. "Ava got it right. You certainly are my precious little Rose." He kissed his hand and touched her tombstone. "I'll be back for you one day … I promise."

James wiped his tears, then finally managed to pull himself away and set out to resume his search for Lily. Considering the details of Ava's story, he rode hard for the rest of the night with a very specific destination in mind. The place he was headed to was further proof that he was truly willing to walk through the fires of hell before he ever gave up on the daughter that Levi Collins mysteriously decided to throw away.

Chapter Twelve

"JEREMIAH! DON'T PULL THAT FUCKIN' TRIGGER!"

The Ghost Rider holding a double-barreled shotgun to James's face suddenly pressed it against his forehead. "Why the fuck shouldn't I shoot this snoop, right here, right now?!" he asked, cocking the rifle.

"If you shoot that man, you'll be throwin' away five thousand dolla's," the man behind him replied. He then quickly walked up beside Jeremiah. "I Just saw his wanted posta's plastered everywhere down in Virginia. He's a fugitive. You'll get a pretty penny for this pretty boy."

James looked over Jeremiah's shoulder and realized that the man selling him out was Austin, the percussionist from Lily's show.

"You sure this is him?" Jeremiah asked, his shotgun still pressed against James's head.

"Just as sure as the fact that flies love shit," Austin replied.

James lowered his eyes and gave Austin a hateful glare.

Austin glared back, looking just as evil. He then pulled his pistol out and aimed it James. "Go on and get Tex," he told Jeremiah. "I'll keep watch ova' him."

The Ghost Rider trotted up the steps of the dilapidated log cabin that James had been hiding behind.

"Hit me," Austin murmured as soon as Jeremiah was out of earshot.

James looked confused. "What?"

"Hit me and run! Hurry up dumbass! I'm tryna get you outta this shit!"

By the time James realized that Austin was an ally, Tex was trotting down the steps.

"Shit!" Austin exclaimed under his breath, looking angrily at James for not listening while they had the chance.

Eight Ghost Riders filed out of the house behind Duke's cousin, Tex. They all surrounded James.

"Caught this fucker snoopin' around here, listenin' in on our meetin'," Jeremiah told Tex. "Austin says he's a fugitive worth five thousand dolla's."

"It's true," Austin confirmed.

"What's y'ur name, boy?" Tex asked.

James refused to answer.

"I said, what's y'ur goddamn name?!"

"His name's Jake. I think that's what the wanted posta' said," Austin lied.

Toby, another Ghost Rider, stepped up and held a lantern near James's face. "I'll be damned. This sho' is that fucker we saw on them wanted posta's. Had his goddamn face plastered everywhere down in Virginia. Convicted of murda'. Adams, I rememba' that posta' sayin' … James Adams."

Austin closed his eyes. *Shit!* he mouthed, angry that another Ghost Rider recalled that information.

"*Adams?*" Tex snickered. "Well, well, well, boys we done lucked up on a treasure."

"Sure did! This fucker's worth five thousand dollars!" Toby replied.

"Naw," Tex replied. "We ain't turnin' this little shit into no authorities."

Toby looked at Tex like he was insane. "Why the hell would you pass up on that kind of money?"

"To hell with that money," Tex replied. "You and Jeremiah were here when this man's fatha' came here wantin' help findin' this nigga' lovin' thief."

The memory immediately came back. "Adams?" Toby turned to look at James again. "This is Jesse Adams' son? The one who dragged that slave all ova' the country playin' piano?"

"Thee one and only," Tex replied, turning to glare at James. "Gentlemen, this man here is the nigga' lovin' son of a Ghost Rida' grand wizard," he explained. "Not just any grand wizard ... the goddamn founda' of the Ghost Rida's. And he wasn't just convicted of murderin' some meaningless pieces of shit." Tex walked up to James and stared him dead in the eyes. "He murdered three of our brethren ... ova' a *nigga!*" he snarled.

"I don't know what the hell you're talkin' about," James replied.

"Don't lie to me fucker! Duke's son came up here and told me about the shit you done caused down in Virginia. Duke's stuck in prison now waitin' to stand trial for all the shit you caused! Can't be no fuckin' coincidence that anotha' James Adams is now a fugitive."

"I *said*, I don't know what the hell you're talkin' ab-"

"Shut the hell up!" Tex yelled, cutting James's words short with a fist to his diaphragm. "I heard about the romp you had with Duke in the woods. He should've finished the job for killin' three of our own! But I'll be happy to finish it for 'em. My brotha' died on that old rich white nigga' lova's estate! Duke's always said y'ur daddy's too much of a pussy to scar y'ur pretty little face. But I can promise ya', I won't fuckin' hesitate! I'm gonna make you pay for what happened to my brotha'!" Tex turned to look briefly at his brethren. "Turns out we ain't gonna need to catch no nigga' to fry at the rally t'night afta' all! Y'all start erectin' the cross and get the nooses and knives ready," he demanded to a few of the new recruits. He then turned back to glare at James. "And tie this piece of shit up in the shed. I'm gonna give y'all a show t'night worth far more than that five thousand dolla' reward money!"

Twisted cheers erupted in unison as everyone scattered to start preparing for the night's "entertainment." Austin, though, was fighting the intense urge to vomit. He thought using the money offered in the wanted posters would buy him some time to save James's life. His stomach was now punishing him for putting him in even more danger. As the Ghost Riders began hooting and hollering around him, Austin stood there helplessly watching as Jeremiah chained James up and manhandled him into the shed. *Shit! Shit! Shit!* erupted in Austin's mind repeatedly as he tried to figure out his next move.

Austin watched Jeremiah carefully, paying close attention to the fact that he had placed the keys to the locks in his right coat pocket. He then followed behind Jeremiah into the log cabin when he was done. While waiting on the new recruits to erect the sixteen-foot cross, Jeremiah and several other tenured Ghost Riders were partaking in their usual pre-rally drinking ritual. Normally, Austin would be drinking too. On this night, however, he wanted a clear head. He wanted just the opposite for Jeremiah. Austin kept an endless amount of moonshine flowing down Jeremiah's gullet. In the midst of a bunch of loud, rowdy, inebriated men, no one ever noticed the way he was slyly switching out Jeremiah's tin cups every time one was near empty. The one-hundred eighty proof backwoods elixir had Jeremiah's head bobbing on the couch within the hour.

"Can't hold y'ur liquor boy!" Austin teased, playfully slapping Jeremiah in the face as he stood up to go outside. A few Ghost Riders nearby laughed at the pathetic sight of Jeremiah slumped over. Austin then walked through the rowdy crowd of filthy men. He stepped outside on the porch and walked down the rickety stairs in between a few Ghost Riders powwowing on the steps.

"The fuck you goin' youngsta'?" one of the drunk men slurred to Austin.

"I gotta report to you when I need to take a piss," Austin replied.

Austin then walked calmly behind the cabin into the darkness. He looked around to see if any other Ghost Riders were around. He then scurried over to the small shed where James was imprisoned. With shaky hands, he pulled out the keys that he had slyly stolen out of Jeremiah's pocket while sitting next to his inebriated body on the couch. Despite how badly he was shaking, he quickly unlocked the padlock on the shed. He looked behind him before opening the door. With all clear, he ducked inside and shut the door behind him.

"I can't see shit in here!" Austin said, nervously fiddling with the keys.

"Your eyes just need a minute to adjust," James replied.

"I don't have a fuckin' minute! These crazy fuckers'll barbeque my ass along with you for this shit!" He cracked the door to the shed to let some light in and then quickly unlocked James's chains. "Take this," he said, handing James one of his pistols.

"Thanks," James replied. He got up and walked to the shed door and peeked out. When he did not see anyone, he slowly pushed the door open.

A Ghost Rider near a tree stopped his urine midstream when he noticed the shed opening out of the corner of his eye. "HEY!" he yelled.

"SHIT!" Austin exclaimed when he saw the man approaching.

The Ghost Rider was reaching for his gun as he began running toward James. James sprinted toward the man and tackled him before he could unholster his weapon. He then pistol-whipped him into unconsciousness. The sound of the man crying out in pain caught the attention of the Ghost Riders on the porch. They all ran around to the back of the cabin and saw James and Austin take off running into the woods. A hail of bullets began ricocheting off trees as the two of them hopped and skipped over the rough terrain to get away. The gunfire summoned every Ghost Rider from inside the cabin. Suddenly, over twenty men were in pursuit of the escapees.

Sprinting hard, James and Austin disappeared into the darkness with a commanding lead over the group. Despite it, the entire posse continued to give chase. Some had hopped on horses, some split up and searched on foot. Austin knew the backwoods area well and guided James to a steep bank that led down into a rushing creek. "There's a cavern off to the side of the creek about a half mile down! If the current isn't too strong, we can pull ourselves inside and hide in there!"

James didn't even question it, he followed right behind Austin. They slid and stumbled their way down the bank, jumped into the freezing water, and let it sweep them down stream. James quickly lost sight of Austin once they were submerged in the water. He popped his head up and heard Austin repeatedly screaming, "keep right!" James followed the sound of his voice and finally caught sight of him. The strong current constantly dragged them under, scrapping and tumbling them over rocks, tree branches and debris. James was able to get his head above water in time to see Austin grip on to a low hanging tree branch near the hidden cave. Just before running into Austin and knocking him further downstream, James was able to grip onto a branch as well. Both men then struggled against the fast-moving stream to pull themselves inside the cave where the water was calm. Outside of the chattering of their teeth, they kept quiet and could hear men's voices and horse's hooves beating near the creek. Fighting hypothermia, they both climbed up on the short ledges of the cave and shivered there for nearly half an hour until they felt confident that the Ghost Rider posse was no longer a threat.

When all was quiet, James peered out to be sure the coast was clear. He and Austin then carefully gripped onto tree roots and rocks to climb up the muddy bank of the creek and back onto flat ground. Huffing and puffing, they both laid on their backs for a moment to catch their breath.

Crawling to his knees and then steadily getting to his feet, James finally stood up. "I gotta go back for somethin'."

"*What?!*" Austin spat. "Are you Crazy?! The fuck you goin' back for?!" he asked after slowly making his way to his feet too.

"Trust me, if it wasn't important, I wouldn't botha'. Just meet me behind the men's dormitory at the school. There's an old unused storage shed in the woods covered by brush and weeds back there that I've been hidin' out in durin' the day. We can hide out in it tonight. If I'm not there within an hour, you can go on about your business."

Austin shook his head and threw up his hands. "I'll make sure you're dressed real pretty at your fuckin' funeral!" He then turned and ran off into the night, headed toward the school.

Being as cautious and quiet about his movements as he could, James began making his way back toward the Ghost Riders' cabin. Just as he was closing in on the horse that he had left tied near there, he stopped. He noticed a lone Ghost Rider curiously walking up to the horse. The man looked around first and then began snooping in the horse's saddlebags. James ducked behind a tree, drew his pistol, and peered back around at the man. Not wanting his gunfire to draw the attention of others, he decided to put the pistol back in the holster. He picked up a massive tree branch laying nearby instead. The rustling of the leaves caught the attention of the Ghost Rider snooping in

James's belongings. He stopped digging in the satchel and drew his weapon. He cautiously started pacing toward the sound with his pistol raised. James quietly and swiftly maneuvered from behind the tree and bashed the man in the skull while he had his back to him. He collapsed immediately. James took off his Ghost Rider robe and hood and put them on. He then took the man's weapons and ammunition. Before mounting the horse, James checked inside the satchel to be sure that what he had gone back to retrieve was still inside. Levi's journals and all the other items Colt had given him were indeed still there. He then quickly mounted the horse and rode off toward the school.

By the time James made it to the storage shed, Austin had stripped down to his thermals and had wrapped himself in some dirty blankets that he found. He was sitting on the floor warming his hands over a lantern that he had found there as well. James followed suit. He stripped down and pulled out some canned chili for the both of them while he hovered near the small flame.

"Thanks for gettin' me outta that shit back there. I owe you big time," James said as he cut the lid off his chili.

Austin nodded as he shoveled food into a stomach that was loudly begging for sustenance.

"So, I take it the Ghost Rida's have no idea you were part of Lily's show?" James asked as he began to shovel food into his mouth too.

Austin laughed. "Those ain't the kind of men you'd catch at a damn symphony. If there ain't banjos, fiddles, moonshine, and nooses, they don't want no parts of the festivities."

"Why the hell are you runnin' around with those fuckers any damn way?" James asked in between bites.

Austin briefly glanced up at him. "Your face is on wanted posta's for *murda'* and you're questionin' *me* about my actions?" He shook his head and took another bite of his food. "I guess that explains where you've been all this time. Griff said he searched for you and Lily for weeks. He said it was like the two of ya' disappeared off the face of the earth. I couldn't believe my eyes when I saw your face on them damn wanted posta's last week. I been lookin' for Griff so I could tell 'em, but I ain't had no luck findin' 'em. I considered writin' to William, but I ain't sure where he's stayin' these days."

"I believe he's still up in Manhattan."

Austin suddenly stopped eating. "Did you really do it?" he asked, sounding hesitant to ask.

"You're eatin' with a cold-blooded murderer," James replied, still calmly chewing his food.

Austin glared at him for a moment and swallowed hard. "Is that the reason you neva' escaped with Lily as planned?"

"I's in the midst of gettin' 'er to the trade-off spot when it happened."

"I assume you did it to protect 'er then?"

James nodded. "My whole life, all I've eva' wanted to do was protect Lily. It felt like instinct to blow all their heads off."

Austin just stared at him, bewildered as to how he was so matter of fact about it.

"In the moment it made sense," James continued explaining. "Thought I'd be right back by Lily's side afta' that. But in the midst of the chaos, we got separated. Now, I haven't done anything but make 'er feel as though I abandoned 'er some damn where."

"So, you have no idea where she is?"

James shook his head. "I recently got a lead as to where she might be, though. That's why I's out at the Ghost Rida's cabin. I lucked up on a woman who told me Lily was there at her clinic…"

"At a clinic? Was she havin' the baby?"

James shook his head again. "Lily gave birth to 'er the night we tried to escape."

"*Her?*" Austin smiled. "You got y'urself a daughter now?!"

"Not anymore."

The smile instantly faded from Austin's face. The words hit him so hard that he lost his appetite. He sat his can of beans down. "James, I-I'm so sorry," he said, sincerity evident in his tone. "Damn, what the hell happened?"

James sighed. "It's just a really long story that I don't feel like relivin' right now. The short of it is that we tried to escape, everything went to hell, I went to prison, I lost my daughta', and now I've lost Lily. The woman at the clinic said their little village was raided by a bunch of men in white robes and hoods. I knew that signature attire well. So now I'm here, followin' the lead in hopes of findin' Lily."

"Neva' figured you for one who knew anything about the Ghost Rida' organization. Damn near shit myself when I heard Tex say y'ur fatha' was one of the foundin' memba's. Is that true?"

"Not just *one* of the foundin' memba's. He's *thee* foundin' memba'. The name, the codes, the attire … all my fatha's *brilliant* ideas," James replied sarcastically.

"Y'ur shittin' me!"

"I wish I was."

"I bet he was just *thrilled* about your relationship with Lily."

"Ova' the moon!" James replied just as sarcastically.

"So, what otha' info did the lady at the clinic give you?"

"She said men in white robes snatched up all her patients, including Lily. She said they raid vulnerable Negro communities like hers and sell the people they catch to unda'ground slave trada's or straight to plantations. That's the reason I's hidin' out at the Ghost

Rida' camp for the last few days. I's hopin' to hear who or where those fuckers are sellin' people."

"Ironically, that's why I been runnin' with 'em too."

"*To sell slaves?*" James asked with disgust in his tone.

"No! To put an end to what they're doin'!"

Recalling the contentious relationship Austin initially had with Lily, James could not help but pause and look at him in shock. "Are you serious?" he asked, sounding genuinely surprised.

Austin nodded and stared at the small flame in the lantern, suddenly embarrassed to look James in the eyes. "I'm ashamed of the way I treated Lily when I first met 'er. I think about it every day and it sickens me. But afta' all the ugly things I said to 'er, and the way I tried to ruin 'er show, she was the only person who was there for me when my motha' passed away," he sighed. "She *literally* gave me a shoulda' to cry on. She opened her heart to me that day, and it made me wanna open mine to her. She honestly became like a sista' to me afta' that. Hell, wish my real sista's *were* like her. Afta that day, I's adamant that I's gonna do all I could to help 'er achieve her musical dreams. It was like Lily's dreams had suddenly become mine.

"It crushed me the day y'ur fatha' came and took Lily away. Just like that, she was gone … and so were my dreams. Your damn daddy manhandled her and my dreams right out the back door of Winta' Garden. And there wasn't a damn thing I could do to stop that bastard from layin' claims ova' her, like she was some damn horse! It sickened me that he owned not only *Lily* … but 'er *dreams* too. And the stupid slave codes say he has every right to crush 'em if he so chooses." Austin looked directly at James. "I can't lie. I's mad as hell at you too for not doin' anything about it."

"I don't blame you. You had every right to be," James replied.

Austin shook his head. "I left Winta' Garden feelin' lost and hopeless. When I walked onto my pa's plantation, suddenly there wasn't a slave there that I could look at without wonderin' what dreams they had for themselves. What kind of talents did they possess? What incredible things could they offa' the world that my pa's keepin' bottled up on his goddamn farm, because an auction receipt legally says that he can? I's so tortured by that question, I got sick to my stomach every time I looked at one of my fatha's slaves," he confessed, sorrowfully hanging his head low again.

"Forgive me if this stirs up your emotions, but I got me a baby girl now," Austin smiled faintly. "Prettiest little thing on earth if ya' ask me. She's got my eyes, but hers are far more innocent. The day they put 'er in my arms, she looked at me with those eyes and stole my heart. I didn't know it was humanly possible for somethin' so tiny to break a man down into tears. Got me wrapped around 'er tiny little finga'. I wanted 'er to have a name that meant just as much to me as she did ... Georgia Lily." He looked up at James. "Georgia was my motha's name. And Lily ... well, I guess it's obvious where I got that from."

"I'm sure Lily will be honored to hear that Austin," James sincerely replied, his emotions stirring slightly.

Austin nodded. "Lily told me that 'er fatha' sold 'er away from her motha'. The house slave who helped nurture and raise me and my siblings had many of her children sold away from 'er too. Her name was Bernice, but we called 'er mammy. I grew up thinkin' it was normal for mammy's children to be sold. I neva' even gave it a second thought until Lily told me that bein' sold away from 'er motha' was like mournin' her death. I just *think* about somebody takin' Georgia away from me and I feel a rage buildin' inside of me! I'd want heads to roll! Then I sit back and realize that mammy and Lily's stories have happened hundreds of thousands of times ova'. Thousands of fatha's just like me have mourned the loss of their children. Even children mournin' their motha's. And all these years, I's foolish enough to believe it was the most normal thing in the world ... until I met Lily. She was like a giant mirror, forcin' me to see how narrow-minded and stupid I've really been all my life ... how stupid *anyone* is who believes enslavin' folks is right.

"I don't know how it is we eva' became a world that justified playin' God and determinin' the fate of people's lives in such despicable ways. But the guilt of it all weighs heavily on me every damn day now. I wanna atone for it all somehow, James. I wanna somehow do my part to make amends. I wanna help the people like mammy who raised us with love and compassion, hell, even nursed us. I wanna give back to the people who fed us, diapered us, and cleaned up afta' us, built our homes, stitched our clothes, and plowed our fields without complaint, despite all the horrible things we've done to 'em. I just somehow wanna atone for how despicably our country has treated the very people who have been an intricate part of buildin' it and helpin' it to thrive. Slaves have served this country for centuries. The least I can do is spend the rest of my life servin' them.

"Afta' your damn daddy snatched Lily outta Winta' Garden that's all I been hell-bent on doin'. I been workin' with abolitionists eva' since then. That's why I infiltrated the Ghost Rida's. I get much-needed intel at their rally meetin's about when and where they might be plannin' raids. I pass the info along to folks runnin' the unda'ground railroad. That way they know ahead of time where our men might be stakin' out, so they know what routes to avoid and where not to build their camps at night. I bring food, wata', goods, and knowledge. I offa' any kind of support I can to help slaves on their journey to a life where they're free to unleash their dreams, and all the otha' wonderful things they can bring to the world."

James was damn near brought to tears by the evolution of Austin's mind. He had to clear his throat before speaking. "I can't say that I'm the least bit surprised by the way your life and your mindset has changed, Austin. I know all too well the effect Lily can have on a person."

"She seems to have that powa' ova' everyone she meets, doesn't she?"

"Without a doubt," James replied. "The person she's helped you evolve into is exactly the sort of man I need on my side right now. Sounds like you're the answer to my prayers, actually. If you know who or where the Ghost Rida's are sellin' slaves, then maybe you can help put what's left of my family back togetha'."

"You can trust that I'll tell you everything I know. I want Lily back just as badly as you do. I want my little Georgia to meet the woman who inspired her middle name ... the woman who inspired her pa to fight for the rights of *everyone.*"

"I want that too, Austin. Trust me, I do," James said, patting him on the shoulder. "We'll find Lily somehow. I won't eva' lose faith in that."

"Neitha' will I."

Both men then discussed what Austin had learned and settled on a plan to enact the following night. Austin then laid down to try to get some sleep. As usual, though, James's curious mind harassed him into reading more of Levi's journal before allowing him to rest ...

Chapter Thirteen

Slave Code
Article II Section XI

Be it enacted that every master shall provide all slaves, including the sick and the elderly, with a competent diet, yearly health examinations, and adequate clothing and lodging. Owners refusing to abide by this code are to be fined for the first and second offenses. A third offense shall result in permanent forfeiture of slaves.

Maya would be lying if she said that she did not absolutely love Levi's comical new morning routine. His daily expression of excitement about their impending arrival was infectious and kept her fears about her baby's unexpected conception at bay. It was a far cry from the terror she felt while concealing her condition. She never outwardly admitted how much Levi's routine meant, but the internal serenity it brought her was something she felt her words would never do justice to anyway. The smile that instantly emerged on her face when she heard Levi enter the barn on this morning was proof of how truly at peace she now was.

"How're you feelin'?" Levi asked her, per usual.

"I'm fine," Maya replied. Her smile broadened as Levi then knelt and rested his head against her belly.

"How about you? You behavin' in there?" Levi asked, pausing as he pretended to listen to the baby's reply. "I know, I know! I'm eaga' to play with you too. But you're just gonna have to wait! You got

212

anotha' two months, three weeks, and five days before you're allowed outta there. And don't you even *think* about arrivin' any earlier than that, ya' hear?!" As he did every morning, he kissed Maya's stomach after his fatherly chat.

Maya always shook her head and laughed at his playful delivery day countdown.

Levi stood and smiled, always happy to start his morning with the sound of Maya's laughter. "You need anything?" he asked, as always.

"No, thank you," she replied.

"You sure?" Levi prodded, ready to abandon his work for any of her requests.

"I'm sure."

"Promise me you'll let me know if you do, okay?"

"I promise ... but you've already given me all I could eva' ask for," Maya replied, touching her belly.

Her words caused Levi to reflexively caress her cheek and close his eyes to hold back an unexpected surge of tears. His body electrified with warmth as soon as his skin connected with hers. He opened his eyes in time to see Maya's flutter close as she melted into his gentle touch. The surge of warmth running through her gave away how much she had missed his affection. Despite the unrelenting urge to press his lips against Maya's in that moment, Levi found the strength to refrain. "Well, know that I'm always here if eva' you need anything else, okay?" he said.

Maya looked into his eyes and quietly nodded.

After depriving himself of Maya for so long, Levi was happy that the baby gave him an excuse to touch her again in some limited capacity. But this morning, it damn near took an act of God to ignore his burning desire to touch her in more passionate ways, especially with the way she was gazing at him with her beautiful doe-like eyes.

He quietly gazed at her in return with genuine appreciation dancing in his eyes. He then gently brushed the back of his hand along her cheek before forcing himself to walk away to start his duties.

But even an act of God could not stop Levi from secretly buying every baby item he laid his eyes on. As the weeks rolled by, baby blankets, yarn, cloth diapers, rattles, and baby clothes always seemed to mysteriously appear in Maya's cottage. Unbeknownst to Maya, Levi had spent his late-night hours secretly working away at his final two gifts. Two weeks before her due date, she walked into her room and found a rocking chair and a crib, both with bows on them. Her tears pelted the railings of the crib as she ran her hand along the place her baby's loving father had handmade for her to sleep. Levi's beautiful morning routine, his expressions of love, and all his precious gifts indeed made Maya feel as though she already had it all. Her eyes full of tears, she sat down in the rocking chair and cursed herself for ever believing that an incredible man like Levi Collins would ever have expressed anything less than extreme love for the life they had created together.

****

The night before the predicted due date of Levi's countdown, he was barely able to sleep. Before dawn, he sprang out of bed and skipped breakfast. Like a child on Christmas morning dashing to the tree, he hurried into the barn as if his gift would somehow be there magically waiting for him. Maya was already there, standing with her back to him near a horse stall. Instead of a baby, though, she only held her aching pregnant back. Levi quietly approached her. "How're you feelin'?" he asked, per usual. When Maya turned around, the color drained from his face.

For two days, Maya had not been feeling well, but she had pushed herself to carry on with her duties as usual. Her fever had suddenly spiked the night before, though, making her short trek to the barn feel like a voyage up Mount Everest. "I'm fine," Maya forced herself to reply to Levi per usual, her breaths coming in short pants after using what remained of her energy to speak.

"My God, Maya, you're nowhere near fine," Levi replied, his heart plummeting over the way she seemed to be deteriorating right before his eyes.

Suddenly quivering with tears welling in her eyes, Maya dropped to a knee when intense pain exploded near her pelvis. Just after midnight, her labor pains had begun coming on and off like clockwork. The onset of illness, fever, and mounting excruciating pain had now nearly crippled her. Levi scooped her up before she fell over. He quickly carried her across the field back to her cottage and frantically yelled for help from another female slave. As Nora dashed into the room to help, Levi slowly stepped backward out of the cottage in a daze. Realizing that he was partially responsible for Maya's current torture had him on the verge of vomiting. He had looked forward to this day but was now dreading the way in which Maya would have to suffer prior to the most joyous moment of his life.

Knowing that Maya's pain was a natural part of the birthing process, Levi tried to get some work done in the barn to distract himself. His efforts were in vain, though. Maya was constantly bombarding his mind. His constant worry over her well-being robbed him of the ability to concentrate. He could not get through five minutes of work without nearly losing control over his emotions, and his stomach for that matter. He had never been so overwhelmed by anxiousness and worry while waiting for his other children to arrive. His genuine love for Maya seemed to cause the stark contrast.

After an hour of trying to work, Levi finally abandoned his duties altogether and left the barn. As he stepped closer to Maya's cottage, a sudden shrill pierced his ears. He froze, snatched his hat off, tilted his head back, closed his eyes, and said a brief prayer. When he opened his eyes again, they were full of tears. He began pacing outside Maya's cottage, straight-faced and nervous, feeling it deep in his gut every time he heard Maya scream in agony. As he marched back and forth, wearing a hole in the ground, he continuously asked God to end Maya's suffering as quickly as possible. While in the midst of praying, it seemed that God had answered. After a half hour, Levi suddenly halted his incessant pacing. His heart nearly leapt out of his chest as he quickly swiveled his head toward the sound of angelic cries.

A wave of euphoria hit Levi that propelled his legs toward the front door of Maya's cottage. He opened the door, but his shaky knees caused him to stumble slightly while trying to step over the threshold. He caught himself just before his jittery body hit the floor. He stood tall then exhaled sharply, but it did nothing to untie the knots in his stomach nor to calm his racing mind. Stepping slowly on wobbly knees, he slowly entered the room where his latest arrival lay wrapped up, already nestled in her mother's arms. As he approached, he could not pull his eyes away from Maya. Despite the effects of exhausting labor, she somehow had never looked more beautiful to him than in that moment. With an erratic heartbeat and a lump in his throat, Levi cautiously approached and stood towering over Maya, finally getting a peek at the life he had helped to create. He could not seem to remember how to speak at first but cleared his throat and said the first thing that came to his mind. "Is he alright?"

"*She*," Maya corrected, keeping her eyes pasted on the baby that she had instantaneously fallen in love with.

Levi's smile broadened. "A *girl?*" he responded in happy disbelief. He squatted down to get a better look, the beautiful sight stirring his tears. "I finally got myself a little girl," he whispered, pure joy in his tone. "I can hardly believe it."

"Yes, I'm sorry to say that she's broken your streak," Maya replied, extreme exhaustion evident in her faint words.

"That's nothin' to be sorry about. It's reason to celebrate," Levi sincerely replied. He then reached his arms out toward Maya, eager to hold his first daughter. His excitement dissipated and immediate hurt set in when Maya flinched and pulled the baby in closer to her. Her motherly instincts were already overpowering her. Suddenly, she questioned whether she should trust Levi.

Maya's reaction surprised Levi, but after the way he had sold other slave children, he understood why she had suddenly become so protective. But it hurt him, nonetheless. "Maya, I swear I would *neva'* hurt her," he whispered.

The weeping sound in Levi's voice stole the attention Maya was giving her baby. She looked up at Levi and saw in his eyes how her refusal had genuinely hurt him.

"Please?" he begged.

Maya searched Levi's eyes for reassurance that her daughter would be returned to her. Seeing the tears brimming in his eyes, she suddenly cursed herself for thinking, even for a second, that he would ever do anything to harm her. With that, she carefully handed him his newborn.

Cautiously, Levi gathered his very first daughter into his arms. Through half-lowered eyelids, Maya watched as tears cascaded down his cheeks, rolling by the genuine, loving smile on his face. "You're as pale as a Lily…" Levi said, kissing the baby's forehead. "And just as beautiful," Maya heard him whisper before the illness that had invaded her body began to take a serious toll. While Levi's attention was on the gift that Maya had delivered for him, she lost consciousness and slowly slumped over.

*****

June 1st, 1835,

Today, the love of my life gave me the most sacred gift any man could ever ask for ... my very first baby girl. She came into the world at 8:45 this morning. I've dreamt a long time about this moment, but by God, the feeling of holding my daughter for the very first time shattered every last one of my expectations. I knew I'd probably shed a tear, but I was not expecting the sea of joyous emotions streaming nonstop from my eyes. I knew I would smile, but I wasn't aware that this smile would not fade for hours. I smile now as I glance down at her nestled in my arms. I can't even bring myself to put her down as I write this. I feel my tears brewing once again, simply glancing down at this little miracle sleeping peacefully in my arms, looking to me like the most precious little angel. I can hardly believe I had anything to do with creating something so perfect. I may not know her name yet, but I can say with confidence that this precious little girl is not just a <u>part</u> of my heart ... she <u>is</u> my heart. And so is her mother. Maya is dreadfully ill at this very hour. Half of my heart will be forever shattered if she slips away from my world permanently. I pray now that God brings her back to me and our beautiful little creation.

*****

For the fourth straight day following that journal entry, Levi knelt at Maya's bedside at midnight, holding one of her limp hands in both of his. He had his eyes closed and his head bowed, begging God to heal her. Since giving birth, Maya had been in and out of consciousness. An extremely high fever had her babbling incoherently and hallucinating to the point that she could not decipher dreams from reality. Her odd illness kept her from eating and drinking enough to sustain her own life, let alone a baby's. Levi, therefore, asked Nora for her help again. She had, fortunately, given birth several months before Maya. Nora happily took over nursing and caring for the baby while Maya was sick.

Despite the baby being well taken care of, Levi was still emotionally unsettled. He worried about Maya around the clock, so much so that he had literally scraped together change to pay a doctor to stop by and treat her. Despite the medication the doctor administered, Maya's prognosis remained grim. She still laid there all day looking like a breathing corpse. The lack of answers and remedies to her bizarre ailment left Levi feeling frustrated and helpless. After four days with no change in her symptoms, his hope was now fading as well. The possibility that his daughter might grow up without her mother began to slowly creep into his spinning mind. The mere thought of losing the woman who had brought so much joy into his life caused Levi not to be able to eat or sleep. He had snuck out of his house every night and spent those sleepless hours at Maya's bedside, his eyes closed and his head bowed, tearfully begging God for another miracle.

After his prayers on this evening, Levi sat next to Maya dabbing a cool cloth on her chest and forehead. "I need you to get well. We got ourselves a beautiful little girl who's eaga' to get to know her mama," he whispered. Levi suddenly turned his head toward the door when he heard the baby crying in the other room. He turned back to look at Maya. "See, I told ya'. She's cryin' for you now," he teased, kissing her on the cheek before heading into the room where the baby was.

"Hey, my little Lily, what's all that fussin' about?" Levi playfully asked, caressing her head.

"I done fed 'er and cleaned 'er up already. Don't know why she's so fussy tonight," Nora explained, swaying the baby in her arms.

Levi took the baby into his arms and kissed her. Her fussing immediately transitioned into soft coos.

Nora smiled. "I guess you were all she needed." She caressed the baby's cheek. "She must've just been missin' you."

"I missed her too," Levi smiled, kissing the baby on the cheek again. "You can go and get some sleep for a little while. I'll keep watch ova' her for now."

"Alright," Nora replied. "Wake me if ya' think she needs anotha' feedin'."

"Will do."

Nora nodded and turned to go lie back down.

"And Nora…"

"Yessa'," she replied, turning back around.

Levi swallowed hard before saying what was on his mind. Her two oldest sons were among the three children he had sold years prior. He knew she had every right to spitefully abandon his newborn, but she had graciously stepped in without expressing an ounce of resentment. "You owe me no kindness … not an ounce. I'm very aware of that. So, I just wanted to say thank you so much for bein' willin' to take such good care of the baby, despite my transgressions against you. I'm foreva' indebted to you for keepin' her alive and thrivin'."

"No, you're not. It's my pleasure. No matta' your transgressions, I'd've neva' had the heart to sit by and watch that precious baby die."

"Well, I still want you to know how grateful I am. Your kindness will neva' be forgotten."

"Thank you," Nora nodded, genuinely feeling moved by his gratitude.

Levi turned to leave but turned back around when Nora called out to him again.

"Despite the past, I-I just want you to know that I've always believed you were a good man," she nervously confessed. "You just have the misfortune of bein' in a world that ain't worthy of a man like you."

Unexpected tears began to christen the newborn in Levi's arms. "And I'm certainly not worthy of your words. But they mean more to me than you'll eva' know."

Nora nodded and turned to go lay down.

Levi closed Nora's door and turned his attention back to the baby. He walked carefully with her back into Maya's room and shut the door. "You're worried about your mama too, aren't ya'? Is that why you up fussin' this time of night? I know you'd ratha' be in your mama's arms. But don't you worry. You'll be back in her arms again soon," he said, looking down at Maya as she lay there looking lifeless. "At least that's what I've been prayin' for."

On cue, the baby started to fuss again as if she was saying that soon was still not fast enough.

"Shh," Levi said, trying to settle her again. He pulled the rocking chair next to Maya's bed and sat down with the baby. He opened all the buttons on his pajama shirt, removed the baby's blanket, laid her against his bare chest, and placed the blanket back over the top of her. Her fussing immediately ceased the moment she felt her father's skin against hers. She melted into his warmth, snuggled close to the rhythmic thumping of his heart, and her rigid body instantly relaxed. Levi closed his eyes and melted too, feeling the love for his daughter grow just by the simple pleasure of being so close to her. He began rocking slowly, humming his favorite melody as of late, while caressing her back. When he felt her body grow heavy, he slowly tried to get up to take her back into Nora's room, but the baby shifted her head. She woke up just long enough to grasp her father's finger tight with her tiny hand. It felt to Levi as if she was begging him to stay there with her. He happily granted her wish. He kissed her head, sat back down, and rocked her and *himself* to sleep.

During his lunch break the following day, Levi could not get his feet to move fast enough to go and see the baby. He entered Maya's cottage ready to read his daughter one of the many children's books he had purchased for her.

As soon as Nora saw him walk in, she smiled at the way Levi's face lit up upon seeing the baby. "Fed and clean and ready to see 'er daddy," she said, as she handed Levi the baby.

"Thank you, Nora," Levi said, smiling at the baby. "How's Maya?" he then asked.

"I gave her the medicine the doctor prescribed, just like you instructed." Nora shook her head. "She was barely able to swallow it. As usual, she was still babblin' like she ain't even speakin' English."

"Not a single change then, huh?"

"No sa', I'm afraid not."

"Well, thank you anyway."

"Yessa'," Nora nodded, stepping out of the cottage to do her chores.

Levi walked directly to Maya's room when Nora left. He sat down next to her makeshift bed and propped the baby up on his knees. He held Maya's hand, said a prayer, and then turned his attention back to the baby. "Here we are again," Levi smiled, looking down at the baby who was staring at him with eyes that Levi now realized were identical to his. "You're wide awake today, huh?" He smiled and caressed her cheek. "You know this is my favorite part of the day, comin' in here holdin' my little Lily. Levi and Lily … Lily and Levi," he sang. "I like the sound of that. Levi and Lily." He smiled as the baby continued to stare at him. "You're lookin' at me like you're sick of hearin' me call you that. Sorry, but I don't know what else to call ya' for now. We gotta wait on your mama to wake up and give you a permanent name," he said, glancing over at Maya as she lay there unconscious sweating out the mysterious bug that had a tight grip on her weakened body.

Still, the baby had yet to blink. She had her mouth partially open, looking as if she was in awe of what she was seeing. "What you lookin' at with those bright beautiful eyes, little flowa'?" Levi asked when he turned to look back at her. "You're starin' at me like you just gotta figure out who this strange man is. Well, I'm sorry to break it to ya', but this funny lookin' pale man is your daddy. You're stuck with me." Levi laughed at the fact that she had still yet to blink her eyes. He pointed to his ears and his nose, naming each body part. The entire time the baby stayed focused on his every move like a curious kitten. "I done been around a lotta babies, but I ain't neva' seen one so bright-eyed and full of wonder at five-days old in all my life. Be lucky to keep one awake long enough to get finished with a feedin'. I can already tell you're gonna be curious and smart, just like your mama," he smiled. "It's okay to blink, little flowa'. I promise you won't miss much if you do." On cue, she finally did. Levi laughed at her perfect timing, raised her up and kissed her forehead. He lowered her onto his knees and laughed again when she went right back to staring at him.

He ran his fingers through her tendrils of hair as he gazed at her with just as much awe. "My God, I'm so happy you're here ... and so proud to be your fatha'," he said in a tender tone, as he started to become emotional. "Afta' five straight boys, I's startin' to think God would neva' bless me with a little girl, let alone one as beautiful as you. Sometimes, I can't hardly believe I had anything to do with creatin' somethin' so perfect," he whispered, still running the tips of his fingers gently through her curly hair. "I honestly can't believe that me and your mama created you at all for that matta'. Let them foolish doctors tell it, you ain't even supposed to be here. But against all odds, here you are, lyin' in my arms, lookin' at me with those big bright beautiful eyes." He kissed her again. "I may not know your name yet, but I'm convinced God wanted you here for a reason. You're gonna be as special to the world as you are to me … I just know it. I can feel it in my soul." He held Maya's hand again. "There's no way God would bless me and your mama with such a beautiful miracle for nothin'."

Levi quickly turned his head toward Maya when he felt her squeeze his hand. "Your daddy is right," she slowly grumbled. She swallowed and took a deep breath before continuing. "You're our miracle baby," she added in a raspy tone.

Hearing Maya utter her first coherent words in days caused Levi's eyes to instantly flood with tears. "Thank you, God," he whispered, kissing her on the forehead. "Where you been?" he jokingly asked, gazing at her through the tears in his eyes.

"Lord help me, I sho' don't know."

"I don't know eitha', but I sho' am happy you're back."

"I come back just in time to see that you done found yo'self a new love," she whispered, her words still extremely raspy.

"Mm-hmm, now I got myself two beautiful ladies to love," he replied, looking down at their baby and then back at Maya. "This little one said she misses you." Levi held the baby up for Maya to get a better look.

Maya instantly started crying. "My God, she's so beautiful."

"I miss you holdin' me mama," Levi said, playfully speaking on behalf of the baby.

"I wanna hold you so bad too sweetheart, but I just don't have the strength. Feels like a horse is sittin' on my chest."

"Don't push yourself too hard. I'll have Nora sit with you and take care of the baby while I ride into town and get the doctor. Maybe there's somethin' else he can give ya' to help you get your strength back."

"Th-thank you," she replied weakly.

"Thank *you* ... for comin' back to me," Levi replied. He let another kiss linger on her forehead before heading into town.

****

The first Sunday after Maya had awakened, Levi walked up the steps to the stage in his church and stood near the piano. It was within these church walls that his musical talent had been trapped since conceiving Wyatt. Levi took a moment to scan the familiar faces in the church he had attended his whole life. The congregation knew him well ... or so they thought. The man they stared back at was actually far more of a mystery to them than the inner workings of his gifted musical mind. Levi briefly glanced in the front row before taking his seat at the piano. His wife and boys were there, including seven-year-old Wyatt, sitting in the spot where his father's musical mannerisms would become ingrained in his young mind. Levi smiled pridefully at his boys, but the thought circulating through his mind when he looked at his wife was further proof that the man he presented himself to be was a facade. Nobody within those walls would ever have guessed that Levi was currently glaring at his wife wishing that a woman he beheld as a Nubian goddess was sitting there instead. A newborn baby snuggled in the protective arms of her oldest brother would complete the imagery of perfection in Levi's mysterious mind. He sighed deeply as he stood there; his sorrow was suddenly heavy, knowing the family he envisioned would never take their rightful place in that coveted front row pew.

The facade of Levi's life would be further evident to the congregation if they knew the true motivation behind the song he was about to play for them. Levi had not jotted down a single note of this particular song. Despite never having rehearsed it, he was confident that he could play it flawlessly. The song had ignited in his mind and played on a joyous loop since the day he discovered he had conceived a child with Maya. He often hummed the melody to a certain little person while he held her on his chest and rocked her to sleep at night. Every note, every key change, and every dramatic pause was now solidified in his mind ... and so was the title. "I call this song..." Levi paused a moment as he thought about the newborn who had inspired it. "A beautiful miracle."

When Levi sat at the piano bench and closed his eyes, a precious little face with eyes identical to his materialized in his mind. He had to clear his throat before he began, already fighting to choke back tears. Despite his efforts, his prideful emotions slowly began to emerge the moment he struck the keys. The complicated notes flowed effortlessly down to his fingertips. The slow, angelic tune sounded even more magnificent to Levi than he had imagined in his mind. Hearing the sentimental melody for the first time echoing within the church walls further ignited his emotions.

The heavenly sounds caressing Wyatt's youthful ears began to stir his tears for the first time ever while watching his father play. He sat unblinking in the front row, entranced by the way his father poetically danced and swayed, adding to the sentimentality of the melody. He was simply mesmerized, in much the same way that he would be twenty-five years later by the sister his father now played in honor of. Wyatt was not alone. The entire congregation was hypnotized by the passionate way in which Levi played the highs and lows of the inspirational ballad. They watched intently as he musically painted the beautiful moments that inspired his angelic melody. They, too, became over-emotional seeing Levi's tears stream past the joyous smile on his face, a smile that gave away the fact that he was witnessing the most glorious visions in his mind.

With a sudden dramatic key change in the melody, Levi's tears transitioned into that of anguish and the smile faded from his face.

Like a waterfall, his tears began to flow onto the piano keys as he thought of the numerous songs he had played that were inspired by Maya, ones he could never bring her to his church to hear. He cried for the fact that there would never be a day when he stood proudly waiting for Maya to walk through the pews and meet him at the altar currently beneath where he sat. He cried knowing that he would never be able to proudly introduce everyone to the precious little miracle Maya had delivered for him either. As he gallantly played, many people in the congregation were sobbing … including little Wyatt. Never had they seen Levi so overcome by emotion during a song. Nor would they ever know that the deluge spilling from his eyes reflected the heartache of accepting that his expressions of love for Maya and his newborn would remain as trapped in his heart as his music was within those church walls.

When he finished the enchanting eight-minute ballad, Levi stood and wiped the tears from his eyes. He walked to the forefront of the stage and bowed to a congregation that was already on its feet, a congregation who felt as though they had indeed just experienced the myriad of magical emotions after witnessing … *a Beautiful Miracle*.

****

Nora was sitting next to Maya in her bed, both of them staring at the baby. "Thank you for takin' such good care of her while I's sick," Maya told her.

"You're very welcome!" Nora replied. "I's happy to."

"Can't believe this poor baby done been in this world all this time with no name," Maya commented, sounding much stronger than when she had first awakened.

"Masa' Lee been callin' 'er little Lily all week. He say she just as pale as one … and just as beautiful."

"He's got a point! She sho' is mighty pale," Maya laughed.

227

"She'll get a little more color soon. Just takes time."

"Lord, I hope so, or I'll be convinced y'all done gave me the wrong baby!"

Nora laughed. "Naw, she's most definitely yours," she said, caressing the baby's hair. "Beautiful, just like 'er mama."

"You say Masa' Lee been in here all week?" Maya asked curiously.

"*Every* night … *all* night. Been right here by yo' side prayin' for ya', holdin' onto that baby like he can't breathe without 'er. Truth be told, seems to me like he couldn't breathe without you eitha'."

Maya kept her eyes on the baby, trying hard to prevent her rising emotions from allowing a smile to creep onto her face. "Well, you can't blame 'em for worryin'. No masta' could stand to lose a slave he done paid good money for," she replied.

"Hmph, now that's funny, 'cause I could've swore masa' Lee got you from Emily's daddy as a gift."

Maya smiled sheepishly. "Well, free or not, I'm sure he can't afford to lose a slave," she replied defiantly, despite knowing she was caught.

"Mm-hmm, that's the story I promise I'll *pretend* to believe."

Maya continued hiding her smile in silence.

Nora breathed a heavy sigh and ran her hands through the baby's curls. "Sho' is amazin' the beautiful things that *love* can create," she added slyly.

"You're relentless, you know that?" Maya laughed.

"I know," Nora smiled. "It's one of my *finer* qualities."

Levi stepped into Maya's cottage, delighted to hear the sound of laughter coming from her room. "Hello ladies," he greeted. He was still dressed in his church attire.

"Hello masa' Lee," Nora replied, standing up to leave them alone. Before departing, she turned back to give Maya a telling glance with a smile and a wink. Maya smiled back sheepishly as she shook her head.

"I'm happy to see that smile on your face," Levi said, her smile igniting his. "You look like you're feelin' much betta'."

Maya's smile broadened over how much more handsome he looked clean shaven with his hair cut and styled and dressed in fine attire. "I'm feelin' stronga' every day. I don't know what they put in them drugs, but they sho' do work wonders. I feel like a new woman today, actually."

"Certainly glad to hear that!" Levi sat down on the bed next to her and put his arm around her. He caressed the baby's hair as he gazed at her. "You thought of a name for our little one yet?"

"No." Maya looked at Levi. "But her daddy did."

Levi looked perplexed.

"*Lily*," Maya smiled as she turned her attention back to the baby. "Such a beautiful name for the beautiful little girl you blessed me with."

Levi's face lit up with a brilliant smile. "Lily," he whispered. "Turns out you're my little flowa' afta' all." He leaned down and gently kissed her forehead.

When Levi looked up, Maya was gazing at him. She then took a hold of his hand. "Thank you for makin' me a motha'," she said, her emotions stirring.

"It was my pleasure," Levi whispered, kissing her tenderly on the forehead as well.

Maya smiled devilishly. "And most *certainly* mine too!"

Levi laughed as his pride swelled. And so, too, did his heart. Maya's words gave him complete confidence that her health had finally returned, right along with her sensual sarcasm. He kissed Lily again and then departed, finally feeling at peace that his daughter would now be raised by her loving mother.

Levi walked out of the cottage and was immediately knocked off the happy cloud he was drifting on. His haggard looking wife, Emily, was standing there staring at him with her hands on her thin hips. Just hours out of church and she was already reeking of alcohol, per usual. Emily was only twenty-two, but years of daily alcohol consumption had taken a serious toll on her features. She now easily looked twice her age. Her once supple, taut skin was prematurely sagging and thinning, looking as though it might slough off at the slightest touch. Her once lustrous, flowing brown locks were constantly pasted to her face in thick oily strands. The dirty clusters of hair always seemed to be constantly getting trapped in the deep crevices near her mouth that had formed from years of scowling. Years of squinting harshly at Levi had cemented crow's feet around once lively blue eyes. The mesmerizing color of her eyes was now barely visible through the alcoholic glaze that had formed over them. Those glossy, bloodshot, beady eyes were now pasted on Levi.

Levi was instantly enraged to find Emily standing there. She only ever set foot in the fields when she was ready to stir up trouble. Levi closed his eyes, pinched the bridge of his nose, and let out an exasperated breath, preparing himself for the drunken argument he was convinced his wife was about to incite on the Lord's day. "What do you want now, Emily?" he asked, annoyance evident in his tone.

"Done seen you headin' in and outta this cottage three times or more every day for the last week," Emily spat, her usual scowl firmly in place. She folded her arms across her chest, alcohol lending to her fidgety movements. "I finally got a peek at that baby when I saw Nora walkin' with it. He sho' is awfully fair-skinned for a nigga'." She squinted even harder than usual. "He's *yours*, ain't he?"

Levi should have known that's what Emily was there to ask. She had accused him of fathering every newborn birthed by a slave on their plantation. His stark denial was always proven true once the children's features and skin tones were prominent. Emily stood there now expecting him to deny her accusations as usual but that was nowhere near the case. "Yes. She's mine," Levi proudly confessed.

Emily scoffed and took a step back, the news seeming to punch her in the gut and quickly sober her. "*She?!*" Her mouth fell open. "You gave that lowly slave *a girl?*" she said with the utmost disgust in her tone.

Levi was completely apathetic to his wife's anger. Her words and the jealousy in her tone only reminded him of how badly she had hoped for a girl. As much as Emily hated him, he knew Lily's gender was a far bigger offense than the sinful misconduct that had brought her into the world.

"What the hell you in here takin' care of that little nigga' for anyway, huh?!" Emily suddenly erupted.

"Her mama's sick! It's my duty and *the law* to take care of sick slaves residin' on this farm."

"*Duty*, huh?" Emily barked, looking her husband up and down with scathing eyes.

"Yes, nothin' more!" he lied, trying to diffuse what had the potential to be a far more volatile situation.

"I don't believe you! That's probably the reason you's sittin' up at that piano in church cryin' like a little sissy today! Your whore's too sick to suck your cock tonight!" Emily taunted, a devilish smirk on her face.

Levi lowered his eyes and took a deep breath to keep from verbally erupting.

Emily stepped forward and put a finger in her husband's face. "You let them otha' nigga's take care of your bastard and your cock suckin' whore! It ain't a damn thang you can do to stop that morally corrupt Jezebel from dyin' anyway! You ain't no doctor! You're too damn stupid to be one!" she slurred. She then turned and stumbled away after adding to the pile of demeaning insults she had hurled at her husband over the years.

Levi typically never bothered to retaliate nor even respond to his wife's baseless insults. He felt her foolishness was not worth the expended oxygen. However, internalizing her spirit-killing words had just allowed her to flee the scene with yet another sliver of his sanity.

Chapter Fourteen

December 24, 1860

William's face remained void of emotion when he opened the door of his sons' Manhattan apartment and did not see Lily standing alongside James and Austin. He peered over their shoulders and looked down the corridor of the building, hoping for the faintest chance that Lily was hiding around a corner ready to surprise him. After seeing that the hallway was empty, he solemnly looked back at James and Austin without uttering a word. James and Austin said nothing either. They were equally hoping for the slim possibility that Lily had somehow made it to Manhattan on her own. William's silent actions quickly extinguished that hope. The disappointment seemed to temporarily strip them all of the ability to even speak. The only sound next was all three men sighing their frustration in unison.

Considering the fact that William had not seen James and Austin since April, one might have viewed William's emotionless welcome as being annoyed by their presence. James and Austin knew better, though. Only someone who had come to love Lily as they did could understand how her absence seemed to be causing everyone's hearts to deteriorate. James had been through this before during the many years he was away at Ohio University. He was, therefore, not at all offended by William's cold welcome. Such behavior was minor on the scale of bizarre ways that James had acted out his frustrations during the six years he was away from Lily while at school.

After their collective sigh, James and Austin both quietly followed William into the apartment. Emerson was already setting out five glasses on his dining room table when they entered. He then filled them with the only known liquid prescription powerful enough to numb a man's emotional pain. He left the bottle of whiskey in the middle of the table, knowing they would all need a second dose ... and maybe even a third.

Isabel was already sitting in the dining room when they entered. She was the only one to outwardly express excitement when she saw James and Austin. She immediately sprang from her seat and gave each of them a hug. Isabel had been relieved when William received James's letter weeks earlier. When she found out that James and Lily were a no-show on the night of their planned escape, she immediately suspected that her brother had had something to do with it. She had yet to forget Elijah's vehement hatred for James and his outspoken desire to avenge their parents' barbaric murder.

After pretending to assist the bandits in the search for James and Lily back in April, Elijah had briefly come back to Manhattan. Isabel immediately noticed her brother was behaving more oddly than usual while he was at home. When she calmly asked why James and Lily had failed to show, Elijah became instantly enraged. "I don't have to explain a damn thing to you!" he had erupted, screaming the words just inches from her face. Isabel felt his belligerence further justified her suspicions. A few days later, Elijah packed all his belongings and left Manhattan without a word to anyone about where he was headed. Isabel had only heard from him via occasional letters in the months since then.

Isabel now hugged James tight, feeling comforted by the fact that her brother had not left town to fulfill his vengeful desires as she had feared. Still though, there was something about Elijah's odd behavior that had left her wondering if he knew where Lily was. But extreme fear of her brother's volatile temper, once again, kept her from mentioning her suspicions to everyone as they sat down to discuss their plans to find Lily.

After Wilson finished pouring every man a much-needed drink, he sat down at the dining room table and the discussion commenced.

"Where have you and Austin searched for Lily thus far?" William asked James.

"Austin here was brave enough to infiltrate the Ghost Rida's and gathered some valuable intel about where and to whom they sell black market slaves. We followed a few leads and posed as interested black market buyers down in Mississippi, but we came up empty with any furtha' leads."

"We searched damn near every plantation down there known for illegal purchases too," Austin added. "But everything was a dead end. Seems like Lily just vanished without a trace."

James was mindlessly spinning his liquor glass in a circle on the table. "At this point, everything's gonna seem like a dead end since we got started with our search seven months afta' Lily went missin'. She could be anywhere by now."

"Griff and the bandits searched for the both of you back in April," William said. "Before receiving your letter a few months ago, Griff and I just assumed that perhaps you and Lily didn't want to be found and that you'd changed your minds about going to the Old World."

"Neva'. That was Lily's dream and there was no way I was gonna deprive her of that."

"I actually think I knew that then as well, but I wanted to tell myself that little lie to keep myself from fearing the worst. I nearly hit the floor when I read your letter and realized that things were far worse than I had ever suspected." William shook his head to ward off a sudden urge to cry when he recalled reading about Rose. "And may I say that I'm so sorry for your loss, James."

James nodded but kept staring at his now empty liquor glass. He could sense the emotions in William's tone and feared that he, too, would become emotional if he looked over at him.

"There's one thing I haven't mentioned," Austin said, staring at his glass too.

"What's that?" William asked.

"When the Ghost Rida's can't sell a slave, they're useless to 'em, and they don't hesitate to ... to..." He shook his head, blew out a frustrated breath and looked at William. "What if Lily's dead?" he blurted.

An instant rage pulled James to his feet. "SHE ISN'T DEAD!" he yelled, hurling his glass into a nearby fireplace.

"How do you know?!" Austin fired back.

"'CAUSE MY GODDAMN HEART'S STILL BEATIN'!" James yanked Austin up from his seat by his collar. "And don't you eva' utta' those words in my presence again!" he growled, shoving Austin back down into his seat.

"I-I'm sorry," Austin stuttered, staring up at James whose face was beet-red. "Y-y'ur right, I sh-shouldn't've said that. It's just ... I'm just frustrated that we can't find 'er!"

James's sudden explosive temper reminded Isabel of her brother; it rattled her into tears. His outburst further solidified her decision to remain silent.

"Look, everyone's emotions are running high right now, but let's not turn on one another because of it," William said, trying to restore the tranquility. "The fact that we all care so deeply for Lily should make us a united front in ensuring her safe return ... not bitter enemies."

James finally pulled his eyes away from Austin, looked over at William and then sat back down.

"That being said, I refuse to even entertain the idea that Lily is dead," William continued. "I just don't believe that God would deliver a woman like Lily into this world just to callously snatch her away before she's done what He sent her here to do. Perhaps this nightmare is meant to make us all stronger somehow. Whatever it is, there just has to be some good reason that God is dragging us all through this bloody madness. I hold dear to that belief with all of my heart … and so should all of you."

"I already do," James replied, suddenly glaring at Austin. "And I *always* will."

"Me too," Isabel whispered.

The twins and Austin nodded in agreement as well.

"Well, we can only learn the meaning of all this when we find Lily," William continued. "So, let's vow to be a united front and make a solid plan to bring her home. Let's renew our search for Lily with hope, confidence, and optimism. Can we do that?" William asked, taking a moment to glance at all the frustrated faces in the room.

"Yes, of course," James replied first. "You're right, we don't need to turn on each otha'. We need all the manpowa' we can get right now. Austin, forgive me for gettin' angry. Afta' everything you've done to help me, you certainly didn't deserve that. So, I apologize."

Austin nodded. "It's alright I unda'stand. I'm just as frustrated as you are."

"Austin and I can only do so much to find Lily, though. I'm a wanted man in the south. My wanted posta's are plastered everywhere," James explained. "I'm a fugitive whose crime was lovin' a slave. I'm sure bounty hunta's wanna do far more to me than make a few thousand dolla's before they turn me in. Because of the circumstances, Austin and I were forced to do most of our searchin' late at night. I'm riskin' gettin' rearrested every time I set foot in the south ... especially in Virginia. That's why we cut our search short and came here to regroup and figure out what to do next. We were hopin' you knew where Griff or the otha' bandits might be. I'm sure they'd be willin' to help."

"I most certainly do," William replied.

"You do?"

"One floor down." William turned to Emerson. "Go on to Griff's apartment and tell him that James is finally here."

Emerson nodded and got up to do as his father wanted.

"I looked for Griff for weeks afta' I saw James's wanted posta's. He's been here the whole time?" Austin asked.

"Not the whole time. He's come and gone over the last several months." He turned to address James. "Griff searched for you and Lily for weeks. Even though we surmised that you two did not want to be found, it just wasn't sitting right with him that Samuel was missing too."

"Samuel still hasn't turned up?" James asked, sounding equally baffled by the mystery.

"No. He, too, seems to have vanished without a trace."

"Somethin' definitely doesn't smell right. He was as loyal a security bandit to Lily as Griff," Austin added.

"I know. That's what kept Griff's search goin'. He'd search for a few weeks and then come back here to give me updates on his progress every now and then," William replied. He then turned toward James again. "I just so happened to receive your letter while he was in town. After reading the details, he decided to wait here for you, so that you could all formulate a plan to search for Lily together."

"Griff always did love Lily like she was his own," James stated.

"As do I," William replied. "All of us love her. And, together, we *will* find her. Even if I have to spend the rest of my life and every bit of my resources to do it ... we *will* find her."

Griff came over shortly thereafter and formulated a plan to do just that. He broke everyone up into pairs. James and Austin were to search together. The twins were paired, and Griff felt it was best that he and William searched as a team. He gave each group weapons, money, and maps of areas that were notorious for stolen slave purchases, assigning James the states that were least likely to have his wanted posters. Isabel was then assigned the duty of handling the correspondence of letters between everyone.

Griff's love for Lily and his desperation to find her was further proven by the last item he gave everyone to aid in their search. "I went to see that French fella' that did Lily's paintin'. I had 'em draw these," he said, as he passed out 4x6 color pictures of Lily. "Figured y'all could show 'em to people to let 'em know who y'ur lookin' for."

When James was slid Piers LeRoux's stunning depiction of Lily, his mind went blank. He no longer heard a word Griff was saying. All his emotions were suddenly fighting to escape all at once, much like the way he suddenly had an unrelenting desire to escape that room. He needed to breathe fresh air. He needed to breathe, period, something he suddenly felt he couldn't do while staring at the lifelike picture of a missing woman who he loved beyond measure. He struggled to inhale while considering the *thousands* of square miles that a mere *six* men had to scour with only the *slightest* chance of finding her. The enormity of it all had him ready to jump out of his skin ... and Emerson's apartment window for that matter.

As soon as their meeting was over, James immediately grabbed his coat. He resisted the urge to jump out of the window and instead walked downstairs and out onto the snow-lined roads of Manhattan.

He wanted to walk out in the cold all alone. He could have taken his horse, but he hoped the walk and the fresh air would alleviate the pent-up emotional pressure in his chest that Austin's angering statement about Lily had ignited: *What if Lily's dead?* James tried to walk until that looping phrase ceased and the unbearable pain of such a thought began to subside. But even after walking all the way to the Manhattan train station, the tightness and ache in his chest remained.

James stepped onto the train platform and stared blankly into a particular empty corner of the station. Despite the fact that train whistles blew loudly, and people moved briskly around him, he suddenly felt as if he was standing there alone with Lily. His mind had completely abandoned reality and drifted away to the unforgettable moment from a year prior that had drawn him to the sentimental section at the Manhattan train station ...

"You were right all those months ago, ya' know," Lily called out to James before he had gotten too far.

James stopped just feet away from her and turned around.

"I've always felt it," she continued.

James looked at her a bit confused. "Felt what?"

Lily approached him and ran her hand down the front of his overcoat. "How much you've always loved me," she answered. *"And I hope you've always felt it too."* Her eyes were suddenly fixated on his. *"How much I've always loved you."*

James froze for a moment and let his eyes drift across the softness in Lily's face after she had spoken the words. "Always," he finally assured her, in a faint whisper.

"Good. 'Cause I do," she admitted, blinking away the tears she could no longer hold back. *"I really do love you, James Adams. Through everything all these years ... I always have."*

... That moment replayed with such precision in James's mind that he felt a surge of tears threatening to fall, much like on that night. Lily's invaluable words meant far more to him than just a declaration of her love. He had kissed her that night with a finesse that conveyed how grateful he was that she had finally granted him full access to her heart after he had once broken it. He had then ridden away on the train committed to fiercely protecting her life and handling her vulnerable heart more delicately after being given a second chance. But now, as the train horn sounded behind him, it seemed to be blowing the whistle on how he had failed at honoring that vow. The consequences of his failures caused the pain in his chest to intensify and turned up the volume to the torturous words looping in his head: *What if Lily's dead?*

Still desperate to nullify that taunting phrase, James walked solemnly back into town, passing by high-rise buildings that he had watched Lily gaze at through eyes of wonderment. When he reached his destination, he halted and looked up. The words he currently saw placarded on the Winter Garden Marquee suddenly blurred and faded into "The Dream Symphony." In his mind, he could see the joy on Lily's face as she stood in that exact spot a year ago, proudly reading those very words.

While on his walk down memory lane, James wanted only to relive Lily's momentous accomplishments and their cherished moments from their time in Manhattan. But a brief flashback of the disaster that had occurred a year ago in the back hallways of Winter Garden made him hesitant to enter. He feared walking inside would trigger the pain of his failures tenfold. Still though, he was unable to resist the unrelenting need to revisit the places where glorious memories were made on the path paved by his incredible woman during her unprecedented journey. Upon stepping inside, he looked around and easily understood how the meticulously designed interior had caused a look of awe on Lily's face like no other theater before it. He marched up to the balcony seats and rested his hands on the railing. His eyes swept from one side of the massive facility to the other. After absorbing the breathtaking view, he was not stung by the pain of his failures, but by envy. He was envious of those who had once sat in the seats surrounding him and had witnessed Lily's last performance. It was then that the pain in his chest intensified, an ache so acute that he felt a need to sit down. He lowered his head into his hands, suddenly mourning the fact that he had missed those magnificent final hours of the Dream Symphony.

Startled by the sudden sound of workers preparing for this year's Christmas show, James lifted his heavy head. He stood up again and looked toward the stage. The grand piano sitting centerstage stole his attention. All the workers surrounding it faded away as a memory of him and Lily in Jamestown, New York came into focus...

After the last of the student orchestra and dancers left the theater, Lily sat down at the grand piano and began playing a new melody with James watching on. A few days before, she had finally realized she was with child. Since then, she had obsessively thought of a unique way to tell James. Her creative mind had naturally composed a song instead. Lily wanted to tell James with something far more unique than music, though. She wanted to give him something commemorative that he could touch and see to memorialize a first in his life. Until she could think of something more sentimental, she kept the secret of the life growing inside her tightly wrapped in the notes of her angelic melody. So there James stood, watching Lily play, completely unaware that she was divulging through her very fingertips that he was about to become a father. He may not have known what, or rather *who*, had inspired the song, but it brought him just as much happiness as it seemed to be bringing Lily as she played.

"That's a new one," James remarked with a smile when she finished.

"Felt like my finga'tips were gonna burst if I didn't get it out," she smiled back.

"Very heavenly soundin'."

"Perfect description! That's definitely what I's aimin' for." She then stood and walked to the front of the stage.

James walked up behind her and wrapped his arms around her waist. "What inspired it?" he asked, kissing her on the neck.

You just wrapped your arms around it, she thought to herself. "Just the fact that I'm on a journey with a man who loves me … playin' shows in all these beautiful places," she said instead, looking out at the interior of Jamestown Performing Arts Theater.

"Hmm, I hadn't noticed," he teased. "Your beauty has been far too much of a distraction."

Lily smiled as she turned around and wrapped her arms around James's neck. "Is that why you were starin' at me non-stop durin' rehearsals?"

"I can't help myself."

"Any particular reason?" Lily asked, maneuvering his hand onto her buttocks.

James replied with a soft moan. His eyelids slowly lowered and his shaft instantly hardened.

"So just what was on that mischievous mind of yours while you were starin' at me?" Lily asked in a lustful tone.

"I was…"

Lily put a finger to his lips. "I don't want you to *tell* me." She closed the curtains to the stage and walked back over to James, gazing at him with want in her eyes. "I want you to *show* me."

James immediately picked her up, carried her to the grand piano, and sat her on top of the lid. "I visualized you sittin' here."

Lily leaned back and crossed her legs as she gazed down at her man. James stepped back to gaze at her in return. Her sensuous pose looked even more to him like an Egyptian queen than he had envisioned.

"And then what?" Lily purred.

James stepped toward her again and slid his hands under her dress. He gently glided them up her thighs, slowly spreading her legs apart as he gazed into her eyes. "And then I kissed you here," he said, caressing her hidden jewel through her underwear.

Lily's eyes fluttered closed and she let out a soft moan as wetness flooded her nether region. Feeling the rush of moisture on his fingertips, James's mouth began watering as he quickly slid her undergarments down. Alternating left to right, he kissed his way up her thighs. Lily gasped and tilted her head back when he reached her precious pearl and began gently French kissing it. James grunted and suckled harder when she spread her legs even further. As the feeling intensified, Lily began thrusting her hips toward the pleasure. James grabbed hold of her waist and greedily drove his tongue inside of her, the heat of her folds pleasantly singeing his lips. Lily, in turn, grabbed a handful of his hair and forced him to plunge deeper. In harmony with one another, deep groans of delight escaped them. Lightly grazing her skin with the whiskers of his beard, James made his way back up to Lily's swollen nub and devoured it. He simultaneously slid his fingers inside of Lily's dripping cavern. Knowing just the way to tickle and tease her, he quickly milked her of her nectar. Lily amassed her hands in his hair again, arched her back, and unleashed a climactic moan along with an eruption of her sweet elixir. After the eruption settled, Lily leaned down and thanked her man with a kiss, taking each of his swollen lips into her mouth one at a time, sucking the taste of herself from them. "And then what?" she panted seductively afterward.

James carefully lifted Lily off the piano and put her feet back on the ground. He sat down with his legs on either side of the piano bench. "You were sittin' here," he replied, the throbbing bulge in his pants pointing out exactly where.

A subtle moan rumbled in Lily's throat as she unbuttoned the top of James's pants and unleashed the hardened part that awaited her. She gazed into his eyes and a sensual smile emerged on her face as she lifted her dress and straddled the piano bench. She placed her hands on either side of James's face and leaned down to kiss him. There was a softness in the way she moved her lips that suddenly made him want to touch her with equal tenderness. He, too, placed his hands alongside her face and gently caressed her cheeks. He pulled her closer, moaning when Lily suddenly deepened their kiss. The sweet taste and feel of her soft tongue intensified the throbbing in his groin. The throbbing turned into a merciless ache when the heat from Lily's abyss began to singe the tip of his hardened flesh. Slowly, she filled herself and set both their bodies aflame. The jolt of pleasure tore their lips apart as guttural moans simultaneously roared through both their vocal cords.

The usual aggressive lioness in Lily was far more tamed as she rode James this time. The movement of her hips was of a slow grinding nature that left James submerged in the searing heat of her chamber as she erotically danced on his lap. James briefly opened his eyes to find Lily's closed, looking completely lost in the rapture of their union. The glistening tears on her eyelashes spoke of how intensely the passion had affected her. He reacted to her beautiful expression with a kiss that was equally as intense as the look on her face. He gently held her face close as they kissed, moans and sighs reverberating in their mouths as their lips and tongues made love. It was only a sudden explosive climax that had enough power to tear their lips apart again. Lily's back arched, her mouth fell open, and deep moans erupted from her throat as her body spasmed again and again. The erotic sight and sound nearly caused James's stones to explode as he burst inside of her seconds later. Both stayed suspended in a state of euphoria, their entire bodies throbbing with immense pleasure. Had their performance been part of Lily's shadowed show, their erotic silhouettes would have had every patron's jaw on the floor, every maiden's hand-fan flailing at full speed, every man's erection at full attention, and *all* their eyes wide with envy. A standing ovation most certainly would have followed.

In his mind, James was most certainly giving Lily a standing ovation for her outstanding erotic performance. "Are you okay?" he asked when he opened his eyes and noticed tears trickling down her cheeks.

We're just fine, Lily wanted to say as she thought about the little person growing inside her that had ignited her joyous tears. "I'm just so happy," she said instead, gazing at James with a smile on her face.

"Me too," James replied, wiping her tears. He then kissed Lily tenderly on the lips, further igniting her joy as she continued to contemplate the unique way in which she wanted to reveal to the loving man before her that he would soon be a father.

… James now sat in a sea of seats alone at Winter Garden, thinking about the fact that he had not been able to experience that sort of beautiful lovemaking with Lily for eight months now. That crushing reality, once again, made the swell of emotions in his chest expand a little more. Solemnly, he stood and walked toward the exit with Austin's words, *what if Lily's dead?* echoing even louder as he made his way out of Winter Garden.

Preston Mills was about to lock the doors to the Manhattan Art Gallery, where Lily's magnificent portrait hung. However, he stopped when he saw James plodding up the stone steps. Preston immediately recognized James but could not recall his name. "Oh hello, Mister umm ..."

"Adams. James Adams. You're Preston Mills, the curator of the museum, correct?"

"Yes, I am. Very nice to see you again," Preston replied.

"You too."

"I'd ask how you were doing, but from what William's told me, I assume that you're not in the greatest of spirits."

"So, he told you Lily's missin'?"

"Yes, very horrible news to say the least. I can only imagine the heartache that you probably feel. Just from watching the two of you for those few hours while you were here last year, I can tell that you both had a special bond."

"Without question. Our lives have been intertwined since we were kids. She's *everything* to me." James sighed and shook his head. "It's eatin' a hole in my soul not to know when or where I'll see 'er again."

"I can only imagine. I'm so sorry for the tragic turn of events. I'd encourage you to never give up hope, but I'm quite certain that's not necessary."

"Only death can cease my hope."

"*Hope* will get you far ... and so will *prayer*, which I will most certainly be doing for you both. Seems God brought you two together for a grand cause as children. So, I'm apt to believe that God will pull you both back together again when the time is right. Perhaps in the most unusual of ways."

"Thank you for that. I believe that with everything in me too Mr. Mills."

Preston patted James on the shoulder. "Take your time here. I'll close up whenever you're through."

"Are you sure? I don't mean to be a botha'."

"It's no bother at all."

"Thank you. I truly appreciate that."

Preston already knew what James was there to see. He had experienced this phenomenon on several other occasions with William. In lieu of sitting near his wife's gravesite, William began coming to the art museum often. Being within the walls of a place that Emma loved helped him feel close to her again. Every time he visited, William had gone to the music-themed exhibit just to sit before Lily's portrait and pray for her. Preston had no doubt that that was exactly where James was headed. His prediction was accurate. James made a beeline for the expansive portrait that Piers LeRoux had rendered of the Dream Symphony. He walked in to find that *Musical Dreams* still hung as the centerpiece of all the other music-themed art, just as Preston had promised it would during the unveiling. Even though Lily was only an image, her beauty stunned James to the point that he froze the moment he saw her. Yet again, he swallowed his emotions as he stepped closer to her lifelike portrait. He then slowly sat on a bench in front of the painting and just gazed at Lily for the longest time. All the while, he was silently praying for God to bring her back into his life and to keep her safe until then.

After praying for Lily, James finally forced himself to get up. He tried to walk out of the art gallery altogether, but he just could not bring himself to do it yet. Before he knew it, he was standing in the grand ballroom where a bidding war had taken place for tickets to

Lily's show. He gazed at the dance floor, visualizing Lily's arms around him again. He recalled how at peace he had felt with her head on his shoulder as they danced together. He then walked into the center of the room and gazed at the podium on the stage. He closed his eyes and his mind transported him back to the moment Lily read her letter from the Queen of England. A euphoric feeling suddenly shot through his body, like he was in the midst of the student orchestra's hysterical celebration all over again.

James then turned and looked at the spot where Lily was standing when she had called on him with her eyes, enticing him into a playful chase. He suddenly found himself following the memory of her down that corridor again. He walked into the room that he had snatched Lily into. When he glanced at the couch in the corner, it instantly brought back the erotic memory of the lovemaking session they had there. When that glorious memory finished playing in his mind, he walked over and looked out the window at the full moon. He sighed, knowing Lily was somewhere on the vast land beneath it.

In the very spot James now stood, the decision to start a new life in the Old World was solidified between him and Lily. As he stared out the window, he was struck by how different his life would currently be had his father not found them. He realized that he would now be a world away, sitting in a rocking chair with his baby napping on his chest. Had his father not found them, his baby would still be *alive*. Had his father not found them, Lily's career would still be thriving. Had his father not found them, he would not be on the verge of having spent a year of his life without his wife. Had his father not found them, he would have given Lily a wedding fit for a princess in the land of kings and queens by now.

Unbeknownst to Lily, James had been planning a sentimental wedding proposal after her performance at Winter Garden. Backstage, he was prepared to get down on bended knee and ask her to marry him, in front of all their adopted family members. He had hoped to turn their journey across the sea into a massive week-long engagement celebration, complete with pyrotechnics and endless fine wines. As James stood there thinking about his failed proposal plan, the emotional tide in his chest rose a little higher.

Had my fatha' not found us, how different would life be? That question was suddenly added to the one already plaguing James: *What if Lily's dead? Had my father not found us? What if Lily's dead? Had my father not found us?* Relentlessly, those questions began torturing James's mind, causing the pressure in his chest to rise to unbearable levels. He suddenly tilted his head back. "SHE'S NOT DEAD!" he shouted out the window, tears erupting from his eyes. He then angrily sat down on the couch nearby and dropped his head into his hands. "Where are you, Lily? God, please help me find 'er," he begged as he continued to weep uncontrollably. He wept with such intensity that Preston Mills nearly broke down in tears himself as he stood outside the door, listening to the sounds of a man who had just shattered under the extreme weight of his excruciating emotional pain.

Chapter Fifteen

Three months into their painstaking search, William and Griff arrived in the town of Galveston, Texas. It was among the cities that Austin had overheard Ghost Riders speaking of often during the months he had infiltrated their organization. It was the twenty-ninth city on Griff and William's assigned plotted map that was rumored to be inundated with black market slaves. The twenty-eight towns they had searched prior to arriving in Galveston had only produced frustration and extreme exhaustion. Traveling for ninety grueling days without producing a single lead was beginning to fray their confidence that Lily would ever be found. But still, the pair pressed on, clinging to hope for dear life.

Holding on to that shred of hope, Griff began his usual sly investigation tactics in Galveston. With his rough exterior, he fit in well at town pubs. By now, he had become a master at striking up conversations with inebriated patrons and getting them to verbally vomit town gossip. Through that gossip, he had learned that nearly every politician in Galveston seemed to own more slaves than was listed on slave registries. Griff did not know if it was just the usual hatred for greedy town politicians that had led to such gossip, but he did not want to leave any stones unturned. He and William, therefore, got a list of all the politicians in town and began paying them a visit.

On the third day of their search, they arrived at the massive estate of the seventh politician on their list, Atticus Atkins. Atticus's sprawling land and mansion rivaled William's. While Griff fit in well at pubs, William always provided the image of importance and trustworthiness when knocking on the doors of the well-to-do. His affluent air, British charm, and intellect was always useful in talking their way past some of the security detail standing guard at many of the politicians' estates. Such was the case at the Atkins residence. After William's charm and quick-thinking lie easily gained them access to the grounds, they plodded up the steps of the beautiful manor home and rang the doorbell. A thirteen-year-old, blonde-haired, blue-eyed girl answered the door with a cheerful smile and a personality that was equally as bubbly as William's. "Hello, may I help you?" she asked.

"Well, hello little lady," William smiled. "I'm William. William Werthington. May I ask your name?"

"Well, hello Mr. Werthington!" she replied respectfully. "I'm Allison! Are you here to see my fatha'?"

Typically, William was eager to speak with adults, but most were reluctant to answer questions to two strangers. He figured he may have better luck getting answers out of the sweet little girl in front of him. "Actually, I was hoping that a wise little lady like yourself would be willing to help me," William smiled.

"Sure! How can I help?"

"I'm searching for a young lady." William dug inside his interior coat pocket looking for the picture he had of Lily. When he failed to find it, he turned to Griff. "I think I've left the picture of Lily in the carriage. Would you mind fetching it for me?"

"Sure?" Griff replied, trotting down the porch steps to retrieve it.

William turned his attention back to Allison. "The woman I'm searching for is a slave. Your family may have recently purchased her within the last year or so. Her name is Lily. She has fair skin, light eyes, dark hair, and is about so tall," he explained, motioning with his hand. "Has your family recently acquired anyone of that likeness?"

"My fatha' actually bought two new slaves within the last year or so, but their names are Olivia and Bella."

"Well, would you mind if I speak with the both of them?"

"Not at all," Allison smiled. She then turned around. "BELLAAA! OLIVIAAA!" she yelled.

Allison's yelling only ended up summoning her curious mother. "What in God's name is all this yellin' about?" she confronted after arriving in the foyer.

"Sorry mama," Allison replied sheepishly. "This man just wanted to ask Bella and Olivia some questions, and I was tryna call 'em up here."

Her mother turned to William with embarrassment written all over her face. "Please forgive my daughta's manners, or lack thereof, I should say."

"No worries ma'am. She was polite as can be. It's apparent that you've raised her well," William replied, hoping that the compliment would make her as eager to help as her daughter.

"I'm not so sure about that," she said, forcing a smile and then turning back to scold her daughter with her eyes. "Go on upstairs to your room, Allison! You know betta' than to meddle in adult affairs!"

"Yes mama," she replied, trotting off to do as she was told.

Her mother turned back to William when her daughter was gone and introduced herself. "I'm Evelyn Atkins. May I ask who you are?"

"William Werthington. Pleased to make your acquaintance, ma'am."

"Yours as well," Evelyn smiled. "Now, how may I help you?"

Just then, Griff returned with the picture of Lily and handed it William. "We're here looking for this woman," William explained as he handed it over to Evelyn.

The smile slightly faded from Evelyn's face when Griff's rough exterior made her slightly uncomfortable. She stared at him for a moment before finally glancing at the picture of Lily.

William noticed the change in her disposition but pressed on with politeness, hoping to maintain her cooperation. "You see, there's been a mix-up," he explained as Evelyn studied the picture. "This was a slave of mine who wasn't supposed to be sold," he lied, pointing to the picture. "And I was hoping to purchase her back from you if she's here … or from the person who may have her, if you know who that would be. I'm willing to pay triple the price paid for the inconvenience."

Evelyn suddenly rudely tossed the picture back at William. "There's nobody here with that likeness," she stated coldly.

William caught the picture. "Okay, well, your daughter said there were two recently acquired slaves here on your plantation that I could speak to. Bella and Olivia. I was wondering if I still might have a word with them. Perhaps they would know of Lily's whereabouts."

"No! Get off my property! All of our slaves were purchased legally!"

"I never accused you of purchasing them otherwise, ma'am," William replied, looking confused.

"I said get off my property! If you have a problem with any slave purchases, then you need to contact the Negro auction that was responsible for your slave transactions. You have no right to trespass on people's property and harass law abidin' citizens about such issues!" Evelyn looked at Griff with disgust. "So, if you and your oddball friend trespass on this property again, I'll be forced to report you to the authorities!"

"No need to involve the authorities. Have a wonderful day, Mrs. Atkins," William calmly replied before walking away.

Rude treatment and scathing words of that sort were all James, Austin, Griff, William, and the twins left a plantation with as the months rolled by and the daunting search for Lily dragged on. On frustrating days, James continued to distract his aggravated mind with the journals of Levi Collins ...

Chapter Sixteen

June 1, 1838

I've been blessed enough to have six strong sons to carry on my name. Like every man would be, I am incredibly proud of that fact. Despite the great fortune of my sons, I still always felt like my life wasn't complete, as if there was always something missing. I never could quite figure out what that something was. I now realize that that something was actually a someone. Every day, I now see that little someone dashing around my farm at lightning speed with a smile on her precious face. Every morning, I watch her fearlessly playing with frogs and lizards. I stand at a distance in awe, proudly listening to her brilliance shine as she speaks and expresses herself like someone ten times her age. I smile at the way her eyes light up in amazement and curiosity over every new thing she encounters. As I stand here watching her run by me today, I think back to the way I bathed her in tears of love and pride the very first time I ever looked into those bright, beautiful curious eyes of hers. Because today is the third anniversary of that moment, the moment when my first and only little girl, Lily Collins, came into the world. At this very hour, she was laid in my arms and finally answered what it was that had always been missing from my life. God, how I wish I could pick my little flower up, squeeze her tight in my arms, and tell her how truly grateful I am to her for completing my life three years ago today. After witnessing the brilliance of her mind, I have no doubt she is intelligent enough to truly understand the magnitude of that sentiment.

After writing that entry, Levi closed his journal and watched Lily dashing across the field. "Daddy! Daddy!" she screamed as she then ran and jumped into his arms ... at least that was what Levi *wished* Lily was about to do. Instead, she kept on running past him like he was a stranger. As sad he was about that, Levi managed a smile at the fact that Lily never seemed to walk anywhere. She seemed to have twice the energy of a normal three-year-old. That was all Levi seemed to know about her these days, things he could see and hear from a distance. His smile began to fade as he tried to recall the last time he had any meaningful interaction with his only daughter. His stomach turned when he realized that it had been two years to the day...

While Emily was on her daily trek into town, Levi had snuck over to Maya's cottage to spend time with Lily, just as he always would whenever his wife was gone. Nearly every day during the first year of

Lily's life, Levi would make time to sit her on his lap and read her a story. He always hurried over, eager to see the way Lily now toddled toward him with a four-toothed, vibrant smile on her face the instant she saw him. She had learned how to wave, but the backward hand motion looked more like she was signaling him to come closer. Her greeting proved she was just as eager to spend time with her father as he was with her. "Wead" was one of her very first words, one she said repeatedly with enthusiasm as she climbed onto Levi's lap, begging him to "wead" her a story. Lily undoubtedly owed her explosion in vocabulary to her father's daily reading sessions. Levi loved how genuinely amused and receptive she was throughout every story, laughing hysterically at his funny voices, and even turning the page when prompted. During his daily time with Lily, he had also taught her how to blow him a kiss goodbye. Upon his departure, he would pretend to drop the kisses she blew and make her blow him another one, again and again, until he finally caught one. Lily never ceased to erupt in a fit of endless baby giggles over his playful routine. Her laughter and enthusiasm easily made Levi's daily visits with her the highlight of his day. So, as he knocked on Maya's bedroom door on this particular day, he was looking forward to those short-lived treasured moments with his daughter. "Hello Maya," he greeted when she opened the door.

"Hello," she replied flatly.

Levi eagerly looked over Maya's shoulder in search of Lily, itching to scoop her up in his arms, kiss her on the cheek, and tickle her until she was laughing non-stop, just as he always did. Today, however, Lily was not toddling toward him; she was trapped in her crib. She was excitedly bouncing up and down, a smile on her face as she waved backward at him. Levi smiled back as he took a step toward her. Before he could take another, though, Maya blocked his path. Surprised by her bold action, Levi looked at her oddly. The expression on her face instantly caused his heart to plummet into his stomach. "What's wrong?" he asked, concern heavy in his tone.

"No more Levi."

Levi genuinely looked baffled. "No more what?" he replied, slightly shaking his head in confusion.

"No more sneakin' in here to see Lily."

"Maya, why not?"

"I have my reasons."

"Well, I wanna know what they are!" Levi demanded, his heart suddenly galloping.

"I don't want Lily to know you're her fatha'!" Maya blurted.

Her words hit Levi in the gut with such force, he did not have the breath to conjure a reply at first. As he fought to fill his lungs, he glanced over Maya's shoulder at Lily. She was still joyously bouncing up and down, her face still lit up in a four-toothed smile, as she waved backward. The thought of never again being greeted with that excitement immediately began to stir Levi's emotions. He then solemnly glanced into Maya's eyes. "What did I eva' do to deserve such a thing?" he asked, his quivering voice sounding just as shattered as the sight of him.

Upon seeing the tears suddenly forming in Levi's eyes, Maya became emotional as well. She lowered her head before the heart-wrenching sight made her change her mind. "Please just ... just pretend like Lily don't exist," she said, refusing to explain herself any further. She closed the door and Lily immediately erupted into tears.

Too numb to react, Levi stood speechless on the other side of the door, the lump in his throat swelling as he listened to the sound of Lily hysterically crying. In his hand was *The Little Mermaid*, the new book he had purchased for Lily's first birthday gift. He glanced down at it and his waiting tears rolled down his cheeks.

For three days after that moment, Levi refused to utter a word or to even look at Maya. He worked as far away from her in the barn as he could manage. His silence and distance spoke volumes about how angry he was. Maya had tried to prepare herself for how heartbroken Levi would be over her decision, but the devastating way that it seemed to have broken him far superseded what she had anticipated.

After days of seeing how hurt Levi was over the matter, Maya finally approached him in the barn, hoping that an explanation for her decision would ease his sorrow. She gently touched him on the shoulder.

"Don't touch me!" he said, snatching away from her grip. He turned around and looked at Maya, still wearing the forlorn look on his face that had been there for days.

Finally seeing him up-close caused an immediate lump to form in Maya's throat. His eyes were stained a deep red and were swollen from tears and a lack of sleep. She cleared her throat, trying not to cry over the disheartening sight of him. "Levi, I just wanted to…"

"In all the years that my wife has spent insultin' me, her words have neva' *crushed me* the way that yours did the otha' day," he interrupted, his voice quivering with raw emotion. "I *love* my little girl with *everything* in me! She means more to me than anything in this whole damn world! And you want me to *pretend she doesn't exist?*" he said, angrily furrowing his eyebrows. "You may as well rip my *lungs* outta my chest and demand that I keep breathin'!"

"Levi, please, I…"

"Please tell me that what you're about to say has to do with you changin' your mind about lettin' Lily know that I'm her fatha' … or at least about me spendin' time with 'er again," Levi interrupted.

Maya was paralyzed by the sight of his lip quivering as tears trailed down his cheeks.

"Does it?" Levi pleaded softly, a hint of hope in his tone.

With tears now in her own eyes, Maya sighed and slightly shook her head. "No."

"Then I don't wanna hear it!" Levi suddenly tossed his rake across the barn. "Whetha' you like it or not, she's my baby too!" he erupted, piercing Maya with tear-filled eyes before breezing past her.

Tears were jolted from Maya's eyes when she heard him kick an empty pail against the barn wall as he stormed out. "Please God, give me the strength," she whispered as she began to weep uncontrollably.

Strength was indeed what Maya needed while dealing with Levi's coldness. For nearly a month, he remained silent and distant. He could not even bring himself to *look* in Maya's direction whenever Lily was strapped to her back as she worked in the field. It caused the pain of being denied that sort of closeness with Lily to multiply tenfold. It was the one time in Levi's life that he contemplated using his authoritative powers as Maya's master to *force* her to let him spend time with Lily. But he knew that it was nothing more than his anger conjuring up his dictator-like thoughts. But still, he remained too stubborn to listen to her reasoning, feeling as though no excuse would be good enough for his own child not to know who he truly was, or to at least be allowed to spend quality time with her.

Maya missed the warmth Levi exuded toward her and their silent camaraderie, but she was equally as stubborn. Though it hurt her to see Levi on the verge of tears whenever he glanced at Lily, Maya remained strong in her convictions. She felt as though the reason for her decision trumped everything ... including Levi's shattered heart.

But even Maya's heart-shattering words and stubbornness did nothing to destroy what Levi felt for her. In the months that followed, his love for her prevailed and he eventually calmed enough to resume speaking to her. Still though, he could not bring himself to accept or forgive her decision about Lily.

... I don't want Lily to know you're her fatha'! Just pretend like Lily don't exist. Even two years later, those insulting phrases felt like a knife in Levi's heart whenever he thought of them. The knife twisted during moments like now as he watched Lily run past him like a stranger, instead of running to jump into his loving embrace. The hurt over being left to learn about his daughter from a distance just refused to subside.

It did not help that Emily did all she could to further push Levi toward the edge of insanity. After learning of Lily's paternity, the insults and complaints from Emily about Levi's failures as a man had risen to unprecedented levels. Her anger led her to show up at random moments in the barn on a daily basis. Without saying a word, she often paced back and forth, her inebriated eyes scrutinizing every move Levi and Maya made as they worked. Emily got as much of a rush from making them uncomfortable as she did after polishing off a bottle of whiskey. Her presence was far more of a nuisance to Levi than the horse flies and gnats that relentlessly buzzed around him. Desperate to end her unwanted visits and their tumultuous feuds, Levi tried to give Emily the daughter she wanted. He was willing to do anything to create a diversion and restore some sense of peace in his life. But his plan was an abysmal failure. Disappointment loomed in the room when the child referred to as Delila in utero turned out to be their sixth son, Dallas. Dallas's birth further added to Emily's fury. With her new baby on her hip, Emily resumed her random visits to the barn, pacing like an overzealous foreman overseeing the demolition of the relationship between Maya, Levi, and Lily, content to remain until destruction was complete.

Between Maya's baffling refusal to allow Levi near Lily, and Emily's silent objection to such a thing, they had indeed succeeded in destroying the father daughter bond he had hoped for with his only little girl. That fact was evident as Lily ran past him like a stranger as usual. But with his wife and sons out of town attending another family event, Levi could not resist the chance to close the distance between him and Lily, especially since it was her birthday.

While Maya was distracted with work in the barn, Levi approached Lily as she stood gazing up at an apple tree. "Hey there, little flowa'. Would you like an apple?" Levi asked her.

Lily turned around and gazed at the towering man behind her. The moment those little eyes beamed up at him, Levi's face lit up in a brilliant smile. "Yessa', I would really love to have one! But I'm just not tall enough to reach up there." Lily perched her hands on her tiny hips. "Hmm, I think I'm definitely gonna need a ladder, but I'm just not strong enough to carry one quite yet!"

Levi laughed at his precocious child's ability to problem solve and verbalize the solution with such clarity at such a young age. He knelt to Lily's level. "You're right, a ladder would definitely work, but I think I have an even betta' way."

"Whoooaaa!" Lily exclaimed as Levi suddenly lifted her up. "This will *definitely* work!" she giggled.

"Pick the biggest one you can find," Levi told her as he held her up near the apple tree branches.

"Okay!" she said as she scanned the array of apples now easily within her reach. "I got one!"

"Alright!" Levi said as he lowered her back down. "A little teamwork, huh?"

"Yup! We did it!" Lily said excitedly as she held her apple high above her head. "Thank you masta' Lee!"

"You're very welcome, little flowa'." Levi could not resist reaching over and running the back of his fingers down her soft little cheeks, the way he had when she was just a baby.

"LILLYYY!" Maya yelled in the distance. Startled, Lily turned around and saw her mother trotting toward her. She approached nearly out of breath. "I'm so sorry," Maya said, picking Lily up. "Seems every time I blink my eyes these days, she done run off and got into somethin'," she said to Levi, giving a laugh of embarrassment.

"It's quite alright. She's just curious," Levi replied, still smiling at Lily.

"Yes, mama, I'm just very curious." She shrugged her shoulders. "That's all."

Levi and Maya both laughed.

"You two teamin' up against me, huh?" Maya remarked.

"Yes! We! Are!" Lily replied.

"We make a great team, don't we?" Levi tickled Lily's neck until she broke out in laughter and dropped her apple.

"What you done gone and took now, girl?" Maya asked, reaching down to pick up the apple. She then tried to hand it back to Levi.

"But Masta' Lee helped me get it," Lily replied, looking over at Levi.

Maya looked at Levi for confirmation.

"Maya, you know she's welcome to play with or eat anything she can get her little hands on on this farm … anything at all. You know that."

Maya nodded sheepishly.

"As a matta' of fact, I'll tell you what, Lily. Do you see that basket ova' yonda'?" Levi asked, pointing to it.

Lily turned to look at the wicker basket near the base of the apple tree. "Yessa'," Lily nodded.

Levi took Lily from Maya's arms and set her back down on the ground. He squatted down again. "Well, now that basket is all yours. So anytime you find any apples layin' out here, you can pick 'em up and fill up your basket with as many as you can carry, okay?"

Lily smiled. "Okay! Thank you!"

"Same with that ol' orange tree ova' yonda'. Those oranges'll be nice and ripe and sweet in a few weeks, and soon there'll be more on the ground than hangin' on the branches. So, you be sure to pick up just as many of those as you want, too, alright?"

"Thank you, masta' Lee!" Lily suddenly threw her arms around her father's neck to hug him.

Levi smiled and hugged her back. "Go on and see what you can find, okay?"

"Okay!" Lily took off running, grabbed her new basket, and went in search of little orange and red treasures.

Maya and Levi both watched their daughter scamper away with smiles on their faces. But the smile suddenly faded from Maya's face when she turned to look at Levi again. "Levi, what're you doin' ova' here with her?" she asked, giving him a disapproving look over his interaction with Lily.

Levi did not see the look on her face, though. His eyes were still on Lily as something else distracted his mind. "*Masta' Lee,*" he said somberly. "Feels like shards of glass in my ears every time I hear Lily refer to me that way. It literally turns my stomach that my own little girl has absolutely no idea who I really am."

"You know that's the way I want it to stay, Levi."

"And I pray every day you'll change your mind," he replied, finally turning to look at Maya.

"I truly believe it's best this way."

"And I truly believe this will *always* be somethin' that we agree to disagree about. I just don't see how it could eva' be best for a little girl not to know her fatha'."

"Unda' normal circumstances, I'd completely agree with you. But you can't keep pretendin' like this is anything close to normal. As much as it may hurt, I'm hopin' one day you'll admit to yourself that this is *indeed* what's best."

"I highly doubt I'd eva' be able to get my mind or my mouth to form such a statement."

Maya sighed and shook her head after hitting a brick wall over the issue yet again.

Levi slid his hands into his pockets. "Despite how differently I feel, I know this is the way you want it, and I promise I'd neva' dishonor your wishes, but..." He shook his head and sighed. "It's killin' me inside, Maya." He turned and watched Lily still searching for fruit. "There's hardly eva' a minute in my day when that little girl isn't weighin' heavy on my mind and my heart. I miss readin' Lily stories. I'd love to let 'er climb on my back for a pretend horse ride. I wish she'd ask me to a pretend tea party, ask me to dance with 'er, or whateva' otha' fun things little girls love to do with their fatha's. I wanna tuck 'er in bed and kiss 'er goodnight. I wanna pick 'er up and hug 'er wheneva' I feel like it." He exhaled to steady his emotions. "And God knows I'd give anything to hear her call me daddy," he said, his voice slightly cracking. "I wanna tell 'er how much her daddy loves her..." Levi turned back toward Maya. "And how much I love 'er motha'." He touched Maya's face. "I want 'er to know that even through this entire situation, my love for you has been unwaverin'. I want my little girl to know that she was made outta love. But here it stands, the woman I love beyond measure has given me the little girl I thought I'd neva' be fortunate enough to have..." He took his hand off Maya's face and turned to look at Lily again. "And I can't even show 'er how precious she is to me ... and it's killin' me inside," Levi whispered. He then turned back to look at Maya. "And so is the fact that I'm missin' you." He softly caressed her face. "I miss you more than you can possibly imagine."

Maya could not logically comprehend how it was possible for her to feel the way she felt about a man who had sold other people's children. But there she was, returning his gaze, feeling a wonderful surge of butterflies fluttering through her stomach after hearing his words and feeling his gentle touch. She suddenly broke her fixation on Levi when she heard Lily calling to her.

"Mama! I found an orange for you!" Lily exclaimed, running back toward her. She took the fruit from her basket and handed it to Maya.

"Thank you, baby," Maya said, smiling down at her. She was glad to have a way to hide the tears Levi had caused to flood her eyes.

"You're welcome!" Lily then turned to Levi. "I found one for you too, Masta' Lee!" she said in a voice that exuded pure innocence. She reached in her basket and handed an orange to her father with the brightest smile on her face, as if she was handing him a rare treasure.

And to Levi, that's exactly what it felt like Lily was handing him: a precious gift from his precious little girl. He looked at Lily and could feel a lump growing quickly in his throat. Such a small gesture nearly brought him to tears. He kneeled, touched Lily's cheek, and looked into a tiny set of eyes that mirrored his. He wondered how on earth the laws could ever punish him for creating a child so beautiful … in every sense of the meaning. He wished that the man who had the audacity to create such an offensive law could kneel the way he was and come face to face with the sort of child whose existence he was trying to prevent. "Thank you, little flowa'," Levi finally said, unable to take his eyes off his daughter.

"You're welcome," Lily smiled, not knowing how her simple gesture had triggered her father's emotions, nor how her father's nickname for her would trigger this very memory twenty-two years later. "Ma-ma, can you help me find some more apples?"

"Sure baby," Maya replied, walking off hand in hand with Lily as Levi watched on, feeling unbridled envy.

****

Just after ten p.m, Levi finally tossed his comforter aside. After lying in bed unable to sleep, he sat up, put his feet on the floor, and exhaled. From the nightstand, he picked up the orange that Lily had given him. He sat on the edge of his bed mindlessly twisting it, while thinking about the little girl he had created with a woman who inspired him to write his thoughts daily. Still holding his cherished orange, Levi got up and walked across the hallway. He leaned against the doorframe of the bedroom directly across from his. In the secret world of his mind, this room was Lily's, decorated in whatever artful colors her heart desired. Many a bedtime story he had read to her there with a goodnight kiss that followed. Knowing such a thing would always be just a fantasy, though, Levi sighed and walked back to his bedroom. He leaned against the doorframe while staring at his empty bed. He closed his eyes and pictured Maya lying in his embrace as he dozed off after making love to her. That vivid imagery had comforted him for years as he laid feeling lonely and unloved next to his wife.

The loving thoughts of his fantasies with Maya and Lily drew Levi to his bedroom window. Like it was a priceless artifact, he carefully sat his orange on the window ledge and gazed out at the place that housed the two beautiful subjects of his daydreams. Minutes later, he suddenly exited his bedroom. With a relentless nagging voice in his head tugging him, he was trudging across the fields in nothing but his work boots and pajama pants. He stopped in the barn, retrieved something from his hidden compartment in the horse stall, and took it to his bedroom. He then quietly tiptoed into Maya's cottage and into her room. Maya had her arms wrapped tightly around Lily with her face nestled into her curls. Both were sleeping soundly. Levi just stopped and stared at the beautiful display of motherly love. It was yet another moment that amplified the love he felt for Maya. But it also amplified his envy. He often wished that Lily could curl up on his chest and nap with him on the couch, just as he had done countless times with his boys when they were her size. Unable to resist the urge to hold Lily that close, Levi reached down and took her from her mother's arms.

Maya immediately roused. "Where you goin' with her?!" she said, panic in her voice as she sat straight up.

"Shh, it's okay." Levi caressed Maya's face. "Everything's okay," he reassured her.

Lily did not move a muscle or open her little eyes at all as Levi gently laid her head on his shoulder. He held her dead weight with ease as he ran his hand gently up and down her back. He embraced her tighter, closed his eyes, rested his head in her hair, and swayed gently with her as Maya watched on. When she saw the way that Levi held her, she immediately relaxed after realizing that her fears were not warranted. Levi opened his eyes after a moment and reached his hand out to Maya. She hesitated at first and then placed her hand in his. He got a firm grip on her and helped her to stand. "Come with me," he said.

"Wh-where we goin'?" she asked, confused.

Levi gazed lovingly at her. "Where you belong," he whispered, his eyes communicating his sincerity.

Maya was not sure what he meant by that, but the tender tone of his voice made her decision to join him an easy one. Levi held Maya's hand the entire way across the field while holding Lily in his other arm. He guided both of them into the house and quietly closed the door before taking Lily upstairs to the bedroom he had just imagined her sleeping in. He gently laid her down on the mattress. For the first time in his life, he then tucked Lily into bed. He placed the comforters just right and then sat down next to her. Lily still had yet to budge. "Does she always sleep this hard?" Levi asked Maya, as he ran his hand over Lily's hair, feeling a ping of sorrow over the fact that he did not know something so simple about her.

"Always. She refuses to nap in the afta'noon. She fights it hard, but pays the price at night," Maya answered. She smiled and sat down on the opposite side of the bed and played in Lily's hair along with Levi. "You could run a train through here, horns blarin', and she wouldn't move a muscle," Maya laughed. "She plays hard and sleeps even harda'."

Levi laughed quietly. "I miss the days when I could sleep like that."

"Me too."

Levi leaned down and lightly kissed Lily on the cheek before rising and going around to the other side of the bed. He took Maya by the hands and guided her out of their daughter's temporary bedroom. He then guided her across the hall to his master suite and locked the door behind him. He took a moment to light several candles in the room. He then turned around and stood there quietly gazing at Maya for a moment, happy that he had given into the nagging voice in his head that had led him to now be alone with this woman. He reached both of his hands out to Maya, inviting her to place hers there. When she obliged, he gently pulled her toward the center of the room.

"What're you doin'?" Maya asked, starting to feel her heartbeat accelerate.

"Somethin' I know I shouldn't ... but I can't seem to help myself when it comes to you." Levi walked over to the dresser and retrieved what he had taken out of the secret compartment in the barn earlier. "I made this for you," Levi explained as he handed Maya a plain wooden box.

Maya opened it and pulled out what looked like a large white jewelry box. She looked confused. "What is it?"

"Open the lid," Levi said, as he took the empty wooden box from her and set it aside.

Maya slowly opened the lid, and the sound of a piano melody began to play, while the tiny sculptures of a Caucasian man and a Negro woman spun around in a circle, dancing to the music.

"It's a music box," Levi explained, gazing at the look of awe on Maya's face. "That's supposed to be you and me dancin' in there. I'm no artist, so I know it's not the most perfect lookin' thing eva'," he said, laughing lightly at his own attempt at artwork. "But since I don't have a piano here, I figured this was the best way for you to hear the song it's playin'. It's one I play in church often and I really wanted you to hear it." He touched Maya gently on the face. "Because you inspired it."

Maya looked up with tears welling in her eyes. "Levi," she whispered. "This is beautiful."

"Wheneva' I play this song, in my mind, I can see little Lily walkin' down the aisle of a church, droppin' flowa' petals on the floor. She has a big smile on 'er face, lookin' so pretty in her little dress with 'er hair all fixed up. And then I see you…" He caressed Maya's face again. "You're in your weddin' gown, makin' your way down the aisle toward me as I stand at the altar, waitin' eagerly for you." Levi briefly closed his eyes. "In my mind, you're far and away the most stunning bride on earth." He paused a moment and listened to the melody. "This part of the song always trigga's an image of me pledgin' my vows to you. When the ceremony is ova', I always imagine us at our reception…" He looked down at his handmade gift. "I'm holdin' you close to me, dancin' just the way we are in this music box."

"I'll always cherish this," Maya whispered, tears now cascading down her cheeks.

Levi took the music box from Maya's hand and set it on the dresser. He closed then opened the lid and restarted the music. He drew the curtains back and opened the window all the way. He then took Maya by the hand, guided her to where the full moon was casting its light into the room, and pulled her close to him. Maya rested her head on his shoulder and wrapped her arms around him. Her tears ran in streams down Levi's bare skin as they danced under the moonlight, just as gracefully as the figurines he had carved.

"I missed holdin' you this close to me," Levi whispered when the song was over. "More than I can possibly explain." He placed his hands on either side of Maya's face and let the sensuousness of his slow kiss express that for him.

The feel of Levi's lips and the warmth of his skin melted Maya just as quickly as the first time he had touched her in that way. "I missed havin' you this close too," Maya whispered back, resting her forehead against his. "But I want you even closa'," she added, her supple lips grazing his as she spoke.

"How much closa'?" Levi lustfully replied, his lips grazing hers in return.

Maya caught his lips in a kiss again, as she slowly unbuttoned her dress and let it fall to the floor. She then confidently stepped back into the moonlight, letting it illuminate her nude body to perfection. All the while, she watched Levi's unblinking eyes as they roamed the landscape of her body in awe. His parted lips and jagged breaths made her nipples harden and set her nether region ablaze. She kept her eyes trained on his captivated face as she untied his pajama pants and unleashed the rock-solid mass that was clearly begging to escape. When Levi stepped out of his pants, Maya took him by the hand and pulled him toward the windowpane. She turned to face the stars in the sky and made him put his arms around her waist. She then placed her hands on the ledge, leaned over, maneuvered her hips backward, and slowly filled herself with his erection. "This close," she moaned.

Feeling pure elation after sliding into the silky wetness of Maya's abyss, Levi let out a long, satisfying groan. For nearly four years, he had fought this sinful sexual temptation that was as strong as the devil's will; but no more. He now wanted to erupt inside of Maya, even if he was sentenced to hell for it.

Levi did not want to move at first while standing in the window reunited with Maya, bathing with her in the soft glow of the moonlight. He needed time for his mind to photograph such a picturesque moment with the woman he loved. He bathed her neck in gentle kisses as his hands slid up her waist and onto her breasts. Gently, he began tugging her hardened nipples as his tongue and teeth playfully teased her earlobe. Not knowing if he would ever be blessed with another moment like this, his hips remained still. He simply wanted to enjoy the feeling of melting inside the heat of Maya's paradise. The pleasurable feeling radiating from Maya's nipples eventually turned on her hips, though. But her tamed slow movements proved that she, too, wanted the feeling to last. Levi began moaning in response to Maya's soft sighs as her slick internal folds began to massage his erection. Softly, he bit her neck as the pleasure escalated within him. Perfectly matching Maya's rhythm, he began meeting her thrusts with slow gentle strokes. Despite their patient pace, Levi's pleasure began to elevate quickly. He leaned his head back and let out a groan to alleviate the mounting pressure. He then grabbed Maya's waist and drove himself deeper, picking up speed. Maya immediately fell in sync, the plump cheeks of her posterior now slapping hard against Levi's pelvis. The sudden spike in intensity built into a sensual melody of moans that drifted out the window like an erotic duet.

Just seconds away from exploding, Levi suddenly withdrew from Maya and turned her around to face him. He descended on her mouth with fervor, completely covering her lips with his, dancing his tongue around hers. Maya gently bit each of his lips when he slowly tried to break their kiss. The twinge of pain sent a pulse of pleasure to his groin and stirred a carnal growl. As if her bite had turned him into a beast, Levi suddenly began savagely suckling on Maya's neck. He then kissed his way down to her breast and softly bit her nipple in return. Moisture pooled between Maya's thighs as she unleashed a carnal growl of her own. She grappled the back of Levi's head, silently begging for more pleasurable punishment. Levi happily followed her orders and devoured her other nipple while driving two fingers inside of her abyss. Maya's head fell backward as the shock of immense pleasure sent a primordial roar ripping through her vocal cords. With her head hanging slightly out of the window, she rode Levi's fingers as he feasted like an untamed caveman on her breast.

Levi and Maya's starvation for one another was evident in their hasty, manner-less movements. After nearly four years of deprivation, they were suddenly torn between wanting to extend the experience and rushing to satiate each other. Levi's ravenous hunger caused him to tear away from Maya's breast. He was starving for another part of her. He slid his tongue down her abdomen and onto her swollen nub, quickly sucking it into his mouth. Maya's cries elevated, pleasantly piercing Levi's ears. He growled again when she gripped the back of his head and began thrusting her southern lips against his tongue, forcing him to have his fill. With intense sensations now shooting through her body, Maya's purrs were non-stop and so, too, was the heated pleasure rising in her core. Sitting on the windowpane illuminated by her beloved starlight, she suddenly tilted her head back and howled at the full moon as she came with intensity. Levi grunted over his appetizer, happily syphoning her sweet honey as it rushed down into his mouth and delighted his tongue.

Maya's unapologetic hunger for Levi remained evident by the way she then quickly pulled him over to the bed and mounted him. Being manhandled in such a way had a certain part of Levi standing as stiff as steel; he nearly erupted in tears of pleasure as Maya's heated abyss slid down over it. Pleasantly overwhelmed by the feeling of having him buried inside her, Maya erotically exhaled and her eyes fluttered closed. She slowly opened them and felt a surge of butterflies rush through her stomach after seeing the loving way that Levi was gazing up at her. He continued to gaze at her in awe as he gracefully slid his hands down her sides. His eyes then began following the path of his fingertips as he feathered them across Maya's soft brown skin. With such a vivid memory of her body, he immediately noticed her breasts were larger, her buttocks was rounder, and her hips were slightly wider. Levi immediately fell in love with the beautiful natural enhancements that childbirth had given her; he felt as though her new voluptuous curves made her look even more like a Nubian goddess.

Maya was most certainly feeling like a goddess, one who was sitting astride her Adonis. Her eyes surveyed Levi's brick hard body as she slid her hands lovingly along the ripples of his abdomen. His gentle touch had brought her back to serenity, and she was, once again, in no rush to end their passionate connection. Slowly, she began rocking her hips, her hands continuing to peruse Levi's muscles as she rode. Levi was absolutely and utterly entranced by the smooth erotic way that Maya danced on top of him, her eyes closed, and her lips parted, letting soft moans escape. He, too, continued gracefully sliding his hands along her curves, inhaling sharply every time she suddenly thrust hard and buried him deep inside her warmth. He could not fathom that there was any more heavenly sight, nor any more magical feeling, than what he was experiencing with this woman at this very moment.

That magical feeling was quickly becoming too much for Levi to bear, though. But after depriving himself of Maya for so long, he was nowhere near ready for this experience to end. He suddenly sat up to stop Maya's movements before he erupted too soon. He then glided his hands from her hips to her breasts, and onto her face. He froze and just gazed at her in the most loving way before satisfying an intense need to taste the sweetness of her lips again. He then gathered his arms tightly around her, pulled her close, and put all his emotions into the passion of his kiss. The way Levi's lips danced with hers brought forth a sudden surge of tears to Maya's eyes.

With their lips still locked together, Levi slowly laid back down and brought Maya with him. He wanted her soft skin to melt into his. He slid his hands down her back and gripped each of her rounded cheeks, prompting her hips back into motion. Levi then began slowly thrusting upward into her. The sudden intensity of pleasure caused Maya to break free from their kiss. The strength of his strokes then suddenly escalated into powerful pounding, catapulting Maya into a pleasurable bliss. She kept her hips frozen in place, roaring like a lioness as Levi filled her over and over again, until there was no stopping the rain of hot orgasmic liquids that spilled out of her onto his abdomen. The heat of her juices glistening on his body, the tightness of her insides repeatedly constricting around him, and the sound of her elated cries, brought Levi to an end just seconds after Maya. He howled her name from the pit of his stomach as he exploded deep inside of her.

Quickly succumbing to the lightning bolts of pleasure, Maya immediately collapsed down on Levi. The aftershocks of ecstasy were revealed in their shaky breaths, sweaty bodies, and quivering legs. Levi laid silently with Maya pressed close to him, stroking her back. His eyes were closed, imagining that this was his normal, that at any time he could make love to the woman he was now holding onto for dear life. He held Maya tight and pretended as though the life he had dreamed of had finally come true.

Just like the night he had helped conceive Lily, Levi did not feel an ounce of regret for his actions. His sudden confession to Maya further proved that. "I felt this way the last time we were togetha'," he said as he continued softly caressing Maya's back with his fingertips.

"Felt what?" Maya asked, enjoying the way he was touching her.

"This sense of peace that I ain't neva' known before. Feels like it ain't nothin' missin' in my life when I'm holdin' onto you like this. I feel it even stronga' this time around now that we have Lily." Levi kissed Maya's forehead. "It honestly scares me to think that I might live the rest of my life and neva' know this sort of peace again … not without you and Lily."

Maya opened her eyes and saw the way Levi was looking at her. It was that look of sincerity that always captivated her. As with his other bold confessions, there was not a thing she felt she could say in return that would rival his words. She tenderly kissed him instead.

When Maya laid her head back on his chest, Levi gathered her tighter in his arms and the feeling of completion immediately enveloped him again. "Tell me more about Lily."

"What do you wanna know?" Maya asked, as she got comfortable on his chest.

"Any and everything. All the things I don't get to hear or see."

"My God, where do I start with that curious little ball of energy?" Maya smiled. "First thing that comes to mind, as of late, is her natural love for animals … especially reptiles. Every time I turn around, that girl done dug up some filthy four-legged creature, from God knows where!"

"Now *that* I have noticed her doin'," Levi laughed.

"I don't know why she can't eva' find a cute furry little bunny or a puppy! It neva' fails to be somethin' hideous with scales, fangs, and claws!"

Levi burst out laughing. "Reminds me of me as a boy, actually. Those were always my favorites too! Guess it runs in the family."

"So, I have you to blame for all the frogs, lizards, and turtles she drags into the cottage insistin' we name and make pets out of, huh?"

"Guilty, your honor!"

"Well, I sentence you to *life* for passin' on that skin-crawlin', appallin' trait to our child!"

Levi broke out in laughter again. "Well hopefully, she'll get your love of the celestial skies to balance 'er out as a nice, well-rounded, respectable young woman," he teased.

"Lord, I hope so! I'd much prefer her to name the stars with me, ratha' than those filthy little critta's!"

"Name the stars?"

"Mm-hmm, it's a little ritual I have wheneva' I'm usin' the magnificent telescope you gave me."

Levi suddenly pulled Maya back and looked her in the eyes. "Really?" he asked, thoroughly intrigued.

Maya smiled and nodded. "And tonight would be such a perfect night to use it. It's so crystal clear in the sky right now," she said, gazing out the window. "I see my two favorite stars so clearly," she pointed. "There's Lily and Levi right ova' there."

Feeling honored that she had done such a thing, Levi replied with a gentle kiss.

Warmed by his affection, Maya snuggled closer to him. "I can't wait until Lily's old enough for me to take 'er on my secret excursions into the woods late at night." She suddenly had a distant look in her eyes as she gazed out the window. "I look forward to seein' the look on 'er face when she peers through that telescope for the first time and sees the moon, and all those beautiful stars up-close. I'm still in awe at the way it makes everything seem close enough to reach out and touch. I'd be curious to hear all the names Lily chooses, and the brilliant way she'd express the sheer amazement of our grand universe."

Levi was nearly at a loss for words listening to Maya express her own brilliance. "Lily is so incredibly intelligent, isn't she?" he replied.

"No doubt about it. That girl's mind works in a way I ain't neva' seen at her age. That's one of the reasons I ain't showed 'er that telescope yet. That girl talks circles around folks non-stop all day, every day. If I showed 'er that contraption, everybody from here to Georgia would know about it by sunrise."

Levi broke out laughing again. "She sho' does talk like a grown woman," he concurred. "Her conversations neva' cease to amaze me."

"You?!" Maya laughed. "I can't tell you how many times I've foolishly found myself in full on grown folks' conversations with 'er. I always have to pause and remind myself that I'm talkin' to a toddla'! She's like a word tornado, suckin' up big words and spittin' 'em right back at me with ease."

"Every word so clear and concise too! Makes 'er brotha's seem like a bunch of babblin' morons."

"Don't say that!" Maya laughed, playfully hitting him.

"Just preachin' the truth! She's brilliant." He kissed Maya's forehead. "Just like 'er motha'."

"Says the brilliant prodigal pianist," Maya smiled.

Levi suddenly sighed. "That's one thing I wish I could share with Lily. You wanna teach 'er about the stars, and I'd love to teach 'er about music. It'd be the ultimate dream come true for me to teach 'er how to play piano. Somethin' tells me she'd love it. I'm convinced she's brilliant enough to soak it up with ease, just like she does with words."

"I couldn't agree with you more."

"I can only imagine how those beautiful, curious eyes of hers would light up the moment she touched the keys."

"It'd definitely be a moment to cherish."

"Cherish is an unda'statement. I'd be ova'come with emotion if eva' I could give 'er such a grand experience."

"Impossible dreams," Maya sighed.

"Many a man and woman have ova'come what seems impossible."

"I can't argue with that."

"I pray every day that the impossible happens for Lily. Maybe I'm the one who'll sound insane this time, but I'm convinced there's somethin' special about her ... *uniquely* special. I don't just say that because I'm her fatha'. I feel it in a way that I neva' felt with my boys. I've felt it since the moment I held 'er as a baby and I looked into those big, bright, curious eyes of hers ... she's here for a reason. And now, seein' how brilliant she truly is, that belief has embedded itself in my soul."

Maya lifted her head and tenderly kissed Levi on the lips. "No strait-jacket needed, Mr. Collins. That doesn't sound insane to me at all. I believe that about our baby girl with all my heart too," she said. She then snuggled back into his embrace.

Levi felt like he was in heaven, lying there with Maya nude in his arms, as they talked and laughed until well after midnight. He did the best he could to live in the moment and enjoy living out his rare fantasy evening with Maya. But that proved difficult for him knowing that such a thing was very temporary. With the hours rolling by so quickly, it kept him bouncing back and forth between joy and sadness. The latter suddenly won the battle when Levi released Maya for a moment while he scooted over to retrieve a glass of water from the nightstand. For the few seconds his back was turned, Maya had gotten out of bed. Levi whipped his head around. "Where you goin'?" he asked.

"I betta' get on back to the cottage," Maya answered as she got dressed. "With my luck, this'll be the first night Lily wakes up before sunrise, wonderin' where she's at. Or worse yet, wonderin' where *I'm* at, and what I'm *doin'*. Lord! We *certainly* don't need 'er to know that," she laughed.

Levi suddenly hopped out of bed. "No, please don't go," he said, quickly putting on his pajama pants. He then took a hold of Maya's hands. "I was hopin' you and Lily would stay here with me for the weekend."

"In *this* house? The *whole* weekend?" Maya shook her head. "No, I don't think that's a good idea, Levi."

"Maya please?" he begged, a sudden sorrowful look on his face. "I just wanna know what it feels like?"

"What, *what* feels like?" she asked, looking thoroughly confused.

"To be a husband to you. To be a fatha' to Lily. To have you both as my family. I wanna know what it's like to wake up next to you and make love to you in the mornin'. I wanna know what it's like to lay down next to Lily in the mornin' and let 'er tell me about 'er dreams. I wanna know what it's like to eat breakfast with 'er ... just *once*."

"Absolutely *not,* Levi," Maya replied, seriousness now having returned to her tone. She then turned and opened the door to leave.

Levi grabbed Maya gently by the arm and closed the door back. "Maya, I'm beggin' you to stay. If not the whole weekend, then just stay until mornin'. Let me at least have breakfast with Lily and read 'er a story ... just one. Please? She doesn't have to know that I'm her fatha'. I just wanna spend the day with her ... with *both* of you."

"Levi, it's beautiful that you wanna have that experience with our daughta', but you know how I feel about that." Maya placed her hand gently on his shoulder. "Maybe you can just have me in this way wheneva' you need me."

"BUT THAT AIN'T ALL I WANT!" Levi suddenly erupted.

"AND YOU THINK THIS IS ALL I WANT?!" Maya angrily snapped back.

Silence.

"DO YOU?!" she demanded.

Levi still just stood there, stunned into silence.

"Trust me, I want more than just remnants and scraps of your love! I *know* I deserve more! Me and Lily *both* do, damn it! But you only come to me when it's convenient for *you!* You give me these incredible gifts and make me feel loved to the core of my soul, just to turn around and rip my heart clean outta my chest the minute your wife sets foot back on this plantation! So how dare you have the audacity to get upset when you can't have what you want for a change!"

Levi still stood there silently taking Maya's verbal blows like a man.

"You're sorely mistaken if you think I haven't ached ova' the things that I can't have! But quietly and completely *alone*, I just deal with the emotional pain of havin' those few incredible days with you years ago … and not a damn thing since!

"The absence of your love has left a void in my heart that you can't possibly measure! It took me two damn years to stop yearnin' for you to hug me and kiss me wheneva' you walk in that damn barn!" she yelled, her anger escalating. "Two years to stop gettin' mad as hell wheneva' I saw you on the porch with your wife, feelin' like that's supposed to be *me* you's kissin' goodbye! Two years to let go of my envy every time I saw you through the window sittin' down to eat dinna' with your boys, laughin' and talkin'. Two years to stop wishin' that I's the one makin' meals for y'all every evenin' and sittin' there along with you! Two years to stop wishin' you'd make love to me and hold me in your arms every night! Just a few beautiful days with you, and I was left dreamin', and cravin', and achin … for *two! damn! years!*"

Levi still could not bring himself to utter a word in response.

Maya angrily wiped away an escaping tear. "You don't think I'm crushed by the fact that my daughta' can't call you daddy? Or that I'm not angry ova' the fact that Lily don't even know it's her own brotha's she's playin' with some days?! Hell, I've lost count of how many times I've cried watchin' you roll outta here with your boys on the way to church, wishin' that me and Lily could get dressed up and go with you!" Maya suddenly broke down sobbing. "It should be *me* and *Lily* sittin' there with her brotha's in the front row of the church watchin' you play piano. *I* should be your wife! It should be you and *me* buildin' a life ... *togetha'!* Your sons should be *my* boys! Lord knows I love 'em more than their own damn mama! This should be *our* home, *our* traditions, *our* family! But it ain't!" She held up two fingers. "And it took me two painful years to accept the fact that it neva' will be!" she sobbed.

Levi tried to gently touch her, but she stepped back and evaded his hand. She shook her head and let out a brief sarcastic laugh. "I swear I'm goin' *mad* on the inside, wonderin' what the hell kind of woman I am to feel this way about anotha' woman's husband?!"

"A woman who loves me just as much as I love her," Levi quickly replied. "You may not eva' say it, but that's what I feel when I'm with you," he whispered. "It's what I wish I could hear," he admitted.

"It doesn't matta' how I feel, Levi!"

"Of course it does!"

"No! It doesn't! My feelin's will neva' change anything about our circumstances! Not a damn thing!"

"Yes, it will!"

"Oh really?" Maya said, throwing her hands on her hips. "Will my feelin's change the fact that you'll go right back to barely lookin' at me when your family returns?"

Levi lowered his head.

"Will it change the fact that I'll spend anotha' two years hurtin' and yearnin' for you afta' tonight?" Maya paused and waited for his reply. "Will it?!"

Still, Levi could not bring himself to look at her.

"When you subject me to these fleetin' beautiful moments and go back to ignorin' me, it's the worst kind of bitta' sweet torture in the world," Maya confessed. "Especially when the source of all the beautiful moments is right there in front of you every single day, pretendin' that you don't even exist.

"If I'm bein' honest, I'd only eva' made baby steps in gettin' ova' you," Maya admitted. "The longin' and the pain was still there, but I'd finally numbed myself to it. But now, here you are subjectin' me to anotha' sweet moment with you. And I can assure you that it's already revitalized all the feelin's I'd managed to numb. In a few days, the bitta'ness will set in, and I'll have to fight to crawl my way back to numbness. Afta' tonight, it'll be anotha' two years of fightin' to suppress my pain and envy all ova' again. For anotha' two years, I'll be cryin' wheneva' I see you rollin' away to church, knowin' that me and Lily will neva' see you play piano. For anotha' two years, I'll be lyin' in my bed all alone, cravin' to feel your arms wrapped around me and the warmth of your bare skin next to mine. I'll spend anotha' two years dreamin' and achin', tryna accept that this ain't our house, that your sons ain't mine, and that I can't be your wife … and that we'll neva' be a family, no matta' how hard I wish, and I pray, and I cry for it to be that way.

"For the next two years, I'll look in the mirror and see the sobbin' pathetic mess that I now *refuse* to let my daughta' be! Through swollen eyes, I'll see reflectin' back at me the very reason that I don't want Lily to know what it's like to feel the full extent of the love you're capable of showin' her! *Eva'!* I'm a grown woman and I can barely handle bein' deprived of your love afta' feelin' the true powa' of it! I don't even wanna *think* about how it would devastate a little girl!"

Maya wiped her tears again and looked straight at Levi. "But yet, here you are insistin' on puttin' Lily through that torture. She may be just a toddla', but Lily rememba's *everything!* She'll rememba' every detail of the day *Masa' Lee* made 'er pancakes and let 'er sleep in a fancy house in a real bed. She'll rememba' how wonderful it felt for you to read to 'er, dance with 'er, and play with 'er all day. You'll give 'er one beautiful day that her brilliant little mind will neva' eva' forget! But even as smart as she is, she'll neva' unda'stand why you then suddenly snatched it all away from her ... just like you always used to do to her when she was a baby!

"So many times back then, you heard your wife comin' back home unexpectedly and you tossed Lily aside like garbage. You always scampered outta there and left me alone with a cryin' baby in my arms. And I's unable to give 'er the one thing that she was hollerin' for, because he was too busy fleein' from the room, so his wife didn't catch 'em there! As wise as Lily is now, do you really think she'll be okay with a few stolen moments that you're only willin' to give 'er while your *wife* is in town? Do you think she's just supposed to accept the fact that 'er own daddy goes runnin' out the door the minute his *wife* returns?!"

Levi swallowed hard, but it did nothing to hold back the tears that suddenly began trickling down his cheeks.

"Do you?!" Maya demanded.

Levi subtly shook his head.

"I don't want Lily to go to bed at night in a puddle of tears, cravin' the sort of fatherly love that you show your boys! I don't want 'er lyin' there wonderin' why she only eva' gets small pieces of your love thrown at 'er wheneva' it's convenient for you!" Maya continued. "But that probably doesn't matta' to you, does it? Because you ain't the one who'd have to deal with the heartbroken look on 'er face every time you leave. You wouldn't have to see those tears in her eyes when she starts askin' why she can't go to church with 'er brotha's, or why she can't sleep in the fancy house like 'er brotha's. Why won't my daddy let me eat dinna' with 'em? Why don't my daddy treat me like my brotha's? Why's my daddy always runnin' away from me? Why doesn't he love me as much as my brotha's?! Afta' you shatta' Lily's heart into a million little pieces and toss 'er aside like garbage, *I'd* be the one who has to answer those questions with the cold-hearted truth! That she's nothin' but her daddy's secret bastard love child ... an *abomination* created in sin! *I'd* be left to look 'er in her innocent little eyes and tell 'er that ... not *you!*"

Maya's words hit Levi like the force of a tornado, immediately ceasing his selfish desires and self-pity. Her confessions having beaten the strength out of him, he slowly sat down on the bed without a word and dropped his face into his hands.

"So, unless you wanna be the one to explain these god-awful things to a child, I'm *beggin'* you to respect my wishes, Levi ... *please!*" Maya pleaded. "It just ain't right for a child to bear the heavy burden of adult secrets."

Maya caught her breath, wiped the tears out of her eyes, and looked down at the heap she had reduced Levi to. "One of the hardest things I've eva' had to do was tellin' you not to be a part of Lily's life anymore. It used to bring joyous tears to my eyes to watch you play with her as a baby. I *loved* the way you loved her. It crushed me just as much as it crushed you to deprive her of your love. And I still see it in your eyes when you look at Lily. I can feel how much you still love that little girl, Levi," she said, her tone finally softer. "But you love and you love *hard*. And if you express that to Lily, even for a little while, and then snatch it all away, you'll devastate her for a lifetime. Bein' ignorant to your love is bliss. Trust me ... I speak from experience."

Levi still could not find the strength to lift his head. He continued staring at the massive puddle of tears near his feet. Still too numb to talk, he held out a hand toward Maya. It was the only way he could express that her two-minute confrontation had immediately put to rest two years of anger and inability to forgive her decision about Lily. Maya walked over and slid her hand into his without hesitation. He pulled her closer, wrapped his arms around her waist, and nestled his head against her abdomen. It was as if he needed to be close to her to regain the strength to speak. "I'm so s-sorry, Maya," he finally said, his quivering voice raw with emotion. "I neva' meant to h-hurt eitha' one of you. That's neva' been m-my intention. I swear that to you," he said, his tears soaking her dress.

Maya squatted before Levi, held his face and made him look her in the eyes. "I don't have one single solitary doubt about that. Not one. I've neva' thought for a second that you would eva' *intentionally* hurt us. And I neva' will ... that I swear to you too."

Levi nodded as Maya wiped his tears. "The happy life you described with me, Lily, and my boys ... that's the life I've been cravin' to have with you too. But no matta' how hard I try, I can neva' figure out the right answer to this situation," he sighed.

"That's because there is no right answer. We'll both always be victims of our circumstances ... and so will Lily. And we both have to find a way to accept that."

Her words suddenly made Levi's tears flow harder. His mind and his heart were nowhere near ready to accept that painful truth. Maya continued holding his hand and caressing his face until his tears subsided.

After a few quiet minutes, Levi finally found the strength to stand. He exhaled, took Maya by the hand again, and quietly led her over to the room that he wished was permanently Lily's. He let go of Maya's hand and sat down on the bed next to his daughter again. He just stared at her for a moment as she slept peacefully. "My little masta'piece," he choked out past the lump in his throat. "I still can't believe I had anything to do with creatin' somethin' so perfect," he said, as he softly stroked her hair. "I'm convinced we made the most beautiful little girl in the world," he added, his voice beginning to quiver again.

Levi picked Lily up and she roused slightly from her sleep. She shifted in her father's embrace, snuggled her head into the crook of his shoulder, gathered her arms tighter around him, and fell right back into a deep sleep. After two years of being deprived of hugs from his daughter, her involuntary show of affection caused a surge of emotion to suddenly rush to Levi's chest. He closed his eyes and hugged her tighter. "I adore her. She's the most precious thing in my life. She's *not* an abomination in my eyes, Maya … she's my *beautiful miracle*. I wish the world could see that," he said as he suddenly began sobbing uncontrollably, weeping in a way that most men would never dare in front of a woman, or even in the absence of one for that matter. "I want s-so desperately to be a p-part of h-her life. A-and it f-feels like a d-dagger in my h-heart to accept that I can't." He was crying so hard that Maya could barely understand him.

Now sobbing uncontrollably too, Maya walked over to Levi. Knowing that no words could ever ease his level of sorrow, she attempted to comfort him with her embrace.

Levi pulled Maya close to him too and kissed her on the forehead. "I'll still always wish I could give you the world," he whispered.

"You already have," Maya replied, touching Levi gently on the face. "You made me a motha'. You gave me Lily," she said, kissing her on the cheek. "And to me she *is* the world. Otha' than her freedom, there ain't nothin' else I could eva' want in my life."

Levi nodded, her words giving him a sliver of peace.

After a few minutes, Maya reluctantly stepped out of Levi's embrace. The devastated look on his face made it nearly impossible to look him in the eyes as she began to speak. She lowered her head before proceeding. "You need to let us go, Levi. Let go of this idea that we can eva' be a family. It'll eat you alive inside," she sniffled, the words difficult for her to say out loud. "So long as Lily and I have each otha', we'll be alright."

Upon hearing those words, Levi's heart finally shattered completely. He gathered Lily tighter in his arms, holding her like letting go was a physical impossibility. He was not ready to accept that he would never read Lily another book, hear about her dreams when she awakened each morning, walk her down the aisle, dance with her at her wedding, or experience any of the other unique things that a daughter could bring to his life. Lily would never hear or even know how much her own father loved her, because Maya was right … he needed to let them go.

As painful as it was, Levi gave Maya her music box and walked her back to their cottage, carrying Lily next to his shattered heart the whole way there. With great reluctance, he gently laid Lily back down on her mother's makeshift bed and kissed her cheek. "Dream beautiful dreams, my sweet little flowa'." After staring at Lily for a moment, he stood up, walked over to the music box and opened the lid. When the beautiful piano ballad started, he took hold of Maya's hands. "Will you dance with me one last time?"

With her eyes full of tears, Maya wrapped her arms around Levi's neck and laid her head on his shoulder again. With tears still flowing in his own eyes, Levi laid his head on top of Maya's. He then swayed slowly to every note of the melody that he had composed for the beloved woman he now held in his arms. The song stopped long before Levi was ready. Another ten years' worth of notes would not have sufficed, in his estimation. But with silence now in the room, Levi had to accept the abrupt ending to the sentimental song, like a painful metaphor for his desired fantasy weekend with Maya and Lily. After reluctantly releasing Maya from his embrace, he stepped back and gazed lovingly at her, just as he always did. With tears still sparkling in his eyes, he took her by the hand. He guided her to her makeshift bed and helped her lay back down next to Lily, officially putting the subjects of his fantasies back the way he had found them. Maya wrapped her arms around Lily and softly kissed her cheek while Levi watched. He then leaned down and kissed Lily's soft cheek. "I'm sorry I can't be the fatha' that you deserve," he whispered, his words still broken by emotion. "S-so sorry." He ran his fingers through her soft tightly curled hair. "But your daddy loves you more than you'll eva' know," he whispered in her ear, hoping maybe that fact would make its way into her dreams. He looked up at Maya and caressed her face. "I love you *both* to your precious stars and back."

"If anybody in this world believes that wholeheartedly, Levi ... it's me," Maya replied, letting a gentle kiss linger on his lips thereafter.

When their lips parted ways, so did Levi. After literally kissing his dreams goodbye, he finally forced himself to leave Maya's cottage, against his heart's will. He then reluctantly dragged himself across the field alone, his head hung in pitiful sorrow. He finally lifted his head near the porch steps to look up at his big empty house. He suddenly could not bear the idea of walking back into it without Maya and Lily inside. Instead, he walked up onto his porch and leaned against the railing. He stared out at the night sky, wondering if there was a world out there that Maya had seen through her telescope that would accept them both with open arms.

After standing there a while, Levi finally sat down on the rocking chair behind him, closed his eyes, rested his elbows on his knees, and clasped his hands together. "Lord, I know I've sinned, but please don't let the world take it out on my little girl. God, I'm beggin' you for anotha' miracle. Please make a way for Lily to have an incredible life, one that's far granda' than what I could eva' possibly give to her in a world like this. I'd give my life for you to bestow such a miracle in hers." Levi put his head in his hands and broke down crying again, attempting to let his tears flush his beloved child and her mother out of his soul, just as Maya had begged him to do.

Part Two

The Cornerstone Speech

The new Confederate States of America constitution has put at rest forever all the agitating questions relating to our peculiar institution—African slavery as it exists among us—the proper status of the Negro in our form of civilization. Our new government is founded upon exactly the opposite ideas; its foundations are laid, its cornerstone rests, upon the great truth that the Negro is not equal to the white man; that slavery, subordination to the superior race, is his natural and normal condition. This, our new Confederate government, is the first, in the history of the world, based upon this great physical, philosophical, and moral truth. This truth has been slow in the process of its development, like all other truths in the various departments of science. May we not therefore look with confidence to the ultimate universal acknowledgement of the truths upon which our system rests? It is the first government ever instituted upon the principles in strict conformity to nature, and the ordination of Providence, in furnishing the materials of human society. Many governments have been founded upon the principle of the subordination and serfdom of certain classes of the same race; such were and are in violation of the laws of nature. Our system commits no such violation of nature's laws. Our Confederacy is founded upon principles in strict conformity with these laws. This stone which was rejected by the first builders has now become "the chief of the corner"—the real "Corner-stone"— in our new edifice.

Alexander H. Stephens –

Vice President of the Confederate States of America

Savannah, Georgia March 21, 1861

Chapter Seventeen

The Emancipation Proclamation

*I, Abraham Lincoln, President of the United States,
do declare on the first day of January, in the year of
our Lord, one thousand eight hundred and sixty-three,
that all persons held as slaves within any State, or
designated part of a State, the people whereof shall then
be in rebellion against the United States, shall be then,
thenceforward, and forever free ...*

President Lincoln began scripting those words in January of 1863
with the intention of freeing slaves who were being forced to fight
against the union, therefore, weakening the Confederate army.
Though his proclamation was heavily motivated by war strategery,
there was a particular slave lingering in the recesses of his mind as he
stroked his quill that fateful day. Three years prior, he had sat in a
Chicago theater mesmerized by her emotional music and the dancing
shadows of her unique symphony. It was a masterpiece he deemed
grand enough to later take his family to witness as a Christmas gift at

Winter Garden. President Lincoln recalled how honored he had felt to later meet the beautiful Negro woman responsible for the symphonic brilliance. The Dream Symphony, and the story of Lily Adams, further enhanced the prideful feeling President Lincoln had as he signed his name on the Emancipation Proclamation, knowing that such a woman would likely be as deeply affected by his actions as he was by hers.

Two years before the Emancipation Proclamation was written, that same lovely woman was heavily on another man's mind when he, too, scripted a letter regarding the war:

May 27th, 1861

William,

After several months of searching desperately for Lily, my heart is shattered by the fact that Austin and I have still yet to find her. As we have searched, there are battles breaking out all around us, and people are fleeing their small towns as troops march in to take over. A few months ago, Austin and I attended the speech of a man named Alexander Stephens, who claims to be the vice president of the Confederate States of America, a new country the south is attempting to form. He has cited that their new constitution and country will be founded upon Negro subordination, therefore cementing the institution of slavery in the south. Many states in the south are seceding from the union to join the Confederacy in order to maintain the right to own slaves. It seems our country is on the verge of being severed forever. In this new battle to maintain the union, there is great debate that the United States may very well be on the eve of the abolition of slavery. Both Austin and I can think of no greater cause worth putting our lives on the line. Therefore, our decision to enlist as privates in the Union army was an easy one. Harrison has also decided to enlist along with us. I now fight this war in Lily's honor. If I have to die to free her then so be it. Her life and her freedom are worth just that much to me.

With a war of this magnitude spreading across the land, I know that it may be impossible to continue your search for Lily. For that reason, I fully understand if you must suspend your efforts. Please know that I have greatly appreciated everything that you, Griff, the other bandits, and your sons have done to try to bring Lily home. If I still have breath in my lungs when this war is over, I believe that God will find a way for me to hold my beloved wife again. But, this time, as a *free* woman.

P.S. For necessary anonymity, I have enlisted as Michael Adams. Please address any correspondence with that name and direct it to my brigade.

Sincerely,
Private Michael Adams
First division, Iron Army Brigade of the East

In the three years since writing that letter, James had gone from witnessing the dreams of Lily's symphony, to witnessing the daily nightmare of slain men surrounding him like fields of wheat. Month after grueling month, James had set up camps near piles of decaying bodies. He slept in tents pitched on top of dirt that had been fertilized with the blood of soldiers. His stomach had become numb to constant pangs of starvation, his skin just as numb to frost, heat, wounds, and bug bites. Using his medical training, he had treated severe burns, permanent facial disfigurements, and slashed abdomens with protruding organs. Stoically, he endured the sight of bullets piercing men, bayonets severing limbs, decapitated heads rolling near his feet, and true friends bleeding to death in his arms, as he rushed them to overrun medic tents. The savage nature of war made his father's butchery seem like a lovely daydream in comparison.

In the face of the hellish world James was being tortured in, Lily was the sole reason he forced his eyes to open every morning. She was the reason he bothered to inhale and exhale. She was his motivation to put one foot in front of the other, as he marched miles and miles on blistered feet from one camp to the next. She was the reason he accepted the harsh weather conditions, the deprivation of food and fluids, his growing collection of scars, and the irreparable mental trauma. In honor of Lily and Rose, it became his personal mission to help ensure that there would never be another baby, like his, who was born and died as a slave. Every cannon he launched was so that no other family would be torn apart because of business deals and greed. Every bullet he fired was to permanently cease the legality of shackling and whipping the innocent. Every hatchet he swung was to see every Negro auction closed forever. James marched, starved, slayed, and mercilessly killed without remorse, knowing that it was a means to freedom for Lily and others, who had suffered far worse for centuries at the hands of the very country they had helped to build. James's courage, pride, and willingness to die for what he believed in, made him stand out as a man worth leading and encouraging the masses. He, therefore, quickly climbed the army ranks from a private to a revered lieutenant. He led by his inspiring examples of loyalty to the vow he made to fight until the bitter end, or until he was carried away among the fallen, in his pursuit of a utopian America that was truly *united*.

Three years of living an untamed, barbaric life had naturally toyed with James's sanity, though. In times when he was emotionally teetering, memories of Lily and her music had a mysterious way of materializing in his mind, just in time to coax him back from leaping over the cliffs of insanity. The beautiful visions of Lily dressed elegantly, playing her songs at a grand piano, had the power to damn near bring a smile to James's face while drowning in a sea of dying soldiers and madmen wielding axes. While tightly gripped by the ever-lasting effects of Lily's altruistic love and music, nothing seemed to break Lieutenant James "Michael" Adams ... except for mail-call.

As often as he could, James sent a package to William. Inside was always a brief note to William and another large sealed envelope that he instructed William to store away for Lily. Lily's envelope contained weeks' worth of daily letters that James had written to her. Inspired by Levi's writings, his letters read much like a diary. The content covered an array of topics. He wrote about his experiences as a soldier, the good and the bad, as well as the places he had traveled to. He elaborated on all the constant dreams he had of her and Rose, how her music inspired him, how he desperately missed her, fond memories of them from the past, and his grand hopes for their future. He ended every letter to her the same way:

I pray every day that God will keep you safe and see you back into my arms soon. Until then, I promise to you my eternal love and loyalty.

Forever your soldier,
Lieutenant Adams
Iron Army Brigade of the East

James always received a response to his letters in return. Such was the case on this cold October day during mail-call. The moment his name was called, three common recurring questions began spinning in his mind: Had Lily been found? Had William received correspondence from her? Was the letter being handed to him actually *from* Lily? The potential answers always had James's hands shaking uncontrollably as his envelope was handed to him. Considering that President Lincoln had technically emancipated all slaves, James's hopes of hearing from or about Lily had been especially high as of late.

James refused to glance at the letter after it was handed to him. As always, he wanted to be alone in his tent before he even looked at who it was from. His hopeful heart still pounding, he sat down on his cot, closed his eyes, and blew out a nervous breath. "Please God," he whispered, before opening his eyes again. His hands still shaking, he turned the letter over. He sighed when he saw the name of the sender. He was not unhappy to hear from William, but the heartache of not seeing Lily's name suddenly drained his eagerness to read the contents that lay within the envelope. James slowly opened it and pulled the letter out. After years of receiving William's letters, he already knew the opening line:

Lieutenant Adams,

I hope this letter finds you well...

Through William's letters of the past, James had learned that he and Griff had continued to search for Lily for several more months before suspending their efforts. After taking a month off, Griff and the bandits regrouped and continued to search in areas of the country that were not war-torn. William stayed behind with Isabel, not wanting to leave her while the country was in such dire straits. Isabel was especially distraught because it had been years since she had seen or heard from Elijah. William had also written to James about the fact that Wilson and Emerson had joined another brigade in the north, both voluntarily serving in their mother's honor. William also always relayed any political information regarding the war that he thought would be helpful to the Iron Army Brigade. Such verbiage was indeed included in the letter that James now held. Today, though, James glossed over that information and his eyes quickly found their way to yet another familiar sentence included in every letter from William for the past three years:

I regret to inform you that I have no new news as to Lily's whereabouts ...

Without fail, reading those words always instantly cast James into an emotional pit of despair. It always felt to him like he had lost Lily all over again. He had numbed himself to all of the slayings he had witnessed, but there was simply no numbing himself to the fact that his wife seemed to have vanished without a trace. It was the one thing during the war that made him want to immediately hurl himself over the cliffs of insanity.

Austin walked into the tent and saw the way that James sat on the edge of his cot, his face buried in his hands with the crumpled letter beside him. Austin was all too familiar with that body language and the nasty attitude that accompanied it. "No news of Lily, huh?" he asked James, despite knowing the answer.

Without a word or so much as a glance in Austin's direction, James snatched his satchel and left. He stepped outside of his tent into the putrid smell of blood and death lingering in the air like a toxic fog. No matter how much the wind blew, the stench remained pungent and ever-present. The suffocating atmosphere prevented James from taking a much-needed deep breath to help calm his nerves. His nerves were further frayed as he walked past the overcrowded medic tent of delirious men with missing limbs and pus-filled gangrene wounds, who were screaming, groaning, and begging to be shot to alleviate their suffering. Normally, James was putting his medical training to work and assisting with the battered bodies of his fellow soldiers. But, today, the torturous sounds coming from within the medic tent only made his mind pick up pace as it raced toward the cliffs of insanity. He plugged his ears to drown out the sounds, and then began banging his fists against the sides of his head as his mind continued to spiral out of control. Just as he was nearing insanity's edge, Lily's music suddenly erupted in his mind and snagged him by the arm, just as he began to fall. The incessant banging on his temples stopped immediately and the sound of dying men no longer grated his ears. He froze, closed his eyes, and tilted his head back to let the sun warm his skin, while Lily's beautiful melody warmed him inside and caressed his damaged mind. He took a long deep breath as if the horrid odor in the air was suddenly non-existent. He slowly opened his eyes and exhaled as Lily's music decrescendoed and faded away. He then proceeded to walk to a nearby creek for his post-letter calming ritual. He sat under a tree and briefly listened to the flowing water. He reached inside his satchel and pulled out a children's book that he now knew by memory. After four years of toting it and turning its pages, it was now rather tattered, but it had become too sacred to James for him to part ways with.

Just before joining the war, James had gone back to Ava's little town to place fresh flowers at Rose's grave. By then, he had finished reading Levi's journals and now knew every intricate detail of his love affair with Maya. After learning about the tribulations of his life, James realized that he had aspired to be the sort of father to Rose that Levi *wished* he could have been to little Lily. His respect for Levi's sentimental journals made James feel as though they were worth keeping safe in the bunker beneath Ava's barn, along with the rest of his treasured belongings. James could not bring himself to part ways with the Little Mermaid children's book, though. Whenever his mind was frayed, it brought him peace to read it aloud to Rose.

Convinced that Rose could hear him from heaven, James now read the Little Mermaid aloud to her as a post mail-call ritual, to help soothe his irritated nerves. In the midst of a brutal war, he just wanted a few minutes to feel bathed in innocence. He wanted to keep Rose's memory alive and feel as close to her as the hour she had spent nestled against his chest. Reliving that memory, while reading a story about two people from different worlds, who triumphed despite their obstacles, was exactly what James needed to renew his hope after every frustrating mail-call incident.

As always, James tilted his head back toward the sky when he finished reading. "I love you, my little angel," he said as a tear slid down the side of his face.

Unbeknownst to James, he had a secret admirer watching him, who was warmed by the secret ritual for his daughter, much like the admirer Levi once had during a secret ritual of his own ...

Chapter Eighteen

August 17th, 1838,
I never knew I could get so much joy from picking apples...

Helplessly drawn to Maya's jubilant mood, Levi laid his rake down and walked over to her as she brushed a horse in the barn. "I just gotta know what's got you smilin' that big beautiful smile this early in the mornin'?" he asked her, a smile now on his face as well.

Maya stopped tending to the horse, looked Levi in the eyes, and touched him on the cheek. "This man right here." She gently kissed him on the lips. *"Definitely* smilin' about this incredible man," she whispered before walking out of the barn to tend to her other chores.

Maya's bold confession left Levi standing there happily baffled, now unable to stop smiling himself. He was unaware that Maya had happened to wake up earlier than usual that morning. On the way to fetch a glass of water, she had glanced out of her cottage window. In the pre-dawn hours, she caught sight of a shadow walking toward the orchard. When her eyes adjusted to the moonlight, she realized it was Levi carrying a ladder. She stood there and watched as he then used the ladder to climb up into an apple tree. He picked ten apples and dropped them to the ground and then went to an orange tree and did the same. Such a thing may have been meaningless to others, but Maya suddenly felt tears cascading down her cheeks.

For nearly the entire summer, Lily had woken up and dashed out to the orchard with the basket Levi had given her. She filled it with apples and oranges and then proudly handed them out to the other slaves on the plantation. It was a ritual little Lily looked forward to, but she never knew that the ease of her morning mission was because of her father. After weeks of Levi's secret pre-dawn ritual, the bottom of his fruit trees were bare. He now had to resort to climbing a ladder to pick the fruit at the top. Until glancing out her window, Maya had no idea that every apple and orange that Lily collected was put there by a man who was secretly going to extreme measures that proved he loved his daughter dearly. Maya accepted right then that there was nothing she could ever do or say to stop Levi Collins from expressing his love for Lily in any small ways he could manage. Such a thing warmed Maya enough to kiss him gently on the lips before she exited the barn to finish her other chores.

That same warm feeling was completely absent in another woman who just so happened to witness Levi's secret ritual that morning also. "Awfully odd how many apples and oranges are fallin' off of them trees every day here lately," Emily stated to Levi as he sat down to eat lunch that afternoon.

Levi was just about to take a bite of his food but paused and looked up to meet his wife's scathing eyes. Her words and the smug look on her face made him instantly lose his appetite.

Several times throughout the summer, Emily had roused briefly from her drunken stupor, and noticed Levi slipping out of bed earlier than usual. Curious about the odd trend, Emily had managed to get her alcohol-infused brain to carry her feet toward the window after Levi left on this particular morning. When she finally gathered the wherewithal to focus her eyes, she watched him intently, certain that she would catch him headed to Maya's cottages for sinful reasons. However, she was confused to find him picking apples and oranges. She did not understand the purpose of her husband's odd routine, until she just so happened to be sweeping the porch later and saw Lily running toward the orchard, placing the fruit in her basket. Emily then glanced over at her husband and watched his reaction.

Much like he did every morning, Levi was taking pause to watch Lily collect all the fruit she assumed had fallen from the orchard trees. He was leaning against the frame of the barn door with his arms folded across his chest. He had a prideful smile on his face as he watched how Lily meticulously figured out just how much weight she could carry. She added or removed fruit from her basket and lifted it to be sure she could haul her load with ease. When it was just right, she then trotted off on her quest to hand fruit out to everyone. The daily tradition brought a genuine smile to Levi's face, in much the same way that rainbows did for Maya. It lifted his spirits knowing that he was finally able to do something special for Lily, even if it was in secret … a secret that turned his wife's stomach as she watched on from the porch.

The sneer on Emily's face was just as prominent as Levi's smile in that moment. Emily hated how much pride she saw in her husband's eyes when he watched Lily. She hated that Levi was showing any interest in his daughter at all, especially on a level that hinted at the fact that he loved her. She wanted nothing more than to turn her husband's joy into a misery that was equal to her own. That was precisely her goal as he sat down to eat his lunch. "Looks like I'm gonna have to go out to that orchard every mornin' now and collect them apples myself, before your little mulatto monsta' gets to 'em," she told Levi, glaring harshly at him while he sat at the kitchen table. "I'm gonna scold 'er good the next time she touches what ain't hers."

"She's a three-year-old child!" Levi yelled, slamming his sandwich back down on his plate.

"And I'm gonna whip that little thief like a grown woman the next time I catch 'er stealin' my fruit!"

Levi suddenly flung his plate against the wall and stood up. "If you so much as *step* toward Lily with a whip in your hand, I *promise*, she won't be the female gettin' the most brutal *whippin'* of her life!"

"You don't have the intestinal fortitude to lay a hand on me, you weak cowardly son of a bitch!" Emily fired back. "In the bizarre case that you grow a big enough pair of testicles to touch me, I swear to God, I'll mar your little demon until she's unrecognizable! The sight of her will give *you* nightmares for the rest of your pathetic life!"

Levi overturned the entire kitchen table and stepped toward Emily. "Touch that little girl, and you'll be the only one in this house with permanent nightmares." He suddenly leaned in within an inch of Emily's face. "I warn you not to test me," he snarled through gritted teeth, glaring at her with pure hatred.

Emily swore she was staring into the eyes of the devil. Having never once seen such evil in her husband's eyes, she nearly wet herself after his threat. "Just keep that little heathen away from my orchard!" she replied, trembling with fear.

Levi huffed, stepped past Emily, and stormed out of the back-kitchen door. His rage led him to slam the door so hard, he shattered the glass in the windowpane. Too enraged to even look back, Levi kept on walking to the barn. The beautiful music in his mind inspired by Maya's earlier kiss had now transitioned into violent visions inspired by his wife. He jumped on his horse and sped off the plantation to escape the rage-driven urge that would have immediately ceased oxygen from escaping his wife's trachea ever again.

Emily had never seen or heard such savagery from a man who typically absorbed her threats without so much as changing the expression on his face. Genuinely fearing her husband for the first time ever, Emily's body finally relaxed when he was gone, and so too did her bladder. She stepped over the puddle and bolted up the stairs in search of a liquid that would quickly refill it. She slammed and locked her bedroom door and retrieved what she needed from the back of her closet. Her hands shook uncontrollably as she sat on the bed and raised the bottle of whiskey toward her mouth. Once she pressed it to her lips, her tears ceased quicker than a baby siphoning from its mother's breast.

Levi did not return to the farm until late that evening. Even then, he slept in the guest bedroom for the night. He needed as much distance as possible between him and the woman who had just caused his beautiful mind to erupt with the ugliest images of violence he had ever envisioned.

The following morning, Lily darted over to the orchard with the basket her father had given her. For nearly half an hour, she searched for her little orange and red treasures, but she could not find any. When Lily failed to return with her fruit, as usual, Maya walked to the orchard in search of her. She found Lily humming and playfully drawing in the dirt with a stick, her basket just as bare as the ground. "What you doin', baby?" Maya asked her.

"I'm just waitin' on the apples to fall, ma-ma," Lily replied, standing up and grabbing her basket.

Maya looked around beneath all the trees and noticed how bare the ground was. She then suddenly got the feeling she was being watched. She turned toward the main house and saw Emily on the porch, her eyes pasted on her. Wearing her typical devilish expression, Emily's arms were folded across her chest as she glared at Maya and Lily. Maya watched as Emily then turned to look at Levi and caught the hateful glare the pair exchanged. When Levi turned back to look at Maya, she gave him a telling glance. He lowered his head as if to acknowledge the fact that she was right about Emily affecting his actions.

Maya suddenly took the basket from Lily's hand and placed it back near the base of the tree, where it originally was when Levi had given it to her. The sight made Levi's heart sink. "I don't think it's gonna be any more apples or oranges, baby," Maya explained to Lily.

"But perhaps I just have to wait a little longa'," Lily surmised.

"I don't think waitin's gonna help, Lily."

"But why not?"

"It just ain't," Maya stated firmly.

"But everybody's gonna be so disappointed," Lily replied, her eyes suddenly flooding with tears.

"I know, but they'll have to get their own fruit now." Maya picked Lily up, guided her away from the orchard, and put an end to Levi's secret tradition.

Levi's heart remained lodged in the pit of his stomach as he watched Maya carry away a tearful Lily. He then turned and glared with pure hatred at his smirking wife, praying that the grim reaper would make room on his current daily schedule to pay her a visit. He figured Emily would feel right at home spending an eternity in hell snuggled up next to the devil. Levi then ducked into the barn and distracted himself with chores before his rage-driven urges compelled him to do the grim reaper's dirty work on his behalf.

Chapter Nineteen

Halloween
October 31, 1864

"ROSE!" James shrieked, waking up in a panic. Panting and sweating, he quickly sat up in his cot, looking confused as to where he was. He slung his legs over the edge of his rickety army cot and rested his face in his hands after realizing he had just had another one of his recurring dreams about Rose. Throughout the years, Rose had grown in James's dreams. She now looked to be four years old, as he playfully chased her toward her towering treehouse. In every dream, James still froze before he could catch her. And not once had Rose ever turned around or reacted to the sound of his voice as he called to her. James's inability to hug, or to even see Rose's face, still frustrated him every time he awakened from the bizarre dream.

James's frustrations were evident to the soldiers lying nearby; they were constantly subjected to his ear-piercing screams in the middle of the night. His shrill screams had roused a few soldiers on this occasion, but they were used to the random names of flowers flying from their lieutenant's mouth from time to time. They now thought nothing of his night terrors. After being rocked from their sleep, many of them just groaned and rolled back over. However, there was a new soldier amongst them who was especially annoyed by the screaming on this occasion. "Who the hell is Rose? Anotha' low-life slave you fuckin'?" the soldier asked.

With panther-like reflexes, James pounced on Elijah and began pounding away at his face, grunting with every punch he landed. Elijah was so caught off guard, he could do nothing but take it at first. After several blows, Elijah was finally able to wrap his hands around James's throat. He squeezed tight, but even cutting off his air supply was not enough to stop James from pelting him in the face. Elijah resorted to using his legs to launch James off him. He landed hard in between two cots. As soon as he hit the ground, Elijah hopped on top of him and reciprocated with several blows to his mouth. The savage grunting, and the force of their violent blows, easily proved they were unleashing years of pent-up rage and hatred for one another. That was further evident by the fact that it took the brute strength of six soldiers to pull the pair apart. Once untangled, the damage they had inflicted on each other was clear to see. Elijah had a swollen right eye and a gash over the other, blood pouring from it. James had a split lip, and a nose dripping with blood as well. However, their boiling rage seemed to make them completely oblivious to their throbbing faces. Both savages were still desperate to fight to the death, each thrashing wildly to break free of the soldiers holding them.

Unable to break free, Elijah verbally erupted instead. "THE FUCK IS WRONG WITH YOU?!" he yelled at James, his words insinuating an unjustified attack.

Harrison, Austin, and another soldier tightened their grips on James when he suddenly tried to lunge. "Lieutenant calm down!" they yelled. They had a death grip on him, but James still managed to drag them all over the place as he thrashed.

"What the hell'd you say to him?!" Harrison asked Elijah.

"I didn't say shit! This crazy fucker just woke up and pounced on me!"

James finally wrestled himself free and stood a hair's breadth away from Elijah's face, his bloodshot eyes lowered into angry slits as he glared at his nemesis. His chest was visibly heaving as he breathed hard, forcing spit through his tightly clenched, blood-covered teeth. Standing there foaming at the mouth, James looked very much like an animal infected with rabies. Fearing he had truly gone mad, Harrison and Austin tried to grab James once more before he attacked Elijah again. But James shook them loose and stormed out of the tent before his rage resulted in the vicious death of one of his own new soldiers.

Austin approached Elijah when James was gone. "I heard what you asked him, you lyin' sack of shit."

"So fuckin' what," Elijah replied, snatching his arms free and wiping the blood off his sliced eyebrow.

"Rose is his *daughta'* … his *dead* daughta'." Austin scoffed and shook his head. "You deserved to get your fuckin' ass whooped," he said before walking away.

Years ago, it had taken Elijah very little time to burn through the money that he had stolen from Lily. He had ended up with nothing to show for it except the clothes on his back. He had spent most of the cash traipsing from city to city, brothel to brothel, and drinking heavily, drunkenly bragging to bar patrons about the heinous crimes he had gotten away with. Despite the fact that murdering people became a joyous sport for him, he was initially angry over the fact that he had been drafted into the war. When given the choice between prison and serving his country, he chose to serve. He much preferred the option that allotted him the opportunity to legally take more lives, especially those of white people. He had no idea that years later, that choice would then lead him to the very white man who had ignited his passion for killing … a white man that he wanted to kill above all others.

Weeks before Elijah's arrival, James had learned through intel that a massive confederate troop was allegedly marching their way. It was he who had then written a letter requesting assistance from another brigade. He then assigned five of his men to deliver it to their allies and guide them back to their camp. James could never have known that his loyal soldiers had guided his nemesis right back into his life in the middle of the night, ironically delivering such a nightmare on Halloween.

James's dismay over being stuck with such a man was now clear to see on Elijah's swollen face. It was clear for the Iron Army's general to see as well. As another soldier was guiding Elijah to the medical tent, General Blackshear grabbed Elijah by the arm and stopped him when he saw the extent of the damage to his face. "I just saw you last night when you got here, and I don't rememba' your goddamn face lookin' like that! What the hell happened to you?!" he demanded to know.

Neither Elijah nor the soldier beside him spoke. Elijah was far too angry that he had not been allotted the time to finish his fight.

"One of y'all betta' get to goddamn talkin'!" General Blackshear erupted.

"Lieutenant Adams just lost it on 'em when he woke up this mornin', sir," the other soldier confessed.

"Is that true?" General Blackshear asked, looking at Elijah.

"Yessa'," Elijah replied, trying to hide his aggravation.

"You!" He pointed to the assisting soldier. "Go and find Lieutenant Adams!" He then pointed to Elijah. "You go and wait in my goddamn tent."

After quickly being found, James stepped inside the general's tent and stood at attention. "General, you wanted to see me, sir," he said, making the statement as if he was ignorant as to the nature of his request.

"Don't play like a dumbass in my presence, lieutenant! You know goddamn good 'n well I was gonna wanna see you afta' this shit!" he said, motioning his hand toward Elijah, who was also standing at attention, still bleeding badly from the gash above his eye.

"Oh that," James callously replied.

"*Oh that?*" General Blackshear mocked. "He ain't been here six hours and you're already fightin' like two goddamn little pussies on a schoolyard!" he yelled. "Maybe you haven't noticed, but we have a war to fight! We're short enough on men as it is, and here you are tryna kill the very men we requested help from! I expect more out of a lieutenant! This ain't the kind of damn example I need you settin' for the rest of my men!"

"Yessa', my apologies. It won't happen again," James lied. "Are we finished here, sa'?" he asked, eager to get away from Elijah.

"Did I say we were finished?!" General Blackshear growled.

James quietly exhaled to settle his annoyance.

"Now, I want you two to spend some *brotherly* quality time with each otha', until you can learn to play nice togetha' on the playground," General Blackshear said, smiling devilishly. He pointed at James. "You go on and stitch 'em up, *doctor*. I want you to put his face back just as pretty as you found it! Make an *accidental* slip-up on 'em, and you'll be stitchin' up the second hole I put in y'ur ass!"

"Yessa," James replied.

"Now both of ya' get outta my sight!" the general barked.

James much preferred the extra hole in his ass over helping heal a man whom he hated nearly as much as his father and brothers, but he saluted his general and went to do as he was told.

Elijah saluted as well and then followed James with a smirk on his face. He lay back on the cot in the medic tent with his hands behind his head, enjoying the fact that the white man he hated had no choice but to serve him like a slave. "Put me back togetha' just like the general said … *doc*. I wanna be nice and pretty again … just the way Lily liked me," he provoked.

James had his back turned collecting the supplies he needed when Elijah made his statement. His inner beast was still very much awake, thirsty for more blood. But James quietly exhaled and swallowed hard to find the strength to maintain control over his rabid inner monster. Instead, he forced the doctorly side of himself to emerge. He was then able to start diligently cleaning the gash over Elijah's eye without so much as a grimace on his face.

"So, you think Rose was *your* daughta', huh?" Elijah snickered, taking the free moment to try to rile James up again.

Silence. James set his towel down and picked up his needle and thread.

"I guess Lily neva' told you the true extent of our relationship while we had free time afta' all of her rehearsals, did she?"

Silence. James initiated the first stitch above Elijah's eye.

"Let's just say, that dead little girl might very well have been mine," Elijah continued to torment.

Silence. James knew Lily. He did not believe a word Elijah was saying.

"Heard you was havin' a hard time findin' your sweet little Lily years ago," Elijah continued.

Silence. James continued to concentrate on sewing the gash above Elijah's eye.

"Well, I saw 'er in the back of that wagon with that old man you left 'er with," he suddenly confessed.

James instantly froze. The words rang too true for him to dismiss Elijah this time.

Finally garnering a reaction from James, Elijah smirked. "Maybe if you stayed by Lily's side to get 'er to safety like a real man, you wouldn't be wonderin' where the hell she's at right now. That's what I would've done. But *you*," he scoffed. "You passed 'er off into the hands of some decrepit old man to do your dirty work like the pussy you are," he taunted.

James clenched his fists and locked his jaw to keep his raging inner beast from attacking again. "You betta' tell me if you know where she is!"

"You're here fightin' this war in Lily's honor, ain't ya'? You wanna feel all proud and patriotic while you're fuckin' 'er as a free woman," he snickered again. "Well, I got news for ya', doc. You're wastin' your fuckin' time tryna free her ..." He sat up and got close to James's face. "'Cause that fuckin' whore is dead," he said smugly.

"You're a liar!" James screamed, his blood now boiling. "Tell me where she is!"

"Don't know. Might wanna ask the wolves and coyotes. I'm sure they enjoyed pickin' apart her dead body."

"WHERE THE FUCK SHE IS?!" James yelled, grabbing Elijah by the neck. He then began repeatedly slamming his head against the metal rail of the cot as he asked that question over and over again. The back of Elijah's head was split by the time Austin and two other soldiers were able to drag James off him.

The two soldiers wrestled James outside. Austin stayed behind and glared at Elijah with hateful eyes, convinced that he had enticed James into another fight somehow. "What the hell is wrong with you?!" Austin asked, as he loomed over him.

"Get the hell outta my face!" Elijah erupted, holding on to the back of his aching head.

Austin turned to another medic. "Come and finish stitchin' this fucker up!" He then stepped outside to find James incessantly pacing with his fists balled up.

"He knows somethin' about Lily, Austin!" James pointed toward the medic tent. "He knows! That piece of shit *fuckin'* knows!"

"How do you know?"

"Just trust me, he does!"

"Okay, okay, calm down."

"*Calm down?!* That asshole knows information that he couldn't possibly be privy to unless he actually saw Lily with his very own eyes, and you want me to *calm down?!*"

"Well, we're not gonna get any answers while y'ur in an uproar. So yes! You need to take a walk and calm down first. I'll cova' for you if General Blackshear starts askin' questions."

"No! I want answers outta that fucker *now!*"

"You're just gonna end up in anotha' fight! Just go on and get outta here for now! Go calm yourself down somehow before Blackshear bashes your head in too! I'll try to talk to Elijah in the meantime."

Without another word, James angrily stormed off and made his way to the creek. He kicked and threw rocks into the water, trying desperately to diffuse his anger. His mind rushed back to the bullet wound that had taken Gideon's life. He now wondered if Elijah knew who had shot him and why. As James continued to fire rocks into the water, a plethora of other questions suddenly bombarded his mind: Where was Samuel? Why wasn't he at the first trade-off spot as planned? Why was Elijah there instead? James felt his knees begin to buckle under the extreme mental weight of those unanswered questions. He suddenly sat down against a tree with his elbows on his knees. "She's not dead! She's not dead! She's not dead!" he ranted incessantly while literally trying to bang the thought out of his head with his fists. "FUCK HIM!" he suddenly erupted. He was beyond furious over the fact that he had allowed Elijah to make him spiral out of control. He exhaled, tilted his head back, and closed his eyes. It was then that he recalled Ava's words: *Your Lily was alive when she left here, if that's any consolation to you.* James took comfort in that all over again. That's what he continued to focus on: *Lily alive* and in his arms during a masquerade party on Halloween, exactly four years prior …

Lily immediately made her way into James's arms after the curtains closed on her show in Chicago. She was locked in his loving embrace when chants of "ENCORE!" began to ring out loudly in the theater. Lily pulled back and looked at James with a look of happy surprise. It was the first time any audience had done such a thing.

"Seems they haven't had enough of you yet, Miss Lily," James replied, kissing her hand. "I certainly know the feelin'," he smiled.

Lily laughed and turned to look at William as he approached. "What should I do?" she asked, valuing her mentor's opinion.

"Well, that is certainly up to you m'lady, but I've always been in favor of giving an audience what they ask for." He was silent for a moment to let the continued chants of encore take over.

"I guess I have to give them what they want then, don't I?"

"Wise decision," he smiled proudly.

James, William, Austin, and the entire student orchestra all watched on as Lily made her way back out onto the stage. She walked with a confident stride and a sultry sway in her hips, feeling much like a queen in the red designer gown that Anna Mae had tailored to accentuate her curves. The sight of her returning to honor the crowd's request brought them all to their feet again. Lily stopped near the front of the stage and curtsied, feeling her excitement rise along with the audience's drawn-out applause. Lily had no plans to play any of her old material the way the audience wanted, though. She suddenly asked if there were any pianists in the crowd. She lucked up on three who were brave enough to come up on stage. At Lily's request, she had them play just the short chorus of their favorite piano songs. Lily thanked them for their contributions and had them take their seats again. James, William, Austin, and the orchestra all looked at each other curiously, perplexed as to what Lily was doing.

Lily strolled toward her grand piano and turned to face the crowd. "And now ... the encore will begin." She sat down at the piano bench, draping her dress tastefully at her side. When she was seated as perfectly as a living sculpture, she glanced over into the wings. She was immediately warmed by the immense amount of pride she saw on James's face as he gazed lovingly at her. Lily smiled at him and then closed her eyes.

There was complete silence in the theater as Lily gracefully lifted her hands and struck the keys. Slowly, she began replaying the chorus from the first pianist she had invited on stage, then the second, and the third. Her fingers then picked up speed as she began blending all three choruses together. A brand-new song was being born, every reworked combination of notes quickly conjured up in the musical birthing chambers of Lily's mind. The mystical melody then flowed seamlessly down through her fingertips, as if she had played it dozens of times before. The audience sat in awestruck silence as Lily's new melody pleasantly graced their ears with a variation of speeds, soft lows, and intense highs. When her imagination decided the song was complete, Lily opened her eyes and smiled as she slowly repeated each original chorus again. She let the last note slowly fade away, the way her gifted mind had just cleverly commanded her to do. Her astonishing feat yielded an extraordinary commendation from the audience … including a powerful man sitting in a balcony seat who would soon become president.

James, William, and the rest of Lily's entourage thought that they had already seen the extent of Lily's unique abilities. But, yet again, they found themselves flabbergasted by what she had just accomplished. They, too, erupted in applause as she stepped to the front of the stage and gracefully curtsied. "I hope to see you all at our masquerade ball at the Chicago Convention Centa' lata' tonight." Lily said, blowing a kiss to the crowd and touching her heart before she exited the stage.

Lily walked backstage to the sight of her entourage evenly lining both sides of the hallway. She lit up with a smile when everyone suddenly erupted in applause and whistles. "Aww, thank you," she said, blowing kisses to everyone as she sauntered between them. She laughed at Austin, who was playfully bowing, as if a queen had just crossed his path. She then made her way into her dressing room to change for the masquerade ball. James entered just seconds behind her and locked the door. Lily looked up at him in the mirror and smiled as she took off her earrings. "You stalkin' me?" she teased.

"Mm-hmm," James replied, wrapping his arms around her waist. "Not even ashamed to admit it." He turned Lily around and kissed her lightly on the lips. "It's nights like this, I'm convinced you're a goddess who descended straight from the heavens," he joked. "There's no way you're truly of this world."

Lily laughed. "Sorry to disappoint you, but I'm just plain ol' Lily from Virginia."

"There's definitely not a damn thing *plain* about you, Miss Lily from Virginia. And I'm in no ways disappointed by who you are … especially knowin' that I'm the one lucky man on this earth who can call someone as extraordinary as you my woman."

Lily wrapped her arms around James's neck. "And I'm afraid you're stuck with me."

"Is that a promise?"

She nodded. "I'm yours for a lifetime..." She moved his hands down to her buttocks. "Every inch of me." The way James gently squeezed her posterior cheeks sent a rush of heat to her core. She turned around and pressed her buttocks against his pelvis. "Be a gentleman and help me outta this dress," she said, her words motivated by the hardened bulge she felt throbbing beneath his pants.

James glided his hands up her sides and began unbuttoning her dress, placing light kisses along the nape of her neck as he slowly slid the right side down. Lily watched his every movement in the mirror, moaning lightly over the feel of his lips. James then moved on to her left shoulder, pulling the sleeve down, until the dress cascaded onto the floor.

"Take off your pants," Lily demanded.

Far too eager to do as he was told, James could barely get his mind to remember how to loosen his belt. Lily smiled devilishly at the desperation on his face as he finally freed himself. Still watching his expression in the mirror, she lowered her lace undergarments, maneuvered her hips backward, and slowly slid his throbbing shaft into her aching abyss. She moaned over the sight of James's mouth parting and his eyes rolling back into his head. She then placed her hands on the vanity and began smoothly gliding him in and out of her. She was slow, at first, intensifying her own pleasure by watching the glorious expression on James's face. She then guided his hands onto her breasts. Still looking at him in the mirror, she conveyed her desires to him with her eyes. The growl that escaped James at that moment made her purr with delight as well. She closed her eyes and her head fell slightly back as James began to drive himself hard into her. He now was the one who watched her intensely in the mirror, feeling his ego swelling the closer Lily looked to her impending eruption.

With a hallway full of people, Lily bit her bottom lip to keep the overpowering pleasure from singing out through her vocal cords. James took it as a challenge to hear those lovely sighs, though. A loud rhythmic clapping sound ensued as he drove himself deeper and faster into her tight folds. He, however, was the first to give in to the pleasure. His willpower to remain silent was no match for the feel of Lily's insides. Her slick internal walls quickly began to launch him toward the skies of ecstasy. His infectious, guttural groans caused Lily to reciprocate. The sound of James's grunting intensified after hearing Lily's beautiful moans pleasuring his eardrums. His grunts further deepened when she suddenly began thrusting her hips back on him, equally meeting his strokes with force. The deep pounding instantly pushed Lily to the brink. Her insides forcefully spasmed and flooded her body with intense pleasure, forcing James's name through her vocal cords in an erotic moan.

Landon happened to be walking past the dressing room and heard James helplessly cry out for God after exploding inside of Lily. Landon paused, raised a single eyebrow, and smiled enviously. "Damn lucky man," he said to himself before he walked off in his usual relaxed strut.

That's exactly what James was thinking to himself after pulling Lily into his arms and gazing at the two of them in the mirror. "Encore, encore, encore," he chanted softly in her ear while gently caressing her breasts and nibbling at her earlobe.

Lily laughed lightly and turned around to face James. She wrapped her arms around his neck and placed her forehead against his. "I'll be more than happy to give you an epic encore performance afta' the ball tonight." She kissed him. "But only if you do every little thing I tell you to do."

"I'll crawl into that ball on my hands and knees and bark like a damn dog if that's what you command me to do."

Lily burst out laughing. "While I'd surely be tickled by such a spectacle, I think I'll give you a far less humiliatin' task."

"Name it and it shall be done."

"Be my prince at the masquerade ball tonight."

"As you wish," James replied, as he bowed and kissed her hand, already embracing his new role as prince.

Lily laughed lightly. "Well then go on and get outta here and let a lady get dressed."

"Yes, m'lady," he teased with another bow.

James then put his clothes back on and went down the hall to clean up and get into his masquerade costume. An hour later, he stepped out of the carriage along with Landon and William and stood outside the Chicago Convention Center. They welcomed the hundreds of costume-clad patrons who began making their way inside. However, James suddenly stopped greeting people when Griff stole his attention; he knew Lily was inside the carriage he was guiding their way. Griff halted the horses just in front of the building's entrance, climbed down, opened the carriage door, and took Lily by the hand. Before Lily could even exit, a welcoming roar of applause erupted from the patrons who were still standing in line. The noise of the ovation faded away from James's ears altogether, though. When he saw Lily step down from her chariot, the sight of her left him far too mesmerized to focus on anything other than her stunning beauty.

Isabel had designed her a gown fit for a princess. She had styled Lily's hair into loose spirals and crowned her head with a sparkling tiara, further adding to her look of royalty. But to James, Lily far superseded that. "Truly a heavenly goddess," he whispered, gazing at her in awe as he lifted her hand to his lips and graced her dainty white glove with a gentle kiss.

"Thank you, my prince," Lily replied. She flashed an alluring smile at James, who was indeed dressed very much like an English prince, complete with a sword and monarchy-style patches on his jacket.

James then extended his elbow to the beautiful woman in his sights and guided her through the large crowd. Lily took her time walking, greeting as many people as she could before entering the building and waiting in the wings of the ballroom for Landon to make announcements.

Landon had already made his way to the podium. From his elevated position, he was taking a moment to scan the audience for a woman who had the potential to make him praise God, in much the same way as he had overheard James doing earlier. He gazed in wide-eyed delight when he found a unique-looking, olive-toned woman with dark hair, and piercing multi-colored eyes. The curvaceous creole woman turned and caught Landon's eyes on her. She flashed an alluring smile and then placed her feline mask in front of her face, inviting him to chase a naughty pussycat. Landon's manhood instantly stirred to life, signaling that it was ready for the chase. A wicked smile emerged on his face as he discreetly nodded, accepting her challenge. Eager for the chase to begin, he wasted no further time beginning his brief announcement. "Ladies and gentlemen, may I have your attention." He reluctantly pulled his eyes away from his potential conquest to make sure he had everyone's attention before he continued. "Thank you all for attending this evening. Please feel free to continue enjoying the fine wines, food, and festivities. But, more than anything, I know all of you are eager to meet the composer, creator, and star of The Dream Symphony. And so, without further ado, I give you … Miss Lily Adams," he said, extending his arm toward the corridor where she had been waiting. As James and Lily emerged, Landon breezed right past them; he was far too hungry for his very first taste of creole cuisine to even glance in their direction.

Like a true prince guiding a princess into a ball, James escorted Lily toward the dance floor, entering to the grand sound of the applauding crowd. After making their way to the center of the room, James held one of Lily's hands high, as she gracefully curtsied to the humbling commendation from the audience. James then turned to Lily, placed one hand behind his back, and the other across his heart, as he bowed toward her. He took her by the hand and kissed it, then rose and looked her in the eyes. "Before every man in here fights to get to you, may I have this first dance?" he whispered.

"But of course," Lily smiled.

After the applause settled, the orchestra began to play, and James began waltzing Lily across the dance floor. They were simply doing their typical short, choreographed dance, to present Lily to the audience in an artistic, tasteful way. But the way James and Lily gazed into each other's eyes made the audience feel as though they were watching something far more authentic. The elegance of the entire scene served to make everyone completely blind to the contrast of their color. The loving way they were entranced by one another suddenly made the masquerade party seem more like the ball of a true prince and princess at their fairytale wedding reception.

James very much had Lily feeling like a princess bride. She was completely lost in the moment with him, until the music finally faded. When the audience began to applaud, James took a step back and bowed toward Lily again while holding her hand. When the next song began, many other attendees found a dance partner and flooded the dance floor with costume laden bodies. Before parting ways with James, Lily put her feathered masquerade mask up to her face and gazed at him through the eyeholes. "Don't botha' lookin' for me when this ball is ova'..."

James looked confused.

Lily leaned in close to his ear. "Not unless you're ready for that encore," she whispered, grazing his earlobe with her lips. She pulled back and smiled devilishly at the hungry look on his face. Her wicked smile broadened after briefly glancing down at his crotch and seeing that her words already had him beyond prepared for another epic performance. After teasing him, Lily then galivanted off into the arms of another eagerly waiting gentlemen. As James watched Lily drift away, he blew out a breath to calm his body. He feared impaling his next dance partner with the steel Lily had just caused to rise between his thighs.

Through her mask, Lily discreetly watched as James became further aroused by dancing so closely with a multitude of desirable women throughout the night. Lily was no fool. She knew it was every man's ultimate desire to bed as many women as his body would allow throughout his lifetime. If given the opportunity, she knew that even the strongest of committed men would cave easily to their unrelenting carnal cravings for a woman's flesh. She felt there was something mysterious about a man's urge to spread his seed that seemed to temporarily inhibit his conscience. Lily had learned that it was extraordinarily rare to find a man who had built the strength to overcome such mental weakness on behalf of the woman he loved. Lily was confident that the man she stared at from behind her mask was indeed one of those priceless anomalies. Despite being teased by a variety of shapes, colors, sizes, looks, and scents, James Adams chose loyalty every time ... for Lily's sake. Lily's appreciation for such fortune always moistened her eyes, as well as the abyss between her thighs. It had ignited her fetish for watching the moments when James was tempted by the flesh of a woman. She was turned on by witnessing his brutal bodily fight between the overpowering need to copulate and his desire for faithfulness. James's hard-fought choice to remain faithful always suspended Lily's body in a heightened state of arousal.

Despite a variety of females enticing him with sinful desires, Lily was confident that all the women fawning over James were nothing more than three hours of foreplay, priming his body for action they would never experience. As she continued to follow James with her eyes, Lily's devilish smile returned and her insides dripped with anticipation, knowing confidently that the erection between his thighs would only ever be slid between hers.

James watched Lily too. His glances at her were far more overt, though. He gazed at her with an ever-present hunger in his eyes, his need to devour her intensifying the longer she playfully ignored him while in the arms of other men. Though playful as it was, James could not tamp feelings of *real* jealousy. Logic told him it was all a game, but his aching loins did not want to play. He knew the power of the appendage dangling between every man's thighs. The very second it flooded with blood, he knew a man's mind would simultaneously flood with erotic visions of fucking his prey. So, while entranced by the mind-altering spell of lust, there was nothing playful about the persistent naughty thoughts that Lily's essence was igniting in the minds of the men she danced with. Every smile, every clever sentence whispered in Lily's ear, every joke told, and every drink they handed her was motivated by their brick-hard appendage's incessant begging to erupt inside her body. Seeing so many men flock to Lily with that goal had James's jealousy at peak levels. But witnessing the phenomenon was also the ultimate reminder of the precious treasure she was to him, a treasure that he did not want men thinking about in such savage ways. The mere thought of the ways in which they might be envisioning fucking his woman had James's jealousy teetering on the verge of a blinding rage. It was only during those rare moments when he briefly caught Lily glancing at him that immediately brought him back from the brink of madness. The sparkle in her eyes, the alluring smile she flashed, and the sudden blush of her cheeks all seemed to say: *no matter what these men may want, I am faithfully yours ... always.* It was a collection of those simple moments that had built

James into a one-in-a-million, mentally strong man, with cemented loyalty and faithfulness to the woman he loved.

As intently as James had watched Lily throughout the evening, she had somehow managed to escape his sight by the time the festivities were coming to a close. He politely excused himself from the lady he was dancing with and walked over to speak to Landon. He was sitting at a table, genuinely enamored by the beauty and conversation of his creole catch. "Have you seen Lily?" James asked him.

"I believe she's already back at the hotel," Landon answered, not taking his eyes off the woman he hoped to have in his own hotel room by the end of the night.

James went and stood on the stage and quickly scanned the crowd. When he was unable to spot Lily, he went outside and saw that Griff and her carriage were indeed gone. Samuel then gave James a ride back to the hotel. He hopped out of the carriage before it even came to a complete stop in front of the hotel entrance. He trotted up the steps, two at a time, toward Lily's suite on the top floor. Heavily panting, he fumbled with his keys in his haste to open the door. He stepped inside and found Lily lying on her side in bed with a sheet draped over her body, holding her masquerade mask up to her face. James shut the door and tossed his keys on a table nearby, while gazing at Lily the entire time. The way the light from the fireplace illuminated her body made her look like a living work of art in his eyes.

"Took you long enough. I's startin' to think I'd be performin' an encore all alone," Lily teased.

"That may very well be the case … I'm afraid I'm gonna have to punish you for runnin' off on me," James teased in return as he unbuttoned his jacket.

Lily pulled back the sheets. "You will do no such thing."

James hardened immediately after she unveiled her nude body. "You're right, I won't," he quickly admitted, his eyes widening in awe.

He made his way toward her like a magnet to metal, his eyes fixed on the landscape of her sensuous curves.

Still having yet to blink, James sat down on the bed and began gliding his hand along Lily's hip. Gently, he caressed the soft skin of the lady he revered as a living portrait of womanly perfection. His lips then followed the course of his hands. He kissed her from the side of her neck, down to her waist, and then lightly bit the side of her buttocks. Lily purred with each bite, her core constricting and moistening her insides. She then rolled over onto her back, wanting him to moisten her in an even more erotic way. The very second she spread her legs, James began to drool. He tore out of his shirt and got on his knees in between her thighs. He raised up on all fours, crawled near her face, and hovered over her. He gazed at her for a moment before slowly lowering himself down to kiss her lips, pressing the bulge in his trousers between her thighs, to give her a preview of what was later to *come*. He then slowly kissed his way down her body, his mouth watering incessantly as he made his way toward his destination. He was drooling heavily by the time he slid his tongue into Lily's heated abyss.

"Yeees," Lily moaned, arching her back and thrusting her hips toward James's mouth. She erotically exhaled as she threaded her fingers in his hair. She pressed his head closer and began rocking her hips toward the pleasure. James moaned as he ate, drool continuously seeping from his mouth, much like the semen quickly collecting in his underwear.

After Lily's antics at the masquerade ball, James now wanted his chance to playfully tease her in return. He suddenly stopped tasting her and used his tongue to tickle the sensitive skin of her interior thighs, until she began laughing lightly. As soon as she laughed, he went back to suckling hard on her hidden jewel, turning her laughter back into deep moans. Back and forth, he toyed with her that way, moaning every time he heard her pleasure-filled sighs.

The pleasurable feeling of James's whiskers brushing against Lily's sensitive skin began to bring out her aggressive lioness. She forcefully took hold of his head again, hooked her leg around his neck, and began grinding herself against his face. Her savage nature nearly made James erupt in his pants. Like a lion king laying claim over his jungle, he was roaring as she forced him to ferociously suck every drop of sweet essence from her body. James happily drank to the sound of his name escaping Lily's lips in a low raspy growl.

When James finished with his ravenous feeding, he finally emerged from his trance and looked up at Lily. She was smiling devilishly at him. "You gonna punish me now?" she asked, petting his hair like she was calming a rabid animal.

James shook his head. He kissed Lily's inner thigh and removed her leg from his neck. He then began lightly kissing her skin, from her stomach to her neck, and then up to her ear. "I don't wanna punish you," he whispered, his lips grazing her earlobe. He then pulled back and looked her in the eyes. "I wanna make it clear how much I love you," he said, gently caressing her face.

His statement softened the expression on Lily's face. Her playful, devilish smile faded away altogether as she gazed back at him. She suddenly felt a flurry of butterflies and a surge of warmth rush through her that ignited her tear ducts.

Usually, James let Lily have her way with him every night. He thoroughly enjoyed the sexual games she played. But every now and then, he wanted to remind her that his desire to bury himself inside her was motivated by far more than lust. His *need* for her was something he felt even the greatest poet could not adequately describe. That indescribable feeling pulled his lips toward Lily's again. He kissed her even more gently this time, as he wiped the tears cascading down her cheeks. He then softly kissed her forehead, took a pillow, and tossed it on top of a plush rug near the fireplace. He picked Lily up, carried her over to the rug, and gently laid her down on top of it. Lily laid there watching James as he towered over her, unable to take her eyes off him as he stripped down. It was yet another moment when she appreciated how truly fortunate she was to have a man with a rare heart, one that beat inside the sculpted body of an Adonis.

Despite the immense pressure throbbing in his groin, James was in no rush. He walked over and retrieved a bottle of body oil. He poured some in his hands, rubbed it into his palms, and then let the fire heat his hands slightly. He got down on his knees in between Lily's thighs and placed his heated hands on her legs. Lily sighed softly as he began a gentle massaging motion, spreading the oil up her hips, onto her stomach, and then her breasts. He traced the outline of her nipples with his finger, tugged at them lightly, and then covered the right one with his mouth. He suckled softly on it while he slid two fingers down the side of her body and into her abyss. Lily gasped, pressed his head tighter against her breast, and began to ride his fingers. Her sensual moans and bodily thrusts instantly put an end to James's desire for foreplay; he was now desperate to be inside his woman. He quickly removed his fingers and sucked the taste of her off them, as he slowly slid his erection into her heated cavern. The loud erotic moan that suddenly escaped Lily in that moment nearly made James erupt upon entry. He closed his eyes and breathlessly whispered Lily's name as rapture swaddled his body.

James slowly opened his eyes and gently kissed Lily to thank her for the pleasure currently causing his nerves to electrify. As his lips still massaged hers, he took her right leg and placed it over his shoulder. The oil that James had applied to Lily's skin allowed his body to glide effortlessly across hers, as he then began gently burying himself inside her. Suddenly, he increased the power and depth of his strokes. The sudden intense sensations ignited more fire in their kiss. Their tongues moved wildly, as if they could not taste one another enough. Throughout every deep stroke, James only pulled back from

Lily's lips long enough to allow her soft sighs to escape, using the sound of her pleasure to refuel his stamina.

... Lily's moans were playing joyously in James's mind as he pleasured himself alone in the woods. Vividly, he recalled himself on that rug with her leg slung over his shoulder. As he massaged himself now, he envisioned the sight of her beautiful face, as her breathing began to quicken and her hips fell in sync with his. With clarity, James could still see the way that Lily broke their kiss, pressed her head back into the pillow, and called out his name in the ultimate climactic moan. Just seconds after hearing that glorious sound, James recalled the way his seed had rushed inside of Lily's womb, much like the way it rushed from within him now, as he stroked himself to the rhythm of that glorious memory.

When his body settled, James leaned back against a tree to catch his breath. He rested his head against the trunk, closed his eyes again, and began thinking about how his Halloween had ended that night. He had laid on his side on the plush rug with his arms around Lily, facing the fireplace. There was no need for a blanket. Between the crackling fire and James's strong arms, Lily was perfectly warm. Both drained from an extremely long day, their eyes had grown heavy quickly. Just before Lily faded away into sleep, James whispered in her ear, "you are so loved."

"You *definitely* proved that tonight," Lily whispered back as she snuggled closer to him and drifted off to sleep.

All these years later, James's fury over Elijah's words *definitely* proved that those intense feelings for Lily were still alive. He sat in the woods alone, wishing he could whisper those same sentiments into Lily's ear while she was lying in his arms again. That Halloween memory further strengthened his determination to fight for another moment like that with her. It also managed to settle the boiling rage that Elijah had caused. Now feeling rather calm, James blew out a breath. He then stood up, dusted the leaves from his clothes, and walked back to camp ... and so too did the person who had been watching him.

Amelia Morrison waited for James to get a good lead before she began making her way back to camp. As many times as she had followed him, she knew exactly how long to wait, and which route to go, so as not to get caught spying. As she walked, the fire James ignited in her nether region was blazing hotter than in times past. That fire began as a spark two years prior when she first began her stint as a nurse with the Iron Army Brigade, and one Lieutenant Adams walked into the medic tent. Amelia was one of dozens of dedicated nurses to the brigade. She made meals, treated soldiers, and did any other things necessary to support the troops. Considering that the men she tended to had not had the comforts of a woman in years, Amelia's presence alone was often the medicine they needed to maintain their will to live. She could damn near heal a man with one sweeping glance of her hazel bedroom eyes. Many men could not even bring themselves to blink, or close their drooling mouths, with her in their field of view. She was a strikingly beautiful brunette with perfectly proportioned curves, naturally tanned skin, and a full, even smile. Many men had attempted to win her affections after her warm disposition had completely melted them ... but Lieutenant Adams was the one man who had remained as cold as ice.

James's lack of warmth toward Amelia seemed ironic since the pair often worked long grueling hours together, tending to the needs of battered soldiers. Working frantically under extreme pressure, their combined efforts had tugged many a man back from the brink of death. Accomplishing such miraculous feats together made Amelia feel a bond with James that would typically be reciprocated by any normal man ... but her lieutenant seemed far from normal. He was often like a mute while working with Amelia, his conversations with her strictly limited to the medical needs of their patients.

From Amelia's perspective, James always seemed lost in thought, the expression on his face leaving her to believe that he was haunted by whatever he was envisioning. After the euphoria of saving a life, she expected to see a hint of joy, or at least a small sign of life in his eyes. But in such cases, all she ever saw in James was an even further plunge into sadness. She could not help but wonder why. Her only clue was the children's book she sometimes saw him reading alone in the woods immediately after every man they pulled back from the edge of death. The fact that he sometimes wept uncontrollably as he read made her assume that there was a child in his past that he was unable to save. Her assumption was accurate. Only she did not yet know that the child was his. Still though, she found James's emotion over the matter incredibly endearing, and it further added to her intrigue.

The same quiet mystique and rugged good looks that had captivated women about James in his school years, had now undoubtedly infected Amelia like some incurable virus. The symptoms had led to an unrelenting curiosity that had her stalking her lieutenant into the woods and eavesdropping on him in his most vulnerable moments. Her sneakiness was the only way for her to learn anything about James, since the ice he had encased himself in seemed impenetrable, even by a stunning woman who normally had the power to turn a man into a puddle. The mysteriousness of Lieutenant Adams only served to make Amelia Morrison even more eager to conquer the challenge of melting the icy wall he had erected around himself. Her nurturing nature lent to a burning need to mend his ice cold, broken heart, and to care for him like the wounded animal he seemed to be.

In quiet ways over the years, Amelia had made her interests in James known, always going above and beyond for him. She made his meals extra special and was always the first to diligently tend to any of his battle wounds. But still, James remained withdrawn and quiet. He offered her no smile or meaningful conversation, just a genuine thank you before he escaped back behind the solitude of his icy wall. Amelia would have felt a victory had he even gazed at her for more than a second. But even after all her efforts and the many life-saving successes she had achieved with James, he hardly glanced in her direction. Amelia would have been surprised if James even knew the color of her eyes. She certainly knew his. Every one of his exterior features had been thoroughly examined and filed away in her mind. What she now wanted to file away were the things about him that she could not see, things that were trapped in a mind that she surmised was equally as beautiful as he was. She wanted to know what made his intelligent mind tick, and perhaps even his fantasies ... *especially* those she could help him fulfill.

Now, after two years of giving James subtle cues, Amelia suddenly could not fight her urge to be bolder with him, especially after watching him at the creek today. The erotic show he was unwittingly putting on had turned her spark of lust into a raging inferno. She was now dying to know what occupied the thoughts of Lieutenant Adams ... dying even more for a certain part of him to occupy her body.

An hour after James had returned from his rendezvous in the creek, Amelia was in the medic tent cleaning medical utensils along with him. As usual, he was quiet as he went about his work. The flask in Amelia's inner coat pocket had been full prior to beginning her work. She dug inside to sneak another sip and realized that the blood-warming elixir was now empty. She had wanted to calm herself before capitalizing on the rare moment while all was quiet and she was alone with James. But even with an entire flask full of alcohol coursing through her veins, her heart suddenly began racing as she summoned the courage to speak to him. She swallowed hard, but her throat remained parched from her sudden onset of nerves. On wobbly legs, she turned around and saw two of James before she got her intoxicated eyes to focus. "Lieutenant?" she finally choked out.

Torn from his thoughts, James jumped when he heard his name. He turned around, looking surprised to see Amelia, despite the fact that she had been there with him for over an hour. "Yes, can I help you with somethin'?" he replied dryly, as usual.

Amelia moved closer, bringing her utensil with her to continue cleaning it next to him. "Nothin' important," she stated, managing to hide her tipsiness well. "I just umm ... I-I's kind of wonderin' somethin'?"

"What's that?"

"Do you..." She nervously looked down and then back up at James again. "Do you eva' get lonely here?"

James thought it was an odd question to be asked out of the blue, but he answered anyway. "Don't we all? I'm sure there's not a person in this camp who hasn't felt a twinge of loneliness bein' away from their family."

"I guess that's true," Amelia laughed nervously, still scrubbing a utensil that was now beyond clean.

"Loneliness seems to go hand in hand with war, I suppose. But why're you askin'?"

"Well, it's just that loneliness weighs heavily on me every day too. I just thought that sometimes it'd be nice to have a little company."

"I see."

"I figured the same would especially be true for a man," Amelia stated boldly.

"I certainly can't deny that," James replied.

"I figured as much. I'm quite sure the *comforts* of a woman would definitely help ease a man's loneliness."

Now realizing where her conversation was heading, James paused a moment. "What're you sayin', Amelia?"

Amelia looked down for a second, then found the confidence to gaze into James's eyes, and bravely step closer to him. "I'm sayin' that if eva' you're feelin' lonely, I'd love to be a *comfort* to you ... in the most important way a man needs *comfortin'*," Amelia said, the alcohol now finally controlling her words.

James stared at Amelia for a moment and then set his utensils down. "I'm not blind, Amelia. You're a beautiful woman ... but I'm married."

"Oh, I see. I didn't know. I-I'm sorry," she said, lowering her head in embarrassment.

"No need to be sorry. But I do thank you for the offa'." James then began to walk out of the tent, wanting to extinguish the sudden awkwardness of the moment.

Amelia, however, was far more eager to extinguish the fire James had set in her nether region. "Your wife wouldn't have to know," she said boldly, just as he was about to exit. A wave of surprise and shock then shot through her after realizing that the strapping man before her had driven her to spew such scandalous words. She swallowed hard when James stopped in his tracks and turned around. She felt her heart beating wildly against her ribcage as James approached her. He froze when he was within a foot of where she stood. Like she had always wanted, Lieutenant Adams was finally looking deep into her eyes with a prolonged gaze. She was the one who now found herself melting under the eyes of a man, the entire puddle seeming to pool between her thighs. His first sentence further heated her insides.

"I *desperately* miss the warmth, the taste, the feel, and the scent of a woman." James's eyes momentarily fluttered closed over the thought. "More than I have the words to adequately express." He opened his eyes and looked straight into Amelia's again. "But I don't wanna experience such things with any otha' woman than my wife. If eva' I did, Lily *would* know. Make no mistake about that. She'd sense it. She'd feel it. Without me eva' utterin' a single word about it, she'd know. She knows me just that well ... knows me betta' than I know myself," he said, a sudden rawness in his voice and a distant look now in his eyes. "Many times in the past, I've hurt my wife. I've broken promises to her and torn her heart clean outta her chest. I've made major mistakes that have crushed her *whole* world, in ways you couldn't possibly imagine. So, I'll be damned if I dishonor my vows to her and crush her world all ova' again in one foolish moment of indiscretion." He shook his head. "So quite frankly, Amelia, I don't care how beautiful you are, or how lonely I get, you'd neva' be a *comfort* to me ... you'd be a *mistake*. You and any otha' woman for that matta'."

The moisture that had pooled between Amelia's thighs had now risen to her eyes. Embarrassment crawled over her like a horrid skin rash, and she flushed a deep shade of red. She now wished to not only escape James's harsh gaze but to escape the Iron Army camp altogether.

When James turned around to leave this time, Harrison was standing near the exit of the tent. He had not caught the entire conversation, but after seeing the tears welling in Amelia's eyes, he feared his college fraternity brother had unintentionally broken another heart. He shook his head at James, berating him with his eyes about his lack of compassion when dealing with women in such circumstances. James ignored him, though, and stepped outside when he saw Austin in the distance.

Harrison approached Amelia when James left. "I've known the lieutenant for ova' a decade. He's an odd bird. Has feathers like no otha' damn bird I've eva' seen, actually," he joked. He placed a comforting hand on Amelia's shoulder. "Try not to let 'em get to you."

Too late for that, Amelia thought to herself. But she nodded, genuinely appreciating Harrison's comforting words. She then lowered her head and scurried away with her embarrassment in tow, after James had crushed her with a response that proved he was indeed the one-in-a-million faithful man that Lily had always deemed him to be.

After Amelia left, Harrison jogged to catch up with James, who was walking toward Austin.

Austin turned around after James tapped him on the shoulder. "There you are! Me and Harrison were lookin' for you earlia'," he said.

"Did you get any information out of Elijah?" James asked.

"Nah," Austin replied. "Fucker literally wouldn't say a word. Hell, even Harrison's lawyer integration methods were useless."

Harrison nodded. "The coward just laid there on the cot, holdin' the back of his head with his eyes closed, poutin' like a sissified little shit."

"What the hell'd he say to you to send you into a rage like that twice in one day?" Austin asked.

"It doesn't matta'," James replied, waving his hand dismissively. "Fuck 'em! Whetha' he confesses about the rest of what he knows or not, I'm gonna find my wife one day ... *alive*. And there's nothin' that arrogant, lyin' prick can say to convince me otha'wise."

Austin and Harrison both patted James hard on the back. "We're with ya'."

*****

The Iron Army Brigade of the East had marched for four hours to merge forces with the large brigade that Emerson and Wilson were in. They arrived just as night fell. Exhausted from their journey, nearly every soldier sat huddled around a bonfire, drinking heavily and exchanging insults. James refrained from drinking for a change. He sat there quietly as usual. Amelia was on the outskirts of the group, taking care of several men with blistered feet. After her mishap with alcohol

338

earlier, she also refused to drink. She was finally sober, but noticeably sadder than usual to everyone, except for James. He was solely focused on sharpening his bayonet.

As James mindlessly sharpened his weapon, a drunk soldier stumbled over and sat down close to him, landing with an uneasy thud. A pint of whisky had finally given the soldier the liquid courage to ask James a question he had been curious about for months. "Lieutenant?" he slurred.

"What do ya' want, Private Bradshaw?" James replied, sounding annoyed by his presence. He never even raised his eyes from his blade as he continued to sharpen it.

"Why the hell you always dreamin' about flowa's?"

"What?" James asked, sounding confused.

"Y'ur always hollerin' like a banshee about roses and lilies when ya' wake up some days. I'm just curious, what the hell's so nightmarish about flowa's?" Private Bradshaw asked, letting out a whistly drunken laugh. In his intoxicated state, he found his own rhetoric far more hilarious than it should have been.

James suddenly stopped sharpening his bayonet. The banter from all the other soldiers around the fire suddenly ceased and their eyes were on their lieutenant. Amelia refused to look in James's direction, but her ears perked as well. Other than a few tidbits about where James was from, the brigade did not know much about him. During his entire stint in the war, he had been far more focused on his mission than making friends and holding leisurely conversation. From the way everyone was suddenly staring at him, it was clear that the mysteriousness of his life had not only piqued Amelia's curiosity, but that of all his troops as well.

Knowing how the topic of Rose and Lily tended to affect James, Harrison and Austin suddenly glanced at each other, wondering if they should find a way to intervene. Just as Harrison decided it was best to change the subject, James suddenly spoke. "Lily is my wife," he stated calmly. "Rose is my daughta'. She passed away shortly afta' she was born." He gazed at the ground as he thought of them. "I guess it's natural for a man to dream about his family when he's away from them … especially since they're my motive for bein' here."

"Why the hell would they have anything to do with you fightin' against the south's rights to own slaves?" Private Bradshaw probed, while liquor still gave him the guts.

"Lily's a slave," James boldly replied. "Accordin' to the laws, that meant my daughta' was born and died one as well. So, I'm here in hopes of settin' my wife free."

Crickets and the crackling of the large bonfire were suddenly the only sounds in the entire camp. Knowing the shock that would be written all over everyone's faces, James did not even bother to look up, until he suddenly heard Private Bradshaw burst out in a fit of hysterical laughter. He was the only fool drunk enough to do so, though. Everyone else was wise enough to keep their silence after remembering what James had done to Elijah earlier. Amelia was especially silent. Hearing about Rose made her feel ten times worse about her earlier actions.

"You're wife's a goddamn slave?!" Bradshaw said through his drunken, whistly laughter. "That's a good one! You had me goin'!"

James looked at the cackling man out of the side of his eye and tightened the grip on his weapon. Harrison and Austin suddenly tensed, both looking ready to grab James before he did something he regretted. But James took into consideration that the man was thoroughly inebriated, and he responded calmly, "it's the truth."

Bradshaw finally sobered and ceased his laughter. "Wait a minute … that' ain't no joke?"

James just stared at the man with a serious look on his face.

"If she was a slave, then how in the hell is she *legally* your wife?" Bradshaw asked, looking perplexed.

"There's no law that takes precedence ova' a vow I made to God. In the eyes of our immortal Lord, Lily's my wife." James looked straight at Bradshaw. "And I'm here doin' my part to change our inhumane backwards mortal laws … and to free my *wife*."

"And so am I," Austin added, wanting to make it known that he was James's ally.

"Why? You married to 'er too?" Bradshaw joked, attempting to lighten the mood.

Austin proceeded to speak over everyone's laughter. "I's a percussionist in 'er symphony, actually."

"*Symphony?*" one of the new brigade members questioned, looking at Austin oddly.

Austin nodded. "The Dream Symphony," he said, a great amount of pride in his voice. He motioned his head in James's direction. "The lieutenant's wife composed the entire show and played piano."

"A piano playin', music composin' slave?" Bradshaw replied with another hearty laugh. "Now, I ain't buyin' that shit this time."

"I tell no lies, my friend. She's the single greatest piano playa' I've eva' laid eyes on," Austin replied. "Hell, probably the best that's eva' walked this earth."

"Wait a minute. *The Dream Symphony?* The show with the dancin' shadows?" another soldier asked Austin.

"Thee one and only!" Austin replied.

The soldier turned to look at James. "The composa' of that show is *your wife?*"

James nodded. "She is," he boasted proudly.

"Well, hell's bells! I saw that show up in Chicago!" the soldier further explained, a hint of excitement in his voice as he reminisced about it. "My wife dragged me to see it. I didn't feel like sittin' through no damn symphony... was just doin' what the wife wanted for a change." He shook his head. "But I'll be damned if I wasn't left mesmerized by the time it was ova'. I don't think I blinked through the whole show. Damn show was so good, I tried to buy tickets on the way out, so we could go back the next night and see it all ova' again." He laughed at himself. "I's mad as hell when they told me they were sold out."

"That doesn't surprise me. There were neva' any empty seats at 'er shows," James replied.

As Amelia discreetly watched James, she saw a genuine smile emerge as he spoke of Lily. It was the first time she had ever seen such an expression on his face. Despite being rejected by him earlier, she could not help but wish he would smile at her that way.

The more Bradshaw listened, the more he seemed to sober. "Wait a minute! So, you mean this fucker's tellin' the truth?" he asked, pointing to Austin.

"He sure is!" another soldier answered. "My wife dragged me to the Dream Symphony when it was playin' in Jamestown. We even got to meet Lily at the post-show gala. Your wife's truly a lovely lady. You're one hell of a lucky guy," he said, nodding in James's direction.

James nodded in return. "Tell me somethin' I don't know."

"Me and my wife saw the show *twice* in Pennsylvania!" another random soldier bragged. "I scrounged up the money to take the kids on the second go-round. I felt they just had to see it!"

"My wife and I took our kids to the show too," another soldier added. "My little girl came home sayin', 'I wanna play piano like that pretty lady, daddy. I wanna play piano just like her!' You know kids, though. They'll be fascinated by somethin' for a day or two and then it passes … but not with this. For weeks and weeks, my little girl begged me every day to play piano, until I finally caved and got 'er some lessons. She was only four. She's nearly nine now, and she's been playin' damn near every day since. Says she wants to put on her own symphony one day," the soldier smiled as he thought about his ambitious daughter. He looked over at James. "I owe my little girl's life dream to your wife."

James nodded, his proud grin still in place.

"I unda'stand why it stuck with my little girl the way it did," the soldier continued. "That was far and away the greatest stage show I've eva' seen. Your wife told such captivatin' stories. To this day, I still rememba' 'em all with such detail. And I've neva' heard music like that eva' before in my life. It was truly spellbindin'. I can still hear it playin' in my head. It's the kind of music that you hope neva' fades away from your mind."

"Thank you," James replied. "Lily'd be humbled to hear that."

"Any of the stories in the show true?" the man curiously asked.

James nodded. "The story of how we became friends as children." His voice trailed off and his eyes hovered to the ground as he thought of Lily.

"I rememba' that! You were the sneaky kid spyin' on 'er from behind trees," the soldier laughed.

James shook his head and laughed lightly. "That was me."

"Hell, my wife would've portrayed me as that goddamn fire-breathin' dragon!" another soldier joked.

Everyone suddenly burst out laughing.

"I rememba' that dragon too!" a different soldier announced. "Them goddamn explosions eruptin' on the sides of the stage almost made me shit myself!"

The entire brigade roared with laughter.

"All you fuckers are lucky," another soldier added after listening to everyone's stories. "I tried to get my wife tickets for the Christmas show at Winta' Garden in Manhattan, but an old fucker in front of me bought the last damn pair."

"I lucked out and saw it there!" another soldier bragged. "You missed one hell of a show!"

"Rub it in, ya' little shit! I knew I should've whupped that old man's ass in the street and snatched his tickets!" the man replied, riling up another hearty round of laughter.

The way the first few soldiers recounted their Dream Symphony experiences with such enthusiasm was infectious. Suddenly, one barbaric soldier after another began sharing how they unexpectedly became emotional as they watched Lily's show. Their vibrantly told stories made it seem as though the brilliant light, music, and shadows were playing and dancing before everyone's eyes all over again. In a freezing place, covered in blood stains and heavy with the stench of death, the Dream Symphony managed to bring warmth, camaraderie, laughter, and a much-needed boost in morale to a band of battered, broken soldiers. As James absorbed the love his men expressed for Lily and her show, he was now the one who felt himself becoming unexpectedly emotional.

From a distance, Amelia gazed at James. He was lost in a hypnotic trance, reliving the show in his mind. As everyone spoke fondly about his wife, the joy on his face was easy for Amelia to see. She had become teary-eyed after hearing the hint of emotion in his voice when he briefly spoke about Rose and Lily. The love she heard in his tone further deepened her guilt for her earlier actions, yet, simultaneously, made her want James more. She so desperately wished it was her that was motivating the look of pure pride she now saw etched into his features.

James suddenly came out of his trance when a question was directed at him.

"What the hell eva' happened to your wife's show, lieutenant? When I couldn't get tickets to the Winta' Garden performance, I tried to find out where her next show was gonna be, so I could surprise my wife with a trip. The show was so popular, but it's like it vanished without a trace."

"In a way it did. That Christmas night was Lily's last show. When my fatha' found out about 'er symphony, he showed up at Winta' Garden and dragged 'er back to his farm. He had a bill of sale that gave 'em the right to end it all ... right there in the back hall of that theata'."

"Why the hell would any slave owna' be against a show that could've made 'em a boatload of money?" the soldier asked, looking bewildered.

"My fatha' isn't exactly the kind of man that would be ova'joyed by a slave makin' a name for herself ... money or not."

"Well, no offense, but y'ur fatha' sounds like a damn fool if he prefers for a brilliant pianist to pick cotton on his farm, earnin' dimes ova' dolla's."

"*Fool* is an unda'statement. He's a goddamn *demon* ... a demon I tried like hell to help Lily escape from, so she could get back on the life path she deserved to be on."

"*Tried?*" the man questioned. "And succeeded ... I hope."

James swallowed hard. "Yes and no."

"What do you mean?" the man asked.

"I tried to help 'er ... but such a thing is nearly impossible when you're livin' in a country that's constructed invisible barriers for people like Lily."

"Aww hell, now our country's government is to blame, huh? I ain't heard that one before," Private Bradshaw laughed, attempting and failing at a joke.

No one found the statement funny, especially James. "It's a fact that the laws and slave codes written by our nation's government have bred demons like my fatha'. Men like my fatha' know every loophole in the laws that allow them to get away with whateva' they want ... up to and includin' cold-blooded murda'," James stated, not bothering to even glance at Bradshaw. "Those laws emboldened my fatha' to feel as though he was well within his rights to beat Lily half to death for tryna escape the hellish life he had her imprisoned in. The laws gave 'em every bit of confidence that there would neva' be any consequences for it ... nor for killin' our baby eitha'. For the entire thirty-six minutes my daughta' lived, slave codes stated that a demon owned her, and every breath she fought to take. Loopholes allowed a purebred demon to strip 'er of her life, without so much as a monetary fine, or a disapprovin' glance in his direction.

"Those laws have now bred an army of self-righteous Confederate monsta's with cannons and guns, ready to kill to maintain the right to snatch a woman's dreams away on a whim, to viciously beat the woman you love without so much as a slap on the wrist ... to kill a man's only child and get away with it. Our nation's laws have led the Confederacy to feel as though oppressin' those they deem inferior is their fundamental right. Southerners now feel entitled to have this nation built on free labor, to have their children nourished by the breasts of their chattel, to have their food cooked and their fields plowed without forkin' ova' a penny to their workers ... not even afta' back-breakin', life-givin' services have been rendered. Laws that have managed to sway an entire nation to see humans as profitable products has even given rise to money-hungry, backwoods slave trada's, one's who felt Lily was an object valuable enough to steal, no different than a thief in the night, sneakin' off with a trunk full of jewelry. The unjustifiable laws of this land have cost me *everything* ... even the knowledge of what new piece of shit demon now owns my wife."

James stood up and began looking every soldier in the eyes who had previously spoken about Lily's show. He stopped when his eyes landed on the man in front of him. "The woman you just deemed as a brilliant pianist couldn't even walk past 'er plantation gates without a goddamn permission slip, because of the backwards laws of this land." He turned to the man on his left. "The woman you were willin' to beat an old man's ass to see was nearly beaten to death for wantin' to continue her dreams." He turned to another man. "The woman your little girl longs to be just like had her own little girl senselessly murdered." He glanced at another soldier. "A woman whose dream stories you paid twice to see, is now likely livin' in a daily nightmare." He turned and glanced at everyone. "The woman whose show you were all dragged kickin' and screamin' to see by your wives, was dragged away kickin' and screamin' by slave trada's in the dead of night."

He finally glanced at drunken Private Bradshaw. "And so yes, the laws and codes written by our nation hold some responsibility for the unspeakable things my fatha' and brotha' did to Lily and my daughta' the day I tried to help them escape. Yes! Our nation holds some responsibility for the horrific circumstances that led to Lily and me bein' separated that night. Yes! The government holds some responsibility for why I don't know who or where my wife has been sold to. Yes! Backwards laws are why I haven't held my wife for years. Yes! Backwards laws are partially to blame for why there's nothin' left of my daughta' but a skeleton and the memory of 'er tiny face. Yes! Our nation's laws are responsible for the hauntin' nightmares I now suffa' afta' watchin' 'er die in my arms!"

James took a deep breath to calm his rising rage, his chest visibly heaving before it slowly settled. "Laws that only eva' ensure huge financial profit and political gain. Laws that ensure slaves only eva' be compensated with pain and sufferin' for all their hard work. Politically and financially thrivin' off the brutal free labor of otha's … that's the sort of powa' and control the Confederacy is fightin' for. They're willin' to slash the hearts of every Union soldier to maintain that level of powa' ova' a class of people they've deemed inferior … includin' one of the most brilliant women eva' born on this earth.

"My Lily and my little Rose. They're the reasons I'm here. I wanna rob the Confederacy of the powa' they have to get away with the despicable things my fatha' and brotha' did to my wife and daughta'. I wanna help us move toward a nation where *everyone* in these United States has the right to open a store, stay home and be a lovin' motha', or an artist, a teacha', or present her musical dreams in a symphony to a bunch of bums like us, without the laws of this country standin' in the way like a goddamn brick wall. Anyone who has a dream in this country should have the right to decide to pursue it. That should neva' be decided by some demon who owns them.

"We need to win this war. There are no ifs, ands, or buts about it. We need to win. For every woman like Lily, who wants to maintain owna'ship of their dreams. For every fatha'…" He paused and swallowed hard. "For every fatha' like me who wants to experience the joys of fatha'hood without fear of their child bein' taken away … or senselessly murdered." He again swallowed the lump in his throat. "We *need* to win this war … there are no otha' fuckin' options."

The last of his words seemed to harmonize beautifully with the chirping crickets and crackling bonfire. His whole speech resonated like Lily's music in everyone's ears, bringing a hint of tears to their eyes in much the same way too.

James walked away before his own tears had a chance to escape in front of his men. He breezed past Amelia, who hid her face as she wiped away the tears in her eyes. There was no need to hide her face, though. James had not noticed her; he had locked eyes with Elijah. He was sitting on a tree stump on the outskirts of the group, sharpening the blade on his bayonet as he glared at James with lowered eyelids. James reciprocated the glare, daring him with his eyes to use his weapon. James was not surprised that Elijah seemed unaffected by his words. However, James was surprised that a drunken question had revealed how the Dream Symphony had impacted such hardened soldiers. Such a touching thing led James to feel equally unaffected by Elijah for once. He breezed past him with no urge to choke the man for a change.

James walked back to his tent on a high, his pride at immeasurable levels. The fact that his men still remembered Lily with such fondness all these years later reaffirmed to James that she was a woman born for greatness. He reached in his backpack and took out the book that was meant as Lily's first birthday gift. James suddenly had an epiphany as he gazed at it. In some ways, the man who bought it was responsible for the mesmerizing symphony that had inspired a band of barbaric soldiers. One tragic day had been a critical turning point in Lily's life that set the wheels in motion for the beginning of her musical journey. It was a journey that ultimately had a ripple effect on him, Austin, his soldiers ... and even a president. It was one tragic day that caused James to weep the day he read about it through the tear-filled eyes of Levi Collins ...

Chapter Twenty

January 13, 1845

Twenty-four hours, most often an innocuous time period that drifts by without a second thought. On busy days, some people wish they had an extra sixty minutes, but today I wished I had an extra sixty years. Every microsecond of the next twenty-four hours will undoubtedly be the most excruciating of my life ...

Levi tiptoed into the chicken coop and quietly snuck up behind Maya. "Feelin' any betta'?" he suddenly asked.

Startled, Maya quickly turned around, dropping her empty basket. "Oh lord!" she laughed at herself, placing her hand over her heart. "You're as sneaky as a cat, I swear."

Levi laughed. "I's hopin' my sneaky ways could get this beautiful smile to emerge," he said, softly brushing the back of his hand along her cheek. "I ain't seen it much since that nasty cold took a hold of ya'. Your symptoms subsidin' at all yet?"

Maya's smile broadened. "Yes, definitely! I feel *much* betta' today. I owe that to your cat-like ability to sneak me some medicine ... and that amazin' homemade soup!" Levi had snuck the old family remedy into Maya's room and left it at her bedside while she was napping with Lily. She had opened an eye and caught him leaving as he hurried out.

"You liked it then?" Levi asked.

"*Loved* it! It was really good. Worked wonders for my sore throat."

"I'm glad to hear that. I'm not well unless you are," Levi said, tenderly placing his hand on Maya's cheek. His gentle touch sparked warmth from Maya … but sparked instantaneous rage inside his wife, who just so happened to catch a glimpse of the rare, fleeting moment.

Emily had forgotten her purse while heading into town and had returned to retrieve it from the kitchen counter. She glanced out of the back window just as Levi placed his hand on Maya's cheek. She then slowly stepped out onto the back porch to get a better view, and saw the way that Maya covered Levi's hand with hers as it rested on her cheek. With her mouth agape, Emily continued to glare at the pair as Maya closed her eyes, tilted her head, and melted into Levi's touch. The way Levi then gently kissed Maya on the forehead, and embraced her, turned Emily's smoldering rage into an inferno.

Surprisingly, in all the years that Maya had been there, Emily had never once seen an interaction like that between the pair. It was a moment like that that Emily was trying to catch during the months she had randomly shown up in the barn after Lily's birth. But she had never caught them doing anything more exciting than milking cows and shoveling horse manure out of stalls. They were such an excruciating bore that Emily finally ceased her efforts at literally trying to catch her husband with his pants down. However, she never knew that the boring scene in the barn was a facade.

For years, Maya and Levi had been extraordinarily careful with their actions around all the children, especially Lily. Keeping their feelings a secret was a responsibility they both took very seriously. But Levi's loving nature made it impossible for him to refrain from expressing his emotions for Maya in small ways whenever he was confident they were alone. As they stood in the chicken coop together, he assumed it was one of those moments. As misfortune would have it, Emily had caught a glimpse of an extremely rare moment when Maya and Levi had let their guards down. The display of affection was over in seconds, but their brief encounter would soon prove to carry hefty, lifelong consequences.

Levi emerged from the chicken coop, walked toward the barn, but froze when he saw his wife still on the farm. He was certain she had already left to take Dallas to the dentist in town. His heart picked up pace when he noticed the anger in Emily's body language as she scurried up the steps to Maya's cottage. Levi glanced back at Maya, who was still gathering eggs, oblivious to the fact that they had likely been spotted. He then began trotting toward the cottage to see what trouble his wife was about to cause.

A few times in the past, Emily had snooped in Maya's room in search of more proof as to her husband's continued infidelity. She was certain that she would find prophylactics or perhaps some of Levi's clothing. However, her random sneaky searches had never yielded any damning evidence. Maya had created a secret compartment inside her wall that she was always sure to keep her telescope and music box hidden in. In Emily's state of hysteria this time, though, she began ransacking Maya's room like a mad woman. As she tossed items around in a blinding rage, she accidentally loosened the plank on the hidden compartment. The music box immediately fell out. Emily nearly threw up when she opened the lid and saw the color of the two figurines dancing to the piano tune. Even though Emily hated Levi, the beautiful creation in her hands suddenly caused her to burn with jealousy. Never had her husband expressed his feelings for her in such a way. In fact, it had been years since he said that he loved her at all. Even then, she could feel his words to be more out of obligation than truth. He had certainly never bothered to hand make her anything, *ever.* Only Emily's desire to keep digging inside the wall stopped her from hurling the music box across the room and shattering it into pieces. As she was pulling out the telescope, Levi finally entered Maya's room.

Emily quickly turned around, her face fire red as she glared at Levi. "Did you make this for your whore?!" she shouted, thrusting Maya's music box in his face.

Levi just stared at his seething wife without saying a word.

"What about this telescope?! Did you spend *our money* to buy this for her?!"

Again, Levi did not reply.

"You had the audacity to spend *money* on that whore?!" she screamed, slamming the telescope down on the bed.

Levi pinched the bridge of his nose and blew out a frustrated breath.

"DO YOU LOVE HER?!" Emily suddenly spat.

"Lily's my daughta'! Of course I love her!" Levi fired back.

"I don't mean that little heathen! I'm talkin' about your whore!"

"Why the hell do you care, Emily? You've neva' loved me!"

"ANSWER THE DAMN QUESTION!"

"YES, I LOVE HER!" Levi erupted.

Burned by Levi's bold confession, Emily gasped, took a step back, and stared at him with scathing eyes. Loving Lily was one thing. But now, learning the true depth of his feelings for Maya instantly plunged her into madness. Emily tossed the music box onto the bed and stepped toward her husband, her eyelids lowered into angry slits. "For nearly ten years, I've kept quiet about the fact that your demon spawn is runnin' wild around this farm! And now you have the audacity to look me in the eyes and tell me you're in love with her motha'! I refuse to take any more of your blatant disrespect! You've humiliated me

353

enough!" She put a finger in Levi's face. "I want you to get rid of 'er," she said through tightly pursed lips.

"Jesus Christ, Emily! Don't you think you're overreactin' about this!"

"*Overreactin'*?!" She threw her hands on her hips. "My husband fucks a slave, has a baby with 'er, and now I find out he's in love with 'er, and you think I'm *overreactin'*?! You're lucky I don't divorce you, take your boys, and throw you off this property! There ain't a court in the United States that would grant you a thing on this farm afta' I tell 'em about the cheatin', nigga' lovin', son of a bitch that you are! I want 'er gone or that'll be your future!"

"I'm not gettin' rid of Maya! We hardly have any help on this farm as it is!"

"Not your *whore!* Your *illegitimate mutt!* I want 'er gone!"

"Have you gone mad?! Lily's innocent in this!"

"I don't care! I don't wanna spend anotha' day starin' at your *abomination!*"

Levi pinched the bridge of his nose and blew out a frustrated breath while trying to think of a way to deescalate the situation and silence the irritating sound of his wife's voice. *As long as we have each otha', we'll be alright*, Levi suddenly recalled Maya telling him years before. Selling Maya and Lily was the last thing he wanted to do, but he was certain that he would have some semblance of peace, so long as they remained together. "Fine Emily. If it'll give you peace, I'll take 'em both down to the auction this weekend. That's the end of this conversation. I don't eva' wanna hear a word about this again," he replied, taking a step to leave.

"Oh no," Emily replied. "I neva' said anything about sellin' your whore."

Levi froze. "What?"

"You heard me. I only want that heathen outta here. *Not* your whore!"

"Goddamn it, Emily! There's no way in hell I'm sellin' that little girl away from 'er motha'!"

"Don't you mean sell 'er away from *you?!* Don't think I neva' saw you sneakin' in here to give that little mongrel all the stupid presents you made 'er for Christmas! I saw you wakin' up at the crack of dawn to pick them damn apples off the tree for her! I see the way you stare at 'er now with that stupid grin on your face, gazin' at 'er with pride in your eyes, like you were responsible for producin' the world's next queen, when Lord knows she ain't gonna do nothin' but grow up and be a whore just like 'er motha'!"

Levi suddenly gripped Emily hard by the chin. It took every bit of his strength not to slap every drop of saliva out of her mouth instead. "Watch your goddamn mouth!" he snarled through gritted teeth. "Don't you have a bottle of liquor to shove in this filthy trap of yours instead of standin' here insultin' my daughta'?!"

"Take your damn hands off of me!" Emily yelled, slapping him across the face. "I want your little creature gone!"

"For what?!" Levi bit back, unfazed by the blow. "Maya's the one you're bothered by!"

"That's *exactly* why I want 'er to stay right here on this plantation! I know how much she loves that little bastard! I wanna watch 'er suffa' without 'er daughta', just the way I've had to suffa' *with* 'er! I wanna watch 'er kick and scream and holla' as you drag that little mongrel away from here. I wanna see 'er drop to her knees in agony and wail like a dyin' animal. Day afta' day, I wanna watch as she slowly shrivels and dies without 'er daughta'! And *you* too! I wanna watch you *both* mourn the loss of your little mutt! It's my turn to watch you *both* ache the way I have! I wanna see those pathetic tears in your eyes as you drag your little bastard outta here! I wanna see the way your whore recoils at your touch. I wanna see the coldness in 'er eyes every time she glares at you! I want 'er to *hate* you as much as I do!"

"I don't give a damn what you want, Emily! So, I'm gonna say this one more time! I *refuse* to tear Maya and Lily apart! I'll sell 'em both *togetha'!* Now, this conversation is ova'!"

"If you don't get rid of that little creature, I swear to God, I'll ruin you! I'll spread it all ova' this town that you're a *nigga' lova'!* I'll see to it that you rot in prison for procreatin' with a slave!"

"I'll do the hard time with a smile on my face before I sell that little girl away from 'er motha'!" Levi snarled. He then turned around to leave.

"I figured you'd say that ... *nigga' lova'!* Don't think your noble sacrifice of doin' hard time is gonna save your mutt and your whore from bein' torn apart. While you're rottin' in prison, I'll sell the little heathen my damn self!"

Levi froze near the door but kept his back turned, too disgusted to look at his wife.

"And I'll be sure to give 'er that long ova'due whippin' before I sell 'er off to a place where you'll neva' find 'er," she added coldly.

Levi spun around, his face fiery red as he glared angrily at his wife.

"Hmph, I figured that would stop you in your tracks," Emily snickered, glaring just as hatefully back at him. "One way or anotha' ... she's leavin' this damn farm."

"What happens to Lily, happens to you," Levi said through gritted teeth. "I already warned you."

"Be kinda hard for you to retaliate behind bars, now won't it?" Emily taunted.

"Take your anga' out on *me!* Not Lily! Not Maya! *Me!* Leave them outta this!"

"Hell, you're so caught up in tryna be your whore's hero that you haven't even once thought about the impact all of this will have on your own sons, have you?"

Levi's eyes hovered to the ground when his sons suddenly bombarded his mind. His facial expression softened, and his demeanor instantly changed.

Emily smirked when she noticed her words had finally taken the fight out of him. "If there's anything you love more than your whore, it's those snot-nosed little boys. And I know how much they respect and love you too. I hear you preachin' to 'em all the time about bein' respectful to women, tryna teach 'em to be upstandin', God-fearin' gentlemen who abide strictly by God's laws! You always prancin' around here on your moral high horse! Got your boys lookin' up at you like you're some kind of *god.* They probably swear you shit roses and piss holy wata'! But little do they know, you ain't nothin' but a sinna' shrouded in a holy robe! I'll snatch you down off that horse, rip that robe clean off you, and unveil the *devil* you really are, right before their very eyes! I'll destroy all the respect they have for you in a heartbeat! I'll tell 'em how their fatha' is a self-professed God-fearin', hypocritical adulterer! A *nigga' lovin'* adulterer at that! I wonda' how they'll feel when I tell 'em the little slave girl they been playin' with all these years is actually their bastard half-sista'?!"

"What the hell kind of motha' would consida' hurtin' her own sons that way?"

Emily threw her hands on her hips and cocked her head to the side. "One who doesn't give a damn about the little monsta's you ejaculated into me. They ruined my life ... I'd just be returnin' the fava'," she replied smugly.

Her vulgar statement made Levi's face twist in utter disgust. "You're *clearly* the only *monsta'* in this family."

"JUST GET RID OF YOUR BASTARD!" Emily huffed and stepped closer to Levi. "And if I have to lift a finga' to do it, you can rest assured, I'll drag her outta here without an ounce of flesh left on 'er back! If you wanna maintain the respect of your sons and keep your bastard's back unscathed, I suggest you get 'er outta here with your own two hands! If not, your little mulatto mistake *and* your sons will suffa' dearly! The choice is yours!" She stepped toward the door and turned around one last time before exiting. "You have twenty-four hours!" she warned before storming out of the cottage.

With a deep-creased scowl ingrained on his face, Levi glared out the window of the cottage as his wife fled following her ultimatum. But Lily and Maya quickly stole his attention. They were far off in the distance, folding a sheet together that they had just taken down from the clothesline. The mother and daughter were talking and laughing as they went about their duties, completely unaware of the fact that a life-altering countdown had just begun. For the time being, Levi wanted to keep them both floating in the bliss of ignorance, while he thought of how to resolve the situation. He quickly began putting Maya's room back in order, so she did not suspect anything was amiss. *As long as we have each otha', we'll be okay,* replayed in Levi's mind as he straightened up the room. That notion had been proven for nine years at that point. Despite their circumstances, Maya and Lily seemed happy, blissfully so. Seeing how much they loved each other had helped ease the pain of not having the father-daughter relationship with Lily that he had yearned for. Despite being forbidden to interact with her, he still cherished watching her grow. He picked up one of the many stuffed ragdolls that he had made and secretly left in Lily's room for Christmas. The one in his hand seemed to be her favorite. She had carried it everywhere when she was smaller. Its missing eye and tattered ends were further proof of how attached she was to it. Seeing her joy over such things from a distance had given Levi solace. But now Lily's joy and his solace were in jeopardy ... and so, too, was

Maya's. As that fact crossed Levi's mind, teardrops suddenly landed in the cloth eye socket of the ragdoll in his hands.

Levi's attention was stolen again when he glanced out of the window and saw Emily screaming at Dallas. When the eight-year-old was not moving fast enough for her taste, she snatched him by the arm and dragged him back to the wagon. She was being unnecessarily nasty to him, like she so often was with all her boys. Emily's unwarranted outbursts were one of the things that made Levi hate her with an extreme passion, and so too did the fact that this was not the first time that he had to contemplate selling a child because of her foolish actions ...

Early in their marriage, Levi arrived home one day to find a foreclosure notice inside his mailbox. It was not the first. It was the third and final one. Emily had gone about hiding the other foreclosure notices, along with all the other bills she had failed to pay for months. She would have hidden that final foreclosure notice too, had she gotten to it first. Levi trusted his wife with handling their finances. He, therefore, assumed the notice was a mistake, or that there was a logical explanation. But that was far from the case.

After Levi confronted Emily about the foreclosure notice, she had no choice but to come clean about the true depths of their financial disaster. The revelation led to Levi learning that his wife's addiction to alcohol not only made her mean and cold, but reckless and stupid as well. Instead of paying their debts, Emily's drunken trips into town were spent squandering their meager income on frivolous shopping sprees, and even sometimes gambled away on horse races. After their confrontation, Emily finally led Levi to the stockpiles of liquor, clothes, jewelry, shoes, and gambling receipts she had hoarded away in their attic.

An internal rage kept Levi from speaking to his wife for days. Knowing she was the sole cause for nearly losing everything, he feared the sort of venomous words he may spew at her. Fueled by his fury, he tore angrily through the attic instead. He threw everything that Emily had accumulated into his wagon and spent the weekend reselling every bit of it to various thrift stores. He even peddled off the liquor for cheap to any wino he could find drifting through town. But the money he reclaimed for the items barely put a dent in the amount he owed on his mortgage. For two weeks thereafter, he worked around the clock in the fields, and sold every pound of cotton and tobacco he could haul. Still, he was short on his mortgage. He then resorted to doing odd jobs for people in town. Even so, he was just days away from having no place for his three little boys and his then-pregnant wife to live. Levi Collins was beyond desperate.

With three days remaining until the bank seized his property, Levi got out of his bed after tossing and turning for hours. He went downstairs and sat alone at his kitchen table, with only the moon shining through the window as his light. The light beamed directly onto the glass of whiskey he was nursing. It was the first time his tongue was numbed by liquor since the night he had impregnated Emily at the church retreat. The life-altering decision that alcohol had led to that night had cemented his distaste for numbing elixirs that impaired his rationale. But on this night, the horrible thing he was contemplating doing made him *want* to impair his mind. He wanted to feel nothing, to deaden all his pain, especially the excruciating pain in his heart.

After hours of drinking, Levi was indeed numb. He could barely feel his feet beneath him as he stumbled drunkenly across the fields that morning, headed toward Nora's eleven-year-old son, Timothy. With whiskey fueling his courage and tears brewing in his eyes, he wrestled Timothy away from Nora and sold him at an auction. When Timothy did not earn enough to cover the rest of what he owed to the bank, Levi took another slave's little boy to auction the following day. On the final day that his home was due to be repossessed, he then sold Nora's younger son, Daniel. When the auction ended, Levi walked into the bank with a heavy heart. He then handed the bank teller a stack of bills that he felt was not even close to the true value of the three little boys he had just snatched away from their parents. However, in the bank's eyes, that money held enough value to cease the repossession of his farm.

Levi had wanted to sell the parents and children together, but the adult labor was vital to keeping his farm afloat and his children fed. The irony of destroying families to take care of his own nearly gave Levi an ulcer. For weeks after selling those children, he could barely bring himself to eat or sleep. He was easily irritated and hard to be around as he fought to emotionally heal from his acts of cruelty.

Maya had only been working at the farm for a year at that point, but she easily sensed the shift in Levi's demeanor. The kind-hearted, calm Levi she had come to know seemed to have disappeared overnight. And Maya was confident that selling those children had triggered the drastic change in his mood. It left her believing that it was never something he actually wanted to do. Still though, like all the slaves on the plantation, Maya was angry with Levi for his decision. At the same time, however, she was unable to shake a deep feeling of empathy for him. Her empathy led her to approach Levi after she saw him kick a pail of cow's milk clear across the barn for seemingly no reason at all. But Maya was certain she knew the source of his agitation. After seeing Levi sit down on a stool and bury his face in his hands afterward, Maya bravely walked up behind him and placed a comforting hand on his shoulder.

Levi jumped and stood up. "What do you want?!" he yelled, thinking it was his wife who had just touched him. He turned around and immediately felt guilty for his actions when he saw Maya standing there with her head lowered, her body quivering, looking deathly afraid.

"I-I just come to say that I-I'll finish up the c-cows and cleanin' the stalls … i-if m-maybe you'd like to go on and t-take your boys f-fishin' for the afta'noon instead." Maya kept her eyes aimed at the ground. She knew that her offer had the chance of being met with a punishment, but she hoped that Levi would show mercy for her empathy.

A punishment was far from Levi's mind. All he could think about at that moment was how he wished that Maya had not removed her hand. He had secretly wanted that touch for months. He now *needed* that touch. He needed to feel the hand of someone who was empathetic to his plight. He was floored by the fact that, of all people, that empathy had come from someone who owed him nothing but vehement anger. With tears suddenly stinging his eyes, Levi gazed at Maya and fell even more in love with her than he already secretly was. "Afta' what I did, I don't think I deserve such an honor with my boys," he whispered, his head weighed down by shame.

With her head meekly lowered too, Maya never saw the way Levi's lips quivered as he spoke, but she indeed saw his tears as they pelted his shirt before he solemnly walked away.

… The three sons that Levi could not bring himself to take fishing that afternoon had appeared as flashes in his mind when he auctioned off the three young boys from his farm. As the bids came in, he had envisioned his sons standing on the auction block instead. The imagery made his stomach do violent flips. He had felt a blend of guilt and gratefulness that the fortune of his race prevented him from ever having to experience such a devastating loss against his will. At the time, he had thanked God for the fact that he would only ever have to imagine a scenario so painful. But now, all these years later, Levi Collins was having to face the possibility of knowing full well what it was like to have his very own child staring down at him from an auction block. With minutes suddenly seeming to pass like seconds, Levi glanced at his pocket watch. The following day, his wife had demanded that he live out that scenario in living color ... at precisely 12:32 p.m.

With only twenty-four hours to make a decision, Levi stepped out of Maya's cottage, suddenly feeling keenly aware of time. He swore the watch in his pocket was ticking as loudly as a grandfather clock. He swore every movement of the pocket watch's hands were thumping against his leg like a sledgehammer, painfully counting down the most agonizing hours of his life.

Levi stood in a trance outside of Maya's cottage, thinking about how brief moments in time, and split-second decisions, could prove to have lifelong consequences, either for the better ... or for the worse. As he watched Emily riding off in the wagon to take their son to the dentist, he was reminded of the latter part of that fact. He then glanced back over at Maya. It took a millisecond for him to fall in love with her. It had taken seven seconds of euphoric pleasure inside her body to conceive a child with her. Though fleeting as those moments were, they had changed Levi's life forever ... for the *better*. And now, an affectionate exchange in a chicken coop, lasting less than a minute, had led to a twenty-four-hour ultimatum that had the power to dramatically change a little girl's life, for the rest of the days she spent on Earth. Yes. Time, and life-altering decisions, were all that Levi Collins could think about on January thirteenth of 1845.

12:34 p.m.: Levi had watched Emily leave the farm to take Dallas to the dentist.

12:40 p.m.: Levi was angrily sifting through Emily's liquor cabinet for the strongest thing he could find. The smell of alcohol usually only reminded him of the night that led him to be shackled for a lifetime to a woman whom he now detested. The last time he had had any liquor was the day he sold the three boys on his farm. But at 12:42 p.m., after several years without a drop of alcohol in his system, Levi proceeded to drink ... *heavily.*

12:45 p.m.: Levi wearily wandered upstairs with a full whiskey bottle in hand, went into his bedroom, and locked the door. He sat down next to the window and watched his only daughter in the distance, as he began contemplating what to do to remedy his situation, in a way that would satisfy all parties.

1:00 p.m.: Levi was still sitting at the window, guzzling whiskey, contemplating what to do about his predicament, and watching his daughter. He was recalling the many times he had peered in the window of Maya's cottage, and seen Lily and her mother playing the song in the music box, and dancing ... *together.*

1:27 p.m.: Levi momentarily stopped contemplating, watching Lily, and reflecting while he refilled his glass with more whiskey, for the *third* time.

1:28 p.m.: Levi resumed guzzling whiskey, contemplating, watching Lily, and reflecting on the times he had seen her and Maya sneaking away at night with their telescope to name the stars ... *together.*

2:16 p.m.: While still sipping, contemplating, and watching Lily, Levi recalled how every Christmas "Santa Claus" would quietly sneak into Lily's room and deliver a gift for her. When she was four, "Santa Claus" had handmade her a rag doll with Lily's light brown skin tone, with hair and eye color that resembled hers as well. Years later, Levi still saw Lily holding onto that ragdoll as she slept cuddled up in her mother's arms, both looking comfortable and happy ... *together.*

2:17 p.m.: Watching Lily, contemplating, and guzzling whiskey suddenly ceased. Levi quickly sat his liquor glass down, and violently threw up in a trash can the very instant he thought about the woman he loved and his beloved daughter no longer being ... *together.*

2:20 p.m.: Levi laid on the bed and stared at the ceiling, his skin too numb to feel the stream of tears rolling down the sides of his face. The room was spinning ... along with the wheels in his head.

3:05 p.m.: Levi was *still* contemplating what to do, *still* thinking about his beloved daughter ... still too numb to feel a damn thing as the room spun violently around him.

3:33 p.m.: Levi was shaken from his trance when he heard his sons storm into the house after school. He then fell into an alcohol-induced slumber. He slept hard and was awakened for dinner at 6 p.m.

6:11p.m.: With a head-splitting migraine, Levi sat at the dinner table with his head hanging low. He was usually engaging his sons in conversation. But on this evening, the sound of silverware clinking against plates dominated the noise in the room. Levi only stared at his meal, too nauseated to eat, having yet to say a single word, clearly looking dejected.

"Pa, wh-what's wrong?" fifteen-year-old Colt was finally brave enough to ask, after the uncomfortable silence became too much for him to tolerate.

Levi did not even attempt to open his mouth, for fear he would spew vomit instead of words.

"Oh, I'm quite sure around noon tomorrow, your fatha' will be rid of what's weighin' heavily on his mind," Emily interjected, her eyes focused on the steak she was cutting.

Emily's words finally triggered Levi to move. He lifted his throbbing head and glared at his wife through bloodshot eyes, fighting the sudden urge to jump up and choke her in front of their children.

Emily returned the glare and bit into her steak, chewing with a smirk on her face. "You boys go on and finish up your homework, get your chores done, and then get cleaned up for bed. Leave your good *God-fearin'* daddy in peace. He's got a big decision to make t'night."

6:31 p.m.: Levi's contemplating suddenly ceased. As he stared at the sickening sight of his wife, he had indeed made a decision that would resolve his problem ... *permanently*.

11:30 p.m.: Levi sat up in bed and looked over at his wife, who was lulled into a deep sleep by alcohol as usual. Anger heated his entire body when he saw the slow rise and fall of her chest. He then silently cursed the grim reaper for having yet to answer his prayer to cease her heartbeat.

11:33 p.m.: Levi left his bedroom. He leaned against the doorframe of his three eldest sons' room and watched sixteen-year-old Wyatt sleep. Although he had accidentally conceived him with a woman whom he now hated, Levi could not imagine his life without him. Levi then turned and gazed at fifteen-year-old Colt, and thirteen-year-old Dylan, sleeping peacefully in bunk beds. He could not see himself without those two young men either.

11:38 p.m.: Levi quietly cracked the door to his youngest three sons' bedroom. He gazed upon the resting bodies of twelve-year-old Lucas, eleven-year-old Bo, and eight-year-old Dallas. The thought of life without them was crippling as well.

11:42 p.m.: Levi wandered outside and peered through the window of the child who he was supposed to subtract from his life in order to solve his difficult life equation. Even at nine-years-old, that little person still found comfort sleeping nestled in her mother's arms, while holding on to the rag doll created in her image. Levi was curious about the contents of Lily's dreams at that moment. He wondered if he had ever played even a small role in her dreams, the way she had countless times in his. Even though he had limited interaction with Lily, the thought of subtracting her from his life, and worse yet, from her mother's, nearly brought Levi to his knees at that very moment. The thought of such a thing had helped solidify what Levi felt was the one true answer to all his current problems.

Levi was a logical thinking man. It was what always drove his decisions as head of the household. Logic and numbers. Currently, Levi had the option of tearing apart the lives of six little boys, or the life of one little girl. Six and one. Two numbers. One number greater than the other. Damage one or damage six. All seven of those little lives were on his mind when he stepped back into his house at 12:05 a.m.

12:10 a.m.: With lightning and thunder suddenly rumbling in the distance, Levi stood over his wife as she lay on her back, passed out. The haggard sight of her turned his stomach and intensified his current urges. Quickly, the storm seemed to roll toward Levi's house, thunder clapping noticeably louder. Another strike of lightning illuminated the room, revealing the empty liquor glass on Emily's nightstand. As lightning lit up the room again, Levi cursed under his breath when he saw his wife's chest *still* rising and falling. Lightning suddenly struck again, rocking the house. This time, Levi caught a glimpse of himself in the mirror as he lowered a pillow onto his wife's face. He was ready to finish the job that the crushed sleeping powder he had laced her alcohol with had failed to do. With such heavy sedatives coursing through her veins, Emily did not even flinch as Levi began to smother her.

"Pa?" Levi suddenly heard. He slightly lifted the pillow from Emily's face as his bedroom door squeaked open. With the pillow still near her face, Levi looked up to find Dallas standing in the doorway, rubbing his pasty eyes. "Pa, can I sleep with you and mama? The storm is scarin' me," he said, sounding and looking like he was sleepwalking.

With his mouth agape, Levi only stared at Dallas as he proceeded to wearily crawl into bed and cuddle up next to his mother. The sleeping powder had put Emily into such a deep sleep that she did not budge as Dallas laid on her chest and quickly drifted back to sleep himself. Lightning lit up the room again. This time, it illuminated the tears that suddenly trickled down Levi's cheeks as he gazed at his wife and son. When Dallas snuggled up next to his mother, it was the first time in years that Levi had ever bothered to view Emily as human, one who was *somehow* loved by the little boy on her chest … a beloved human whose life he was about to ruthlessly take.

12:15 a.m.: The storm ended just as quickly as it began. Thunder rumbled far off in the distance as Levi slowly backed out of his bedroom. Levi was indeed a logical thinking man … except when it came to Maya and Lily. His homicidal urge was just as impossible to resist as scratching the world's most intense rash. His racing mind was ready to justify anything to keep Lily in his life. Not even the consequence of rotting hell could halt Levi's overwhelming need to commit murder on his daughter's behalf. The sudden storm that had blown in and awakened Dallas seemed to prove that it had literally taken an act of God to cease a homicidal impulse that would have indeed ended Levi's troubles … *permanently*. He sat down at the top of the stairwell, lowered his head in shame, and let his soft murder weapon fall from his hands and tumble down the steps.

12:20 a.m.: With Emily Collins miraculously still breathing, Levi solemnly got up off the stairs and dragged himself to the barn. He went into an empty horse stall, kicked aside a pile of hay, and lifted the lid to a hidden compartment that housed all his journals, and other treasures that were sentimental to him. He pulled a small tin lockbox from within the secret compartment and sat down with his back against the stall wall. He then unlocked the small metal chest and took out a series of grainy, eight by ten photographs. The photograph on top of the pile was one of Lily at three-years-old, sitting in Maya's lap. Not long before Lily was born, many slave owners had begun the practice of photographing their slaves for insurance purposes. After Lily was born, Levi claimed to be doing the same. But his motives had absolutely nothing to do with insurance. Levi simply wanted time-stamped memories of his daughter and the woman he loved. He had to pay a significant amount of money to have every slave on his farm photographed to cover up his ploy. But Levi felt every penny was worth it to have the priceless frozen images of his daughter that he now held in his hands. Every year of Lily's life, he had new photographs taken. He sat there treasuring all nine of them now, scrutinizing each one for the longest time, while sipping straight out of a bottle of whiskey. In every photo, Maya was straight-faced, sitting tall, looking like a lovely Nubian queen with her little princess on her lap. At age five, a flock of birds had caught Lily's attention and she happened to look up and smile as the photo was snapped. That picture of innocent childhood wonderment was Levi's favorite. It was in that photo that he finally realized Lily was a splitting image of him.

As Levi slowly shuffled through his time-stamped treasures, he suddenly halted altogether and laid eight of the photos down. Left in his hand was the very first picture ever taken of Lily as a baby. He stared intently at it, recalling how something so tiny had completed his life. At 12:32 a.m., with exactly twelve hours remaining in his ultimatum, tears began trickling down Levi's cheeks, as he then thought about how completely meaningless his life would be without the precious baby girl whose photo he gazing at. His tears flowed even more at the thought of destroying the beautiful woman in the photo who was holding her. He cried even harder still when he realized that there was no other logical solution to the difficult life equation his wife was forcing him to solve.

6:25 a.m.: "Levi, are you alright?" he suddenly heard Maya ask in his sleepy haze. He thought he was still dreaming, until he opened his pasty eyes and saw her towering over him in the horse stall, where he had drunk himself into unconsciousness.

"I'm fine now," Levi would *usually* say to Maya whenever she found him there. He would always let a kiss linger on her forehead, to let her know that it was the sight of her lovely face that instantly made him forget about his troubles. But this time, he did not utter a word. Levi only peeked at Maya briefly through swollen, bloodshot eyes as he lay limply against the stall wall.

As Maya watched him struggle to stand, she knew immediately that something was seriously wrong. She had never seen Levi intoxicated following any arguments with Emily. The true weight of his burdens was further proven by the fact that he staggered past her without giving her his usual forehead kiss. Instead of being warmed by Levi's affections, Maya felt a cold chill race down her spine when he did not leave her with a sign of his love, only the putrid smell of alcohol wafting from his pores as he stumbled away.

Levi's cold actions proved that not even Maya had the power to cease the splitting migraine caused by the ultimatum countdown clock, that was chiming as loudly as church bells inside his aching head. Only one thing could stop the sledgehammer of time that was pounding away at him. At 6:28 a.m., Levi was on his way to beg for that very thing.

Just as Levi entered the house, Emily had roused from her alcohol and drug-induced sleep and immediately began screaming at Dallas to get out of her bed and get ready for school. Her gift to her youngest son for unknowingly saving her life was an earful of obscenities. After Dallas scurried out of the room, Emily laid back down, not knowing that attempted murder was the reason her hangover was worse than on other days. Her headache, and the sick feeling in her stomach, immediately worsened when she heard Levi enter the room and drop to his knees near her side of the bed. Still in a haze, she slowly sat up and glared down at her husband, the look in her eyes silently asking him why he was annoying her with his presence.

Levi ignored her look of disgust and took hold of her hand before he spoke. "Emily, I know I've sinned, and that I've hurt you in the worst possible way any husband could. I've dishonored our vows and for that, I could neva' be more sorry. I've asked God for his forgiveness, and now I kneel before you and ask the same. I swear to you, I'll spend the rest of my days tryna make things right between us. But for now, I'm beggin' you to change your mind about me sellin' Lily ... *please*," he pleaded, his eyes beginning to brim with tears. "Despite how she got here, Lily's still my daughta', and it'll kill me to neva' see 'er again."

Emily looked over at the clock behind him and then glared back at her now weeping husband. "Six ... hours ... left," she replied coldly. She then callously tossed his hand aside and walked out of the room, leaving Levi and his tears in a sorrowful mess alone on the floor.

Levi knelt there on the floor with his face buried in his hands, until his legs began to go numb. Using the little strength he had in his weakened arms, he held onto the nightstand and pushed himself up. When blood returned to his tingling legs, he slowly made his way over to the window, peered out, and saw Lily emerge from her cottage. She was energetically skipping over to the barn to begin her chores with her mother. Levi then looked back at the clock: 6:42 a.m. In less than six hours, he was expected to begin a life without seeing Lily happily skipping that way ever again. The thought of such a thing made Levi tear himself away from the window, and head straight down to his wife's liquor cabinet again. Emily peered around the kitchen corner, saw him sifting through her supply, and devilishly smirked. Pure joy was coursing through her over watching the sight of her husband emotionally unravel before her very eyes. She was proud to know that he could now commiserate with the level of pain that would drive a person to drink. The thought of her husband's anguish had her preparing breakfast for the sons she hated with a glorious smile on her face, for the first time ever.

Levi found a bottle of moonshine, snatched it from the cupboard, and proceeded out to the porch. Like a hopeless-looking hobo, he sat slouched in a porch rocking chair with the bottle perched in his lap. He had no idea about the true power of moonshine. It numbed his lips and tongue on the very first sip. Despite the disgusting taste, he refused to stop drinking it, until his soul was just as numb. He continued to sip and rock and watch his precious little girl through swollen, bloodshot, tear-filled eyes.

7:30 am: Levi's boys all filed out of the house to begin their assigned chores before school. The first five were oblivious to their father sitting there as they trotted down the steps toward the field. Wyatt, however, happened to look over and see his father drowning his sorrows. Stunned by the way he looked, Wyatt immediately stopped in his tracks. "My God. Pa, you alright?"

Levi kept his eyes on the only thing that mattered in his world at that moment. He sat in stone-cold silence and never even turned in his son's direction. It was the first time Wyatt had ever seen his father drink. Worried about his despondence, Wyatt turned back to look at his mother with questioning eyes.

"Don't you worry about him, son," Emily said, leaning against the doorframe with her arms folded, a joyous smirk still planted firmly on her face. She glanced at her watch. "In just about five hours, your fatha' will be just fine."

Wyatt looked as confused by her statement as by his father's demeanor.

"Go on out into the fields with your brotha's. You'll have to be the man of the house today. I'll need you to stay home from school and do your fatha's chores for 'em."

"Yes ma'am." Wyatt glanced at his father again. The strong man that he knew him to be was gone. Through Wyatt's eyes, his father looked completely broken. Before the heart-wrenching sight brought him to tears, Wyatt trotted down the stairs to begin doing the work that his father was clearly too broken to do.

When Levi heard the door slam behind him, it brought his sense of awareness back and he glanced at his watch again: 7:32 a.m. Exactly five hours to go. This time, Levi did not sip from his bottle; he guzzled.

8:32 a.m.: Levi watched Lily skipping behind her mother to go hang wet clothes on the clothesline together. It was sinking in that this may very well be the last time that he sees his precocious daughter, merrily bounding across the fields in her jubilant childlike manner. All her firsts suddenly began rolling through Levi's head. He recalled the dates and the moments like they were only yesterday. He began with the first time he ever saw her walk. To his and Maya's astonishment, Lily's first steps were sudden. At ten-months-old, she had suddenly gotten up off the floor the moment she saw her father walk into the cottage to read to her. She toddled three steps and fell, got up, and did it again. It was as if she was determined to get into her father's waiting arms the quickest way possible. She stumbled her way toward him with a grand smile on her face and her arms outstretched, eager for him to scoop her up for a big bear hug. Lily's eagerness to be in his arms was another sign of how her love for him was growing, just as quickly as she was. Such a thing brought joyous tears to Levi's eyes as he hugged her that day. But only tears of misery trickled from them now as he sat recalling the precious moment that he had motivated his daughter's very first steps. It was killing him to know that if he did not figure out what to do, he would never again witness another of her grand life achievements.

9:32 a.m.: contemplating, thinking of Lily, and sipping on moonshine.

10:32 a.m.: contemplating, thinking of Lily, and sipping.

11:32 a.m.: contemplating, sipping … tears trickling as Levi thought of Lily.

12:27 p.m.: With five minutes left in his ultimatum, Levi had yet to conjure up a single solitary solution to his ordeal. Outside of serious regret about not smothering his wife, nothing had come to Levi's mind as to how to save all his children from senselessly having their lives torn apart.

12:30 p.m.: Wyatt trotted up the steps for lunch. He hurried into the house when the sight of his broken father was still too much for him to bear. As Wyatt passed by, all of Levi's children came crashing to his mind again. *Save six and hurt one,* he thought to himself. He then glanced over at the daughter that he deemed as his beloved miracle. *Save one and hurt six.* Levi turned around and glanced through the window of his home. Heavy with hatred, his eyes nearly squinted shut when he glared at his wife, who was mindlessly going about her chores, like it was just an ordinary day. He touched the pocketknife on his hip. *Kill one and save all seven* … But Levi Collins was a logical thinking man.

Levi looked at his watch just as the long hand landed on the twenty-fourth hour: 12:32 p.m. The pocket watch's hand moved in slow motion in his eyes. He swore the solitary tick shook his entire body and chimed as loudly as a massive bell on a church tower at high noon. Emily suddenly stepped onto the porch behind him. He could feel her presence looming over him like an evil spirit, but he was too disgusted to glance back at her. He knew he would only turn to find a look on her face confirming that the time had come.

Without ever glancing at the woman he loathed, Levi wearily gathered enough strength in his legs and arms to rise from his porch rocking chair. The depths of his inebriation hit him hard when he finally stood up after sitting there for hours. With his world spinning, he began marching down the porch steps, holding onto the railing for dear life. With no more railing to support him, he stumbled when his feet hit the dirt and then struggled to keep himself from falling flat on his face. Under wobbly legs, he began making his way toward two blurry figures near the clothesline.

Just like any normal day, Maya took a sheet down off the clothesline. But the sight that came into her view after she removed it was far from normal. By the way Levi was stalking toward her and Lily with staggered footsteps, she knew immediately something was very wrong. Lily had her back turned, folding a pair of trousers, oblivious to what was transpiring behind her. Maya, however, had stopped her duties altogether. Levi's bizarre behavior in the barn earlier immediately flashed in her mind. With a pounding heart, she glanced over Levi's shoulder and saw Emily standing on the porch, glaring at her with cold eyes. When Maya saw the look on her face, she knew immediately to stand in front of her daughter to block Levi's path. As he closed in on her, Maya's terror escalated when saw the bizarre expression on his face. It looked to her like nobody was truly home behind his eyes.

Lily suddenly yelped when she felt her mother grip her arm tightly. "Mama, you're hurtin' me," she said, but Maya's terror made her oblivious to her daughter's words.

Maya gripped Lily even tighter and pulled her in close. She looked over at Emily again as she began stepping backward with Lily. She then locked eyes with Levi and began shaking her head, tears already stirring in her eyes. "Levi! Don't you listen to Emily! Whateva' she said, don't do it! You'll regret it!" she warned. "This ain't you, Levi! What're you doin'?! This ain't you!" she screamed, as he staggered toward them looking catatonic. "Levi, stop! Don't listen to Emily! Lily's yo' daughta' too! Don't you dare forget that! Whateva' she told you to do, you'll regret it! Don't you dare hurt your own child!" she yelled, attempting to snap him out of his bizarre trance.

Upon hearing her mother's pleas, Lily's mouth fell open and she looked up at her in confusion. The confused look still remained as she then glanced at the man she had only ever known as "Master Lee." That very man then tried to reach around Maya to snatch her.

Levi's sudden movement was met with the ear piercing shrill of his name and a fierce blow to his jaw by Maya's fist. "YOU PROMISED ME! YOU SWORE YOU'D NEVA' HURT OUR BABY!" she erupted. She suddenly became insanely combative, striking Levi repeatedly with a closed fist as he continued to try to grab Lily. Levi felt nothing, however. Moonshine had indeed succeeded in numbing both his mind and body. He was seeing double and was uncertain which child to even grab. Despite repeated blows to his face, he kept reaching for Lily, until he finally had her in his grip. He lost his balance and stumbled when Maya began yanking Lily away. While on his knees, he grabbed Lily's ankles before Maya could drag her too far. He stood up and pulled Lily toward him, but Maya's motherly brute strength kept her daughter firmly in her grip. Lily cried out in agony when her wrists and ankles then became the gripping points in a merciless tug of war. Maya's desperate, unfiltered pleas accompanied her battle. Her words had no ability to penetrate Levi's severely intoxicated brain, though. The haze of his mind was equal to the dirt cloud they were now shrouded in. Only Lily seemed to be absorbing the repeated phrases that revealed the true identity of the man who seemed to be trying to rip her feet clean off her body.

The brutal battle and Lily's shrill screams of pain had commanded the attention of everyone on the entire farm. Her heart-shattering cries even drew Wyatt from the kitchen to the porch. With the massive dust cloud surrounding the scuffle, he could not see clearly, though. "What's goin' on?" he asked his mother, looking confused.

"Maya's fightin' with your fatha'! Go help 'em!" Emily screamed.

"What do you want me to do?"

"Get the whip!"

"*Whip?*" he asked, looking confused. "What whip?"

"It's hangin' in the barn!"

"But I don't wanna whip Miss Maya!"

Wyatt's neck cracked from the force of his mother's hand across his face. "Don't you dare disrespect me, you worthless heathen!"

Wyatt held his aching cheek, his chest heaving as he glared at his mother with disdain.

"NOW DO WHAT I SAY!" Emily screamed, shoving him.

Wyatt stumbled slightly and caught himself before he fell down the porch steps. As he went in search of the whip, his secret hatred for his mother was running rampant on his mind. From the time he could comprehend words, he knew his mother equally loathed him. He could not ever recall her telling him that she loved him. But he had most certainly internalized the countless times she had told him that he was a regretted, unwanted mistake. The pain of her words was now embedded in his nerves, muscles, and every bone in his body. His body was one that his mother had only ever touched with the sting of a leather strap, and never the warmth of a motherly embrace. Her constant belittling and brutality had caused Wyatt's hatred for her to fester in his soul for sixteen years. His mother's callousness was the reason he looked forward to working with Maya in the barn every morning before school. She never failed to greet him and his brothers with a smile and a much-needed hug. He loved that Maya even spoke to them like they were human. Her warmth and simple affections were the antidote for the constant mental poison his mother injected into his mind that sometimes made Wyatt want to hang himself. Maya's loving, motherly medicine was indeed his saving grace. Now, here his mother was, asking him to brutalize the only woman on the farm who had ever shown him any compassion. The thought of such a thing had Wyatt seething inside by the time he found the whip. His mother's blow to his face seemed to have caused sixteen years of simmering anger to transition into a boiling rage. As he yanked the old, dried out whip off the wall, that rage was now ready to erupt with volcanic force. He stormed out of the barn with it, wishing it was his mother's back he could lash it across nonstop, until he stripped the demon from her soul.

Anger had temporarily stripped Wyatt's youthful mind of rational thought as he exited the barn. He angrily glared at his mother and then marched out to the middle of the field where his father was still wrestling to get Lily away from Maya. Wyatt stomped into the dust cloud with tears in his eyes, his face red, and his teeth clenched. With explosive anger propelling his arm, he hurled the whip across Maya's back with all his might. The shock of the sting immediately caused her to lose her grip on Lily. Maya dropped to her knees and Wyatt dropped the whip. He then kicked Maya in the back, sending her into the dirt on her stomach. With vengeful fury clawing to escape his body, Wyatt turned her over and straddled her. For the countless times that his mother had called him stupid and unwanted, he began beating Maya about the face. For all the times his mother had unnecessarily spanked him, he continued to pummel Maya. Long after Maya had ceased all movement, Wyatt burned her with the frothing rage that was intended for his mother. In the throes of temporary insanity, he mercilessly beat into unconsciousness the one woman who had always given him the warmth and love that his mother had denied him.

Once the vengeful rage was purged from his body, Wyatt's sanity suddenly returned. He stood up over Maya and froze. He looked down at her like he had just returned from an out-of-body experience. Had it not been for his aching fists and his legs straddling the limp body beneath him, he would have sworn it was someone else responsible for the battered face he was staring at. Mortified by what he had done, he began sobbing uncontrollably. When he was finally able to get his body to respond to his brain, he looked up at his mother in the distance and glared at her with contempt. He then quickly fled the scene, trying to run from the instant regret he felt for brutalizing a woman who he loved, in the way a son should love a mother.

While Wyatt was bolting into the woods in tears, Levi was fleeing with Lily, guiding his horses into town in a drunken haze. Wyatt had returned from his out-of-body experience, but his father could not say the same. Levi was still mentally detached from reality as he fled the scene with Lily. In his alcohol-induced, catatonic state, he was completely oblivious to his daughter's desolate sobs and her pleas to be returned to her mother. Lily looked through the wagon cover at the man she had just learned was her father. Through her nine-year-old tear-filled eyes, he seemed as emotionless as a well-oiled cotton gin, mindlessly carrying out its programmed duty. Lily perceived that her very own father was intentionally ignoring her pleas to know where he was taking her. She could never have known that Levi's mind was unable to rationally comprehend anything at all in his frazzled mind.

When Levi arrived in the town square, he may very well have been parking his wagon with bales of cotton in the back; his mind was too far gone to interpret the difference. He could have signed the president's name into the slave registry, instead of Lily's, and he would never have realized his mistake. Like a walking dead man, he was going through the motions of preparing to sell his only daughter. Through every "i" dotted, through every "t" crossed, Levi's brain was failing to absorb any of it.

After signing one of his own children's names into the Negro auction registry, Levi went back out to the wagon. Perceiving Lily no differently than an inanimate object, he lifted her out of the back of the wagon and took her by the hand. Levi's catatonic mind left him completely impervious to the soft hand that had once curled around his finger as a baby and melted his heart. He now held that same hand to march his little girl up the auction block steps to put her on display, like a piece of antique furniture, ready to be sold to the highest bidder.

Levi trotted back down the auction block steps, still too lost in an absent-minded haze to absorb the fact that he had just left his only daughter there helplessly alone. He mindlessly squeezed into the middle of the crowd, turned, and stared up at her. This time, flashes of his own children did not have to appear there on that auction block. Live and in living color, there one of them stood amid a sea of strange, raised hands, eager to take her away. He stood there in an unblinking trance, watching the tears cascading through the light tint of dirt on his daughter's face. He looked callous and unconcerned through Lily's nine-year-old eyes. Unbeknownst to her, though, she was a blur to her father. In his intoxicated state, the chanting crowd sounded distorted and the world was spinning. The heart-wrenching sight and sound of his daughter's shoulder-heaving sobs had no visible, or even internal, effect on him whatsoever. Levi Collins was simply in a state of pure, unadulterated shock.

Levi's brain continued to operate like that of someone with a single digit IQ. If asked, he would not have been able to verbalize what was happening around him at that moment. His ears worked no better than a deaf man's. He did not even hear how much the auctioneer announced his daughter had sold for when the bidding was over. His legs worked no better than someone who was paralyzed. He seemed unable to move, until a worker at the auction prompted him to come and escort Lily to her new owner. Still numb to Lily's touch, he could not even feel her soft little hand in his, as he held it and ushered her toward Jesse's wagon.

"Are you really my fatha'?" Lily asked Levi as he dragged her along. He heard the words, but somehow his brain failed to comprehend the simple question. Still perceiving her like an inanimate object, he lifted her into the back of Jesse's wagon. "A-are you?" Lily sniffled, still hoping for an answer. But Levi remained totally disconnected from the world as he kneeled and placed shackles around his daughter's tiny ankles. He stood tall after shackling her legs and came face to face with a set of eyes that were undoubtedly his. *"Daddy?"* Lily suddenly whispered with a quivering bottom lip and eyes full of tears, as she gazed at her father with the most sorrowful expression on her face. A word that Levi had longed to hear, she had just whispered in a solemn tone that begged to know why he would do this to her.

Daddy. That single word processed in Levi's brain with the utmost clarity and brought reality crashing back to him. With that one word, Levi finally felt the impact of everything he had just done at full force. That one word had instantly sobered him. It suddenly restored and magnified every one of his senses. He comprehended where he was, and the world finally stopped spinning. That single word had yanked him from the depths of a dark blinding abyss and brought him into the light to finally see his little girl with great clarity. Eyes that Lily swore were glaring at her coldly were actually gazing at her with immense compassion. Levi was now fully aware that he was staring into the sparkling eyes of the beautiful child he had created out of pure love, a child who he loved beyond measure … a child he would now never see again.

By the time Levi was finally able to absorb the magnitude of his actions, his daughter was being dragged away by a brutal demon. According to the law, he could now legally do nothing to stop him either. Like a coward, Levi turned his back, and listened to his beloved daughter repeatedly hollering the one word he had been desperate to hear since the moment she could speak. As he walked away with his head lowered in shame, he recalled how he had once told Maya that he would give anything to hear Lily call him daddy. Never, in his wildest imagination, did he ever think that *Lily* would be the *"anything"* he was forced to give away.

Levi now no longer had to imagine what it was like to sell one of his own children. He had answered that question for himself. The sickness that it caused to stir in his stomach led him to go to a remote creek on the outskirts of town, where there were no inhabitants for miles around. He climbed down from his wagon, immediately dropped to his knees, and vomited violently into the rushing water, his body purging what was left of his sanity. After clearing his stomach, he sat on his knees, wailing like an animal with its leg caught in a trap. He stayed there paralyzed in pain like one as well. Weakened by sorrow, he eventually fell over onto his side. His body had finally succumbed to the exact moment when Levi Collins was never again the same man: January 14, 1845 … 1:53 p.m.

Chapter Twenty-one

Emancipation proclamation continued

... And as Commander-in-Chief of the Army and Navy of the United States, I further declare, and make known, that the military and naval authorities of the United States will recognize and maintain the freedom of all persons held as slaves. And as a fit and necessary war measure, I further declare that such persons of suitable condition, will be received into the armed service of the United States to garrison forts, positions, stations, and other places, and to man vessels of all sorts in said service. And upon this act, sincerely believed to be an act of justice, warranted by the Constitution, upon military necessity.

I have hereunto set my hand and caused the seal of the United States to be affixed.

President Abraham Lincoln

December 25, 1864

Just after midnight, the popping sound of gunfire tore Mary Jo Parker from a dead sleep. Her father, Joseph, was awakened as well. He glanced out his window to find that a miniature war had broken out on his plantation. He had expected as much, though. While doing business in a neighboring town, he was warned about a brazen group of men, who were sneaking onto plantations and freeing slaves in the dead of night. After seeing the battle outside his window, Joseph was certain that that very group had made its way into Fayetteville and was now descending on his property. But Joseph Parker had prepared in advance to meet the group's late-night thievery with force. He had hired a team of armed men to guard his plantation around the clock. But the money he had spent proved worthless on this night. The small group of hired men were disarmed, bound, and shackled together in a matter of minutes by the midnight crusaders currently invading the farm.

With the security team rendered useless, Joseph and Mary Jo were now completely vulnerable to the onslaught of men, who were rounding up their slaves and ushering them to safety. Trying desperately to defend his daughter and his property, Joseph loaded his pistol and bravely went outside. He quietly tiptoed to the back of his wraparound porch and hid. He peeked around the corner and shot a man who was headed toward his house. The sound of the shot blast prompted several men to charge toward Joseph. He panicked and quickly tried to run back inside his house. But he turned around only to find a gun aimed at his face. To Joseph's shock, he was staring down the barrel of a man whom he had known since birth. "James!" he shouted.

"I'm not here to hurt you, Mr. Parker. I'm just here for Ms. Claudine," James explained, referring to Joseph's house slave.

"Sh-she ain't here!" Joseph answered, nervously raising his pistol.

Before Joseph could straighten his arms to shoot, the handle of James's rifle connected with his skull. The force of the blow immediately rendered Joseph unconscious. He dropped to the ground, blood pouring from the massive gash near his temple. When James leaned down to take Joseph's weapon, his peripheral vision picked up movement. He turned, looked inside the back door, and saw a trembling Mary Jo. She was standing a way back in the kitchen, staring down at her father as he lay bleeding on the porch. Slowly, her head panned up to find that the person crouched over her father was a man she once loved. James stood tall and stepped toward the door. Still paralyzed with fear, Mary Jo could not get her feet to work as James closed in on her. He froze near the entrance and slowly raised his gun. Just as the barrel was lined up with Mary Jo's face, a fireball erupted behind James in the distance. A newly freed slave had just torched the slave quarters. The burning building illuminated James to perfection as he glared at Mary Jo with pure hatred in his eyes.

"P-p-please, d-d-don't sh-shoot," Mary Jo begged, trembling so hard that her words were barely intelligible. Her tears were flowing just as fast as the river of urine running down her leg.

"MISS CLAUDINE!" James yelled. He kept his weapon aimed at Mary Jo, enjoying the sight of terror on her face too much to turn away. "You have the choice to leave here for good, if you want," James explained to Claudine when she arrived, still refusing to remove his eyes from a tearful Mary Jo as he spoke.

The shock of seeing James with a gun aimed at Mary Jo's face made Claudine slow to respond. "I-I can just l-leave?" she asked nervously.

"Yes ma'am. You can stay here, if you want. But, by orda' of the President, you're now free to go. Which do you prefer?"

Claudine took one look at the self-centered woman, who had spent years rudely demeaning her, and her mind was instantly made up. "I'll go!"

James motioned his head towards the door. "Go on out to my troops. They'll help ya' out to the wagons and take you to safety."

"Yessa'," she replied, stepping over her master's unconscious body on the porch as she made her way to freedom.

"Anything, you wanna say?" James asked Mary Jo once Claudine was gone.

Mary Jo's knees suddenly buckled. She dropped down into the praying position, landing in a pool of her own urine. Her body quaking with fear, she glanced up at James. "I b-b-beg your f-forgiveness. P-please, I'm so s-sorry for e-everything I d-did to you and L-Lily," she choked out.

Even though the word was stammered, it was the first time James had ever heard Mary Jo address Lily by the correct name. But he knew her sudden show of respect was selfishly motivated by a need to preserve her useless life. Disgusted by her insincere apology, he pulled back the hammer on his gun.

Mary Jo winced and closed her eyes when it clicked it into place. "Pl-please, God n-no!"

Silence.

After a moment, Mary Jo cautiously opened her eyes to find herself alone. She breathed a heavy sigh, crawled over to her father, and collapsed on his chest in a sobbing heap.

If James was callous enough to kill a woman, he would have shot Mary Jo straight between the eyes on Lily's behalf. Instead, he hopped on his horse and briefly glanced back at her as she wept on her father's unconscious body. As much as he desired to murder her, he was satisfied knowing that a life without her slaves was equivalent to a torturous death for her anyway.

James snapped the reins on his horse and sped toward the exit of the Parker plantation. Before leaving for good, he stopped at the front entrance, climbed down from his horse, and hammered a large stake into the ground. Attached to it was a massive American flag. James climbed back on his horse and looked down with pride at the star-speckled, red, white, and blue symbol that signified that *the Freedom Riders* had succeeded in yet another mission. He then sped away on his horse, with one more *very personal* mission to conquer in Fayetteville.

Despite the Emancipation Proclamation, the south had refused to emancipate their slaves, per President Lincoln's orders. Instead, the Confederacy had begun forcing even more slaves to fight on behalf of the south. Frustrated that the President's orders were being ignored, James asked and received permission from General Blackshear to form a special task force. The sole purpose of the alliance was to extract slaves from their owners to prevent them from being forced to fight against their own freedom. Knowing James's story of Lily and Rose there was no shortage of troops who wished to be part of the coalition. The most surprising person who wished to join the team was Elijah Ridley. Even more surprising than that was the fact that James did not deny his request. As much as he hated the man, James could not deny that Elijah was one of the most skilled soldiers of the entire brigade.

James, Elijah, Harrison, Austin, the twins, and many other soldiers then began their crusade together as *the Freedom Riders*. James named the group specifically as a retaliatory antonym to his father's racist cult. Much like the Ghost Riders, the Freedom Riders also snatched slaves in the dead of night, but for far more honorable purposes. James's dedicated team of men had marched south through various states, releasing thousands of slaves to groups of people that could help them begin the process of rebuilding their lives, as *free American citizens*. They ushered women and children to safety and gave weapons to the men who wished to fight to put an end to the institution that had held their families captive for centuries. Instead of burning crosses like his father's group, the Freedom Riders planted American flags at the entrance of every plantation that they emptied of slaves. The name of their organization was beautifully branded into the wood of every stake they hammered into the ground. After nearly a year of successful missions, well over two-hundred flags had flown gallantly outside the homes of slave owners, as a symbol that their captives had been officially freed. With every rescue mission, James hoped to hack away at his father's so-called legacy and eventually obliterate it altogether. While on his monumental journey, James ultimately hoped to find the woman who had inspired him to fight on behalf of freedom in the first place. Despite hundreds of missions, James had yet to succeed in that goal. But only death would have prevented him from continuing his efforts.

Having arrived in his hometown, death was indeed on James's mind ... but not his own. It was a major rule among the Freedom Riders that no innocent civilians were to be harmed during their late-night raids. Joseph Parker had been the first civilian ever injured. But James had no plans for him to be the last in the town of Fayetteville. Right after leaving the Parker plantation, James made his way onto familiar grounds.

"*Masa' James*?!" Corrina yelped. She had been startled awake when she heard him whisper her name. When her eyes adjusted, and she realized who he was, she jumped up to hug him.

"Shh," James said, reciprocating her embrace.

"Lord, I feel like I'm dreamin'," she said when she pulled back and looked at him again. The commotion began to rouse the other slaves from their sleep. They woke up to the sight of dim lanterns and several uniformed men standing in the slave quarters.

"How's Lily?" Corrina asked James.

"I wish I could tell you. I don't know. We got separated the night we left here. I haven't seen 'er since then."

A look of disbelief came over Corrina's face. "Lord, that was my worst fear. That Griff fella' came by here askin' 'bout y'all years ago. He left before I could tell 'em what happened. I been prayin' he'd find y'all every night since that day."

"And I'm convinced that your prayers and mine will lead me back to Lily when all this war madness is said and done."

"Me too."

"But listen, we don't have a lot of time to talk. I need you and Henry to wrangle everyone togetha'. Y'all take your blankets and load 'em up with food and clothin'. Make sure it's light enough for y'all to throw ova' ya' shoulda' and carry easily." James pointed to a few of his troops. "These men are gonna lead y'all to a group that're waitin' to take ya' to safety, okay?"

"Yessa'," Corrina replied.

She, James, and Henry then began waking up all the other slaves and helped them gather their things as quickly as possible. When they finished, James's men began guiding everyone out the back exit of the plantation, toward several wagons that were waiting for them.

Corrina and Henry stopped on the way out and stood before James. "Masa', James. This mean we free now?" Corrina asked.

James put his hand on her shoulder. "I'm no longa' your masta', Corrina … and neitha' is my fatha'. Accordin' to the orda's of the President of the United States, you're *free*." He looked over at Henry. "You're *all* free."

Corrina's tears were instant. "Thank you for all your sacrifices," she said as she embraced him.

"I'm honored to now be the one at your service," James replied, reciprocating the hug.

Henry then shook his hand. "Thank you, Mas– James. Thank you, James."

James nodded, feeling proud to have delivered on a promise that he had made to them years ago. "Hurry, I want y'all to get to safety before daylight."

"Yessa'," Henry replied, his eyes welling with tears.

Corrina hugged James one final time. "You take care of yo'self, ya' hear?"

"I will."

Corrina finally released him and followed behind one of his soldiers toward a new life.

When all the slaves on his father's plantation were gone, James stepped back inside the dilapidated slave quarters and went into Lily's old room to look around. It triggered a flood of memories, some fond, some not. He recalled laying down with Lily as a boy, while she hummed lightly and ran her fingers through his hair to help comfort him after his mother's death. They were huddled together under the blanket he had given her, one they made love under years later. James then glanced in another section of the room and recalled that Auntie had passed away there … and so too had Rose. With that memory, an instant blend of sorrow and rage began to twist James's insides and constrict his lungs. He suddenly tore himself from the room when he began to feel like he couldn't breathe. He bolted out of the exit, bent over, and placed his hands on his knees, fighting to catch his breath.

Harrison rushed over when he caught sight of James appearing to hyperventilate. "You all right?" he asked, placing his hand on James's back.

James stood up straight after a moment and looked up at the slave quarters again. "Where's the kerosene?" he asked Harrison, rage evident in his eyes as he glared at the run-down dwelling.

Not bothering to question his motives, Harrison went to retrieve a can of kerosene and returned to the slave quarters with it. He stood next to James, who was still staring at the building in a trance. Austin, Wilson, and a few other soldiers walked up behind James, all waiting for him to set the slave quarters on fire. With Rose's final moments playing in his mind, James snatched the kerosene from Harrison's hand. He then suddenly walked away, leaving his fellow soldiers baffled.

James most certainly wanted to torch *something*. But this *thing* was no inanimate object. This *thing* walked, talked, breathed, and killed for entertainment. This *thing* was responsible for creating the catalog of memories that still tortured James's mind. This *thing* was responsible for taking the life of his only child. This *thing*, James was convinced, had crawled its way out of the nightmarish place that every Christian feared being condemned to burn in for eternity. James was now ready to send that *thing* back to where it had slithered from.

"What the hell's the lieutenant doin'? We gotta get outta here," a soldier said to Austin. The soldier made a move toward James to stop him.

Austin grabbed the soldier's arm and halted him. "This is his fatha's plantation," Austin explained.

Knowing the extent of what his father had done to Lily and Rose, the soldier relaxed. He immediately understood the personal nature of this particular mission for James. Austin told the few troops left to go back to the wagons and finish helping get all the slaves to safety. Harrison, Austin, and Wilson then began following behind James, ready to back him up, if need be.

On the way toward his father's front door, James walked past the whipping tree, where Lily once hung by her wrists limp, nude, and bleeding badly. The visions of her being violently beaten by Jesse began to remind James of the words of William Werthington: *In some rare instances, it would better serve the whole of society to put a vicious, rabid, animal down to save us all from being unnecessarily infected with its disgusting disease … always remember that.* James certainly had not forgotten those wise words. In fact, they played on a constant loop in his mind, along with the visions of the extensive damage his father had caused to Lily's body. It had James's rage brimming to boiling levels by the time he bounded up the steps of his father's front porch. When he reached the top, he dropped the canister of kerosene. He walked around the sides of the house and began bashing in all the windows with the handle of his rifle. Just as he had wanted, the shattering of glass awakened the *thing* he had come for.

Jesse flung his front door open and was greeted by a man whose inner beast had broken free from its chains. The vengeful look on his son's face startled Jesse a bit, but as usual, he did not let it show. Instead, he reciprocated with an ice-cold glare of his own.

"I could blow your head off right now…" James began.

Jesse raised his shotgun in response. Before the muzzle was aimed at him, James smacked his father in the face with the handle of his rifle. The blow fractured Jesse's jaw. He stumbled backward and dropped his weapon as he grabbed his face in agony. James reached down, took his father's shotgun, and tossed it behind him into the grass. James then aimed his rifle at his father's head. "I'd highly advise you to cherish these last few breaths…" He grabbed his father by the hair and forced him to look him in the eyes. "'Cause I'm sendin' you back to hell tonight." He then threw his weapon aside too. "But I'll be damned if you go easy."

A bullet suddenly grazed James in the shoulder. He looked up and saw his brother, Jacob, standing at the top of the stairwell, his smoking pistol still raised. Jesse used that moment of inattention to attack James. He lowered his shoulder and charged at him. Jesse was still surprisingly strong for his age. The force of his blow sent him and James flying from the porch onto the ground. Jesse landed on top of his son and began punching him repeatedly in the face. James took his father's blows like he was being fed candy, though. He suddenly stopped Jesse's flying fist with one hand and began squeezing his neck with the other. James's eyes were squinted into hateful slits, as he glared up at the sight of his father struggling to breathe. He then rolled his father over, got on top of him, and began choking him with both hands. The more Jesse struggled, the tighter James squeezed. He did not want to stop until his father's lips turned purple and blood vessels burst in his eyes. James wanted him to feel what he had put his mother through for twenty miserable years. When Jesse's eyes began to roll back in his head, James suddenly released his grip. "Catch your breath, you sack of shit." He leaned down in his father's face. "I ain't nearly finished with you yet."

Jacob had finally made his way downstairs and rushed out of the house to come to his father's aid. The very second he exited, Harrison lowered his shoulder and tackled him in the side. The blow caused Jacob to drop his weapon. He and Harrison then began to tussle on the porch and eventually fell over the railing. The force of the fall caused them to break the grip they had on each other. Jacob took the opportunity to scramble toward his pistol, but Harrison placed his boot on his back and stopped him. He grabbed Jacob by the hair, rolled him over, and let him come face to face with his revolver. Austin and Wilson ran over with some rope, dragged Jacob to a tree, and tied him to it. Knowing James would want to determine his brother's fate, they left him there, alive. For now, Jacob could do nothing but watch his father suffer, much like he had forced James to do the day his father had beaten Lily.

After Jacob was disabled as a threat, Harrison, Wilson, and Austin collected all the weapons that were dropped. They then trotted over toward James, who had finally stopped choking his father.

"Get up, you son of a bitch!" James demanded. Coughing and gagging, Jesse rolled over and tried to crawl away. Before he got far, James kicked him in the gut and knocked the wind out of him. "I said, get up!"

When Jesse fell over onto his side, James began kicking him repeatedly in the ribs, offering the same mercy that he had to Lily while she was with child. Jesse had fractured *one* of Lily's ribs during that assault. James violently shattered *all* his father's. Grunting with every blow, he then suddenly began to stomp his father's face, like a cockroach that refused to die. Over and over again, he stomped until he was completely winded. When he suddenly stopped to catch his breath, Jesse tried to cowardly crawl away again. The fact that he still had the strength to move further angered James and refueled his energy. He snatched his father by the hair and dragged him like a rag doll over to the whipping tree. He tied a rope around Jesse's wrists and tightened it until his hands began to turn purple. James then hoisted him up into the air with a single pull, took his knife out, and sliced every stitch of clothing off his father's frame.

Breathing hard through clenched teeth, James suddenly froze and stared at his father, looking as though his soul had suddenly departed from his body. Jesse was all too familiar with the coldness in his son's eyes as he stared unblinking at him. That soulless death glare was one that preceded every brutal killing Jesse had ever committed. He realized in that moment that he had passed that wicked trait on to his son. Cowardly tears then suddenly appeared in Jesse's eyes. Because, with that wicked trait, he knew the barbarism that was next to come.

Boiling rage suddenly snapped James out of his death glare trance. He walked over and grabbed Jesse's signature whip; one he had used to maim the backs of countless slaves over the years. James stepped directly behind his naked father and drew his favorite torture weapon back as far as it would go. An explosive need for vengeance then propelled his arm forward, as he growled like a savage madman. The initial lash landed with a violent snap across Jesse's back, stripping him of a thick layer of skin. Years of pent-up rage fueled every brutal sling of the whip thereafter. James refused to stop until he evoked the same desperate pleas he had often heard from his mother while being brutalized by Jesse's fists. He wanted to draw from Jesse the same pain-filled tears that he had constantly caused to cascade down his beautiful mother's cheeks. He wanted to revel in the look of terror on his father's face, like those of the many slaves he had tortured for sport. For the lifelong mental scars his father had given him, James lashed his back. For every slave he had ever killed, James lashed. For killing his mother, he lashed. For destroying his friendship with Lily, he lashed. For the near-death beating he had given Lily, he lashed. For killing his baby … again, again, and over again, he hurled that whip across his father's back, with the unbridled strength of a man who had gone completely insane.

The thought of holding his lifeless baby had tears streaming down James's cheeks, as he continued trying to strip every ounce of skin off his father's back. When he succeeded, James fell to his knees with exhaustion, and dropped a whip that was now saturated in his father's blood. As if it was a work of fine art, James joyously gazed at the massive open wound on his father's back. He then closed his eyes, tilted his head back, and reveled in the sound of him wailing like a slowly dying creature.

Austin, Wilson, and Harrison stood nearby in utter shock, after watching a son so ruthlessly try to kill his own father. They had seen James show more mercy to Confederate soldiers. But the brutality they had just witnessed made it seem as though mercy was now a foreign concept in their lieutenant's world. This was not the James they knew. This was a conscienceless madman, one who was *still* not nearly finished inflicting his punishment. They watched as James slowly got up from the ground. He walked over, cut the rope that held his father, and let him crumple to the ground. He then dragged Jesse's bloodied body over and slammed his back against the whipping tree. The rough bark further inflicted intense pain on Jesse's open wound, causing him to cry out for mercy. Again, James froze and looked down at his father; that soulless death glare was back. There was not an ounce of empathy coursing through James while looming over his weeping father. In fact, a twisted form of pride was rising inside James's chest, as he watched a river of tears coasting through the blood on his father's face. In that moment, James indeed looked very much like a conscienceless madman, as he stood there quietly, chest heaving, teeth clenched, refusing to blink. After admiring his butchery for a moment, James suddenly walked away.

Jesse was left there alone with Harrison, Wilson, and Austin towering over him. They were unable to pull their eyes away from the disfigured pulp in front of them. Had they not been there to witness the entire event, they would have questioned whether they were looking at a man or a mangled animal. A small part of them actually felt sorry for Jesse. But they knew that James would only ever inflict this sort of damage on a man who well deserved it. The sight of Jesse was so gruesome, Austin had to look away for a moment to keep from throwing up. When he turned, he saw James returning with the canister of kerosene. It was then that Harrison finally learned why James had requested it. Jesse screamed in misery again as the unbearable burn of kerosene seeped into his open wounds. Prepared to get a preview of his father's future in the eternal pits of hell, James then snatched a torch from Austin's hand.

Struggling to see through his swollen eyes, Jesse suddenly looked up at his son. "Y-you t-turned out t-to be the s-sort of m-man that I could n-neva' be ... d-despite havin' a p-piece of shit f-fatha' like m-me," he said, struggling for air between every word. "Y-you're the only r-reason my l-life eva' ended up bein' w-worth a damn anyway." He fought hard to take another breath. "So, go on and kill me," he panted, sounding defeated.

James was momentarily stunned by his father's authenticity. In his entire twenty-nine years, Jesse had never once told James that he loved him. He knew it was the closest thing he would ever get to hearing such words. But the sincere confession was way too little and many, many years too late.

"COME ON AND DO IT!" Jesse suddenly demanded.

In some rare instances, it would better serve the whole of society to put a vicious, rabid, animal down to save us all from being unnecessarily infected with its disgusting disease ... always remember that, James heard echoing in his head again as he wiped the sweat from under his nose. Ready take William's advice, he raised the torch and was suddenly tackled to the ground. The blow temporarily knocked the wind out of James. When he turned to see who had tackled him, he instantly became belligerent. "What the hell're you doin'?!" James yelled, trying to toss Elijah off him.

Panting hard, Elijah turned back toward Jesse. James followed Elijah's eyes to see what he was looking at. His eyes were met with the sight of Jacob on his knees. Jacob was directly in front of Jesse, staring at the axe that he had accidentally lodged in his father's chest cavity.

From afar, Elijah had watched James brutally torturing his father. He had steadily crept closer to the scene to get a better view of the unbelievable sight he was witnessing. The way James beat his own father forced Elijah to second guess whether he had any part in his parents' murder. From where Elijah was standing, he was the only one who saw that Jacob had slipped out of his rope, got an axe, and went barreling at James with it from behind. Elijah tackled James just seconds before Jacob lodged the axe in the back of his skull. When Jacob missed, the weight of the metal carried through and lodged in

Jesse's chest cavity. It lodged so deep that only the handle was visible. Blood now shot in spurts out of the sides of the gaping wound, in much the same way that tears shot out of Jacob's eyes, while watching the life drain from his father's face. Jesse looked directly into the eyes of his murderer, blinked for a final time, pushed the last of his tears out, and never opened his eyes again.

While Jacob was collapsed in overwhelming grief, Harrison, Austin, and Wilson walked toward Elijah and James to help them up. James slapped Harrison's hand away and ran his hand through his hair in frustration. He was legitimately angry that his brother had accidentally stolen a moment that was meant to serve as justice for Lily, his daughter, his mother, and every slave that his father had murdered. James did not care that it was a sick and twisted form of justice either. He wanted it for his loved ones. And he wanted to be the one who delivered it.

After sitting there a moment, James suddenly hopped to his feet, pulled his pistol from his holster, aimed it in Elijah's direction, and pulled the trigger. The bullet sailed over Elijah's shoulder and struck his brother square between the eyes. Jacob dropped dead on the spot. Austin, in turn, dropped to his knees. He immediately went into shock after seeing his arm dangling by nothing but muscle tissue. Jacob had yanked the axe out of his father's chest and wielded it toward all five men in a blinding rage, nearly hacking off Austin's right arm. James ran to his aid and quickly tied a tourniquet around it to stop him from bleeding out. Everyone then helped rush him to the medical tent back at their base.

Once James helped the medics stabilize Austin, he felt an unrelenting need to return to his father's home for unfinished business. He made it back just before dawn with Harrison, Wilson, and three other Freedom Riders escorting him. They kept a lookout on the perimeter to watch for any impending trouble. As they stood guard, James walked over and looked down at Jacob's lifeless body.

He was not the brother whose brain he wished to put a bullet through. He knew Jacob was intellectually subpar, with an IQ that barely exceeded his pants size. He was an impressionable follower, only able to mimic others to navigate his way through life. He had, unfortunately, chosen J.R. and Jesse as his life guides. He loyally followed behind them like a lost, lonely puppy, hoping for a proud pat on the head from time to time. James felt Jacob lacked the intelligence to understand how horribly misguided he was. For that fact, James actually had a bit of sympathy for the man, and even a lingering ounce of love. Wanting to show him a bit of decency, he dug his brother a shallow grave, buried him, made a cross out of sticks, and said a prayer for him before he walked away.

The same could not be said for Jesse, though. James had not an ounce of respect, love, or sympathy for a man who had taken pleasure in ensuring the misery of others throughout every second of his life. Without a single prayer whispered, James laid a torch between his lifeless father's legs and watched his body go up in flames, along with his torturous whipping tree. Much like Jesse at his Ghost Rider rallies, James stood there staring at his victim's dead body with nary a tear in his eyes. As he watched his skin bubble and melt, he felt some semblance of peace, knowing that his father's soul was now suffering the very same fiery fate in the eternal pits of hell. The only thing that would have been more satisfying for James, at this moment, was if there was still breath in his father's lungs as he slowly roasted. To have seen him flailing and wailing, like the countless slaves he had tortured, seemed a fitting way for his father to go. His brother had robbed him of that. He now just had to be content with the fact that a rabid vicious animal had finally been put down, like a wise man had once advised him to do, as a service to society.

James tossed Jesse's signature whip into the flames and watched it burn to a crisp as well. "I'm sure you and the devil will get along just fine," he said. Treating his father with the same kindness that he had shown to all his slaves upon their deaths, he callously walked away, leaving his remains to be feasted on by wild animals.

James picked up the kerosene canister on his way toward his childhood home. He trotted up the porch steps and set the canister just outside the door, near the planter that he and Lily had once hidden crickets in to scare Mary Jo. He looked out into the field and let out a faint laugh as the memory returned of little Mary Jo face-planting in the mud, as she fled from the crickets. James then walked into the parlor and a vision of Lily sitting at the piano materialized in his mind. He walked into the kitchen and recalled all the times that he and Lily had laughed as they scrubbed the floor there, together. He stepped into the guest bedroom, recalling the way he and Lily had made love there after reconciling. The beautiful memory made his eyes flutter close as a surge of warmth ignited his insides. He then stepped into the living room and gazed at the special spot on the sofa, where he used to sit and comfort his crying mother as a toddler. Just above that spot was a portrait of her.

As James gazed at her image, he heard Harrison and Wilson enter the house to check on him. "Help me," James said to them, still staring at his mother. Minutes later, they were all carrying his mother's piano into Lily's old room in the slave quarters. James then went back into the house one last time and retrieved the portrait of his mother from the wall. His tears pelted the glass of the frame as he gazed at her. He wiped the tear away, walked out to the slave quarters, placed the portrait inside the piano bench, and covered it all with Lily's old blanket. He then walked back out to the front of the main house and gazed up at the old, rickety dwelling one last time. His childhood home indeed held many very special memories … but Jesse Adams had managed to taint them all. He left a dark cloud that constantly rained misery and sorrow, flooding everyone with tears. The cloud drifting over that house never cleared, no matter how much laughter and love tried to shine through it. For that reason, James let go of the torch in his hand and dropped it in the trail of kerosene that he had poured all throughout the house.

With a massive inferno blazing behind him, James Adams walked off his father's plantation for the very last time. He stopped at the entrance and planted an American flag, branded with *the Freedom Riders* emblem. But this time, it symbolized an ironclad guarantee that Lily would never again have to set foot in that house of horrors or be taken prisoner by the man who had made it the nightmare that it was.

Chapter Twenty-two

James was standing at the end of Austin and Emerson's cots in the medical tent. Emerson was among the few who had been shot on Joseph's plantation during the brief battle there. James and his medical team were forced to amputate Austin's arm that same night. After recovering for nearly a month, James had just declared both men well enough to go home. Wilson was leaving too. During a recent mission to retrieve supplies and ammunition, their troop was attacked, and he sustained a knife injury to the face that nearly cost him his right eye. James felt it was wise for all three men to travel back home together. Emerson agreed and got up to gather his belongings along with Wilson.

"So much for eva' playin' percussion again," Austin joked while looking at what was left of his bandaged arm.

"I'm really sorry we couldn't save it. I promise, we tried like hell," James replied, lingering guilt still in his tone.

"I know, and for that I truly thank you," Austin said, still looking at his arm. "I guess I can look on the bright side. It gives me a legitimate excuse to finally go home and see my little girl again. At least I still have one good arm to hug 'er with." He quickly looked up at James. "I'm sorry I didn't mean to…"

James put a reassuring hand on Austin's shoulder. "It's alright. I love hearin' you talk about little Georgia Lily. I get to live vicariously through you," he said sincerely.

Austin nodded. *"Danny* ... that's what Georgia used to call me before I left home. She had it confused with the word *daddy*. It was the most adorable damn thing eva'," Austin said, smiling at the memory. "Hard to believe she's almost five now. Afta' all these years, I just hope she still rememba's that I'm her *danny*."

"I don't think anyone could eva' forget you, Austin. I know I certainly won't."

Austin nodded his appreciation for the kind words and stood up to get his backpack.

James helped him put it on when he struggled to put the straps in place. "Is that everything?" he then asked.

"I think so," Austin replied, looking around. "This may sound insane, but in a way, I might actually miss bein' here."

"I don't think it's insane at all. As gruesome as it's been, these battlefields have been your home for four years now."

"It's not the battlefields I'll miss. The Freedom Rida's are like my family now."

"Afta' everything we've been through, I think we're all bonded for life now, wetha' we wanna be or not," James replied. He exhaled and looked Austin in the eyes. "But truth be told, you've felt like family to me long before we eva' formed the Freedom Rida's ... I mean that sincerely."

Austin looked James in the eyes as well. "The feelin's been mutual ... for just as long."

Both men stood there silently for a moment, neither of them ready to say goodbye, especially James. He was still astounded by Austin's evolution from arrogant young man to a man that was now worth honoring. A man he once loathed for hurting Lily was now one he greatly respected for trying to free her. The fact that their friendship had evolved to that degree was hitting James at full force, making a simple goodbye seem impossible.

"Will you write to me and let me know when you find Lily?" Austin asked.

"Absolutely."

"You make sure you bring your ass home to her in one piece. I'm sure she'd much prefer you that way," Austin teased.

James laughed. "Tell that to our enemies!"

When their light laughter subsided, Austin looked around the tent one last time and exhaled. "Well, I guess I best get goin'. Emerson's waitin' on me." He then extended his only remaining hand to James.

"You both be careful on the journey home," James replied, shaking his hand. "I'll be prayin' for ya' both."

"I appreciate that. I'll be prayin' just as hard for all of you too." Austin adjusted his backpack, put on his hat, and made his first steps toward home. He suddenly paused, though, and turned back around. He nervously looked down at the ground and then up at James. "When you find Lily … will you please tell 'er that I tried my best to help find 'er and officially set 'er free?" He lowered his head, looked at his arm, and began to tear up. "I tried," he whispered.

"You can damn well believe I already had every intention of doin' just that."

Austin nodded and quickly turned around to depart before his tears could fall.

"Austin!" James called out before he exited the tent.

He stopped and turned around again.

Despite Austin being a lower ranking soldier, James stood at attention, slowly raised his hand to his head and saluted him.

Despite the overwhelming emotion of the moment, Austin straightened up, stood at attention, and absorbed the honoring moment like a true patriotic soldier. He then nodded his head, turned, and began the long journey back home to his wife, and the little girl he had named in Lily's honor.

Chapter Twenty-three

W illiam stood inside the Manhattan museum's music themed room, staring up at the portrait of Lily in Piers LeRoux's painting of the Dream Symphony. He was about to sit down to start his usual silent prayers for all his loved ones, until he suddenly heard a familiar voice behind him.

"Isabel told us we'd find you here, perusing the halls of our mother's favorite museum."

William turned around and was instantly stunned into tears. "Emerson! Wilson!" Tears spilled from his eyes as he gazed at his twins. "Please tell me my old mind isn't playing tricks on me," he whispered, his bottom lip quivering.

"We're here father," Wilson said as he embraced him.

William's tears seeped onto Wilson's decorated military jacket as he embraced his beloved son tightly. He only released him to embrace the other. The tears on Emerson's jacket proved how grateful he was to be holding him as well. Emerson reciprocated the hug as best he could with the sling on his arm.

William pulled back, wiped his eyes, and gazed at his sons with pride again. The joy of having them both home alive had made him oblivious to their injuries at first. "Will you both be alright?" William asked, after noting the dressing on their wounds.

"No worries. Bullet broke a bone in my shoulder and lodged in the muscle, but James removed it and stitched me up well. He said I'd regain full use in a few more weeks."

"James stitched me up too. I won't know how badly my vision has been affected until I'm healed enough to remove the stitches and the gauze in a few weeks. But James was optimistic."

"You both still have breath in your lungs and capable minds. That's all that should matter."

"Indeed," Emerson replied, exhaling to ward off tears. "More importantly, how are *you* fatha'?"

William refused to blink his tear-filled eyes as he gazed at his sons. "Two pieces of my heart have just returned home from the bloody fields of battle. Now, all I need is for James, Elijah, Harrison, and Austin to return in one piece. Only then will my heart feel whole again."

"Well, you can cross one of those off your list."

"Austin!" William erupted, after turning to find him standing near the entryway next to Preston Mills. Austin's daughter, his wife, and Isabel were there as well, their eyes filled with tears after watching a loving father reunite with his sons.

Austin approached William. "I neva' really had much of a capable mind." He lifted his amputated arm. "Nor can I say that I'm in one piece anymore," he joked. "But I'm definitely here with breath still left in my lungs."

"And for that I'm truly grateful. It's wonderful to have you back home as well," William said, his tears fresh again as he embraced Austin like a son.

"Certainly a homecoming deserving of a celebration," Preston expressed as he approached. "I have just instructed my staff to put together a gala for all of you in the coming weeks. Please feel free to invite friends and family to celebrate your homecoming and your service to our country. Food, drinks, and entry will be free for all. Your dedication to mending our divided nation is sincerely appreciated, and we here at the Manhattan Museum would like to show our gratitude for all your heroic sacrifices. I'm sure many of the residents here in our town will as well."

"Your gesture is equally appreciated Mr. Mills," Emerson replied. "Thank you very much."

"It's an honor to do so," Preston replied, shaking Emerson, Wilson, and Austin's hands. "Unfortunately, I'll be leaving town this evening, but it will be my first order of business to finalize all plans when I return to Manhattan in a few days."

"You're a brave man to venture outside of this town in the midst of a war," William joked.

"*Brave?* I think *insane* is the word you're looking for," Preston joked in return. "Unfortunately, I'm being *forced* to deliver several very expensive portraits to a family down in Texas. The wife is a very particular socialite and art connoisseur. She *demands* that I deliver them personally. She refuses to pay otherwise. Seems the delivery of her fanciful decor trumps the safety of a man traversing a war-torn country."

"Sounds like you're dealing with a truly *selfless* woman with very sensible priorities. Oh, how I envy you," William joked, wrinkling his nose.

"Well then, I'll gladly trade places with you, my friend," Preston sarcastically replied.

"I think I'll pass," William laughed. "But I bid you safe travels, my good friend."

"Yes, safe travels, Mr. Mills. And thank you again for the homecoming celebration," Wilson said.

"Yes, thank you," Austin added.

"It will be my pleasure, gentlemen. Now, if you'll excuse me. I must set off on my journey to meet the world's most selfless socialite," Preston joked. He gave a slight nod before departing to the train station.

When Preston was gone, Austin took a moment to look around the music themed exhibit. He stopped and looked up at the painting of the woman who had inspired him to become a soldier. "I'm appreciative of Mr. Mills wantin' to celebrate our homecomin'." He briefly glanced over at his wife and little Georgia. "I'm ova'joyed to be back with my family, but…" He looked back at Lily's portrait again. "But part of me is devastated that I wasn't able to see the war through 'til the very end."

"Your sentiments definitely mirror mine," Emerson added.

Austin looked down at his missing arm. "Still hard to believe I spent years fightin' on battlefields, only to end my stint as a soldier durin' a routine rescue mission on a plantation field instead."

"I can imagine that such a thing is truly devastating. But we must accept that all things happen for a reason … reasons that are often beyond our earthly comprehension," William replied.

"Much like the fact that we rescued thousands of slaves … and not a single one of 'em was Lily." Austin shook his head. "That's indeed beyond my earthly comprehension."

Wilson walked over and stood beside them. "I know how you feel. Felt like we scoured every nook and cranny in the south. Seems impossible that we never crossed paths with her. Makes me feel like her existence was just a figment of our imaginations."

"Those are words from a mind on the verge of defeat. Let us not lose hope," William replied.

"I haven't," Austin quickly replied. "I may not be a part of the Freedom Rida's anymore, but that certainly won't stop me from doin' my part to find Lily." He turned again and gazed up at the portrait of her sitting centerstage in the Dream Symphony. "The show ain't ova' yet."

"Not even close, my boy," William replied. "Not even close."

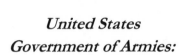

Chapter twenty-four

United States
Government of Armies:
Rules of War

Section I Code II

Commanders, whenever admissible, must inform the enemy of their intention to bombard a place, so that the noncombatants, especially the women and children, may be removed before the bombardment commences.

Section I Code XI

The laws of war do not condone cruelty, or the infliction of suffering for the sake of suffering, or for revenge. Unjust retaliation removes the belligerents farther from the mitigating rules of regular war and nearer to the barbaric wars of savages. Therefore, acts of cruelty for individual gain, or revenge, shall be severely punished, and especially so if committed by officers.

January 30, 1865

"Red, puffy eyes … *check*. Distant and withdrawn … *check*. Refusin' to smile … *check*. Accordin' to that list, it's clear that the old Adams heartbreaker has returned and crushed anotha' heart."

Confused by Harrison's random statement, James suddenly stopped putting away a new shipment of medication and looked at him oddly. "What the hell're you talkin' about?"

411

"Amelia," Harrison replied, as if it was obvious. "I guess you unda'estimate the powa' of the Adams' charm, and how it has this mysterious ability to make women abandon their morals," he teased. He motioned his head toward Amelia. "I assume she's made some kind of mistake with you that she now regrets. She's been avoidin' you like the plague lately. Don't tell me you haven't noticed?"

James turned and looked at Amelia, who was sitting in the far corner of the tent. She had her back to him, kindly tending to a patient. The aftereffects of humiliation had indeed caused her to keep her distance from James, something only Harrison seemed to have noticed. That fact was further proven by the sheepish look on James's face when he turned back to look at Harrison.

"Of course you haven't noticed … just like all the otha' fragile carnage you left in your wake back in school," Harrison replied. He then patted James lightly on the shoulder. "Go easy on Amelia, huh. Don't fault the woman for carin' about you."

James briefly glanced over at Amelia again and then turned back to Harrison. "I'm sorry. I honestly didn't realize I's so harsh. I don't mean to be that way. It just …" He ran his hands through his hair and blew out a breath.

"Just what? *Lily?* C'mon Adams, it's been four years."

"And your point?!" James angrily shot back, instantly incensed by his words.

"Sorry, I…"

"Do you know what it's like?" James interrupted, his eyes suddenly lowered into angry slits.

"What *what's* like?" Harrison responded, looking confused.

"Bein' forced to watch your fatha' nearly beat your wife to death? To watch your baby die in your arms?"

Silence.

James took a step toward him. "DO YOU?!" he demanded, his face now fire-red.

Harrison swallowed hard, wishing it was his words that he had just re-ingested. He nervously looked around at all the eyes in the tent suddenly turning in their direction. He then sheepishly glanced back at James and lowered his head in shame.

"Yeah, I didn't figure you had much experience on havin' your *whole world* ripped apart! You may know laws backwards and forwards, but you're no goddamn expert on when a person's grief is supposed to expire! You don't have the *slightest clue* about this level of pain!" James replied, his voice shaking with emotion. "You're ignorant as to how just the *thought* of your own flesh and blood takin' 'er last breath in your arms can sometimes feel like someone's suckin' the air clean outta your own damn lungs! Let me guess! You've neva' felt a stabbin' pain in your chest ova' the memory of your fatha' tryna beat the life outta your wife! You've neva' once felt like a monsta' was tryna claw its way outta you to brutally murda' your own brotha', anytime you think about 'em defilin' the woman you love! If you'd eva' experienced even *one* of those things, you'd unda'stand why the pain from that day has its hooks in my heart, and it won't let go! You'd know how it can weigh a man down, and stifle 'em from damn near *everything!* You'd unda'stand why the memories of the way I failed that day makes me wanna put a bullet in my goddamn brain!

"I failed Lily, Harrison! I failed the woman I loved! I failed my little baby!" he exclaimed, his agitation rising. "All day, every day, my mind is haunted by what my fatha' and brotha' did to Lily! I'm constantly tortured by the memory of her danglin' on the verge of death in the back of that wagon, because I failed to protect 'er! I failed as a husband! I failed as a doctor! I failed as a fatha'! I failed as a goddamn *man* ... and it's eatin' me alive inside! Where's Lily?! Is she okay?! Is she still sufferin' because I failed! Ova' and ova' and ova' and ova' again that's all I hear runnin' through my goddamn head!" James suddenly began banging his fists against his temples. "Fail! Fail! Fail! Fail! It's devourin' my sanity!"

"James, calm down," Harrison said, nervously looking around again at all the flabbergasted eyes pasted on James as he unraveled.

James suddenly stopped hitting himself and looked directly at Harrison, tears now glistening in his eyes. "And yes! Even *four years* lata' that day is just as fresh on my mind as the day it happened … and so is the pain. And there's nothin'…" He glanced at Amelia. "And no *one* in this camp that can ease the weight of this pain!"

Harrison placed a hand on his friend's shoulder to calm him. "James, it'll be alright."

"NO, IT WON'T BE ALRIGHT!" James yelled, knocking his hand away. "UNLESS I CAN FUCKING GO BACK IN TIME, I CAN NEVA' MAKE IT RIGHT!" he screamed, suddenly overturning a tableful of medical supplies and storming out of the tent.

Harrison nervously glanced at all the patients staring in his direction, their mouths agape. He then looked at Amelia. Both were too uncomfortable to hold each other's gaze for long. After a moment, Amelia walked over to pick up the scattered supplies, but Harrison stopped her. "No, please don't. I'll clean it up." Quietly, he went about placing the supplies back on the medical cart. All the while, he was praying that James's outburst had helped to alleviate even a fraction of his repressed pain.

Unfortunately, that was not remotely the case. Prior to their interaction, James had already been teetering emotionally after receiving another disappointing letter from William regarding Lily. Harrison's statement had easily nudged him over the edge. He stormed out of the medic tent and went to retrieve his satchel from underneath his cot. He grabbed *the Little Mermaid* and went to find a place to be alone for his post-letter ritual. However, he was so irate, the book barely settled his racing heart. Not long after, he was back in his tent with his failures still rampant on his mind. To cease the looping torturous thoughts, he angrily laid down in his cot and forced himself to go to sleep for a good portion of the day.

Later that night, Harrison walked into the tent to find James sitting on the edge of his cot, sharpening the blade on his weapon. James stopped sharpening it when a flask was suddenly thrust into his view. He looked up to find Harrison sheepishly standing there holding it out toward him. "Peace offerin'," he said to James, trying to hand him a flask full of his favorite whiskey.

"For what?" James replied, sounding annoyed by his presence.

"For insinuatin' that your grief is supposed to have expired by now," Harrison sighed. "I feel like the biggest jackass on the planet for bein' so callous."

"You should."

"I know. That's why, man to man, I wanted to say that I'm sorry. I should've neva' disrespected Lily that way … nor your marriage for that matta'. I'm sincerely sorry for that. I guess I just wanted to see you back to your old self. But my words didn't reflect that, only insensitivity … and *definitely* ignorance. For that I beg your forgiveness."

James gently snatched the flask from Harrison's hand as a sign that he accepted his apology. He took a swig, exhaled to let the burn out, then wiped his mouth with the back of his hand. "Thanks, and I'm sorry too. I know I ova'reacted. I shouldn't expect that everybody unda'stands how special Lily is to me."

Harrison nervously chuckled. "Ya' damn sure made that blatantly clear to me today … and to damn near everyone else in this camp."

James took another swig from the flask, then offered it to Harrison. He accepted, sat down next to James, and took a sip.

James laid his weapon down, rested his elbows on his knees, and stared blankly at the ground as he thought of Lily. "My pain is so great because the love was so great. Lily loved me in a way that I've neva' experienced before … in a way I fear I neva' will again. She's such an extraordinary human being. I've neva' met anotha' woman even remotely like her. I don't think I eva' will again in this lifetime. And quite frankly…" He turned to look Harrison in the eyes. "I don't even have an interest in tryin', because I'm convinced that no otha' woman could eva' live up to her."

James took the flask back from Harrison and took another sip. "I know how Amelia feels. I know what she wants from me. And hell, I don't blame ya' for thinkin' I belong in an asylum for not wantin' 'er that way too," he joked. "And maybe you're right. Logically, I probably should be able to let go of the past, move on, and give Amelia a chance. But it's like every part of me is numb. Too numb to tell my body and my mind how to feel, what to think, what to do … too numb to move on. I dunno how to explain it." He shook his head. "It's like my emotions are unda' lock and key and there's only one thing that'll unlock it all."

"Findin' Lily," Harrison answered.

James nodded. "*Exactly*." He sighed as he stared at the flask in his hands. "Hundreds of rescue missions we've done. Thousands of slaves we've freed. And I'm proud of that, but…"

"But what?"

"But it pains me to say that not a single one of the slaves we've freed has been Lily," James answered. "It's made every successful rescue feel so bitta'-sweet. My heart is always in my goddamn throat every time we step onto a plantation. I can't stop my mind from racin' in those moments. Is this the place? Is this the day? Will I hold my Lily again? Prayin', beggin' God every step of the way. My chest swells with hope before we open every slave quarta' door, only to feel the hope deflatin' with every person we usha' outta there. Afta' everyone is gone, and Lily's nowhere to be found, the sweet moment of success always manages to turn into bitta'ness. Wheneva' we walk away without 'er, I feel just as empty as every slave quarta' we clear out." James sighed and took another gulp of whiskey. He absorbed the burn without a reaction this time, as he lowered his head in misery again.

"When the bitta'ness sets in on those nights, it always makes me wish I'd neva' taken Lily off my fatha's farm to meet William," James continued. "My fatha' rarely bothered Lily before then. Hell, he hardly even looked at 'er. She may have been livin' in a shithole, but at least I knew where she was, and that she was relatively safe," he sighed. "At least I knew for a fact that she was alive. But now I don't know any of those things. I'm stuck with nothin' but torturous thoughts of the hellish places she *might* be, or the ways in which she *might* be sufferin'. They're the kind of gruesome thoughts that would make even a sane man wanna fling himself off a cliff to escape. And the fact that I hold some responsibility for what Lily may be goin' through is unbearable some days, Harrison." He paused and glanced at his weapon. "It's all I can do to not set that musket between my legs and blow my own damn head off."

"Responsible? How so?" Harrison asked.

"Because all this turmoil started when I went and upset the applecart. I tried to lead Lily to a betta' life. But I only led my fatha' and brotha' to unleash their demons on 'er instead. Makes me regret eva' takin' Lily to meet William. If I'd've just left well-enough alone, she'd've been among the slaves that we set free on my fatha's plantation the otha' night. She would've finally had 'er freedom," James sighed. "*Freedom* … and givin' Lily the life she deserves. That's all I eva' wanted for her since I's a kid." He shook his head. "Can't eva' seem to succeed in that. All I've managed to do was destroy the life of a beautiful soul. Some days that fact is too much to live with."

"Destroyed her life?" Harrison replied, looking thoroughly perplexed. "Hindsight is twenty-twenty, as they say. You did what you thought was right at the time. And what you did for Lily was the most selfless thing I've eva' seen a man do for a woman. And I gotta be honest. Neva' in a million years would I have grown a big enough pair of testicles to do what you did for her. Considerin' Lily's status, your efforts were beyond magnanimous. With tears wellin' in my eyes, I rememba' watchin' the grand finale of the Dream Symphony. I recall glancin' at you when it was ova', feelin' proud to know that my good friend was the one God had chosen to help carry out such an extraordinary miracle. Seein' all that you were willin' to sacrifice for Lily impacted me in ways that I have no words to explain. But I can say that I certainly wasn't watchin' a man destroy a woman's soul. I was witnessin' the most *altruistic* display of love I'd eva' seen in my whole damn life ... And I'm *confident* that Lily would say the same."

Harrison's candid words compelled James to finally raise his head and look his good friend in the eyes again.

"James, I don't know why God is testin' you and Lily like this, but I'm convinced it's for a grand cause. And I'm just as convinced that God'll reward you *both* with anotha' miracle when He feels the grand cause is complete."

James breathed a heavy sigh. "Your words mean a lot, and I pray you're right, but I'm reluctant to get my hopes up. I've learned, in the most tragic ways, that you neva' truly know what God has in store. That's the scary part. With Rose everything is so final. For His own good reasons, God decided to bring 'er back home. I'll probably neva' stop grievin' ova' her death, but I have to learn to accept His decision, and find the strength to move on, with my pain in tow. But with Lily, it's still so open-ended. Everything is *still* an unanswered question. Maybe God decided we should neva' be togetha' again ... that's very likely. But it's the *not knowin'* that's eatin' me alive. If Lily's moved on and has decided she neva' again wants me as a part of her life, I'll have to respect that, and somehow learn to accept it. But one way or anotha' ... I just need to know. At the very least, I wanna know that she's okay. Just that alone would give me some semblance of peace."

"I know it's probably impossible not to let your faith start slippin' away unda' these circumstances but try to hold on to it. Because I find it impossible to believe that God brought two kindred spirits like you togetha' as children just to tear you apart foreva'."

"I hope you're right. Because, at this point, it's eitha' Lily or no one. *Faithfulness* and *loyalty* ... 'til death do us part. If I didn't mean every word, I neva' would've spoken 'em. Someone would have to show me Lily's cold dead body before I eva' break those vows, or even *contemplate* layin' with anotha' woman." James took another sip from his near empty flask. "Besides, it seems incredibly unfair to be with anotha' woman while, in the back of my mind, I'm thinkin' that she'll neva' live up to Lily. Seems selfish and wrong to me. I know I may sound like a nutcase to most otha' men, but that's just the way I feel."

Harrison took the flask and drank the last of the whiskey. "Ya' know, I didn't think I could eva' admit that I admire anotha' man..." He looked James in the eyes. "You just proved me wrong. You're one hell of a noble man, James Adams. Crazy as hell!" he joked. "But *definitely* noble."

"Well, I can't deny the crazy part," James laughed.

"Nor should you the noble," Harrison replied, patting him hard on the back.

Harrison was not the only one feeling like the biggest jackass on the planet. Elijah was standing outside the tent eavesdropping. He had overheard every word of James and Harrison's conversation. Prior to merging with the Iron Army Brigade, Elijah was convinced that James's claims of love for Lily were merely lust, that he was a typical possessive master, obsessed with the flesh of his property. But over the months trapped there together, Elijah was forced to see and hear the real James. His actions and authenticity regarding Lily had slowly begun to shift Elijah's beliefs. Even his hatred for the man could no longer blind him to the truth. Now, to his own surprise, Elijah suddenly heard his inner voice agree with Harrison's stance on James's nobility. Along with that voice came a sick feeling in his stomach. In the midst of war, Elijah had slain many a man. He was no more affected by ending a man's life than if he had crushed a cockroach. But suddenly, the sick feeling in his stomach had him on the verge of vomiting, when he thought about the death of three men in particular: Samuel, Tucker McCormick, and that of a kind-hearted old man, who became an innocent victim of Elijah's vengeful rampage ...

On the night that James was attempting to escape his father's farm with Lily, a panicked Dr. Gideon Whitfield had finally arrived at the X on the map that James had provided. With Lily still unconscious in the back of the wagon, Gideon nervously looked around for a man named Samuel, as he had been instructed to do. A campfire was burning, but nothing else was there except for a few empty cans of beans, and a team of horses hooked together. After being caught up in gunfire with James, Gideon was now jumpy and leery of everything. He grabbed his pistol and quickly turned his head to the left when he suddenly heard leaves rustling. "A-are you Samuel?" Gideon stammered when Elijah came into view with his gun drawn.

Elijah hesitated a moment, staring at Gideon oddly. "Yes, I'm Samuel," he lied. "Who the hell're you?"

"No need for the pistol then. I've got Lily with me in the back," Gideon replied, lowering his gun and relaxing a bit.

When Gideon put his pistol back in its holster, Elijah did the same. "Where's James?" Elijah asked, looking around.

"He ran into some trouble while we were on the way here. He said he'd catch up with us as soon as he could. He wants you to just take Lily for now."

"*Trouble?* What kind of trouble? And where's Lily any damn way? Lily?!" Elijah called out.

"She's injured," Gideon explained.

"The hell you mean, she's *injured?*"

"I'm sure James can explain all this to ya' betta', but there was some kind of debacle on his farm with his fatha' before they could leave."

Elijah looked at Gideon with leery eyes. He then snatched a lantern and began making his way to the wagon to see if Gideon was telling the truth. As he began to climb up the back of the wagon, a sliver of early morning sun peeked over the ridge of a hill. As dawn's early light illuminated the campsite, an unsettling sight caught Gideon's attention. He saw what looked to be a pool of blood on the nearby terrain that he had not noticed in the darkness. As the sun brightened the area more, Gideon's eyes then followed drag marks that led from the pool of blood to an area covered in loose brush and leaves. The moment he saw that mound, Gideon's heart rate accelerated. There was no doubt in his mind that a body lay beneath that makeshift grave. His gut instinct made Gideon suddenly snap the reins, prompting the horses into an immediate gallop. As the horses surged forward, Elijah lost his balance and fell backward off the wagon. He landed awkwardly on his right arm, popping his shoulder out of its socket. As he rode away, Gideon shot the team of waiting horses, leaving Elijah with no way to give chase. Despite the excruciating pain of his injury, Elijah managed to wrestle his pistol from its holster. While lying on the ground, he then began shooting wildly at Gideon, until he emptied the chamber of his revolver. Elijah saw Gideon lurch forward after the last bullet was fired.

Despite the searing pain from the bullet that Elijah had lodged in his shoulder, Gideon kept his horses galloping at full speed. His only focus was on carrying out James's plan for Lily. He recalled that James told him to get Lily to Harrison, if all else failed. *Fail* was now an understatement. Gideon's shoulder was bleeding too badly to carry on to Harrison's home without treating it. Once he was certain that Elijah was no longer a threat, he pulled over and hid in a cave. He bravely removed the bullet from his own wound, stitched it, and carried on trying to find Harrison. As misfortune would have it, Harrison was out of town indefinitely, on account of an important murder trial. Assuming he would return soon, Gideon had hidden in Harrison's barn and waited. In that time, he did all he could to take care of Lily, who was now drifting in and out of consciousness. But Gideon, himself, suddenly felt his own body beginning to fail as he waited. When Harrison did not return home by nightfall, Gideon felt he had no choice but to take Lily to his good friend, Ava. Out of desperation, he then began making his way to her tiny, hidden hospital. He was weak and disoriented by the time he arrived, but Gideon was determined to get Lily to safety and to save her life ... just as determined as James had been to save his little boy's. Gideon's determination and Elijah's bullet, however, had ultimately cost him his life.

... Dr. Gideon Whitfield was the final victim of Elijah's vengeful killing spree. He had senselessly taken three lives out of jealousy and anger, while on his quest to avenge the death of his parents and to destroy the relationship of a couple that he now realized never deserved it. Regret for his actions slowly began to devour him the night Elijah sat around the bonfire, listening to the way James spoke so passionately about his love for Lily and Rose. His words brought clarity to the reason James had attacked him in a blinding rage when he spoke ill of Rose the morning he arrived at camp. Elijah now believed he deserved to have his skull bashed in for it. In fact, whenever he recalled what he had said about Rose, he got sick to his stomach.

Witnessing the way James had tortured his father further opened the floodgates of regret about Elijah's role in the destruction of James and Lily's lives. Worse yet, he had to accept that he even bore some responsibility for the death of their beloved child. Now, after eavesdropping on James's conversation with Harrison, all those regrets had finally eaten away his insides completely and had begun nipping away at his soul.

As Elijah stood there reliving his life regrets, an explosion rocked the ground and jolted a single tear from his eye. James and Harrison both halted their conversation after hearing the distinctive noise too.

"It's afta' midnight. That can't be what it sounds like," Harrison commented.

"It shouldn't be, but I think that's damn sho' what it is," James replied, grabbing his musket and bolting out of the tent. Harrison was quick to follow. He and James stood alongside Elijah, their eyes wide in disbelief as the sounds continued in rapid succession. All three tried to convince themselves they were in the throes of a nightmare when their eyes were then met with the hellish sight of cannonballs raining from the sky, that began pelting their massive campsite like a meteor shower. Far off to their right, several cannonballs landed directly on tents of sleeping men, exploding on impact. The blood-curdling shrieks of injured men were quick to follow. James took off running to help, dodging other soldiers, who had been torn from their sleep by all the noise. There were dozens of men emerging from their tents with weapons in hand, trying to make sense of the chaos that was suddenly erupting in their besieged campsite. James felt as though his legs could not propel him forward fast enough to assist the wounded, but shock suddenly stopped him on a dime. "Holy shit," he murmured when his eyes caught sight of a horde of men, rising up over the ridge of a hill. After lighting their way with fires set by cannons, a tidal wave of growling Confederate soldiers had come storming toward the Iron Army Brigade.

The Elite Confederate Infantry of Virginia had received intel that finally led them to the Union troop responsible for the secret nighttime thievery of slaves. Their raid was in direct retaliation to the so-called *Freedom Riders*, embedded within the Iron Army Brigade of the East. *The Elite Infantry* was hell-bent on putting a stop to their tradition of freeing slaves and planting American flags on the sacred grounds of the new Confederate country they were fighting to build. Mimicking the midnight ritual of the Freedom Riders, the Elite Confederacy's infantrymen had also strategically hidden until nightfall and attacked in the dead of night, in an unwarlike fashion. The warning of an impending battle was never given to General Blackshear. Their blatant disregard for the rules of engagement was to ensure that the Freedom Riders would be left just as vulnerable as the innocent civilians they had stolen property from. The Confederate Elites felt that the Freedom Riders' lawlessness made them unworthy of the fair rules of war.

With a meteor shower of cannonballs as their only warning, the Iron Army Brigade was indeed caught off guard. After sleeping soldiers were jolted awake, they chaotically scrambled out of their tents to the nightmarish sight of their enemies swarming them. Before Iron Army soldiers could attempt to defend themselves, angry Confederate Elites began savagely tossing them into the massive fires that were now ravaging their camp. With his campsite now completely under siege, James now had no choice but to abort his mission to help his fellow injured soldiers. He suddenly dropped to a knee, lined a man up in the sight of his musket, and fired the only round in the chamber. The single shot was enough to literally blow the man's brains out. With the horde of Confederate soldiers now surrounding him, engaged in hand-to-hand combat with Union troops, James had no time to reload his musket. Acting on unadulterated rage, he picked up an axe out of tree stump and hurled it, end over end, directly into the chest cavity of a man running toward him at full speed. He pulled the axe out of the dead man's chest and proceeded to drive it into the face or chest of any man who dared to come within his vicinity.

Harrison and Elijah had quickly joined in fighting close to James. The trio had their backs to one another, protecting each other as they slaughtered dozens of southern troops. With their axes swinging, heads had literally begun to roll. The fire-ravaged camp easily illuminated the face of a man that rolled near James's foot. He then briefly glanced at several other dead bodies nearby. He had grown up seeing some of their faces when they were not cowardly hidden behind masks with distinctive eye holes. He had no doubt he was staring at deceased Ghost Riders. Their ghostly white robes had been traded for Confederate uniforms. His father's brethren were swarming his men. That fact sent James into a homicidal rage. He bared his blood-stained teeth, grunting and growling as he commenced to slaying men who had been loyal to his father. Amid his blinding rampage, James savagely butchered over a dozen men in minutes, reveling in the glory of sending his father's henchmen to burn alongside him in the devil's paradise.

As the battle waged for nearly an hour, the so-called *Elites* proved only to be superior at dying at the hands of *Iron* soldiers. Despite being caught off guard by the sneak attack, the Iron Army Brigade was slowly reducing the number of Confederate Elite Infantrymen left alive. His long hair now dripping with the blood of those he had slain, James leaned over his latest victim and snatched his axe from within his chest, ready to continue his killing spree. In the vulnerable split second that he took to retrieve it, an Elite infantryman began approaching swiftly from behind him. With the blade of his musket leading the way, the Elite soldier came barreling toward James at full speed, hell-bent on impaling him through the chest the very second he turned around. With the infantryman's blade just feet away from James's heart, Elijah swung his axe and chopped the man's arm off. Simultaneously, Elijah's name erupted from James's mouth in a blood-curdling scream, as the world suddenly seemed to slow down in his eyes.

In the very same moment that Elijah had turned to defend James, a bayonet had been driven into his back and out the front of his chest. With his boot, the confederate soldier then kicked Elijah off his blade and watched him slump to the ground. Growling like a primordial beast, James swung his axe and sliced the head clean off Elijah's attacker. When the headless man fell to the ground, so too did James. He dropped to his knees, picked up his fallen brother, and held him in his arms. "Hang on, Elijah, it's gonna be alright," James tried to reassure him, despite seeing the life start to drain from his eyes. "Keep your eyes open, Elijah!" James prompted him, trying desperately to keep him conscious. "Look at me!"

Elijah used what little strength he had left to do just that. "P-p-please t-take care of my s-sista'," he coughed. "T-tell 'er, I l-love h-her."

"For what? You'll be able to tell 'er yourself soon."

"I'll t-tell your l-little Rose her f-fatha' loves 'er," he promised, just before he took his final breath.

"ELIJAAAH!" James screamed, trying to shake the life back into him.

"Just the way I figured I'd find ya' ... all snuggled up with a *nigga'!*"

James looked up at the man who had just uttered those words, only to find himself face to face with the barrel of a musket. It was held by someone he had longed to torture to death for four grueling years.

What had guided *The Elite Confederate Infantry of Virginia* to the Freedom Riders was a letter that was delivered to one of the leaders of the troop:

Lieutenant Jesse Adams Jr.

January 3, 1865

It is with tears in my eyes and a truly heavy heart that I must relay the sorrowful news of your father and brother's passing. My sorrows run even deeper knowing that their deaths were not by accident, or by an act of God. Your cherished father, and my beloved husband, were both senselessly murdered. In a matter of days, thousands of slaves were stolen from dozens of Fayetteville plantations. The Parker plantation was among the victims. On the night their plantation was raided, Mary Jo was a witness to her father's heinous beating. She is certain that the man who brutalized him was your youngest brother, James. Hours after Mr. Parker's unjust beating, your father's slaves were also stolen. Your father and brother's lives were both ended that very night. I have since learned that your youngest brother, James, is the leader of a group of men embedded in a Union army brigade. They call themselves "The Freedom Riders." I have no indisputable evidence, so I am only left to speculate that James, or a member of his despicable group of bandits, was likely responsible for the unspeakably gruesome way that your father and brother were murdered. I am eternally sorry for the loss of your family. Please know that I have buried them at your family's gravesite, following the honorable ceremonies they both rightfully deserved.

Praying for your safe return,
Analyse Adams

James's greatest mistake as a lieutenant was leaving Mary Jo Parker alive. After his serious head wound, Joseph Parker had no recollection of what had happened on his plantation Christmas morning. Mary Jo had not forgotten a single detail, though. After staring down the muzzle of James's rifle, she was finally able to name the man at the helm of the notorious group who had emptied nearly every slave quarter in Fayetteville. Mary Jo retold an over-exaggerated version of her harrowing experience to anyone willing to give her the attention she craved. As usual, the salacious gossip about Fayetteville's most wanted outcast quickly spread like a raging inferno. It was through such rampant gossip that Jacob's wife, Analyse, had learned the identity of the person who was likely responsible for murdering her husband and father-in-law. That gossip was scripted by Analyse and sent to a man who was also a leader in his own right.

Just as hard as James was fighting to dismantle the institution of slavery, J.R. was shedding blood to maintain it. Much like James, J.R.'s dedication to his infantry had earned him the rank of Lieutenant. That position gave him the power to make decisions, including those involving strategery. "To hell with the war rules of engagement!" J.R. had angrily denounced, during a motivational speech to his troops. "These nightcrawlin' so-called Freedom Rida's ain't worthy of respect! Them cowardly sons of bitches been sneakin' 'round, tormentin' innocent families in the middle of the night, stealin' their slaves and burnin' their homes! When we find these cowardly pieces of shit, we lie low and attack while they're curled up like babies, dreamin' about the pussy they ain't had in years! What's good for the goose, is good for the fuckin' ganda'! LET'S DESTROY THESE FUCKIN' FREEDOM RIDERS!"

The eruption of cheers that followed let Lieutenant Jesse Roscoe Adams Jr. know that his men stood behind him on his mission. However, they were unaware that the true motive for the attack was far more of a personal mission than anything else. After reading about how "unspeakably gruesome" his brother and father's deaths had been, J.R. was not left speculating about who their true murderer was, like Analyse. He was convinced that James had succeeded in half of the promise he had made to kill him and his father the day they had stood face to face in court. The driving force behind the plan for J.R.'s nighttime raid was to avenge his family, and to see to it that James failed at carrying out the other half of his deadly threat.

J.R. now stood looming over his youngest brother, with a raging need to satiate his thirst for spilling vengeful blood. With the vulnerable position James was in while holding Elijah, J.R. definitely had the upper hand. When James tried to make a move to get up, his brother kicked him in the jaw. He nearly lost consciousness as he fell backward. Just as his dizzy haze cleared, a sudden searing pain in his right upper thigh caused James to cry out in agony. J.R. had snatched a bayonet out of a nearby dead body and drove it straight through James's thigh, pinning him to the ground. James then looked up and saw the handle of J.R.'s musket coming toward his chest. When he tried to maneuver out of the way, he cried out again, as he ripped even more muscle and flesh in his thigh. Unable to get away, J.R. repeatedly pile drove the handle of his musket into James's chest, hitting him in the diaphragm and ribs. The repeated blows fractured a multitude of James's bones and left him gasping for air. A savage urge for more up-close and personal torture motivated J.R. to toss his weapon aside and spit on his brother. He then dropped to his knees on top of James, pinned his arms down, and began choking him with every ounce of force he could muster. J.R. squeezed so tight that his own face flushed red. The blue tint now painting James's lips gave J.R. near orgasmic pleasure. But, *still*, that was not enough to satisfy his wanton lust for torture. Baring his rotten, yellow teeth, J.R. repeatedly slammed his brother's skull against the frozen ground, grunting with every blow, as he split a deep gash in the back of James's head. James was beginning to fade into unconsciousness when J.R. suddenly eased the tension on his neck and looked his brother in the eyes. "Your whore had the best pussy I eva' had in my life. Makes me hard just thinkin' about the way I rammed my cock in her sweet little cunt, ova' and ova' again. I'd buy 'er just to fuck 'er in the ass like a mad dog until she's bleedin' and beggin' for mercy," he grimaced. *"Please James, help me, help me,"* he said, mocking Lily.

J.R.'s unsightly smile broadened, and he let out a sinister chuckle when his words prompted James to start thrashing and trying to get up. James's movements began to shred even more of the muscle tissue in his leg, but his rage made him oblivious to the pain. Still unable to unpin himself, James spit blood in his brother's face. J.R wiped the blood off and began punching James in the face for his disrespectful actions. "You nigga' lovin' son of a bitch!" he growled, repeatedly pummeling his brother. James was completely numb to the heavy blows, though. Killing his brother suddenly trumped everything, even the pain of his now fractured eye socket.

Killing James dominated J.R.'s mind as well, but he was determined to do it in a way that would make his father smile up at him from the fiery depths of his new eternal home. After blackening both of James's eyes and damn near breaking his nose, J.R. was now ready to fulfill his murderous goal. He suddenly stood up and straddled his youngest brother's body. He flashed another wicked grimace, proud of the bloody, black and blue living work of art he had just created. He then reached down and picked up the axe that James had slaughtered a multitude of his men with. "Nothin' good eva' comes of a nigga' lova'," he said as he raised the axe over his head, ready to slowly pick his brother's body apart.

With the axe hovering high above his head, J.R. suddenly grunted and froze. An intense pain had erupted in his groin and ricocheted through every nerve ending in his body. When the shockwave of pain exploded into his fingertips, he dropped the axe by his side. J.R. looked down to find the blade of James's hunting knife buried deep in the soft tissue between his legs. James had snatched the weapon off his hip and drove it with wrathful force into the part of his brother that he had used to violate Lily. The repulsive thought of his brother, forcefully stealing pleasure from the pureness of Lily's insides, had sent James spiraling into the pits of madness. His desire to annihilate J.R. had stewed for four unbearable years and had now erupted with volcanic force through the tip of his knife. Baring his bloody teeth, James began twisting his blade deep in the recesses of J.R.'s bowels, raping his scrotum with murderous intent. He then yanked the knife out of his brother's body, slicing through the front of his pants when it exited.

With tears in his eyes, J.R. grabbed what was left of the body part he had used to invade the delicate walls of Lily's insides. It now dangled loosely from his skin, severed into two bloody pieces. With the pain having paralyzed J.R., James easily used his free leg to kick him backward. He then sat up and snatched the bayonet out of his leg, finally unpinning himself. Despite his gaping wound, James effortlessly stood up and glared down at his brother, his soulless blood-red eyes speaking of what was next to come. Trying to evade further torture, J.R. used the little strength he had left to cowardly crawl away. James put his heavy boot on his brother's back, easily stopping his escape. He wrapped J.R.'s thick mane around his hand and pulled him up. With blood now pouring from the gaping wound between his legs, J.R. sat weakened on his knees, shivering like a frightened puppy.

For four years, James had envisioned slaying his brother in a slow, demonic fashion that would have made his father seem like a saint by comparison. But their surrounding conditions did not allow the time for the sort of torture that James truly wished to inflict. He, therefore, quickly straddled J.R.'s back like the useless animal he was. James then gripped his hair tight again and yanked his head back, exposing every critical vein in his throat. "Now, *you* beg for mercy," he grunted through gritted teeth.

"M-make it q-quick," J.R. begged, his true cowardice revealed in his quivering voice.

Years of pent-up rage suddenly ripped through James's vocal cords, erupting as a primordial growl. Vengeful fury ignited his hand as he then sliced his brother's neck from ear to ear. As the blade glided across J.R.'s throat, James's archaic screaming continued. The anger and pain, from all that he had lost at his brother's hands, then suddenly came gushing from James's eyes, much like the blood from J.R.'s life-ending wound.

Upon his brother's slaying, pain finally returned to James's body. His right leg suddenly felt like it was continuously being trampled by teams of wild horses. After his brother's lifeless body slumped to the ground, James dropped his blade and fell to his knees. Every muscle in his body suddenly went limp. He felt his own life draining. With his ribs now crushed, he was sure that his final breath was near. He found the strength to pray, accepting that it would not be long before his mother welcomed him into heaven, where he would once again hold his precious baby girl. He gave in to weakness and fell over, just feet from his dead brother. Blood, mud, and grass caked James's face like camouflage, leaving only his crystal blue eyes visible beneath. As he lay there fading away, the battle raged on around him, guns blazing, and cannons erupting. Unblinking, James laid there, unable to bring himself to move. His stare was as empty as the emotional volcano that had just erupted and cleansed his soul. Four years of war, four years of mourning, four years without his love, and the triumph of revenge had now completely drained him. James knew of only one person who had the power to heal him and reignite his strength. But that beautiful woman was lost somewhere, too far away to comfort him and refuel his desire to breathe. Without the love of his life, he gave up and closed his crystal-blue eyes. With Lily's inspiring music playing in his head, James Adams faded away into the light.

Seconds later, James opened his eyes and all was calm. Guns and cannons were no longer erupting around him. The fields were barren. Mangled dead bodies and flaming tents had disappeared. The mud and blood that caked the grass was no more. James, too, was completely clean. His strength had returned. His bruises and scars no longer existed. Even the excruciating pain in his leg had ceased. James slowly stood up and tilted his head back. There was nary a cloud in the sky. He closed his eyes and inhaled the fresh air around him, as he bathed in the warmth of the sunlight. He suddenly opened his eyes and turned toward the beautiful sound of a familiar laugh, a laugh that he was only ever graced by in his dreams. In the distance, he spotted the source of the jubilant sound, flying high on a treehouse swing. Her white summer dress and long brown curly locks were flowing behind her, as she soared back and forth into the sky.

With a racing heart, James cautiously began walking toward the angelic sight. As he got closer, the child's giggling began to subside, and the swing suddenly slowed. When the swing stopped altogether, James did too. With tears stirring in his eyes, he just stood there and watched as the child got out of the swing. Fearing that she would run away if he took another step, he remained frozen, unable to take his eyes off the little person he was gazing at. He saw the child suddenly glance up, as if someone was speaking to her. She then turned to look over her shoulder, as if she had been prompted to do so. It was at that moment that James realized his fears were unwarranted. The precious little girl, who had spent every minute of her life cradled in his arms, suddenly started running toward him. With her arms outstretched, she ran as fast as she could, yelling a word that James had longed to hear. "Daddyyy!" Rose erupted repeatedly. She had the grandest smile on her face as she leapt into her father's arms.

James erupted in tears the very second his daughter locked her little arms around his neck. After years of war, James was now an extremely hardened man, but the simple embrace of a child, *his* child, literally brought him to his knees. He held Rose as tight as he could without breaking her. He closed his eyes and gently rubbed her back as she lay with her head on his shoulder. Such a simple pleasure tapped deep into James's well of emotions; Rose's hair was saturated with his tears within a matter of seconds.

After praying for years for the chance to hold Rose, James was reluctant to let her go. But he had been equally eager to finally see the beautiful little face that his and Lily's love had created. Slowly, he released Rose from his embrace and set her feet on the ground. He remained kneeling and just gazed at her in awe. She now looked to be four years old. He studied her features carefully and was astounded to see his own eyes staring right back at him. But he felt as though hers sparkled with so much more innocence. Her golden skin and the texture of her hair were the perfect blend of his and Lily's. But in all other ways, James realized she was a tiny replica of her mother, just the way he had prayed she would be. That fact brought fresh tears to his eyes as he caressed Rose's soft cheek.

Rose reached out and played with a tendril of her father's hair, finally breaking his fixation on her face. "You have long hair like mine, daddy," she commented, her sparkling eyes lighting up as she smiled.

"I know, but yours is much prettier," James smiled as another tear ran down his face.

"Don't cwy daddy," Rose replied, speaking with a slight impediment, just like James had as a child. "It's gonna be okay," she smiled, wiping a tear off his cheek. He should have been comforting her, but she bravely took on that role, just the way James had with his mother when he was her age.

"I can't help it, sweetpea. I've missed you so much. I've been worried about you for a long time."

"You don't have to worry, daddy. Gwampa takes good care of me."

"*Grandpa?*" James asked, sounding a bit confused. He was certain that his father was in a far hotter place than where they stood.

"Yes, he said he's mommy's daddy," Rose explained.

The revelation instantly warmed James's heart. "Oh, I see. *That* grandpa, huh?" he smiled.

"Yup! I'm *gwampa's girl!*" Rose boasted proudly. "That's what he calls me!"

"He does?" James replied, his face still lit up in a grand smile.

Rose gave one big nod. "Mm-hmm!"

"I bet grandpa does all kinds of fun things with you, doesn't he?"

Rose nodded again. "Yup! And your mama does too!"

James's chest instantaneously swelled with emotion again. "M-my motha's here with you too?" he whispered, fresh tears glistening in his eyes.

"Yup! She said she's the one who brought me here when I was a baby."

The thought of his mother there by his side during the most tragic hour of his life instantly caused James's waiting tears to spill down his cheeks. "She did?" he whispered, his lip quivering with emotion.

"It's okay daddy, don't cwy," Rose said, wiping her father's tears again.

"I'm not sad, sweetpea. I'm just so happy grandma takes care of you."

"Me too! I have so much fun with her and gwampa! Gwama always does my hair weally pwetty and makes me pwetty dwesses! When we go on walks togetha', she tells me funny stowies about you and mama. She said you and mama would wun away to pway with each otha' all the time when you were little. She said you were tryna keep it a secwet, but gwama said she knew aaall alooong," Rose laughed. "She said she has motherly intu- ... intra- ... umm, intermission?"

"*Intuition?*" James smiled.

"Yeah! That's the word! She said that means mamas know *everything!*"

"They sure do!" James laughed, instantly infected by her enthusiasm.

"She said she even knew that you always loved mama."

"She's right. I loved your mama from the very first moment I saw her," James smiled. "Grandma sure does know everything, doesn't she?"

"Yup! You can't hide anything from her!" Rose shook her head. "I don't eeeven twy!"

"You're a wise girl!" James replied, tickling her neck.

Rose began laughing uncontrollably, igniting James's laughter as well.

"What otha' fun things do you do with grandma and grandpa?" he asked when her laughter subsided. "Tell me *everything!*"

"Gwampa built me a biiig tweehouse! He said you always wanted to build one for me, so he did it for you, since you weren't here. And now he pushes me on the tweehouse swing, hiiigh up in the sky!" she said, motioning with her hands. "And he takes me fishin', and swimmin', and weads me lots and lots of stowies!"

A blend of envy and pure joy caused another tear to trickle down James's cheek. "Nothin' but the best for *grandpa's girl*, huh?"

Rose gave another big nod. "Mm-hmm! I love it when gwampa weads to me..." She suddenly leaned over and whispered in her father's ear. "But I love it even more when you wead me the stowy about the mermaid." She pulled back and her innocent eyes lit up as she smiled. "It's my favwit!"

"You can hear me readin', sweetpea?" James smiled, his joyous tears still steadily trickling.

Rose began giggling. "Yes, I like it when you do all those silly voices! It's so funny!"

"I'll be sure to read that more often then."

"And guess what else, daddy?!"

"What's that?" James smiled.

"Gwama and gwampa are teachin' me how to pway piano!"

"They are?!"

"Yup! And sometimes when gwama pways piano, gwampa dances weally silly with me," she laughed. "He's so funny!"

"I bet he is!" James smiled, tickling Rose's neck to entice more of her sweet laughter.

"Gwampa said he taught himself to pway the piano, just like mama."

"I know. One of your uncles told me."

"Gwampa said he loves all of mama's music!"

"Your grandpa can hear her?"

Rose nodded. "He said her music made him cwy ... but not because he was sad."

"I know how he feels. It makes me cry sometimes too."

"Auntie said it makes her cwy sometimes too."

"Auntie's here with you too?"

Rose nodded her little head again, as she reached out to play with another tendril of her father's hair. "And Miss Anna Mae and Mista' Benjamin too. They all said mama's music is weally pwetty."

"It truly is," James replied, his emotions surging again as he thought of the people she mentioned.

"I wanna hear mama's music too ... but she neva' pways anymore."

"She doesn't?"

Rose suddenly stopped playing in her father's hair and sorrowfully shook her head. "She doesn't wanna pway anymore without you," she whispered, sadness having overtaken her tone. She then suddenly looked behind her as if something, or *someone*, had just called to her. James looked over her shoulder and saw nothing. After a few seconds, Rose turned back to her father. "I have to go now, daddy."

James instantly felt a lump forming in his throat. "No, c'mon, not yet." He pulled her into another embrace and gently laid her head back on his shoulder. "I'm not ready for you to leave."

"But he said you can't stay."

"Who?"

Rose turned and looked over her shoulder again at something that James still could not see. "You have to go now, daddy," she insisted when she turned to look at him again.

"I'm not ready to let you go yet."

"I don't want you to go either, but you can't stay..." With tears sparkling in her innocent eyes, she looked directly into her father's. "Mama needs you," she whispered.

The statement instantly caused James's tears to erupt again. "Well, will you promise me somethin' before I go?" he asked, gently touching Rose's cheek.

"Yes," she nodded.

"Promise me you'll always rememba' how much I love you?"

"I promise," she replied, throwing her arms around her father's neck and hugging him with all of her strength. "I love you too, daddy," she whispered.

"I love you too, sweetpea," James whispered back, letting a kiss linger on her forehead as his tears fell in streams. "More than I have the time to express."

"I know, daddy … I hear you tell me all the time."

James suddenly felt his strength fading. Despite how hard he tried, he suddenly no longer had the ability to hold on to his daughter.

"Bye daddy," Rose whispered, kissing him softly on the cheek. She then easily stepped out of his embrace.

James could not bring himself to say the same. He found the pain of saying goodbye far more excruciating than the massive hole that his brother had put in his leg. But even if he wanted to reciprocate the words, he suddenly found that he was unable to speak anyway. As desperately as he wanted to pull Rose back, he could no longer move either. Frozen on his knees, he could do nothing but watch her walk away through the blur of tears in his eyes. After walking several steps, Rose reached her hand up, and placed it into the hand of someone that James still could not see. She then turned around one last time and waved at her father. When she turned away from him again, she placed her other hand into the hand of another. In the protective hands of two beings that James could not see, little Rose turned again and walked away for good.

As Rose faded away from James's sight, searing pain instantly returned to his leg. He slowly emerged from unconsciousness, surrounded by a sea of dead bodies. After hours of lying there, his throat was parched, every inch of his face was throbbing, his chest felt as if it had caved in, and his stomach was cramped in knots. The force of gravity felt like a boulder sitting atop his body, making any movement feel like an impossibility. He had only the strength to open his heavy eyelids and stare up into a sky thick with dark clouds. As soon as his eyes adjusted, the curtain of clouds slowly pulled back and exposed the sun. The beaming rays felt like a much-needed warm hug. James basked in the warmth, as he watched dozens of buzzards circling hundreds of *elite* and *iron* men. Despite the sneak attack, *iron* men had prevailed. It was overwhelmingly the carcasses of *so-called* elite men that the buzzards happily feasted on.

Like the buzzards picking apart the flesh of elite carcasses, James could taste death on his tongue. In fact, he was convinced that he *had* died. The place he had just returned from felt too real to have been merely a dream. His neck still tingled where Rose's soft hands had hugged him. His cheek was still warm where she had kissed him. He could still smell the sweet scent of her hair overpowering the stench of death permeating the surroundings he had awakened in. He was convinced that he had indeed been allowed to hold a true angel, one who was being cared for with extreme love, in the sort of utopian paradise in which he had always prayed he would be able to raise her. He now believed that that prayer had been answered in the most heavenly way. James's eyes suddenly misted over with tears. "Thank you, God," he whispered, for the mysterious celestial experience that had just instantly halted his mourning and given him instant inner peace.

James's peace was reinforced when his weakened body caused his head to suddenly fall to the right. Directly in his line of sight was a flower. Amid a sea of decaying bodies, it stood tall and unscathed, as if every soldier had taken great care not to trample it. Right before James's eyes, the sun began to tickle its petals open. As it slowly blossomed, James's tears suddenly began to pour in streams, when he realized that the flower was indeed a single rose.

Mama needs you. Despite gravity feeling like a boulder on James's body, the angelic voice echoing that phrase in his mind gave him extraordinary willpower. He used it to extract the rose from the ground and lay it upon his chest. The simple task left him extremely winded. His battered chest seemed to barely be able to push air through his windpipe. Despite the lack of oxygen, he used the last bit of strength in his dying body to raise his hand in the air to signal for help. The feat felt as strenuous as lifting a wagon off his body. *Mama needs you*, was repeating in his mind, fueling his strength to hold his shaking hand in the air. With that motivational phrase replaying, James was content to die before he allowed his arm to fall.

In the eyes of iron soldiers scouring a sea of dead bodies, the sight of a solitary hand in the air stood out like a glorious ray of sunlight peeking through the clouds after a catastrophic storm. Within seconds, a longtime loyal friend was by James's side, scooping him up. After desperately searching for James and miraculously finding him clinging to life, Harrison had tears in his eyes, as he trotted away with his dear friend toward what was left of the medic tent. James lay limp in Harrison's arms, holding the rose on his chest, and the words of a little angel in his heart ... words that renewed his faith in the fact that Lily *still* needed him, as much as he needed her.

Chapter Twenty-five

Judging by the wide-eyed look of astonishment plastered on Preston Mills's face, one would assume he was gazing at the expensive artwork he had just traveled across a war-torn country to deliver to the Atkins estate. But those expensive portraits were nowhere near his current field of view. However, in Preston's expert opinion, he would undoubtedly appraise the statuesque work of art in front of him as priceless. Preston's expressive words to the beautiful sight had brought everything to a standstill in the Atkins' formal dining room. For several uncomfortable seconds, there was stone-cold silence. Suddenly, not a single piece of fine china was touched by the roomful of upper-class guests who had been eating their artful cuisine. Finely aged glasses of wine were ignored as dozens of rich eyes stared bewilderedly at the Manhattan Museum curator. Preston, in turn, had his eyes transfixed on *Bella*, one of the Atkins' servants. Her presence had compelled him to slowly rise from his seat as he spoke to her, his eyelids refusing to shut in the process. Bella stood there uncomfortably returning Preston's gaze with an empty tray in her hand, unable to bring herself to utter a word in return. Preston was only able to pull his eyes away from Bella after she discreetly shook her head and scurried away into the kitchen without a word. It was only then that Preston snapped out of his trance, nervously looked around, and realized that he had completely shifted the atmosphere in the room. His eyes swept across the room of well-to-do guests, until they landed on the displeased face of Atticus Atkins, the enigmatic politician who had purchased Bella four years prior ...

For decades, Atticus Atkins had reigned supreme as a powerful figure in Galveston, Texas. As an experienced attorney, Atticus had perfected the art of lying, colluding, and hiding his underhanded ways from every good-natured Texan. They were none the wiser to the fact that he was the sort of man who took great pride in hiding his money from the government. His combined talent for deception, and consistent record of courtroom victories, had easily convinced an overwhelming majority of Galveston patrons that he was worthy enough to be voted in as their mayor. Voters were completely ignorant to the fact that they had just elected a man who was about to take even greater pride in siphoning from the pockets of every fool who had cast a ballot on his behalf. Despite having the brilliance to maintain his affluent lifestyle legally, Atticus simply had a passion for cheating and breaking the law for personal gain. That mentality even applied to acquiring his slaves. Every one of them had been purchased on the black market, including his absolute favorite ... *Bella*.

Atticus was sub-par physically in comparison to the average man. In fact, in his early years as a single man, the only attractive attributes about him were his intellect ... and his money. His bland appearance and enigmatic ways left him struggling with women in his youth, until his financial assets suddenly turned him from a frog into a prince in the eyes of eligible women. His money drew the eyes of the McCoys, another wealthy Texas family. Their daughter, Evelyn, proudly married Atticus for money and power, just as she had been raised to do.

Evelyn made Mary Jo Parker seem like a saint in the world of socialites. She was ruthless and held her societal status and family image far above everything, even marital happiness. The only mutual love the couple expressed was for the goal of achieving elite status together. For twenty-five years, Evelyn gladly stood side by side with

Atticus as his beautiful, prized wife. She *tolerated* her marriage to him with a smile, so long as he funded her socialite lifestyle with an equally fake smile. She took pride in maintaining their family's perfect image, while they both worked toward their ultimate goal of residing at 1600 Pennsylvania Avenue, in Washington D.C. In Evelyn's mind, becoming the country's most adored first lady would have been equivalent to being crowned queen of the socialite world. She would have sold her three children's souls for pennies on the dollar if that was the cost of achieving such royal status. Her extraordinarily selfish goal made maintaining all of her husband's dirty secrets a breeze ... including the most scandalous of them all.

Ten years into his marriage, Atticus was attending a small gathering of businessmen at the home of a client that he had won an important case for. As a bonus for winning his case, the client gave Atticus the choice of any, or all five, of his Negro pleasure girls. Atticus was ignorant to such experiences before then. He was afraid to even accept the offer at first. Had it not been for alcohol, and assurance from his client that his evening of indulging would be kept secret, Atticus might have declined. With alcohol giving him the courage, he took a risk and chose two pleasure girls from the group. The two exotic ladies seductively smirked, both eager to toy with a man who seemed so hesitant and naive. They then guided him back to their pleasure palace, their hips swaying provocatively in front of their inexperienced new toy as they walked.

Atticus's nerves had him so frozen when he entered their room that both women had to remove his spectacles and clothing on his behalf. After guiding him to the bed, the pair of beautiful servants slowly began dancing out of their clothing. Atticus's wide eyes nearly dried out from his refusal to blink, as he watched them strip. Never in his life had he seen naked bodies built like goddesses, posteriors and breasts so plump, and hips so round. Once his seductresses were unclothed, they began showing him the skills that had earned them the label of *pleasure girls*. Soft tongues and thick lips caressed nearly every inch of Atticus's skin, until his manhood stiffened with anticipation. He let out a breathy moan and his eyes rolled back when a set of thick lips suddenly slid over his erection and began trying to suck the life out of him. He was near eruption when the girl's oral pleasuring suddenly ceased. She backed up and made way for the other goddess to mount him. Atticus breathlessly cried out for God when she slid her slick folds down over his hardness; he certainly felt as though he had been catapulted into heaven. He never realized what he was missing sexually until his member was submerged deep between the thick thighs of a Negro woman. The wetness, warmth, and tightness of her insides was unlike anything he had ever felt with his wife. The erotic dancing of her body, as she pounded his hardened flesh, caused Atticus to have an explosive, climactic eruption that ignited an instant obsession with Negro women.

After leaving the pleasure palace, Atticus was indeed a different man. He did nothing but fantasize about burying his penis in the tight, wet folds of beautifully colored bodies. His constant daydreams left him desperate to find a way to satiate his ravenous craving for the terrifically sinful feeling of thick lips, plump rumps, and the smoldering insides of a Negro woman. His throbbing penis was literally aching for more. His obsessive desires even began disrupting his work and changing his life in a way that his wife easily noticed.

It was *not* the sudden lack of intimacy from Atticus that led Evelyn to care about the fact that he began returning home unusually late from work, in the weeks following his secret experience with the pleasure girls. It was *only* the speed with which money was suddenly disappearing from their safe that made Evelyn raise an eyebrow about Atticus's unusual behavior. She assumed he was gambling. Gambling, he was. But not in the ways that Evelyn had predicted. Oddly, Evelyn was not angry about the sinful sexual affairs that she soon learned her husband was having. Even the fetish that had compelled his actions did not bother her. What angered her most, was the ease with which the private investigator she hired had found him at a secret, upscale brothel where he was spending thousands of dollars. Despite the masks provided for the affluent customers at the brothel, Evelyn feared her husband's secret would easily be discovered by their affluent town. Becoming First Lady was all that eclipsed Evelyn's mind. She was just as obsessed with maintaining her polished socialite status as her husband was with his unique new fetish. Evelyn, therefore, did not care how many Negroes she had to endure her husband sleeping with to get to the White House. But if his scandalous secret jeopardized her chance at being crowned queen of the United States, there would be hell to pay.

To continue *enjoying* the freedom from her intimate "wifely duties," Evelyn came up with a solution that would help feed her husband's fetish, maintain his secret, and keep her polished image shimmering. A week after discovering her husband's transgressions, Evelyn guided Atticus into a bedroom in their basement that she had secretly remodeled just for him. His jaw nearly hit the floor when he saw what his wife had beautifully decorated the room with. Evelyn stared at the profile of her husband's face while he continued to stand there unblinking, shocked into silent awe. "You set anotha' foot into one of those filthy whore houses, and I'll hire somebody to kill you myself," she warned Atticus.

Her words finally got Atticus to turn and look at his wife, his heart immediately galloping. Up until that very moment, he was not aware that Evelyn knew the truth about his secret late night "meetings."

"And if you impregnate one of these whores … well." Evelyn glanced down at Atticus's crotch and then looked him in the eyes. "Let's just say, you'll wish you were dead." She handed him a box full of prophylactics, then glanced over at the three "whores," who were all standing quietly across the room in lingerie. "He's all yours now, ladies," she stated. "And don't botha' bein' gentle." She then turned to look at her husband again. "I heard he likes it rough." Evelyn smirked and walked out, gladly leaving the responsibility of satisfying her husband to the three slave women she had just purchased on the black market. She went to her room, sat on the bed, and began reading a novel. She sipped from a glass of wine as she read, feeling as relaxed as a mother, who had the evening to herself, after dropping off her children for a playdate. She read with a smile on her face, confident that her plan would help preserve the reputation of her rich and powerful family, as they stair-stepped toward the White House.

Atticus was smiling as well. His smile, however, was driven by devilish lust. His flesh hardened as he gazed wide-eyed at the array of beautiful, voluptuous, Negro women in front of him, who stood there ready to satisfy his fetish. The love that had once faded away for his wife suddenly came roaring back, as he drooled with delectable delight at the unbelievable gift she had just given him.

With Evelyn's blessing, Atticus's collection of black-market slaves began to grow over the years. However, he soon began selecting his bevy of brown beauties on his own, assuring himself that he would always have an array of colors, shapes, and sizes that suited his particular tastes. He surrounded himself with variety, disguising them as cooks, maids, and nannies, until the late-night hours when he would select one as his lover. For years, Evelyn turned a blind eye to his late-night activities. For the way she quietly allowed his sinful behaviors, she simply asked that her husband always abide by her strict rules. But much like a child who was given an inch, Atticus took a mile. His desires eventually trumped his ability to reason. His disrespect would eventually test how serious Evelyn was about the consequences of breaking her rules.

A month before purchasing Bella, Atticus had awakened looking forward to being with a slave named Clara. She was like his coffee. Every part of his body would rise in the morning, eagerly anticipating the taste of her, and the lively energy she infused in him afterward.

Atticus walked down to the basement, toward the bathroom where Clara met him every morning. She was usually sitting nude in the bubble bath she had prepared for them. With a certain part of him visibly ready for his sultry morning routine, Atticus opened the bathroom door. But when he looked inside, his erection immediately began to soften. There was no bubble-filled bath water ... and no Clara either. His wife stood there staring him down, instead.

"Year afta' year, I ignore the fact that my husband has an acquired taste for the filthy pussies of *Negro whores!*" Evelyn berated. She suddenly stepped toward Atticus with lowered eyes. "All that I've done for you, all that I've let you get away with, and you have the *audacity* to disrespect me by impregnatin' one of your *whores!*"

"Evelyn, let me explain..."

"Shut up! There is no explanation for what you did! Were you stupid enough to think I'd neva' notice?"

Atticus stood there looking like a frightened child being scorned by his mother.

"Answer me!"

"I-I was gonna tell you. It's just..."

Evelyn suddenly slapped him so hard that his ears began ringing. As Atticus stood there holding his cheek, she put her finger in his face. "I told you there would be consequences! You're lucky I didn't walk in here with a butcha' knife! But this is your last warnin'. If you bring shame to this family again..." She grabbed his penis, twisted, and squeezed with all her might. "I can promise you, it won't be one of your precious whores you wake up missin'," she whispered in his ear. She yanked hard on his member before releasing it and storming out of the bathroom. Atticus grabbed his crotch and dropped to his knees, his eyes filled with tears of excruciating pain.

Atticus's fury over finding Clara gone that morning was immeasurable, but he could not remotely begin to argue the fact that he rightfully deserved the consequences of his actions. What his wife had done with Clara and his unborn child remained a mystery, one that genuinely broke Atticus's heart, especially considering that he would never get to meet his child. Despite the painful loss, he never dared question his wife about it. Seeking to numb the heartache, he instead began focusing on finding a replacement for his favorite lover. Wanting to buy a woman of similar shade, shape, and sparkling eye color, Atticus boarded a train and set out to Mississippi, to meet with the usual backwoods, lowlife, black market slave traders with whom he secretly made his purchases.

For Atticus, purchasing slaves on the black market had nothing to do with getting deep discounts on humans. Legal auctions just never had a wide assortment of women to choose from that were suitable for his eclectic preferences. After so many dirty dealings in the past, Atticus's usual slave traders now knew his eclectic tastes extremely well. They always brought a dozen or more female slaves, with the array of skin tones and hair textures that he preferred. Though the slave traders considered Atticus a peculiar man, he was by far their most favorite, loyal client. He paid top dollar for their inventory and, most importantly, for their silence. With the profits they made, the underhanded men never failed to arrive early with their load of stolen humans.

Right on schedule, Atticus arrived at their secret meeting spot. As usual, the slave traders were already there. Most backwoods deals were made at night, but Atticus paid extra to do his selection in the early morning sunlight. He wanted the sun shining just right, perfectly illuminating the array of shackled, barefoot women. After being wrestled away from various places in the dead of night, the women all stood there with their heads hanging low, trembling with fear over the prospects of what their futures held. They prayed it would not be any worse than the conditions they had just been snatched away from.

Atticus walked slowly down the line, gently raising the head of each potential purchase, carefully examining each and every one. He had a knack for seeing past their tear-stained, filthy faces and recognizing the beauty that lay underneath. The slave traders normally brought women who were in acceptable physical condition, but that was hardly the case on this particular morning. Many were so battered, bruised, and emaciated that Atticus was finding it hard to see their beauty this time, until he lifted the head of the seventh woman in line. "I'll take this one," he said to leader of the sellers as he gazed into the woman's eyes.

"You sure? You still got five otha's to look at," the backwoods seller replied.

"I *said* I'll take this one," Atticus adamantly expressed, without ever taking his eyes off his new replacement. He knew immediately that she was truly a precious diamond in the rough. "What's your name?" he asked her, still having yet to blink while gazing at her.

His new prospect was too paralyzed with fear to reply. She did nothing but continue to tremble as a tear ran down her bruised cheek.

"He asked your name!" the backwoods seller yelled, lifting his hand to slap her.

Atticus grabbed his wrist and stopped him before it reached her face.

The seller snatched his arm out of Atticus's grip. "I don't think you wanna buy her! I'm convinced she's fuckin' retarded!"

"If you think I'm here shoppin' for a genius, then you're the one who's *fuckin' retarded!*" Atticus replied. He then turned his attention back to the slave he wanted and gazed at her with lust in his eyes. "Besides ... she's just scared. If you didn't know where the hell you were, or where the hell you were about to end up, you'd be scared to death too." Atticus wiped the tear away that careened down her bruised cheek. "What's your name?" he asked her again.

Again, she failed to reply or to even glance in Atticus's direction.

"*Bella,*" the slave trader interjected. "She told us earlier that 'er name was Bella."

"*Bella,*" Atticus repeated. "French for beautiful. So perfectly fittin' for you," he whispered lustfully, while caressing her cheek. "I'll take Bella then," he reiterated to the trader, without turning his eyes away from her.

The backwoods trader shook his head. "It's your money." Which is exactly what Atticus paid the black-market thief ... and lots of it.

After making the illegal transaction, Atticus placed a box of food and several canteens of water in the back of the slave trader's wagon, for all the other stolen slaves to eat. He then walked up and put a finger in the slave trader's face. "The next time you bring me a batch of slaves just barely clingin' to life, it'll be the last time we eva' do business! These women look like they haven't eaten in weeks! You're makin' pure profit off these slaves! Hell, with the money I'm payin' you alone, you can certainly afford to feed 'em, for Christ's sake! Unless you're plannin' on sellin' to necrophiliacs, you're gonna have a hard time turnin' a profit off dead bodies!"

When Atticus walked away, the lowlife slave trader turned to his partner and asked, "what the hell's a necrophiliac?"

His toothless partner shrugged. "Hell, long as he keeps payin' big money, that rich fucker can use all the goddamn big words he wants." He snapped the reins on their team of horses and rode away with pockets full of cash and their load of stolen, starving women.

Atticus's threatening final words to the slave traders were proof that he wanted his women in pristine condition. He further proved that after arriving back in Galveston, Texas with his new, illegally purchased property in tow. In anticipation of seeing what was laying underneath all Bella's cuts, bruises, and swelling, Atticus took her immediately to his trusted doctor. The doctor was paid handsomely to keep his services a secret, and to meet all of Atticus's high expectations. After years of treating his slaves, the doctor knew the list of those expectations like the back of his hand. Once Bella was left in his care, the doctor gave her a thorough exam, to ensure that she was free of lice, disease, and any other major ailments. The doctor then called on a trusted dentist to clean Bella's teeth and tend to any of her oral issues. For nearly a month thereafter, a team of nurses were then handed the daily task of scouring and moisturizing Bella from head to toe, to soften her skin. They painstakingly tended to her wounds and bruises, mending them in a way that made it seem like they never existed. All along, Bella was fed well, to help add weight to her emaciated frame. Once she was back to a healthy size, a seamstress was called on, to measure her and provide her with an array of well-fitted undergarments, lingerie, and dresses. When Bella was given a clean bill of health, the doctor sent Atticus notice to come and pick up the new diamond that his nurses had polished.

Within an hour of receiving notice, Atticus eagerly returned to retrieve his property. When he laid his eyes on Bella, he froze. For the first time ever, he realized that his assessment about a slave's potential beauty had been inaccurate. With freshly styled hair, nary a bruise in sight, and Bella's healthy frame now covered in a form-fitting dress, Atticus swore he was looking at a completely different woman altogether. The look on his face was proof that he was awestruck by how greatly he had underestimated how truly stunning she was.

Atticus was literally salivating as he rode home seated across from his newest "plaything." Bella did not know where to place her eyes, or how to situate her body, to alleviate the discomfort of being gazed at like she was a meal for a dog who had not eaten in weeks. She could easily sense the repulsive thoughts that were dominating her new master's mind. She was silently praying to God that he would not act on those desires.

Bella continued praying as the carriage pulled through the gates of Atticus's estate. Once it came to a halt, Atticus took her by the hand and helped her down. Had Bella bothered to raise her head from its submissive position, her eyes would have taken in the grand sight of Atticus's mansion. The massive structure could have easily been mistaken as the three-story home of a British royal. The golf course and lake on the sprawling acres of land would have contributed to such a belief. Bella's head hung too low to notice the unique English architecture, or even the fine details of the handcrafted double doors that she was being marched through. She never raised her head to see the dual staircase in the foyer either. She only noticed that the house had stairs at all when her feet were forced to march down them toward "the whore floor," as Evelyn had aptly named it. The entire basement belonged to Atticus's women. Evelyn considered Atticus's whores as beneath her, and she wanted to be sure they lived that way as well.

Atticus starkly disagreed with his wife's terminology, though. In his mind, the basement was his pleasure paradise. He considered the stairs he was descending as the hallway to heaven. He certainly had the basement lavishly designed like a paradise on Earth. It could have been considered as the most warm, inviting place had it not been for the fact that it was technically a prison for his illegally purchased whores. His captives were living in a beautifully decorated home within a home, featuring several bedrooms, a kitchenette, and even a massive bathroom with a garden tub. Atticus believed that if he treated his women like goddesses, they would naturally treat him like a god in return. He had no desire to use whips, chains, or forceful ways. There was never any marring, scarring, or brutalizing his women to achieve what he wanted. Such a thing, he felt, would obscure the colorful beauty that he admired so much. He simply provided his women with a lifestyle that would make them want him, just as badly as he wanted them. The way the original pleasure girls seemed to genuinely want him was a caveat that he now *needed* in order to garner the ultimate pleasure from his sexual servants. The simple thought of a harem of exquisite women, *desiring* to dote on him like a god, always had a certain part of him rock solid, whenever he set foot in his personal pleasure paradise.

That part of Atticus was indeed rock solid as he marched down the hallway to heaven and entered his kingdom with Bella. Several Negro women there immediately ceased their conversation, the very second they saw Bella. They quietly eyed her as she walked by, each with an unreadable expression on their faces. All their curious eyes continued to follow the new addition as Atticus guided her through his palace. Bella was ignorant to the goddess-like ways she would be treated while there. Fear of the unknown was clear to see in the way she seemed to resist every step toward one of the bedrooms. As every Negro woman there studied Bella's face, they all noted the silent plea for help written on it. But each woman simply glared back at her, without so much as a twitch in their facial muscles. Bella even swore she saw a smirk on one woman's face as she swirled the wine in her glass.

Atticus did not say a word to Bella after they entered one of the bedrooms and he locked the door. She was not given any food, wine, nor even a formal introduction. But there Atticus stood, methodically disrobing her near the door, breathing harder as he slowly unveiled her bare skin. Atticus's entire body followed the movements of Bella's dress as he slid it down. Bella's trembling and shaky breaths did nothing to stop his unwanted actions. She covered her breasts and her vagina the best she could after he fully disrobed her. He rose up slowly, eyeing every inch of her on his way up. He suddenly slowed when he reached her vagina. The look on Bella's face easily gave away how repulsed she was by the way he deeply inhaled the scent of her essence. Like a dog who had sniffed a female in heat, Atticus began to pant as his erection swelled to capacity. Disgusted by his bizarre actions, Bella winced and recoiled slightly. Atticus was too entranced to pay her actions any mind, though. He simply stood tall and stepped back to take in the entire sight of her. The fear written all over her face did not deter him from slowly removing her hands from her private areas. His mouth gaped open as he moved her hands aside. After finally seeing an unobstructed view of his new plaything, he let out a deepthroated, anticipatory growl and his erection turned blue with excitement.

Bella's entire body visibly shook with fear. She quickly covered her private areas again. "P-p-please don't do this," she begged, tears running in streams from her eyes.

Atticus took a step forward and gently wiped her tears away. "Relax and you'll enjoy it," he whispered in a lust-driven moan. Once again, he then stopped her hands from obstructing his view.

"P-please, I'm b-beggin' you not to do this," Bella pleaded. She winced when Atticus took her by the arm and began ushering her toward the bed. She resisted, forcing him to pull her along. Her bare feet slid across the cold hardwood floor until they were near the bed. "Please don't," she begged again.

"Shh, don't force me to tie you up," Atticus said, gently caressing her face. "I only wanna make you feel good."

"B-but I don't w-wanna do this," she cried.

"You'll learn to love it," he moaned in her ear. "They *all* do."

Atticus was no stranger to the resistant behaviors of some of his new purchases. Some had started off flailing in fear, leaving him with no choice but to tie their wrists and ankles to the bedposts. Within weeks, though, they had slowly evolved into the sort of women who were willing to cater to all his needs, some even with an air of pride. Their slow transition into willing participants was the part of the game that aroused Atticus the most. All day, he wondered just when his new plaything's pleas to stop would become begging and pleading for more. He was eager for the fear in her eyes to become a gaze of wanton lust. Anticipation of the day her cries transitioned into moans had his erection nearly blue with excitement, at every waking hour.

Atticus's confidence in the metamorphosis of his new slaves left him numb to their tears and pleading during his first encounters with them, much like how he now was with Bella. Like taming a wild horse, he looked forward to the challenge of breaking her. He was confident that there would soon come a time when a single look, or command of his eyes, would have her surrendering on her knees, or any other position he so desired. The beginning of Bella's transition had him on an intense high, so much so that he did not get upset over how extraordinarily resistant she was. None of his other slaves had given him such a challenge, though. Bella's panic-induced strength and endless flailing made it difficult to tie her arms and legs up. By the time Atticus was finished wrestling her into position, sweat was pouring from his body. When he finally had her secured, he crawled off her and stood at the end of the bed, panting hard as he gazed lustfully at the sight of her legs spread wide.

Imagining that Bella was eager to see him nude, Atticus began making a show of himself. He slowly took off his shirt, revealing a chest sprinkled with graying hair, and a once-solid frame that was beginning to sag in his middle age. He unlatched the button on his pants, slid them down his legs, and stepped out of them. Still fantasizing that Bella was enjoying the show, Atticus slowly lowered his boxers. With his eyes fixated on her, he then began to stroke his member. His eyes suddenly rolled back, his breaths deepened, and his mouth began to water as he imagined her body creating the pleasurable sensations currently rushing through him. Taking his time before getting to that moment, Atticus stopped stroking himself and kneeled at the end of the bed.

Not bothering to wipe the drool seeping from his mouth, he began suckling Bella's toes. After savoring the taste of each one, he crawled atop her and gazed down at her flawless face. The tears running in streams from her eyes compelled him to kiss her tenderly on the forehead. He then nipped at her earlobe. "Relax," he moaned in her ear. It was something that Bella could not fathom doing, especially as he began to sniff her hair and neck, like a ravenous dog getting to know the scent of his mate's pheromones. Her trembling intensified as Atticus began perusing her body with his hands and mouth, kissing, licking, and sucking nearly every inch of her. While Bella lay there feeling tortured, Atticus was thoroughly enjoying the feel of her soft skin against his lips, as he worked his way toward the erogenous kingdom between her thighs.

Saliva flooded Atticus's mouth and spilled from his lips the moment he thrust his tongue inside of Bella's intimate abyss. Like a connoisseur of fine wine, he let the taste of her insides linger on his tongue, savoring it for a moment. He moaned loudly after her sweet nectar permeated his taste buds. Her distinctive taste shot straight into the sensory system of his brain and was filed amongst the flavors of his other pleasure girls. The catalog of their various scents and flavors was pleasantly locked away in his long-term memory, making it easier for him to select which dessert would best satiate his cravings on a nightly basis.

After cataloging Bella as by far his favorite flavor, Atticus dove in to finish ravenously devouring her. However, Bella did not derive an ounce of pleasure from what would normally be extremely erotic stimulation. It only escalated her cries for him to stop and caused her to struggle even harder to free herself. Her actions still did nothing to cease Atticus's invasion, though. If anything, her struggles only added to the excitement of his first encounter with her. He was now dying for the day when he would eventually feel her quivering give way to erotic trembles of pleasure. His ears were eager to hear her sobs decrescendo into raspy, deep-throated moaning. Her defiance simply made him crave the day when Bella would be excited to have him stroking inside of her, lost in the throes of passion along with him.

Desperate for that day to come, Atticus finally lifted his head from between Bella's thighs. He then sheathed his pulsating member and began kissing his way up her body. Nary a goosebump raised on Bella's skin, nor did a single butterfly flutter through her stomach as he pressed his lips to her. She was becoming more and more panicked the closer he grew to her face. Once parallel with her body, Atticus began breathing harder and harder. Bella, in turn, began sobbing uncontrollably, as she continued thrashing and begging him to stop. Atticus paid her pleas no mind, though. He only cared to listen to every nerve, muscle, and urge in his body that was screaming for an orgasmic explosion. Even as Bella's demands to stop were being shouted near his ear, Atticus still insisted upon kissing her on the forehead. He kissed her softly as if that's all it would take to stop the river of tears from coursing down the sides of her face.

With Bella's screaming at a fever pitch, Atticus finally introduced her to the only part of himself that he felt she ever needed to become acquainted with. Overcome with pleasure as he slid into her, Atticus's moan came out like the carnivorous growl of a wild animal. He began pumping forcefully inside of her much like one too. After sliding inside of her against her will, the only thing Atticus had turned on in Bella was her defense mechanism. His unwanted invasion into her body was tantamount to injecting her with a powerful anesthetic. Her thrashing suddenly ceased. She laid there as stiff as a porcelain doll. The tears rolling down the sides of her face were now the only thing moving. But she could not feel the moisture. Her senses had completely shut down. Her vocal cords muted her ability to plead. She became deaf to Atticus's heavy grunting, a hair's breadth away from her ear. Her eyes remained open in a glaring trance, but she was unable to comprehend what she was seeing. She could no longer smell

Atticus's breath and his odd natural body odor. She could no longer feel his drool, as it fell in a stream from his mouth and cascaded down her cheek. Nor could she feel Atticus's sweat-slicked body slithering across her skin as he stroked inside her. She was even numb to his forceful penetration. Bella's natural mental defense mechanism was working overtime to keep Atticus's heavenly dream from being her hellish nightmare.

Despite Bella lying there like a corpse, Atticus continued trying to launch his body into the clouds. The way he moved within her proved how every first encounter with a new slave revitalized his youthful virility. He pumped hard inside of Bella, deriving the ultimate satisfaction from her misery, so much so that his pleasure-filled grunts echoed loud enough to be heard on the entire whore floor. With every thrust of his hips, he was confident that he was bringing Bella closer to being the sort of pleasure girl who would beg to have an erotic moment with him like this one. He began imagining Bella standing quietly among all the other pleasure girls in her custom-designed lingerie, hair perfectly styled, make-up precise, and thick lips glistening. The thought of Bella gazing at him, seductively begging him to choose her with her eyes, suddenly made Atticus burst inside of her. He howled uncontrollably from the intense rush of pleasure, as his first test ride came to an abrupt end. After only a few powerful strokes, it was over.

Atticus momentarily laid there buried between Bella's thighs in a weakened heap, after completely draining his stones. After gathering his strength, he raised up and gazed appreciatively at her for temporarily suspending his body in the heavens. For Atticus, the pleasurable ride was twenty-three seconds of pure bliss. For Bella, however, it felt like being paralyzed in a surreal out-of-body experience, witnessing twenty-three *years* of her own torture. The moment Atticus pulled out of her, Bella quickly returned from her out-of-body experience, just in time to feel him kissing her passionately on the lips. Repulsed by the sheer gall of his so-called affection, Bella's lips did not reciprocate his movements. But the way Atticus smiled at her and kissed her forehead proved that he had enjoyed her, nonetheless. Despite her disgust, her restricted hands left her unable to wipe away the residue his lips left on hers.

Atticus slithered off Bella and stood at the end of the bed. He continued to gaze at her as he unsheathed himself and put on a robe. He then sat on the side of the bed, ran his hand slowly down Bella's stomach, and dipped his finger into her abyss. "Your pussy was far betta' than I imagined," he professed, having the audacity to say such a thing while she was still tied up against her will. "And your flavor is unlike anything I've eva' tasted before," he said as he withdrew his finger from her and slid it into his mouth. Her sweet flavor made him moan and caused his eyes to flutter close. When he opened them again, he gazed at Bella in an erotic trance. "I can't wait to taste you again," he moaned in an eerie tone that made her skin crawl.

After reluctantly pulling his eyes away from Bella's flawless face, Atticus finally untied her. He then took her by the hand and helped her out of bed. Bella's extremities had gone numb from her constant struggle to free herself. But her mind was too flushed with anguish to notice the pins and needles feeling suddenly prickling her hands and feet, as blood finally began to circulate in them again. Atticus suddenly caressed her face and kissed her lightly on the lips, tasting the salty trail left by her non-stop tears. "If you're good to me, I promise I'll always be good to you," he stated. "Go ahead and get dressed."

Bella still just stood there trembling, with tears spilling down her cheeks, unable to get her racing mind to command her body to move. When she failed to pick up her dress, Atticus helped her into her clothing. He then held her hand, emerged from the pleasure room, and escorted her through the main room of his paradise. This time, Bella's head hung too low to notice the expressions on the faces of the Negro women she had been dragged past earlier. They stopped doing their chores again and discreetly looked her up and down, understanding all too well what she had just endured. Their sympathy for her, however, was nearly nonexistent. They were *confident* that she would soon grow to have their unique mentality about their circumstances.

"This room is yours," Atticus explained to Bella, as he opened the double doors of a massive bedroom, one that was equal in magnificence to a royal suite. He guided her to a queen size canopy bed draped with sheer white curtains. It was decorated in extravagant custom-made linens and an array of soft pillows. "This bed'll be yours," he told her. "These are yours as well," he said, pointing to a basket of soaps, lotions, and sponges placed neatly on the bench at the end of her bed. Atticus then promptly left without another word.

Bella looked down at the basketful of soaps and sponges and wanted to use them to scour herself while submerged in a bathtub full of scalding hot water. But she felt so heavy with grief that her knees became weak. She suddenly collapsed and sat with her back against the nightstand. She pulled her legs up to her chest, buried her face between her knees, and began sobbing uncontrollably.

"Oh, hush up all that damn cryin', girl!"

Startled, Bella suddenly lifted her tear-soaked face to find a fair-skinned Negro woman with a neatly styled, reddish-brown afro glaring at her from across the room. The woman had a flawless, milky complexion that looked soft to the touch, the sort that begged to be caressed by a man. She was sitting on the bench near her own bed, with one leg slung over the other in a suggestive pose, exuding a sexual seductiveness that seemed natural to her. Bella's eyes were suddenly drawn to one of the woman's long toned legs, as it peeked out from the slit in the erotic dress she was wearing. Following the line of the slit, Bella then surveyed her body, slowly raising her head until she locked eyes with the exotic woman. Her bedroom eyes were glaring at Bella over the top of the wine glass she was sipping from. Bella recalled she was the same woman who had smirked at her on the way in. She had been so lost in her own sorrowful world this time, though, that she had not even noticed the woman had been sitting there the whole time.

Bella's sniffling and trembling continued as the pair stared at each other.

"I *said*, hush up all that damn cryin'!" the woman demanded again, uncrossing her legs and leaning forward as she spoke this time.

The woman's scolding tone and icy glare suddenly made Bella feel foolish for crying. She huffed and angrily wiped the tears from her face.

"That's betta'." The woman took another sip of her wine and relaxed back into her seductive pose. "So, you're Bella, huh?"

Bella nodded.

"Well, I'm Ryla. Now, get ya' ass up off the floor and sit in that bed. You look like a damn fool sittin' there shiverin' like a little mouse."

Bella did not budge. Her tears suddenly erupted again. "That d-disgustin' m-man just had me tied up, forcin' himself on me! Don't you th-think that g-gives me g-good r-reason to be cr-cryin'?!" she replied, nearly hyperventilating.

"Maybe. But I can certainly think of far worse things worth cryin' ova'," Ryla replied calmly, taking another sip of her wine.

"What?!" Bella fired back, stunned by her dismissive reply.

"Hell, he didn't have to tie you up. You shouldn't've resisted. Should've just gave 'em what he wanted."

Bella tilted her head to the side and her mouth fell open. "A-are you mad?! Or has that d-disgustin' man brainwashed you?!"

"Get yo' ass up off the floor, sit on that bed, and at least throw your insults while you're lookin' at me eye to eye!"

"I don't wanna sit in that d-despicable m-man's bed!"

"She's just fine on the floor!" another woman suddenly interjected. Startled yet again, Bella quickly swiveled her head to the right to find the woman suddenly springing from her bed. She took a few steps toward Bella, lowered her eyelids, and threw her hands on her hips. "Why'd Atticus have to buy her any damn way?! We don't need no mo' slaves in here! And I certainly don't want 'er sleepin' next to *me!*"

"Oh, shut up and get the hell outta' here, Lola!" Ryla demanded. "Don't nobody give a damn what you want!"

Lola glared at Bella a moment longer and then stormed out of the room.

Ryla turned back to Bella. "Don't pay that crazy heffa' no mind. She's always findin' some petty reason to bitch and moan about every new girl who comes here. She wants Atticus all to herself. She used to be his numba' one pick every night, but he don't hardly glance at 'er anymore. She's angry all the time now. I suppose she done fell in love with his stankin' ass. For the life of me, I can't unda'stand why. Turns my stomach every time he drops his pants and turns his cock loose. Smells like rotten goat cheese to me! Don't matta' how much that man bathes and douses himself with cologne, his natural body odor ova'powa's it, and has him reekin' of sweaty ass on a hot summa' day."

Bella thought she had been imagining Atticus's odd pungent odor. At the time, she could not remember what it reminded her of. She realized that Ryla's goat cheese comparison was spot on.

"But to each his own, I guess," Ryla continued. "What one thinks smells like sweaty ass, anotha' inhales as the fresh scent of cologne." Ryla's sarcastic rhetoric suddenly eased the tension in the room. She took another sip of wine, then lifted a finger from the glass, and pointed at the bed. "Now I said, get up and get yo' defiant ass in that bed."

Bella angrily wiped her tears again and reluctantly sat on the edge of the bed with a scowl on her face. She folded her arms across her chest and refused to look in Ryla's direction.

"At least listen while you sittin' ova' there poutin'." Ryla drank the last of the wine in her glass and got up to refill it. "You need to find a way to deal with the scent of ol' goat cheese, Atticus," she said, as she poured herself more wine.

Bella whipped her head around and glared at Ryla. "I don't wan-"

"Shut up, girl!" Ryla interjected, quickly swiveling her head toward Bella. "Close that hole in your face and just listen!" She sat back down and continued to glare coldly at her. "Every new girl walks in here quiverin' just like you, sittin' ova' there thinkin' to themselves, how can I escape this place? How can I stop this stankin' ass man from forcin' himself on me every night? There's just gotta be a betta' life for me than this? I'm quite sure there is a betta' life for a Negro woman out there, but you'd be hard pressed to find it while you're a slave.

"Trust me, Bella, I get it. I unda'stand the initial urge to escape this place. Don't no woman wanna spend 'er life bein' forced to submit to a man she don't love. Hell, especially one she can't hardly stand the smell of! But Atticus believes in givin' the finest to all his illegally purchased whores. Most masta's would have you workin' in a filthy field in the blazin' hot sun, or in the house takin' care of his little demons, scrubbin' his floors, washin' his nasty ass unda'wear, and cookin' his meals, while you damn near starve. Some'll even strip ya' bare, and whip ya' half to death when they're angry, and then have the audacity to fuck ya' while ya' still bleedin', 'cause the sight of your naked ass done made his cock hard! Ol' goat cheese, Atticus, ain't nothin' like that. He's eccentric as all hell. He's certainly got bizarre fetishes … and that goddamn awful odor! But he's incredibly

464

particular about the way he treats his slaves. He's possessive and greedy. He don't want nobody touchin' his whores. He even wants us healthy and clean. Lemme guess, he's already put you in the hands of a doctor, a dentist, a seamstress, and a slew of nurses?"

Bella nodded.

"Mm-hmm, I ain't surprised. His bizarre fetishes lead 'em to do things that no otha' masta' would eva' waste his money on. He'll dress you in fine clothin', feed you the finest cuisine, and drown you with fine wines," she said, pausing to take a sip of that very wine. "You'll have the softest threads wrappin' your body at night, on that custom-made mattress you're ova' there poutin' on! And you can even bathe as often as you want. That's 'cause Mr. Goat Cheese wants fresh clean pussy to slide his cock into, and soft skin to glide his stankin' body across. Those same doctors, dentists, and seamstresses you met will be back here dotin' on you every single year. Like clockwork, his crew of money-hungry minions will be here caterin' to us, like we're a goddamn harem of princesses. Mr. Goat Cheese *needs* eye candy. He wants to see to it that our teeth always sparkle like fine china, that our pussies are always in fuckable shape, and that we're always adorned in the sort of custom-made dresses and lingerie that'll keep his decrepit cock solid as a rock! But his motives don't fuckin' matta' to me! The fact is that we reap the rewards of his bizarre fetishes!

"But Atticus only spends that kind of money to cater to slaves that he feels are worth it. He quickly gets rid of the ones who ain't. He must've liked yo' pussy a lot to give you Clara's old bed. She was his favorite fuck. Seemed to wanna fuck that girl mornin', noon, and night. She had him walkin' around here with his cock as hard as sixteen-year-old boys'."

"Well, I'd be just fine with 'em gettin' rid of me!" Bella defiantly replied.

"I unda'stand why you might feel that way. It's *neva'* a glorious thing to open your legs to some strange man, when you don't want to. I certainly ain't tryna make light of a man forcin' himself on a woman. No matta' how well you're treated, it's evil ... *always* evil. But I can assure you this is the beautiful side of evil, compared to the ugly shit that damn near *every* slave woman is bound to suffa' in her life. Trust me ... I know."

"I don't care! I hope he gets rid of me! *Today!*"

"Oh, you think that'd be best, huh?"

"I *know* so! I don't care about no fancy clothes and fine doctors!" Bella angrily replied, her tears starting to flow again. "I don't wanna be tied to a bed against my will with that man crawlin' all ova' me every night!"

Ryla snickered, shook her head, and took another sip of her wine. "Oh, you gonna be one of those, huh? Defiant, hard-headed, think you fuckin' know it all. Got your nose turned so high up in the air that you can't see the truth when it's right in front of ya'. Got your ears plugged so tight that you can't hear the truth when it's bein' screamed at ya'! You can be a defiant fool if you want to. But I'm tellin' ya, if you don't find a way to tolerate and satisfy Atticus Atkins, you'll end up in a place that would make you wanna crawl back here on your hands and knees and beg to suck his cock! That's a guarantee!"

"I can't imagine *anything* that would make me that desperate!"

"Well, since you can't imagine it, lemme paint it for you in pretty colors," Ryla sneered, lowering her eyelids. "Atticus'll sell you straight to a whore house, just as sho' as his ass stanks! That's where all his disappointments go. And he'll sell ya' there in a heartbeat! I've seen 'em do it, time and time again ... some right afta' his first test ride. Atticus's leftova's sell for top dolla' in a whore house. It's like his way of gettin' back at ya' for wastin' his money. Figures you gonna do what he purchased you for one way or anotha' … whetha' it's with *him* or a whole *slew* of filthy pigs!

"Atticus may smell like rotten goat cheese, but in a whore house, I can promise ya', you'll be smellin' and dealin' with far worse. In this pristine mansion, there's only *one* man fuckin' you every night, instead of *dozens!* In a brothel, you'll have an endless flow of filthy, stankin' men crawlin' inside of ya', smellin' like they ain't touched bath wata' in months! Their breath smellin' like they eat shit for breakfast, lunch, and dinna'! They don't give a damn about protectin' themselves eitha', so you're bound to wind up spittin' out some stankin' ass man's baby! And your guess about who the daddy is will be as good as the tiny face starin' back at ya'. That's only if you weren't too drunk to recall the faces of the hundreds that done fucked ya'! If you're one of the lucky ones who can't bear children, then it'll eventually be some god-awful disease they ejaculate into yo' body. You'll pull your unda'garments down one day, catch a whiff, and swear you just shit yo'self. Won't take ya' long to realize it's actually the smell of yo' pussy, rottin' away from the inside out!"

Ryla smirked when she saw the look on Bella's face instantly transition into one of pure disgust. But still, Ryla was far from finished. "Mm-hmm, keep up that defiant bullshit and that'll be your life. If you ain't willin' to satisfy Atticus's needs, he'll drop you off at a brothel, and ride off to handpick himself anotha' whore to suck his cock, and sleep on that custom-made mattress you sittin' there shiverin' on."

Ryla took a moment to examine Bella's body. "Long legs, round ass, curvy hips, cocoa-colored skin, supple titties, and long, soft hair. Those whore house owna's would be salivatin' the minute they lay eyes on you. I'm certain they wouldn't even botha' to negotiate Atticus's price demands down. They'd pay him whateva' he wants, knowin' they'd have a line of filthy old men wrapped around the buildin' willin' to pay top dolla' to fuck a pretty young thang like you.

"So, it might seem like the worst thing on earth to be trapped here, but this is paradise compared to the hell that Atticus Atkins won't hesitate to cast you into. So, I highly advise you to use your body to your advantage. Slave nigga's like us ain't got money, but we got somethin' far more valuable between our legs. When I realized that, I stopped whinin' about men that wanted to fuck me and started appreciatin' the powa' of my pussy.

"My last masta' had fifteen kids, eight of 'em girls, five of 'em menstruatin'. I's assigned laundry duty while I's livin' there, and I got sick of washin' all them damn bloody unda'garments. Hell, I don't wanna wash my own bloody unda'wear, let alone somebody else's! But there I was, week afta' week, scrubbin' them nasty thangs. I'd have a pail full of red wata' by the time I's done. My nails always seemed to be a permanent shade of pink. Shit had me nauseated by the time I's finished. I's willin' to do anything, and I do mean *anything*, to neva' have to submerge my hands in a pail full of piss, shit, and blood eva' again. Bein' the simple fuckers that men are, I knew *exactly* what it would take to get outta doin' that damn laundry. As horny as my masta' was all the time, I knew that racist bastard wouldn't hesitate to fuck me if I let 'em. Even a man as racist as him wasn't gonna pass up good pussy, no matta' what color it was. And I was right. It didn't take but a moment alone with 'em in the barn and the sight of my naked body. I fucked 'em good that night and damn near every night thereafta'. I'm convinced I fucked the racism right outta his dark heart. His old racist ass even had the nerve to wanna cuddle up with me afta'ward, goin' on and on about his life troubles, like I really wanted to hear that bullshit. But I took the opportunity to tell 'em my troubles too..." Ryla took another sip of her wine and smirked. "I haven't touched a pair of bloody unda'wear eva' since.

"That simple laundry situation made me see with such clarity how much powa' pussy really has. That revelation changed my life. I realized that the men who had forced themselves on me in the past were nothin' but weak pieces of shit who yearn for powa', but don't possess the ability to achieve it. They've walked around their whole life wishin' women didn't recoil at the sight and smell of 'em. I's convinced they stole pussy from me because they knew they could neva' have a woman like me otha'wise. So, from then on, I refused to let any man break me. Instead, I take pity on 'em, because I realize that *they're* the ones who're broken.

"If every woman unda'stood the powa' their pussies possessed, they'd all realize that it's really *us* who truly rule this world, and *everything* in it. Men think they control us when it's really *us* who literally have them by the balls. Men are delusional enough to think they want money and powa', for the sake of money and powa'. But, subconsciously, their ultimate goal is to attract as much pussy as humanly possible befo' they die. They're too stupid to realize that they ain't nothin' but a bunch of mindless ejaculatin' morons, lookin' to make a deposit in every pussy open for business. From the time they wake up, 'til the time they go to bed, fuckin' is all that dominates their minds. Men wanna fuck! And they'll do anything for pussy! Pussy drives men to be rich and powa'ful, just to ensure they have access to plenty of it! They work long hours to pay for their pussy. They plow fields to feed their pussy. Every nail a man hammers into a house is to have a nice warm place to keep his pussy. Men start wars and fight ova' pussy. They'll steal it when they can't have it or drop to their knees and cry like a bitch when their woman gives it to anotha'. Pussy even has the powa' to heal a man. He won't need no doctors or preachers prayin' for 'em. Don't matta' what's ailin' 'em, if you fuck a man right, it'll be the only medicine he eva' needs. And hell, if he *is* about to die, I'm quite sure he'd prefer it be with his wrinkled cock crammed into a pussy, so he can be fucked to death.

"Men are simply bred to fuck! They have strong backs, strong hands, strong bodies … but *weak* minds. They're easily controlled by the ugly appendages danglin' between their legs. The minute their cocks gets hard, it instantly robs 'em of every ounce of intelligence and common sense in their pea brains. And us women should be wise enough to use that weakness to our advantage." Ryla paused, squinted, and pointed at Bella. "That's *exactly* what I'd encourage your defiant ass to do! Betta' start thinkin' of yo' pussy like a horse's reins. We're in the driva's seat, guidin' men to do whateva' the hell we want 'em to do.

"And don't let all these gospel-preachin', bible thumpa's make you feel an ounce of regret about fuckin' eitha'! I don't care what they say! Fuckin' a man is natural! Them holy books was surely written by a bunch of repulsive men, who could neva' get any pussy ... or men who were actually smart enough to figure out that pussy is a man's ultimate weakness! They'll sell us anything to put the powa' back in a man's hands. But God didn't give us this kind of powa' between our thighs for nothin'!

"So, I'd advise you to stop lookin' at sex as somethin' that can ruin your life and start viewin' it as a way to get whateva' the hell you want. Money, a home, food, *love* ... if you believe in that bullshit," Ryla snickered. "Whateva' tickles your fuckin' fancy." She looked Bella up and down. "Hell, especially a woman like you, with them sparkly eyes and angelic features ... Put yo' youthful pussy on a man right and you could rule this fuckin' world.

"Just take a moment and put it all in perspective, Bella. Ol' stankin' goat cheese, Atticus, is the one who has to work his ass off to afford buyin' top shelf pussy. And all we really eva' have to do is lay on our backs, spread our legs, and let 'em elevate his body into pure bliss for seven seconds every few days. In exchange, he's crazy enough to let us drink fine wines, lay in fine linens, and wear even fina' clothes, all while livin' in the luxurious house he paid for. Hmph ... seems like a fair trade to me. This life we livin' furtha' confirms my belief ..." Ryla took a sip of her wine, leaned back into her natural, seductive pose, and smirked. "Pussy is quite simply God's most immaculate *masta'piece*."

Ryla paused for a moment, intently examining the expression on Bella's face as she waited for a potential reply. Bella only stared at the floor, seeming to search there for another defiant response to fire back at Ryla. When she found nothing, she slowly raised her head and met Ryla's eyes. When Ryla saw the look of defeat in her expression, she smirked and drank the last of the wine in her glass.

Ryla exhaled when she finished her drink, stood up, and walked over to a serving table full of various wines and wine glasses. She continued purging the thoughts on her mind as she worked to open a new bottle of Chardonnay. "Look, I know there's neva' any genuine glory or pride to be takin' in fuckin' a man you don't truly wanna be fuckin'. Like I said, Bella, it's neva' my intention to make light of a man forcin' himself on a woman. But, unfortunately, that's an inevitable truth for women like us. It's not a matta' of *if* … it's only *when* and with *who*. Anytime that happens to a woman, it's wrong and evil. That's a stone-cold fact. But it's also a stone-cold fact that, before we came here, we had no food, no clothes, no shoes, not a sip of wata' … not a damn thang. Atticus could make you leave here just as empty handed…" She turned and looked seriously at Bella. "With a hellish whore house as your final destination.

"So, while you're stuck in this situation, you do what you gotta do to tolerate ol' goat cheese. When you find yo'self nauseated by the whole ordeal, the best thing you can do is pour yo'self a drink, numb yo' body, and let yo' mind drift into anotha' world. Fantasize and escape to your wildest, exotic dreams. Use Atticus, just the way he's usin' you. In yo' mind, don't think of 'em as Atticus, the lowlife, cheatin' snake. Make 'em the man of yo' dreams. Pretend he's some man you once loved, or the sort of man you dream will love you one day. Hell, pretend he's some ol' masta' you thought was handsome enough to fuck. I don't give a damn which method you choose, just do what you gotta do to stay within these walls, and tolerate the pretty side of evil, until you're *certain* you have a far betta' option than bein' sold to a filthy whore house." Ryla stopped twisting the corkscrew and waited for Bella's eyes to meet hers. "You unda'stand me, girl?"

Mortified by Ryla's speech, Bella finally conceded. She swallowed hard and slightly nodded her head.

"You can thank yo'self for it lata' or forgive yo'self … whicheva' makes you fuckin' feel betta'," Ryla added as she finally popped the cork on the chardonnay. She filled two wine glasses and walked toward Bella. With wine glasses in hand, she stopped and loomed over her as she sat quietly on the bed, her body slumped in a defeated posture. "Besides, that pussy ain't yours anyway. Accordin' to our backwards laws, Atticus Atkins owns it. Ain't shit you can do to leave here right now any damn way. So, for now, you betta' heed my warnings, rub some sandpaper on those sensitive emotions until they're calloused, and keep the tears off ya' cheeks … Look at me!"

Bella slowly raised her head again and met Ryla's serious eyes.

"Tears are for weak bitches. You don't strike me as weak … maybe a little soft from time to time, but definitely not weak. But if I'm wrong, don't let that weak shit show around here, ya' hear? Put on a fake smile and pretend to be a happy memba' of Atticus Atkins' elite harem of colorful nigga's. You're one of nine of the finest handpicked nigga's any slave trada's have to offa'," she said, extending her hand to give Bella a glass of wine.

Bella hesitated for a second before removing it from her hand. She then just stared at it.

"Oh, go on and drink it, girl. Don't be a sissy about it," Ryla said. "That shit'll calm your nerves."

Bella drank slowly at first, then tilted her head back and finished it all without stopping. Having not eaten in a while, the alcohol immediately warmed her entire body.

Ryla snickered. "Good lord, girl! You *definitely* ain't no weak bitch!" She took the glass from Bella and handed her a handkerchief. "Get outta that bed and go on and clean ya' face up."

The alcohol hit Bella so hard, she nearly lost her balance when she stood up to walk to the mirror.

"I told you!" Ryla laughed, taking hold of Bella's arm to keep her from falling. "Top shelf wine for top shelf pussy. That expensive shit'll hit you quick. You'll get used to it, though."

Bella glanced at herself in the mirror. Had she not been violated less than an hour ago, she may have considered the hair, dress, and makeup a wonderful sight. But it only reminded her of the way in which it had all aroused a disgusting man. She dipped the rag into the water and began wiping all the makeup away, wishing she could wipe away the memory of that disgusting man's actions with it. She scrubbed hard, the way she planned to do to her entire body later. Ryla understood all too well what the hard scrubbing was about. It led her to quickly refill Bella's wine glass and hand it to her. Bella swallowed it all, again without stopping. She sat the wine glass on the dresser with a hard thud, opened her eyes, and saw two of herself in the mirror.

Ryla stood nearby and waited patiently for Bella's spinning mind to settle. "Well, now that you're feelin' all warm and fuzzy, lemme give you a grand tour of ... *the whore floor*," she announced, mocking the hospitable southern dialect of a Texas socialite.

Bella nodded after regaining her balance and walked alongside Ryla.

"You eva' ate pussy befo'?" Ryla suddenly asked as they walked to the corner of the room.

Disgusted by the thought of such a thing, Bella whipped her head around and looked at Ryla like she had just spoken in tongues. "God no!"

Ryla laughed. "Oh, don't be such a prude, girl! You might wanna acquire a taste for it. Ol' goat cheese won't let you go anywhere fo' sho' then. He keeps all his best whores until their pussies dry up. But it don't matta' how old I get. He ain't neva' gonna get rid of me. I eat pussy and suck a cock like nobody's business. Hell, I'll be far more valuable to 'em the day I lose all my teeth."

Bella suddenly burst out laughing. She was shocked that she was capable of such a thing after her ordeal earlier. She knew for sure then that the top shelf wine had indeed taken full effect.

"Just preachin' the truth, girl!" Ryla replied as they arrived at a set of double doors. She opened them and revealed a closet the size of a small bedroom. Ryla looked Bella up and down. "You look to be about a size four. The clothes on this side'll fit you," she said, pointing to the area. "You can use anything here you'd like, until Atticus's designa' brings you some more custom dresses." She looked down at Bella's feet. "Shoe size is six." She pointed to an array of footwear lining the wall. "All these in this row will fit ya'." She then turned to look at Bella. "Don't eva' once ascend these stairs in pajamas, hair undone, teeth unbrushed, or lookin' like hell just woke you up. Primped, pressed, and smellin' fresh before your feet hit the first floor. Lingerie is a *must* unda'neath your dress at all times. Atticus's designa' will bring you a custom collection of lingerie as well. Got it?"

Bella nodded.

Ryla nodded back, shut the doors to the closet, and continued taking Bella on a tour. "Go anywhere you like in this house, except for Atticus's den, and his masta' bedroom, unless the housekeepin' slaves need extra help with cleanin'. Same with his children's rooms. His kids are away at boardin' school, except some weekends, summa's, and any otha' school breaks. You'll meet the spoiled little heathens then, but their rooms are usually off limits too. We're usually only responsible for keepin' this floor tidy, and providin' service at all dinna' parties," she explained as they exited their bedroom. "Speak freely amongst us slaves, but outside of sayin' *good mornin'* or *good night*, you only speak to the Atkins family, or any of their guests, when you're spoken to first, unda'stand?"

"Yessum."

The pair carried on their conversation until they reached another set of double doors at the end of a hallway. Ryla opened the doors and revealed a massive bathroom with a garden tub. "In this house, we keep clean asses and fresh pussies at all times. Your makeup and nails should always be done, and your hair should smell sweeta' than fresh cut flowa's." She opened a small closet with dozens of soaps and shampoos. "Choose any scent to your likin'. Atticus is fine with any of these. Makeup and nail polishes are kept in these vanity drawers," she said, showing her. "I can help you apply it, if you don't know what the hell you're doin'." She walked over to a rack near the tub. "All clean towels are kept here. You can bathe as often as you like, but minimum once a day and twice in the summa'."

"Yessum," Bella replied as they were leaving.

Ryla suddenly stopped walking. "Look here, that *yessum* shit ain't necessary with me. Save that for shit for crazy *Devilyn*."

"Who's *Devilyn?*"

"Atticus's wife. Her name's Evelyn. But she's an evil, two-faced bitch. I'm convinced she's the *devil's* daughta'. So, I can't help but call 'er *Devilyn*. She don't speak to people she deems beneath her, and *beneath her* doesn't even begin to describe the way she views us. She wouldn't wipe 'er feet on us if we were floor mats. We're lowa' than a pig-pen full of shit in her eyes. You'll see the ugliest side of her two faces wheneva' she's hostin' her grand, social events. She's as sweet as apple pie to all her rich snooty guests, but the devil will raise up outta her in a millisecond when us servants don't meet her high service expectations ... which seems to *always* be the case."

"I can't believe Atticus is married," Bella stated, looking bewildered.

"Mm-hmm. Been married twenty *glorious* years," Ryla replied sarcastically.

"Does she know about 'er husband's, umm, you know ... his *activities?*"

"Know about it? Honey, she's the one who purchased me and the first two girls *for* him!"

"*What?!*"

"Mm-hmm, she surprised 'em with his little *playroom.* She designed everything down here, and affectionately named it *the whore floor.* When she was done, she lined all us ladies up, dragged Atticus down here, and danced outta here like an exhausted motha', who gladly left 'er baby sucklin the titty of a wet nurse."

Bella's mouth gaped open as her eyes widened in disbelief.

"I tell you no lies," Ryla added.

"As bad as Atticus smells, I guess I can't blame 'er for buyin' someone else to do her dirty work," Bella joked.

Ryla burst out laughing. "Chil' preach! I'd spend every dime I had not to smell that stankin' ass man eva' again!"

"I certainly can't wait to meet this *lovely* wife of his."

"Well, ya' won't catch 'er down here ... *eva'!* Hell, you may not even lay eyes on 'er until she's screamin' in your face at one of 'er dinna' affairs. I *guarantee*, she'll show you every reason she well deserves her nickname."

"Sounds like fun. I can't wait," Bella replied sarcastically. Considering what had happened to her less than an hour before, Bella was stunned at her ability to even get out of bed, let alone conjure up the strength to speak. There was just something about Ryla that had eased her emotional pain … temporarily anyway.

Ryla continued filling Bella in about the odd dynamic between Evelyn and Atticus on their way to another room down a long hallway. When they arrived, Ryla opened yet another set of double doors, and walked inside of what looked to be a luxury lounge. Fancy decorations lined the shelves on the walls, and expensive sofas and lounges were strewn about the room. A billiards table was the centerpiece of the room, and a bar sat just off to the right of it. Ryla walked behind the bar. "Most of the wine and liquor is kept here. The liquor is for Atticus. We're allowed red or white wines only. No hard liquors allowed in your system. Help ya'self to any of these, but don't eva' exceed your limits. Just enough to calm your nerves and moisten your pussy … and your mouth for that matta'," she joked. "This is also the room where we all meet for Atticus's nightly selection."

"*Nightly selection?*" Bella questioned, looking puzzled.

"Mm-hmm. Atticus chooses who he wants to fuck for the night," Ryla answered nonchalantly, like such a thing was not the least bit odd. "We have to be in here by nine p.m. sharp, or ten p.m. when Atticus's kids are back from boardin' school. We line up ova' here accordin' to our complexion," she further explained, pointing out the area. "More than likely, you'll be in between Olivia and Esther. We'll know for sure when we line up tonight."

Bella followed Ryla with a dumbfounded look on her face as they exited the lounge. Ryla then guided her to Atticus's "playroom," the very place Bella had had her first unwanted encounter with him. "Don't eva' once let ol' goat cheese finish his business inside of you, ya hear? No matta' how drunk, or outta control, forgetful, or stupid he may get when he's in the throes of fuckin' you. You need to *always* make sure he's wearin' one of these," Ryla explained, opening a drawer full of custom-made, sheepskin prophylactics. "Clara, the girl you just replaced, slipped up and got pregnant. We ain't seen 'er since the day

Devilyn found out she was carryin' her husband's baby. We *still* don't know what happened to her or the baby. But if hateful Devilyn had anything to do with it, I'm convinced she condemned her and that baby to suffa' for the rest of their natural lives in some shithole."

Bella was barely able to comprehend what Ryla was saying. Her eyes were suddenly fixated on the bed that Atticus had her tied to earlier. She suddenly felt her body temperature rise, along with a surge of tears, as flashbacks began torturously replaying in her mind. She stood there paralyzed by the memory of struggling to free herself from the silk ties around her wrists, while a stranger invaded her body.

Showing empathy for the first time, Ryla placed a comforting hand on Bella's shoulder when she saw tears cascading down her cheeks. "Look at me." She waited patiently for Bella to turn toward her. "The day Atticus Atkins ceases to breathe, he's goin' straight to hell. For *every* injustice he's eva' committed, the devil will derive the utmost pleasure from drivin' a pitchfork deep into the pit of his ass for all eternity. He *will* suffa' dearly for what he did to you, and every otha' woman within these walls … make no mistake about that."

Bella glanced back at the bed she was tied to just an hour before and swallowed back another sudden surge of tears.

Ryla gently touched Bella's face, and turned her back toward her before speaking again. "Atticus Atkins is a *weak* and *broken* man. Don't you *dare* give him the victory of breakin' you too. You unda'stand me, girl?"

Bella suddenly commanded her mind to turn off the horrible memory of Atticus. She then wiped away the very last tear that she would allow to escape her eyes. "Tears are for weak bitches…" She looked directly into Ryla's eyes. "*Right?*"

A prideful expression illuminated Ryla's face. "Damn right," she nodded.

With a renewed sense of strength, Bella held her head high and walked out of the playroom. Side by side, she strolled confidently next to a unique woman, who took pride in empowering the minds of the oppressed.

Atticus's arrogance led him to believe that it was his expertise as a lover that had suddenly caused the women in his harem to willfully reciprocate his affections. But the credit for their transitions actually belonged to Ryla and her abrasive, no nonsense speeches. Her harsh, vulgar words had an unorthodox way of quickly penetrating their minds. She empowered them not only with her words but by being a shining example of a woman with strength and resilience. Had it not been for Ryla and her zero tolerance for emotional weakness, Atticus Atkins may have found many of his slaves hanging by the neck, from the ends of the silk ties he had used to bind them with.

Whether or not Bella had truly been empowered by Ryla's words was about to be put to the test as the nine o'clock hour neared. Like the backstage chaos of getting into costume for a show, all of Atticus's women had gathered in the bathroom together. Some were scouring themselves in the garden tub, some traipsing around naked, some sitting at the vanity tables with towels on, doing their hair and makeup. No matter what stage of preparation they were in, *everyone* was guzzling wine, thoroughly numbing themselves before the show was set to begin.

"I don't know why the hell all of us are botherin' to get ready tonight. You know who Atticus is gonna choose," Lola complained. She was standing in the corner naked, swirling the wine in her glass, glaring at Bella through a set of jealous eyes.

"Shut yo' drunk ass up and cova' up those saggy titties!" Ryla fired back, throwing a towel at her. "If I's Atticus, I wouldn't want yo' withered, dried-up pussy eitha'!"

Everyone erupted in laughter … except for Bella. She actually agreed with Lola. Her words had instantly caused Bella to stop doing her hair and gaze emptily into the mirror. She was suddenly in a trance. She could no longer see her reflection. Instead, the flashbacks of Atticus forcing himself on her were gazing back at her.

Sensing her distress, Ryla walked up beside her and refilled her glass with wine. She then squatted down and waited for Bella to return her gaze in the mirror. "He ain't Atticus Atkins, Bella," she whispered. "He's whoeva' the hell you want 'em to be. Drift away in your mind and use that broken rat bastard for your own pleasure, just the way he's usin' you."

Bella nodded in appreciation for her reminder. She then sat there quietly as Ryla put the finishing touches on her hair and makeup for her. When she was done, Ryla stepped back and faintly smiled at Bella's beauty. Bella would have smiled too, but she felt the occasion was not worthy of an expression that represented joy.

"Let's go ladies," Ryla demanded after glancing at the clock.

Ten minutes before nine, everyone filed out of the bathroom and headed to the lounge. Just as Ryla had predicted, Bella's skin tone led her to be placed in the lineup between Ester and Olivia. Bella was slightly trembling as she stood there. She quietly inhaled and exhaled, trying to muster the strength to calm herself down, something that three glasses of top-shelf wine had failed to do. Her nerves escalated tenfold when Atticus walked through the door precisely at nine. The strong odor of his musky cologne wafted in with him and immediately overtook the room. His salt and pepper hair was damp and his body was covered by a navy-blue, custom, silk robe with his initials embroidered on the breast pocket.

Atticus stood there with a glass of bourbon in his hand, his eyes slowly sweeping across the line of lingerie-clad beauties before him. He sat his glass of bourbon down and slowly walked down the line, gently caressing various erogenous body parts of his mistresses as he passed them by. The entire routine was Atticus's foreplay. He loved to let the sight, scent, and softness of their bodies light the fire in his groin. The fabric rising just underneath the tie on his silk robe proved his method was quickly working. As he groped the candy dish of women before him, his mouth began to water. His salivary glands were always activated by the array of various colors and flavors he had to choose from: white chocolate, caramel, toffee, dark chocolate, and every blend in between. Atticus usually kept his pleasure girls on a flavorful rotation. But, despite already having had a taste of her earlier in the day, he stopped when he got to Bella. He looked deep into her eyes. She coldly stared back. Atticus caressed her cheek with the back of his hand, his lust-filled eyes silently speaking of how badly he wanted her. That wanton look was nowhere to be found on Bella's face, though. Her glare was empty, as if she was looking right through him. Her only focus was on not letting a look of disgust creep into her facial expressions. But the overpowering smell of liquor, from Atticus's lustful heavy breathing, suddenly caused her to wince. She reflexively blinked her eyes, recoiled slightly, and her stomach began to turn. Atticus's arrogance made him dismiss her reaction to him as nervousness. "Don't be scared. Come with me," he whispered lustfully, taking her by the hand and guiding her out of the lounge.

Lola quietly scoffed and rolled her eyes after seeing that her prediction was accurate. In turn, Ryla gave Bella a telling glance, discreetly trying to remind her of her words. *He ain't Atticus Atkins. He's whoeva' the hell you want 'em to be. Drift away in your mind and use that broken rat bastard for your own pleasure, just the way he's usin' you.* Bella discreetly nodded back when she heard those words again in her head.

Words were one thing, but the thought of putting those words into action had perspiration seeping rapidly from Bella's pores, as Atticus held her hand and guided her to his playroom. She closed her eyes and prayed for strength when they entered. *He ain't Atticus Atkins.*

481

He's whoeva' the hell you want 'em to be. Drift away in your mind. Those sentences kept echoing in Bella's head as Atticus laid her down on the bed. Instead of the softness of a mattress, though, Bella suddenly felt the prickle of hay beneath her back, from the makeshift hay bed in her old slave quarters. She kept her eyes tightly shut. Bella was now blind to Atticus's skin-curdling, fetish-driven glare. Instead, she was warmed by a set of calming, beautiful eyes. They were gazing lovingly at her in the fantasy world of her mind. Her nose was suddenly impenetrable to the stomach-turning odor that seeped from Atticus's pores. Instead, Bella felt her nether region moisten over the memory of a manly scent, one that always pleasantly aroused her sense of smell, and all other parts of her for that matter. In the world where Bella's mind had drifted, Atticus Atkins was no longer lying on top of her. Instead, she was wrapped in the warm embrace of a man who once loved her immeasurably. The memory of that night with her lover in the slave quarters began to replay vividly in her mind ...

Just after midnight, Bella was jarred from her sleep by a bizarre dream. Her lover had his arms wrapped tightly around her and was awakened when she shuddered. "You okay?" he asked, sounding groggy.

Bella rolled over to find him gazing appreciatively at her. "I'm fine," she smiled, tracing her finger down his bare chest.

"You sure?" he asked, kissing her gently on the forehead.

"Mmm, maybe a little hungry," she replied.

Her man caressed her cheek. "Want me to rustle you up somethin'?"

Bella propped herself up on her side and let a kiss linger on his lips. "You already have what'll satisfy my cravin's," she whispered, sliding her hands down into his pants. She began slowly stroking him, and seductively bit his neck when his erection began to pulsate in her hand. The graze of her teeth triggered a moan and further ignited the pleasure in his groin.

"Shh!" she laughed quietly. "You'll wake everybody up."

He gently pulled her down on top of him and wrapped his arms around her. "I can't help myself. I lose all my self-control when you touch me like that," he whispered.

"Well, since you can't control yourself..." Bella placed his hand on her buttocks. "I guess you can't have any of this," she teased. She broke free from his embrace, threw the blanket on top of him, and quietly trotted out of the slave quarters.

"We'll see about that," her lover replied. He quickly untangled himself from the blanket and put his pants back into place. Like a lion after a lioness in heat, he then immediately gave chase. By the time he made it out the slave quarter doors, Bella was halfway across the field. She began laughing hysterically when she heard her man's footsteps closing in on her. She playfully screamed when he caught her. He scooped her into his arms and carried her into the barn.

"The punishment for teasin' a man and runnin' off is severe, ya' know?" he joked, gazing down at her in his arms.

"There is no punishment that'll stop me from doin' it again," she jokingly defied.

"I think otha'wise," he replied, suddenly tickling her neck mercilessly with his lips.

"Okay, okay, I give up!" she spat through a fit of uncontrollable laughter. "You win! You win!"

Her infectious laughter had her lover laughing as well. "What did I win?"

"Put me down and I'll show you."

The sudden, sultry tone of her reply immediately made her lover's mouth water and his member harden again. After he placed her on her feet, Bella lit an oil lamp and closed the barn door. She then turned and walked back toward her man, slowly undoing the buttons of her dress along the way. His breaths deepened as he stood in a wide-eyed trance, watching her every movement. Bella stopped five feet away from him and continued to undress. She gazed at him as well, equally turned on by the way he watched her erotic show with his mouth agape. She loved the way his eyes lingered with appreciation on her bare skin as it was slowly revealed. The awestruck look on his face made her feel as though he viewed her like a priceless work of art.

After Bella's dress hit the ground, her lover's eyes slowly careened upward, wanting a second appreciative viewing of her body. Once he panned up to her face, he gazed into her sparkling eyes. He stepped forward to touch her, the way her eyes were silently commanding him to do. Still entranced by her beauty, he stared intensely at her as he approached. He then gently placed his hands on either side of her face and descended on her lips. As he caressed her lips with his, he slowly slid his hands down her angelic face, to her hourglass-shaped hips, and onto the curvature of her buttocks. The way he gently massaged her posterior cheeks invoked a moan from Bella that broke their kiss. The sound of her pleasure garnered a deep-throated groan from him in return. *Needing* to hear her sighs elevate, he suddenly dropped to his knees, spread her legs, and voraciously sucked her pleasure seed from its hiding spot. He gripped her buttocks tight, holding her firmly in place as he feasted. The strong suction of his lips instantly made Bella's knees weak. She gripped his head and hers fell backward, allowing her deep, raspy purrs to escape with ease. Rhythmically, she then began grinding her hips against his lips, and instantly succumbed to the intense sensations. The hot, climactic explosion roared through her vocal cords, tore through her core, and turned her legs to putty. Her lover's tight grip on her posterior kept her firmly on her feet as he ravenously drained every drop of her erupting juices.

Only when her lover was certain that he had extracted every ounce of pleasure from Bella did he release the stronghold he had on her southern set of lips. He then quickly stood to kiss the bee stung lips on her beautiful face. The ravenous movement of his mouth seemed to translate how extraordinarily aroused he had become after getting drunk off the sweet taste of her nectar. Bella's body, too, seemed to burn with equal need. She pressed her pelvis flush against his. Her lover immediately reacted. He slid his hands down her back, grappled the cheeks of her buttocks again, and hoisted her up. Bella immediately wrapped her legs around his waist, pressing the heat of her abyss directly against the bulge in his pants. Still kissing her with fiery lust, he carried her over to the tail end of a nearby wagon and sat her down. He reluctantly pulled his lips away from hers and quickly grabbed the oil lamp. He placed it inside the covered wagon, wanting to be sure he could see every erotic expression on Bella's face while he was submerged deep within her body. He then laid a blanket down and took Bella by the hand to help her inside. He laid on his back, inviting her to do whatever she pleased: use him, abuse him, or make love to him tenderly. It did not matter to him, so long as the woman he loved garnered the pleasure that her actions had confessed she was hungry for.

Bella mounted her lover and ran her hands slowly up his hardened abdominal muscles, while he, in turn, slid his down the soft sides of her body. She hovered above him and began teasing him with her tongue on the sensitive skin between his neck and shoulder. She kissed her way downward, stopping to tease her lover's nipples, ravenously sucking each one. The sudden, intense pleasure caused his member to pulsate. With every suck and kiss down his core, the pressure mounted in his stones. He welcomed the intensifying pain, though, knowing that the pleasure soon to erupt would be equally as intense.

As Bella removed her lover's trousers, her mouth continued to suck and tease his skin in a way that caused his vocal cords to constantly hum with delight. The low rumbling sound was like music to her ears, so much so that she took her sweet time sliding his trousers off. After stripping him bare, she paused and gazed at the Adonis-like body before her, beautifully illuminated by the firelight. Bella's eyes slowly coasted up her lover's nude anatomy, appreciating every muscle, ripple, and scar that composed his artistically sculpted physique. When she reached his face, she became slightly emotional over the innocent set of eyes gazing back at her with pure love and unbridled adoration. They both remained fixed in a loving gaze for a moment. Then Bella's eyes hovered to his midsection. She smiled seductively at the rock-hard appendage that was standing at attention, eagerly awaiting entry into her heavenly kingdom. Her eyelids suddenly lowered, and she looked back into her lover's eyes. The way she gazed at him with burning lust caused his member to begin seeping semen. Eager for a taste, Bella began kissing the innermost sensitive parts of his legs. The tickling sensations left him equally torn between the need to laugh and to moan. However, any hint of laughter quickly transitioned into deep-throated groans when Bella gently wrapped her lips around the soft, fleshy tissue between his thighs. The groans elevated as she slowly slid her tongue north along his hardened flesh. An animalistic growl tore through his vocal cords when she then wrapped her lips around the tip and began ravenously sucking away. When the sound of his beastly moans ignited an inferno in her own groin, Bella suddenly stopped sucking altogether and kissed her way up his abdomen. Like a gluttonous wild animal, her lips bit and suckled his chest, neck, and lips before forcefully submerging her tongue into his mouth. Insatiably, she kissed him as she slid her lover's pulsating member into the raging inferno between her thighs. The roar that suddenly erupted from him was muted by Bella's mouth as she continued to devour his lips.

Bella refused to part ways with her lover's lips; her tongue was far too happy to be entangled with his, much like her body now was. She only broke their kiss when her lover suddenly began bucking his hips upward, his body now relentlessly chasing the pleasure. Bella steadied her hands on his chest and fell in sync with his motions. Knowing her man well, she could tell by the deepening tone of his moans that their swift motions were about to bring forth his eruption. However, she was not ready for the ride to end. Like a jockey, she took control over her wild animal, forcing his body to obey her commands. She abruptly halted her hips and gazed down at her beautiful beast, her hands petting his chest as she waited for his panting to subside. She could tell that his calm had returned by the way his eyes suddenly opened and met hers. He then began gracefully sliding his hands up the sides of her body and onto her face. The loving way he gazed at her as he tenderly caressed her cheek, unexpectedly made her feel a need to cry. With a slow, rhythmic grind of her hips, she began reciprocating the immense love she felt. Perfectly seated on him, like a rider on a horse's saddle, she continued the subtle motions, letting the intensity build slowly this time. She closed her eyes when the pleasure began to rise, along with a more intense desire to cry.

Seeing Bella's emotional reaction made her lover completely forget about his own pleasures. In another expression of his altruistic love, he now selflessly wished to focus only on hers. Like a goddess had just materialized before him, he gazed unblinking at her. He watched intently as acute, pleasurable sensations propelled her movements like a hypnotic belly dancer. The exotic show taking place on top of him certainly had him hypnotized. He refused to take his eyes off the alluring sight of Bella's torso, rhythmically dancing to the waves of ecstasy flowing from his body to hers. The visual from outside the wagon would have been equally as captivating to his eyes. The firelight from the oil lamp had cast her shadow on the cloth cover of the wagon, displaying her movements like an erotic version of the Dream Symphony.

Much like the patrons of the Dream Symphony, Bella's lover was equally spellbound by the live show taking place before his eyes. He was mesmerized by the glorious sight and sound she exuded as she passionately rode him on her way to climatic deliverance. She had her back arched, her head tilted, with tears trickling down the sides of her face while erotic cries escaped her luscious lips. Overloaded with pleasure, Bella's tears suddenly flooded from her eyes and her body blissfully exploded, finally succumbing to the intensity of the physical and emotional love she felt. The explosion of pleasure radiated through her vocal cords, sounding much to her lover like angels singing. The heavenly sounds quickly triggered his body to burst inside of her with a powerful climactic eruption that damn near brought him to tears too.

... The misfortune this time, however, was that that beautiful moment was merely a glorious memory for Bella. This time around, she did not open her eyes to find her loving man gazing appreciatively at her, just as he had that night. Instead, she reluctantly forced herself to peek between her eyelids to see that she was lying with a man who disgusted her. Instead of her current need to cry being triggered by the bliss of pleasure, they were triggered by the feeling of betrayal. She closed her eyes quickly, trying to ward off impending tears. *Tears are for weak bitches*, she heard echoing in her mind. She searched for the strength to accept that this moment would never blossom into a cherished memory, but, rather, would remain a nightmarish moment that she wanted to banish from her fragile mind.

It was a moment that Atticus, however, had already filed away as one he wanted to relive in his mind again and again. Just seconds after their intimate encounter, he already wanted more. The sighs and moans that erupted from Bella during her fantasy had him absolutely captivated. Her erotic movements left him perceiving her passion as love, causing him to become instantly addicted to her, like no other pleasure girl before. He caressed her face and gazed longingly at her, through a set of mesmerized eyes. However, the eyes that glared back at him harbored not a single ounce of mutual emotion. Atticus's lust and arrogance left him blind to that, though. If he could see through the fog of his lust, he would see with clarity that Bella was weighed down by shame. She was sick to her stomach as he panted on top of her, offensively forcing the odd odor of his breath through her nasal passages. The smell of his breath caused a stray tear to fall from Bella's eye. Atticus wiped it away and kissed her, thinking that the single tear was yet another indicator of her love for him.

Love was hardly Bella's motive for her contrived passionate exchanges with Atticus that night, nor in the intimate sessions she was forced to have with him as the weeks rolled past. While scouring her skin raw in the bathtub after every unwanted encounter with Atticus, Ryla's words played on a continuous loop in Bella's head: *Don't leave here until you're absolutely certain you have a far betta' option than bein' sold to a filthy whorehouse.* Though it was emotionally daunting, Bella took her words to heart. But she indeed had all intentions of escaping to that far better option that Ryla spoke of … as soon as humanly possible.

During her first month in the Atkins' residence, Bella discreetly learned the layout of the mansion. As she slyly strolled through the house, she noted a den, decorated in eighteenth century style antique furniture. Atticus's desk and books stood out to her far above any of the other fanciful decor in the room, though. Bella filed that information away in her mind and began paying keen attention to Atticus and Evelyn's daily routines. She mentally noted the days that they were absent from the house the longest. Every Wednesday, Bella had learned that there was a four-hour window of opportunity to put her devised escape plan into action.

Two months in, Bella was now confident about her Wednesday, four-hour window of opportunity. She could hardly sleep the Tuesday night before she planned to make her move. She lay tossing and turning, trying to summon the courage to move forward with her idea.

Having not slept a wink, she got out of bed at six a.m. and went about her morning chores as usual. She could not even bring herself to eat. With nervousness eating away her insides, she waited with great anticipation for Evelyn to traipse off to her meeting with a women's affairs committee, and for Atticus to go to work. As predicted, the pair left the house precisely at nine a.m. With the four-hour countdown ticking, Bella tiptoed upstairs. She cautiously looked over her shoulder to be sure nobody saw her as she made her way into Atticus's den, a place she knew full well was off limits to her. Perspiring and jittery, Bella shut the door, and frantically made her way over to the desk. She then began going through the drawers, looking for a blank sheet of paper. When she found one, she sat down and picked up a pen from the corner of the desk. With a shaky hand, she dipped it in ink and began to write a letter, one that she was certain would lead her to that far better option that Ryla had spoken of.

The tick tock of the grandfather clock in the corner of the den had never felt so significant in Bella's life. She swore the ticks and tocks were chiming far faster than they should be. The loud countdown caused her hand to shake so hard that her words looked as though they had been scripted by a child. But her horrible handwriting was the least of Bella's concerns. Finishing her two letters quickly, and finding two very important public addresses, was all she cared about. She hoped the leather-bound encyclopedias lining the walls of the den held the particular addresses she sought. Her shaky hands were eager to begin thumbing through every single nonfiction book in Atticus's collection to find both addresses. She did not care if the feat took her months. She planned to leave no page unturned.

Despite sweat pelting the page, Bella finally finished her first letter. Silently, she read it to herself and was satisfied that it would suffice. She then pulled out another blank piece of paper to begin writing an identical copy. "What the hell're you doin' in here?!" she heard, just as her pen touched the paper. Bella's heart dropped into the pit of her stomach when she turned to find Atticus standing near the door. She sprang to her feet and hid her papers behind her back. She glanced to his right and saw Lola's head visible just over his shoulder. The smirk on her face spoke volumes.

Atticus stepped inside of the den and slammed the door, leaving Lola outside. He walked up to Bella slowly, never once taking his eyes off her. "What you got there?" he asked, reaching behind her and snatching her papers away. He took a moment to read the contents to himself. He looked coldly at Bella when he was finished. "You can write … very eloquently, I see." His eyelids then lowered into angry slits. "But I don't remotely like the subject matta'," he said, crumpling the papers and throwing them into the fireplace. Atticus's extreme obsession with Bella caused the contents of her letter to instantly catapult him into a blinding rage. He suddenly grabbed her by the chin. "Haven't I treated you well?"

Atticus was squeezing her chin so tight, she could not move it to respond.

"HAVEN'T I?!" he snapped, finally easing his grip.

"Y-yessa'," Bella stammered, tears flooding her eyes.

"Then what's your rush to leave here?"

"I-I don't b-belong h-here," she boldly replied, tears now rolling in streams down her cheeks.

"I *own* you," he replied, penetrating her with an icy glare. "Accordin' to the law, you belong where I say you belong."

Bella lowered her head in despair, closed her eyes, causing another tidal wave of tears to rush down her cheeks.

Atticus suddenly grabbed her hard by the wrist and gripped her fingers tightly. "If I catch you so much as pickin' up a pen and paper in this house again, you'll be diggin' your fingers outta the ashes in that fireplace." He tilted her chin up and forced her to look at him.

"And if I eva' find you in my den again, I'll write to your little friend on your behalf. I'll even be kind enough to provide the address to the morgue where he can retrieve your corpse."

Now trembling uncontrollably, Bella nodded as a waterfall of tears saturated her dress.

Still gripping her wrist tight, Atticus yanked her hard and ushered her out of his den. As Bella was whisked away, she passed by Lola, who was still standing outside the door with a smirk on her face, not even bothering to hide her betrayal. Lola had initially just planned to tell Atticus that Bella had been fiddling around in his den when he returned home later that day. But in a stroke of luck, he had returned to the house to retrieve a briefcase he had forgotten in the kitchen. Lola took that opportunity to let him see Bella's misdeeds with his very own eyes.

Lola had been just as eager for Bella to leave as she was. However, she had no desire for Bella's next residence to be a better place than where they were now. For weeks, Lola had watched Bella, hoping to find some reason why Atticus should sell her to a brothel. After witnessing her blatant disregard for the house rules, Lola was confident that Atticus would immediately take Bella straight to a whorehouse. But such a thought never once crossed Atticus's mind. Lola's jealousy-driven betrayal only served to make Atticus far more possessive over his new prized slave. That very day, Atticus bought a mailbox with a lock. The gates were locked any time he and Evelyn were off the premises. Windows were sealed shut, double-sided deadbolts were added to all doors … including on the door to Atticus's den. Pens, paper, stamps, and envelopes were four things that Atticus now knew were as valuable to Bella, as jewelry was to his wife. Their value led him to store them in his safe next to expensive diamonds and gold. The four things that had the power to take Bella on to that far better life were now kept under lock and key … and so too was her hope.

Bella had given herself a deadline of only dealing with her circumstances for six months. However, Lola's betrayal turned that six months into a year, then two, and then four. As the years rolled by, Bella was overcome with grief. Atticus's threats and prison warden ways doused her inferno of hope, leaving it as a tiny smoldering ember. Now feeling like a true prisoner, Bella reluctantly submitted to the fact that this was her life now, and there was not a thing she could do about it. Her sadness grew exponentially every time she looked out the window and saw the postman in the distance, knowing that he was the key to her salvation.

... Despite *knowing* she deserved a far better life, Bella carried on for years performing mundane duties, submitting to Atticus intimately, and serving meals to Evelyn's guests at her monthly grand dinner affairs. On this random day in February 1865, Bella was doing the latter. Mindlessly, she went from person to person at a massive dining room table, placing dinner rolls on the plates of the rich guests at one of Evelyn's social events. It was a boring task that Bella had done countless times while her mind wandered to another world, so much so that she could have been serving rolls to cows and never noticed the difference. On this particular evening, however, a gentleman speaking to Atticus from across the table had indeed noticed *her*. The gentleman halted his conversation mid-sentence just as Bella placed a roll on Atticus's plate. The sudden way his mouth gaped open, as he stared wide-eyed at her, made it seem as though she had suddenly cast a hypnotic spell on him. The befuddled look on the man's face made Atticus wonder if his heart had stopped beating, or if he had taken an interest in one of his pleasure girls ... or perhaps *both*. He knew all too well that Bella had that sort of power over a man.

Lost in the beautiful world of her mind, Bella did not notice the way she was being gawked at, until she turned to walk back to the kitchen, and suddenly heard a word that she was convinced she would never again hear in her life. *"Lily?!"*

Bella froze ... and so, too, did the music she was composing inside her beautiful mind. She immediately spun around and met the bewildered gaze of a man who knew her face all too well. Her face was one that he had walked by every single day, while going about his duties as the curator of the Manhattan art gallery. Her face immediately brought back the heart-wrenching memory of overhearing a distraught James Adams at his gallery, weeping over the devastation of losing her. That face, hanging as the centerpiece of the music themed exhibit, had stirred emotions in thousands of visitors, and had brought his good friend, William Werthington, to tears.

"Lily Adams?" Preston Mills repeated, still gazing at her in utter disbelief as he rose slowly from his seat. "My *God*, it is you!" he exclaimed, the sight of her portrait-worthy face now causing a glisten of tears in his own eyes.

The look on Preston's face, and the tone of his voice, had completely ceased all conversation and movements in the room. Every guest stared at Bella and Preston as they silently gazed at each other, both looking equally entranced. The guests were stunned by Preston's raw emotion and the hint of tears they now noticed in his eyes, all stemming from the presence of a mere servant. Atticus was intensely watching the odd exchange too, getting more and more angry at the way that Preston was gazing at his most prized pleasure girl. His anger could not eclipse Evelyn's, though. As she stared at both of them in confusion, she was unable to hide the devilish facial expression she was known for. During her social events, Evelyn demanded that her servants be as transparent and inanimate as wine glasses. This situation, therefore, made her instantly irate. She did not want her party overshadowed by rampant speculative gossip as to why a powerful white man had risen to his feet on behalf of a menial slave. Evelyn's furrowed eyebrows and pursed lips clearly indicated her displeasure over the unwanted attention that might now be brought to her husband's harem of illegally purchased whores. She feared this bizarre exchange between Bella and Preston would ignite the sort of salacious gossip that had the potential to tarnish her family's pristine image.

Bella had yet to notice the devilish glare on Evelyn's face, though. The ironclad memory vault of her mind was far too busy flooding her with a plethora of beautiful memories, all unlocked by the face of a man she immediately recognized as well. As she stared at Preston, she swore he was still holding the tickets to the Dream Symphony, as he auctioned them off to the audience in the ballroom of the Manhattan art gallery. The memories were so vivid, she swore she was standing at the podium in the art gallery's ballroom, reading the Queen's invitation to perform at Buckingham Palace. In Bella's mind, the guests at Evelyn's party had turned into the student orchestra, chanting "say yes!" in response to the Queen's letter. The memories had her heart racing, as an intense need to cry began to burn her eyes.

"My God, Lily, is this where you've been all this time?" Preston suddenly asked, his words finally pulling her back to her current surroundings.

Her visions of James wrapping his arms around her, as they celebrated her decision to sail to the Old World, instantly faded away. Through a blur of tears, she looked around and finally noticed all of the bewildered eyes pasted on her, *especially* the cold glaring eyes of Atticus Atkins.

"Lily, William's been looking f- …"

With Atticus's threats terrorizing her mind, she discreetly shook her head at Preston to halt his words.

"You must be mistaken, Mr. Mills," Atticus interjected. "Her name is *Bella*."

"But I'm certain that…"

Bella subtly shook her head at Preston again.

Preston was confused, but finally accepted Bella's cues this time. "Oh, my mistake," Preston replied, still trying to read the expression on her face. "I'm so sorry. I'm horribly embarrassed. It's just that, umm … she, umm, looks exactly like another young lady that worked as a house slave for a friend of mine."

"I see," Atticus replied, staring intensely at Preston, easily sensing his lie. "I certainly unda'stand how easy it can be to confuse one Negro with anotha'. Happens to me often. They all look so alike," he said, attempting humor.

"Or perhaps my wife is right to hound me about having my eyesight checked," Preston tried to joke in return. Now sweating profusely from the heat of true embarrassment, Preston sat back down just as slowly as he had risen. All the while, he kept his eyes on Bella as she scurried into the kitchen. The moment his posterior hit the seat, everyone slowly returned to their meal … everyone except for Atticus.

After reading the scowl on his wife's face, Atticus knew she was silently demanding that he begin damage control. He guzzled what was left of the alcohol in his glass, wiped his mouth, threw down his napkin, and then got up from the table once everyone was distracted by conversation again. He stormed into the kitchen and grabbed Bella her by the arm when nobody was around. She gasped after being startled by the sudden force of his grip. He dragged her into an empty room, shut the door, and turned her loose with a slight shove. "Do you know that man?!" he asked in a harsh but hushed tone.

"No sa'!"

"Don't lie to me!" Atticus erupted.

"No sa', I-I swear I ain't lyin'. H-He said he had me confused with someone else."

"You're a liar! Do you think I've forgotten?"

"Forgotten what, sa'?"

"*Lily* ... that's the name you had written at the bottom of that letta' you were writin' to ask some man named *William* for help all those years ago. And now that art gallery lunatic just so happens to mention *both* names!"

Bella - or rather *Lily* - lowered her head and remained silent. She knew she had no way to defend such a coincidence.

Atticus stepped closer to her. "Who are you?"

Lily began trembling as he closed in on her, tears now forming in her eyes. "B-B-Bella," she replied.

"Wrong!" Atticus snapped, causing Lily's tears to suddenly careen down her cheeks. "I said, who are you?"

"I-I-I'm *y-yours*."

"I'd highly advise you to rememba' that. Or do I need to remind you again of the only way you're leavin' this house?" he asked, burning her with a glare that was just as devilish as his wife's.

"N-no sa'."

"Good," Atticus responded softly. His devilish facial expression faded into one of lust as he suddenly began gazing at his prized pleasure girl with hunger in his eyes. Lily flinched when he suddenly reached out to touch her face. Atticus smoothed his fingers down her cheeks and wiped away an escaping tear. "I've dressed you in the finest linens. You've known nothin' but the softest of mattresses against your back. I've purchased nothin' but the most expensive soaps and lotions to soften this skin," he said, still caressing her face. "This tongue…" he said, kissing her on the lips and grazing her tongue with his, "has tasted nothin' but the finest of wines and the fanciest of foods. You've lived a life fit for a queen. Which of those has given you reason to wanna leave here?"

"N-n-none of them, s-s-sa'," Lily stammered, her body mercilessly trembling.

"Good. I want you to be as happy and satisfied as you make me," he said, now speaking tenderly to her.

Lily nodded.

"Your work is done for tonight. Go on downstairs and draw yourself a bath and have a glass of wine to help soothe your nerves. I'll join you as soon as I can." He gently kissed her lips again. "You'd like that, wouldn't you?" he whispered lustfully, caressing her tear-stained face.

"Y-yessa'," she forced herself to say.

Atticus then took her by the hand and guided her to the servant's stairway. He kissed her tenderly on the lips again before allowing her to make her way to her room. Lily somehow got her feet to carry her to her bed. She collapsed onto the mattress, curled up in the fetal position, and erupted into a shoulder-heaving fit of tears. She lay there crying over the ironic fact that it was Preston Mills she had intended to send her second letter to, during her failed escape plan. She had never thought to learn William's personal address during the time she resided with him. Knowing there was no way to find it, she felt the next best thing would be to scour through all the Encyclopedias in Atticus's den, in hopes that she could find the address of the popular Manhattan Art Gallery. Wilson and Emerson would also have received a correspondence, if she could have located the address of New York University, where the twins worked as professors. She wanted to send them all letters, hoping that one of them would pass the message on to William as to where to find her. It was Lola who had prevented Lily from rescuing herself all those years ago, but now she only had cowardice and fear to blame for not going upstairs to beg for Preston's help.

While Lily was crying uncontrollably downstairs, Ryla was upstairs watching the way that Atticus and Evelyn continued to glare at Preston throughout the evening. Their forced smiles and disapproving glances in his direction easily proved that they wanted him gone, sooner rather than later. Ryla saw the way Atticus lingered near Preston as the evening went on. She was convinced that he was intentionally trying to absorb every word of his conversations, and to make certain that he did not interact with any of his other pleasure girls.

Preston was also very aware of the fact that he was being discreetly watched, and that his presence was no longer welcome. He could only guess that Atticus's surveillance had everything to do with the debacle regarding "Bella's" identity. While Preston could only make assumptions regarding that matter, he was *absolutely certain*, beyond a shadow of a doubt, that "Bella" was *not* the true name of the woman who damn near brought him to tears at dinner. For that very reason, Preston's desire to leave the party quickly was equal to that of the Atkins'. He had been desperate to escape the social event the very second that "Bella" scurried into the kitchen. For another two hours, though, he remained at the party, doing his best to recover from the awkward moment during dinner. When he felt he had sufficiently recovered, he thanked Evelyn and Atticus for the wonderful evening, and for purchasing the art he had delivered. He then left just as quietly as he arrived.

From a distance, Ryla watched Preston leave, noting the heated whispers between Evelyn and Atticus afterward. She then tiptoed away from her duties and walked down to the whore floor to check on a woman whose identity she was now unsure of. Upon entering the room, Ryla lit two oil lamps, and quietly walked over to Lily's bed. Lily still lay in the fetal position, sniffling from time to time, her tears still saturating her pillow. She could feel Ryla staring at her, but she refused to roll over and look in her direction. With this being the second time she had been denied a chance to communicate with Preston, Lily was not in the mood to hear one of Ryla's lectures about crying. But there Ryla was, looming over her, swirling the wine in her glass. As soon as Lily heard the swishing of the liquid, she knew that Ryla was about to purge what was on her mind anyway.

Ryla exhaled and sat down on the edge of Lily's bed. "Years ago, I asked you if you had a story to tell. Do you rememba' what you said to me?"

Lily refused to reply.

"*We all got a story to tell, don't we?'* was all you replied," Ryla reminded her. "I left it alone and neva' hassled you about it again, even though I could feel in my bones that you were hidin' somethin'. Hell, it didn't take me but a few days to realize there was somethin' different about you. I could tell by the way you carried yo'self. In all my life, I ain't neva' seen a slave naturally walk with they head held high the way you do sometimes, like you some damn show pony. Ain't neva' met no slave talk with so many big fancy words eitha'. And when ol' goat cheese caught you readin' and writin' years ago, it furtha' confirmed that there was somethin' unique about you. But ... *We all got a story to tell, don't we?'* was all you were willin' to say when I questioned you." Ryla took a sip from her wine glass. "I don't wanna hear that bullshit now, though. Afta' what happened in that dinin' room tonight, I'm convinced that you got a story that'll blow everybody's mind."

Still not wanting to hear any of Ryla's rhetoric, Lily suddenly hopped out of bed and headed for the door.

"Where you goin', *Lily Adams?!'* Ryla shouted.

Lily stopped near the door and spun around. "Don't call me that!"

"Why not?!" Ryla sat her glass down, jumped up, and walked toward her. "That's yo' *real* name, ain't it?!"

"No, it ain't!"

"Liar! I saw you spin around the very second that rich white man said yo' *real* name!"

"You heard him! He mistook me for anotha' servant," Lily deflected.

"He was clearly lyin' to save your ass! That man knows you somehow! And you must be important to 'em, 'cause ain't no rich white man gonna look at no servant in the face long enough to recall who she is *years* lata'! Even if he did, he damn sho' ain't gonna rememba' yo' first *and* yo' last name!" Ryla walked closer and glared at the woman she had only ever known as Bella. "I know you got a story to tell … now come on with it!"

"No, I don't!"

"Then who the hell is Lily?!"

"I don't know anymore!" she screamed. She lowered her head and tears suddenly exploded from her eyes. "I th-think she's d-dead," she whispered as she continued sobbing uncontrollably. She then opened the door and ran off to be alone.

Lily indeed felt as though her true identity began a slow painful death the night James attempted to escape with her back in April of 1860. After sustaining such severe head trauma, she had virtually no recollection of that day, nor of the shootout between Elijah and Gideon at the planned tradeoff spot. She was even ignorant as to how she had ended up in Ava's care in her tiny Negro hospital. Her memory of holding her dead baby, however, was strikingly clear. For years, that tiny, motionless, baby doll-looking face had silently haunted her. The hows, the whys, the wondering if James knew his beloved baby was dead, had damn near eaten away her soul completely. The devastation of that moment left Lily scrounging for answers as to how she had ended up with a lifeless child in her arms, and James nowhere to be found. She was baffled as to why the ironclad memory vault of her mind refused to unlock the memories of those life-altering events.

Even her memories of being wrestled out of Ava's hospital by Ghost Riders were spotty at best. She barely recalled having a cloth sack placed over her head and being shackled to several other women who had been stolen from various places as well. For days, Lily's sickly body drifted in and out of consciousness as she traveled in those conditions, not having the mental clarity to even ponder what her fate might be.

With her body still struggling to heal from childbirth and a severe beating, Lily could barely sit up straight as she was tossed about the bumpy roads, with her battered face cloaked in darkness. She was cold, deathly ill, dehydrated, and underfed to the point that she was constantly dry heaving, making it nearly impossible for her internal wounds to heal properly. She and the other stolen slaves were treated so poorly that two of them perished as they made their way from buyer to buyer. Ironically, Lily would have been amongst the dead, in just a few short days, had it not been for Atticus purchasing her. She was so close to death before then that she had lacked the strength to even utter her own name when Atticus asked her. With the combination of an assigned name and Atticus's anal-retentive medical routine, Lily was revitalized as a different woman and reborn into a life that she did not want. The tale of her journey to that point was part of the incredible story that Ryla was desperate to know. It was also something she now felt the need to apologize for *demanding* that Lily tell her.

Hours after Evelyn's social event was over, Ryla went to find Lily. While everyone in the house was fast asleep, Lily had walked upstairs to the main floor. She was standing by a massive picture window that overlooked the sprawling land of Atticus's estate. Desperate for fresh air, she had wanted to stand on the back porch. She needed the cool breeze to help dry her tears and clear her mind. But with all the doors to her "prison" deadbolted, the picture window near the back porch was as far as she was able to go. Being denied such a simple pleasure had her tears flowing again as she stared out the window, silently begging God for her freedom. Lily suddenly sensed Ryla's presence behind her, but she could not bear to pull her eyes away from the beautiful star-filled sky. The sight of it brought back fond memories of her mother and of her first performance on William's amphitheater.

"Forgive me for pushin' to know who you are … or who you *used* to be," Ryla said to Lily. She spoke with an uncharacteristically soothing tone, as she stepped beside her good friend and gazed at the sky with her. "Yo' life story ain't none of my damn business. I know betta' than to be so pushy. Most folks here don't wanna dwell on their past. They got enough to worry about right here within these walls. It's just with you, I can't let go of this feelin' that you're someone special, Bella. This place … this *life* … it's *all* beneath you. Far, far beneath you compared to the rest of us. I can feel that this place has dimmed the beautiful light you normally shine. And now, I'm startin' to fear that that beautiful light within you will fade away altogetha'. Somehow, I *know* that would be among the world's greatest tragedies." For once there was no wine glass in Ryla's hand. She used the free hand to touch Lily on the shoulder and gently turn her around. Ryla then waited for her eyes to meet hers. "I just want so badly for you to shine again … *Miss Lily*."

Lily's tears instantly ignited again when Ryla's last two words triggered the beautiful memory of a particular man.

Ryla gently touched her dear friend on the cheek. "Lily ain't dead. She's alive … just barely, but she's still alive. And I believe, deep in my heart, that she *will* shine again…" She briefly turned to look at the sky. "Even brighta' than them goddamn stars."

Lily turned and watched as Ryla suddenly walked away. She swore she saw a glimmer of tears sparkling in her friend's eyes before she departed, *sincere* tears. Lily then turned back toward the window and gazed at the star-filled sky, through the blur of sincere tears in her own eyes. She exhaled as she stood there alone, holding on tightly to words that had managed to instantly reignite hope that had been snuffed out, four long and lonely years ago.

Chapter Twenty-six

Army of the United States
Honorable Discharge

This is to certify that

Michael Adams

Lieutenant of the Iron Army Brigade of the East

is hereby honorably discharged from the military service of the United States of America.

This certificate is awarded as a testimonial of honest and faithful service to this country.

Given in

Summersville, West Virginia

Carnifex Ferry Battlefield

Given on this

20th day of February 1865

Edward R. Blackshear

General of the Iron Army Brigade of the East

General Blackshear loomed over James while he lay in his cot in the infirmary with a brace on his leg. "Lemme get this straight. You have the chance to leave this Godforsaken place, and you're tellin' me you don't wanna go?" the general questioned, a puzzled look on his face.

"I have reasons, General … *very personal* reasons why I *need* to be here. I had no intention of eva' leavin' this war until the bitta' end… or until I'm tossed into a pile of bodies no longa' breathin'." James inhaled sharply. "I can still smell the stench of rottin' flesh. Seems to me my lungs are still in perfect workin' orda'."

"Your lungs may be … but you know good 'n damn well you can't say the same thing about that leg of yours. Lieutenant, I unda'stand and greatly appreciate your passion, but you're no good to any of our troops now. That's just a fact that you have to accept."

"General, there must be some otha' way I can serve in some capacity."

"No! There isn't! You can hardly walk, let alone protect yourself or any of your troops."

"Maybe here in the medical tent? The men can surely use my medical expertise."

"You can hardly stand long enough to take care of y'ur damn self, Lieutenant! Y'ur no longa' an asset to any of us … y'ur a liability! That's just the brutal truth! You're limpin' y'ur ass home as soon as you're healed enough to go. That's an orda'!"

James exhaled and lowered his head in defeat. "I don't have a home," he mumbled under his breath.

"What?"

"I said I'm healed enough to go home now."

"Lieutenant, don't be a jackass! I'm no doctor, but I can clearly see that you're not ready to travel a long distance with that mangled leg of y'urs."

"Well, no disrespect, General. But I *am* a doctor. And I'm fine to go now."

"Amelia?!" the general suddenly called out, still glaring at James.

"Yessa'?" she said, scurrying over.

"Do you think Lieutenant Adams is healed enough to travel?"

Whether he was or not, Amelia had the same answer. "No sir, General Blackshear. Not remotely."

"Again, no disrespect meant. But I'm the lead doctor here," James replied. "My word is final. I can treat my leg along the way, as long as I have the propa' medication and bandages. Besides, if I can't be of assistance here in some capacity then I need to make room in this bed for soldiers who truly need it."

The general blew out a breath of irritation. "Somethin' tells me that you're the one who still needs this goddamn bed a few more days, but I'll trust your judgement." He turned and looked at Amelia. "Go on and find 'em a walkin' cane, supplies, and medication."

"Yessa'," she replied, briefly glancing over at James. After hearing that he was leaving, she suddenly found herself fighting the urge to cry. James's head hung far too low to notice the sorrow in Amelia's eyes. Just as her tears began to fall, Amelia turned and went in search of the items the general had requested.

As the general stormed out of the tent, he breezed past Harrison, who had been looking on from the corner. Once the general was gone, he walked over to James.

"I don't need any goddamn medical supplies. I need to stay," James complained, letting his body fall back on the bed in frustration.

"Neva' ceases to amaze me that doctors always make the most hard-headed patients," Harrison replied.

"And you lawyers always have a smart remark locked and loaded and ready to fire at the weak and helpless."

"Weak and helpless, *precisely*. I know you're probably in a rush to resume lookin' for Lily, but it's gonna be hard to find 'er on a leg that isn't remotely ready for such a gruelin' journey. I think the general's right. You need to regain some strength and let it heal a little longa'."

"I'll heal just fine on the road. If I can't be of use here, I'm leavin'," James fired back defiantly. "I don't wanna just lay around here bein' coddled like a damn baby."

"More proof that every doctor has an impenetrable noggin," Harrison said, shaking his head. "I guess it's natural to be angry about not reachin' a goal. But deep down, you know bein' discharged is for the best."

"Makes me sick to admit that you're right," James reluctantly replied, staring blankly at the roof of the tent.

Harrison could not bring himself to look directly at James. Internally, he was glad he had pulled through and was now free to leave. But the thought of fighting a war without his best friend by his side was suddenly causing an extreme tightness in his chest. "So, uh, you headed to Ohio or Manhattan?" he asked, as he fought to settle his emotions.

"Both," James replied, sitting up again and carefully putting his feet on the ground. "I'm gonna regroup with Griff and William in Manhattan and resume our search for Lily. But I wanna stop in Ohio first. Got some business to attend to there and then I wanna check on my godchildren."

"I can't believe I've only eva' seen my little girl in pictures," Harrison replied, his emotions reigniting again over that thought.

"Zach's four. Harriet's three." He shook his head. "First steps and first words. I've missed it all. Hell, they don't even know me."

"I'll be sure to tell 'em everything about their fatha' while I'm there … well, *excludin'* some of your *activities* durin' our university years, of course," James joked.

"Yes, please pick and choose your stories carefully," Harrison laughed.

"No worries. Your children will only hear of the true hero their fatha' is," James said with sincerity.

"Ah!" Harrison waved his hand dismissively, trying to stave off his emotions more so than James's words. "Fraternity brotha', brotha'-in-arms, yes! But I think tellin' my kids I'm a hero may be ova'doin' it just a bit, don't ya' think?" he jokingly replied.

"Fraternity *brotha'*, *brotha'*-in-arms. You're my *brotha'* alright." James looked his best friend in the eyes. "Harrison, you're the only *true* goddamn brotha' I've eva' had. And you damn sure betta' believe your children will hear the story of how my one true brotha' saved my life. Until the end of my days, I'll tell 'em that story again and again, so they neva' forget that their fatha's a hero."

Amelia suddenly approached with a walking cane for James and interrupted the moment. Harrison was glad for the distraction. It gave him a chance to settle the swell of emotions that were threatening to explode out of his chest. "I'll, uh, go and get a horse and wagon ready for ya'," he said. He then stepped away to give Amelia the privacy he could sense she wanted with James.

For weeks, James had lain in the infirmary tent fighting for his life. Fever and infection had him in and out of consciousness for most of that time. Amelia had spent nearly every moment by his side, treating his wounds, keeping him cool with a damp cloth, and tearfully whispering words of encouragement. When James began regaining consciousness, it was Amelia he had awakened to holding his hand.

After days of weakness, James finally had the strength to speak and to squeeze her hand in return. "Lily?" he had whispered repeatedly, still too lost in a delusional haze to realize who he was speaking to, or whose hand he was holding. Even though Amelia knew he was hallucinating, the utterance of his wife's name was enough to stir her tears. Despite her envy, she still pretended to be the woman James loved, feeling as though such a small thing would give him the strength to heal faster.

Amelia's selflessness was not in vain. After days of nursing him, the way his wife would have, James had indeed returned to full consciousness. He had awakened completely unaware of how he had further broken Amelia's heart. He was far more concerned with evaluating the damage that his brother had done to his leg. When he struggled to even move it, he knew it would not be long before General Blackshear sent him packing. With his potential discharge looming, Amelia was not a thought on James's mind. Instead, he spent days trying to strengthen his leg enough to avoid being sent home. Amelia helped in any way she could; she, too, did not want him to leave.

Amelia was now just as heartbroken as James over his impending departure. She could not bring herself to even look him in the eyes as she handed him his walking cane and placed a satchel full of food and medical supplies near his cot. She then quickly scurried away before her emotions got the best of her again.

Surprisingly, the heaviness of her sorrow did not go unnoticed by James for a change. "Amelia," he called out, just as she was about to exit the tent. She turned around and watched James struggle to his feet with the help of the cane she had just given him. Slowly, he limped his way toward her. "I wanna thank you for all you've done for my men … and for *me*. Your kindness has not gone unnoticed, and certainly not unappreciated. I'm truly grateful to you for takin' care of me so diligently all these years. In fact, I somehow get the feelin' that I literally would not be standin' here healthy enough to go home had it not been for you."

Amelia's eyes quickly filled to capacity with tears. "Well, I don't feel you're healthy enough to leave quite yet," she teased. "But it's been my pleasure, Lieutenant. And I thank you for the kind words," she said, as her tears overflowed and ran down her cheeks.

James gently wiped a tear from her face. "Your future husband betta' cherish havin' an incredible woman like you..." He raised a fist in the air. "Or he'll have these bare knuckles to answer to."

Amelia let out a genuine laugh. "I suggest you let that leg heal first before you go hurlin' those fists at anybody."

James reciprocated the laughter. "I think I definitely need to follow that advice," he replied, groaning as he struggled to bend over and pick up his satchel.

Amelia helped him lift it onto his shoulders. She felt the need to cry again once the satchel was secured. "You take good care of yourself on the way home, ya' hear?" she said, swallowing back her tears.

"I promise, I will. And you do the same for the remainda' of your time here, okay?"

"I promise I will too. Goodbye, lieutenant."

"Goodbye, Amelia."

After Amelia walked away, James hobbled out of the infirmary into the warmth of the sunlight. Slowly, he made his way to his tent to collect the rest of his belongings. He was sure not to miss a single sentimental thing, especially what he now believed was Rose's favorite story. When he finished packing, he breathed a heavy sigh as he looked around the tent. He now completely understood how Austin was feeling before he left. There was an unexplainable heaviness about leaving his brothers-in-arms, as if he was deserting them. James looked down at his stitched leg and silently cursed J.R. for the fact that he was now being forced to abandon his iron brothers, and for ruining yet another one of his life plans. But he quickly realized that he should be appreciative of the fact that he was still alive, a claim he was happy that his father and J.R. could no longer make. As the sole survivor of their family, he no longer felt tainted by the evils of the Adams name. And with his military discharge, he was now free to resume searching for the woman with whom he wanted to rebuild the Adams family legacy. James steadied himself on his cane again, prepared to spend the rest of his life dedicated to doing just that. Before he took his first step to leave, though, a familiar soldier stepped inside the tent to speak with him.

"Heard you're leavin' this paradise today," the soldier said.

James breathed a heavy sigh. "Unfortunately, that's true."

"Well, can ya' do me a favor?"

"What's that?" James asked.

"When ya' find Lily, can ya' ask 'er if I can get a pair of front row tickets to 'er next show? I'll pay any damn price she wants! I don't wanna have to resort to whuppin' an old man's ass and stealin' his ticket just to see 'er perform … But I won't hesitate next time!"

James burst out laughing. "I think that can be arranged. Certainly don't need any old men with black eyes layin' in the streets outside of her shows."

"Much appreciated," the soldier laughed. He then stood tall and saluted his lieutenant. "Y'ur damn sure gonna be missed around here, lieutenant. Safe travels to ya'."

"Thank you," James nodded.

"Lemme help ya' with all that," he said, picking up all of James's bags for him.

"I appreciate that."

After the soldier left to load up his bags, James slowly limped out of the tent to a sight that hit him like the force of a cannonball. The instant tightness in his chest nearly constricted his ability to breathe, as he stood there frozen in awe, absorbing the patriotic sight of all the Freedom Riders in his troop. They were evenly lined up across from one another, standing at attention with their hands held in the salute position.

Harrison walked up to his best friend. "Through school, through life, through this war, I now know what's driven your honorable actions all these years ... or should I say *who*. We *all* know." Harrison suddenly stood tall and raised his hand to his head. He saluted and slowly lowered his hand down to his side. "For Lily and Rose," Harrison whispered, swallowing back his tears.

James pursed his lips tight and swallowed hard to keep himself from breaking down in front of his men. Fearing his tears would fall, he refrained from replying verbally. He nodded to Harrison instead, stoically raised his head, and began slowly making his way to his wagon through the long patriotic corridor of his men.

"For Lily," James suddenly heard from a Freedom Rider on his left as he passed him by. The soldier then saluted and lowered his arm back to his side, standing perfectly at attention. "For Rose," James then heard from the Freedom Rider on the right. The soldier saluted and stood back at attention as well. "For Lily ... for Rose." As James limped his way down the corridor of his men, his ears were graced by the beautiful sound of his wife and daughter's names, proudly uttered by every Freedom Rider as they saluted him.

As slowly as James walked, it took him nearly five minutes to get to the end of the long line of Freedom Riders, who had patriotically honored their founder. When he finally made it, General Blackshear stood proudly awaiting him. "Every man here vows to see to it that everything your wife and daughta' suffered through wasn't in vain. In honor of Lily and your little Rose, we all vow to fight with every ounce of strength in our bodies ... until the bitta' end." He shook James's hand, handed him his documents, and officially discharged Lieutenant Michael Adams from the United States Army with honor.

James saluted his General for a final time. He then turned to find Harrison there waiting to help him up onto his wagon. Both men stared at each other, neither wanting to be the first to say goodbye. Harrison refused. Instead, he embraced James in the way that a *true* brother would. He then pulled back and looked James in the eyes. "I'm proud to have you as my brotha'," he said, his emotions causing his voice to crack slightly.

"Just as I am you," James replied, miraculously holding his emotions together.

"Take care," Harrison said, patting him hard on the back.

"You too."

Harrison helped James into the wagon. After settling into the seat, James turned around to look at the hundreds of troops still standing at attention. A single tear finally drifted down his face when he realized that his wife was not there in the flesh, her beautiful music could not currently be heard, her dancing shadows could not be seen. But Lily Adams, composer of the Dream Symphony, still had the power to inspire an entire field of soldiers, simply by the *memory* of her monumental journey to Winter Garden.

Chapter Twenty-Seven

James brushed aside a pile of hay and opened the trap door on the hidden compartment in Ava's barn. Considering the condition of James's weak leg, Ava and one of her nurses pulled out his old trunk for him. Apart from being covered in dust and cobwebs, it was perfectly preserved. James did the honors of unlocking the trunk and opening the lid. He immediately pulled out Lily's wedding ring and proudly placed it on his necklace, along with his metal military identification tag. After securing the necklace clasp, he held Lily's ring up and stared at it for a moment, silently praying that he would soon be able to put it back in its rightful place.

"Told ya' everything would be just fine down there," Ava commented as she too gazed at the ring.

James nodded. "I'm certainly glad it all managed to survive the madness in this country." He then looked up at Ava. "And you too." He touched her shoulder. "I'm truly glad to see you're okay."

Ava smiled. "I owe that to the grace of God … and brave men like you."

"More God than savage men like me."

"You prefer *savage*. I prefer *brave*."

James nodded his appreciation.

"I'm sorry you've yet to find your Lily. But I feel in my heart that God's about to reward you for your courageousness."

"I certainly hope so, Ava. I really do," James replied, picking up the picture of him and Lily dancing together.

"It'd seem awfully *savage* of *Him* not to bestow you with such a blessin' afta' all your sacrifices."

"I agree. But the Lord works in mysterious ways, as they say. You neva' truly know how His plans may diffa' from yours. I've learned that the hard way."

"You and me both!" Ava smiled.

James suddenly closed his eyes and felt his body start to sway.

"You alright?" Ava asked, when she noticed he was slightly off balance.

"I'm fine," James lied, shaking his head to clear his sudden dizziness.

"I ain't tryna be disrespectful, but ya' lookin' awfully gaunt and ghostly. You're welcome to stay here in my hospital and let me nurse you and that leg back to health for a few days. Sho' looks like it needs more time to heal. And your body looks like it's cryin' for nutrition."

"I'm fine," James replied defiantly. "I just wanna collect my belongin's and visit Rose's grave. I wanna get back to searchin' for Lily as soon as I can."

"Again, I ain't tryna be disrespectful, but you'll neva' find 'er if you're dead. That leg don't look right. *You* don't look right. Your woozy body's tellin' you to rest."

"Thank you for carin', Ava. I truly appreciate your concern. But I'll be fine. I've got medical supplies with me and plenty of food."

Ava blew out an exasperated breath and shook her head. "Hmph, we doctors sho' do make the most hard-headed patients."

"You sound just like my brotha'," James laughed, thinking of Harrison.

"Well, he's a wise man!" Ava laughed. "But since you refuse to listen to wisdom, I'll help you get on your way then." She and one of her nurses loaded his trunk in his wagon, then stood behind James to be sure he climbed up in the seat safely. "Last chance to admit I'm right and stay for a while," Ava said, smiling up at James.

"I admit, *you're right* ... about the hard-headed part!"

Ava laughed and shook her head. "Well then safe travels, Dr. hard-headed Adams ... and good luck!"

"I'll be sure to bring Lily back here again when I find 'er. I have no doubt she'll wanna thank you in person. So, we'll see you again ... *soon!*"

"Soon indeed! I have faith in that! Until then," she smiled.

James tipped his hat and prompted his horses to carry him to the cemetery. His eyes instantly flooded with tears the very second he saw the grave marker bearing his daughter's name. Ignoring the pain in his leg, he slowly climbed down from his wagon and sat next to her tombstone. Through the blur of tears in his eyes, he read her favorite story aloud and then placed a fresh bouquet of roses in the stone vase. *Mama needs you,* he heard Rose saying in his mind as he stared at her resting place. Those echoing words finally gave him the willpower to pull his emotions together and leave. He struggled his way back up into the wagon and turned to look at Rose's tombstone again. "I need your mama, too. We'll *both* be back here soon to get you, my sweet girl," he whispered, finally snapping the reins to depart.

****

James stumbled as he limped along the dirt pathway to the blurry cottage in front of him. His fever-ravaged body affected his eyes' ability to function properly. The extravagantly colorful flower garden on either side of the walkway was the only thing he managed to see clearly. He used it as his guide toward the steps of the cottage porch. As weak as he was, he struggled to make it up the three rickety stairs.

Desperate for help, he pounded on the door. It cracked open the third time his fist hit it. The motion of the door carried his body weight forward. With no strength to stay upright, he immediately collapsed on the floor. Everything in James's mind then instantly went black.

Hours later, an older woman entered the cottage. She looked down at James's cane laying by the door. Her eyes then followed the drag marks through the dust on the hardwood floor, where James had slithered his way across it. The path led to the couch where she found this strange man passed out. Scattered on the floor nearby was all the medication and supplies he had used to treat his oozing, infected wound. The open opium bottle gave away the reason this strange man was likely deep asleep; so, too, did the fever he looked to be sweating out. Desperate to cool his body, he had taken his uniform off and laid it over a chair. He had nothing on but his thermal underpants and his leg brace. His bruised chest and weakened condition made her feel as though he was no threat. She sat down in a rocking chair nearby and diligently watched over him as he lay shivering, sweating, mumbling in his sleep, and screaming occasionally from his night terrors.

James woke up when a ray of morning sunlight hit him in the face … two days later.

"I don't recall placin' an ad for a new tenant," the strange older woman said to James when he finally opened his eyes.

In James's pasty eyes, she was a strange, hazy figure looming over him. In his state of delirium, he suddenly thought he was at Harrison's house with his wife. "My memory isn't that great, but I'm fairly certain you're not Lauren," he said, his voice extremely raspy.

"I'm fairly certain I'm not Lauren eitha'," the lady joked.

"Where am I?" James murmured.

"Safe."

He opened his eyes wider and let them adjust to the light. "I know you. Feels like I've seen you somewhere before," he said after finally having a good look at the woman.

"Oh, I'm certain you have." She waved her hand dismissively. "I've been hangin' around here for years. All my husband's students call me Miss Em."

"Well, hello Miss Em, I'm..."

"Lieutenant Adams," she finished.

James looked baffled.

She pointed to the uniform bearing his name that was still laying over a chair.

James managed a weak laugh. "Ah, I's convinced you were a mind reada'. Thank you, Miss Em. I can't rememba' how I got here, but I know I owe you my sincerest gratitude ... for lettin' a hard-headed idiot like me stay here and rest."

Miss Em laughed. "No problem. I'm used to it. I gave birth to two hard-headed idiot boys of my own," she joked.

"What town am I in?"

"Athens ... Ohio."

"Well, at least I'm in the right town. Don't rememba' how I made it. Just glad I did."

"May I ask why the wind done blew you this way?"

"Just passin' through on my way to look for someone."

"Anyone in particular."

"A woman."

"Got plenty of those 'round here," Miss Em laughed. "Might wanna be a little more specific."

"My wife. Motha' of my child … my best friend. Her name's Lily. Been searchin' for her for four years, ten months, and two weeks."

"She sho' must mean the world to you, if you've got the days and months locked in your head that way."

"She sure does."

"How'd you manage to lose 'er?"

James exhaled. "It's a long and sordid tale with a war in between."

"Well, if you haven't given up afta' all these years, I certainly can't say you aren't persistent!"

"Only one thing will cease my persistence. And thanks to you lettin' a hard-headed idiot like me rest … *death* hasn't got me yet."

Miss Em laughed. "If you don't learn to let your body rest more often, death gon' catch you long before it really needs to."

James laughed lightly. "You sound just like Ava."

"Don't know who she is, but she's a wise woman! Betta' take her advice more often!"

"I certainly will from now on. It took this hard lesson to get through my impenetrable noggin!"

"Afta' raisin' two boys, I know all too well about how verbal wisdom rarely penetrates a man's noggin! Seems hard lessons are the only way you stubborn men eva' learn!"

"I certainly won't botha' tryna argue against that fact anymore," James laughed as he sat up, his body now feeling reinvigorated.

"No argument back from a stubborn man?! Victory is sweet!" Miss Em joked.

"And so are you, Miss Em. I truly thank you for lettin' me stay. I think I've burdened you long enough, so I'll get dressed and let you finally have this here comfortable couch back."

"Thank heavens! Been sittin' in this hard rockin' chair prayin' for ya' for so long, I can't feel my posterior anymore!" she teased.

James laughed again. "Before I go, what can I do to thank you for your bodily sacrifices? Name it and it shall be done!"

Miss Em smiled warmly. "You can escort an old lady like me to church."

"It'd be my pleasure! That's the least I can do for literally bein' a pain in your posterior!"

"Me and my bum would certainly appreciate that!" Miss Em laughed. "I'm gonna see to it that you get lots more prayer while you're there. As big as this world is, only almighty God has the powa' to help you find your beautiful Lily. Togetha', we'll pray for Him to see 'er back into your arms."

"You certainly won't get an argument outta me about that eitha'."

"Victory two times in a row! Hallelujah! I'm on a roll!"

James laughed again as he grabbed his clothes and his satchel and hobbled into a back bedroom. He pulled out a can of chili and finally managed to eat it all without getting sick to his stomach. It gave him the strength he needed to go outside and fill a pail of water. He went back to the room and cleaned and redressed his leg wound. He then gave himself a quick sponge bath. When he was finished, he set the pail of water on a dresser nearby. He then glanced at himself in the mirror and froze. It was startling to finally take a good hard look at his own reflection and absorb what four years of war had physically done to him. He hardly recognized the thick-bearded, long-haired man gazing back at him. He wondered how Miss Em had not been scared off by the sight of him. He was astounded at the amount of dirt that seemed permanently embedded in the crevices of his skin. He figured it would take a box full of scouring pads and several more buckets of soap and water to remove it all. The baby-faced, muscular, head turning, esteemed country doctor was indeed long gone. James viewed the person in the mirror with sun-chapped skin, a malnourished frame, and a collection of battle scars as a beat down mountain man who had lived a hard life. The visual was so hard to digest, he suddenly had to turn away from the mirror. When he did, his eyes fell on his uniform laying nearby. He limped toward it. Despite the struggle it was to place his leg in his pants, he managed to dress himself without help. He then went back and glanced at himself adorned in the uniform that he had proudly worn while pursuing an honorable cause. He suddenly stood tall, now feeling as though his drastic physical transformation had been worth all the years he spent helping to transform his broken country.

Miss Em could immediately sense the pride in James's steps when he emerged from the backroom hobbling on his cane. She smiled proudly as if it was one of her own sons standing before her. "Let's get it movin' lieutenant! Got a church full of folks waitin' to pray for you and your Lily."

"Let's not keep 'em waitin' then," James smiled. He then escorted Miss Em out of the cottage to head to the church.

As the pair approached, they could easily hear the powerful sounds of the choir escaping the walls of the small rundown church. The angelic sound of their uplifting music made James ignore the pain in his leg as he cautiously climbed down from the wagon. Side by side, he and Miss Em then entered the crowded church. As packed as it was, the pair were forced to stand in the back among some other people, who were also looking for a place to sit. The praising, clapping, and energy from the choir made sitting feel impossible anyway. Even the people in the pew rows were on their feet clapping along. The clapping and singing suddenly halted, though, when the preacher announced, "those of you in need of prayer, please come forward now." With the organ playing softly and the choir humming lightly, attendees wanting prayer began making their way toward the altar, while all others sat and bowed their heads to pray silently.

With a slow gait, James made his way down the church aisle with the warm feel of Miss Em's hand on his back, helping him keep his balance along the way. The pair fell in step with dozens of other people shuffling their way to the front of the church. When James made it to the altar, he reached his left hand out to hold Miss Em's before the prayers began. He suddenly looked to his left when she failed to grab hold of it. He looked further down the line of people, thinking maybe she was standing next to someone else, but he did not see her. He looked to his right, scrutinizing every face. Again, she was not there. James then turned around and looked behind him. No Miss Em. Left and right his head quickly darted. Instant panic set in when he scanned the remaining bodies in the pews and saw no sign of Miss Em there either. There was something about her sudden absence that triggered an instant terrifying state of confusion for James. He began to sweat, and his breathing quickened, his chest visibly heaving. He felt as though he was suddenly awakening from one of his bizarre night terrors. The sound of the organ and the faces of churchgoers became distorted. He closed his eyes when he felt the room spinning. The way he began to stagger and hyperventilate finally commanded the attention of church leaders. One by one, choir members ceased humming and began to stare at James's odd, paranoid behaviors. Complete silence then fell on the entire congregation. Sensing something was off, those in the pews who had their heads bowed in prayer, suddenly ceased praying. One by one, they began to lift their heads, until every single person in the room was staring at the bearded, long-haired soldier who was leaning on his cane, looking like a lone, frightened deer in a field.

When the room stopped spinning in James's damaged mind, he began slowly scanning the sea of Negro faces staring bewilderedly at him. He nearly jumped out of his skin when the pastor placed a comforting hand on his shoulder from behind. "Are you alright, young man?" he asked.

James turned around and stared at him, unsure how to answer in his state of confusion. "Wh-where's the lady I came with?"

"What lady?" the preacher replied, now looking equally confused.

"She was right here," James said, glancing to his left at an empty space.

"Sir, you came here by yo'self."

"No! She was right here!" he said defiantly.

The pastor's reply again made James feel like he was trapped in one of his bizarre dreams, but this time unable to rouse himself. His head quickly turned to the left to look down the row of people waiting on prayer. Nothing. With his panicked state still escalating, he quickly turned around to survey the entire room. As soon as he faced the crowd, James caught sight of a woman rising slowly from her seat, in the far-right corner of the room. Her mouth was partially agape, and her eyes were trained on him. The moment James locked eyes with her, his paranoia instantly ceased. With her head bowed in prayer, the woman had not noticed him until now. But the moment she laid eyes on James, she was instantly pulled to her feet. It was clear by the look on her face that she, too, felt like she was trapped in a dream ... one she did *not* want to wake up from.

Despite being cloaked in a beard and long hair and having sun-chapped skin that was marred with scars, this woman was certain she knew the man those crystal blue eyes belonged to. She suddenly could not bear to turn away from the eyes gazing back at her. In fact, she *needed* to be closer to them. Those innocent eyes had immediately pulled her from her seat and were now tugging her toward the aisle to get a better look. She slowly sidestepped past the patrons in her row. She was far too entranced by the face she was seeing to remember to say excuse me as she passed. Still gazing at James in a hypnotic trance, she stepped out into the aisle and froze. With him directly in front of her, a mere ten yards away, she now had the perfect vantage point.

The very second she got a perfect look at those crystal blue eyes, an explosion of tears suddenly rained from hers. She now had absolutely no doubt that it was indeed those eyes that had rendered her speechless near a creek as a child while she held onto a turtle. Those eyes had given away the secrets of his love for her, long before his words ever had. Those were the same piercing eyes that had given her comfort and a sense of peace countless times throughout her life, in much the same way that they were now as they gazed upon her. If he was not an illusion, those stunningly beautiful blue eyes indeed belonged to the man that she had desperately missed for four years, ten months, and two weeks.

The blue eyes that had pulled this woman from her seat now stared at her with just as much awe as the very first day they had met as children. James stood in the middle of the aisle, his eyes wide, his mouth agape, while every patron in the church curiously watched in complete silence. James did not notice all the eyes on him anymore, though. He was far too entranced by the sight of a woman he had only been able to see in his dreams as of late. If it was not one of his realistic dreams, this woman's angelically flawless face, and entrancing spindle-colored eyes, belonged to the woman who had consumed his fantasies, dominated his thoughts, and motivated his actions for nearly his entire life. His arms had longed to wrap around her, his hands had itched to gently touch her face, and his lips had been desperate to caress hers … for four years, ten months, and two weeks.

Despite years of yearning for one another, there they both stood, unmoving, staring at each other like they were figments of their imaginations. Fear that they were in the midst of an enchanting dream kept them both frozen like statues decorating the ground. So many times over the years, this woman had fantasized about this glorious man, only to come back to the painful reality that she was in the arms of a man who owned her. She was afraid that if she made another move, this incredible man would now vanish as quickly as a realistic dream and return her to the nightmare of her reality. That fear kept her feet firmly planted. A similar fear gripped James. For years, he had screamed the name of this stunning woman in his sleep. He now silently prayed that this would not be another moment when he would awaken heartbroken over the fact that he was not able to hold her in reality, the way he could in his dreams.

Despite his fears, James finally took a step toward her. The audience did not know these two people, but they could easily sense the sentimental depth of the moment. They watched with bated breath as James began slowly limping toward the woman whose music had kept him sane in the darkest days of his life. He had marched hundreds of miles during his tenure in the war, but no journey had ever felt longer than the few feet left between him and the love of his life. When he was within arm's reach of her, though, he stopped. Suddenly, there was no pain in his leg. There was no audience ... there was just *Lily*.

James's eyes had filled to capacity with tears and his body suddenly began to tremble with uncertainty. He stood before the woman he loved, still praying silently that she was not an apparition. "A-are you r-real?" he finally found the strength to ask, his voice quivering. "P-please t-tell me you're real. I've b-been dreamin' about you f-for so long, I-I'm afraid you're not real."

Finally conquering her own fear, Lily found the strength to move too. She reached down and took hold of James's hand. Without breaking their mutual, loving gazes, she slowly raised his hand, and gently placed it on her face. James exhaled with great relief when the softness and heat of her skin sent a shockwave through his body, draining all his fears, right along with a waterfall of thankful tears. Lily's eyes fluttered closed as she melted into his palm, his warmth confirming that this glorious man was no figment of her imagination either.

Lily's mere touch seemed to heal every inch of James's body, making him completely oblivious to the weakness in his leg. He dropped his cane and had the instant strength to pick Lily up off the floor and hold her as close to him as possible without crushing her in his loving embrace. As he held her, James felt his lungs inflate to full capacity for the first time in four years. The pressure in his chest pushed another deluge of tears from his eyes. He held his woman in that strong embrace for several minutes as they both wept in a way that ignited the tears of nearly every stranger in the room.

After infecting the congregation with their emotional display of love, James reluctantly eased the strength of his embrace and placed Lily back on her feet. He held her face in his hands and rested his forehead against hers. He was dying to feel her lips against his but held off for the moment. Despite how difficult it was for him with his injured leg, he kneeled before Lily. He took off his necklace and removed her wedding ring. He took hold of Lily's hand and looked up at her through eyes that were still overflowing with tears. "Will you still have me?" he asked, holding up her ring.

Lily took a deep breath, trying to settle her emotions enough to speak. "Every day for four years, I've gotten down on my knees and begged God to bring me one thing ..." She reached down and caressed James's face. "And he just answered my prayers." Lily held her ring finger out. "I'm yours, James Adams ... until the end of eternity. That's what I vowed to you nearly five years ago. So, I'm afraid you're stuck with me," she smiled.

"I wouldn't want it any otha' way," James smiled in return, as he finally slid his mother's treasured ring back onto his wife's finger. He then struggled to his feet and gently held onto the sides of Lily's face. After nearly five years of deprivation, he satisfied his craving for the sweet taste of love. With tenderness, James slowly caressed Lily's lips with his, savoring the flavor of their tears as they cascaded from their eyes and christened their first kiss in years. As his mouth slowly made love to hers, his mind noted that he had not forgotten the taste and feel of her. The sweet taste immediately began extracting a catalogue of sentimental memories from their fantastical life journey together that had cemented his love for her. The gentle way her lips caressed his in return now quickly added yet another moment with Lily that would imprint itself in James's mind forever.

The new, unforgettable moment took great strength for James to end. But he slowly pulled back from kissing Lily and opened his eyes to appreciate the sight of her angelic face again. Still in disbelief that she was indeed real, he refused to blink. It was not until he heard sniffling from a woman in the audience that he even remembered that there was a roomful of onlookers. He and Lily both smiled sheepishly at each other when they finally realized that they were interrupting the church service.

After unwittingly testifying to the congregation about the power of prayer, James picked up his cane, took Lily by the hand, and proceeded out of the church doors to let the service proceed. They walked in between men who had placed their hats over their hearts. They appreciatively nodded their head toward James, as a show of gratitude after seeing his uniform. James nodded back, feeling proud to have served, and even prouder to be holding the hand of the woman who had inspired him to do so.

Carefully, Lily helped James descend the church steps. She then guided him toward her carriage. When the carriage door opened, Griff's eyes were torn away from the newspaper he was reading. He squinted and pretended to wipe the crust out of his eyes. When he was still not convinced of who he was seeing, he shook his head. "Little flowa', umm, do I need a set of spectacles, or is this bearded man who I think it is?"

"I'm happy to confirm that your eyes are workin' perfectly," Lily smiled.

"I'll be damned." Griff stepped down from the carriage to look James directly in his eyes. "Welcome back lieutenant," he said with sincerity, giving him a proud pat on the shoulder.

James looked at Lily. "Truly great to be back."

Griff helped James into the carriage. He then transferred his belongings from his wagon to their carriage. "I'll come back and get your horse and wagon lata'," he told James.

James nodded. "Thanks Griff."

"Not a problem," he replied, closing the carriage door.

"And thank you too, God … for finally answerin' my prayers," James whispered, gathering his arms tighter around Lily. She rested her head on his chest and melted against him. The pair seemed content not to say another word to each other for most of the ride. The closeness was all they needed for the time being. Lily only felt compelled to speak after James suddenly lifted his head off hers. She looked up at him and noticed him staring oddly out the window. He had his eyes fixated on the yard of Miss Em's tiny cottage. Her colorful flower garden in the front yard was now covered in tall weeds, and the windows were boarded up.

"What's wrong?" Lily asked after noticing the look of confusion on his face.

"The flowa' garden's gone."

Lily glanced at the rundown shack. "What garden? I've rode past here a few times ova' the last few days. That house has always been abandoned."

James looked utterly perplexed.

Lily touched his face to garner his attention. "Hey … you okay?"

James was still baffled but shifted his focus to Lily. "I'm holdin' my wife again." He let a kiss linger on her forehead. "I'm more than okay

… I'm in heaven." He raised her hand to his lips and kissed her ring bearing finger, christening it with a stray tear. "I came home prepared to spend the rest of my life searchin' for you, so I could finally put this ring back on your finga'."

Lily smiled and caressed James's face. "Well, you have William and Griff to thank for sparin' you all that trouble."

"We searched for you for years. How did they find you?"

Chapter Twenty-Eight

Two weeks earlier

Dear William,

When last we spoke, I mentioned to you the expensive artwork I was to deliver to a family in Texas. At the last minute, I was invited to their dinner affair as a thank you for my personal services. What I saw at the dinner event, or rather, who I saw, still has my mind reeling. Before reading further, I would caution you to sit down. For years, I have walked past Piers LeRoux's portrait of Musical Dreams in my art gallery. Countless times, I have recalled you sitting before that portrait, praying to God to help you find Lily. Day after day, I see the beautiful face of Lily Adams perched at that grand piano. Because of the way that portrait has etched her exquisite features into my memory with perfection, I have no doubt that it was Lily's face I saw this evening at the dinner party here in Galveston, Texas. It seems she is owned by a man named

Atticus Atkins, and she has been forced to live by the name Bella. She seemed incredibly terrified by the fact that I had accidentally revealed her true identity, almost as if her very safety depended on maintaining the secret of who she truly is. Considering her well-being, I did not want to pursue the matter further without your input. I am staying at the Astoria Hotel at 75 Main Street in Galveston, room 203. Please let me know what further action you would like me to take.

Sincerely,

Preston Mills

"My God," William whispered. He had not heeded Preston's warning to sit down and his knees nearly buckled when he read the assumed name Lily was living under. He had not forgotten that beautiful name, nor the peculiar name of Atticus Atkins. It stood out like a sore thumb on his list of politicians in Galveston. Reading the name now immediately sparked the memory of his contentious interaction with Evelyn Atkins and her vehement denial of Lily's presence on her property. It was all too clear now why she had rudely tossed Lily's picture back at him and threatened to report him to the authorities for trespassing. He and Griff had calmly walked away unaware that they would be leaving Lily behind to rot … for *four years.* Evelyn's rudeness was not very different from the way others had treated William as he and Griff searched, so he had not thought much of it at the time. But now, unbearable guilt leveled William like an unexpected blow to his stomach. The force stole his breath and caused tears to gush from his eyes. They careened in streams down his cheeks and blurred the ink on the letter that he held in his shaking hand.

William did not bother replying to Preston with a letter. He used that time to take a series of nonstop trains to Texas. Within forty-eight hours, he was banging on the luxury double doors of an extremely crooked politician. With Preston, Austin, Griff, and his sons by his side, William stood on the porch staring down Galveston's most infamous socialite.

Evelyn's hospitality was just as "warm" as the last time. "I thought I told you and your oddball friend not to trespass on my property! Now leave immediately before I summon the authorities!" she spouted.

"Well, I'm afraid you'll have to do just that, because I'm not leaving here unless you forcibly remove me," William boldly replied.

"What the hell do you want that could possibly be that important?!"

"The same thing I wanted the last time I came here! You have a woman living here by the name of Bella. I need to speak to her urgently! I'm certain that she knows the whereabouts of the woman I came here looking for four years ago," William said, handing Evelyn the picture of Lily again.

Evelyn tossed the picture back at William. "Like I told you last time, I don't know who this woman is!"

"Maybe you don't, but I'm *positive* that Bella does!"

"Bella no longer resides here! Now get off my property!" Evelyn tried to slam the door, but Griff stopped it.

"He said we ain't leavin' here 'til we speak to Bella," Griff snarled, his eyelids lowered as he glared coldly at Evelyn.

Petrified by Griff's dark presence, Evelyn suddenly screamed for her husband.

"Is there a problem here gentlemen?" Atticus asked when he arrived at the door.

"There will be if you don't get Bella to this door in the next two minutes," Griff barked.

"Who the hell're you?" Atticus demanded.

"We're looking for this woman," William explained, handing him the photo of Lily.

Evelyn's husband snatched it and tossed it back at William. "I've neva' seen this woman before!"

Preston Mills suddenly stepped into view. "Still care to make that claim, Mr. Atkins?" he challenged, glaring coldly at Atticus.

Furious, Atticus glared back at Preston, his face beet red. His lips were pursed so tight that another lie would not have been able to escape his lips if he tried.

"Now it is *I* who will be reporting *you* to the authorities, about the illegal purchase of this so-called Bella, if you don't let me retrieve her at once," William threatened. "In the midst of their investigation, I'm quite certain they'll uncover just how many other illegally purchased slaves a prominent member of their community has residing here." William slightly tilted his head. "Should do wonders for your future political aspirations, don't you think?" he asked sarcastically.

"You're not going to threaten me!" Atticus fired back.

"I just did."

Atticus put his finger in William's face. "You're not takin' Bella any-"

Griff smacked Atticus's hand out of William's face. "Her name is *Lily!* And we ain't leavin' without 'er!" he barked.

"How dare you lay your hands on me!" Atticus bit back.

"Shut up and let 'em in!" Evelyn intervened, her public image now at the forefront of her mind.

Atticus whipped his head around and looked at his wife in disbelief. "What?!"

"I said, let them in!" Evelyn squinted her eyes at her husband, quickly glanced down at his crotch, and then met his eyes again. "Let ... them ... in," she reiterated through tightly pursed lips.

With great reluctance, Atticus stepped aside to allow them in. He then looked at his wife with disgust and angrily stormed off.

Evelyn stood there quietly as everyone walked into the foyer. William glanced up to find Ryla and two other slaves standing at the top of the dual staircase. They had stopped cleaning to come and see what the ruckus was all about.

"Ryla!" Evelyn said. "Show these ..." She looked Griff up and down with disgust in her eyes, *"gentlemen* ... to the library."

"Yessum," Ryla replied, descending the stairs.

Evelyn then trained her devilish eyes back on William. "Retrieve your property and get outta my house! And don't you dare set foot on this estate eva' again!"

William paid her no mind. He knew that Evelyn just needed to feel some sense of power before ultimately letting him have his way. He simply turned his attention to Ryla after Evelyn sauntered away.

"Right this way, gentlemen," Ryla said as she began guiding them through the corridors of the massive mansion.

With every step, William's heart picked up speed. It was racing at a gallop pace by the time they reached the double doors of the library. After arriving, Ryla stepped aside, knowing full well that it was unnecessary to point out who they were looking for. The woman William had traveled over sixteen-hundred miles to see was standing in the far corner of the library with her back to everyone, dusting a grand piano of all things. With his entourage standing behind him, William stepped just inside the library and froze, now mere yards away from her. When he glanced across the room, he pushed his spectacles up higher to be sure his old eyes were not deceiving him. After his eyes focused, he just gazed at the lovely young lady before him, as if she was a magnificent sunset. "I'd much prefer to hear you play that piano … not watch you dust it," he finally said, after absorbing the stunning view.

That familiar British accent caused every muscle in Lily's body to immediately cease functioning. With the feather duster still in her hand, she stood there as stiff as ice, unable to turn around. The only active part of her body seemed to be her tear ducts; they suddenly began flooding her eyes with moisture.

After summoning the strength to wrangle his emotions, William walked toward the woman who had tears stirring in his eyes as well. "Lily," he said softly when he was just feet away from her.

Still, she could not bring herself to turn around.

"Lily," William said softly again.

Now certain that she was not hearing delusional voices, she began trembling uncontrollably. Still, though, she could not manage to turn around.

With his own hand now trembling, William gently took hold of her shoulder and turned her toward him. The sight of her beautiful face immediately confirmed the words in the astounding letter that he had received. "My dear, Lily, it is you," he whispered, as tears suddenly spilled from his eyes.

Lily dropped her feather duster, lowered her face into her hands, and wept with body-shaking intensity as William gently embraced her.

"It's okay, Lily. It'll be alright," William comforted, holding her tightly.

"I don't know who Lily is anymore. I don't know, I don't know, I don't know," she sobbed, unleashing years of pent-up mental anguish. "I d-don't know who she is. I-I can't f-find her ... I can't f-find h-her."

"We'll find her," William assured her. "*Together* ... I promise, we'll find her again," he whispered, as she continued weeping in his embrace.

It seemed to take an eternity for Lily to gather the strength to raise her head from William's shoulder. When she looked up and saw Griff, the twins, and her dear friend Austin, her tears ignited again.

All the other female slaves in the house began entering the library, passing by Atticus, who stood just outside the door with a scowl on his fire-red face. Their intrigue left all the ladies oblivious to the anger in his body language as they filed in and stood next to Ryla. They watched with curious eyes as everyone took a turn hugging Lily, each man on the verge of tears as they embraced her. Their raw emotion made it very clear how precious Lily was to them. Even as hardened as she was to life, Ryla found a hint of raw emotion stirring in her as well. She struggled hardest to hold back her tears seeing how reluctant Austin was to let go of Lily with the one good arm he had left.

Lily, too, was reluctant to pull back from Austin's embrace. When she finally did, she cautiously looked around for the one man who had kept the ember of hope burning inside of her while she was imprisoned there. She felt her heart plummet when she did not see him. "James?" she whispered, fear preventing her from even forming a complete question. She lowered her head and braced her heart for an answer.

"Look at me, Lily." Austin gently raised her head when she seemed unable. "I have *Lieutenant* James Adams to thank for why I only lost an arm ... and not my life. On the train ride home, I'm gonna flood your ears with all our epic tales." Austin gently caressed Lily's face. "It'll leave you with no doubt that your husband *still* loves and misses you more than anything in this entire world."

Lily erupted in tears again and fell back into Austin's embrace.

When Lily finally got her grateful tears to subside, she stepped over to Preston. "I know I h-have you to thank f-for this, Mr. Mills," she sniffled. "You h-have my s-sincerest gratitude."

"No thanks necessary. I truly feel honored to help reunite you with your family and friends. Trust me when I tell you, they've missed you an awful lot," Preston sincerely replied. "In fact, I think William may have had me murdered if I had left this town without you," he joked.

"Certainly right about that," William replied sarcastically.

"And he wouldn't've had to pay me a penny to do the *goddamn* murderin'!" Griff added, not so sarcastically.

Everyone erupted in much needed laughter.

After Lily's laughter subsided, Ryla suddenly caught her attention. She had never once seen a twinge of sadness in Ryla's face until now. After so many years, Lily was overjoyed to finally see all the men in her life, who were like her family. But she suddenly felt the same bittersweet sadness that she could sense Ryla was feeling. Wanting to comfort her friend, Lily wandered over to her.

"So, it really is Lily, huh?" Ryla said, still trying to be her usual hard self.

Lily nodded sheepishly.

"I knew you had a story to tell. By what I've seen here today, it must truly be epic."

"And you've added to my story, Ryla ... in the *greatest* of ways."

Ryla nodded in appreciation. "Just as you have mine." She suddenly felt something foreign rolling down her cheek. "Tears are for weak bitches," she murmured as she quickly wiped away the escaping tear.

"Or for those who're gonna miss their cherished friends," Lily replied, wiping away fresh tears of her own.

Ryla nodded. "I'm damn sho' gonna miss you. But you go shine bright again, ya' hear?" She turned to look at William. "Somethin' tells me this man here will stop at nothin' to be sure you're twinklin' like a star."

"You truly read people well," Lily said, smiling at William. She then turned back to Ryla. "I'll be back for you soon." She turned to look at all the girls. "For *all* of you."

"No, you won't," William interjected.

Ryla and Lily both looked at him confused.

"Because you're all welcome to come now, if you'd like," William explained. "I don't want to *force* any of you to do something you don't want to do." He turned and sneered at Atticus. "Seems your *captor* has spent far too many years doing that already!" He turned back to all the ladies. "So, you're all free to decide if you'd like to join us and leave today."

Furious, Atticus finally stepped inside the library. "You will not be…"

"Oh, shut up, you blathering old fool!" William interrupted. "Don't bother objecting, unless you look forward to answering lots of questions in court as to the acquisition of your slaves! Questions that I'm certain a politician like yourself wouldn't want to be public knowledge!"

To further encourage Atticus to keep his mouth shut, Griff walked over and just stared at him without saying a word. Atticus nervously swallowed, suddenly ingesting every word he was about to spew.

As Atticus silently accepted his fate, the ladies were excitedly chatting amongst each other to determine theirs. Everyone quickly decided to depart along with Lily ... except for Lola. She stood in a corner alone, a look of shame dragging down her facial features. Lily walked over to her. "You don't have to stay, Lola."

"Don't much think I deserve to go."

"Yes, you do. Everyone makes mistakes ... and I forgive you for yours."

Lola looked at Lily with tears in her eyes. "Thank you," she replied sincerely.

Lily nodded. "You're more than welcome to come."

Lola swallowed hard and glanced at Atticus. "I-I still think I'll stay," she said, her pride preventing her from any other decision.

Lily nodded and left her alone to live with her decision ... and with Atticus.

Lily wandered over to the other ladies, who were now cheerfully congregating in the hallway. With all the men trailing behind them, they then headed for the front door. One by one, they all filed out of the Atkins estate, breezing past Atticus and Evelyn, who stood there silently emitting their vexation over the entire matter. Lily was the last of the ladies to step outside. When she did, she closed her eyes, and tilted her head back in the sun. To her, the rays of sunlight felt far more glorious on her face when she was free.

When Lily opened her eyes, she smiled at the awestruck look on Griff's face while he gazed at Ryla. Ryla saw his expression too and could not help but entice him further. "How you doin', cowboy?" she asked as she sashayed by him with a sweep of her bedroom eyes.

Lily never thought Griff, the consummate storyteller, could ever be rendered speechless, but Ryla quickly proved her wrong. Griff could not get his mouth to form words to reply to her, but his delighted, wide eyes and giddy grin spoke volumes.

Lily wandered up to her favorite security bandit and put her arm around him. "Sorry to be the bearer of bad news, Griff. But I doubt you have the strength or the stamina to tame all that," she whispered in his ear.

Griff put his arm around Lily in return. "That may be true, little flowa' … but that damn sure ain't gonna stop me from tryin'," he whispered back, without ever taking his eyes off Ryla.

Lily let out a laugh. "Well, much luck to ya'!"

"Thanks. I'm gonna need it … and *coffee!* Lots and lots of coffee!"

The way Griff had Lily laughing, made her feel like she was already home.

Chapter Twenty-Nine

Sunday
February 26, 1865

The man whose humor had made Lily feel at home was now truly guiding her there. Griff sat proudly at the top of Lily's carriage after church, guiding her and James through the steel gates embossed with the famous Werthington name. Today, her ride with James was far different from the first time they had entered Werthington Estate together back in 1859. This time, Lily was not riddled with the fear of being turned into a breeding animal. William was no longer an unknown man for whom she harbored a premature hatred. James was no longer an enigma. It was not a strange unfamiliar place that evoked terror for Lily; it was a warm inviting place that had changed her life forever.

In stark contrast to their initial journey to Werthington Estate, there was now no coldness or question about James and Lily's feelings for one another. This time, their silence was intentional. For now, they did not want to question any more of the whens, whys, and hows of their long separation. They now knew instinctively to just absorb each other's healing energy. They wanted to feed off the love they emitted in order to, once again, become an unbreakable, united front. They knew they would need that level of strength, if ever they were going to tackle the trauma they had each endured during their years apart. For that reason, James had Lily gathered in his arms with his head

542

resting on top of hers, not saying a word as he gently caressed her back. His eyes were closed, but his tears still managed to escape and soak Lily's hair. He was completely lost in the essence of her, her scent arousing every memory of the times he had held her this close. Lily had melted into James's chest, laying there in absolute silence as well. She did nothing but weep and appreciate his warmth. Her continuous flow of joyous tears had now soaked his well-decorated military jacket. There was simply not an inch of measurable space between the couple as they entered the place where their love for one another was reignited, a place they both considered *home*.

William had been under the weather for the last several days and was not up to going to church with Lily. Isabel had stayed behind to take care of him, Emerson, and Wilson. After receiving a certified letter about her brother's death, she had no desire to leave the house anyway. Wanting some fresh air, Isabel had helped William make his way onto the porch. Ryla, Emerson, and Wilson had joined them as well. They all sat chatting and drinking lemonade as Griff guided the carriage toward them. He halted the horses just in front of William's porch and climbed down to open the door. Lily reluctantly pulled herself away from her husband's embrace, took Griff by the hand, and allowed him to help her down.

When William saw how swollen and red Lily's tear-filled eyes were, he abruptly ceased his conversation with Isabel. "What's wrong m'lady?" he asked her.

Lily was still far too overcome with emotion to speak. She simply looked toward the carriage.

Despite how weak he had been feeling over the last few days, William suddenly rose from his seat with ease. Isabel followed suit. Two normally chatty individuals stood there utterly speechless when they saw the reason Lily was so overcome with emotion. William pushed his spectacles up higher on his face, just to be sure his illness was not causing him to hallucinate.

After being helped down from the carriage by Griff, James steadied himself on his cane, took hold of Lily's hand, and made his way toward the porch. Griff walked up beside James, patted him gently on the back, then looked up at William. "Picked up this scraggly drifter on the way back home. Figured you wouldn't mind lettin' 'em stay a while," he joked.

James gazed up at the two people standing there staring back at him awestruck. "William ... Isabel," he said, turning to greet each of them.

Finally convinced that he was not hallucinating, William blinked and tears cascaded down his wrinkled cheeks. Isabel put her hand over her mouth and began crying too.

James slowly limped his way up the porch steps, approached William, and extended his hand for him to shake. William bypassed his hand and embraced him like a father would his son. "Welcome home, my boy." He pulled back, held both of James's shoulders and just gazed at him in disbelief. "If this is a dream, I pray I do not wake up."

"You and me both," James replied.

Over William's shoulder, James glanced at Isabel. By the way she was standing quietly off to the side alone, he was certain that her deceased brother was weighing heavily on her heart. By now, he assumed that Elijah's remains were buried near his parents at the family plot there on Werthington Estate. His assumptions were accurate. Isabel's posture, tears, and facial expressions easily gave away how her emotions were swinging back and forth between gratefulness and devastation. She was subtly glancing at everyone on that porch, only to be met with the reality that her mother and father were not there as they should have been ... and now neither was her brother. Despite his mistakes, Elijah was all she had left. Everyone else's sons and brothers had made it back from a horrific war, but she had no brother to hug, nor a mother or father to comfort her over that fact. She was now fighting to express gratefulness for everyone else's happiness, but James could easily see that devastation over her losses was currently winning her emotional battle.

James limped over to Isabel, looked her in the eyes, and gently placed his hand on her face. The warmth of his empathetic touch caused her to immediately break down into heavy sobs. James laid his cane down and hugged her for the longest time. "I'm so sorry about your brotha', Isabel ... so incredibly sorry," he reiterated, feeling genuinely saddened by the fact that she had not a single member of her family left. James pulled back to look at her. "With the last few breaths he could muster, your brotha' laid in my arms and told me to tell you that he loved you."

Isabel lowered her head when another rush of tears surged from her eyes.

"He also asked me to take care of you," James continued. "I wouldn't be standin' here conveyin' that message to you if it wasn't for him. He died protectin' me, Isabel. I owe my very life to your brotha's sacrifice. He's a hero in my eyes." James gently touched her face again. "So, I vow to you, I'll spend the rest of my life honorin' his wishes."

Isabel's sobs erupted again.

"I know I'll neva' replace Elijah ... and I'm not nearly as handsome," he joked, managing to pull a hint of laughter through Isabel's sobs. "But from now until the end of my days, I'll be as much of a big brotha' to you as humanly possible."

Feeling as though a thank you would never suffice, Isabel threw her arms around James and hugged him as tightly as she could, her tears soaking his shoulder as she wept. Emerson approached Isabel and handed her his handkerchief. After patting her eyes with it, she took hold of James and Emerson's hands and then looked over at

Wilson. "I guess now I have three pesky brotha's again," she said, managing to let a hint of humor shine through her pain. Her adoptive brothers all smiled in return.

William took a quiet moment to let his eyes linger on everyone standing there on the porch. His chest suddenly swelled with pride. "Every one of you has made every second of my life worth living. Whenever God sees fit to bring me home, I want all of you to know that I'll be ascending into the heavens with a heart that stopped beating completely at peace."

"None of that death talk, father," Wilson replied, waving his hand dismissively. "You'll get past whatever's ailing you soon, and live to be a stubborn, ornery old centenarian!"

Everyone chuckled lightly.

"Well, even as a stubborn centenarian, I'm sure this day will still be filed away in my ornery old mind as one of the grandest days of my life."

"I think that goes for all of us," Isabel replied. "Which is why I think a *grand* dinna' affair is certainly in orda' to honor that fact. As an official way to welcome home my three brotha's, I wanna cook a special meal for all of you tonight. Dinna' will be served promptly at six!"

"Well, seein' as how Lily's probably gonna be, uh ... *preoccupied*," Griff said sarcastically, looking over at her and James. "I'll give ya' a hand in the kitchen."

"You just wanna impress Ryla!" Isabel teased.

Griff winked at Ryla. "Damn right I do."

"Well, I'll take the help any way I can get it," Isabel replied.

"Okay, I'll warn ya', though. I don't know a thang about cookin'! But I've certainly mastered the art of doin' whateva' the hell a woman tells me to do … my three daughta's damn sho' made sure of that!" Griff said, igniting much-needed laughter as always.

"*Whateva*' a woman wants?" Ryla looked Griff up and down. "That's *definitely* my kind of man!" she said, further prompting the laughter as everyone headed into the house.

Isabel turned to William. "You want help gettin' back to bed?" she asked.

William shook his head. "I definitely need to rest up to have the strength for your impromptu grand dinner affair this evening. But you go on and start on your masterpiece. I'll get myself back to bed just fine."

"You sure?"

"I'm sure." He turned to look at James. "I suddenly feel much stronger."

"Alright then," Isabel smiled.

"Rest well, William," James said.

"I certainly will now." He touched James on the shoulder and smiled. "I'm so happy to have you back safe, Lieutenant Adams."

"Thank you, William. I'm happy to be back."

"I know you two have lots of catching up to do, so I'll leave you to it."

"Call on me if you need me," Isabel replied, kissing William on the cheek.

"Will do, sweetheart."

Lily kissed William on the cheek as well before he slowly departed back to his room with Wilson and Emerson by his side.

As William walked away, James caught sight of Griff holding Ryla's hand as they headed to the kitchen. "Very unique couple," James commented.

"That's puttin' it mildly," Lily smiled. "But once you get to know Ryla, you'll realize they're a match made in heaven."

James shrugged. "They say there's somebody for everybody. Guess they certainly prove that's true."

"Boy, do they!"

James peered inside the double doors and could not help but notice how slowly William was walking. "Is William okay?"

"He will be. I refuse to believe otha'wise."

Before entering the house, James exhaled, took Lily by the hand, and steadied himself on his cane. Hand in hand, they then stepped inside the double doors to a home that was once like their own private paradise. They had entered William's home feeling a great deal of apprehension back in 1859, both for very different reasons. This time, however, the reason for their trepidation was mutual. James suddenly paused in the foyer and looked around the massive mansion. It had been rebuilt relatively the same, yet he felt it was so different.

"You okay?" Lily asked him.

"I guess I'm just surprised that William finally found the strength to come back here. It's hard for me to walk in these doors without it triggerin' horrendous memories. I can't imagine how he must've felt."

"We've only been here a little ova' a week. Afta' the Ghost Rida's caused such tremendous loss here, he did admit that it was excruciatingly painful to set foot back in this place. But he suddenly couldn't stand for them to have that sort of victory ova' him. He said they may have burned all his treasures … but not all the wonderful memories in his mind that made this place home. He thinks our heavenly family will be lookin' down on us with great pride, watchin' us prove that the darkness of trauma from the past does not have to keep us from shinin' now and in the future. So, he said he now refuses to let all the ugliness from the past trump all the wonderful things that have occurred here. He wants us to go about addin' to the amazin' memories our family left imprinted on our minds. He feels it's the best way to prevail ova' the cowardly demons that were hell-bent on destroyin' our spirits."

"William and his damn wise words. Always givin' the sort of wisdom worth livin' by. That man neva' ceases to stop inspirin' me." James turned and placed his hand on Lily's face. "And neitha' do you," he whispered as he gazed lovingly at her.

Lily closed her eyes and melted into his touch. "What do you say we follow William's wise advice and go start fillin' this house with more beautiful memories," she said in a sensual tone that James had desperately missed.

"My God, I would love that," he breathlessly replied, a certain part of him instantly reacting with extreme excitement.

"So would I," Lily whispered, tenderly kissing him on the lips. "Will it be easier for you to stay in a room on this floor?" she asked, considering his injured leg.

"Maybe, but I much prefer makin' memories with you in our old room."

"Okay," Lily smiled, sliding her hand into his.

Hand in hand, James and Lily made their way upstairs. Every step was grueling for James. He needed a moment to let the pain in his leg subside halfway up. Lily waited patiently by his side, while encouraging him to push further. It seemed a metaphor for the uphill battle they had both prepared themselves to fight as they rode quietly in the carriage together. The pain of the ascent made James's limp more pronounced after he reached the top. Lily put her arm around his waist to help him to the bed. He collapsed onto the mattress, breathing hard and sweating. The look of excruciating pain on his face instantly made Lily's eyes well with tears. "I'll get you some medicine and run you a bath with Epsom salt. It'll help with the pain."

"Thank you," James replied, while trying to catch his breath.

Lily returned quickly with the medication and a glass of water and gave it to James. She sat on the edge of the bed and placed his empty cup on the nightstand after he swallowed the pills. She then turned and gazed at her man. "Relax for now," she smiled, playing with a tendril of his long hair. "I'll go fix your bath." She kissed him softly on the lips before getting up to do so.

When Lily was finished fixing the soothing bubble bath, she sat back down on the bed again. She quietly gazed at James as she ran her hands through his hair and beard.

"This face of mine's been itchin' to escape this bushy thing for years … literally," he joked, scratching his jaw.

Lily laughed lightly. "I'll shave it for you, if you want." She played with a tendril of his locks again. "But the long hair stays."

"You like it?"

"I love it," she smiled. "Just as much as the man unda'neath."

James closed his eyes and kissed her hand.

"I sorta missed you all these years, ya' know," Lily said, gazing lovingly at him.

"Did you now?" James smiled, reciprocating the loving gaze.

"Just a little," she teased.

"What did you miss?"

"The way you always ran your hands through these locks when you were worried," she said, stroking his hair. "The way you always slid your hands into your pockets when you were nervous. The fact that you always seemed to know when I's in dire need of a hug. The way you used to gaze at me in a crowded room, remindin' me with your eyes how much you loved me. I missed your strong arms wrapped around me, keepin' me warm at night." She interlocked their fingers. "I missed the way these strong hands managed to caress my skin so tenderly. I missed the feelin' of your lips against mine, and the passionate way you always kissed me." Her eyes briefly fluttered closed. "And Lord knows, I *desperately* missed the feelin' of you inside of me," she said as a tear slid down her cheek. "I missed absolutely and utterly *everything* about you, Lieutenant Adams," she whispered, touching the name stitched on his coat.

One of James's strong hands reached out and caressed Lily's cheek. The feeling of his soft touch was indeed just as tender as she remembered; the sensation ignited more of her tears. James gently wiped them away as he pulled her in close to press his lips against hers, the way that he had missed too. After their lips parted, Lily began unbuttoning James's uniform. Her tears then began christening his skin, as she unveiled a torso scattered with old wounds. Trying not to inflict any pain, she carefully removed his shirt, while gently kissing his chest and abdomen. Pain, however, was not remotely an issue. The warm feeling of Lily's soft lips had already anesthetized his skin. An unexpected rush of intense pleasure then suddenly shot with force to every corner of James's body, causing Lily's name to roar through his vocal cords. As Lily was working to remove his pants, she had simultaneously wrapped her lips around his hardened flesh to distract him from any pain. Feeling the heat and moisture from her mouth after so many years nearly caused him to instantly succumb to the glorious sensations. When he was on the cusp of explosion, Lily slowly slid her lips off. She gently kissed the tip and then kissed her way down his inner thighs as she slid his pants all the way off. She then sat beside James on the bed and gently stroked his erection. "I'll give you more of that lata'," she whispered lustfully. James savagely grunted, his overly aroused mind unable to respond in any other way. Lily smiled seductively, her body igniting with warmth after seeing the sudden, intense want in his eyes and hearing his breaths become more jagged.

Lily then helped James out of bed and moistened his lips with a passionate kiss. When she managed to pull her lips away, she helped him into a robe and handed him his cane. Hand in hand, they walked to the new bathroom that had been added to her room during the rebuild. She closed the door and turned around to look at the strapping man sitting before her. She walked over and touched his beard. The ruggedness of his looks actually turned her on even more. She almost hated to see the beard go. But at James's request, she shaved him clean and trimmed just the dead ends of his long tresses. Ten years seem to fall from his age along with the hair on the floor. After soothing his face with aftershave, Lily stepped back and looked at James. A sensual moan escaped her when she touched his now smooth skin. The moisture suddenly pooling between her thighs proved she did not regret his decision to unveil the strikingly handsome face that had been hidden behind his beard.

The beautiful sight of James suddenly ignited Lily's desire to slowly remove her clothing, like that of a showgirl. Watching him watch her, she began unbuttoning her dress. James's heart and breathing quickened in anticipation of seeing the only woman whose nude body was perfectly etched in his memory. He refused to blink, and his chest began to swell with emotion as Lily slowly unveiled every inch of her body. Like a blueprint in his mind, James remembered precisely where her neckline began to curve into her shoulder, and just how much her collarbone protruded. His mental map still knew the exact plumpness of her breasts, the nickel-sized, dark color of her nipples, and the four abdominal muscles that slightly protruded underneath the firm skin of her belly. He knew the exact depth of her navel, the small birthmark on the left side of her hourglass hips, and the precise length of her long, toned legs. Every inch of Lily was etched in James's mind as if he had been the sculptor who had created such a masterpiece. It was for that reason that his chest had begun to swell with emotion. The faded gash above Lily's right eyebrow, the cut mark that curved along the upper ridge of her lip, the circular scar just beneath her breast, the two light brown stripes across the right side of her torso, the two barely visible stretch marks on her lower abdomen, and the slight discoloration that looked like permanent bracelets around her wrists were all very subtle, faded, and old. However, to a man who had the map of Lily's body photographed in his mind, her scars were huge ... but only in the metaphorical sense. Those scars and stretch marks were permanent reminders of a day that James felt he had astronomically failed as a husband and father. But, more importantly, they were now visual reminders of how fortunate James was that the woman he loved had survived his father's barbarism. James mentally photographed each and every one of Lily's new scars and quickly stored the new blueprint in the treasure vault of his mind. The fact that Lily stood before him now completely nude, scars and all, still willing to share her body with him, was proof of her unconditional love and her ability to forgive him. Those scars, therefore, enhanced the beauty of the masterpiece in James's sights in a major way, and further justified the reason his heart set his beloved wife's value at *priceless*.

James traced his finger along one of Lily's subtle scars, then wrapped his arms around her waist and gently rested his head against her belly. His tears began moistening her skin when the cause of her scars began flashing in his mind.

"It's okay," Lily whispered, sensing what had stirred his tears. She lifted his head toward her. "It's okay. It's not your fault," she reassured him again, looking him in the eyes as she caressed his face.

James subtly nodded in response, shaking the tears further down his cheeks.

Wanting to return his mind to the present, Lily removed the bobby pin from her hair and let her tresses fall to her shoulders. James's mind indeed quickly refocused on what stood before him. With her body silently calling him, he easily rose to his feet without his cane. He stepped forward, ran his fingers through her soft hair, and rested his forehead against hers. Lily then untied his robe and slid it down his body.

"God, I missed the feelin' of your skin against mine," James whispered, slowly sliding his hands around Lily's waist. He gently pulled her in and pressed her body flush against his. The rush of warmth made him feel as though his bruises had instantly healed. "I's afraid I'd neva' hold you like this again," he confessed, tightening his embrace.

"So was I," Lily whispered back, laying her head on his shoulder.

The transfer of heat to one another's skin had them mutually melting. The tender caress of James's powerful hands sent an explosion of butterflies rippling through Lily's stomach. Her warmth and softness naturally ignited a need for more erogenous stimulation in James. He descended on her lips, tenderly sucking them into his mouth one at a time, slowly savoring the flavor of each. He pulled back and glided his tongue along the curve of her upper lip before devouring them both again. The fiery way their mouths then began making love set their bodies ablaze.

With the heat in James's body quickly rising to boiling levels, he had to force himself to pull back from kissing Lily. Panting heavily, he gazed at her, feeling disbelief that he had yet to wake up from what felt like a dream. The way Lily reciprocated his gaze proved that her mind was in sync with his. Overjoyed that he was no illusion, she sensually smiled as she ran her finger across his swollen, red lips. James kissed her hand, then took hold of it and guided her toward the massive garden tub to help simmer their flaming bodies.

Normally, when they bathed together, it was James who held Lily in his arms, washing and caressing her like she was his queen. But just as James was about to step inside the tub, Lily stopped him. "Me first." She touched his face. "I wanna take care of my soldier this time."

James smiled back at her and nodded as he helped her into the tub first. Lily then returned the favor. She held his arm to help him stay balanced as he carefully stepped inside. Lily immersed her body in the warm, bubble-filled water and waited for James to join her. He slowly settled in between her legs, resting his back against her chest, careful to keep his wound above the water. He moaned lightly when Lily wrapped her arms around him and kissed the side of his neck.

As they relaxed in the soothing suds this time, Lily began washing James's hair, just as he used to do for her. When she was finished, she slowly ran a sponge up and down his sunbaked skin, kissing his neck and shoulders all the while. She gently cleaned his leg wound, then let him lay back and relax against her again. She suddenly let the sponge float away, slid her hands down James's chest, to his stomach, then in between his thighs. James's breathing quickened when Lily began gently suckling his neck while stroking his erection. She intentionally took her time, wanting to ensure his pleasure overrode his pain. The way his head fell back onto her shoulders, his mouth agape and his eyes closed, seemed proof that there was not an ounce of pain riddling his body. The sound of his manly groans so close to Lily's ear, easily coaxed her inner lioness to come out and play. Her soft suckling immediately turned into playful bites and nips, as her stroking hand picked up pace. The deepening sound of James's moans signaled to Lily that he was nearing eruption. With his earlobe clenched in her teeth, she quickly ceased all stroking and let her man's body calm from a rolling boil back into a simmer. "Can't wait to feel this inside of me," she whispered seductively, finally letting go of his erection.

Another guttural grunt escaped James as his rock-hard appendage suddenly protruded from the water, proving he could not wait either.

Lily devilishly smiled at the pulsating toy that awaited her. She kissed James's neck, then slid out from behind him and exited the tub.

James stayed put for the moment and watched her with his mouth agape. His eyes remained pasted on her as she provocatively dried herself. She then intentionally turned around and slowly leaned down to dry her legs, placing the most treasured part of her body directly in James's line of view. After so many torturous years without her, James literally began to drool over the glorious sight. "My God," he moaned, momentarily frozen in wide-eyed wonderment.

Desperate to reunite with his beloved woman, James's hardened flesh began mercilessly throbbing. The overpowering need to bury himself between her thighs caused him to effortlessly rise and step out of the bathtub, like he had two perfectly good legs. His hands were quickly drawn to Lily's posterior cheeks, like metal to powerful magnets. He slid them from her buttocks, up her back, and onto her shoulders. At that moment, it was all James could do to refrain from slamming himself inside of Lily and unleashing his seed in a single stroke. With the ounce of willpower he had left, he quickly turned her around and devoured her lips, kissing her like his hunger for her would never be satiated. The fervor of his prolonged kiss left Lily's insides pulsating just as mercilessly as the brick hard erection pressed against her pelvis.

"Did you miss makin' love to me?" Lily breathlessly moaned, after breaking the intense meeting of their lips.

James pulled back and gazed at her, his eyes suddenly brimming with tears. "I missed *everything* about you too, Lily ... absolutely *everything*," he whispered, caressing her face.

Not expecting such a reply, Lily's eyes instantly misted with tears as well. She took James by the hand and guided him back into the bedroom. His limp seemed far less noticeable with his woman by his side, leading them back to the first place they had ever made love. Hand in hand, they made their way up the two steps of the stage-like platform where the king-size bed sat. Considering his condition, Lily let James lie back on the bed first. He laid there gazing up at Lily's nude body through a set of mesmerized eyes while gently caressing her buttocks. The awestruck look on his face was equivalent to a man witnessing an angel materializing before his eyes. "Forgive me for starin'," he said. "I'm afraid to blink. I keep thinkin' I'm gonna wake up from the most glorious dream of my life."

"It is a dream … one that's finally come true." Lily leaned down and gently kissed his lips. "And my body has the most *glorious* way to prove it," she whispered, her lips grazing his.

Her words alone had James's stones nearly threatening to erupt. "Prove it then," he moaned.

Lily smiled seductively, sat down on the bed, and gently ran her hands down James's abdomen. Her eyes trailed down his body, gazing in disbelief that her man was close enough for her to touch in such a way. It was a simple act that she had prayed to do for years. Knowing his body as well as she did, she easily noticed the amount of muscle and weight that was now gone from James's frame. The way his rib bones were now visible under his skin made it clear that he had willfully endured years of malnourishment. Fresh tears began to sting her eyes as she surveyed the minefield of bug bites, fading bruises, and scars in various stages of healing. When she glanced down at the catastrophic damage on his leg, her tears surged forward, gushing like a broken dam. In Lily's estimation, his battered, marred body served as permanent evidence of what James was willing to go through in her honor. It further strengthened her resolve to do whatever was needed to take the utmost care of him during his time of need, and for the rest of his life for that matter. From home cooked meals prepared with love to restore his vitality, to offering the love of her body to restore his virility, Lily was ready to give James *anything* he needed. With all that Ryla had taught her, she knew that the euphoric pleasures of her body would *by far* be the most important for a man who needed healing, and the reassurance of his woman's love.

With that in mind, Lily climbed in bed and hovered above James. One soft kiss at a time, she then began her quest of expressing her eternal love and gratitude for all that James had sacrificed on her behalf. Her tears began christening his skin as she gently pressed her lips to his wounds, praying that something so simple could help heal them. Whether her intimate affections had that sort of power or not remained a question. But the love James felt every time her lips touched his body was undeniable. As Lily's lips roamed his body, the delicate sensations began to stir his emotions again. Rather quickly, the pillow beneath him found itself saturated in the moisture of his tears, his entire body equally saturated with the overwhelming feeling of being immensely loved by his woman. For nearly five years, James had feared that the chemistry, friendship, and bond that he had with Lily may have been destroyed by their time apart. But one tender kiss at a time, his insecurities began to fade away. His fears melted away altogether when Lily kissed her way up his body and her lips finally met his. The soft, slow way her mouth passionately caressed his left no doubt that her love had not faded; it had intensified.

Just as the intimate meeting of their lips came to an end, Lily carefully lowered her pelvis toward James's waist. She was gentle with her movements, fearing she might inflict more pain on his healing body. But her fears were unwarranted. James was completely oblivious to the aching in his leg while gazing up at the stunning goddess atop him, about to sit gracefully on her throne. She gazed at him in return, now suddenly feeling as though she, too, was experiencing a glorious dream. She now felt the need to convince *herself* that the dream of being reunited with the love of her life had indeed come true.

"I'll be gentle ... I promise," she whispered.

James smiled at the memory of saying that to her while she lay in that very spot before they made love for the first time, when potential pain was at the top of her mind. "I trust you," he replied, reciting her same response from all those years ago.

"If you need me to stop, I will," she smiled, restating yet another promise James had made to her that night.

With his throbbing rock-hard flesh now just a hair's breadth away from her heavenly kingdom, James looked Lily in her eyes and softly wiped her tears away. "There's *no way in hell* I'd want you to stop," he stated with emphasis, his burning want for her causing him to modify her original reply.

Lily smiled at his response. "I didn't think so," she seductively replied, leaning down to gently kiss his lips again, her heavenly entrance now grazing the tip of his aching erection.

After so many years of dreaming, fantasizing, wishing, and begging God to be with his beloved wife again, here she was now slowly sliding him inside of her. As James's erection began to part Lily's velvety folds, her breath suddenly caught. She broke their kiss and let out a raspy moan when the feeling of his rigid flesh instantaneously set her insides ablaze. The pleasure jolted her body to sit straight up, driving her pelvis down with force, instantly burying James inside of her. The sudden intense sensation caused an explosion of pleasure to tear through James's entire body. After years of extreme intimate deprivation, he had absolutely no strength to hold back. The very second his body was reunited with his beloved woman, he erupted inside of her. The glorious sound of him singing Lily's name caused her core to immediately begin a succession of powerful spasms. The pleasure ricocheting in every corner of their bodies, composed a perfectly harmonized duet of moans. After the heightened pleasure receded, Lily collapsed down onto James, and their moans quickly transitioned into a sentimental duet of weeping. James wrapped his arms tightly around Lily and let her body melt against his skin as they wept. For minutes, they stayed locked in that loving embrace, both sobbing tears of euphoria over a surreal moment that proved, in the most *magnificent* way, that a four-year long dream had indeed come true.

When Lily's tears finally ceased, she sat up and gazed down at the man she was overjoyed to be reunited with again. "Let me know when you're ready for more," she said, playing with a tendril of his hair.

"Then you may as well not even botha' gettin' up," James replied, caressing her cheek.

When Lily felt his body suddenly answer the reason for his statement, she seductively smiled and passionately kissed him, eager to send him soaring back to the pinnacle of ecstasy.

 Chapter Thirty

With his eyes frozen open, Harrison's decapitated head came to a halt near James's foot. James had run in a full-on sprint to defend his friend from being slain from behind with an axe, but his attempt was futile. He dropped to his knees and let out a blood curdling scream as he looked into the lifeless eyes of his best friend. James then suddenly heard his name being called repeatedly, but the sound transmitted through his ears as if he was hearing it underwater. He looked in the direction of the distorted sound to find Lily quivering on her knees, a blood-covered sheet wrapped around her body, tears coursing through the mud on her face. James looked down at Harrison's head again, then jumped when he heard the sound of a cannon. He plugged his ears, looked to the left again, and saw Lily still mouthing his name. James screamed her name in return and suddenly tackled her before the confederate soldier behind her could sever her head with his axe as well.

"James! Please stop! You're hurtin' me! Please!" Lily screamed.

But James remained on top of her, valiantly trying to protect her from death. He looked over his shoulder to be sure the soldier was no longer a threat, but the fireplace was the only thing in his sights. He then quickly turned toward Harrison's head again and saw nothing but a pillow.

"J-James, it's j-just a dr-dream … pl-please, you're h-hurtin' me," Lily whispered, tears now running in streams down into her ears. She had been jolted awake by the deafening sound of James screaming at the top of his lungs. She had scurried to the far end of the bed, her heart pumping a mile a minute. Confused by the sight of James acting out a nightmare, she had called his name repeatedly to calm him down, only to be tackled by him seconds later. She now lay there trapped under him, being held so tightly that she felt as if her bones were about to snap.

Breathing hard, James continued to frantically look around, trying desperately to differentiate between a hellish nightmare and reality. Once the confusion cleared, he looked down at Lily again. Tears began to well in his eyes when he realized that the only reality was that he had unintentionally hurt her. Smothered by guilt and embarrassment, James quickly got off her, sat on the edge of the bed, and dropped his face into his hands.

For the previous three days, there was not a single soul in William's house who had any desire to deal with the weight of the past four years. There were no talks of war, loss, separation, or tragedy. Everyone had distracted their minds with food, wine, and spirits, to celebrate the joys of being reunited as a family again. But this current issue was now too much for James to ignore. The daytime hours were like heaven, but the nights were beginning to turn into hell for him. Every night, gruesome dreams of war had him thrashing and screaming in his sleep. Lily had woken him up and soothed him on every occasion. But this was the first time he had physically attacked her. James was now extremely disturbed by his own bizarre behavior. After attacking Lily, his uncontrollable night terrors now felt just as debilitating as his leg wound. The emotional impact was clear to see by the way he sat slouched in humiliation on the edge of the bed, unable to even look at Lily.

Lily quickly scooted up behind him for comfort. She softly ran her hands down his shoulders, wrapped her arms around his waist, and laid her head on his back. "I'm here. It's okay," she whispered.

The very second Lily's soft hands caressed his body, James felt his misery start to melt away. "I'm sorry. I didn't mean to hurt you," he whispered.

"I know. It's okay," she reassured him, as she continued to caress his skin.

James grabbed hold of Lily's arms and pulled them tighter around him. "You got me through every dark moment of my life ova' the last four years, Lily. In times that I didn't think I could carry on anymore, I'd hear your music in my head. I'd see your face. I'd even dream about you when I needed you the most. Without even bein' there in the flesh, you kept me sane ... you kept me alive. Thoughts of you kept me believin' that we'd see our way back togetha'. And now, feelin' your touch like this again..." He kissed her hand. "Makes me feel like I can conquer anything. Just like always, you make me wanna be the best man I can be for you. But..." He let go of Lily's hand and lowered his head again.

"But what? Talk to me," Lily prompted.

"I'm startin' to question if that's possible anymore. It feels like somethin's terribly wrong with me. It's like my mind is broken, Lily. At any given moment some days, it's like I suddenly can't tell what's real and what's not. I can't control it. Sights, sounds, dreams, anything can trigger it. And I'm petrified to let you keep seein' this side of me. I'm afraid it's gonna scare you off." He swallowed hard to get the lump out of his throat. "And I'd be devastated if I lose you ova' this. I honestly think I'll give up and die if I have to spend anotha' minute of my life without you again. But I'm scared my mind is too damaged to eva' be the sort of man you deserve ... one you can be proud of."

Lily got off the bed and dropped down to her knees in front of James, so he did not have to hold his head up to look at her. She held both of his hands as she gazed up at him with tears in her eyes. "I know we have a long, tumultuous road to navigate to conquer nearly five years of healin'. Both of us are foreva' changed in some ways. But one thing that hasn't changed an ounce is how much my love for you continues to grow. So, at this very moment, right here, right now, as you are…" She touched James's face. "I am and always will be proud of you as a man, as my best friend, and as my husband. Afta' what you just did for me for the last four years, I would neva' *eva'* have the audacity to walk away from you. I'll do whateva' I have to to help you ova'come that fear and reassure you that I'll always be here for you. So, me leavin' you is a fear you can let go of right here and right now, okay?"

James nodded.

"I know how hard it might be to let go of your fears and strange, sorrow-driven beliefs. Your mind will use every dark trick durin' your most vulnerable moments to convince you that your fears and beliefs are warranted. I'll neva' forget how my vulnerable mind convinced me that you had abandoned me as a punishment for losin' our baby…"

James quickly locked eyes with her. "Lily, I would neva'…"

"I know betta' now," she interrupted, gently touching his face. "I know you would neva' do such a thing for somethin' that was beyond my control."

"*Neva',*" James emphasized, a tear rolling down his cheek as he touched her face in return.

"I know." Lily's eyes closed as the warmth of his touch penetrated her. "It's just that I's feelin the way you may be feelin' right now. My mind was broken afta' losin' you and Rose … not to mention all the things I's forced to deal with afta'wards. But when I…"

"Things? Wh-what things?" James asked hesitantly, preparing himself for the worst.

Fresh tears began to well in Lily's eyes. She looked down and exhaled.

"No secrets, Lily. Tell me ... please."

"This may be hard to hear ... and even harda' for me to say, but…" Lily exhaled again. "Ryla and the otha' ladies you met, we were personal slaves for a rich politician. We were handpicked by him to…" She momentarily lowered her head in embarrassment.

"To what?"

"To ... to *submit* to him in whateva' way he wanted," she said, thinking of the least graphic way to explain.

James lowered his head as anger swelled his chest and pushed tears from his eyes. "I tried so hard to find you before anything like that could happen to you ... I swear I did!"

"I know. I believe you," Lily replied, caressing his leg to calm him.

James angrily wiped the tears from his eyes. "Did he hurt you?! I swear to God, I'll kill 'em!" he said, his sudden rage seeping into his tone.

Lily shook her head. "He ain't worth killin', James," she said, touching his face to help his anger subside. "You and I have dealt with the sort of demons worthy of sendin' to hell before their time. But I can promise ya', Atticus Atkins doesn't remotely compare. Don't get me wrong, he was a disgustin' pig, and a disgrace to the institution of marriage ... and to *mankind* for that matta'. He was extraordinarily peculiar with bizarre fetishes. But, ironically, it was those very same peculiarities that I have to thank for the reason I'm still breathin'."

"What do you mean?"

"Before Atticus bought me, I don't think I had much life left in me. Doubt I would've made it anotha' few days. In fact, a few of the stolen slave women with me didn't make it. And I'm certain I wasn't far behind 'em. Couldn't remema' the last time those backwoods slave trada's bothered to feed us or give us anything to drink. The world was fadin' away from me so fast. I doubt I'd've had the strength to chew even if they had. I's in just that bad of shape. The fact that Atticus bought me when he did actually saved my life. I truly believe that. He was the first person to give me any food or wata' in days. He then took me to doctors and nurses, who put weight on me and mended my wounds. I know his motives were selfishly driven by his peculiar ways, but I's definitely gettin' the kinda care that my body desperately needed.

"I know for a fact my fate could've been far worse. Those slave trada's could've easily sold me off to live in squalor, to a place where I's treated like an animal, while bein' used and abused as a grand bonus. But Atticus actually took care of all us slaves like we were his collection of expensive porcelain dolls, dressin' us and primpin' us no different. It was the most bizarre thing I've eva' witnessed. His twisted mind is one I'll neva' unda'stand. I don't care to try eitha'. I'm absolutely and utterly disgusted by the fact that he used us women like his toys. But I can't deny that his twisted ways kept me alive. So as much as I loathe 'em for the evil acts he committed, I think we should let God ... or the *devil*, determine his fate. All I wanna focus on is the fact that I'm still here to look my husband in the eyes," she whispered, gently touching James's face again. "And I hope that's all you'll focus on too."

James nodded and his tears rolled onto Lily's hand. Her strength was like an instant anesthetic for his rage. He kissed the inside of her hand and then held it close to his heart. "Did you have any children?" he asked, gently caressing her face. "If you did, in my heart and my soul, they're mine. I'll find 'em, and love 'em and raise 'em like they're my own flesh and blood."

Lily suddenly froze and looked at James with the same awe as when he had confessed to praying for her to see her mother again when they were children. "Just when I thought there was no otha' magnificently selfless way for you to prove how unconditionally you love me."

"Your children are a part of you, so I couldn't help but love 'em like we created 'em togetha'."

Lily got up, sat next to James on the bed, and kissed his hand in return. "It's so comfortin' to know that. But fortunately, I didn't have any of his children. He was careful as far as that was concerned."

James nodded. "You're sure he didn't hurt you?"

"Physically, no. Emotionally, though, I think it's impossible not to be affected in some ways. But in those unwanted moments, I'd drift away in my mind to all my memories of you. It was like I stepped outside my body and into the warmth of your lovin' arms. I'd stay wrapped up there 'til it was ova' with." She squeezed James's hand. "I's willin' to suffa' a hundred years of abuse if it meant bein' here with you for just anotha' minute."

James raised her hand to his lips and let a kiss linger there, moistening her skin with his tears again.

"Until then, I's doin' all I could to maintain my sanity. I put a wall up in my mind to hold it all togetha'. It wasn't until William walked in and embraced me that I felt safe enough to let my protective wall crumble. Once he wrapped his arms around me, I felt all the pent-up emotional pain rush in and crush me all at once. He finally freed me from playin' a role. But I'd played that role so long, I felt like I didn't know who I truly was anymore. I wondered if it was eva' possible to be *Lily* again. The bond I had with music. The bond I had with you. All the things that made me who I was. I questioned whetha' or not it was all gone. I think I's afraid to return to bein' Lily, and finally have those questions answered. I began to doubt whetha' I could have music in my life again ... but mostly *you*. Did I deserve to have you afta' all the things I's forced to do, afta' losin' our baby, afta' so much time had passed ... would you even want me any more?"

James touched Lily's face and gently turned her toward him. "There was neva' one second, in all these years, that I stopped wantin' to be with you again," he assured her as he wiped away her tears. "Not one."

"The answer to that seems so clear now. But I had allowed the sorrow demons to whispa' the worst things in my ears again. Their horrible loopin' words started to ravage my mind. I allowed it to break me inside. Not in the awful ways that war could break a man, of course. But I's certainly broken in my own way. But when we got here Austin, Emerson, and Wilson began tellin' me one heroic tale afta' the otha' about their lieutenant," Lily expressed, tearing up over the memories. "I's inconsolable through every story, knowin' you were out there literally puttin' your life on the line for me, James Adams ... just like you always have. I ain't neva' been so scared for you in all my life. I cried and prayed, damn near every minute of every day, that you'd make it through alive and come back home safe. With all the incredible tales they shared with me, my mind began to fight back against all the demons that were whisperin' doubt in my ears about you and me. I finally gained the strength to slay every last one of those damn monsta's, the day William walked in here with a box full of letta's from one Lieutenant Michael Adams," Lily said, breaking down into tears just as she had that day. "Like clockwork, William said he'd find your letta's for me in the mail on the first Monday of every month," Lily smiled. "Despite not knowin' where, when, or even if you'd eva' find me, he said you neva' missed a beat writin' to me.

"For days, I sat here cryin', smilin', and laughin' while readin' years of letta's from you. There's not a single piece of paper that ain't been stained with my tears, be it tears of laughta', or tears full of the love your words filled me with. Those letta's reminded me that the man who wrote 'em is kind, compassionate, understandin', and forgivin' ... and pretty damn funny!" she smiled.

James laughed lightly.

Lily looked James in the eyes. "Every sentimental word in those letta's was visual proof that my husband would *neva'* give up on me … and especially not on *us.*"

"*Neva',*" James whispered, bringing Lily's hand to his lips again.

"Your letta's instantly mended everything that was broken inside of me." Lily got up and walked over to the nightstand, retrieved an envelope out of the drawer, and sat down next to James again. "When I finally finished readin' all your letta's, I started writin' replies. There's still so many for me to respond to, but this is my reply to the very first one you eva' sent me," she explained, handing the envelope to James. "I had planned on mailin' it to you the day afta' we happened to meet again in church." She touched his face. "There's obviously no need for that now."

Eager to read her letter, James quickly tore open the envelope.

Dear my beloved Lieutenant Adams,

Well, now that I know where you've been all these years, I guess I can't yell at you the way I wanted to…

James read that first line and it immediately made him laugh. As he read through the rest of it, his reaction bounced back and forth between laughter and tears, just the way Lily's had while reading his letters.

… You have my love for a lifetime and beyond.

Praying for your safe return,

Your loving Wife,
Lily Adams

When James finished reading, his finger slowly coasted down the page, like he was touching the most precious artifact he had ever seen. "Every mail call, I's prayin', by some miracle, that I'd receive a letta' from you one day. I can't even put into words what it would've meant for me to receive this on the battlefield," James stated, his voice quivering as tears trickled from his eyes.

"And I'm hopin' that my letta's will still mean just as much to you now. I know the sorrow demons are whisperin' doubt into your mind about whetha' or not I'll stand steadfast by your side in your time of need. Your letta's helped destroy the demons of doubt in my mind … and now I'm hopin' my letta's will help destroy yours. So, I'm gonna write a reply to each and every one of your letta's, and put 'em right here in this drawer, envelope and all, until it's spillin' ova' with paper. So wheneva' your broken mind is torturin' you, or makin' you fear that you're gonna lose me, I hope you'll open this drawer, pull out one of my letta's, read through it, and let it remind you of how desperately I love you. One letta' at a time, let it heal you from the inside out, the way your letta's did for me. Let my words slay your inner demons and remind you that I ain't *neva'* givin' up on you, James Adams … not *eva'!*"

James nodded, trying desperately to swallow back the raging emotions that were on the verge of breaking through the dam in his chest.

Lily then got down on her knees in front of him again and held both of his hands. "Since I's a little girl, you've been fightin' for me, James. Fightin' for me to get ova' losin' my motha', fightin' to let me live out my musical dreams, fightin' to rebuild our friendship … fightin' to prove how much you love me. And now, ova' the last few years, you were willin' to lose your life, and fight to give me my freedom. You've been my soldier nearly my whole life." She gently touched his face and made him look her in the eyes. "Now let me be yours. Now it's *my* turn to fight for *you*. No matta' what mistakes you feel you've made, no matta' how broken and battered you may feel, no matta' how long it takes, or how gruelin' things may be, I'll always be your soldier, fightin' to help you feel whole again … mentally *and* physically," she said, softly touching his temple and his damaged leg. "I'll fight for you with all my might … until the bitta' end."

Her words instantly obliterated the dam in James's chest. Tears that he had held back, the day his troops made the same vow, now came surging forward like a tsunami. His tears came in tidal waves, soaking the first of Lily's reassuring love letters. Lily slid her arms around James's waist and quietly held him as he wept with body-shuddering force. After his tears washed away his fear of abandonment, James lifted his head and gazed at the strong woman before him with an immense amount of love emanating from his tear-filled eyes. "Thank you," he whispered, now feeling rock-solid confidence that she would always be by his side.

Lily nodded, tears coursing down her cheeks as well. "I'm happy to do whateva' it takes to heal you. I'll comfort you in every possible way a man needs comfortin' from his woman," she said, lightly kissing his lips. "Wheneva', whereva', and howeva' you need it," she whispered, her lips grazing his.

James gently held the sides of Lily's face and just gazed at her for a moment, the loving look in his eyes having intensified tenfold. He pulled her lips to his and tenderly made love to her mouth. The same pressure he had felt in his lungs earlier had now traveled to an organ further south; it, too, was ready to rupture and cleanse him, in a much more pleasurable way. Lily ran her hand slowly up his thigh, slid it into his pajama pants, and let it come to rest on the hardened flesh hidden beneath. The stimulation of her slow strokes sent a rush of heat through James's body that emanated to his lips and ignited a more fiery passion in the way he moved his mouth. He pulled Lily closer and moaned as he deepened their kiss. The juices Lily began pumping from his pulsating organ seeped onto her hand, making her eager to taste. She suddenly tore her mouth from his and gently pushed him down onto the bed. Hungrily, she began kissing her way southward. Her lips moistened the side of his neck. She grazed her teeth along his skin as she moved her mouth from place to place. She snaked her tongue into his ear and bit his lobe, drawing another growl from James. His beastly noises further turned on Lily's animalistic nature. She bit and kissed her way down to his nipple and forcefully sucked it into her mouth, her teeth clamping down until she heard James roar with delight again. She released him quickly after the sound made her even more eager to reach her hardened destination.

Lily's lips carried on southward. The exquisite taste of James's skin had her mouth watering and refusing to let too much time lapse between every kiss. The specific scent of his pheromones reawakened every intimate moment of their past. As the memories of their pleasurable rendezvouses flooded Lily's mind, her heart rate increased and rapidly flooded every tissue in her body with blood. It caused her senses to become extremely hypersensitive. James's natural musk was now an even more glorious scent as it breezed through her nasal passages. Her tongue was now easily able to savor his manly flavor. The sound of his moaning was massaging her ears like a sensual melody. Lily's overloaded senses then began driving the intense way she sought to physically express her love for her man. Ravenously, she sucked, kissed, and licked his body, desperate to hear and taste *all* of him.

James could indeed feel the warmth of Lily's love in the way she fervently perused his skin, feasting like she could not get enough of him. Her expression of love emanated through his body, increased his heartbeat, and quickly pumped blood to his core. It had his erection rock solid before Lily's lips were anywhere near it. His manhood was far too impatient to wait for her to unleash it. It had escaped and rose out of the hole in his pajama pants on its own, eagerly anticipating the warmth of her soft tongue. The quickness with which Lily slid her lips around it proved she was just as eager to taste. The heat of explosive pleasure shot straight through James's vocal cords. The manly roar instinctively caused Lily to reciprocate the moan and increase the power of her suction. Had she not immediately gained control of herself and eased the tension, James would have quickly erupted in her mouth.

Knowing that years of trauma had ravaged James's mind and body made Lily suddenly want to take her time. She wanted to meticulously massage away the pent-up torment that resided within him. Therefore, the gentle movement of her lips, up and down his shaft, was not only to caress his flesh but to ease the agony of his invisible war wounds as well. The slow pace of her motions was to ensure that pleasure had more time to permanently disable his mind's access to horrific memories and apprehension. With the soft glide of her tongue, she was attempting to tickle every nerve in his body and to flood them with the sort of euphoric sensations that had the power to completely anesthetize his anguish. The drawn-out, sensual moans escaping James proved that pleasure was certainly dominating every facet of his being. Agony was quickly being purged through the tears flooding his eyes, as he gently thrust his hips toward the blissful sensations. Lily's loving massage was indeed healing James's fractured mind and body in a way that music and medicine combined could not possibly rival.

After her long, exotic mouth massage, Lily slowly slid her lips to the tip of James's shaft. Seeing how blue it now was, easily proved how immensely he had enjoyed it. The erotic sight caused Lily's heavenly abyss to begin pulsating with a need to be filled with the rock-solid appendage in her view. While hungrily kissing the interior of James's thighs, she slid his pajama pants all the way off. She then stood up at the end of the bed, gazed down at the ruggedly handsome man before her, and locked eyes with him. While intently watching him, she then slithered her lingerie over her head and slowly slid her panties off in a sensual manner. James's refusal to blink as he watched her seductive show caused wetness to begin dripping down Lily's inner thighs. She, too, refused to blink as she gazed at her man while climbing back into bed. The closer she got the more jagged James's breaths became. As she mounted him, more tears began to sparkle in his eyes. Emotional tears were present in Lily's eyes as well when she took hold of her man's hands. "Touch me," she whispered sensually, guiding his hands onto her buttocks. The strength with which he gripped her cheeks caused her core to pulsate with want again. It pumped wetness from her insides, the heat of her juices running down onto James's erection, as it waited for entry into the warmth of her kingdom. Pleasurable heat then began creeping through his body, just as slowly as the way Lily lowered herself onto his rock-hard flesh. A drawn-out deep moan erotically rumbled through James's vocal cords during her entire slow descent. Once buried completely inside her, his tears overflowed down the sides of his face.

With tears now on her own cheeks, Lily descended on James's parted lips. She passionately kissed him, sat up, and then began rocking her hips to the rhythm of his moans. As beautiful as the sight was, James no longer had the strength to keep his eyelids open; intense pleasure had snapped them closed. Lily would not have known, though, her body had caused her eyelids to do the same. Pleasure had even weakened the muscles of her neck. Her head fell backward, and her mouth fell open. All the strength in her body had transferred to her hips as she slowly rode James, guiding his mind and body back to sanity. Her thrusts were long and deep. She buried him for prolonged moments, grinding gently and intentionally slow, letting him dangle near the pinnacle of satisfaction. She kept his damaged mind lingering in the realm of bliss, while letting the pleasure of her body slowly obliterate the pain in his.

After minutes of slowly trotting him toward the clouds, Lily raised up on her knees and began forcefully burying James's erection into her pleasure passageway. The erotic sound of skin clapping rose louder as she began riding him hard and fast into the climactic heavens. The drawn-out way that James suddenly called out for God signaled that Lily had just galloped him to the finish line of their heavenly destination. An explosion of his seed set fire to her insides, causing her to reciprocate with a rain shower of hot, orgasmic juices that heated the skin of his stomach, as she called out the name of the stallion beneath her.

Completely depleted of strength, Lily immediately collapsed onto her man's chest. It heaved just as hard as hers as they both fought to catch their breaths. "My god," James said, breathlessly. "Do I get that kinda lovin' afta' every letta' I read?" he panted.

"If that's what my man needs, then that's what my man shall have…" Lily kissed his neck. "Wheneva', whereva', and howeva' he wants it," she seductively reminded him as she nibbled lightly on his ear.

A low rumbling moan escaped James as he smoothed his hands down the sides of her body. "You'll have my mind right in no time, Miss Lily."

"That's certainly the ultimate goal," she smiled.

Lily then carefully dismounted him, laid down, and got comfortable on his chest. She lay there quietly for a moment, listening to the beautiful melody of his heartbeat as he caressed her soft skin. She suddenly sensed a shift in his demeanor when his fingertips grazed one of the faded lines of her whip striations. "Stop dwellin' on it," she suddenly said.

"On what?"

"On all the things you could've done differently to prevent those scars, and to prevent us from bein' separated the day I got 'em."

"Damn." James kissed her forehead. "Scary how well you read me."

"Your heart beats differently when somethin's weighin' heavily on you."

"I won't lie. It's gonna be hard not to dwell on it sometimes. Especially when I think about how many years I've missed moments like this with you." He paused, his mind momentarily drifting away. "And moments with our little Rose," he whispered.

"I can't believe you were right."

"About what?"

"Rose … we had us a little girl afta' all. You won," Lily smiled.

"Say that one more time. A little louda' this time, though. I couldn't quite hear you," James joked, putting his hand up and cupping his ear.

Lily laughed and playfully hit him with a pillow.

"No fair hittin' cripples," James laughed.

Lily settled onto his chest again and went quiet. James was now the one sensing a shift in her demeanor. "What's suddenly weighin' on this beautiful mind?" he asked, softly kissing her temple.

"W-were you there when Rose was born?"

"Yes. I was there to catch 'er."

Lily tried to swallow a sudden lump in her throat. "W-was she stillborn?"

James paused for a moment while he recalled the short time he had spent with his first born. "No," he replied, swallowing back the swell of emotions the memory had conjured up. "She spent her whole life in my arms."

"That's the only thing I've been wantin' to know about that day. I just wanted to be sure she was in the lovin' arms of her daddy when God took 'er soul home," she said as her tears spilled onto the very chest that Rose had lain next to.

"She was. I held 'er as close as my arms would let me. It was the most cherished thirty-six minutes of my life."

The tears that Lily suddenly felt roll onto her skin, proved how sincere James's words were. "I's so eager to see the look of pure joy on your face the day our baby came into the world. Seems impossible that I have absolutely no recollection of even givin' birth at all. I genuinely don't recall a single thing. Kissin' you goodbye on the porch, and you tellin' me that you loved me is the last clear memory I have of that day. My mind usually retains everything so vividly, but I'm glad everything else from that day was wiped clean outta my brain. I don't even wanna know any otha' details. My scars and losin' our baby are enough to make me realize that I should be grateful to have no recollection of what was clearly the worst day of my life."

Thank God, James thought to himself. He kissed Lily's forehead, relieved that she had no recollection of what his father and brother had done to her. He planned to gladly take those horrors to his grave.

"The only otha' thing I wish I knew was where Rose's body is now. I wish we could give 'er a propa' burial."

"I know *exactly* where she is."

Lily quickly looked up at James. "You do?" she asked, sounding stunned.

"Ava, the good doctor in the little Negro hospital you were in, was kind enough to bury her for us. She even made 'er a custom tombstone with a rose on it."

"You were there?!" Lily exclaimed, surprise still evident in her tone.

James nodded. "It's a long story that I'll fill you in on lata'. But I followed the few clues and tips I had about the unda'ground railroad. I also recalled that Gideon used to share supplies with a few Negro doctors in Ohio. It all led me to Ava's little hospital, but you were long gone by then. Ava told me about the Ghost Rida's raidin' that place months before. She said you were one of the ones they stole. Every lead I followed from there was a dead end."

"I'm surprised anybody from the unda'ground railroad would trust you enough to tell you anything."

"They didn't at first. It was my name and my description of you that convinced Ava I was an ally and not an enemy."

"Why your name?"

"Ava told me that you asked to see Rose's body. She said afta'wards, you kept repeatin' that *James* would neva' forgive you for losin' 'er."

Sickened by the memory of her own words, Lily felt her stomach turn. "I-I didn't mean it. I just wasn't in my right mind."

"I know, that's what Ava figured too. But I wanna say this to you loud and clear, right here and right now." He gently put his hand under Lily's chin and made her look at him. "I neva' eva' thought to blame you for Rose's death. Nor is that somethin' I'd eva' expect you to ask forgiveness for ... not *eva'*, okay?"

Lily's eyes fluttered closed when the kiss he let linger on her forehead sent warmth through her entire body. "Thank you for sayin' that," she sniffled. "I know betta' now. Like I said, I just wasn't in my right mind back then."

"I don't think any of us were then. I'm glad Ava realized that too."

"My memories of bein' in that hospital with Ava are spotty at best. But I'll neva' forget Rose's tiny face," Lily smiled. "We sho' did make us a beautiful baby, didn't we?"

"Far and away the most perfect one I've eva' laid eyes on. I eventually wanna bring our beautiful baby home and bury 'er here where she belongs."

"Me too. And I'd certainly wanna thank Ava personally."

"I told 'er you probably would."

"That's certainly the least we owe her for givin' our daughta' a propa' restin' place. Far too many folks aren't even given that."

"That's very true. That's why I'm eternally grateful for her kindness. Which reminds me. Ava was kind enough to keep somethin' else buried for us all these years." James slowly got out of bed and limped over to his trunk full of sentimental treasures. He retrieved a satchel and sat back down on the bed with it. "I have a message to give you."

"A message?"

James nodded. "A very important one."

"From whom?"

"Well, I'd ratha' not tell you just yet. Because before you can truly unda'stand the magnitude of the message, I think you need to read these first ... every word," he said, reaching into the satchel and handing Lily the first of her father's journals.

"What is this?"

"Believe it or not, this is one of your fatha's journals."

Lily quickly handed it back like a snake had just bitten her. "Why in the world would I wanna read that?!" she snapped. "Where did you even get that?" she asked, looking at it with disgust.

"Your brotha', believe it or not."

"*Wyatt?*"

James nodded. "Him and Colt. And they broke me outta prison just to do it."

Lily looked completely dumbfounded. "What? Why? Austin told me you went to prison, but he neva' said how you got out."

"I neva' told Austin. Only Harrison knows. I needed to protect Wyatt and Colt for makin' such a sacrifice. It's a long and sordid tale, one I promise to tell you every detail of. But they broke me out for one reason and one reason only … to expend every breath in my body to find you and give you the message in a letta' they wrote. But if you read your fatha's journals first, I think you'll have so much more clarity about your brothas' motives, and all the otha' gifts in this trunk that they made me promise to pass along to you."

"Certainly speaks volumes about how important this must be to 'em."

"Trust me, it is. I know all this sounds insane, but afta' you read these, I'm *certain* you'll unda'stand why it's so important to 'em."

Lily still just stared at the journal in James's hand, with a look on her face as if she feared the book would open the portal to hell.

"Lily, I don't mean to upset you with any of this. That's the last thing I'd eva' want." James lowered his head, stared at the journal in his hand, and exhaled. "This world seems so ova'crowded with cruel people. I suppose that's why it's been so rare that a person eva' inspires me. My motha', William … and *you*," he said caressing Lily's cheek. "Outta the hundreds of people I've known, you're the only three who have truly inspired me in my life. But now, afta' readin' these journals … I have to add your fatha' to the list."

Lily's eyes shot up to James's face. She was stunned to find sincerity in his facial expression. The thought that her father had the ability to inspire any human seemed an impossibility in her reeling mind.

"I know that sounds preposterous. But you trust me, don't you?" James asked.

His words brought Lily's spinning mind to a halt. "Of course. But you want me to trust that the man who sold me away from my motha' is worth readin' about?"

"I know. So let me make it clear that I still don't condone what he did, nor do I mean to disrespect you with any of this. But please trust that I'd neva' give these journals to you if I felt they'd hurt you in some way. I give these to you because I don't think you truly knew your fatha', Lily." James looked her in the eyes. "Because you were neva' *allowed* to meet 'em. In fact, I don't think *anybody* knew the real Levi Collins at all. He seems to have only revealed his true self to the pages of these journals ... and to your motha'."

"*My motha'?*"

James nodded.

Lily's wall immediately came crashing down. "Well, afta' that intriguin' statement, I certainly can't resist givin' it a chance."

"That's all I ask. Some of this may not be easy to read, but I get this unrelentin' feelin' that it'll help a small bit of you to heal, maybe even bring you some inner peace. At the very least, you deserve closure ... and to get to know who your fatha' really was."

Lily stared at the first journal, feeling just as hesitant to touch it as she would a rabid dog. But she blew out a breath and slowly took it from James. When she finally garnered the courage to open to the first page, James suddenly stopped her. "Hold on," he said, "How about you read these out at your favorite spot on William's lake? I wanna hold you in my arms and listen to you read, just the way we used to."

Lily's face illuminated with a smile. "It's a date!"

"See you there," James smiled in return. He gently kissed her on the lips, then hobbled off to clean up and get ready in another room.

While Lily dolled herself up for their date, James had slowly made his way out to her favorite lakeside oak tree, where he had taught her to read. He laid out a blanket, wine, and food beneath the shade. When James stepped back and glanced at the scene, fond memories of him and Lily laughing, and making love there, began to flash in his mind. He was warmed by the memories of moments that had helped reignite the smoldering embers of their love and turned it into a breathtaking wildfire. For all those beautiful reasons, this little shady slice of paradise now held just as much sentimental value to James as their childhood playground.

James snapped out of his trance when he caught sight of movement in his peripheral vision. He turned to find Lily walking toward him in a white, flowing summer dress. The color contrasted perfectly against her honey brown skin. Her hair was blowing beautifully in the light wind, looking just as elegant as her dress. James refused to blink as he gazed at her. In his eyes, she was equivalent to an ethereal angel floating from the heavens to bless him with her presence.

The smile that illuminated on Lily's face proved she was equally delighted by the sight of her man. She was proud to see that just a few days of intimate sponge baths, home cooked meals, and the pleasures of her body, were already undoing four years of war damage. Hair that was once matted down with oil was now featherlike locks that flowed easily in the wind, under James's hat. His new black trousers were now nicely filled out, and so, too, was the white, long-sleeved shirt beneath his black suspenders. Lotions and oils that Lily thoroughly enjoyed massaging into his body, had already helped to shed dead, sunburnt skin to unveil the youthful skin beneath. Lily's smile broadened to see that even his limp was far less pronounced, as the incredibly strapping man in her sights began to hobble toward her on his cane.

"Excuse me, beautiful lady," James said, smiling as her sweet scent graced his nose.

"Yes, may I help you, sa'," Lily replied, playing along.

"I was wonderin' if an extraordinarily stunnin' woman, such as yourself, would take pity on a broken man, and have lunch with me?"

"Hmm." Lily took a moment to think as she looked around their shaded slice of paradise, trying to decide what she wanted her next sentimental memory there with James to be. "Only if you kiss me first," she finally replied.

Innately knowing Lily's motive, James laid his cane down and granted her wish. He gently held the sides of her face and kissed her in the most loving, memorable, and sentimental way his lips could manage.

"You're *not* a broken man ... you're *perfect* in my eyes," Lily whispered when their lips parted.

"That's all that matta's to me." James took her by the hand, kissed it, and led her to the blanket. "Lunch is served," he said, playfully bowing.

Lily smiled and sat down to enjoy the fine cuisine and aged fine wine. When they finished their meal, Lily got comfortable in James's arms and finally opened to the very first page of her father's journal.

May 7th, 1831

Today, my father-in-law gave us one of his slaves. Her name is Maya. Considering the definition of her name, it is so fitting that she has arrived here in this season. She has undoubtedly enhanced the beauty of spring. I never believed in love at first sight, but after *what I felt when I first saw her, I'm starting to think that I can't make that claim anymore ...*

Lily immediately stopped reading and whipped her head around to look at James with obvious shock. "Is this real?" she whispered, tears already welling in her eyes.

"Oh, you ain't read nothin' yet." James pulled her closer. "Prepare yo'self, Miss Lily. Once you start readin' this, I doubt you'll be able to stop. I'm gonna hold on to you extra tight the entire time, 'cause this is about to be one hell of a wild emotional ride." James wiped the tear that finally slid down her face and kissed her cheek. Lily got comfortable in his arms again and proceeded with reading a story that she was now dying to know about.

Chapter Thirty-One

January 16, 1845
Two days after selling Lily

Twenty-four hours after auctioning off his only daughter, Levi had yet to return home. After feverishly searching for him, Colt and Wyatt finally found their father face down in a pile of leaves at the bottom of an embankment, surrounded by empty liquor bottles. The brothers frantically made their way down the hill and rolled him over. He was pale, clammy, and completely unconscious. They rushed him to the town doctor where he was treated for dehydration and severe alcohol poisoning. Once coherent, Levi still refused to utter a word to his sons or to the doctor about why he had nearly drunk himself to death.

Colt and Wyatt took their father home afterward, all three riding in complete silence. The look on Levi's face and his demeanor was enough to make the boys realize that probing him for answers to his bizarre disappearance would have been met with stern resistance. The boys' mother had been very coy around them as she had gone about pressuring Levi to sell Lily. But Wyatt was now old enough to read between the lines. However, he was convinced that the urgency to sell Lily was due to financial strain, a common issue in their household. Lily's paternity was never even a fleeting thought in Wyatt's mind, let alone the possibility that his father was in love with her mother. Levi's example of high morality left Wyatt confident in his father's faithfulness, even despite the increased tension he had noticed between his parents.

So as young Wyatt guided the horses into the shed of their home, he had deduced that his father's bizarre behavior was caused by yet another financial crisis. But after walking around to the back to help his father down, his confidence in that notion began to unravel. Wyatt and Colt stared at their beloved father laying flat on his back, looking as broken as they had ever seen a human in their lives. The sight had the brothers suddenly fighting to choke back an urge to cry. They were truly disturbed by how debilitated their father appeared. They knew he had sold slaves during financial disasters in the past, so they were dumbfounded as to why selling Lily seemed to have instantly changed him into a man who was now like a shattered, lifeless stranger.

"Go on to school," Levi murmured, refusing to get up from where he lay.

Despite their deep concern, the boys honored their father's wish and left him alone in the shed. As they exited, they saw their mother standing on the porch. Her fury was evident to them by the way she had her hands perched on her hips. Her face was fire red as she glared at them through the slits in her lowered eyelids. Emily had been nonchalant about the fact that her own husband was missing. Wyatt almost got the sense that she hoped he would never return. His mother's dismissive attitude about their missing father continued to fuel Wyatt's rage. As much as he tried to expunge such ungodly emotions, they had already saturated his soul. As his mother stood on the porch, he glared back at her, visions of mercilessly lashing her with a whip still vividly playing in his mind. He now wished *she* was the one to *permanently* disappear. He was certain that he would never have wasted a minute of sleep to search for her. That had not been the case with his father, however. Despite their mother's objection, Colt and Wyatt had snuck out before dawn to look for him. Wyatt was hoping that she would overlook their disobedience when he told her the good news, but that was hardly the case.

"Where have you two been?!" Emily screamed when her sons stepped onto the porch.

"W-we were out lookin' for pa. We finally found 'em," Wyatt replied.

"Nobody told you to do that!"

"I know, but we were worried about 'em. It wasn't like him not to come home. And we were right. When we found 'em, he was really sick."

"You're right! He is *sick!* Sick of bein' a *real* man! Sick of handlin' his responsibilities, the way a *real* man should! So, he tucked tail and ran like the sissy little boy that he is! And I didn't need eitha' of you draggin' that immature little baby back here! He would've come home when he decided to start actin' like a damn grown man!"

"HE ALMOST DIED AND YOU ACT LIKE YOU DON'T EVEN CARE!" Wyatt erupted. He then suddenly felt his neck crack from the force with which his mother slapped him across the face.

"That's because I don't!" Emily replied coldly, glaring at her son as he held his bloody lip. "Just like I don't care about any of you disobedient little heathens! I regret havin' every last one of you disrespectful monsta's! And if you disrespect me again, I'll tie you up to a tree and whip every ounce of flesh off your back!" She pushed both boys toward the steps. "Now go on to school where you damn well should've been in the first place!"

Wyatt felt as though the whip would have hurt far less than his mother's confession. He and Colt ran off to school, both feeling as though her callous words had stripped them of their spirits.

After her boys were gone, Emily glared at the shed, hoping the reason her husband had yet to emerge was because he had perished where he lay. For once Emily and Levi wanted the exact same thing. Levi was laying in the back of the wagon, staring at the barn roof, far too paralyzed by grief to move a muscle. During his severe state of intoxication, his mind had partially blacked out. He did not even recall how much, or even what, he had drunk. But as he laid there now, thinking about Maya and Lily, he suddenly regretted that his sons had found him before his body had a chance to succumb to whatever alcoholic poison he had consumed.

As Levi lay there alone, the weight of what he had done finally hit him full force. It was the first time he had had enough mental clarity to realize that his trip to a Negro auction with Lily was not just a godawful nightmare. It was all real. The one thing that bonded him to the woman he loved was now long gone. He suddenly sat straight up when that fact caused a sudden urge to vomit. He quickly stuck his head over the side of the wagon, just as he began to dry heave. Having not eaten for two days, it was only stomach acid and saliva that flooded his mouth. When his stomach stopped spasming, he swallowed back the bitter taste and wiped his mouth on a cloth.

After gathering the strength to get out of the wagon, Levi walked over and looked out of the shed door at Maya's cottage in the distance. The little person he loved more than life itself was no longer residing within its walls. The reason for that caused his head to lower in shame. As he looked at the very hands that had carried her away, his tears began saturating the dirt. The weight of guilt made it nearly impossible for him to lift his migraine-stricken head. Inside his head, an array of thoughts pounded away at him with as much force as his migraine. Simply thinking about the dark, desolate hole that he had cast Maya into had Levi's heart pumping so fast that he felt it was on the verge of exploding. He felt a desperate need to inhale and exhale deeply, but the massive lump in his throat made him feel as though his airway was constricted. His stomach was suddenly so tightly twisted into knots that even vomiting again felt impossible. Sweat poured profusely from every pore on his body, soaking his filthy clothes. A surge of adrenaline suddenly flooded his muscles, instantly turning on his fight or flight instincts. As desperately as he preferred to flee, Levi forced himself to stay and fight. He wanted to fight to heal the woman he loved, fight for Maya's forgiveness, and fight to feel her love again. But after his unforgivable sin, he knew the only thing he would ultimately be fighting to do would be to accept the fact that Maya would now hate him for the remainder of her life. Despite that painful reality, Levi knew that an explanation and a sincere apology for his actions was long overdue. He blew out a cleansing breath and accepted that logic would never suffice as an adequate reason for his betrayal, nor would it even remotely alleviate Maya's suffering. Still, though, he knew he owed her at least that much. With nervousness rattling his bones, he took his first step out of the shed.

Emily peeked her head out of the window, just in time to see the pathetic sight of her husband dragging his feet toward Maya's cottage. Since he did not perish in the shed, Emily was hoping Maya's homicidal rage would be the cause of his death instead. But at the very least, she was satisfied by the fact that the auctioning off their bastard had savagely murdered any love Maya felt for Levi. That fact brought genuine joy to Emily's vengeful, dark heart. With a wicked smile plastered on her haggard face, she closed the curtains and went back to her household duties with renewed energy.

In stark contrast to his wife's demeanor, a trail of tears marked Levi's somber journey from the shed to the doorstep of Maya's cottage. When he was just yards away from the door, he stopped to catch his breath when he swore he felt himself suffocating in the cloud of misery Maya emitted. He inhaled deeply and then forced his feet to guide him the rest of the way. He placed his hand on the doorknob, but what he heard on the other side of the door made him hesitate to turn it. The sounds within those walls far superseded misery. In fact, Levi could think of no word that could adequately describe the anguished sobbing, piercing the walls and torturing his ears. The despondent, nonstop wailing immediately brought forth another surge of Levi's tears and, once again, turned on his desire to flee the scene. He ignored his cowardly desires, however, and forced himself to turn the doorknob. What his ears had heard did not remotely compare to the agonizing sight of the shattered woman now in his vision. He immediately wished that he had perished in the woods, anything to render him blind and deaf to what he was currently witnessing.

Levi slowly closed his eyes, already wanting to erase this moment from his mind. Maya lay in the fetal position on the floor, clutching one of Lily's dresses. Her wailing and bodily convulsions were equivalent to someone suffering intense bursts of physical torture. She was coughing and fighting to catch her breath, nearly suffocating herself as she inhaled her own mucus and tears. She remained covered in dirt from their scuffle two days prior. Her dress was torn, and dried blood remained on her back from where Wyatt had whipped her. Her eyes were black and blue, the right one nearly swollen shut. The blood and dirt on her face were washed away by a river of endless tears. She looked weak and frail. It was clear to see that just *two days* without food and water - and her daughter - had already taken a *major* physical toll.

"Maya," Levi tearfully whispered, sounding just as sullen as she looked.

Maya's sobbing continued.

Levi approached her, got down on his knees, and touched her. "Maya."

She did not react to his touch. "Unless, y-you're h-here to t-take me to m-my little g-girl, or to p-put me outta m-my misery, I don't w-want you h-here," she coughed.

"Maya, can you please gimme a chance to explain?"

"G-go aw-way."

"Maya, please, it's just that I … I just needed to buy some time until I could figure out …"

"*Buy some time?!*" Maya spat, whipping her head around and penetrating Levi with an icy glare. "*Buy some time?!* At the cost of rippin' Lily's heart out?!"

"Maya, please let me explain, I…"

"I don't give a damn about your explanation!" Maya sat up even taller and squinted her swollen eyes at Levi. "Do you honestly believe there's *anything* you could say to me that would make me *hate* you any less than I do right now?!"

"No, but I…"

"I'm convinced this was a punishment to me for not tellin' Lily who you were!"

"No Maya, that's not it, I swear!"

"LIAR! I saw the way you'd always look at me with disdain every time she called you *masta'?*"

"No, Maya, you don't unda'stand. I just needed to buy some time until I could figure out…"

"I said I don't want your goddamned explanation! I want my baby back, you heartless son of a bitch!" Maya shrieked, suddenly springing to her feet. In a barbaric rage, she picked up her music box and threw it at Levi. She then picked up her telescope and began thrashing everything in the room. Levi took a step back, his mouth agape as he watched her destroy everything within her reach, swinging wildly and yelling like an asylum lunatic. She bashed and beat until her beloved telescope was left as nothing more than a useless scrap of metal. She tossed it aside and advanced on Levi. "You promised you'd neva' hurt her!" she cried repeatedly as she began to beat wildly against Levi's chest with the sides of her fists. He just absorbed every one of her blows in silence without daring to stop her. He felt he deserved far more abuse than what she was capable of giving him. Maya beat him until she slumped to the floor in exhaustion. "J-just p-put me outta my m-misery," she begged, rocking back and forth on her knees, a river of tears pouring from her eyes. "Please, I don't w-wanna l-live without m-my b-baby."

"Maya," Levi reached down to help her up.

She slapped his hand away, buried her face in her hands again, and remained collapsed in an inconsolable heap. "Sh-shoot me. Please! Just p-put me outta my m-misery. I don't w-wanna live no mo' without my b-baby … pleeease. I'm b-beggin' you," she whispered, as she continued to weep uncontrollably.

Levi slowly backed away, accepting responsibility for the devastation he had caused a woman he loved more than anything. He went into the barn and drank himself into another liquor-induced coma, trying to obliterate the images of Maya crumpled on the floor. The visions were just as torturous as the look on Lily's face when she finally called him a word that he had been desperate to hear her say since her birth … *Daddy.*

*****

Daddy … As the years rolled by, that one word began to have a debilitating effect on Levi Collins. At various moments throughout his day, it echoed in his head. The solitary word was always accompanied by a perfectly preserved vision of Lily shackled in the back of Jesse's wagon, her bottom lip quivering, and a sorrowful expression on her dirt-covered face. *Daddy,* he heard as a flash of Lily appeared in his mind, gazing at him with a set of tear-filled eyes that were exact replicas of his. In Levi's head, the sound of confusion and heartbreak in Lily's youthful voice was always just as fresh as the moment she had uttered that single word … *Daddy.*

For fourteen years, there seemed to be nothing Levi could do to escape that visual and that word. While hard at work in the fields …

Daddy. While barely ingesting each of his meals … *Daddy.* While talking to his friends … *Daddy.* While driving his horse's into town … *Daddy.* While sitting stone-faced in the church pews every Sunday … *Daddy.* Seeing the efforts Maya went through to evade him … *Daddy.* Every father he saw with their daughters … *Daddy.* The last sound echoing in his mind before he drifted off to sleep … *Daddy.* The recurring nightmare that always jolted him awake … *Daaaddyyy! Please take me back to my maaama!*

The one word that Levi had been desperate to hear from his only daughter failed to bring him joy, but instead brought him fourteen years of inescapable torture. It drove his appetite away, drove his health to fail, drove his creativity into the ground, and drove his craving to play piano into a craving to try to drink that word away. The nights that Levi was awakened by the nightmare of selling Lily, he often sat in the barn drinking and banging his fists against his temples, trying to beat the haunting memory from his brain before it drove him completely insane.

Levi's downward spiral into insanity was compounded by the permanent shift in Maya's demeanor. For the fourteen years that Lily was gone, he could do nothing but painfully watch from afar as Maya withered away. He had watched Maya carefully whenever rainbows lit up the sky, hoping for the slim chance that her smile would light up too. But she never even raised her head to acknowledge them anymore. That simple absence of emotion, during the rare celestial event, was all it took to convince Levi that he had *completely* destroyed the person that Maya once was. Selling Lily had immediately devoured her jubilant nature. Levi had to live with the fact that he was responsible for Maya's dramatic weight loss. It was he who had caused the ever-present sullen look on her face, and the sunken eyes that seemed to always be on the verge of tears. He had robbed her of her goddess-like, graceful movements and caused her to now seem lifeless and mechanical. Her zest for life and nature were now only present in the beautiful memories that Levi had of her. The vivid memories of the old Maya made him so keenly aware of how she had been swallowed by sadness, and had remained submerged there, since the day she lost her daughter. Levi Collins simply had to accept the fact that the man he faced in the mirror every day had completely destroyed a woman who meant the world to him.

The fact that Maya had quickly withered away into an empty shell of a person brought the utmost joy to Levi's wife. Emily had expected that outcome for Maya. But Levi's mental, emotional, and physical collapse was far worse than she had anticipated. The implosion of her husband's life made Lily's absence all the more worth it for her. Uplifted by the success of her mission, Emily gallivanted around the farm with an air of pride, as she watched Levi and Maya *both* writhe in misery for fourteen long years. She was convinced that there was nothing that Levi could ever do Maya to revitalize the person she once was, or to restore the love that Maya had once felt for him. Levi, however, was convinced otherwise.

From the moment he had cast Maya into an emotional abyss, Levi obsessively thought about the day he would be free to pull her out from the pits of despair. He longed to see life in her eyes and feel her jubilance. He prayed for God to let him live to see the day that Maya, once again, lit up with a smile, as she gazed in awe at her precious rainbows. He looked forward to a future when "yes sir" and "no sir" were not the only words she ever said to him. Just one more time, he hoped to experience the warmth he once felt whenever he caught Maya discreetly smiling at him. The sweet sound of Maya's laughter was now a faded memory that Levi hoped to revive. He often fantasized that there might even come a day when Maya would allow him the honor of touching her, kissing her, and making love to her again. But at the very least, he hoped the day would come when she would forgive him, and look at him with warmth in her eyes, instead of the cold hatred that she had penetrated him with for over a decade.

Levi had once counted down the days that Maya was to deliver the most precious, life-changing treasure he had ever received. And now, for fourteen years, he had been counting down the minutes until he could deliver the very same life-changing gift for Maya. Unlike Emily, Levi knew *exactly* what, or rather *who*, it would take to revitalize the woman Maya once was.

January 24th, 1859

For fourteen years now, there's been a countdown in my head to this moment. This past Saturday, I attended Dallas's wedding. All my boys are now officially grown. They're well-educated, married, and have respectable careers. My mission as a father to them now feels complete. However, I feel no sense of honor knowing that I sacrificed the happiness of my beloved daughter, and of the woman I love, to ensure the happiness of my sons. My heart is heavy with fourteen years of torturous regret. My mind and soul are damn near devoured by sorrow. All these years, I've done nothing but dream of seeing my Lily again. To see her beautiful face would be all the nutrients needed to nourish my soul and save it from withering away altogether. Tomorrow, the long countdown comes to an end, and my dream will finally become a reality.

For two days now, I haven't been able to eat or sleep. I do nothing but think about Lily. What does she look like now? How much lovelier is her smile? Does she still have the same bubbly, outgoing personality? What incredible new things has her brilliant mind absorbed? ... Does she hate me? What awful things will she say to me? I've thrown up twice this morning just thinking about that. I can't imagine how sick I'll be when I finally do hear it. But I know I goddamned well deserve every nasty word she hurls at me ... and so much worse. And I will happily endure such torture, if that's what it takes to reunite her with her mother, the way I've dreamed of doing for all these years.

After writing that in his journal, Levi took out a thick manilla envelope from the hidden compartment in the horse stall of his barn. He then pulled out a sheet of paper that still brought tears of misery to his eyes:

Virginia State Negro Auctioneers
Bill of Sale

Name of slave being sold: **Lily**

Birthdate of slave (if known): **June 1, 1834**

Age of Slave (or approx. if known): **9**

Description of Slave

Hair Color: **Dark Brown**

Eye color: **Green/hazel**

☐ Negro ☒ Negress

Approx. Height: **5ft**

Approx. Weight: **80lbs**

Build: **Thin**

Skin complexion:

☐ Fair ☒ Light brown ☐ Brown ☐ Dark brown

Percentage Negro (if known):

☐ Negro (100%) ☒ Mulatto (50%) ☐ Quadroon (25%) ☐ Octoroon (12.5% or less)

I, **Levi W. Collins** of **Collins Plantation** , located at address **1372 Trickum Road, Charleston VA** ,agree to the sale of the above described slave in the amount of $ **1,125.00** to be sold to **Jesse Adams** on this **14** th day of **January** ,18 **45**.

Levi Wyatt Collins

Signature of seller

I, **Jesse Roscoe Adams Sr.** , of **Adams Plantation** , located at address **2798 Jefferson Road, Fayetteville VA,** agree to the purchase of the above described slave in the amount of $**1,125.00** sold by **Levi Collins** on this **14** th day of **January** ,18 **45**.

Jesse R. Adams Sr.

Signature of purchaser

With that perfectly preserved bill of sale in his hand, Levi sat up against the horse stall and stared at the date through the blur of tears in his eyes. *After fourteen years*, he thought to himself. He then picked up his favorite picture of Lily and gazed at her sitting in Maya's lap, smiling as she pointed to a passing flock of birds. "I can finally get my little girl back," he whispered as his tears began pelting Lily's image. He then reached back into the manilla envelope and took out the money that Jesse Adams had purchased Lily with. Every single dollar had sat collecting dust in that secret compartment for over a decade. Levi was now ready to return it to its rightful owner, in exchange for someone whose value he felt far superseded the dusty bills in his hands, and every bill ever printed on Earth for that matter.

In Levi's estimation, the last few hours of his countdown seemed to roll by as quickly as molasses on a frosty day. He lay wide awake, staring out the window; daylight just couldn't come fast enough. When it finally did, fear, joy, anxiousness, excitement, and every emotion in between, had him damn near ready to jump out of his own skin. He hurried to the bathroom to clean up his appearance. His hand shook so badly while trying to shave that he nicked his face in six places before finally giving up altogether. He managed to comb his hair and dress himself, but shaky hands made such simple tasks take twice as long as usual. He took several deep breaths to calm himself before exiting the bathroom. He considered having breakfast but eating was an impossibility for his knot-tied stomach. He therefore bypassed the kitchen, stepped out onto the front porch, and stared at Maya's cottage in the distance. His mind drifted away to what it might be like in a few hours when he would finally see his beloved daughter in the flesh again. He was convinced that the reality of that moment would bring him to his knees in joyous tears, as he apologized and begged her forgiveness. Even so, he felt those tears would never compare to the ones he would shed when he finally rode back through the gates of his plantation with Lily in tow and reunited her with her mother.

Eager for that moment to occur, Levi rushed to the barn and grabbed Jesse's money and the bill of sale. He then quickly climbed up on his wagon, snapped the reins, and began making his way toward the address on the fourteen-year-old paper in his lap. For a little over three hours, he rode along, his heart galloping far faster than the horses he was pushing hard. As he neared the Adams plantation, a man in a passing wagon tipped his hat to say hello, but Levi was oblivious to the gesture. His mind was far too consumed with seeing his little girl again to notice anything or anyone in his surroundings. Knowing that Lily was not actually so little anymore, Levi constantly imagined what she now looked like. His tears fell every time he thought about what he could say to her that would warrant her forgiveness, because he knew the answer to that question was … *absolutely nothing!* That fact caused him to suddenly halt his wagon and jump out. His feet hit the ground at the same time as the vomit violently erupting from his stomach. The shot of whiskey he drank to calm his nerves nearly burned a hole in his throat as it came back up. The scorching burn had his mucus membranes and tear ducts working overtime to cool his singed pores. With snot running down his face, bloodshot eyes, and patchy facial hair from a botched shave, he could have easily been mistaken for a drunken hobo. He remained on bended knee until his stomach stopped spasming and the world stopped spinning. With the little strength he had, he walked to the back of his wagon to find a rag and a canteen of water. He cleaned his face, swished water in his mouth, and wiped his eyes. He then glanced up. His eyes refilled with tears again when he realized that the address where his daughter resided was now a tiny speck in his field of view.

Now sweating profusely, Levi quickly jumped back in his wagon seat and prompted his horses forward. With a pounding heart, he guided them toward the entrance of Jesse's plantation. Before entering, he halted the horses. With his hand trembling uncontrollably, he held up the bill of sale to double check the address. The trembling paper was nearly impossible to read, especially with a mist of tears blurring Levi's vision. He wiped his eyes and exhaled to calm himself. He then glanced back at the paper, looked at the address on the mailbox, and finally verified that he was indeed at the right place. Levi wiped the sweat from his brow, swallowed hard, and nervously snapped the reins to prompt his team to trot through the gates. As he sat there hyperventilating, his horses quickly pulled him to his destination: the front porch of the home where his only daughter resided.

Despite how desperate Levi was to lay his eyes on his beloved little girl, he was suddenly hesitant to exit the wagon. He feared his shaky knees would be unable to support his panic-stricken body. Sure enough, he mis-stepped as he climbed down from the wagon. He slightly twisted his ankle, but the pain never even registered in his spinning mind. He stumbled slightly as he made his way up Jesse's porch steps. But, again, he was oblivious to his clumsiness. He loudly exhaled as he lingered outside the door for a moment, trying to stop his stomach from expelling its contents again. "Mornin'," he said when Jesse suddenly opened the door. Levi nervously snatched his hat off. He was so overcome with anxiousness that he did not even realize he had already knocked. "Uh, I'm lookin' for, uh…" He glanced down at his bill of sale again. "Jesse Adams … Is this his residence?"

"I'm Jesse. Who the hell're you?"

"My name is Levi … Levi Collins. I doubt you rememba' me. I sold you a slave fourteen years ago. A little girl named Lily."

"What about 'er?"

"Is she here?"

"No." Jesse started to close the door.

"Has she gone into town with your wife? If she'll be back shortly, I can wait."

"I said she ain't here! That's all you need to goddamn know!" Jesse fired back, instantly annoyed by his persistence.

"Have you sold 'er?"

"That ain't none of y'ur goddamn business! Now get the hell off my property! I got work to do!" Jesse replied, suddenly trying to slam the door in Levi's face.

Levi caught the door. "Please sir! This is important!"

Jesse looked Levi up and down. "Who the hell do you think you are?"

"LILY'S FATHER!"

Instantaneous rage and disgust turned Jesse's face a dark shade of red. He pursed his lips tight and lowered his eyelids as he glared coldly at a man that he instantly declared as a disgrace to the white race.

Levi's confession had escaped like he had no control over his mouth, but he suddenly owned up to his slip of tongue with an air of pride. "I'm Lily's fatha', and I wanna buy 'er back from you," he boldly stated, despite noticing the shift in Jesse's demeanor.

"*I* should've been the one knockin' on *your* door years ago, askin' *you* for my money back for sellin' me that worthless nigga'."

Though he was immediately enraged by the statement, Levi replied as calmly and as respectfully as he could manage, for the sake of retrieving Lily in peace. "She's not worthless to me, Mr. Adams. But if you feel that way about 'er, I'm more than happy to give you your money back."

"Use that to buy y'urself anotha' goddamn slave! Ain't no expiration date on purchases! All sales are final!"

"I'll quadruple the money! Hell, I'll pay you whateva' you want! Name your price! I just want my daughta' back!"

"I said she ain't here!"

"Well, where is she? Please, I'm beggin' you, sir. This is important!" The waiting tears in Levi's eyes finally trickled down his cheeks.

Jesse's face hardened when he saw such weakness. "She's dead," he replied coldly, suddenly enjoying the thought of torturing a man who fornicated with Negroes and diluted the superior blood of the white race.

"I don't believe you," Levi murmured, his bottom lip suddenly quivering.

"I killed that lazy bitch myself."

"I don't believe you!" Levi erupted, his tears now falling in streams.

Jesse smirked, his dark heart flooding with joy the more Levi cried. "Worst fuckin' purchase I eva' made. Hung that skinny piece of shit from a tree a few weeks afta' I bought 'er."

"You're lyin'!"

"I tossed what was left of 'er body in the woods afta' the buzzards got their fill."

"I DON'T FUCKING BELIEVE YOU!"

"You can find whateva' the wolves left of 'er ova' yonda'," Jesse sneered, motioning his head in the direction.

"I'M NOT LEAVIN' HERE WITHOUT MY DAUGHTER!" Levi suddenly tried to push his way past Jesse. "LILYYY!"

Jesse shoved him back. "I'll splatta' y'ur nigga' lovin' ass all ova' this porch if you don't get the hell off of my property!"

In a state of blinding madness, Levi suddenly lowered his shoulder, barreled into Jesse, and knocked him to the ground. He then stood in the foyer, repeatedly shrieking Lily's name as he frantically looked around.

Jesse quickly jumped up and grabbed Levi by the throat. He then pulled his pistol off his hip and held it to Levi's forehead. "If you don't get your nigga' lovin' ass off my property, I'll send you to hell to be with your mutt!" He shoved Levi out the door and he stumbled backward down the very steps that Lily had just departed from hours earlier. She was riding in the covered wagon of the young man who had tipped his Stetson hat to him an hour earlier, as he rode by on his journey to take Lily to meet a world-renowned composer.

****

A month after being thrown out of Jesse's house, Levi gathered his sons for a meeting at Wyatt's home. All six of his boys sat quietly in the living room staring at their father. He had his elbows resting on his knees with his hands clasped together. His head was slightly lowered as he glared at the floor in a trance. After a few minutes, his sons all began looking at each other in confusion, wondering why their father had summoned them there but had yet to say a word.

"Pa?" Wyatt said, trying to wrangle his attention.

Levi did not budge.

All the boys looked at each other in confusion again. Wyatt cleared his throat and tried again. "Pa, you said you needed to speak with us urgently. We're eaga' to know what's goin' on."

Levi still did not raise his head, but he finally spoke. "I love all you boys. From the moment you were all born, you've all brought me so much joy. You all finished school. You went out and got yourselves respectable careers. I'm proud of each and every one of ya' for that. I'm proud of the upstandin' men and fatha's you've all become. I'm just as proud that you've all abided by my wishes neva' to own any slaves. I neva' wanted any of you to justify your right to own humans based on somethin' as superficial as race. I *definitely* neva' wanted to hear anybody referrin' to y'all as their damn masta' ... like me. That shit's for the birds. I know I've been a walkin, talkin' contradiction all these years because I've owned slaves myself ... but it's wrong. Had I been able to figure out anotha' way to consistently feed you boys

603

without 'em, I'd've freed all my slaves in a heartbeat," he said, his voice trailing off.

The boys all silently looked at one another again, still feeling confused about their father's odd speech. They felt as though he was not even speaking directly to them. "Pa, you've been preachin' all that to us for years. We know these things already," Wyatt finally said.

Levi sighed and continued with what was on his mind. "The day I first took owna'ship of slaves, I no longa' deemed myself a man. Disgrace to the human race was a more fittin' description. That description's fittin' for *every* slave owna' on this earth, for that matta'. But now, I seek to release myself from that pitiful description and regain the title of a man." He placed a thick envelope on the coffee table. "All the slaves on my farm will be officially free as soon as I turn in these manumission documents to the state."

When Levi went silent, the boys all looked at one another again in confusion. "That's very honorable of you, pa. But what do we have to do with any of this? Do we need to turn the documents in for you or somethin'?" Bo asked.

Levi did not reply. He just kept staring emptily at the floor.

"Pa, you all right?" Colt asked when his father's despondency became too much to bear.

"No." Levi finally found the strength to hold his head up and look each and every one of his sons in the eyes. "I've done things in my life that I'm not proud of ... things I deeply regret." He exhaled, stood, and walked to the center of the living room. "From the day you were all born, I promised myself that I'd always show you with my actions how to be upstandin' men. It was of the utmost importance to me. It *still* is. Which is why I'm standin' before you all now, hopin' to teach you all a lesson about ownin' up to things that you've done in life that you weren't supposed to be doin' ... *especially* things that God would consida' sinful. I want you to always be man enough to admit your sins and pray to God to forgive you for 'em ... no matta' what those sins may be."

"What sins?" Dallas asked. "This sounds serious."

"It is." Levi blew out another breath. "Sellin' all those children on my farm has haunted me for a long time. From the moment I sold all of 'em, it was always my intent to right that wrong one day. Ova' the last several weeks, I've found three of the four children that I sold. They're all grown now, of course, so it may be too little too late. But I've made arrangements and settled financial agreements to have them reunited with their parents soon." Levi exhaled and lowered his head, already feeling himself becoming emotional. "But there's one slave that I've yet to find, and it's weighin' heaviest on me ... far above all the otha's."

"Who?" Colt asked.

"Lily. I'm sure you all rememba' her."

"How could we forget her? Dallas cried himself to sleep for a whole *week* when he found out she was gone!" Colt teased.

His brothers all laughed.

"Hey, cut me a break! I was only eight," Dallas replied. "Lily used to help me catch frogs and lizards. She was my favorite playmate ... more like a sista' to me actually."

Levi looked at Dallas knowing that he had no idea of the irony of his statement. "Well, out of everyone I've sold, Lily's the one that I can't find," he continued. "I spoke to the man who purchased her, Jesse Adams. At first, he refused to tell me anything about 'er. But I refused to leave his property until he told me the truth about where she really was."

"What did he say?" Colt asked.

Levi lowered his head briefly again as tears began to sting his eyes. "That she's dead," he whispered, finding it difficult to say out loud.

The boys were completely silent.

"But I refuse to believe it," Levi continued. "For several days, I sat outside Jesse's plantation, hidin' and watchin', to see if I saw anyone in the fields of Lily's likeness. For hours and hours, I scrutinized every face comin' and goin' from the house and the slave quarta's. But I neva' saw her."

"She's much olda' now. You may not have recognized 'er," Bo pointed out.

"No. The people there were much olda' than Lily would be now. Besides, I'd know Lily if I saw her, even all these years lata'. I'm certain of that. And trust me when I tell you, there wasn't a single person on that farm that even *remotely* resembled her."

"Did you check the slave registries? Maybe her masta' sold 'er," Colt suggested.

Levi nodded. "I did that too. I went to Fayetteville city hall and spent hours goin' line by line through their slave registry. I even checked the registries in every neighborin' city. The records show that Jesse was the last known man to own 'er. For weeks, I searched every plantation in Fayette county just to be sure. I even asked dozens of people if they knew of Lily. But most folks probably just view her as anotha' meaningless slave that ain't worth rememberin' any damn way," Levi sighed. "No matta' what I did, I just couldn't get any answers on where or how to find 'er."

"Well, I hate to say it, pa. But m-maybe her masta' was tellin' the truth," Dallas hesitantly stated.

"No! I don't believe that!" Levi emphatically replied. "I don't know why she wasn't there, but I absolutely *refuse* to believe she's dead! I saw the instant change in her masta's demeanor when I told 'em that … when I told 'em …"

"Told 'em what?" Wyatt prompted.

"That I'm Lily's fatha'," Levi finally confessed.

His words seemed to suck every drop of oxygen out of the room, leaving his sons unable to even gasp.

Levi slowly looked around at all the stunned faces of his beloved boys, as they stared at him with their mouths agape. "That's the truth. I'm Lily's fatha'," he admitted again. "That's part of the reason I asked you all here today. You're all men now, and I felt it was time for you all to know the truth ... and to hear it directly from me."

Gaping mouths and unblinking eyes were still the only responses to Levi's startling confession.

Levi exhaled great relief after finally letting go of his secret. Slowly, he looked at each of his sons again. "There comes a time in a man's life when he has to be true to himself, not matta what his religious convictions, no matta' what the world thinks, or even what the consequences may be. A man might go insane otha'wise."

Levi lowered his head, a distant look suddenly in his eyes. "There's not a day that goes by that I don't think about Lily. There's not a single minute that's passed, in fourteen years, that I don't ache ... *unrelentin'* pain," he said, the pain now evident in his tone. "But what hurts me most is knowin' that I subjected my own daughta' to far greata' pain than I could eva' imagine. Lily's suffered enough, and now I wanna spend the rest of my life tryna soothe her sufferin', in any possible way I can. That's why I've been so desperate to find 'er."

Levi exhaled again and nervously glanced at all the unblinking eyes still pasted on him. "My last day in Fayetteville, I snuck onto Jesse's plantation while he was gone. I wanted to ask his slaves if they remembered Lily, and if maybe they knew where she was. But they were too terrified to let me anywhere near 'em. I think that's because things didn't go well between me and Jesse durin' my first visit there," Levi sighed and shook his head. "I'm embarrassed about my actions, but he and I got into a scuffle. All the slaves were workin' way out in the field when it happened. But they all stopped and stared when they saw Jesse march me off his property at gunpoint. They must've remembered my face, 'cause when I tried to approach 'em to ask about Lily, they wouldn't even let me get a word out. Some kept beggin' me to leave before I got 'em whipped. Hell, some ran off before I got anywhere near 'em. It's like they didn't wanna take any risk of makin' it even *seem* like they were tellin' their masta's business, for fear of what that tyrant might do to 'em. I don't know if that's their reaction to every strange white man, or if it was just because of the fight I had with their masta'.

"Which leads me to the otha' reason I've come to you all today. I's hopin' maybe one of you would be willin' to try to get some answers from Jesse's slaves for me. Maybe they'll talk to one of you. Even if they know nothin', I just need help with this," Levi confessed, his voice now starting to waver. "Because, as it stands, I'm stuck with no clues as to where Lily is … not one. And I don't give a damn what that tyrant told me. My little girl ain't dead! I can feel it in my soul. I know my Lily's out there somewhere. And I'm determined to find 'er. But I'm ova'whelmed, and I don't know where to start. I know I'm riskin' so much by comin' to you all, but I'm truly hopin' you'll all help me look for my daughta' … help me find your sista'. It's eatin' a hole in my soul not knowin' where she is. I've raised you boys into adulthood, now the only otha' thing I wanna do with my life is reunite my little girl with 'er motha'. At the very least, I want Lily to know how s-sorry I am for wh-what I d-did to h-her, a-and that I l-love her," Levi confessed, as he suddenly began to weep.

Wyatt and his brothers had never seen their father cry until that very moment. They were all stunned by how hard he suddenly began sobbing. Despite that as proof of how emotionally traumatizing the entire situation was for him, Wyatt's reaction proved a lack of even an ounce of sympathy. He suddenly sprang to his feet. "Does our motha' know about your abominable sins?!" he asked, pure fury in his tone.

Levi wiped his face as he nodded. "She does. *She's* the reason I sold Lily. Certain threats were made by your motha', and I didn't want you boys to be hurt in any way because of my indiscretions. I did what I thought was best to protect you all. But you're men now. Your motha' has no real powa' to hurt any of you anymore."

"Jesus Christ! So, you've *both* been deceivin' us all this time?!" Wyatt screamed.

"No wonda' why it always seemed as though our motha' hated you!" Colt added, glaring at his father with disdain.

"Trust me, your motha' hated me long before Maya eva' came to that plantation," Levi replied.

"Did you eva' love our motha', or has that all been a facade too?" Dallas asked.

"I love that your motha' brought all of you into my life. For the sake of all of you, I *wanted* to love her for more reasons than that … but it just neva' happened. Your motha's neva' loved me eitha'. She's been sure to let me know that loud and clear ova' the years. You just can't force yourself to lie about love. Your eyes, your words, your body language, your actions will all eventually unveil the truth. Your heart just don't know how to lie. Your motha' and I are proof of that. Your heart's gonna love who it wants to love, no matta' how wrong it may be … *Maya's* proof of that."

"You *love* her?!" Wyatt spat, looking disgusted.

"With every ounce of my soul," Levi confessed, pure passion in his tone. "I'm not ashamed of how I feel eitha'. If that's a sin, I've certainly paid for it and then some. I've done my time. And now, I don't wanna live the rest of my life imprisoned with a woman who doesn't love me. I deserve betta' than that … I *demand* betta' than that," he said, recalling what Maya had said to him years ago. "Your motha' deserves betta' too … and so does Maya."

"You can't *possibly* be sayin' that you're gonna leave our motha' to be with a slave!"

Levi looked Wyatt in his eyes. "The Lord is forgivin'."

Wyatt took an angry step toward his father. "I have to believe you've gone half-ass outta your mind to wanna drag us into your twisted love affair with a *nigga'* and weigh us down with the guilt of your lost or *dead* bastard child!"

"And *then* beg us to do your dirty work, so you feel betta' about the fact that you threw away your little mistake!" Colt added.

"LILY'S NOT A MISTAKE!" Levi retaliated, raising his voice to his sons for the first time ever. "For whateva' God's reason, she was meant to be here! The only mistake I eva' made where she's concerned was takin' 'er away from her motha'! But by no damn means is she a *mistake!* She's my daughta'! And whetha' you like it or not, she's your sista'! And you all have to accept that!"

"We don't have to accept a damn thing! If you consida' that nigga' as your daughta', then you can forget about considerin' me as a son!" Wyatt spat.

Levi was stunned into momentary silence. "Wyatt, you'll *always* be my son," he whispered. He glanced at all his boys. "*All* of you will *always* be my beloved sons ... sons that I gave up one of the most precious things in my whole world to protect because I love you all so much, and I wanted you to have a decent life. But I love Lily too, and I'm desperate to find 'er, and give 'er back the life she deserves. I've gotta get 'er back to 'er motha'. It's the only way I can remotely atone for destroyin' their lives. So, despite the sins you feel I've committed, I'm *beggin'* you boys to help me find your sista' ... *please?*" he pleaded.

"SHE AIN'T OUR DAMN SISTA'!" Wyatt erupted. He grimaced and took another step toward his father. "Honestly, I hope Lily's masta' did kill her! I'd ratha' her be dead than admit I have a *nigga'* for a sista' ... and an *adulterer* for a fatha'! For the abominable sins you committed, you deserve to live with the agony of bein' the root cause of your bastard's death!"

Wyatt's disgusting words were as painful for Levi as being ran over by a freight train. With tears of desperation streaming from his eyes, he slowly turned in a circle to look at all the stone-cold faces glaring harshly at him. He could not believe the men surrounding him, like vicious lions, were the same sons he had raised with pure love for three decades. "Wyatt, please ..."

"ENOUGH!" Wyatt interrupted. "I don't agree that a *real* man needs to divulge his damn dark secrets, no matta' how much it might eat away at his sanity! Some things a man is betta' off takin' to his grave ... and *this* is *definitely* one of those damn things! So, you can send us notice when you find Lily's rotten corpse! We'll be glad to help you dig her grave. But there ain't a chance in hell we'll help you look for your bastard!"

The crackling fireplace was the only sound in the room for a moment. Levi just stared at his oldest son in disbelief. He felt as though he was undoubtedly seeing and hearing the influence that Emily had on him. "Wyatt, this ain't the sort of man I raised you to be," he finally said, his voice trembling with emotion.

"And you're *clearly* not the man you've been paradin' yourself to be all these years eitha'. So, I guess we're even," he replied smugly.

"Wyatt, I..."

"You're no longa' welcome here!"

"Wyatt, this ain't you. You're just upset."

"You're damn right I am!"

"Well, just give this some time."

"I don't need time! I need you to get outta my damned house!"

Levi stared at his eldest son, trying hard not to let his callous words affect him. But in his vulnerable state, every word penetrated his heart like an enemy's blade. With tears still streaming down his cheeks, he spoke with the tone of a man whose severed heart was slowly ceasing to beat. "I've confessed my sins to God … and now to all of you. All I can do now is tell you how truly sorry I am. I neva' meant to hurt any of you. But for the pain I've caused and the mistakes I've made, I beg your forgiveness. I pray that you'll find it in your hearts one day to forgive me. Until then, just know that I love you boys more than I have the words to express." Levi lowered his head and solemnly walked out of Wyatt's house without another word.

Levi's plantation was not far from where Wyatt lived, but it took him over an hour to get home. He had walked slowly alongside his steed, needing the exercise to help clear his mind, as well as the non-stop flow of tears spilling from his eyes. Since the day he had sold Lily, he had not been this overcome with grief. As he walked home, he had to stop occasionally and sit up against trees until he regained the strength to continue on. It was as if all the festering pain of his adult life had now erupted with volcanic force, triggered by the seismic quake of his sons' heart-shattering words. The aftershock of tears now refused to stop coming in intense waves. Levi was so weakened with devastation that every step he took felt like an ascent up Mount Everest. But when he approached his house and thought of the demon who resided within, he suddenly felt as though he had just tumbled into hell.

Levi lingered outside the back kitchen door, staring in the window at the demon he silently proclaimed Emily to be. She had her back to him, preparing dinner. As usual, she did not even bother to turn around when she heard Levi enter. No kiss. No hug. No welcome home. She exuded no warmth whatsoever. Sadly, though, Levi was used to it. He stood behind her thinking about the fact that one night of drunken indiscretion as a teenager had sentenced him to thirty-two years of hard time married to a cold, heartless woman. But, in all those years, Levi was thankful to Emily for one thing … or rather six.

"I'm sorry for breakin' my vows to you," Levi suddenly said to her.

Emily was so oblivious to his presence that she was startled when she suddenly heard him speak. Still though, she did not break stride in chopping vegetables.

Levi stepped behind his wife, gently turned her around, slowly took the knife out of her hand and laid it down. "No matta' how we felt about one anotha', I was wrong for my infidelity. I know I sinned, and for that I'm truly sorry."

Emily scoffed. "You should be," she replied flatly.

Levi ignored her coldness and continued with what was on his mind. "Havin' a baby is clearly no easy task. You had six of 'em for me, and I love each and every one of 'em. They're my pride and joy." He took Emily by the hand. "And they're the six things that I wanna thank you from the bottom of my heart for givin' me."

Emily was so stunned by the sincerity in his voice that she could not even move her mouth to form her usual rude words in response. His words had even managed to soften the scowl lines on her face. She felt a surge of warmth run through her, causing her to squeeze his hand tighter in return.

"I still rememba' each and every one of my children's births like it was yesterday. Wyatt, my firstborn," Levi smiled. "Felt as full of pride as any man would feel to hold his first son. Then there was Colt. That boy was so eaga' to come into the world that I had to help deliva' him myself. Dylan, on the otha' hand, was two weeks ova'due. He neva' seemed to be in a hurry for anything, not even crawlin' or walkin'. Bo hardly cried a lick. Came out lookin' around the new world like a curious kitten. Lucas had more hair on his big head than I did," Levi laughed lightly. "Dallas was the tiniest baby I've eva' seen, and only eva' seemed content in a set of arms." Levi's mind drifted away for a moment. "And then there was my sweet little Lily."

Emily suddenly snatched her hand away from Levi's grip. He could smell the bitter stench of liquor on her breath when she scoffed upon hearing that name. The soft expression that Levi had managed to put on her face instantly transformed back into a tight-lipped grimace.

"June first, 1835 at 8:45 a.m., I rememba' hearin' Lily cry for the very first time. I couldn't get my feet to move fast enough to finally go and lay my eyes on 'er. Felt like lightnin' bolts shootin' through me the first time I got to hold 'er. The very moment I held 'er close to me, I rememba' feelin' such an indescribable amount of love for her, and an *instant* connection. There was an extreme tightness in my chest as my heart melted and filled with pride. I could hardly make out her little features through all the tears blurrin' my eyes. When I finally managed to stop cryin', I saw my own eyes starin' back at me. I still rememba' the feelin' of her tiny hand wrapped tightly around my finga', like she was beggin' me to neva' let 'er go. She didn't have to worry, though. I can assure you I neva' wanted to. Wish I could've held 'er like that foreva'." Levi briefly paused, still lost in the memory. "My words just can't do justice for what it felt like to hold a child I created with a woman I actually loved. Seein' the beautiful little baby Maya gave me made me fall even more in love with 'er. But you..." He suddenly looked at Emily with disgust. "I only eva' felt *obligated* to love you *because* of our children. I rememba' holdin' my boys for the first time and feelin' love for them too. But instead of feelin' more love for you, I felt sick to my stomach, knowin' I had yet anotha' reason to tolerate the torture of bein' married to you."

"Why the hell're you sayin' these things?!" Emily suddenly spat.

"If it wasn't for the fact that you were the vessel that brought my boys into this world, you wouldn't be worth a goddamn thing to me," Levi confessed.

"Answer me damn it!" Emily shouted.

"I swore to myself that no matta' how sick I was of bein' with you that I'd see all my boys through to manhood," Levi continued, still ignoring Emily's fury. "I'm proud to say that I stood by my word. Dallas is grown now. He's the last of the six gifts you gave me. Now, there's not a single solitary reason for me to pretend like I wanna stay married to you."

"Why're you tellin' me this?!" Emily blurted again.

Levi reached above the cabinets where he had a thick manila envelope hidden. He grabbed it and tossed it on the kitchen table. "Consida' yourself served."

Emily picked up the envelope, snatched the papers out, and managed to get her intoxicated mind to focus enough to gloss over the contents. She looked up at Levi with ice in her eyes when she realized what she was reading. "The holier than thou, God-fearin' Levi Collins has ridden in here on his high horse with the audacity to ask me for a divorce. What eva' will the Lord decide to do with you on judgement day?"

"I'd ratha' burn in hell for all eternity than spend anotha' second married to you."

"I'll ruin you! I'll tell your boys everything if you file these papers!"

"They already know. I told 'em *everything* about Maya and Lily. Not a detail missed. So, do what you gotta do, Emily. Ruin me. Destroy me. Put me in jail. I don't care anymore. Our sons are grown, established, intelligent men now. You don't have the powa' to hurt 'em anymore, or to hold 'em against me. Even if you tried, they're old enough now to realize how truly evil their own motha' is for maliciously tryna ruin their lives and have them shunned from the community with town gossip. So, go ahead," he threatened calmly. "Hell, Dallas cried for days afta' Lily was sold. Go ahead and tell 'em the truth about the threats you made, and why he neva' saw his favorite playmate again. In fact, tell 'em why I sold all the children on this farm, for that matta'. Go ahead, if it truly makes you feel betta' about yourself. I truly don't give a damn anymore, not about anything you have to say, and certainly not about *you*."

"What do you think you're gonna do now, huh? Marry your whore?!"

"If I could, I would. That's what a man does with the woman he loves." Levi lowered his eyelids. "Or those we drunkenly impregnate."

"The fact that you'd not only be willin' to marry a slave ... but a *whore*, is furtha' proof that you are *indeed* the most idiotic man on this Earth!"

"*Maya* ... Her name is *Maya*. Show some respect for the only *propa'* motha' your sons have eva' known!"

Levi easily caught Emily by the wrist before her open hand connected with his face. He tossed it back down by her side and glared at her.

"I'll make you suffa' for every word you just said to me, you son of a bitch!" she threatened.

"I put my own child on an auction block and watched a stranga' haul 'er outta my life, just to shut you up! You can skin me alive, and I *promise* I wouldn't suffa' nearly as much as I have since that day!"

"You'll wish you *were* skinned alive if you file these damn papers! I will *not* be shamed by this community just because you want the freedom to fuck your whore in peace!"

"We don't belong togetha', Emily!" Levi erupted. "*You're* not happy! *I'm* not happy! There's no need to *force* ourselves to needlessly suffa' in each otha's presence anymore! Let's just appreciate the lives we've created and go our separate ways amicably!"

Emily lit the burner on the stove and tossed the divorce papers into the flames. Levi never moved. He watched them burn, much like he wished he could when Emily's soul suffered the same eternal fate. He never expected her to sign the papers anyway. But, in his mind, the papers burning to ash seemed a perfect metaphor for the finality of his marriage.

After the papers were completely incinerated, Levi looked into the eyes of the woman he now considered his ex-wife. "I at least had to try to end things peacefully. I figured I needed to expect nothin' less than a fight, though." Levi then tossed a set of keys on the counter.

"What're these for?!"

"I bought you a small cottage in close proximity to where all the boys live. You have thirty days to collect your belongin's and leave here, or I'll have you evicted."

"What?!" Emily snapped. "You can't *force* me to leave here!"

"I *can* and I *will*. My parents put *my* name on this property when they made the down payment, so you don't technically own any of this. Take me to court if you want. I'll be sure to tell 'em how you nearly had this place repossessed by the bank. I don't care how hard I have to fight you. I want you gone!"

"I've built my entire life here! Now you expect me to just start all ova' somewhere else?!"

"You demanded that my nine-year-old daughta' do it! You certainly didn't see the harm in that back then, so I damn sure don't wanna hear your pitiful excuses now!"

"Don't act like you're so damn righteous! It was *your* two hands that threw your mulatto bastard away, like the *worthless garbage* she is!"

"Watch your goddamn mouth!" Levi erupted, his face fire-red.

"No! You watch yours! Don't make me out to be the villain and pretend like you care about your bastard all of a sudden! Your actions spoke volumes about how meaningless she was to you! Your feelings don't matta' anyway! As a worthless piece of property, that little mongrel had no right to decide her fate! But *I* have *every* right to be here! And I *refuse* to leave!"

"And I *refuse* to spend the rest of my life in utta' misery! And, for the life of me, I can't unda'stand why you wanna fight so hard to keep livin' this way! You don't love me! Hell, you don't even *like* me! You should be rejoicin' ova' the chance to find someone who makes you happy!"

"Don't you dare tell me what I should be rejoicin' ova'!"

"Forgive me! I forgot I'm dealin' with someone who hates their life so much that they rejoice in makin' otha's hate their own! *You* may not want betta' for yourself, but *I* do! I *deserve* betta' than this! In fact, I *demand* betta'! So whetha' we officially divorce or not … it's ova'! I've served my sentence for my sins and then some!"

Emily stepped toward Levi and put a finger in his face. "You betta' find yourself a damn good attorney, because I'm not leavin' this house without a fight!"

"So be it." Levi shook his head and exhaled. "Have your attorney contact mine. And don't utta' anotha' word to me in the meantime. We're done. *Permanently*," he said, calmly stepping past her toward the door.

"You ain't fuckin' that whore in this house!" Emily screamed, sounding like a whiny child in desperate need of attention. Even after feeling her new house keys pelt him hard in the back, Levi didn't break stride. "You'll burn in Hell for this!" she shouted, frustrated by his lack of reaction.

With his hand on the doorknob, Levi turned to look at Emily one last time. "Afta' thirty-two years chained to you, Hell sounds like a *glorious* vacation."

After the *failed* meeting with his sons and finalizing the end of his *failed* marriage, Levi walked around to his front porch and watched

Maya in the distance. His heart sank as he accepted that he had even *failed* at his mission to reunite Maya with her beloved daughter. Maya was taking clothes down from the clothesline, a task that she and Lily always used to do *together*. The fact that Lily was not there helping her now made watching the simple task feel like torture. Levi lowered his head and closed his eyes. His thoughts then began to take over the torture instead. In rapid succession, the painful words of Emily, Jesse, and his sons began to viciously pelt his mind: *It was your two hands that threw your mulatto bastard away! Your actions spoke volumes about how meaningless she was to you! You're beggin' us to do your dirty work, so you feel betta' about the fact that you threw away your little mistake. I hung that skinny piece of shit from a tree a few weeks afta' I bought 'er. I tossed what was left of 'er body in the woods afta' the buzzards got their fill. I hope Lily's masta' did kill her! For the abominable sins you committed, you deserve to live with the agony of bein' the root cause of your bastard's death!* The violent mental assault of everyone's words easily fractured Levi's fragile mind. *It was your two hands! It was your two hands! It was your two hands,* he suddenly heard echoing in his head in a distorted, mocking manner. He lifted his trembling hands and looked down at them. Tears suddenly gushed from his eyes as he stared at the two reasons that his daughter may have taken her last breath, dangling from the end of a tree branch. The mental vision of buzzards feasting on Lily's body had Levi fighting to catch his own breath. He shook his head to cease the gruesome images from torturously playing in his mind. He fought to fill his lungs, wiped his eyes, and forced himself to reject the idea that Lily was deceased. There was no way he would be able to breathe normally otherwise.

Once Levi caught his breath, he looked up and saw Maya walk into the barn. He desperately wanted to speak with her, but something she told him fourteen years ago suddenly rang out loudly in his mind. A week after selling Lily, he had approached Maya again, hoping to explain himself, but she quickly cut him off and sliced him with her razor-sharp tongue: *Unfortunately, you own me! Legally, I'm obligated to do whateva' the hell you demand me to! But outside of any menial tasks you command me to do, don't you eva' utta' anotha' goddamned word to me, you demonic piece of shit!*

Before that day, Levi had never once heard Maya use such foul language. It was as if her mouth was incapable of forming such words until his egregious actions shattered her linguistic dam, allowing her to flood his ears with profanity-laced language. Even all these years later, the mere memory of her vile words stung like toxic venom and made Levi hesitant to speak to her. But, today, he was desperate to bare his soul, no matter what he had to endure. He, therefore, exhaled and forced himself to step off the porch. In time with his foot hitting the ground, a rumble of thunder rippled through the sky. The sky suddenly darkened, and it immediately began to sprinkle. Levi paused and tilted his head back, thankful that the light mist of rain would help disguise his tears. The rain on his face reminded him of yet another reason for his fourteen-year countdown. He had looked forward to a storm like this, one whose aftermath would leave the opportunity for a spectrum of colors to stretch across the sky and induce a brilliant smile on Maya's face. But the thunder now only reminded him of his failures and caused a storm of sorrowful emotion to rumble throughout his body.

With a hint of tears still stinging his eyes, Levi entered the barn and stood before Maya. Even now, her beauty still had the ability to stun him into a silent, awestruck gaze. Years ago, Maya was once warmed by that look, but her reaction to him now proved otherwise. She lowered her head and briskly moved to exit the barn, just as Levi's presence had triggered her to do for over a decade. Levi knew he had no grounds to reprimand her for her coldness over the years. Usually, he would just let her walk away, knowing he deserved the intense pain in his heart that her actions always caused. But this time, he could not bear to accept either of those things silently. "Maya wait. Please don't leave," he begged.

The emotion in his voice was not enough to cause Maya to break stride. Even over a decade later, she still could not bring herself to be near him.

"Please ... it's about Lily," Levi added, hoping the topic would change her mind.

That name indeed stopped Maya in her tracks. Now fearing that the emotion in his voice had something to do with bad news, she immediately turned around. "Wh-what about her?" she asked hesitantly.

Levi was momentarily caught off guard. It was the first time Maya had looked him in the eyes in years. He shook himself from his trance before proceeding. "I-I'm gonna bring 'er back to you."

Maya scoffed. "Lily would have to be standin' beside you in the flesh before I believed a damn thing you say."

"And I certainly can't blame you for that. But I just wanted you to know that I've already started lookin' for her. It was my goal to have 'er back to you by now, but I'm havin' trouble findin' her. But I won't stop lookin'. Just as soon as I find 'er, I'm gonna bring 'er back home to you ... I swear."

"Just like you *swore* you'd neva' hurt her?!" Years of pent-up rage began to boil again within Maya. "You swore you'd neva' hurt her, Levi! You looked me in my eyes the day she was born, and you *swore!* But you callously tore my daughta' outta my arms, despite how much I begged and pleaded with you to honor your promise! So, I'll be damned if I eva' believe anything that comes outta your mouth *eva' again!*"

Levi swallowed hard. "Y-you're right. I know I've completely destroyed your trust and faith in me. I know I don't deserve to be believed at all. You're absolutely right," he reiterated, sheepishly accepting that painful truth. "So, I'll prove it with my actions. I'll stop at nothin' to bring our daughta' back home."

"Why?" Maya scoffed. "You done finally used up all the time Lily bought you?"

Levi looked confused. "Wh-what do you mean?"

"*Time*. You said you needed to sell Lily to buy some *time*. Lucky you. I notice she bought you just enough time to love and raise your boys into adulthood in peace … even bought you peace with your wife. How truly fortunate you are," she said with sarcastic bitterness in her tone.

Levi shamefully lowered his head.

"Do you have any money left from that auction to buy me back a day or two of the time you stole from me and Lily? An hour maybe? I'll even take a minute … just *one* minute to experience a special moment with my only daughta'. A minute from a moment she was excited to learn somethin' new or excited about 'er first love. A minute to be there the day she blossomed into a woman. A minute to lay down with her unda' the night sky and hear the name she's chosen for a new star we find togetha'," Maya calmly expressed, tears coursing down her cheeks. "Any money left to buy me back a minute or two to experience a special moment like that with Lily, huh? Maybe a second? Do you have any spare change rollin' around in your pockets? Or are you just as *broke* as I am?"

The steady stream of tears trickling down Levi's shamefully lowered head was his only response.

"Answer me damn it!" Maya demanded, fire returning in her tone. "You took *years* away from me and Lily! Are you gonna buy me back that damn time?!"

"Of course I can't, but…"

"Then it doesn't matta' now, Levi!" Maya interrupted. "I probably wouldn't even recognize my own daughta' if she was standin' right in front of me! I probably ain't nothin' but a faded memory in Lily's mind by now! And I damn sho' hope she's forgotten *everything* about you! Lord knows, I wish I could wipe you clean outta my memory too!"

"I know I deserve that, but I wanna do all I can to make this right."

"*Make this right?!*" Maya squinted her eyes at Levi. "The fact that you think you could *eva'* do *anything* to *make this right* makes me wanna vomit! You ruined the chance to do that the very second you put my daughta' on a goddamn auction block, turned your back on 'er, and walked away! Every day, you've had the luxury of huggin' your sons, talkin to 'em, laughin' with 'em, and tellin' 'em you loved 'em wheneva' you damn well pleased! All I've had was Lily's ragdolls and 'er blanket to ball up and cry in every day! And now, afta' all these years, you think there's supposed to be some goddamn way to *make all that right?!*" she mocked. "As if your sudden grand gesture is gonna magically erase years and years of pain and sufferin'! How dare you insult me like that!"

The moment Maya began to sting him with her venomous words, Levi began to fall apart emotionally. "I-I know what I did was damn near worse than murda', Maya. And trust me, I've neva' been more sorry for anything in my whole life. It's just that the things that Emily was threatenin' to do to my boys, I just..." He paused when words began to twist in his muddled mind and spill out of his mouth in a jumbled mess. He shook his head, knowing nothing he said would ever be an acceptable defense for his logic. "I-I just didn't know what else to do," he said, his voice trailing off.

"Maybe stand up to your wife for once in your goddamn life!" Maya fired back, immediately incensed by the audacity of his proclamation. "Grow a backbone and stop bein' such a weak excuse for a man! There's a few options, you cowardly son of a bitch! If you truly gave a damn about Lily, you would've figured out anotha' way to fight back against whateva' the hell was goin' on between you and your wife! I believe you tossed Lily to the wolves to save your *own* ass ...

not your *sons*! Lily was just a chosen casualty in the war you had no backbone to fight against your wife!"

"It wasn't about *me*, Maya. I swear! I had six little boys whose lives would've been ruined if..."

"If you didn't get rid of your illegitimate mulatto *mistake*!" Maya finished.

"Lily's *not* a mistake! She's the most precious gift I've eva' been given!"

"Right! You certainly proved that when you sold your *precious gift* to the highest bidda'," Maya replied with bitter sarcasm. She looked at Levi one last time with disgust and turned to walk away.

Feeling cut to pieces by her words, Levi dropped down on bended knee. He took Maya by the hand before she could leave. "Please, don't walk away. I'm beggin' you, Maya ... *please?*" he pleaded, looking up at her with tears running in streams down his face.

The sorrowful sight sent a ripple of emotion through Maya that made it impossible to abandon him.

"A-All these y-years, there's always b-been so much I've w-wanted to say to you. Whetha' you believe me or n-not, I beg you to just h-hear me out ... *p-please*," Levi choked out.

Maya nodded, but slowly removed her hand from his.

Levi was so overwhelmed with emotion, he had to exhale sharply and swallow hard before he could form words normally again. "I have worshiped you, Maya," he stated boldly, still tearfully gazing at her in a way that confirmed his confession. "I know I've done nothin' ova' the years but prove that I'm unworthy of you. But despite my actions, I've worshiped you like the goddess that you are. I *always* will. You were always so kind and carin' to me and my boys. You gave my boys the motherly attention and tenderness that they desperately needed. You may have neva' said it, but you always made me *feel* so loved. Lord knows, I desperately needed that too. And despite the little you had, you went above and beyond to give our daughta' the most magnificent upbringin'. And how do I show appreciation and gratitude for all your compassion ova' the years?" He swallowed back tears of humiliation. "I snatched away your happiness and destroyed your whole world. It's eaten my soul alive to know I savagely shattered the heart of the woman I worship…" He took hold of Maya's hand again. "The only woman I've eva' loved."

Maya wiped an escaping tear. To Levi's surprise, she left her other hand in his this time.

"I've loved you from the moment I first laid eyes on you, and I've loved Lily from the very moment I learned you were carryin' her," Levi continued. "I know my words are such a contradiction to my actions. But kneelin' here before you, I swear that's the God's honest truth." He closed his eyes and pressed his lips to the back of Maya's hand. His sorrowful tears moistened her skin as he let his kiss linger there for a moment. He pulled his lips away and looked into Maya's eyes again to find them now flooded with tears too.

"I know I've dishonored you in a way that can neva' truly be reversed. If God damns me to hell for my cruelty, it still wouldn't be punishment enough for what I did to you and Lily. I *deserve* to be hated by you for it. Hell, *I* hate me for it. But still, I wanna at least *attempt* to atone for my major failure as a man to you, and as a fatha' to our daughta'. So, I promise to do all I can to bring Lily back to you, so you can both live out the rest of your days *togetha'* … even if I'm neva' allowed to be a part of that. I just want you two back togetha', where you both belong."

Maya's eyes fluttered closed, pushing another swell of tears down her cheeks.

"But there is one thing I beg God you'll bestow upon me," Levi added.

Maya finally opened her eyes, waiting on his request.

"I'm b-beggin' you for your f-forgiveness," he tearfully pleaded. "'Cause even afta' all these years, I still can't f-find the strength to f-forgive myself."

Maya briefly closed her tear-filled eyes again as she searched her mind for a response. She then opened them, wiped her tears away, and exhaled. "Many times, I've wondered if you sold your heart and soul to the devil the day you sold your own daughta'. 'Cause the man that came back here afta' that ain't the same one that claimed to love me and Lily. A *coward* returned in his place! A coward that I can't even look at without gettin' sick to my stomach! Just as sick as the thought of eva' forgivin' you!" She pursed her lips tight and squinted her eyes. "I *hate* you for what you did! You could deliva' Lily back here on a silva' platta', and I'd still *hate* you until the day I ceased to exist!" She snatched her hand out of Levi's, turned her back, and callously walked away, leaving him completely alone in his most shattered vulnerable moment ... just as he had done with their daughter.

Maya's words and actions were the equivalent to a scorching dagger through Levi's already broken heart. Still on his knees, he shamefully lowered his head in defeat and let her walk away without another word.

Maya briskly made her way out of the barn to escape Levi. The earlier sprinkle was now a torrential downpour. In Maya's mind, the storm seemed to be the perfect metaphor for all that had just escalated between her and Levi. Finally saying things to him that she had held onto, since the dark day he had taken Lily, had completely blown open the floodgates of her emotions. Instead of running to get out of the storm, she tilted her head back, attempting to let the sheets of water wash away her gushing tears. However, the powerful weather system had no effect on the emotional storm inside her body. It had all caused a resurgence of bitter pain that began to weaken her. Before her legs gave out, she quickly made her way across the muddy field and into her cottage. Shivering and soaked, she collapsed in a heap on her bed. The booming sound of earthmoving thunder drowned out the sounds of her heavy sobs, as she lay curled up in the fetal position. She wept with body-convulsing force, feeling as though her tears would never cease this time.

Maya eventually cried herself into a deep sleep. She woke up at dawn with swollen eyes, a raw throat, and a stomach that hurt from hours of crying. After hearing a low rumble of thunder, she glanced out the window at the slow-moving storm system that was still lingering above the farm. She felt that the gloom of the storm precisely matched how she was feeling internally. She was laying there feeling blanketed in heavy guilt. After purging her anger the evening before, she now realized just how disgusting the things were that she had said to Levi. It was not like her to be so cruel. She had unleashed the monster inside her that had fed off years of anger, a monster that grew to want to viciously hurt Levi as badly as he had hurt her. Just like Levi too, though, Maya now regretted her actions. However, she did not want to wait fourteen years to make amends for her mistake.

As Maya summoned the strength to get out of bed, she searched her mind for the right words to apologize to Levi. Just as she sat up, the dim light of the sun broke through the storm clouds. It lit up her room enough for her to suddenly notice two things laying on a table near the door. She was certain they were not there the morning before when she left to start her workday. Curiosity immediately gave her the strength to stand and walk over to the table. Her emotions began to surge again when she realized what she was looking at. The telescope she had destroyed was now laying there in pristine, refurbished condition. The handmade music box that she had thrown at Levi and broken was now back in one piece too. Levi had restored it to pristine condition as well. Maya opened the lid and was warmed by the sight of the tiny figurines of her and Levi, once again, dancing gracefully to the beautiful song that he had written for her. Maya could have gazed at their toy replicas for hours, but her focus suddenly shifted to a new sentimental detail that Levi had affixed inside the lid: a miniature copy of his favorite picture of Lily, smiling at birds while on her mother's lap. After mercilessly crying for hours, Maya thought her body had not a drop of tears left. But the gifts in her hands quickly proved her wrong. The return of her sentimental treasures further proved the authenticity of Levi's regret and guilt, as well as his love. As moving as the gifts were, though, none of them would mean as much to Maya as what she truly wanted. The only sacred, sentimental gift that could mend the hole in her soul sat smiling at birds in the picture she could not stop staring at. Tears of joy continued to careen down Maya's cheeks when she thought about the fact that Levi was now promising to bring that very miracle back into her life.

The gifts in her hands made Maya's regret for her nasty words elevate tenfold. She could now see with clarity that Levi was sincere in his desire to finally atone for his dastardly act. She now wanted to atone for hers. She gazed at the picture of her and Lily for a final time and carefully set it back down. She then hastily stepped out into the pouring rain to look for Levi. On his most emotionally draining days, she always knew just where to find him. Just before she reached the barn door, though, Maya once again tilted her head back and let the sheets of rain cleanse her, much like her tears just had. For the first time in years, she looked forward to the moment the storm passed, and the skies cleared. Just the thought of seeing Lily again already made her want to smile as broadly as the rainbow she was convinced would soon stretch across the clear blue sky. With the way it was pouring outside, it seemed that moment would never come quickly enough, nor could the moment she saw her daughter again.

When a booming rumble of thunder rocked the earth beneath Maya's feet, her eyes suddenly shot wide open and her head quickly swiveled toward the barn door. However, it was not the sky's wrath that had jolted her from being cleansed by the earth's tears. The sound she thought she heard, intertwined with the rain and thunder, had triggered her heart to thump with force, her breathing to quicken, and her skin to go even colder than it already was. For a moment, she stood there frozen, trying to force herself to believe that the sound was nothing more than the powerful rumblings of lightning's aftermath. But her pounding heart knew better.

Breathing heavily, Maya approached and opened the barn door. She barely peeked her head inside. "Levi?" she called out softly, her voice quivering. Trembling, she hesitantly took a step inside. She saw and heard nothing other than spooked horses neighing. "Levi?" she called out again, as she cautiously began searching the barn. Left and right, she turned her head as she walked by each horse stall. She turned to her right as she passed by the fifth. When she looked down, both her knees instantly gave out. Maya swore she was falling in slow motion. As she collapsed to the ground, the world went completely silent in her mind. However, the animals around her could attest differently; the sound of Levi's name escaping Maya's mouth in a high-pitched, shrill scream nearly shattered all their eardrums.

The evening before, it was Levi who had been on his knees begging Maya for forgiveness. Now, it was *Maya* who was suddenly collapsed on *her* knees begging *him* in return. She begged him to get up, despite knowing full well he was incapable of even hearing her. The piercing green eyes that had watched her and worshiped her for years were now fixed on her in an eternal gaze, without an ounce of life left in them.

Maya scooped Levi up into her arms, brought him close to her chest, and began rocking back and forth with him. "What've I done?!" she shrieked repeatedly. For minutes, Maya wept uncontrollably, wailing, and bathing Levi in her tears. While violently weeping, she gazed back into the lifeless eyes of the man who had miraculously blessed her with a child. While thinking of the special place he held in her heart for such a miracle, Maya slowed her rocking motions and placed a kiss on Levi's forehead. "I l-love y-you," she whispered, confessing when it was far too late for Levi to appreciate words he had longed to hear for years. "I f-forgive y-you," she then whispered repeatedly, sincerely stating a phrase that she was convinced would have prevented the massive hole that Levi Collins had just blown into his own skull.

Despite hearing a noise behind her, Maya refused to stop gazing at Levi. She did not even budge when she saw a set of shoes in front of her. As it turned out, Maya was not the only one who had realized the error of their ways. Much like Maya, it had only taken Wyatt a few hours to admit to himself how wrong he was to have spoken to his father the way he had. The shock of his father's revelations had led him to say things that he regretted. He was sick to his stomach over how disrespectful he had been to a man who had made such major sacrifices for him and his brothers. After a sleepless night, he had headed to his father's plantation, wanting to offer a sincere apology and his assistance in finding Lily ... two things that he was now realizing he would never be able to do.

Embedded with the sound of thunder and rain, Wyatt had heard wailing coming from the barn as he approached it. He mistook it for a slave giving birth, one on the verge of dying in the process. He went to offer his assistance, hoping to help a life enter the world. Instead, he found that his beloved father had just left it, in the most tragic of ways. Wyatt now towered above Maya, staring down at his father in a wide-eyed trance, feeling as though a bullet had just pierced him too. He was instantly in shock, so much so that he was unable to cry. His mouth agape, he just stood there paralyzed, inhaling and exhaling in short bursts, as if his body was fighting to remember how to breathe.

"Get out," Wyatt whispered to Maya when he finally got his brain to remember how to conjure up words.

Maya finally managed to pull her eyes away from Levi and raise her head. "W-Wyatt. Please, I..."

"I SAID GET OUT!"

"Please, I didn't…"

"NOOOW!"

Despite feeling completely numb, Maya got her legs to comply and she quickly scrambled away. Wyatt's legs, in turn, gave out from beneath him. He momentarily remained on his knees, trying to convince himself that he was trapped in a gruesome dream. When he finally accepted the fact that there was no waking from this nightmare, he collapsed onto his father's body and began weeping uncontrollably.

****

Unable to come to terms with his epic failure as a son, Wyatt was virtually crippled in the days after his father's funeral. He felt it would be impossible to forgive himself for the fact that the last words to his father were some of the most godawful, venomous statements any son could ever make to a father whose expressions of love had *always* been unwavering. Wyatt was so devastated that he remained confined to his room for days. He would not bathe, work, nor speak to anyone. He lay in bed all day with alcohol as his only sustenance, having constant thoughts of ending it all himself. When he was not chugging whiskey, he laid there looking like an asylum patient trapped in a catatonic state. He simply could not bring himself to get out of bed, until his wife came into the room one afternoon. She sat down beside him, handed him a glass of water, and a piece of mail that had been buried amongst piles of sympathy letters from friends and family. Wyatt was content to ignore the letter until his wife showed him who it was from. The name in the return address section made him immediately sit up and open the letter. After reading the contents inside, he quickly got out of bed, got dressed, and left the house for the first time in days.

With letter in hand, Wyatt hesitantly entered the rundown building where his father had taken his last breath. Flashbacks of his father's dead body brought forth an immediate surge of tears the moment he opened the barn doors. He could hardly bring himself to step inside, but he forced himself to endure the torture because of the contents in his hands. Following the instructions on the letter, he shoveled away the hay in the fifth horse stall and unburied the secret compartment underneath. With one of the two keys that were included with the letter, he unlocked the padlock on the compartment door and opened it. He dragged out the trunk inside and unlocked the padlock with the second key. He opened the lid, and his eyes were greeted by a tiny pink baby blanket that covered an array of items underneath.

Levi had been drinking heavily before his suicide. His body was surrounded by empty liquor bottles. The liquor in his veins made it far easier for him to give in to the urge to instantly halt years of internal pain. Before taking his life, though, he had spent hours preparing and mailing the keys and detailed letter that had guided Wyatt to the very spot he was crouched in now. The keys literally unlocked two decades of secrets, containing a plethora of important documents, pictures of Lily and Maya, Lily's baby blanket, and other memorabilia from their lives. Recently added to the stockpile were brief letters to each of his sons, expressing his love, apologies, and begging once again for their forgiveness and understanding. Also included were the manumission papers for all his slaves, another copy of his divorce papers, and a freshly scripted will for Wyatt to execute.

For countless hours, Wyatt sat against the horse stall wall going through the trunk and reading contents that had him bawling like a baby all over again. But it was not the divorce papers, the will, nor even the letter his father had written to him that had him so overwhelmed with emotion.

... Over several days, Lily sat in James's arms near William's lake, completely riveted by all the journals that had her eldest brother in such a debilitated state five years prior. To learn of the incredible love story between her mother and father was indeed the wild emotional ride that James had warned. In more moments than she had anticipated, Lily paused reading, laid her head on James's chest, and wept uncontrollably over the astounding revelations in her father's journals. She cried tears of joy as she read the beautiful words that her father had scripted about her birth. She lit up with a smile as she learned why Griff's nickname for her triggered the memory of her and her father at the apple tree. Four times, Lily read the passage about the song her birth had inspired her father to compose. In fact, she had to read all the passages about her father's musical abilities again and over again. Her eyes, her heart, and her soul had to absorb it several times before she could truly believe that she had inherited her incredible gift from him. The fact that she had never even been privy to the fact that he played piano seemed to prove that she indeed knew nothing about the gifted and loving man that Levi Collins truly was.

With every page Lily turned, she felt more and more confident that her father truly loved her. The strength of his love emanating from the pages was like a healing potion for her broken heart. What astounded her most, though, was the feeling of love that she found growing for her father in return. It made the very last passage he ever wrote, nearly impossible to read. Much like Wyatt, Lily was barely able to make out the sentences through the sea of tears in her eyes, as she read the last page of her father's words aloud:

February 26th, 1859

I am a failure. I failed at marriage. I failed at music. I failed at being an example of an upstanding man of honor for my sons. I failed the only woman I have ever truly loved. I failed at loving Maya the way she deserved. I failed at healing her heart, revitalizing her jubilance, and giving her a reason to smile at her precious rainbows again. But by far, my most epic failure was in being the loving, protective father I should have been to my only daughter. I have even failed at my mission to find her.

For weeks, I searched for my beautiful Lily. I wanted to bring her home to her mother where she belongs. I've been desperate to return happiness to her and her mother's lives. For over a decade, I've been dreaming of the moment they would see each other again. To see their joyous tears as they embraced would have instantly ceased this pain in my heart for an eternity. I know that no grand gesture or passionate, poetic words could ever make up for my betrayal fourteen years ago. But still, I wanted so badly to tell Lily how very sorry I am for what I did to her. I was ready to spend the rest of my natural life proving that fact to her and her mother, not just with words, but with my actions. I wanted Lily to know that there has not been a single minute of my day, for the last fourteen years, that I have not thought about her. I wanted to tell her that I have missed her more than my words could adequately convey. I have prayed that there would come a day when she would sit with me on the porch and let me share with her my fondest memories of her as a child. I longed to share with her the way that I was literally brought to my knees with joy the moment I learned of her existence. I wanted to tell her how my heart swelled with pride and my eyes flooded with tears the moment I first held her in my arms. Selfishly, I hoped maybe one day Lily would consider forgiving me, and that we might have some semblance of the father-daughter relationship I had always craved to have with her. I would have felt so honored to one day walk her down the aisle and dance with her at her wedding. I would have loved to spoil any beautiful grandchildren she gave me with lots of candy, handmade toys, and adventurous trips. I would have loved to introduce Lily to the piano, play songs with her side by side, and perhaps grow to have a shared love of music with her. I know such things were likely impossible dreams, but I dreamed them, nonetheless. At the very least, I wanted to tell my sweet Lily that I have prayed for her every single day, asking the Lord to give her the extraordinary life that I failed to give her. But what I've prayed for, most of all, was for the chance to finally look my only daughter in the eyes and tell her that I love her more than anything that God has ever created. But I have failed. Despite my efforts, I have been unable to find my little flower, convey these things to her, and return her to her mother where she belongs.

I still wish for these dreams to come to fruition. But I have no help. I'm overwhelmed. And I don't know where to even begin looking for her again. But, if I'm being honest, there's a part of me that is far too riddled with fear to carry on searching. I fear I will spend years searching only to find that Lily's master truly did take her life. I cannot possibly conceive of facing Maya with such crippling news. In fact, I'm certain that I would not be able to face her at all. Because, Emily is right. I would only have my two hands to blame for Lily's demise. Wyatt is also right. I would absolutely deserve to live with the agony of causing her death. But the excruciating pain of such a monumental failure is something I simply cannot live with.

Funny, I have played countless piano show finales throughout my life. But, ironically, the very moment I finish scripting these words and close this book, I suppose I will truly be performing the ultimate grand finale, one that I will not receive a standing ovation for but, rather, one I pray God will forgive me for.

Lily closed the last journal, buried her face in her hands, and wept over the loss of her father, as if she was there watching him pull the trigger. James gathered her in his arms, laid his head on top of hers and held her tight. The length and strength with which she wept stirred his tears as well. For minutes, there were no words spoken, only a sea of tears shed while Lily was consoled by the man who loved her.

The fact that Levi would do such a thing was rock solid proof to Lily as to how truly remorseful he was for his actions. "I wish he was still here," she whispered after wrangling her emotions. "I swear I felt that he loved me when I's a child. He neva' said it … but I felt it. Just by the way he'd look at me sometimes, and the way he'd smile back when I smiled at 'em. It was like he was sayin' it with his eyes, and that crooked grin of his." Lily managed a brief smile over the memory. "But I dismissed it all afta' he sold me. Figured maybe it was just my imagination runnin' away with me."

James lightly tapped the journal in her hand. "These books prove that what you felt was real."

Lily nodded as she wiped her tears. "Not a doubt in my mind about that now."

James reached in his satchel. "I'm sure your fatha' would love for you to have these too," he said as he handed her five more journals.

"There's more to read?" Lily asked, sounding surprised.

James nodded. "But they're written in a language only your brilliant mind can interpret," he said, gently kissing her on the temple.

Lily looked a little confused by his statement, until she opened to the first page of one of the journals. Another wave of emotion hit her when her eyes were met with the sight of bars and bars of musical notes. With a smile suddenly illuminating her face, she flipped through page after page of music that her father had composed. In her excitement, she was quickly turning the pages, but suddenly stopped on a song entitled, "The Goddess of Spring." Curiously, her eyes scanned each bar of the melody. Within seconds, tears began coursing down her cheeks, as the piano inside her brilliant mind played the song from her mother's music box. As she listened to the melody in her head, her mind flashed back to the way she had danced with her mother to that song as a small child. The true identity of the figurines, and the song's composer, now elevated the sentimental value of her cherished memory tenfold. That fond memory had led Lily to incorporate the snippet of that song into the first musical piece she had ever composed at eleven years old. Her tears now dotted the complete original version.

In the third music journal, Lily found "A Beautiful Miracle," the song Levi had mentioned writing for her in one of his journals. After months of humming the tune in his head, Levi had solidified the melody in pen. As Lily's mind now replayed a song that her birth had inspired, she wept tears that tasted as if they had come from her very soul. Levi's music journals held hundreds of other songs. Lily felt as though she was taking a walk inside the artistic world of her father's mind, as she effortlessly comprehended the melodies he had composed. Some, he had actually played on the piano. But most, he had only heard in his mind as he sat writing alone in the barn late nights, needing a way to escape the miserable moments of his life.

"I wish I could've heard 'em play all of these," Lily said when she finished skimming through Levi's music. She looked over at all his diaries. "I just wish I'd've known *all* these things about 'em before he … be-before he…" She shook her head, trying to ward off another surge of tears. "I just can't believe he's gone," she whispered, lowering her head as her tears fell yet again.

"My fatha's cruelty neva' ceases to amaze me," James replied. "Makes me wish he ceased to exist long before your fatha' eva' encountered 'em. Your fatha' was already a tortured man. I know firsthand what it does to a man not to be with the love of his life, and to be deprived of havin' your precious little girl in your life. It'll leave a man on the verge of losin' his mind. My fatha's heartless lies were the last thing Levi needed to hear while he was already danglin' on the edge of insanity."

"Seems there was nobody to pull my fatha' back."

James shook his head. "Seems my fatha' helped push 'em instead. I'm terribly sorry for that."

"Thank you for that. But my fatha' made his own decisions. He made his mistakes, and he chose not to live with 'em. I wish he'd chosen differently, but I can certainly unda'stand how the torture of his mistakes were far too much to take."

"That's the part about 'em that inspired me, actually. His mistakes and his faults. He inspired me to always figure out a way to pull *myself* back from the edge of insanity, no matta' what's pushin' me. He made me wanna always fight to give you the life you deserve. He inspired me to neva' eva' let society convince me not to love you the way you deserved eitha'. And I'd've neva' given up searchin' for you."

Lily lightly kissed James on the lips in response to his words. She then melted into his embrace as his arms tightened around her. "I still can't believe he came back for me," she whispered.

"And judgin' by the date, it seems we must've just missed 'em by a few days."

"Or maybe even hours," Lily replied, not knowing how right she was.

James nodded. "Such a coincidence seems more proof that God had much bigga' plans for the musical gift He blessed you with."

Lily glanced down at her father's journal and shook her head, still in disbelief. "Musical gifts that God had given to my fatha' first."

"Gave me chills when I first learned that. Pretty damn incredible, isn't it?"

Lily nodded, her tears still slowly subsiding. "That's an unda'statement," she sniffled. "Every word in these journals still has me absolutely astonished. I can still hardly believe any of it." Lily turned to the first passage Levi wrote about Maya. "He loved my motha' so much."

James gently turned Lily toward him. "And you too," he said, pressing his lips to her forehead. "Seems he loves our little Rose just as much."

"Rose?" Lily questioned, looking puzzled by his statement.

"I saw her." James suddenly had a distant look in his eyes as his mind drifted away. "On the battlefield."

Lily still looked perplexed.

"When my brotha' put this hole in my leg, I thought it was the end for me, Lily. I felt my body slowly shuttin' down. I closed my eyes and accepted my fate. I laid there prayin' to God to forgive me for my sins. I begged Him to allow me into his kingdom, so I could hold my little Rose again for an eternity."

Lily wiped away a tear as it fell down James's cheek. "It's okay," she whispered.

"Right there layin' in the middle of that bloody battlefield … God answered my prayers. I opened my eyes, and all the blood, the carnage, the dead bodies, the excruciatin' pain in my leg … it was all gone," James continued. "The sound of cannons and gunfire were suddenly replaced with laughta'. The sweetest, most innocent laughta' I've eva' heard. But nothin' was sweeta' than what I heard next …"

"What?" Lily asked, completely engrossed in the story.

"*Daddy*," James replied, emotion causing his voice to crack. "I fell to my knees with joy when I saw who was boundin' toward me screamin' that word ova' and ova' again," he smiled, his tears now trickling faster.

"Rose?" Lily whispered, her tears now falling again too.

James nodded. "She jumped into my arms and wrapped her arms around me with all the force her little muscles could muster."

Lily squeezed James's hand tighter and smiled over the way he was smiling at the memory.

"People may dismiss me as insane or claim that moment was an elaborate dream. But nobody can convince me that what I experienced that day wasn't real. I still rememba' how soft Rose's little finga's were when she hugged my neck. I can still hear the sound of her innocent voice and recall the texture of her soft, curly hair. It was real, Lily. There's no doubt in my mind that I was holdin' our daughta' again."

"I believe you," Lily replied, looking him in the eyes.

James nodded in appreciation. "If it wasn't for the fact that I wanted to get a good look at 'er, I would've neva' put 'er down," he smiled. "She looked to be about four-years-old. And she was indeed the little replica of you that I'd prayed for. She was so beautiful." James caressed Lily's cheek. "Just like 'er mama."

Lily smiled as butterflies fluttered through her stomach.

"Like I's some kind of dunce stuck in a trance, I just stood there starin' at 'er, completely speechless, just holdin' her little hand," James continued. "I should've been the one comfortin' her, but she was suddenly the one comfortin' me with 'er words."

"What'd she say?" Lily smiled.

"She told me not to worry about 'er …'cause 'er *grandpa's* takin' good care of 'er. I's confused at first. I thought she was talkin' about *my* fatha'. But then she explained that it was…"

"*My* fatha'," Lily whispered.

James nodded. "Rose said he dances with 'er, reads to 'er, teaches 'er to fish, pushes her on the swings. Hell, he even built 'er a treehouse!" he exclaimed, shaking his head.

Lily laughed lightly.

"She said your fatha's even teachin' 'er to play piano. It seems all the things he wanted to do for you, he's doin' for *grandpa's girl*, as Rose said he calls 'er."

"*Grandpa's girl*," Lily whispered, the term causing a grand smile to illuminate on her face.

James nodded. "And she said that your music makes your fatha' cry..."

Lily suddenly looked at James with shock in her eyes.

"Because he thinks it's so beautiful," he explained, caressing her cheek.

Lily lowered her head and broke down in joyous tears again. "He can hear me?" she whispered.

James nodded. "Auntie, Mr. Ben, and Ms. Anna Mae. Rose said they're all there with 'er, and they *all* think your music is beautiful ... and so does my motha'."

"Your motha' too?" Lily tearfully whispered.

The thought stirred James's tears again. "She said my motha' makes 'er dresses and fixes 'er hair up real pretty all the time. Rose said she tells her all the stories about you and me as kids. Said my motha' even knew all along that we used to run off and play togetha' in the woods ... even knew that I loved you back then."

Lily smiled as her euphoric tears continued to flow down her cheeks.

"There's one otha' thing Rose told me that I've been wantin' to ask you about."

"What's that?"

"She said she wanted to hear your music, but that you wouldn't play anymore without me." He took Lily by the hand. "Is that true?"

The look of astonishment on Lily's face quickly answered his question. "Furtha' proof that you really did hold our baby girl that day," she whispered.

"No doubt about that now for sure."

"Our little Rose is right where she's supposed to be, ain't she?"

James nodded. "I believe that with all my heart. That fact brings me total peace."

"Me too." Lily slowly looked around the picnic blanket at the children's books her father had bought her, the pictures of her and her mother, and all the other trinkets that were symbols of her father's love. "All of this brings me peace, actually," she said. "It hurts to know that my fatha' is gone. But you were right. All of this has brought so much closure. Wounds I thought would neva' close are now healed completely."

"I'm happy to hear that ... and your brotha's would be too. That's *exactly* what they were hopin' for."

"You think so?"

"I know so." James reached into his satchel and pulled out an envelope. "This was the message that your brotha's literally held a gun to my head and demanded I give you," he said, now able to laugh at the memory.

"Good lord! Guess they know how to ensure their demands are met," Lily joked.

"The urine runnin' down my naked legs was proof that it worked," James joked in return.

Lily doubled over laughing. When her laughter settled, she took the envelope from James's hand. She squinted her eyes, trying to make out the two faded words on the outside of the envelope. "For Lily," she read aloud. She then took out the tattered, four-year-old letter inside and began to read it aloud as well:

Lily,

If you're reading this letter, then you have likely already experienced the same shock as my brothers and me when we first read my father's journals. But if you're anything like your mother, I know for a fact that you have a rock-solid inner strength that will help you overcome the things you've read. And if ever your strength should falter, I'm certain that the honorable man who handed you this letter will help see you through the emotional whirlwind created by our father's true life story.

The stories in his journals impacted all of us boys hard at first. But his writings answered one of the things we had always been the most baffled by: why he was never the same again after the day he sold you. Seems we not only lost you that day, but we lost our father as well. He went inside himself and was a completely different man altogether. A man who once took pride in interacting with us boys at dinner barely raised his head enough to chew his food after that day. From that day on, he seemed to only ever speak when it was absolutely necessary. He developed a distaste for the piano, for church, and for life as a whole. Despite our father's anguish, he mustered the strength to fulfill his obligations to us boys and to love us in the best way he knew how. But we could still tell that it seemed his soul had suddenly been stripped away. We just never understood exactly why. After reading his journals, we now know that it was not his soul that was gone. It was you. It seems they may as well have been one and the same.

Even after me and my brothers put the pieces of our father's life puzzle together, we had a hard time swallowing the truth. I hope you can understand how the shock of these revelations caused my inner foundation to crumble. Our father asked me to be the executor of his estate upon his passing. But I was so angry that I simply could not bring myself to honor his wishes. It took me a long time to come to terms with the fact that the man I knew was an illusion. But I now realize that the only thing that mattered was the fact that his love for us boys was no illusion. Any coldness that he showed you, though, was. That is actually the main reason why my brothers and I decided to pass these gifts and journals on to you. I know some of the content was difficult to read, but we wanted you to know the beautiful parts embedded in between the madness.

You see, my brothers and I had the great fortune of having a father who told us and showed us every day how much he loved us. You, unfortunately, had to live your whole life deprived of that beautiful emotional experience. My brothers and I wish we had the power to turn back the hands of time to allow you to experience your childhood with a loving father, doting on you the way you deserve. Since we lack such God-like powers, we figured the stories about you in our father's journal were the closest we could get you to knowing the feeling of being embraced by our father's warmth, kindness, and especially his love. We know that nothing will ever be a true substitute for the reality of that experience firsthand. But we hoped that at least now, on some small scale, you can feel the warmth, kindness, and love of our father, <u>your</u> father, embracing you tightly. The decision to do this was especially easy when we considered that it was our father's dying wish to tell his only daughter, our only sister, how much she truly meant to him. We all now want you to know how much you mean to us as well.

Much like our father, I have seven children of my own. Six boys and now finally one precious little girl. It only took me looking into the eyes of my own newborn daughter to realize how the mere thought of losing her would make me feel that I, too, had been stripped bare of my soul. Her birth instantly put into perspective how pure my father's love for you must have been. So, as the executor of his estate, I am now honored to pass on to you more proof of how sincere his love for you was. His land, his home, and everything in it were left to you and Maya. So, too, was every penny of his savings and his life insurance. Per my father's request, I have officially submitted your mother's manumission papers. She is now free, just as he wanted. Perhaps it was clear from his journals that he wanted to buy you back and manumit you as soon as he was legally able to do so. That fact was restated in his will. Most importantly, he wanted you and your mother reunited. So, if ever you choose to return, please know that you and Maya have a home here to live in <u>together</u>. My brothers and I feel that you and Maya rightfully deserve these things, and we are now happy to pass them all on to you. Everything here is yours ... and so, too, is your freedom.

Though these material things will never replace the love that our father deprived you of, it is the least he could do to atone for all the injustices he committed against you and your mother. I am so sorry that it took my brothers and me a long time to reconcile these truths. We understand that it may take you even longer, or perhaps never. At the very least, we are hoping you will accept these tokens of his love that he has left for you. With his dying wishes now fulfilled, I hope our father's heart and soul will finally be settled, and that he can now truly rest in peace. We hope that you, too, can one day find some semblance of peace with the past and maybe, just maybe, find the strength to forgive him.

PS. In these journals, my father wrote that you were the most adorable of his brood. After looking at these pictures, I'm afraid I have to agree with his assessment. You were an awfully cute little baby. And you clearly grew up to be just as beautiful, talented, and as special as he had predicted.

With Love,

Your oldest brother, Wyatt

Love ya sis,

Your big brother, Colt

With love!

Your brother, Lucas

Love ya' Lily
Your brother, Bo

Love you little sister
Your big brother, Dylan

With love,
Your little brother,
Dallas (hope to catch lizards with you again one day!)

In the midst of her tears soaking the pages of the letter in her hand, Lily heard her name called from behind her. Startled, she and James both turned to find Isabel towering above them, seeming to have quietly appeared out of nowhere.

Lily could tell by the somber tone in her voice and the brimming tears in her eyes that something was wrong. "Isabel, what is it?" she asked, her heart racing after seeing the sullen look on her face. "Is it William?!" She sprang to her feet. "Is it William?" she asked again, knowing he had not been well as of late.

Isabel swallowed hard. "Just please. We need you inside," she replied as a tear slid down her cheek.

Without another word, Lily and James both hurried into the house.

Chapter Thirty-two

William had his back to Lily as he stared at the double doors of his library. The doors were closed. But, still, he just stood there staring at them as if in a trance. Even when he felt Lily's presence behind him, he did not turn to look at her.

"William? Are you alright?" Lily asked, approaching him cautiously.

He did not speak until Lily was standing beside him, staring at the profile of his face. "When I found you, I remember you telling me that you felt as though you didn't know who Lily was anymore," William responded. He finally turned to look at her.

Lily lowered her head shamefully. "Yessa'. That's the truth."

William took one of her hands in his. "Well, I wanted to introduce you to her again." He turned and opened the massive double doors to his library and escorted her inside. "*This,*" William said, gesturing with his hand held out in front of him, "is who you are."

The visual that William had motioned his hand toward nearly stole Lily's breath. She refused to blink as she absorbed the sight of beautiful dancing shadows, a dragon, a knight, an ethereal floating angel, the student orchestra, and William Werthington. In the center of them all was the composer of that grand show, seated on her instrumental throne in vivid color. Musical Dreams, the one-of-a-kind masterpiece that Piers LeRoux had created in honor of The Dream Symphony, now hung above the fireplace of William's library. On

649

nearly every shelf around it were framed ticket stubs, newspapers, and pictures from that groundbreaking year of Lily's life.

"William," Lily whispered when she was finally able to catch her breath enough speak.

William took Lily by the hand, walked closer to the portrait, and gazed at it along with her. "Meek, shivering, submissive, unsure of yourself, cloaked in heavy layers of fear, seemingly content to remain invisible for the duration of your life." William turned toward Lily. "That was my first impression of you. But it wasn't long after spending time with you that I realized that those things did not truly define you. Those things were what the world *expected* you to be. It was the *world* that had cloaked you in those filthy layers. It was the *world* expecting you to remain invisible. Those who expected that from you, had driven their expectations so deep into your psyche that even you began to believe that that's who you were ... meek, submissive, and only meant to be in the shadows. But, day by day, these old eyes of mine had the honor of watching you slowly shed every filthy layer ever laid upon you. I watched you step out from beneath the darkness and bathe in the sunlight where you belonged. I watched you crawl, then walk, then run, until you gained the strength and confidence to become like an unstoppable steam train. I must say, I've travelled the world and have been blessed to see a great many things over my lifetime. But watching you during that magnificent year of your life, as you morphed into the accomplished woman you were born to be, has been far and away the most inspiring thing these old eyes have ever witnessed."

Lily thought she had not a tear left after her emotional day, but William's words easily tapped into the well of her emotions and had them flowing once again.

William sighed. "But now, for reasons beyond your control, that steam train has derailed. After everything you've been through over the last few years, I do not blame you for feeling lost, confused, and for questioning the purpose of your life once again … and for questioning who you really are. And so, I had hoped that this portrait could be a reminder that there was once a time when the world had beat you down, buried you under layers of oppression, and forced you to live far beneath human standards. But despite all the hell you'd been put through in your past, you were fearless enough to crawl out of subhuman conditions and let who you really were inside emerge. Night after night, you shined on stages like this one, and became the Lily that the masses grew to respect … and to love."

William turned toward the portrait again. "The composer of this mystical symphony moved seas of people to tears, moved stubborn men to break down barriers on your behalf, and completely annihilated an old man's incessant thoughts of suicide after losing his wife," William solemnly confessed, momentarily lowering his head. He looked up again at the portrait. "And she even moved genius artists to create awe-inspiring masterpieces." He took both of Lily's hands and looked her in the eyes. "*That* is who Lily Adams is." He gently touched Lily's tearful face. "She's still in there, maybe a little lost and afraid. But I promise I will expend every last breath in my old body to help you find the courage to let her emerge once again."

"And so will I."

Lily turned around to meet the face of the person who had just uttered that promise. An explosion of tears instantly erupted from her eyes. "Somebody pl-please convince m-me that I ain't hallucinatin'."

Maya stepped forward and gently touched her daughter's face. "I'm here, Lily," she whispered tearfully. "I'm here," she said again as she embraced her only child.

Lily was far too overcome with emotion to verbally respond. But the way she wept in her mother's arms said enough. Everyone surrounding them fought their own swell of emotions as the pair silently conveyed their love for one another. A sudden fear made Lily reluctant to let her mother go on this occasion. "H-How long do I have with you?" Lily asked, wanting to keep her expectations at bay this time.

Her mother opened her mouth to speak but was interrupted before she could say a word.

"She's here for good this time."

Lily glanced over her mother's shoulder and looked in the doorway at the man who responded. He then walked over and took her by the hand. "She ain't goin' anywhere this time, Lily. I swear that on my fatha's soul," Wyatt expressed with a tone of honorable sincerity.

Lily nodded as tears of appreciation streamed down her cheek. "Thank you," she whispered, squeezing his hand in return.

James looked over at Wyatt and nodded, silently conveying his appreciation for responding to the letter he had written to him days ago. His letter was simple and straight to the point:

Wyatt Collins,

I have found your sister. She is safe. As promised, I have passed on everything that you and your brothers wished for her to have.

It seems we are all in consensus that Lily was deprived of her father's love. For far too many years, she has also been deprived of her mother's. It is my sincerest hope that you and your brothers will be willing to remedy such a tragedy, as soon as is possible, by bringing Maya here to our residence at Werthington Estate in Athens, Ohio. Your reply to this matter will be greatly anticipated.

James Adams

Wyatt's reply was just as simple:

James Adams,

Honoring our father's dream of reuniting Maya and Lily has been long overdue. Our arrival time at the Athens' train station is scheduled for this Saturday afternoon at 2:30pm. Transportation from the train station to your residence would be appreciated. I look forward to seeing my sister again. I'm confident Maya is too.

Sincerely,

Wyatt Collins

James had received that letter via Pony express just days earlier. He shared the news with William. The very second William finished reading it, preparation for their arrival began. For days, Lily had been so engrossed in her father's journals that the library transformation and the preparation for her mother's arrival had all taken place without her noticing a thing. While James was sure to keep Lily occupied out by the lake, Isabel and Ryla were in the midst of preparing a special dinner, the twins were hard at work preparing Maya's room, and Griff had polished his carriage, groomed his horses, and headed to pick up Maya and Wyatt from the train station. Despite being slightly under the weather, William waited proudly on the porch, ready to welcome Lily's mother with open arms. Wyatt never uttered a word to Maya about their destination. He had simply helped her pack all her belongings and boarded a train with her bound for Athens, Ohio. The way Wyatt struggled to hide his joy during their trip hinted to Maya where she may be headed. But she kept her expectations at bay. On Isabel's cue, Maya quietly entered William's library to finally see with her own eyes that her suspicions about Wyatt's joy were accurate.

The joy Wyatt felt was magnified by a million inside Lily the moment she embraced her mother. After thanking Wyatt for bringing her, Lily walked over to the man she knew deserved the rest of the credit for yet another magnificent surprise in her life. "You and your grand gestures," she said to James, as she placed her hand in his.

"I just don't eva' feel completely settled inside until I fulfill my promises to you. I'm only eva' at peace when I know you are, too, Miss Lily."

"That's one thing on a looong list of reasons why I love you as much as I do, James Adams," she said, kissing him lightly on the lips. "Thank you," she whispered.

"It's an honor," he whispered back.

Lily then turned in a circle to look at all of the amazing people in her life. "Thank you to all of you …" She took her mother by the hand. "For welcomin' my mama home."

William walked up and held Maya's other hand. "And anyone making this place feel like anything less than your home will have to answer to me," he teased, evoking light laughter from everyone.

"I can assure you that's nothin' you'll eva' have to worry about around here, mama," Lily replied.

"I thank you all for makin' me feel so welcome here," Maya smiled.

James hobbled over on his cane and hugged Maya. "Glad to have you here. It's so wonderful to see you again."

"You too, sweetheart," she replied, reciprocating his hug.

"I'm quite sure you two have lots of catchin' up to do, so we'll leave you to it," James told her.

Maya nodded.

Lily then took her mother by the hand again. "C'mon mama, I'll show you around," she smiled.

After watching the pair walk out of the library, Wyatt turned to James. "I'll take that beer now," he said, recalling that James had offered him one the first time he had brought Maya to see Lily. His sarcasm was a peace offering for their contentious interaction that night.

James smiled and patted him on the shoulder. "I think that can be arranged."

Wyatt followed behind James as he hobbled out of the library toward the kitchen. As they headed there, a delivery sitting in the foyer suddenly stopped James in his tracks. Wyatt froze too, looking puzzled by the strange look on James's face. William walked up behind James as he stared at the new portrait of Emma that Piers LeRoux had duplicated. As James gazed at it, he had an instantaneous flashback of the older woman from the cabin, who had accompanied him to church.

"You look like you've seen a ghost," William joked, after noticing the bewildered look on James's face.

"More like an angel," James murmured, still gazing at Emma's picture with a perplexed look on his face. "What did your students call your wife, William?"

"I'm confident you already know the answer to that," William said, patting James on the back. With a grand smile on his face, he then walked away. When Emerson and Wilson returned home from the war, they both separately told their father that their mother had sat vigilantly beside them during times they were sick. By the look on

James's face, William was convinced that Emma had indeed been a guardian angel to him in his time of need as well.

I've been hangin' around here for years. I'm certain you've seen me before, James recalled her saying. "She damn sho' wasn't lyin'," he whispered, laughing lightly. "Thank you, Miss Em."

"What?" Wyatt said, confused by the entire situation.

"Nothin'. Let's grab those beers. I think I *definitely* need one now," James said.

Wyatt shrugged and continued following him to the kitchen.

After filling their cups with Irish ale, James and Wyatt stepped out onto the back porch. They both leaned on the railing with beers in hand, looking out at Maya and Lily walking arm in arm in the distance.

"I finally get a chance to thank you for what you did to get me outta that prison," James said. "Still can't believe you had me runnin' through those woods ass naked, though," James joked.

Wyatt started laughing so hard he nearly choked on his beer. "Had to give you motivation to stay the course."

"Yeah, your brotha' told me. Damn sho' worked!" James laughed. "The humiliation was worth my freedom, though."

"I'm sure men would be willin' to do far more for such a thing."

"No doubt. I know I make light of what you and your brotha' were willin' to do, but I don't take it lightly by any means. You sacrificed your career and your livelihood. I certainly appreciate it."

"I had a damn good reason to take the risk," Wyatt said, staring at his only sister in the distance. "She was so worth it."

James raised his beer. "That she is."

Wyatt turned to James. "Lily ain't the only one I owe an apology to, ya' know. I owe you one as well."

"Why's that?"

Wyatt sighed and turned to stare at the beer in his hand as his thoughts drifted away. "I let my fatha' down when he asked me to help 'em search for Lily and reunite her with Maya. I angrily refused." He paused and swallowed his quickly rising emotions as he thought about the end result. "I's angry at myself for years ova' that. I took my anga' out on everyone around me ... includin' you."

James looked confused. "How so?"

"I rememba' the day you showed up at my fatha's house, tryna' do the very thing my fatha' had asked me to help 'em do. And then, goddamn it, of all the prisons in Virginia, you ended up at mine. Felt like God was punishin' me again. You were a reminda' of the compassion that I lacked. So, I purposely left you in that prison dungeon for days, because I's too much of a coward to see your face and be reminded of my astronomical failure as a son. I didn't even have an ounce of your courage. It hurt to accept that fact, and I wanted you to hurt too ... so I let you rot. For that, I sincerely apologize."

James raised his glass again. "Apology accepted."

Wyatt nodded. "Back then, I's envious of your bravery." He looked out at Maya and Lily when he suddenly heard them laughing. He then turned to look James in the eyes. "But now I'm grateful to you. I love the way you love my sista'. I have no doubt my fatha' would say the same. I know he's lookin' down proud to see there's a man in his daughta's life willin' to go to the ends of the earth to take care of her the way she deserves."

James nodded his appreciation. "And as a son, you've certainly gone to the ends of the earth to atone for the mistakes you feel you've made. I'm sure your fatha's lookin' down on you, feelin' just as proud of you for that too."

Wyatt sighed. "I sure hope so." He and James then turned back toward the sound of Maya and Lily laughing together in the amphitheater seats.

Having never ventured too far outside the Virginia town she was born in, Maya had been overwhelmed with nervous excitement during her first train ride to see Lily. She was spellbound by the beauty of the countryside during the entire ride. The warmth of William's hospitality and the magnificence of his home further deepened her feeling that she was in a dream. The surrealness continued as Lily took her on a tour of William's mansion. Lily had then led her out to the amphitheater, explaining the controversial reason the stage had been erected, and how James had worked tirelessly to help build it. They then sat down in the theater seats, and Lily proceeded to describe the Dream Symphony in a way that made Maya feel as though she was there watching it unfold before her very eyes. She was nearly in tears envisioning her only child centerstage, not to be sold, but mystifying a sea of people.

Eager to tell her mother about yet another awe-inspiring story, Lily then took her by the hand. She helped Maya from her seat and guided her toward the picnic blanket underneath her favorite tree.

Lily picked up a journal. "I just finished readin' this, mama," she said.

"What's it about?"

"Levi's life."

Upon hearing that name, Maya instantly felt her heart start to race. "*M-Masta'* Levi's?" she questioned, sounding surprised.

"Mm-hmm," Lily nodded. "All these were his personal journals," she explained, glancing over at the rest of them.

"H-How did you get those?" Maya asked, her heart nervously thumping.

"It's a long story, but I wanna teach you to read these one day."

"I'd absolutely love to learn to read," Maya smiled. "But why would I wanna read those?"

"Because I'm *certain* your heart will be warmed by the things Levi had to say. His words changed my perception of him completely … and my life for that matta'."

Maya gently took the book from her daughter, opened to the first page, and gazed at what was complete gibberish to her illiterate eyes. "What could you have possibly learned from these that had that sort of impact?"

"That *you* were his poetic inspiration."

Maya quickly looked from the book to her daughter, shock rendering her speechless.

"These journals started the very first day you came to his plantation," Lily added.

Maya was still too stunned to respond.

"Afta' readin' these, I learned that that old telescope we used to gaze at the stars with wasn't somethin' you found in the woods like you told me. It was a gift from Levi, wasn't it?"

Maya sheepishly nodded.

"That music box … the one we used to dance to togetha'. I know now that Levi carved every inch of it by hand. Mama, the first song I eva' composed on my own was a modified rendition of the song that music box played. All these years, I neva' would've guessed it was a sentimental song that Levi'd written just for you."

Tears suddenly began welling in Maya's eyes.

"And the white figurine dancin' inside the music box wasn't a man they'd forgotten to paint brown, the way you told me when I asked you why he was so pale," Lily said, laughing lightly at the memory.

Her mother smiled and nervously laughed at the quick lie she had thought to tell Lily back then.

"He was supposed to be…"

"*Levi,*" her mother finished.

Lily nodded. "Dancin' with you the way he wished he could at your weddin'."

Maya nodded and tears slid down her cheeks.

"I know now that Levi loved you from the very first moment he eva' laid eyes on you … and that he *worshiped* you."

Maya closed her eyes and began sobbing.

Lily took a hold of her mother's hand. "Mama, I also know now that he's…"

"*Your fatha',*" Maya whispered, shamefully lowering her head.

Lily nodded, tears streaming down her cheeks as well.

"I'm so sorry I neva' told you," Maya sniffled, her head still weighed down by guilt. "I thought it was the right thing to do. I didn't want you wonderin' why your fatha' treated you so differently than your brotha's. Lookin' back on it, maybe that was foolish but…"

"Mama, it's okay. There's not a rule book for a situation like that. I know you were just doin' what you felt was best to protect me."

"I was. But Levi was devastated that I wouldn't tell you. He wanted you to know so badly. Maybe he was right. I probably should've told you."

"Actually, you did."

Maya looked confused. "I did?"

"Mm-hmm. The day you two were fightin' ova' me, I rememba' you screamin' that I was his daughta' too," Lily explained.

"I don't even recall sayin' that. I's in such a fit of hysteria, I'm quite sure I's sayin' whateva' it took just to get Levi to turn you loose." Maya's bottom lip began to quiver as she thought about that moment. "I tried. I swear, I tried so hard not to let 'em snatch you away."

"Mama, you don't have to convince me of that. I know it wasn't your fault. I neva' blamed you for what happened. But for years, I wondered why on earth my own fatha' would eva' do that to me. Part of me was in denial that he was even my fatha'. I just didn't wanna believe that my own flesh and blood would do such a thing. But these journals have finally helped me to unda'stand where his mind was at."

"To this day, I still don't know exactly why he took you," Maya confessed.

"You don't?"

"No. He tried many times to explain it to me ova' the years. But I could neva' let go of my fury enough to botha' listenin' to a word he had to say. No excuse was eva' gonna be good enough for me anyway. I just couldn't live with what he did to you."

"Seems he literally couldn't live with what he did eitha'."

"You know what he did to himself then?"

Lily nodded.

"He begged me to forgive 'em that day." Maya shook her head, trying to ward off her tears. "But I refused. Instead, I said some of the most godawful things to 'em." Tears suddenly gushed from her eyes. "I s-sometimes feel as though I w-was the o-one who p-pulled the tr-trigga'," she sobbed.

Lily embraced her mother and quietly let her purge her pain for a moment. She then pulled back and looked her in the eyes. "Don't blame yourself, mama. Levi was a grown man who made his own decisions."

Maya nodded. "I know I shouldn't blame myself, but it's so hard not to. He was a good man ... one who was ova'whelmed by the weight of the world and his life circumstances. I knew that, but I's so cold to 'em anyway. I've been strugglin' to forgive myself for addin' to the heaviness of his heartache."

"He hurt you, mama. You had every right to be angry. It was up to *him* to forgive *himself* ... not you. His inability to forgive himself ate away at 'em. That's why I hope you'll forgive yourself. I don't want such a thing to devour you too ... I can't lose you too."

"Oh, I'm *confident* that I'll find the strength to forgive myself now." She touched Lily's face and smiled. "I finally got my baby back. I can promise ya', I ain't goin' anywhere. Hell, the Lord's gon' have to drag me off this Earth!"

Lily burst out laughing. "It gives me peace to hear that ... and so did my fatha's journals. I hope they'll give you closure and peace too. Afta' you read 'em, you'll realize that you had nothin' at all to do with Levi's pain. If anything, he makes it clear that you were *always* his source of strength and joy."

Maya smiled and opened to the first page again. "That makes me even more eaga' to relive our lives through his eyes."

"Well, I'll warn ya', once you start you won't be able to stop! Every beautiful word my fatha' wrote about you made it so easy to forgive 'em ... *wholeheartedly*. I don't hold any ill will against 'em anymore ... not an ounce. I missed you terribly afta' he tore us apart, but I just wanna learn from the madness of it all and move on. It certainly taught me that the time we have with the ones we love is precious. Holdin' onto anga', and dwellin' on a past we can't change, seems like an awful waste of the precious time we have left on this Earth to make new beautiful memories ... *togetha'*."

Maya gazed at her daughter with extreme adoration. "Your fatha' used to boast on and on about how wise you were beyond your years.

You certainly just proved that yet again. I just know he'd be smilin' so pridefully at you right now with that crooked grin of his," she smiled. "And he'd undoubtedly have tears in his eyes, knowin' that you forgave 'em," she said, as she hugged her daughter tightly. "It would've meant the world to 'em," she whispered. Maya then pulled back and looked Lily in the eyes. "There's somethin' else that would've meant the world to 'em too."

"What's that?"

"Come with me." Maya took Lily by the hand and guided her to her new, beautifully decorated bedroom. "I wanna show you somethin'." She went over to her trunk and opened it.

Lily's eyes lit up when her mother pulled out the music box. "You still have it?" she smiled.

"I sure do." Maya sat the music box on a nearby dresser and opened the tiny drawer at the bottom of it. "And I still have this," she said, taking out a necklace. She turned around and showed it to Lily. "Did Levi write about this in his journal?"

Lily shook her head. "He neva' mentioned a necklace."

"I've had this hidden away for a long time."

"Mama, it's so beautiful! Did he give this to you too?"

"Yes … but it's not mine."

Lily looked confused.

"The same night your fatha' gave me the music box, he sat down next to you while you were sleepin' and just gazed at you for the longest time. 'My little masta'piece,' I rememba' he whispered. That's what your daddy always used to call you. Said he was convinced that we made the most beautiful little girl in the world," Maya smiled. "He said he couldn't believe he had anything to do with creatin' somethin' so incredibly precious and perfect."

Not even halfway through the story, Lily felt her tears brewing again.

"Then he opened the drawer in the bottom of the music box, took out this necklace, and handed it to me," Maya continued. "'Here's somethin' *precious* for my *precious* little one,' he told me. Then he picked you up off the bed and held you close to 'em. 'I want my little girl's first piece of jewelry to be from her daddy ... even if she neva' knows it's from me,' he said. Your daddy was in full on tears that night. He was heartbroken that I would neva' allow 'em to do all the special things a fatha' does for his daughta'."

Lily was now the one in full on tears.

"So, he asked me to give you this necklace on his behalf. He told me to give it to you wheneva' I felt you were old enough to take care of it," Maya explained. "Well, I certainly think you're old enough ... and I also think you deserve to know who it's from." She turned Lily around toward the mirror, placed the necklace on her, and looked up at her reflection. "You deserve to know that your daddy loved you beyond measure."

Lily could hardly see the details of the star-shaped pendant through the flood of tears blurring her eyes.

"Your daddy always used to say that he loved you to the stars and back. The pendant's made outta alexandrite. He said it's your birthstone."

"I won't eva' take it off," Lily sniffled. "It'll always be a reminda' of how much he loved me."

"That's *exactly* what he's always wanted you to know."

Lily nodded. "His journals made that so clear. This necklace is just more beautiful proof," she said, still gazing at it in the mirror. She then turned to her mother. "Those journals made so many things clear to me ... except for one thing."

"What's that baby?"

"I know my fatha' loved me, and I know he loved you … but did you love him too?"

Maya held both of Lily's hands and tears instantly returned to her eyes. "You were made outta love, Lily Collins. Pure, authentic *love*. That I can *guarantee* you," she said.

Lily smiled and embraced her mother, but their moment was suddenly interrupted by a knock at the door. Lily reluctantly let go of her mother to answer it.

"Sorry to interrupt, but dinna' is served," Ryla announced with a smile.

"Thanks, Ryla," Lily smiled.

"No problem," she replied, strolling off to wrangle everyone else.

Lily and her mother took a moment to freshen up and then stepped out into the hallway together. Wyatt had exited his guest bedroom and was headed to the dining room as well when he suddenly heard his name called. He stopped and turned around. "Hey Lily," he said, smiling as she approached.

"Hi," she said, smiling in return. "I know you're probably beyond ready to eat, but I just wanted a moment alone with you to say thank you for all the treasures you sent me … and for your letta'. It all indeed brought me peace."

"You're very welcome. I'm truly happy to know that. My brotha's will be happy to hear that as well. That's what we were hopin' for above all else," Wyatt said with sincerity.

"You most certainly accomplished your mission," Lily smiled.

"Good," Wyatt nodded. "And before we eat, I may as well utilize this moment alone with the both of you too, if you don't mind."

"We don't mind at all."

"There was somethin' else I wanted to put in that letta', but I much preferred to stand before you and Maya and say it face to face." Wyatt exhaled and turned to Maya. "You always took care of me and my brotha's, and loved us like we were your own. Truth be told, you were more of a motha' to us than our real motha' eva' was." He turned to look at Lily. "I rememba' I's always envious of you when I's a boy." He turned to Maya again, but held her hand this time. "'Cause I's convinced you had the greatest motha' on Earth. And I always wished she was my motha' too."

Maya's tears instantly returned. "In my eyes and in my heart, you and your brotha's were always my boys." She touched Wyatt's face. "*Still* are."

Wyatt exhaled and shook his head, trying to ward off tears. "Your words make it even harda' for me to forgive myself for the role I played in tearin' you two apart the day you were sold, Lily. Don't know if I eva' will forgive myself for it. But from the depths of my soul, I just wanna say to both of you how sorry I am for what I did that day. I hope one day you can both find it in your hearts to forgive me," he said, sounding as sincere as any man could.

"The sincere words in our fatha's journals made it easy for me to forgive 'em." Lily held Wyatt's hand. "And now your sincere words make it just as easy for me to forgive my big brotha' too."

"Thank you, little sista'," Wyatt whispered, his eyes filled to capacity with tears.

"And I forgave you years ago, baby," Maya reassured him. "You were just a youngsta', forced to be entangled in grown folks' business. I neva' held any ill will against you."

"Thank you for that. It means a lot." Wyatt exhaled again, doing his best not to shed tears. "There's more I still need to say, though." He let go of their hands and turned to Lily again. "Afta' our fatha'…"

He paused and cleared his throat, unable to even finish the sentence. "Afta' he..."

"I know," Lily reassuringly touched his shoulder. "It's okay."

Wyatt nodded and cleared his throat again. "Afta' that day, I's angry at myself. For years, I blamed myself for what happened. I took that anga' out on everybody ... even those that didn't deserve it. I's hurtin' inside in a way that my words can't remotely express, and I wanted to hurt everybody else. It's like I wanted the world to feel my pain, or to transfa' it to somebody else ... *anything* to make the pain stop. I don't know why I thought that would make the hurt go away. It was foolish logic ... and wrong. I's wrong to treat you both so badly the night you two got to see each otha' again years ago. I's wrong not to have permanently reunited you then. But, like I said, I's hurtin', and I wanted to hurt *everybody* in my path. I know that's no good excuse for my behavior. I wish I could change the past, but I can't. All I can do is tell you how incredibly sorry I am for mistreatin' both of you that day, and hope that you'll find it in your hearts to forgive me for that too."

Maya wiped a tear from her cheek. "If there's anybody on this earth who knows how that day made you feel, it's me. I know how the pain can eat away at you and have you thinkin' the most illogical thoughts. For years, I's mad at myself and hurtin' just like you." Maya held her daughter's hand. "But today, Lily made me promise that I'd forgive myself for my mistakes that day. She and I have made a pact not to dwell on the past and, instead, spend the rest of the precious time we have togetha' here on Earth makin' lovely new memories." Maya held out her hand toward Wyatt. "I'd love for you to join us in our pact."

Without even pausing to think twice, Wyatt reached over and placed his hand in hers. "I'd l-love t-to," he choked out, fighting hard to swallow back his tears. "*Mama* Maya," he added.

Maya laughed. "I love the sound of that!" she exclaimed, sliding her arm into the crook of his elbow.

"Me too," Wyatt concurred as he guided her toward the dining room.

Everyone in the house also followed the aroma of the feast awaiting them. All at once, they gathered at the massive dining room table with wide eyes and watering mouths, as they gazed at the spread of food. Before taking their seats, they all circled around the table, held each other's hands, bowed their heads, and listened to William thank God for allowing such a miraculous moment to transpire. As they ate their perfectly prepared cuisine, Maya proved herself to be on equal footing as William when it came to the art of nostalgic storytelling. She entertained the entire group, retelling hysterical stories of Wyatt and Lily as children. Emerson, Isabel, and Wilson were not exempt from hilarious and embarrassing stories of their childhood's retold from William's perspective. With the laughter and ease of conversation, one would not have known that there were strangers amongst the group. They, instead, would have been admired as generations of loving family reunited at last.

As dessert was passed around, Wyatt took the opportunity to say something that had been on his mind since he arrived. "I must say, it's truly an honor to meet you, Mr. Werthington."

"Thank you. That's very kind of you to say."

Wyatt nodded. "Because of you, my fatha' always used to say, 'Boys! Always be kind to otha's! Especially those less fortunate than you! Magnanimous acts can impact a person for a lifetime!'"

His impersonation of his father drew a round of soft laughter.

"How ever did I inspire such a thing?" William asked.

"More times than I can count, my fatha' told us the story about how you changed his life foreva' when he was twelve," Wyatt explained. "He said he worked all summa' cleanin' horse stalls to save money to travel from Virginia to Manhattan to see you perform. While he was there, he said you let a poor farm boy like him…"

"Wait a minute!" William suddenly interrupted when the story instantly triggered a forty-two-year-old memory. "Your last name is *Collins*, correct?" William asked, a serious tone now in his voice.

"Yessa'," Wyatt replied, nodding.

Finally putting the pieces together, William turned to Lily. "*Levi Collins* … is he your father?"

"Yes, he is," she replied, looking stunned.

"My God." Though the words came out of William's mouth as a whisper, the curious silence in the room made it easy for everyone to hear.

"You rememba' him?" Wyatt questioned, looking genuinely shocked.

"I will *never* forget that young man," William replied, after the shock subsided from his own brain.

A roomful of intrigued eyes and ears now had William's undivided attention.

"Young Levi told me he had worked on farms all over his community to save money, so that he could pay for himself and his family to watch my first ever performance at Winter Garden," William explained. "A ticket taker overheard his story and passed it along to my manager, who then told me. When I heard that a twelve-year-old prodigal pianist had worked for months to journey from Virginia to Manhattan to see me, I just had to meet him. Levi came back to my dressing room when the show was over. He was such a humble and respectful young man. I will never forget the wide-eyed look on his face when he walked in and saw me, nor the way he touched my heart when he told me that I was his musical inspiration."

"Afta' seein' your show, he said he told you it was his dream to perform to a sold-out crowd at Winta' Garden … just like you," Wyatt added.

William nodded. "He did indeed."

Wyatt smiled. "He said you told him, 'there's no betta' time to practice for that dream than…'"

"'*Right now*,'" William finished, smiling at the memory as well. "When he told me that he had taught himself to play piano, I couldn't resist the chance to hear him play. He walked out onto the stage and looked around that empty theater like he was envisioning a crowd full of people. He had an air about him as if he knew the stage was where he was meant to be. He seemed so nervous, though, when he first sat down at the grand piano. But the moment he closed his eyes and struck the keys, it was as if angels had invaded his body and transmitted the most heavenly melody through his fingertips. He blessed my ears with the most enchanting song … and filled my eyes with tears. All these years, I had wondered whatever became of his career. He was, without question, one of the greatest young pianists I had ever seen." William turned to Lily to find her eyes brimming with tears. "Young Levi was who I *immediately* thought of the first time I ever saw you play … You are *indeed* your father's daughter."

The sincerity of his statement made the waiting tears in Lily's eyes cascade down her cheeks.

William turned to Wyatt. "Seems your sister has fulfilled your father's dream."

Wyatt furrowed his eyebrows in confusion.

"She played a Christmas show at Winta' Garden," James explained.

Wyatt's mouth fell open, and he turned to look at Lily, who gave an affirmative nod. Wyatt's eyes then darted back to William, his stunned mind needing further confirmation.

"Not an empty seat in the *entire* theater," William boasted proudly.

Wyatt looked back at Lily. When she nodded again, he felt all the emotions he had held back during the day threatening to explode from his eyes all at once. With a table full of men, though, he fought to keep his emotions from breaking through the dam. Despite it, Lily could easily sense how much her accomplishment meant to him. It motivated her to stand and embrace her big brother tightly for the first time in her life. As she hugged him, a few of his tears seeped through his closed eyes onto his little sister's shoulder.

Now more eager than ever to share Lily's accomplishments, William guided Wyatt and everyone else to the library. It was a room created not only for Lily, but also to show her mother the incredible achievements her daughter had made during their years apart. Now with the revelations about Levi, William knew that the library would be just as meaningful to Wyatt.

Hand in hand, James and Lily watched with smiles as Wyatt and Maya marveled at the artistically preserved memorabilia from the Dream Symphony that lined the library shelves.

"Your fatha' was convinced that you were gonna be special," Maya said, picking up a framed newspaper article with Lily's picture. "He said he knew it from the very first moment he looked into those big bright curious eyes of yours as a baby. He felt it with all his heart. I have no doubt in my mind that he's lookin' down right now sayin', *I told ya' so!*" she smiled, still unable to pull her eyes away from the article.

"He'd certainly have every right to boast," Wyatt added, glancing up at the massive oil painting of his sister.

Maya walked up beside Wyatt. Fresh tears began forming in her eyes as she gazed at her only child's portrait. "My God. I'd give anything to sit front row and watch you live on a stage like this," she said, her voice suddenly overcome with emotion. "I'd be burstin' with pride."

"I'd love to see this live too," Wyatt confessed.

"You would?" Lily smiled.

Wyatt turned around and walked over to Lily. "Years ago, I had the great honor of seein' you play at Mary Jo Parker's party."

"You were there?!" Lily replied, astounded by the coincidence.

"I sure was. I's standin' in the back, my eyes wide, lookin' just as awestruck as everyone else afta' you easily replayed that young fella's song. You reminded me so much of our fatha' while you played. Your mannerisms, your expressions, your theatrics … *everything*. Felt like I's watchin' 'em play all ova' again. There's one difference between you and him though…"

"What's that?"

"You're far betta' than he eva' was."

"You really think so?" Lily smiled.

"I *know* so," Wyatt quickly replied. "I didn't think it was humanly possible for anybody to play betta' than him, but you damn sho' proved me wrong. But that's the one thing our fatha' always wanted … for *all* his children to go on to be betta' than he eva' was. You've certainly done that already. You've accomplished somethin' that he literally dreamed of doin'. I just know he was lookin' down, his eyes full of prideful tears, as he watched his beloved little girl on that Winta' Garden stage, livin' out the sort of life he prayed you'd have. It damn near brought me to tears just to watch you play at that party all those years ago. So, I know I'd be one hell of an emotional mess if eva' I had the honor of sittin' front row at the Dream Symphony, watchin' you command a sold out theata'." He gently touched Lily's cheek. "'Cause I'd be so damn proud of my little sista' too," he confessed, his sincerity evident by the tears glistening in his eyes again.

Lily closed her eyes at his touch and tears rolled down her cheeks.

Wyatt wiped at his eyes before his tears could make another appearance. He then took hold of one of Lily's hands. "Me and my brotha's may be able to carry on our fatha's name, but you have the ability to carry on his true legacy. I honestly think that would mean more to him than anything else in this world. So, if eva' you decide to resume your musical quest, you can best believe that all your otha' brotha's and I will do whateva' it takes to help you go on to achieve your dreams … that's a *promise*."

There was suddenly complete silence in the library. With all her beloved friends and family surrounding her, Lily walked to the center of the room. With tears cascading down her face, she slowly turned to appreciate a library that a musical legend had transformed into a shrine in her honor. She then walked over and sat down at the brand new, custom made grand piano that was artistically carved with shadowed scenes from the Dream Symphony. Through the blur of tears in her eyes, she looked up at the massive canvas mounted on the wall that depicted a show she had created from the brilliant fantasies of her unique mind. Having just completed reading her father's journals, the oil painting suddenly became even more sacred to her. Even though her eyes remained fixated on the one-of-a-kind artwork, Lily was envisioning a moment in her life that was once a source of extreme pain. But now, standing on an auction block, shivering alone as a child, was suddenly a source of extraordinary strength. Had it not been for her father sacrificing her on behalf of her brothers, Lily realized that the Dream Symphony would never have come to life. She would never have touched crowds of people or touched a man so deeply that he was inspired to paint her with such painstaking precision. She perhaps never would have touched a piano at all. She most certainly would not currently be sitting in the library of a man who helped hone the God-given musical gifts that her father had passed on to her. As tragically as her journey to this moment had begun, Lily was now convinced that God had indeed answered her father's prayers to give her an exceptional life ... in His usual *mysterious ways*.

After returning from her trance-like state, Lily lifted the key cover on her brand-new grand piano. She then took a moment to gaze with appreciation at the eighty-eight smooth pieces of black and white ivory in her sights. She then glanced back up at Musical Dreams, recalling what the eighty-eight keys beneath her fingertips had the power to do. Lily suddenly closed her eyes when she was overcome with a rush of emotions. Music that her mind had composed and locked away, during the years she had been torn apart from James, suddenly began erupting from the repressive mental prison that had held them captive. Tears began to well in James's eyes as he gazed with adoration at the woman he loved. Simply by the smile that suddenly graced her angelic face, he instantly knew that Lily Adams was finally ready to resume her mystical journey.

Chapter Thirty-three

United States of America
Constitution
Amendment XIII Section I

Neither slavery nor involuntary servitude, except as a punishment for crime whereof the party shall have been duly convicted, shall exist within the United States, or any place subject to their jurisdiction.

One year later
June 1866

Lily's hair blew beautifully in the wind as she stood on the bow of a steamship with James loyally at her side, holding her hand. William and Maya were on either side of them. *All* of Lily's brothers, friends, and the rest of her massive entourage were all standing on the upper deck. Everyone was completely silent, entranced by the breathtaking skyline of the Old World as it came into view.

"Please tell me this ain't a dream," Lily said, as her eyes swept across the beautiful city in her sights.

"If it's a dream, I pray we neva' wake up," James replied, looking equally awestruck by the view.

"Welcome m'lady," William said proudly when the ship finally docked. Seeing Lily's joyful tears caused his eyes to mist over as well.

"Thank you," Lily smiled. "I'm so thrilled to finally be here!"

"And I'm equally thrilled to finally show you around my homeland. Which will probably be much easier to do once we get off this boat!" William joked.

"Agreed!" Lily laughed.

William offered his elbow to Maya to help guide her down the exit ramp. James and Lily followed closely behind. Hand in hand, they officially took their first steps onto the land they had once vowed to start life anew in together.

"My ship has been waiting an awfully long time to bring you here, young lady."

Lily turned toward the man who uttered those words. "Landon Von Brandt," she smiled.

"The brilliant and beautiful Lily Adams," Landon smiled, greeting her with a slight bow and a kiss on the back of her hand. "You know full well that I'm an impatient man. How dare you keep me waiting on this port for six long years," he playfully teased.

Lily laughed at his sarcasm. "Proved to be a little tougha' boardin' your ship than we had anticipated. My apologies for the delay," she joked.

"Oh, I suppose I'll accept your apology … *this time*," Landon replied.

Lily laughed lightly. "I've missed you, Landon. You and your sarcasm."

"My, how I've missed you too," he replied, absent the sarcasm. "To see those joyous tears in your beautiful eyes has certainly just made the agonizingly long wait to see you again so incredibly worth it."

"Thank you, Landon," Lily said as she hugged him. She then stepped out of his embrace and took her mother by the hand. "This is my motha', Maya," she introduced.

"Pleasure to finally make your acquaintance, ma'am. I see where your daughter gets her beauty," Landon smiled, slightly bowing as he took her by the hand.

Maya smiled back. "I like you already, Mr. Von Brandt."

Landon offered his elbows to Maya and Lily. "Come now ladies, some drab old lady, who calls herself the queen of some antiquated palace, is eagerly awaiting your arrival." Lily and her mother laughed as they slipped their arms into the crooks of Landon's elbows. They were then guided to the first of a dozen waiting carriages.

After loading everyone up, Lily's entire entourage was whisked away by a convoy of pristine horses, draped in signature royal attire. When the convoy reached London, Lily began gazing out the window. Her face lit up with a smile of sheer wonder as they passed by dozens of billboards and banners hanging from buildings bearing the Dream Symphony logo. The vast array of advertisements for her show proved that Landon was still eager to share the talents of Lily Adams with the world.

James wore a smile just as brilliant as Lily's. However, there was not a landmark in the streets of London that had brought him to such a joyful state. He was infected by the sight of the woman he loved, lost in pure rapture as she gazed with childlike wonderment at the architecture of the Old World. Maya wore a brilliant smile as well, but it was the loving look on James's face, as he gazed at Lily, that had induced her gleeful expression. For over a year now, she had seen daily proof of James's unconditional love for her daughter, from small displays of affection to the monumental efforts of helping Lily prepare for this journey. The combination of it all left Maya convinced that James's love for her daughter was impenetrable. The way James loved Lily reminded Maya of Levi. After Lily taught her to read, Maya had spent weeks immersed in the mind of the man whose love for her and Lily was far deeper than she ever could have realized. Life through Levi's eyes had indeed succeeded in purging years of pain, and made room in Maya's soul for complete inner peace, just the way Lily had predicted.

Peace was hardly the emotion Lily was currently feeling. She was as giddy and restless as a child, who was beyond eager to make it to an exciting destination. But when the team of horses turned a final corner, her restlessness immediately ceased. Disbelief paralyzed her and the childlike smile faded from her face. Her vivid imagination had not even come close to envisioning what she was seeing in the distance. James scooted next to Lily and put his arm around her. She snuggled close to him and gazed out the window at the massive, historic landmark adorned in royal flags, whose majestic elegance had tears coursing down her cheeks.

In normal Lily fashion, she had wrangled her emotions by the time the convoy reached the gates of Buckingham Palace. There was nary a tear in her eyes when the carriage doors opened. As she exited the carriage, though, the view before her nearly reignited her tears. But she took a deep breath and remained stoic after emerging to the beautiful sight of the Queen's staff, standing in royal formation to welcome her. Despite the feet of a former slave suddenly touching regal grounds, Lily was treated like nothing less than princess. She was greeted according to royal protocol. She and her entourage were then escorted through the superlative double doors of the palace entrance. The magnificence of the dual staircase in the grand foyer nearly stole Lily's breath upon entering. But still, she composed herself and carried on in a dignified manner. With James, Landon, her mother, and her beloved mentor by her side, Lily Adams was guided through the elaborately decorated corridors of Buckingham Palace. As they walked, they passed by tapestries, priceless artwork, and generations of royal portraits. Lily's heart was pounding from a blend of enthusiasm, fear, and anxiousness. But the fireworks going off inside her body were not remotely obvious to anyone. She exuded an air of nobility in her external demeanor, as she strolled toward a true noblewoman perched on a throne. When they turned a final corner in the maze of the palace, Lily inhaled quietly to further steel herself for the revered honor that was now only ten steps away. She then reached over and held the hand of the man who loved her enough to take her on this journey, one that had begun in a filthy cottonfield six years ago and had now led to the pristine throne room of a queen. As they approached the end of the hall, James gently squeezed the hand of the only queen in his world. The simple return of affection ignited a sensation of warmth in Lily that radiated throughout her body and instantly melted her nervousness. Hand in hand, James and Lily then took the last steps to the threshold of royalty, and had the double doors opened for them by guards. With distinguished poise, Lily stepped inside the throne room of Buckingham Palace to finally meet the aristocratic woman who had personally scripted the invitation for this once-in-a-lifetime moment.

As emotionally overwhelming as the moment was, to finally be face to face with the Queen of England, Lily presented herself with the reverent etiquette that William had taught her. Respectfulness and humility were paired perfectly in every facet of Lily's demeanor as formal introductions were made.

"Welcome, Misses Adams," Queen Victoria greeted.

"Your Majesty," Lily greeted with a graceful curtsy. "It was an honor to receive your invitation, and I am equally honored to be the first to present a show at the Royal Albert Hall."

"After all I've heard about your life story, and the unique artistry of your show, the honor is most certainly all mine," Queen Victoria replied.

"Your words are truly gracious, ma'am. Such an opportunity will be one of my grandest dreams realized."

The Queen nodded. "I certainly look forward to seeing your show in the coming days. Until then, I should hope that you, your friends, and your family will make yourselves comfortable here. I should also hope to see you all well-rested for the dinner affair this evening."

"We look forward to it as well, ma'am," Lily said, giving another graceful curtsy to the Queen before being guided to her royal suite.

Resting was nowhere near possible with the level of enthusiasm bursting inside Lily, though. William's excitement was on par with hers. He was as eager to take Lily on a tour of his hometown as she was to see it all. William's boyhood home, fine restaurants, and the luxury shops in the town's square, were among the many places he took his twins, James, Isabel, Lily and Maya. In normal William fashion, he had a plethora of well-told nostalgic stories that he excitedly shared during their trip around London. However, the last stop on their tour was one that William had no story attached to. But he most certainly looked forward to the cherished memory it would soon imprint on his mind. When the carriage halted in front of the newly constructed Royal Albert Hall, William's keen mind began to absorb every fine detail in complete silence. Its elegance had stolen far too much of his breath to utter a single word anyway.

James helped Lily out of the carriage. Her bewildered eyes were glued to the splendor of the building as she stepped down. Still having yet to blink, she slid her arm into the crook of William's elbow. William gently patted her arm and, together, they entered the Royal Albert Hall. They walked in to the sight of workers erecting the sets for what would be the first performance to ever take place on that stage. To get the best view, everyone went and stood in the center balcony seats. Quietly, they all looked around at every intricate detail infused into the exquisite architecture. In all the theaters that William had played around the world, nothing came close to the ingenuity of this state-of-the-art facility. Even a seasoned veteran such as himself, was overwhelmed by its magnificence. The sniffling Lily suddenly heard proved that her mother was equally overwhelmed. Lily stepped over and wrapped her arms around her. James, Isabel, the twins, and

William felt their emotions stirring as they watched the pair embrace. They completely understood why two former slaves were moved to tears to be among the privileged first few people in the entire world to be invited by a queen to stand inside the luxurious theater named in honor of a prince.

The emotional day continued as Lily and her entire entourage arrived dressed in formal gowns and tailored suits to the Queen's dinner affair later in the evening. Lily entered the ballroom on James's arm, looking as ravishing as an ethereal empress in a flowing, custom-designed, red ball gown. Light applause ensued immediately after Lily stepped into the room. Confusion was obvious on her face as everyone continued to look in her direction as they applauded. It was not until that moment that she was made aware of the surprise that she was the night's honored guest. Such an honor granted her access to a seat near the head of the table.

As the night carried on, an emotional storm was brewing in James's chest as he proudly gazed across the dining room table at his wife. Noblemen, royal family members, and other esteemed patrons of London sat around her, asking about the details of her life. The story-telling skills that Lily had adopted from William kept her audience completely engaged, as she elaborated on the intricacies of her remarkable life story. By night's end, all attendees agreed that Lily's triumphant journey was indeed worthy of being honored. She further earned everyone's respect when she ended the evening with a sampling of her music on the grand piano. She exited the gala to a lengthy ovation from an audience of well-to-do citizens, who were intrigued to see her show now more than ever.

After spending an entire evening celebrating with a royal court, James and Lily retired to their palace suite. Despite the exhausting day, they were still far too intoxicated with euphoria to sleep. Lily had put on her nightgown and went to stand on the balcony underneath the beautiful glow of a full moon. Overcome with gratefulness, she quietly thanked God as she stared out at the Royal Albert Hall in the distance.

After putting on his pajama pants, James exited the bathroom and gazed at Lily from behind as she quietly took in the view of the city. The marvelous view meant nothing to him in comparison to the mesmerizing woman he held in his sights. He walked up behind her, slipped his arms around her waist, and pulled her close to him. "I guarantee there's not a man on this planet as proud as I am to be a woman's husband," he whispered, softly kissing her neck. "You were incredible tonight."

"Thank you," Lily smiled, his kiss and his words warming her. She got cozy in his arms, leaned her head back against his chest, and then looked over at the Royal Albert Hall again. "I still can't believe I'll be the first to perform in such a prestigious place."

"Feels so surreal to be here at all, doesn't it?"

"That's puttin' it mildly."

"And this is only the beginnin'. I was surprised to hear Landon announce that he's already got countless more grand places in otha' countries booked for you to perform in."

"I was so excited to hear that tonight too!" Lily suddenly turned around to face James. "But that suddenly made me wonda' somethin'…"

"What's that?"

She gently caressed her stomach. "Which country this little one will be born in," she answered.

James glanced down at her belly. When he looked up at Lily again, his eyes were filled with tears. "You're certain?" he asked, caressing her face.

Lily covered his hand with hers. "*Absolutely* certain."

The words caused the waiting tears in James's eyes to careen down his cheeks. Lily felt his joy in the way that he then gently caressed her lips with his. His tears blended with hers as he deepened the kiss that expressed the immense love he already felt for his future family.

A slight limp still remained in James's permanently damaged leg, but he still easily managed to pick Lily up and carry her to their bed. He tore out of his pajama pants and striped Lily from her nightgown, refusing to take his eyes off her body as he unveiled it. Tenderly, his hands slid up her legs and onto her belly. Warmth radiated through every inch of Lily's skin when he then let a gentle kiss linger where his baby was now growing. With his tears christening Lily's skin, James slowly kissed his way up her body. The added plumpness of her breasts was now easily evident to his lips and tongue as he sucked her tender nipples into his mouth. Lily pressed his head down harder, begging for more forceful action. James rewarded her physical wanton pleas with powerful suction that gave her near orgasmic pleasure. That fact was evident in the drawn-out, sensual moan that suddenly sang through Lily's vocal cords. The pulsation of her insides fell in sync with the rhythm of James's ravenous suckling, instantly heating her abyss to searing levels. The sudden, intense throbbing between her thighs left Lily far too impatient to wait for what she was craving. As James feasted on her, she grappled his buttocks and forced his hardened flesh deep into the heat of her pleasure passageway. The slick, molten sensation tore James's lips from her breast as he growled like a beast. The euphoric pleasure surging through Lily's body caused a carnal moan to tear through her throat as well and flow directly into James's ear canal. Her erotic singing turned on a sensual dance in his hips. Lily wrapped her legs around his waist as he began rhythmically stroking inside her. The slow tenderness of his thrusts matched the movement of his lips as he began passionately kissing her. The immense feeling of love emanating from James's lips and hips caused tears to roll in streams down the sides of Lily's face. The warmth of his impassioned expressions quickly spiked the pleasurable fever invading her body and detonated an explosion of orgasmic heat. The erotic cries of her sensual eruption instantly set James's anatomy on fire as well. He grunted loudly as his stones spasmed with force and unleashed a tidal wave of seed deep inside the womb of his beloved woman. Fireworks of pleasure, simultaneously launching their bodies into the heavens, were undoubtedly the perfect end to the celebration of their very first night on the international lands of the Old World.

*****

After a week of grueling rehearsals at the Royal Albert Hall, Lily was awakened the morning of the show by a loving kiss on the cheek. "Mornin'," James whispered.

"Mornin'," Lily replied, her voice still heavy with sleep. She wiped her eyes, sat up, and gave James a peck on the lips. He then handed her a cup of coffee. "Thank you," she smiled.

"You're welcome," he said, sitting down on the bed next to her. "I'll definitely be framin' this and addin' it to our collection of memorabilia in William's library," he then said, handing her the morning newspaper. A massive picture of Lily seated at the grand piano on the Royal Albert Hall stage took up a majority of the front page. The rest of it was an article regarding her and her show.

Westminster Chronicle

Friday, June 15, 1866

The Royal Albert Hall is set to open its doors this evening with a presentation of the much-anticipated Dream Symphony. All 5,272 seats in the new state of-the-art facility were purchased weeks ago by patrons eager to see the mystical, shadowed show composed by Lily Adams, a former slave from the United States. She has been mentored by world-renowned music composer, and London native, William Werthington. William will be at the helm of the show, conducting a symphony that drew instant critical acclaim in the United States. A four-year civil war-ravaged America and halted the progression of the Dream Symphony. The outcome of the war ultimately freed Mrs. Adams from the institution of slavery and finally gave her free rein to make the voyage here to London. Mrs. Adams was personally invited by Queen Victoria to officially resume her musical journey by presenting her spellbinding show as the first-ever performance inside a theater that was built in honor of her late husband, Prince Albert of Saxe-Coburg and Gotha.

Lily looked at James when she was finished reading. "I'm gonna expend every bit of strength in my body to honor Prince Albert and the legacy of his theater the way it deserves. I hope to make William, the Queen, and all of London proud."

James smiled pridefully at his wife. "I have not one single doubt that you will, Miss Lily." He kissed her gently on the lips. "Not one," he whispered.

****

Several hours after reading that newspaper, Lily, Isabel, and Maya were in the dressing room of the Royal Albert Hall as those 5,272 patrons began filling the seats. Overcome with emotion over her daughter's success, Maya had been crying tears of joy on and off throughout the entire day. Lily, too, had been overcome with tears earlier in the evening after seeing her mother dressed in elegant attire, looking very much like the Nubian goddess Levi had proclaimed her to be. Maya was appreciative of Lily's compliments, but her focus was on wanting to help enhance her daughter's natural beauty. She wanted to assist Lily with her hair and make-up, but the task was impossible with tears constantly blurring her vision. She finally had to step back and relinquish those honors to Isabel. With Isabel's painstaking work now complete, she stepped aside and let Lily look into the mirror. Maya stood behind her beloved miracle child staring at her reflection.

Seeing Levi so prevalent in Lily's features instantly ignited Maya's tears yet again.

Lily stood up and held her mother's hands. "You gonna be okay, mama?"

Maya nodded as she dabbed at her tears with a handkerchief. "Forgive me for not bein' able to pull myself togetha'. I'm just so grateful to be here with you for this night. I'm so proud of you."

"That doesn't need forgivin', mama. But ya' can't be proud of me yet, you haven't even seen my show," Lily teased.

"I don't need to see you perform to be proud. You're my miracle girl. I've been proud of you since the day you came into my life … just as proud as your fatha'. I wish he could be here too, but I'm convinced that he's lookin' down at you right now from heaven with his eyes just as full of tears as the first day that he held you."

Lily hugged her mother tightly. "Me too," she whispered, fighting hard to keep her tears from ruining her make-up.

Maya pulled back and smiled proudly at her daughter. "Well, I guess me and Isabel need to get to our seats." She kissed Lily on the cheek. "Good luck, baby. I can't wait to see you on that stage."

"Thank you, mama," Lily replied, kissing her mother on the cheek as well. She smiled as she watched her depart. For months, Lily had been adamant that her mother not see or hear any portions of her show rehearsals. She wanted her to see the full live production on opening night. It had caused Maya's anticipation to manifest into an eagerness to see the show that her words could not adequately explain. But it was certainly obvious in the way she hurried to her seat, feeling as though the Dream Symphony could not start soon enough.

After Isabel and Maya were out of sight, Lily sat back down alone at her dressing room table. She was lost in thought, staring at the printed music in her hands, until a hint of tears caused the notes to blur. She exhaled to settle herself and looked into the mirror. Her eyes immediately homed in on the star-shaped alexandrite pendant on her necklace. Again, it was difficult to make out its elegance with tears distorting the reflection. A knock on her dressing room door forced her to pull herself together. She exhaled again before telling her visitor to come in. There was more than one visitor, however. Lily lit up in a smile as her brothers, Austin, Harrison, Ryla, the twins, and Griff all filed in behind Austin's energetic daughter, Georgia.

"Hi, Miss Lily!" Georgia exclaimed, running over to give her godmother a hug. "I can't wait to see you perform! I know you're gonna be incredible!" She then handed her godmother a long-stemmed flower. "It's a lily! Because your name is Lily!"

"Just like your middle name too!"

"Yup! That's the best name eva'!"

Lily laughed along with everyone else. "Thank you, Georgia!" she said, smiling at her childlike enthusiasm.

"You're welcome!"

"Her excitement rivals mine!" Austin smiled. "And she stole the words right outta my mouth ... well, not the part about Lily bein' the best name eva'," he laughed. "The fact that you're gonna be incredible."

"Thank you, Austin," Lily smiled.

"You're welcome," he replied, giving her a hug. He then handed her another long-stemmed lily and stepped aside for the next man in line.

"We all wanted to stop by and wish you good luck tonight," Colt explained.

"You look really beautiful, Lily," Wyatt then complimented.

Everyone nodded in agreement.

"Thank you," Lily blushed.

One by one, everyone then gave her a hug, whispered good luck, and handed her a lily.

Dallas was the last of her brothers to hug her. "Knock 'em dead, sis," he said. The way he referred to her nearly ignited Lily's tears again.

With wine glass in hand, Ryla stepped up to Lily next. "I knew you had one hell of a story to tell. Sho' glad you neva' told me when I asked, though…" She looked around the fancy dressing room and shook her head. "'Cause I neva' would've believed any of this shit anyway!"

Lily let out a genuine laugh. "Sometimes, I can hardly believe it myself, Ryla."

Ryla handed her a lily. "I can't wait to see you shine up there. Much luck to you."

"Thank you, Ryla," Lily replied, hugging her.

"I'd wish you luck too, Little Flowa', but I know from experience that you don't need it. I'm confident you'll show these goddamn Brits what Americans can do," Griff said, handing her a lily as well.

"Thank you, Griff," Lily replied, hugging her favorite security bandit. She then stepped back and looked at everyone in the room. "Thank you all for the flowa's … and for comin' all this way to support me. It means more to me than my words could eva' express."

"It's our pleasure," Harrison replied. "We wouldn't miss this for the world."

Everyone nodded in agreement and then filed out to head to their seats.

Lily inhaled the sweet scent of her bouquet before she arranged it neatly in the vase full of water that Wyatt had thoughtfully placed on her vanity. A seductive smile then suddenly emerged on her face when she saw the reflection of the man who had quietly tiptoed in and appeared over her right shoulder. "It's about time you showed up."

"I've missed you all day too," James replied, brushing her hair aside and kissing her neck as he wrapped his arms around her waist. He had been extremely busy handling the madness of the press and managing the itinerary for their family and friends. He was happy to finally have a moment alone with his lovely wife. "You look heavenly," he said, as he gazed at her reflection in the mirror.

Lily closed her eyes and exhaled, his words and his touch immediately warming her as always. "Thank you," she whispered. "And thank you for all the flowa's," she smiled, confident that he was behind the beautiful gesture.

James shook his head. "I can't steal the credit for that. That was all your brothas' idea. They wanted a way of showin' their sista' how happy they are for you ... and how much they love you." He kissed Lily's cheek. "I preferred to express that with a different gift." He briefly stepped out into the hallway and returned with a large, wooden box that had a bow wrapped around it.

"What've you gone and done?" Lily teased, smiling as he handed the box to her.

"Open it and see," James smiled in return.

Lily slid the bow off, opened the lid, and froze when she saw what was inside. "Isabel will kill me if I ruin this make-up," she whispered, closing her eyes to hold in her tears. She then dabbed at the corner of her eyes with the handkerchief James handed her. Once she cleared her eyes, she could more easily see the details of Piers LeRoux's beautiful, framed artwork. Just as James had always wanted, he had Piers paint an 11x14 color version of him and Lily dancing together in the Manhattan art gallery ballroom.

"You like it?" James whispered.

"I love it," Lily whispered back, dabbing away another tear before it landed on the glass of the decorative frame.

"This was the moment we were celebratin' the chance to sail to the Old World for this show. And now, afta' all these years…"

"We finally made it," Lily finished. "Thank you for this. I can't think of a more perfect gift to commemorate this occasion."

"You're very welcome."

Lily set the picture upright on the vanity and stared at it. James wrapped his arms around her from behind. His hands tenderly caressed her belly as he kissed her on the cheek. "Did you tell your motha' she's gonna be a grandma yet?"

Lily nestled into his embrace. "No. We're still the only ones with this precious little secret," she said, caressing her belly too. "I figured I betta' wait 'til afta' the show to tell everyone … *especially* my motha'. One thing at a time for her. She's so ova'whelmed with excitement, she's been cryin' tears of joy on and off all day. I'm afraid her poor heart's literally gonna burst with happiness if I tell 'er now."

James laughed lightly. "Your motha's showin' outwardly how I'm feelin' inwardly. My heart's certainly on the verge of burstin' with happiness for you too," he caressed Lily's belly. "And joy that my beautiful wife's gonna make me a fatha' again." He paused briefly. "And a little nervousness too, if I'm bein' honest."

"Hey." Lily turned toward him. "Let go of nerves and shift your focus to joy. I have the utmost confidence that little Jameson junior will make it into the world safe and sound," she smiled.

James furrowed his eyebrows and pretended to look confused. "Don't you mean *Daffy?*"

Lily erupted in laughter. "Oh lord! Here we go again," she said through a fit of giggles.

James smiled at the joyful sound. "Here we go again, *indeed* ... anotha' grand adventure togetha'. And it all officially starts tonight. I'm so nervous and excited to see you perform again," he confessed. "I feel like I'm damn near about to jump outta my skin. Glad to see you don't seem the least bit nervous or scared."

"There was a time in my life when I thought I might not eva' see you again. Afta' bein' tortured by such a thought for years, it gave me real perspective on what's truly deservin' of nerves and fear. You holdin' me in your arms again and performin' in the Old World was all I eva' dreamt about while we were apart. Now, here I am about to step out onto a brand-new stage in London, not far from a palace..." She touched James on the face. "With my very best friend here by my side to witness it all," she smiled. "My most prayed for dreams have come true. So, this moment is certainly not deservin' of fear or nerves ... only pure elation."

James exhaled, trying to settle a sudden swell of emotions. "Do you know what I love most about you, Lily?" he asked, taking her by the hand.

"What's that?" she smiled.

"Everything." He gently caressed her cheek. *"Absolutely* everything," he emphasized, his voice slightly cracking.

Lily melted at his touch, feeling an instant surge of butterflies.

"Your way with words, your strength, your confidence, your bravery, and your ability to instantly make me feel at peace. I love it all," James continued. "It all reminds me of why I have every bit of faith that you'll be stellar on that stage tonight ... just like you always are."

"Honestly, I wouldn't have the strength to do any of this without you. You've always been the fuel that fires my courage. From the bottom of my heart, I wanna thank you for all you've endured to get me here and for always believin' in me."

James rested his forehead against hers. "It's been my greatest pleasure, Miss Lily," he whispered.

"Places everyone! Five minutes until showtime!" they heard William announce from the hallway. They both turned toward the door when they then heard William enter the dressing room. "May I steal her from you for, oh … two hours or so?" William joked.

James kissed Lily on the forehead. "Well, looks like I'll be leavin' you in good hands."

"The best!" Lily exclaimed, slipping her arm into the crook of William's elbow.

"I betta' hobble on back to my seat," James joked, lifting the cane he still used for special occasions, so as not to misstep or fall. "Bring the house down tonight, Mrs. Adams."

"I have every intention of doin' exactly that," she replied with conviction.

James smiled proudly at her and kissed her lightly on the lips before departing.

Lily watched him as he walked away, paying keen attention to his slight lingering limp. "James!"

He turned around to find Lily gazing proudly at him with a glimmer of tears in her eyes.

"I love absolutely *everything* about you too," she said, appreciation for his selfless sacrifices affecting the depth of emotion in her voice.

James inhaled, feeling warmed by her expression. He then nodded and smiled back before proceeding to his coveted center balcony seat.

William patted Lily on the arm and exhaled. "Well, here we go again, m'dear. Are you ready to resume yet another grand adventure together?"

"Born ready," Lily replied confidently.

"You'll get no argument from me about that," he smiled, as he began escorting her down the hallway toward her custom grand piano.

Just one year before taking her final steps toward the stage, Lily had reunited with many of the original dancers and members of the student orchestra. With his daughter always in tow, Austin was among the group. Considering his injury, he was under William's wing, hoping that one day William would pass the baton to him to become the show's new music conductor. In much the same way that Anna Mae had become like a mother figure to Lily, Maya had now taken on that role with Isabel. A mother-daughter bond had grown between the pair as they began working nonstop to design and create costumes for the dancers. As promised, *all* of Lily's brothers came to Ohio to help James, Harrison, and the twins with lighting, stage design, building props, and any other detail that Lily asked of them. William's mansion was overflowing with love, laughter, and determination while everyone worked in concert to bring Lily's show to life. All the while, Lily was once again side by side with her mentor, developing the powerful music that would soon stir the emotion of her new whimsical, shadowed story ideas.

Month after month of grueling rehearsals on the amphitheater and tireless dedication from her family and friends had all led to this moment. William escorted Lily to her grand piano bench. He then took his place as well behind the podium. Lily peered between the curtains and felt her elation rise to unparalleled levels when her eyes swept across the Royal Albert Hall and saw that there was not a single seat unfilled, in the most elaborate theater in the world. What nearly brought on her tears, though, was the sight of Wyatt with his arm around her mother, and James holding her hand as she patted her tears with the handkerchief he had given her. Lily lost sight of them, though, when complete darkness suddenly fell on the theater, bringing the murmur of the crowd to an instant hush. Lily felt an immediate calm as her innate, confident stage presence emerged. When the curtains slowly opened, she immediately harnessed control of the crowd's attention and emotion. She let the silence and darkness linger to build the anticipation and suspense.

On Friday, June 15, 1866 at precisely 7:01 pm, after battling back from near death, tremendous loss, oppression, and abuse, Lily Adams exhaled, closed her eyes, thanked God, and struck the keys to her custom-made grand piano, marking the official return of *The Dream Symphony*. After a six-year hiatus, the brilliant signature show lighting illuminated the translucent sheath that was hanging from the rafters of a majestic stage, just a stone's throw away from Buckingham Palace. A rush of joy flooded Lily's body as her ensemble, once again, took to the stage, casting their shadows out to their first-ever international crowd. Eyes of Londoners lit up as they watched shadowed dancers pirouetting in perfect unison around actors, who began reenacting the royal knighting ceremony of a particular prince. Lily's fingers moved as gracefully as every ballerina, as she projected the deep tones of her grand piano into the auditory systems of her entranced audience. The visuals and the unique symphonic sounds traveled through the crowd's eyes and ears, transmitting a wave of emotions through their bodies that instantly penetrated their hearts. The intensity of the show kept their eyes unblinking as they watched the shadowed prince slowly kneel in an honorable fashion, his body moving in sync with the royal undertones of the symphonic melody. The swan-like dancers suddenly paused around him and the music softened as a sword was ceremoniously touched to each of his shoulders. The newly knighted prince then slowly rose to his feet to the sound of the crescendoing symphony, sending another sentimental wave of emotion through the crowd that impacted Queen Victoria with great force. She was instantly brought to tears by an opening scene that paid homage to the noble man the theater had been named in honor of.

After a sensational opening dedication, over five thousand London hearts were now beating just as rhythmically as Lily's beautiful music. Emphatic applause carried on for so long that it blended with the transition into the next song, one in which the Dream Symphony's most infamous character returned. Massive balls of flames suddenly erupted on either side of the stage as a shadowed, fire-breathing dragon appeared in nightmarish fashion. With an audible gasp, all patrons physically reacted, their bodies jumping in response to never-before-seen special effects. Wielding his sword to the beat of Lily's brilliantly remastered melodies, the shadowed version of Prince Albert then began attempting to slay the dragon on behalf of the princess he loved. The fierce battle that ensued, between blade and flame, gripped Londoners and had their emotions just as tightly intertwined with the enthralling scene as Lily's intense music was with the movement of the shadows. Their captive hearts nearly stopped, along with the dragon's, after the prince threw his sword, end over end, and pierced its chest in perfect timing to an intense symphonic climax. The music suddenly transitioned just as dramatically as the dragon slowly collapsing, his body faltering as roaring flames slowly dissipated into steam. When the beast's body hit the ground, Prince Albert, Knight of the Garter, removed his sword from the dragon's chest and raised it in victory. He then freed his princess, took her by the hand, and gallantly escorted her through the grand entrance of the most hallowed palace on the lands of the Old World. As the prince and princess entered their kingdom, the light and music slowly faded away to the resounding commendation of an enraptured London crowd.

When the light returned, the vibrant music and shadows of the Dream Symphony carried on to feature new fictional fantasy tales, some funny, some adventurous, some filled with new, bewildering combinations of magic and captivating special effects. No matter what story was told, every spellbinding moment suspended the audience in wide-eyed wonderment. As Lily's music effortlessly transitioned between power and finesse, she took the minds and bodies of her first international crowd on an exhilarating journey, from joy to sympathy, butterflies to chills, heart-pounding to heart-stopping, and from tears to laughter.

In the midst of that very laughter, the entire theater suddenly went dark. The laughter ceased just as abruptly as darkness had fallen. With absolutely no sound or light, the audience lingered in confusion, unaware that every second of suspense was harnessed under Lily's complete control. When she felt the moment was right, she suddenly struck the highest key on her grand piano. In sync with the single keystroke, the brilliant light illuminated the translucent sheath, revealing the shadow of a large wooden box. Again, there was complete silence. After several more suspenseful seconds, Lily struck the same key and darkness fell again. Silence. Lily struck the key once more and, this time, illuminated the shadows of a man and woman, standing atop the wooden box, frozen as two lovers dancing. Again, Lily let silence persist to allow the audience's eyes to appreciate the beauty of the dancers' statuesque embrace. Slowly and in an intentionally choppy manner, Lily then began playing her next few notes. The choppy music slowly turned on the movements of the man and woman. When the notes began to pick up speed, Maya suddenly sat up taller in her seat. The familiar melody reverberated through her ears, shot straight to her chest, and began melting her heart. Her eyes instantly flooded with tears as she watched the two ballet dancers, slowly spinning around and around, waltzing stiffly on their massive, shadowed music box. The speed and elegance of their movements matched Lily's musical pace as she began playing "The Goddess of Spring." The very goddess for whom the beautiful ballad had been written now had tears cascading down her cheeks as she watched on from her center balcony seat.

As Lily seamlessly transitioned her mother's song into smooth elegance, the two shadowed figurines came to life and stepped down from their music box. Lily began the song as a solo, but piece by piece, the glorious sounds of the orchestra slowly blended in to accompany her, as graceful ballet dancers began telling the unique love story of a simple man, one who had very little but doted on a special woman with handmade gifts. The passion of the shadowed man and woman was expressed in the emotional choreography as they glided, hopped, and pirouetted across the stage in perfect unison. The intensity of their love built, much like the crescendoing symphony driving their movements. At the climax of the melody, the music paused, and so too did the dancers, both locked in a loving gaze. When the music began again, the shadowed man placed his hand over his heart and got down on bended knee in front of the woman. He kissed her hand, stood again, and briefly lifted his lover in the air to the soft sounds of the symphony. As their dance resumed and the song slowly ended, the orchestra faded out one piece at a time, until Lily was once again left alone playing her father's original piece. With only her grand piano tickling the emotions of the audience, the two figurines ended their dance with a matrimonial kiss, as the light slowly faded away.

In the midst of heartfelt applause, a new song began to play as the shadow of a little boy suddenly skipped onto the stage from the wings. Trailing right behind him were five more little boys, each smaller than the next, all skipping in sync to yet another one of Levi's very sentimental songs. One by one, each little boy then hopped into the arms of the male figurine, who proudly tossed them into the air. The shadowed female figurine then poetically danced onto the stage again, twirling over to her husband with a baby cradled in her arms. With the six boys surrounding them, they all froze to take a picture of a family that was now complete. After a black puff of smoke from a camera's flash, the light on the stage faded away. It faded back in seconds later, and beautiful shadows began depicting the evolution of a humble man, who discarded his musical aspirations and dedicated his life to raising his family. Tender moments were displayed of him reading to his children, laughing with them at dinner, teaching his sons to fish … and teaching his only daughter to play the piano. The little girl sat first as just a toddler on her father's lap. As the light faded in and out, depicting elapsed time, the young girl grew along with her father's love and pride. A multitude of pulsating, shadowed hearts were displayed in the background as the father stood by proudly watching his adolescent daughter play piano on her own. For a final time, the light faded out and lit up again in harmony with a key change in the melody. As the song transitioned, so, too, did the shadowed scene. William and Lily now sat behind the translucent sheath, portraying the loving father and his adult daughter, seated side by side as they played "A Beautiful Miracle."

With the God-given musical gift that Levi had passed on to Lily, she had worked tirelessly to compose the orchestral harmonies to blend with her father's most treasured piano melodies. The story of the life and love that Levi had yearned for, once trapped in the pages of his very sentimental journals, had come to life in the last half hour of the Dream Symphony, all backed by his very own remastered music. And Lily had far more in store for *every* future show. She had sat Wyatt down and asked his permission before proceeding with her new idea. He took hold of Lily's hands and gazed at her with eyes full of tears. His answer was immediate and sincere: *"I'm convinced there could neva' be a more magnanimous way to express the depths of your forgiveness and to carry on our fatha's legacy than sharin' with the world the sort of life he dreamed of havin' with all of us ... especially with his one true love."*

The memory of Wyatt's words were churning the emotions in Lily's chest as the translucent curtain rose on a majestic stage in London, revealing her and William as they played the final notes of a song inspired by her birth. When the song ended, Lily gracefully rose to her feet and curtsied to the sound of roaring applause. After closing the first-ever show at the Royal Albert Hall, William proudly escorted Lily to the forefront of the stage and let her have the spotlight alone in front of a sea of his British countrymen. Their reactions made it clear that they, too, concurred with the beauty of the life her father had dreamed of. Absent color or class, the love story of her mother and father was being received in the way that it should have been in reality, with warmth, tears of joy, and one hell of an epic standing ovation. Lily's eyes slowly swept over the 5,272 applauding emotional patrons ... including a queen. Their long, drawn-out show of appreciation reverberated through to Lily's soul. Her eyes then drifted to the coveted center balcony. Her dearest friends, nieces, nephews, sisters-in-law, and all six of her brothers were gazing down at her. She paused on the faces of her brothers; not a single one of them bothered to hide the prideful tears in their eyes as they applauded the life and love of their father ... and for their sister. Standing huddled between them all was the man Lily loved beyond measure; James was holding onto the hand of her inconsolable mother. As Lily gazed at every face in that balcony, she was deeply impacted by the magnitude of the moment when it suddenly dawned on her that the ripple effect of Levi's love and his music had brought peace and unity to his *entire* family. Lily tilted her head back and closed her eyes as she envisioned her father smiling down from the heavens with Elizabeth Adams by his side and little Rose in his arms. She was certain he had joyous tears in his eyes after witnessing his dreams come true. Tears of pure elation then careened down the sides of Lily's face, feeling as though such a miraculous feat had just defined the *true* meaning of *The Ultimate Grand Finale.*

Werthington Estate
April 1930

... Those were the lifetime of grand memories that a frail ninety-five-year-old James Adams had sat in the library cherishing: Lily's journey to Winter Garden, the dark years after she had been dragged back to servitude in the old world, and the after effects of Levi's ultimate grand finale. For hours, James had sat at the custom-made Dream Symphony antique piano, reliving the saga of his turbulent, yet magical, life with his beloved wife, Lily. Like a moving picture show, the mental catalogue of his wondrous eighty-five-year saga with Lily had easily come to life in his mind the very moment he gazed up at her in the center of Piers LeRoux's portrait, Musical Dreams, a masterpiece now worth millions. Even eighty-five years later, James was still just as awestruck by the sight of Lily as the day he first laid eyes on her as a boy, so much so that butterflies erupted in his stomach.

James felt the same span of emotions every decade when he and Lily would begin this two-week long walk down memory lane, leading up to the renewal of their vows. This year was to be the seventh time that he stood under the tree where he had taught Lily to read. With William's sparkling lake as their backdrop, in front of a lawn full of their massive extended family, they planned to exchange their vows, yet again. But before then, they had a tradition of sifting through hundreds of pictures and memorabilia that they had collected during their life together. It all now filled several trunks, lined shelves, and hung on walls. They pored over well-preserved programs, newspaper articles, tickets, and pictures of Lily with fans and world leaders. The one-hundred and fifty-seven letters that Lily had written in response to all the ones James had sent her during his stint in the war were still there. Among those letters were the pardon papers James received from President Lincoln after Harrison crafted a letter stating the unjust circumstances that had led to his death sentence. Harrison articulately detailed James's dedication to their country, including The Freedom Rider organization he had built to help enforce the Emancipation Proclamation. That pardon letter had been personally handed to James by the president in the White house. It was framed and placed in a glass case alongside pictures of James with his brothers-in-arms, standing pridefully in uniform during the Civil war. In the middle of it all was the Medal of Honor he had received for his valiant service to his country and his distinguished acts of valor.

Sixty-five more years of Lily's memorabilia was added to the collection that William had started in his library in 1865. Now in 1930, the massive collection included the first published book of Lily's sheet music. It had sold millions of copies worldwide and was now a staple in many music schools. An entire photo album chronicled the months she had worked with Thomas Edison, who had approached her about recording snippets of music for his new invention, the phonograph. Their work together led to the first ever mass-produced wax record, one that sold out in stores at lightning speed. A framed copy of the first album now hung on the library wall, reminding them of that special moment in Lily's life history at the turn of the century. Hanging beside that album was the framed poster of the first official cinematic moving picture in 1908, one in which Lily had been asked to compose the music score. Picture books full of students she had mentored over the years were plentiful as well. Richard Wells, the very man who had scoffed at the idea of a slave working in his class, had humbly asked her, years later, to tutor his students. After she stopped touring the world, Lily dedicated herself to assisting music students. For twenty years, she was a source of positivity to malleable young minds, striving to be to them what William had been to her. Her appreciative students were at the helm of surprising her with a very special gift upon her retirement. The bronze statue of her seated at a grand piano became the permanent centerpiece of the courtyard near the Werthington Music Building at James's alma mater, Ohio University.

James and Lily were always moved to tears as they sifted through memorabilia that reminded them of those unforgettable moments of their lives. But nothing brought forth their joyous tears more so than the pictures of the four cherished treasures they had created together: Jameson "Jamie" Michael Junior, a National League baseball star, who went on to become a team owner. William "Will" Alexander, whose telescope adventures with his grandmother led him to become a well-known astronomer. Levi "Lee" Wyatt, a standout pianist in his own right with abilities and looks that certainly warranted his name. And, lastly, Lillian Rose, a daddy's girl who followed in her father's footsteps and became a life-saving physician. Lily was insistent upon naming her sons after all the special men in her life. James was just as adamant about giving their only surviving daughter a name that always rolled off his tongue sounding like *Lily and Rose*: the two special ladies of his life who had inspired him to fight for American freedom. Pictures of James and Lily's four children covered nearly every space of their walls and filled countless photo albums. Rose was not forgotten either. Her tiny casket was exhumed, and she was brought home with the original tombstone that Ava had made. And Piers LeRoux was more than happy to honor James's request of creating an oil painting of Rose from his memory of the moment with her on the battlefield. James's detailed description of her curly hair, her white dress blowing gingerly in the wind, her innocent face, and her sparkling, crystal blue eyes, were all painted flawlessly onto a massive canvas that now hung at the top of their dual staircase.

James and Lily's once-a-decade tradition had grown to encompass two weeks. They spent that time together filling picture albums of their ever-growing family and framing anything new that they had collected in the previous ten years. All the while, they took the time to appreciate all the older trinkets and treasures that sparked memories of the extreme highs and seemingly bottomless lows of their lives while coming of age together. They never wanted to forget that their love had persevered through a war, abuse, years of separation, a turbulent childhood, and even the loss of a child. They used their two-week tradition to honor the fact that they had overcome every tumultuous obstacle ever thrown in their way. All the things that were a testament to the strength of their unique bond would ultimately serve to deepen their appreciation for one another and inspire the words for the new vows they would then each write for their ceremony. Every decade, James and Lily would then stand under their favorite tree by the lake. With their massive family surrounding them, they would read their new vows to one another, snip a locket of each other's hair, and seal it all away with all their other vows from the past.

And so, in April of 1930, at the age of 95, James and Lily's traditional walk down memory lane together was fast approaching. On the eve that they were set to begin their seventh nostalgic voyage together, James had helped Lily into and out of her bubble bath. She was more than capable, but for years, it was just something that James loved to do for her every evening. He lotioned her back, helped her to dress, and straightened the cherished birthstone necklace from her father. James then wrapped his arms around her waist, planted a kiss on her cheek, stared up at Lily in the mirror and smiled. "Day afta' day for the last eighty-five years, you get more and more beautiful to me," he said to her.

Lily handed him his glasses. "Eitha' that or you're goin' blind," she teased.

James put his glasses on. "Whoa!" he exclaimed, feigning shock at the clarity of her face. "My initial assessment was *definitely* wrong!" He touched Lily gently on the cheek. "You're even more beautiful than I thought."

Lily laughed.

James gazed at her for a moment, smiled, then walked to the corner of the room. He then walked back toward Lily as the soothing music he had just started on the phonograph took over the room. He cleared his throat. "Excuse me pretty lady, I saw you from across the room, and I was wonderin' if you'd allow an old man like me the honor of dancin' with you this evenin'?"

"I thought you'd neva' ask, handsome," Lily smiled.

James took a step back, bowed, and kissed her hand. He then wrapped one arm around her waist and held Lily's hand with the other. Lily rested her head on James's shoulder, he rested his on top of hers, and pulled her in as close to him as possible. Slowly and carefully, they swayed, both silently lost in the essence of one another. This was James's way of making love to his wife every night at this stage in their life. Such a small thing was equally euphoric for Lily.

When the song was over, James helped Lily into bed and laid down next to her, feeling just as satisfied as if he had actually made love to her. "I love you," he whispered in her ear, just as he had every night since returning from the war.

Lily felt a rush of butterflies fluttering through her stomach as James gathered her tighter. He intertwined their fingers and kissed her lightly on the cheek, "I love you too," she whispered back before drifting off to sleep.

James woke up the next morning looking forward to beginning the nostalgic voyage he was to embark on with Lily, reminiscing on those decades of ups and downs together that would inspire the new vows they wrote. Before making Lily's breakfast, James kissed her on the cheek, just as he did every morning. This morning, however, his lips were met with a sensation he had never felt before. The odd coldness of her skin instantly jarred him into full consciousness. Slightly alarmed, he kissed her again and said her name softly at first. A rapid heart rate and a burst of adrenaline immediately overcame him when she did not reply as she usually did to his affections. Her name then came out sounding like a question as he suddenly threw back the covers. No movement, no response this time sent James spiraling into panic. He rolled Lily over and yelled her name with intense desperation. Delirium, madness, grief, despair, dismay, distress, horror, dejection ... not a single one of those emotions, nor even all of them combined, was adequate enough to describe James's emotions when he laid his head upon Lily's chest and felt nothing but his tears as they began to pool on her skin. James yanked his head up and glanced at Lily's face in the morning sunlight. Her name escaped him again, this time sounding like it had come from a man whose mind had just completely shattered. Even all the gruesome things he had witnessed during the war could not prepare James for what his eyes were absorbing. To see Lily's supple lips a permanent shade of blue and know they would never again utter her love for him, to know the warmth in her soft skin would never again radiate into his, to realize that her sparkling, kaleidoscope-colored eyes would never again open to gaze back at him with such love, caused James's entire body to go numb. He suddenly collapsed back down on Lily's chest. Only hours before, he was making love to her in his own special way, and now he was holding her limp hand in a grief-stricken, inconsolable heap. To find the woman he had loved for eighty-five years in such a state may as well have been the death of James Adams as well.

Even at age ninety-five, Lily seemed healthy and strong, both mentally and physically. Though expectedly slower at her age, she was still very active in the lives of her family and the community. She had no illness nor any other sign to suggest that her life was in jeopardy. Those facts made her death just as unexpected to everyone as her miraculous conception. As active as Lily still was in the community, it was no surprise that the news of her passing seemed to cause nearly the entire town of Athens to go into mourning. But, shockingly, her death triggered a wave of sorrow that stretched far beyond what their little town could have ever imagined.

In life, Lily had set many precedents. But now, even in death, she proved to still have that ability. She became the very first musician whose death quickly spread across radio waves and international newspapers. As she traipsed across the globe in her youth presenting her art, Lily's story, her music, the Dream Symphony, and of course, the loveliness of Lily herself had burrowed into the hearts of millions. Upon her death decades later, the reaction from her fans made it clear that the love in their hearts was as permanent as cement. Phone calls, condolence letters, sympathy cards, and flowers began to pour into James by the hundreds from around the world. There were so many, in fact, that James decided to delay the date of the funeral just to allow time for those who planned to travel from other states, and even other countries, to attend. Every second of those hours was excruciating for James. Instead of a lawn full of family listening to him recite his new vows to Lily, there was a lawn full of people for a reason he was not yet ready to face. It had him ready to crumble emotionally. His desire to eat, drink, or sleep had completely ceased. Crying in moments when he was alone seemed the only thing his body was capable of. There was no amount of tears that he could shed to alleviate his anguish, but the immense amount of love that people showed for his wife gave James the fuel to push through and give Lily the sort of homecoming celebration that he knew she well-deserved.

Much like they had flocked to see the Dream Symphony, people came in droves to gather around the custom-made amphitheater on the day of her funeral. This time, though, they were there to celebrate the life of the once enslaved woman whose brilliance had begun to shift the world on that very stage. In the very place where she had been introduced to the world, people of all colors, creeds, and from many continents filled nearly every inch of her land to say goodbye to her. A sea of family, friends, fans, and even political leaders listened intently to the eulogy given by Austin's daughter, Georgia Lily, as she told the emotional tale of why her middle name held such significance to her and her father. Her poetic words about her godmother not only sparked streams of tears, but also streams of other people stepping forward to testify about the ways in which Lily had altered their lives as well. In life, Lily had inspired the people who spoke. And now, even after her death, the plentiful stories they shared about their experiences with her consequently inspired a new audience of people, as the homecoming celebration of Lily Adams was the first-ever to be broadcast on live radio. Those listening had the chance to be touched by her music as well. Many of the students she had mentored came together to replay a few of her most popular musical compositions. They ended with the song Lily always played during her famous shadowed angel scene, depicting the moment she was embraced in the arms of her waiting mother in heaven.

The morning after the funeral, James stood in the foyer hugging each of his children for the longest time. Being a daddy's girl, Lillian had hugged her father far more than her brothers during her lifetime. She could easily feel that the once strong man she knew had deteriorated over just ten days. Even the strength of his hug was not the same; she was sure to hug him with the strength he lacked. It took Lillian the longest time to find the heart to pull back from her father's embrace. Even then, she still held his hand in a way that proved she was still a daddy's girl. "You sure you wanna be alone, daddy? I can stay," she said.

"I'm sure, sweetheart. But thank you," James replied, kissing her hand. He then stepped back and gazed with pride at his brood as he slid his hands into his pockets. "Seems I've learned all too well ova' my lifetime how suddenly life can change ... and even *end* at any unpredictable moment," James sighed. "As old as I am now, I suppose such a thing for me is imminent. I don't know when God will call me home, so with the fragile time I have left, I want to be sure you all know how honored I am to be your fatha'."

James turned to his three boys. "You'd be hard-pressed to find anotha' fatha' on this earth who's as proud of his sons as I am of you three. You've been nothin' but the utmost astute gentlemen. Your activism in the community and the way you've taken care of your families has made me so proud. But nothin' has made me prouda' than the way you've taken care of and protected your sista' ... and your motha'. It's what I wanted from my sons above all else. You've all managed to infuse a sense of honor into the Adams family name and made it one that future generations will be proud to carry on."

"No dad," Jamie replied. "The legacy of honor in the Adams name started the day you stepped onto a battlefield and put your life on the line to help free our motha'."

Jamie's words brought instant tears to his father's eyes. "Thank you, son," he replied proudly.

James then turned to Lillian. Despite his sorrow, the sight of his only surviving daughter instantly brought a hint of a smile to his face. "And you, my beautiful girl."

His words caused Lillian to smile as well.

"I always wanted a daddy's girl," James smiled. "I rememba' the day you were born, I was ..."

"Cryin' harda' than me and mama both," Lillian finished.

"And when I held you in my arms for the first time..."

"My little mouth fell open, and I stared at you without a tear in my wide eyes, lookin' utterly shocked that this big cryin' sap was my daddy," Lillian finished again.

James nodded and let out a faint laugh.

"You've told me that story a million times, and I *still* feel like I can neva' hear it enough," Lillian smiled.

"And every word of it is the truth. You were my sunshine from the day you were born. You lit up my life every day. You've made the reality of havin' a daughta' supersede the dream by leaps and bounds. It was such an honor and a privilege to work side by side with you in our medical practice for all the years that we did. I have no words to express the prideful feelin' of watchin' my little girl blossom into one of the finest physicians this teary-eyed sap has eva' seen."

"Thank you, daddy," Lillian replied, her tears erupting again.

James reached over and held her hand. He then looked at his four priceless treasures again. "Quite simply ... you four and your sista' Rose are truly the greatest gifts your motha' has eva' given me."

"You've certainly proven that to us through your actions every single day of our lives," Jamie said.

Levi nodded. "By watchin' you, I've learned how to love my kids."

"The way you loved our motha' showed us boys how to love a woman with complete vulnerability and selflessness," Will added.

"And showed me the sort of love and respect that I should expect from a man," Lillian finished. She squeezed her father's hand tighter. "Quite simply ... the sort of love that you and mama expressed was the greatest gift that all of *us* could've eva' received."

James lowered his head when the warmth of his children's words triggered his tears. He raised his head again only to say, "that means so much to me. I love you all so very much."

"We love you too," they all replied in unison.

Each one of his sons stepped forward and hugged their father again, each verbally expressing their love individually as they embraced him. Lillian was the last to hug him. As she lay her head on her father's shoulder, she whispered heartfelt words into his ear. James then pulled back to look at his youngest child. Just like the day she was born, he saw a strength in her eyes that superseded his. Her astounding words proved that she had indeed inherited her mother's strength. Warmed by her selfless expression of love, James nodded. "I promise, I will," he tearfully replied, as complete peace finally settled within him.

After willing herself to let go of his hand, Lillian kissed her father on the cheek. "Goodbye daddy. I love you."

"Goodbye, my sweet girl," he tearfully whispered back, touching her cheek. "I love you too."

After their goodbyes at the door, James's children reluctantly left him to the solitude that he had begged them for. To be the strong, comforting patriarch of his massive family, James had fought for ten days to repress his emotional pain, until he was numb enough to get through it all. He was now too depleted to carry on with such a charade. When he was finally alone, he walked out to the now barren backyard where the amphitheater sat. He paused and gave a sweeping glance to the sprawling land that William had graciously left to them. He refused to look at Lily's tombstone in the distance, though. It was all he could do to remain upright when they had lowered her casket into the ground. He did not know how William had ever summoned the courage to visit his wife's gravesite weekly. The mere thought of Lily's body buried beneath his feet made James want to vomit.

Being sure to keep the family plot out of his peripheral vision, James walked across the lawn and stopped at Lily's favorite spot near the lake. He looked up at the towering tree that had witnessed the beautiful love he had made to Lily underneath it. In fact, he was convinced that their love had helped nurture its roots, as it provided the shade and the backrest during the many times he and Lily had read stories there together. While standing in its shade, that tree's rustling leaves had served as the beautiful melody playing each time James and Lily renewed their vows. That tree was the backdrop of many family birthdays, picnics, fishing competitions, and the countless times James and Lily had played with their children in the lake. That tree near the glistening lake, Lily's little spot of heaven, was the place she told James about the fantasy life she dreamt of having with him.

That tree now bore the proof of how Lily's fantasy had come true. Four generations of descendants that James and Lily's love had been responsible for creating were now engraved onto small metal placards that had been nailed into the tree. They were perfectly grouped in descending order. With James and Lily as the matriarch and patriarch, their names were now so high up on the growing tree that he would have had to climb a ladder to see it clearly. Countless children, grandchildren, great, and even great-great grandchildren now trailed down beautifully below them. Part of their two-week tradition had been to add the engraved placards of the newest additions to their ever-growing family. Aurora Lily Adams and Rory James Adams were the new twin great-great grandchildren that James hammered into the bark before stepping back to pridefully look at what had literally become a family tree. When he did, a wave of sorrow suddenly rolled over him. On this very day, at this very hour, every person whose name graced that tree should have been surrounding him as he renewed his vows for the seventh time to the love of his life.

The tidal wave of sorrow carried James as far away from that tree as he could get. Before grief caused his knees to buckle, he plodded over to the amphitheater and stood in front of the stage. He then looked down at the now faded scar on his hand that Lily had stitched after he sliced it open during its construction. He closed his eyes when it brought back memories of his youthful self, surrounded by the fresh smell of paint and the sound of hammers, as he worked side by side with Ben in the heat. Helping to construct the Dream Symphony amphitheater was among the top things James had been most proud of in his life. When he had helped build it, however, James never could have guessed that he was also constructing the stage where Lily's funeral would take place. But he felt it was fitting. The place where

Lily had been introduced to the world was the very place that the world had all come to say goodbye to her. He opened his eyes and scanned the beautiful way in which people had chosen to do so. Mounds and mounds of single white lilies were left behind on the stage by family, friends, students, and fans. The flowers were so plentiful that there was not an inch of the stage left uncovered. James thought it was a beautiful metaphor for how completely people loved his wife. But he felt they could have snuffed an ocean dry with lilies and it still would not even come close to the depths of his love for her. Still, though, he was warmed by the way they had expressed their heartfelt goodbye.

Goodbye: a word that James could not bring himself to say to his best friend. After being reunited after the war, James had never spent a single day apart from Lily. Six years of being away from her at school and five years of being torn apart by war was enough to make him have a deep appreciation for having Lily by his side every day thereafter. It was likely a record-shattering streak that most would feel was overwhelming, but not James. He knew all too well that spending every day with the woman he loved had been a fragile privilege that could have easily been destroyed by happenstance ... or death. That sobering thought had made him want to spend every day with Lily like it was his last, and to always view his time with her as an honor.

Unwilling to relinquish such an honor, James wanted to relive his life with Lily all over again. Avoiding the sight of her grave, he had walked into the library that William had decorated in Lily's honor. He took his time as he walked around the room, admiring the many pictures and treasures that lined the shelves. He then sat down at Lily's custom-made grand piano, closed his eyes, and exhaled.

And so now here James was, on this April fifteenth of 1930. He should have been renewing his vows with Lily for the seventh time. Instead, he had begun his traditional walk down memory lane alone, starting with that fateful day when he had returned home from Ohio

University and caught Lily playing his mother's piano. As he relived it in the recesses of his mind, he could feel goosebumps rising on his skin, just like all those years ago when he had listened intently and watched her in awe. Now, though, he looked back on that memory appreciating how that fateful moment had ignited more than just goosebumps and an overwhelming need to shed tears. He now realized that that very moment had been a monumental turning point in their lives. That was the day that began his extraordinary journey with an even more extraordinary woman.

While sitting in the library escaping into his mind, James felt like he was truly reliving his astonishing storybook life with Lily all over again. This time, though, he did not need to look at trinkets and treasures to help him relive his childhood adventures in the woods, adventures to Winter Garden, fantastical adventures around the world, and every other adventure born from the fateful moment he had walked in to find Lily seated at his mother's piano. Every life-altering experience with his best friend that had shaped him as a man, was now as ironclad in his mind as his love for Lily.

After his mental retreat into the past, James opened his eyes to the reality that he had finished his nostalgic journey all *alone*. It was then that he had mustered the courage to gaze up at the portrait of Musical Dreams. Every breath, every step he took, every thought, every decision, every heartbeat for eighty-five years had been for the inspiring woman in that picture. He had relied on her strength when he was weak. Even in the years when they were torn apart, the thought of reuniting with her had kept him thriving. But now, she was no longer by his side, not because she was at his father's home while he was away, or because she was missing, but because she was truly gone … *forever*. Finally accepting that fact shattered the rest of James's broken heart. The subsequent pain suddenly hit him like a speeding freight train. He dropped his face into his hands, and the agony that had been brewing in his chest for the past ten days came spewing from his sullen eyes like an erupting volcano, his body convulsing as he wept with intensity.

Just ten days without Lily's laughter, her smile, her warmth, the sound of her voice, and her daily expressions of love, was the equivalent to starving James of oxygen. He recalled William once saying that breathing felt like an insurmountable task without his wife. James felt that William's statement did not even come close to adequately describing the extreme struggle it suddenly was to fill his constricted lungs, and force air through his singed trachea.

Hours of body-shuddering sobs left James weakened and exhausted. With his beautiful best friend no longer steadfast by his side, he had no desire to replenish his strength to begin trying to overcome the most crippling tragedy of his life. With what remained of his fading energy, he slowly rose from Lily's piano and began making his way toward the grand dual staircase in his foyer, staggering all the way there as if he was drunk off misery. Breathing hard by the time he arrived, he held onto the railing to keep himself upright. When he caught his breath, he gathered the strength to lift his head and gaze at the portrait of the child who had spent her entire brief life in his loving arms. With Rose's tender blue eyes seeming to beam down at him with love, it gave James the needed strength to begin making his ascent. He had been left with a permanent slight limp after the war. But now, in such a weakened state, he climbed the stairs as if his injuries were fresh again. As he dragged himself up the steps, he continued to gaze at his daughter's portrait the whole way for the needed motivation to complete his ascent.

James was starved of oxygen by the time he made it to the top. He leaned on the railing and took a moment to catch his breath. Before walking toward his room, he looked up at Rose and silently thanked her for being his inspiration … yet again. He then limped into the rebuilt bedroom that he had first professed his love to Lily in. He took a moment to look around the sentimental room he had shared with

her for decades. He sighed and then walked over to a shelf and pulled out the very first wax record ever made with Lily's music on it. He then shuffled over to the homophone in the corner of the room, opened the lid, and placed the record on it. After placing the needle on the edge, Lily's melodies overtook the silence in the room. James then turned to look at the bed. Another surge of tears careened down his wrinkled cheeks and butterflies erupted in his stomach, as a vision of making love to Lily for the very first time began playing in his mind with crystal clarity.

James then sat down at a desk and took out a pen and paper. Without one pause or second-guess, he began writing. The words on his mind flowed effortlessly and poetically. By the time the first side of Lily's record was complete, so was James. He got up and turned the record over to side B. Another sea of tears surged from his eyes when Lily's music overtook the room again. As the song gave him strength, James picked up the tear-stained paper he had just written on and folded it neatly. He then walked over to the mirror, picked up a pair of scissors, and snipped a locket of his now white hair. He then placed it in an envelope along with the new vows he had just written, that were inspired by his nostalgic quest down memory lane.

After sealing the envelope with wax, James briefly thought about how the years *without* Lily had affected him just as equally as the special moments *with* her. Anytime they were separated, it had always been the hope and anticipation of seeing her again that had compelled his actions and decisions. That was no different on this day. James suddenly stood and made his way up the two steps that led to the bed. He then sat down on the edge of it. Sitting in that very spot right after the war, James had once tearfully confessed to Lily that he would give up and die without her. Lillian had never been told that story, but it proved to be a sentiment she innately knew to be true: "*You've loved us so unselfishly all these years. Now it's our turn to do the same. Go on home to her, daddy. We'll miss you so much, but we'll learn to be okay without you. Give mama and my big sista' a hug for me,*" Lillian had tearfully whispered in her father's ear that morning before reluctantly letting him go, in more ways than one. With the memory of his daughter's words giving James the final bit of peace he needed, he lay back on the pillow and placed his vows on his chest, vows that proved the precious love he felt for Lily at first sight had remained indestructible during his entire life. Now prepared to prove that his love was just as indestructible throughout the infinite hours of eternity, James closed his eyes, pushing a swell of tears down the sides of his face. When the last song on Lily's record stopped, so too did James's shattered heart. When he exhaled for a final time, a smile graced his face. His tears suddenly morphed into those of joy as he was welcomed into the afterlife with a warm embrace from the only woman he had ever loved, a woman the world first came to know as *the prodigy slave* ... but who died as a cherished, world-renowned, *iconic musical legend.*

Did you enjoy this entire series?

Your positive review on Amazon would be greatly appreciated!

Use your smart phone to scan the QR code below to leave your review or go to Amazon and click "write a customer review."

Thank you in advance!

About the Author

Londyn Skye is a comical, 44-year-old mother of two, ex-all-American collegiate athlete, million-mile lady trucker phenom, and a romance novel junkie! When she was a child, Londyn began creating stories in the fantasy world of her mind as a way to escape life's troubles. As an adult, she decided to challenge herself to turn her comforting fantasies into a novel. That challenge led her to write *The Prodigy Slave* trilogy. Wanting the utmost quality for her readers, she has diligently worked to balance the saga with humor, drama, romance, unpredictable plots, and devious, neurotic characters that are equally as captivating as the erotic love scenes between the fascinating heroes and heroines. She has painstakingly painted her fantasies with words that she hopes will help readers to see the images just as beautifully as her unique mind does. Most importantly, she hopes that everyone will feel just as emotionally moved and inspired by the heroes and heroines in her love story.

Connect with Londyn at www.facebook.com/AuthorLondynSkye